# GRANTA

## GRANTA 74, SUMMER 2001
www.granta.com

EDITOR  *Ian Jack*
DEPUTY EDITORS  *Liz Jobey, Sophie Harrison*
US EDITOR  *Kerry Fried*
EDITORIAL ASSISTANT  *Fatema Ahmed*

CONTRIBUTING EDITORS  *Neil Belton, Pete de Bolla, Ursula Doyle, Will Hobson, Gail Lynch, Blake Morrison, Andrew O'Hagan, Lucretia Stewart*

FINANCE  *Margarette Devlin*
ASSOCIATE PUBLISHER  *Sally Lewis*
MARKETING DIRECTOR  *Claire Paterson*
TO ADVERTISE CONTACT  *Lara Frohlich* (212) 293 1646
CIRCULATION DIRECTOR  *Stephen W. Soule*
FULFILLMENT MANAGER  *Richard Sang*
SUBSCRIPTIONS  *Dwayne Jones*
LIST MANAGER  *Diane Seltzer*

PUBLISHER  *Rea S. Hederman*

GRANTA PUBLICATIONS, 2-3 Hanover Yard, Noel Road, London N1 8BE
Tel 020 7704 9776 Fax 020 7704 0474
e-mail for editorial: editorial@granta.com
Granta is published in the United Kingdom by Granta Publications.

GRANTA USA LLC, 1755 Broadway, 5th Floor, New York, NY 10019-3780
Tel (212) 246 1313 Fax (212) 586 8003

Granta is published in the United States by Granta USA LLC and distributed in the United States by Granta Direct Sales, 1755 Broadway, 5th Floor, New York, NY 10019-3780.

TO SUBSCRIBE call (800) 829 5093 or e-mail: granta@nybooks.com
A one-year subscription (four issues) costs $37 (US), $48 (Canada, includes GST), $45 (Mexico and South America), and $56 (rest of the world). Toll-free customer service line (US only): 1-800-829-5093.

Granta, USPS 000-508, ISSN 0017-3231, is published quarterly in the US by Granta USA LLC, a Delaware limited liability company. Periodical Rate postage paid at New York, NY, and additional mailing offices. POSTMASTER: send address changes to Granta, 1755 Broadway, 5th Floor, New York, NY 10019-3780. US Canada Post Corp. Sales Agreement #1462326.
Printed in the United States of America on acid-free paper. ∞

Design: Random Design.
Front cover photograph: S. Wilde/Stone, back cover photograph: self-portrait by Martín Chambi
ISBN 1-929001-04-5

# GRANTA 74

# Confessions, etc

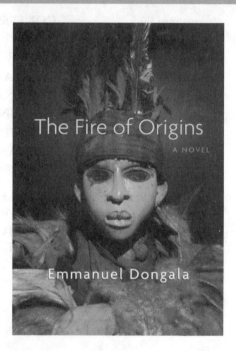

GRANTA

# CONFESSIONS OF A MIDDLE-AGED ECSTASY EATER

Anonymous

But who are they [this whole class of opium eaters]? Reader, I am sorry to say, a very numerous class indeed... I do not readily believe that any man, having once tasted the divine luxuries of opium, will afterwards descend to the gross and mortal enjoyments of alcohol. I take it for granted:

That those eat now, who never ate before
And those who always ate, now eat more.

*Thomas de Quincey, Confessions of an English Opium Eater, the London Magazine, 1821*

To the reader. I hereby present you with a record, of sorts, of a remarkable period in my life. According to my application of it, I trust, as I likewise hope, that it may prove not merely interesting, but, to a considerable degree, useful and instructive. It is in that hope that I have troubled myself to draw it up, even as I feel compelled in advance to apologize for breaching that delicate and honourable reserve which, until quite recently—when certain publishers became aware that there was for the marketing of such breaching an apparently limitless audience, that is, one ripe to be r(e)aped—has restrained me from the public exposure of my own errors and infirmities.

Which makes me no less reluctant to do so, for while there are many whom it would please loudly to dispute it—they do not know me well enough, or know all too well but that certain part of me—I am, at heart, an abashed man. Indeed so alive am I to the professional reproach and public humiliation that such exposure necessarily would arouse that I have for months resisted the prodding of certain parties to permit any part of my narrative to come before the public. And it is not without enormous anxiety, nor an absence of insomniac nights, that I have, at last, reached the decision to do so however constrained I am to remain anonymous in the doing.

This is not, understand, owing to my self-accusation constituting a confession of guilt, any more than it does an expression of hubris. I feel no guilt, none at all. I know this to be true for I am as susceptible to guilt (and shame and self-loathing) as to self-aggrandizement, and in this instance I feel of either, as I do of both, neither tweak nor discernible twinge. As pertains to what follows, such feelings are utterly beside the point.

That said, I am not, thank God, Thomas de Quincey (or Coleridge, Baudelaire, Cocteau, Huxley, Paul Bowles, Carlos Castenada, William Burroughs, Ken Kesey or Hunter S. Thompson, to name but the more usual of the usual suspects), and the irreparable harm that revealing my identity inevitably would inflict, not only upon my professional reputation but upon those whom I love and care deeply for, simply is not commensurate with the benefits liable to redound to me in so doing. Perhaps some day, one day when we all of us are more—what?—grown up? Grown up enough, at least, to be less hysterical and apocalyptic about the subject at hand. But

Anonymous

for now, more's the pity, no. If I do not court censure, neither do I curry accolade, and so for the time being am, as I must be, content to skulk behind the craven's mask.

I am fast—I am tempted to say far too fast, save that it never ceases to strike me as the unlikeliest of miracles—approaching my fiftieth year, and most of my adult life has been lived comfortably upon the right side of the law, first as a journalist, then as a novelist, prose-poet and essayist. I am at present, or so I gather, what I so long ago explicitly aspired to become—a man of letters.

From my birth I was as it seems to me now an intellectual creature first—I emerged from the womb (if one is to believe my mother, and how dare I do otherwise) brow furrowed, face knit in an expression of the most singular concentration and perplexity: 'Where the hell am I and why am I here, what precisely is going on and what, pray tell, if there be one, which seems increasingly unlikely, is the point?' and I do not wonder, for those questions I grapple with still, as still without adequate answers. And so intellectual in the highest sense my pursuits and pleasures have always been, even from my schoolboy days.

I know little for an immanent certainty, but this I immanently, most certainly do (one needn't be Stephen Hawking to appreciate such evident truth)—nothing surpasses the life of the mind, that same mind, as William Gass has rightly observed, that is the 'only claw man has'. And so, if eating Ecstasy be chiefly a sensual, and so a mindless pleasure, and if, as I confess, I have indulged in it to excess, no less true is that I have struggled to understand my habit, if not yet with the religious zeal required properly to get shed of it.

But then, perhaps I do not wish to get shed of it, not really, or not nearly enough. And this is but one of the many lessons, insofar as one may be disposed to receive them, that Ecstasy is wont to impart: that first principles—of life, love, God, beauty—fly apart, and it is not incumbent upon us to puzzle them through that we might piece them together again, but merely do as we might to hold on for dear life, to ride out the storm and, as we may manage it, gather unto ourselves some little enjoyment in the doing. Anything else not only is an utter waste of time, but an exercise in self-deception, deceit and the grossest, most overweening vanity. Ecstasy—and not merely the drug—never was intended to be intellectualized.

10

Order, even creatively ordered order, perhaps especially creatively ordered order—that which it pleases intellectuals such as myself to anoint Art (and oh, how we do insist in the solemnity of our self-congratulation upon the capitalization of that A)—is powerless against the chaos, because that chaos resides not only out there, in the 'real' world, but inside each one of us. It is hewn to the double helix, the anarchic state of our collective soul, and its only counter, its only effective antidote, is death. Against which, I fear, no vaccine—at least, not yet. (Though if science can design for us Ecstasy, can immortality be far behind?)

I have occasionally been asked how I first came to it, that is, how I became a regular Ecstasy-eater, the assumption being, I presume, that I was seeking a cheap (I have paid as little as ten dollars a pill when buying 'in bulk', seldom more than twenty-five dollars) and ephemeral thrill, pursuing a temporary state of pleasurable, if wholly artificial excitement, the craic of that High, the visceral flow of its fix, the ultimate *roll*. And perhaps, at first, I was. I was aware of its reputation as the 'Love Drug', had heard it described—I can no longer recall just where—as a 'four-hour, full-body orgasm', had read Sean Elder's seminal 1986 article, 'On Ecstasy', and all of this I found—what?—intriguing, appealing, alluring? Well, I found it worthy of further investigation.

Which is odd, because ordinarily I would not have condescended to pay it the slightest heed. Even at university, the high times of those heady years—in my case 1969 to 1976—I was not a user, chronic, casual or otherwise. Despite an environment in which experimentation with illegal substances was culturally certified as little more than an alternative form of recreation, indeed in which smoking grass and dropping acid (if not yet snorting coke or shooting smack), was not only benignly accepted, but benevolently smiled upon, I deliberately chose not to indulge. (OK, once. I did some speed. I had fallen behind in a course and was facing an all-nighter. I swallowed the pill, whole—something called a 'white cross' as I for no earthly reason recall—and was up, each of my senses on red alert, my heart a snare drum in my ears, my eyes seeming literally to sweat, the world standing newel-post straight at full attention for the ensuing forty-eight hours. I saw tigers everywhere and heard the incessant wailing of sirens. I learned later I ought to have ingested only half. I never did it again.) And this, one ought not with a measure of humility hesitate to aver, required no fair amount of self-discipline, as it did a right gathering of will. The dope was everywhere, it seemed at times to be in the very drinking water, in the air itself, and everyone—including my friends (my closest was a jazz musician, imagine), more than a few girlfriends, and most of my professors, as they were content enough to broadcast—was doing it.

Except me. I wasn't. And this had nothing to do with feelings of superiority or intolerance (however consistently I may have refused to suffer hedonists gladly), or the bucking of countercultural convention, as it did less with morality or politics or religion. (I was in those days, right down to the black of my beret, an existentialist on the first count, a raving anarchist of the Malatesta school on the second, a crypto-Kierkegaardian on the third—or so I recollect fancying myself.) It had to do solely with fear. Not only was I afraid of 'fucking with my mind', I was petrified of irreparably fucking it up. I took myself seriously, far too seriously—those were serious times for those of us who took them seriously, as seriously as did I—and I steadfastly refused to buy into the druggie/head trip/stoner agitprop of the day. Reading *The Electric Kool-Aid Acid Test* or *Fear and Loathing in Las Vegas*, listening to Hendrix or the Doors, Cream or the Airplane was more than enough for me. I was possessed of no itch to experience the psychedelics of that 'trip' first-hand, as I felt no exigency about making God's more intimate acquaintance.

Not that I was, despite my Midwestern Calvinist upbringing, narrow-minded or uncurious, nor was I unhip. If I was far from some paragon of Mailer's White Negro, well, even the Negroes I knew— I hung out a lot in jazz clubs—were not paragons of Mailer's White Negro. (Indeed, over time, I have come to surmise that only Mailer himself—and perhaps Mick Jagger—ever was.) Simply, I was scared. Small wonder, then, how often those select few with knowledge of my current habit have remarked—less appalled, perhaps, than incredulous—upon my being the 'least likely person in the world' to have fallen prey to it.

Well, yes. And likewise, no. For while I cannot swear with spot-on certainty, I believe that my coming to Ecstasy—or it to me—goes further than mere thrill-seeking. I believe it goes to the centre of my life at the time, a life that, to employ a colloquially turned phrase, was a mess. I was headed south, a south sunless, unlovely and cold.

This is difficult, even now, to talk about. We all have our war stories. Mine is but one more heaped among the remains of the rest. I do not presume to claim for it some vaunted or exalted status. I have no desire to extol what merits no extolling (much less to aestheticize it). If ecstasy is not meant to be intellectualized, neither is suffering intended to be phenomenalized, particularly where it is of no higher order than anyone else's. If it is special, somehow different, that is only because it is mine and mine alone. It was a period of personal devastation. Such periods eventually are visited upon us all. We all encounter those dark fires through which we must walk or perforce self-immolate, and no one who lives his life as it is meant to be lived ought to expect to emerge from them unscathed. One's scars are not chevrons; they are not meant to be brandished like stigmata.

It began with my only child, a son—he was then my best friend, from time to time still is—and I did not see it coming (not that I was looking; I was sitting on a fast ball, not the curve I was eventually served), and it culminated in Ecstasy, and to that I see no end. He was beautiful and sensitive—perhaps too sensitive, more than I knew or he had a right to be, this permeable membrane—and extraordinarily talented, talented enough that at thirteen his poetry had won the notice of university professors and New York book editors alike; the budding Rimbaud. So when he undertook to destroy himself, he took his mother and father with him. That was not, nor is it, his fault. He was thirteen and had neither the capacity nor context to grasp what he was doing. He was then being held hostage to problems of his own, problems he could no more articulate than dogs do long division, trees turn somersaults or thunder parse sentences, and which he would have roundly denied if he could. And if he had been capable of knowing the pain and heartache his behaviour was causing the two people he loved most in the world, he would not have cared. He was not, then, possessed of the wherewithal.

One always can be more specific, describe more, one always can concretize experience. The only issue is how detailed, how concrete, how descriptively specific one wishes to be. So: he attempted suicide.

Anonymous

(The details are unimportant; the very devil is in them.) He ran away, serially. He purchased a handgun from a school friend. He stole, sometimes from stores, more often from his parents, typically in the middle of the night. He was arrested for stealing. He was sentenced to community service. He committed various, not particularly imaginative acts of vandalism. He taunted and cussed at strangers on the street. He got drunk—beer, wine, liquor, whatever he could lay his hands on—and when he got drunk, he got violent. He verbally and physically abused his mother. He attempted, using a pair of candles, to set her hair on fire. The second time he used gasoline. He dismantled furniture, broke china, smashed crystal and, unprovoked, punched out windows and kicked in walls. He shredded his wardrobe with scissors, every stitch of his clothing, and when he had finished, started in on his mother's. He trashed his bedroom down to lathings, shims and cinder block. He graffitied what remained with every racial and sexual epithet imaginable. He slept on the floor amid rotting food, curdled milk, the mouse droppings that appeared in their wake and a rubble of plaster, drywall and broken glass. He refused to bathe. He defecated in the yard and urinated in Coke cans which he deployed about his bedroom in pentagrams, these red metal voodoo dolls. He carved his arms with the filed-down ends of paper clips. He discovered marijuana, then cocaine. Then PCP. Then Special K (an animal tranquillizer, which he called 'catfood'). He fought with friends. One scrape involved a spot of knife play culminating in a facial slash requiring a ten-stitch repair. The few that remained he manipulated and abused, this adolescent Svengali. He was flung through a plate-glass window by a schoolmate, a football player, escaping serious injury, according to the principal, 'only by divine intervention'. He was expelled from high school. He impregnated a girl. There was an abortion. He disappeared for days at a time, often into New York City where he slept in storefronts and abandoned buildings and on park benches; at least twice he was shaken down at knifepoint. He sold or bartered his personal belongings, many of them Christmas and birthday presents—guitars, stereo equipment, CD collections, wristwatches, leather jackets—to raise money to buy drugs. He contracted one sexually transmitted disease, then another. He was under age, so when he drove his friends' cars he did so illegally. High on cocaine, he eventually rolled one on the Interstate while going in excess of eighty mph. That he and his two passengers, one his girlfriend, were not killed outright—the car came to rest on its roof in a creek bed; they climbed out bruised and bloodied through its open trunk—was in the by-now familiar words of the State Trooper, 'only a matter of divine intervention'. He escaped incarceration at the state juvenile detention facility only because the court was inexplicably merciful. He dropped out of a second, 'alternative' school. He worked sporadically, a succession of menial, part-time jobs, none of which lasted more than a few weeks: window washer, hod carrier, gas jockey, bellhop. Eventually he was removed from his home and consigned— exiled, really—first to lockdown in a private psychiatric ward, then to a special school out of state. He was counselled. He was diagnosed with a variety of acronyms: AD, ADD, ODD, ICD, possible BP. He was prescribed medication: Zoloft, Depakote, Paxil, Wellbutrin. When that school and that counsel and that medication did not 'take', he was given different medication and more counselling and sent to yet another school out of state, a private high school with an annual tuition fee of $40,000. While there, during an off-campus weekend, he was arrested and jailed overnight for possession and sentenced to community service. He briefly participated in a scam to pass counterfeit money. He took his exam and got his driver's licence. Two months later he had accumulated thirteen points. His licence was suspended. He kept driving anyway. He was now dealing as well as using drugs and the wheels were essential to what he called his 'livelihood', as they were conducive to his lifestyle, a lifestyle redolent of a vampire's, for he lived upside down, sleeping all day, drugging all night. Eventually, in the course of one five-day spree, he totalled two automobiles, one his father's, pulverizing his ankle so badly in the process that it required twenty-six staples, ten screws and two stainless-steel plates to reconstruct. I would not swear to the precise chronology of any of this—even now it remains a blur—but to this I would: he strewed wreckage everywhere. His was another kind of reality, an unreality perhaps, an anti-reality, and those drawn into the chaos of its orbit, those who found themselves cobbed in its web inevitably suffered damage.

In the meantime his parents' marriage, all twenty years of it, was collapsing. My wife was and remains a beautiful, caring, generous, gifted woman. She is the oldest soul I know, the blithest spirit, and I would not hesitate to give my life for her, and though we no longer live together, have not lived together for years, I admire and, on some level, love her still, as I know I always shall. But sometimes that is not enough. Sometimes nothing is enough, as sometimes everything isn't. The marriage had its long-standing problems, its rifts and fractures and shoals, and when it came under siege and then assault, when our son began the process of so thoroughly, as we took to referring to it, 'flushing himself', the stress was too much. We lost our way, then ran aground, and then, at last, we broke.

We tried over and over again to address the issues, patch the problems, spackle them, caulk them, span them, fill them, whatever it is one does when one senses imminent demolition and doesn't know quite why and is floundering as one flails and hasn't a clue what to do. We tried because we once had had something valuable, because we shared an intimate history of mutual investment, because we once had cherished the sound of one another's laughter, because not trying seemed to us grotesque. We tried because we loved one another and because we loved our son, in the face of whose own self-demolition neither of us could have survived intact. If that sounds melodramatic, it should. It was a melodramatic time.

So we broke, and I left. Oh, not straight away—the break was anything but clean; it was tortured, as it became Byzantine—and I never went far. A basement apartment across the street, a rodent-infested one the next town over. I was in and out, out and in, back in and back out for years. I was at a loss as to how I could properly leave and unsure I wished to find out. But then, I wasn't sure of much, not any more, and that disconcerted almost as much as it depressed me, because being dead certain, even when I was dead wrong, was a quality I had typically hung my hat on. The quintessential male facade, and one behind which I was quaking.

I couldn't seem to stop quaking.

Eventually I found a place just bleak enough to mirror the way I felt, and I felt dreadful, wretched, unsalvageable, I felt vile and violated, and I felt lost. And solitary. And wrong. All of me, wrong. I stopped shaving, bathing, sleeping. In time I stopped eating. (Over one three-month period I shed forty pounds.) I no longer recognized the aesthetics of myself. There are any number of poetic words that lend themselves to the state to which I had descended, but a single, six-letter one seems best: bereft—'void of; taken away, removed, quite gone'. Somehow I had become radioactive, the world a wilderness of asperity, and I was left to maunder it untethered and mapless, self-menaced and heartsore and seared.

The place was a single, windowless room scarce larger than a tool shed, a root cellar space attached to the back of an abandoned garage, and I wallowed in it, in its cobwebs and scum-scrim and filth—I hadn't, naturally, the wherewithal to clean up after myself—alone. And so it was alone that I began to disintegrate. I continued to write, frantically, incessantly, desperately, because writing was the only way I knew to stay afloat, though looking back I cannot say whether I was writing myself out of what I sensed was an approaching madness, or writing myself more deeply into it.

The nightmares arrived on cue. Not images of hell and its hounds—those I might have withstood—but waterfalls and rivers of words. No images, no meanings, just words, disconnected, decontextualized, foaming, alone. Words as onrushing water, whirlpools and eddies and swirls. I was afflicted by freshets and torrents, marooned in the froth of their flow. Cascades, cataracts, outpours, an unending, recurring cadence that streamed forth in syntactical arabesques. I was haemorrhaging rhymes and the metre of verbs, and each morning, 4 a.m., 5 a.m., morning after morning for months, I awoke unbuoyed and drenched to the bone.

And I wondered, as I wonder still, which of us is possessed of the temerity to suggest that we are not drowning? To gainsay that we are not being dragged under, again and again, and forever?

Somehow, I no longer recall just how and prefer even now not to, I completed the 500-page draft of a novel about, of all things, Lizzie Borden, but when I submitted it to my agent he deemed it 'one of the most brilliant pieces of insanity' he had ever read, declared it utterly unmarketable, and declined to take it on. (He was, I see now, as I was incapable of seeing then, perfectly correct to do so. Brilliant it may have been, insane it decidedly remains.) We parted company, upon the heels of which my editor quit his job at a prominent New York publishing house. My marriage was dead—though I still insisted upon thinking of it as merely semi-comatose—my son still very much alive, I was agentless, editorless, apparently unpublishable, was living like a tramp and a recluse, my income close to nil, and slowly, and then not so slowly, I was, I had convinced myself, going mad. Having cast myself out—of home-and-hearth, as from all human contact—I had become in every way imaginable an outcast. Dostoevsky's subterranean man. The ex that prefixes exist.

There is, it bears mention, suicide in my family—my mother's brother (at thirteen, with a .22, to the head)—and while such history, or its spectre, has a way of haunting one's more susceptible moments, I never contemplated cashing myself in. I had peeked at the desolation behind that door years before only to decide at the last possible moment—at such times it always is the last possible moment and one lives in its present perpetually—not to see it through. It simply was not in me. Suicide, permit me to suggest, is an act of vanity, the penultimate gesture of the born narcissist, and while I had, and have, a surplus of the stuff, it is also—let no one tell you differently—an occasion of infernal courage, a gesture of brute bravery. I wanted the mettle, as I hadn't the nerve.

So for the first time in my life I sought help. My therapist was a wise, caring, gentle man, and while he tried—when I scraped fiscal bottom he carried me gratis for months—a year later he had failed to solve me. I continued to dream in words, only now I did so wide awake, this perambulatory radio of the mind, and I powerless to switch it off. I didn't hear voices, no intonation, inflection, insinuation—what I was hearing was characterless, qualityless, robotic, disembodied—I simply heard words, braids and imbrications, interlacings and overleafings, plaited webs and thatched rafts of words, and the organic pacings and tempos of their architecture. Every day deeper into this deep blue sea, its rip tides and undertows. Every day further out, beyond the crest of the next crashing wave, the slough of its swell—bluer, bluing, more blued.

So—isn't it obvious?—I began visiting bowling alleys, dozens of them, month after month. Something about the explosion of the ball and the collision of caroming pins, a sound distinct to my childhood, the only one I could imagine might mute the ones inside my head. I never bowled myself, just sat hunched to whatever bar top I found myself bellied to, nursing a beer and moving my lips to such poetry as I had at hand: Rimbaud and Rilke, Leonard Cohen and Jim Carroll, Heaney and Ashbery and Charles Olson. And Paul Metcalf, with whom I had recently begun a lively and regular correspondence. I read Metcalf—Herman Melville's great-grandson—above all. (A few months later he was dead of a heart attack at the age of eighty-one and I felt not only aggrieved, but oddly accountable.) But eventually it proved too dispiriting. The bowlers began to appear too alien, their displays of team triumph and defeat only underscored my own lack of affect, and at last I ran clean out of bowling alleys. And now I could sense it, the lurking of something hard, and dark as it was cold. It had been decades since I had read, much less thought about Fitzgerald's 'The Crack-up', but now I began to suspect that this might be something much like that: the pending implosion. Something was inside, something outsized and other, and it was stronger than I was, and more potent, and it meant me only ill. My life—this is precisely what it felt like—had cornered me at last.

Perhaps certain questions suggest themselves: what about religion, for example, or sex, their consolation and refuge, the salvation to be had of their purchase. Although I had once had the former in spadefuls—in my early twenties I had been awarded a scholarship to Vanderbilt Divinity School, one that at the eleventh hour I had chosen not to pursue—in time I had come to travel a different path. I became a journalist, a newspaper reporter, and in the process lost what little faith I once had possessed. I was engaged in 'real' life in those days, the quotidian issues driving the lives of others, and by the time I threw over my thriving career several years later I had seen far too much of it for it to engage me further. Not that I experienced my loss of faith in any active or meaningful way. God simply, gradually, imperceptibly became as incidental and finally irrelevant to my life as our lives, I am convinced, are to Him. Those who have faith, those who somehow have succeeded in finding the depth and fortitude of character to keep it, doubtless will deem such a declaration exceedingly sad. I do not. The point is, that particular option was closed to me. The despair I was feeling not even Christ might assuage.

As for sex, despite protracted periods of acquiescent celibacy inside my marriage, I had always liked it, the little I had had, and now I missed it, terribly, became, in fact, abstracted by its absence. Sex tends, I think—deplorably—to be taken for granted when one has easy and routine access to it, but when one finds oneself deprived of that access, well, one yearns. All day, every day. At least I do. Did. Unfortunately, while I have always adored women—to a greater extent than I feel kinship with men—I am constitutionally incapable of one-night stands, casual affairs or even what might these days be considered an acceptable level of discreet larking about. Not that I haven't had my opportunities, but I have never failed, save once, to take a rain check. Infidelity, philandering, debauchery, promiscuity, profligacy, skirt-chasing—call it what one will—none were among the reasons my marriage unravelled, though the meagre quantity and quality of the sex certainly was. And my reticence, if that is what it was, had very little to do with epidemiology—with Aids and its lesser cousins—as it had nothing whatever to do with morality. Indeed, what it had to do with, God knows. The point is, that option was not open to me either.

So: suicide, religion, sex. Three strikes, as is said, and you are out. Quite gone. Void of. Bereft. Thrice over.

And then the unthinkable happened, or rather, two things happened. I met someone, a woman, and while I in my recalcitrant fashion followed up on that meeting so that she might eventually save me (as save me she eventually did), my son was becoming—with a vengeance, which is his own fashion, the only fashion he knows, headlong as headstrong in all things—what is called in the parlance, a 'raver'. And he seemed for the first time in years—he was seventeen by then—happy. Not giddy or euphoric, but content, at peace with himself, within himself. I do not mean to invoke images of Zen and Buddha—my son is roughly as Zen-like as Eminem—but the transformation was as striking as it was palpable, this sea change. Indeed it seemed so definitive that I could not help asking him about it, and when I did, he smiled—I shall always remember that smile, he has the most incandescent smile in the world—and said simply, 'Uh-huh. I am.' And when I asked him why, what had happened, what accounted, he smiled again and said, 'Aw, you wouldn't understand. But it's my whole life now. I know why I'm alive.'

I remember my response. And perhaps had I responded in some other way or simply not responded at all, what was about to happen would never have happened. Or perhaps it would have. Perhaps it would have happened anyway. Perhaps it had to happen, and no matter what I said or left unsaid it was going to happen, because that is the way these things happen. What I said was, 'Congratulations. I'm happy for you. Really. I wish I did.' Because despite everything, my son and I have never withheld, not from one another. He confides, as do I. He tells me things no child ought ever tell a parent, things no parent wants to hear, disgusting things often, morally reprehensible things, nauseatingly cruel things, things that are so appallingly beyond the pale, so rife with risk, rank with recklessness, so absent all human feeling and judgement that I am left, as I seldom am, quite speechless. For one cannot speak when one's teeth are set so on edge, and one is tectonically grinding them.

And so he turned to me and said, 'Seriously?' And when I answered not only in the affirmative, but the declarative, he told me a story and made me an offer, and so was hatched yet another aspect of our relationship, an aspect that is as wholly illicit as it is morally unsavoury, and one that continues to this day.

We both know it is wrong, this part of it, the arrangement, the dilemma it poses, wrong in the most intimate and unholy of ways, as we both know that neither of us care enough about the fact to do anything about it. Why should we? We have disappointed one another so often in the past that it seems to matter less than not at all. It is a shared shame now, something the two of us have that no one else has, and it has become, like the abiding commonness of our blood, a large and integral part of what bonds us—father and son, parent and child. Perhaps no truth is more momentous, as none more difficult to face, than the blackest, most abject one about oneself. My son supplies me with drugs, with Ecstasy, and if I am to be consigned to perdition, if I am to roast in hell, this, it seems to me, is first among the reasons that I shall do so. And it seems to me, further, that it is one damn fine good reason, because reckoned objectively, it is a horror, it is a latter-day horror story, save that it is not a story, it is not fiction, it is about as far from fiction as one can conceivably get. It is as real and true as it is unthinkable, and there are times when the obscenity of it takes my breath away and dizzies that benighted part of me steeped in self-disgust.

Anonymous

And so the first time I ate E—or X, or EX, or XTC, or MDMA (methylenedioxymethamphetamine) or ADAM—it was owing to my having given my son permission to sell it to me. I became his customer, a buyer, a reliable and steady client, the lowest link on the food chain of the multi-billion dollar commerce that proceeds unabated every day, every hour, in every large city and small town in every state in this union, in what is called by those paid to 'war' against them, as likewise those who traffic in them, 'controlled substances'.

You must pardon me—I do not mean to sound smug—but I find it funny. I find it ironic. It tickles and entertains and amuses me. Because I cannot think of a single commodity in our country—one that, meretricious as it may sound, I love dearly, know well and for which my father and his father fought and sacrificed much—that is less controlled than are such substances, nor a single 'war' that is as pathetically futile, vaingloriously chimeric and long-ago-lost as is this one. It is not that I am unsympathetic to those who, after all, are only doing their jobs (often at grave risk to their lives)—however much I might suggest that such frontline foot soldiers would do better to find another line of work—but I am nothing but unrepentedly hostile towards policies and laws (or rather, the sort of tortured, twisted, two-penny logic that produced and continues to pursue them) that, however well-intentioned, are so indefensibly stupid, monstrously ill-conceived, implicitly dishonest, and, in the impracticability and inequity of their application, as unjust as they are dumb.

I went, only last week, to see the movie *Traffic*. Fine film, if not nearly so fine as the critics seem to think, but then the critics, as they so often do, miss the point. *Traffic* is not a movie about the evil of drugs and inhumanity of the drug trade, it is a movie about the idiocy of our drug policy and the evils it not only fosters, but ensures will continue to flower.

Why is this so difficult to apprehend? What prevents us from possessing the humility of character to embrace the lessons hard won of our defeat? Why do we pretend? Is it really necessary to cite statistics or solicit the rhetoric, fatuous as it is fatigued, of 'experts'? We know better, or ought: the handwriting is on the wall, the toothpaste has vacated the tube, Rome is long since burned to the ground, the Emperor is wearing no clothes, and our folly has returned home to roost. You can fight City Hall, but wrestle as you will, you cannot reform or arrest human appetite any more than you can with a wave of the wand make a gay person straight or summon the voice of God that He might shed the ecumenical light of His omniscience upon the subject.

Ecstasy was made a Schedule One illegal drug—for which we can all thank that cynosure of intellect, Texas Senator Lloyd Bentsen—in June of 1985. Which, at present, makes it as illegal as heroin. This, in its preposterous disproportion, is just the sort of run-amock governmental lunacy guaranteed to ensure that those like myself—and more importantly, our children—will write off that same government and those who enforce its drug laws as out of touch, coercive, morally bankrupt and, yes—wake up guys! wake up and smell the poppies!—un-American. Because America is not, or did not use to be, about throwing sixteen-year-old kids in jail for—all in the spirit of free-market capitalism and entrepreneurial enterprise—home-growing a little cannabis, even as the rest of us chain-smoke our Camels, sip our Absoluts with a twist, and devour our Prozac.

Visit a rehab centre sometime. You will learn two things inside that first hour. One, that there are people in this world—some quite admirable, others ostensibly less so—who are more prey to addiction than others; there always have been, always will be, addicts. And two, that the 'gateway' argument is as simplistic as it is spurious. We are not losing our kids to drugs. We have lost our kids because we haven't the time, inclination, strength of character or political will to do the right thing in their name: to eliminate the black market that so mercilessly exploits them—and the runaway violence it spawns—by legalizing, taxing and regulating the trade.

'Controlled' substances? That, regrettably, is but a misnomer meriting our laughter, as it ought to occasion our tears. There is no control. There is a bureaucracy, and a so-called policy, and some laws, and the lot is a sham and a smokescreen that increasingly deceives no one. There is but a single way to 'lick the scourge and eliminate the blight', to win, that is, the so-called war on drugs—to win it so that it might have some chance, however slim, of staying won—and that way consists of two words, words that are more American than any two of which I can conceive (save, perhaps, 'Uncle Sam'): Wall Street.

But then, who cares what I think? Anybody can think anything about everything, as everybody inevitably does. I pretend to no monopoly of wisdom upon the subject. But I know something of Ecstasy, perhaps I even know a lot, or more than most, and certainly more than most of a certain age, which is to say, a comparable, middling one. And what I know I know because I have eaten and continue to eat so much of it. I am an experienced, seasoned, veteran eater of E—I would not hazard a guess as to the exact quantity, though it is fair to say a lot—and it is a fact of which I am neither proud nor mortified.

So here, in a word, a most sober, solemn, even a sombre word, is what I know: *yum*.

Ecstasy is delicious. Or, put it another way, Ecstasy is delicious and I recommend highly, loudly and long that everyone whose health—physical *and* psychological—does not contraindicate or preclude its ingestion, ought to ingest it. Young/old, man/woman, rich/poor, gay/straight, black/white, saint/sinner, genius/dolt, Christian and Jew and Muslim, Democrat, Republican and Independent, lawmaker and lawbreaker, heartbreaker and soulshaker, the sexually degenerate and sexually celibate, the whole damn Rainbow Coalition. (Am I being deliberately provocative? Of course. As I am being entirely serious.)

Go out, I admonish you, all of you, hie thyselves thither, hit the streets or collar that neighbourhood kid, drum up a contact, do a deal, repair thyselves home, soften the lights, put on some music—the best stuff—pour yourself a pitcher of ice water, perhaps two, keep a tin of Altoids handy, as well as a tube of Vicks Inhalant and a couple of packs of mineral ice, make yourself comfortable, lay back and...swallow.

Swallow that pill, let it slide, feel the glide, and relax. Quiet your mind. Calm your soul. An hour from now, perhaps somewhat less, you are going to experience something you have never experienced before. You are going to experience something you will never forget. You are going to experience something that shall forever change such time as remains to you on this earth. You are going to experience something that will halve your life into before and after: BE/AE. You are going to experience something that is, every second of it, delicious—deliciously, positively, unprecedentedly w-o-n-d-e-r-f-u-l.

It is your self-anointing, and I envy you it. I envy you that first time. So relish it, savour, languish in, treasure. Consecrate it, that sacred four hours. You have just swallowed wonder, ambrosia and mead, you have partaken of lustre and grace.

Just make certain that before you swallow you know that the pill is authentic, genuine, the real deal, the goods, and not some innocuous rip-off or inimical knock-off. Do that, and the rest, as they say, is a piece of cake, a piece of cake that, in this instance, is like no other you have ever tasted. Think of the best day of your life, or recall the sweetest, purest, most special thing along the way— person, place, moment, memory, sentiment, experience, accomplishment. Got it? Now multiply that tenfold. That does not begin to describe how impossibly delicious E is.

I am not unaware of how redolent this is of Timothy Leary's often loopy proselytizing for LSD, and I know how out of step is the sort of ethos he once so widely touted—turn on, tune in, drop out—but this has nothing to do with that. Ecstasy is a clarifier. That, ultimately, is its value. That it enables one to see, feel and think, if not more deeply, then certainly more clearly. That it clears the deck of all that is unclear that one might more clearly—and immediately—experience that clarity. And not just in the moment. The high, as all highs do, subsides, but the clarity, the lucidity lingers. The residue of the *roll*.

In that sense, not to mention in its chemical composition, it is quite the opposite of LSD, which at the peak of its use came cauled— for all I know, still does; I never have used LSD and am possessed of no inclination to do so—in all sorts of religious accoutrements and connotations. (One does not, by the way, hallucinate on E, not even mildly, at least I never have. Nor does one become or perceive oneself as having become someone or something else. One remains indubitably oneself, just vastly, profoundly more so.) Ecstasy has nothing to do with religion, save to make clear to its user that such religion—the questing after something more or higher, the meaning of god and existence, the miracle of faith, call it what you will—while understandable (a whole lot is understandable on E, a lot more than is understandable off of it), is mainly nonsense. There is no need to quest, not any more, for what is being quested after is right here, right now—the birth of a state of better being.

Anonymous

Ecstasy is a clarifier, but it is a personal clarifier. It is not—despite all the peace/love/unity/respect hype surrounding it—a universal one. Its lessons may be universal in their implications, but they are intended to be applied to oneself, not to be shared with one's neighbour, friends, colleagues or community. Which is not to say that the drug does not have its social dimensions or that one ought not do E in the company of others. Indeed I would not find it congenial to do, nor have I ever done it, alone. (As close as I ever came was on an unpeopled, night-time side street in downtown London, and it was raining, and it was one of the memorable experiences of my life— neon, glistening, menthol, veneered in layer after thickening layer of thick honey. Lovely streets, London, and lovely, so lovely, its rain.)

But better by far to do it with those one loves, and best of all with one's one-and-only lover. The point is, one must do it oneself to truly 'get it'. Listening to the stories and anecdotes of others or such lessons as they may have drawn from the experience, reading an article such as this one certainly does no harm, but everyone takes from E something different, something as uniquely, idiosyncratically private as the person taking it. And if what one takes in the broadest sense is all about human connection and empathy—E has proven highly effective in certain kinds of couples therapy—it is all the more about connecting with and feeling empathy for oneself. It is, contrary to its image as the current drug of choice among teenagers and the prevalence of its use at their bacchanalian, all-night, tribal dance rites—their 'raves'—the most intimate of drugs.

I did it my first time with the woman I mentioned earlier, the one who saved me. It was her first time as well. Neither of us used or so much as experimented with illegal drugs—we typically limited ourselves to wine, beer and cigarettes, and those in moderation—and we were, as zero hour approached, visibly apprehensive, an attitude, I think, that is healthy, as it is only sane. Perhaps—who knows?—it even exaggerated the impact of what was about to occur.

It was, in our case, a pair of Calvin Kleins. EX comes in a variety of shapes, sizes, colours and brand names—Nikes, Mitsubishis, Motorolas, Versaces, Rolling Stones, etc.—thousands of types, each with their subtle distinctions with respect to the quality and length of the *roll*. I recall their being round, perhaps oblong, about the size of a Tylenol, smaller, and of some somehow comforting amber hue. As I say, I was too apprehensive to register all of the details. My heart, its thumpeting, was in the way.

We had cleared our schedules ahead of time, switched off the phones, and we were in her home, just the two of us, in our bathrobes, in the living room, on the couch—a couch, it is fit to say, with which we were by that time well acquainted. Van was on the stereo, *Astral Weeks*, *Moondance*, *Common One*, *The Best of: Volume One*. A fire was roaring in the fireplace and we were feeding it. The lamp on the end table was turned way down low. It was mid-evening, and we had ready, as my son had taken care to instruct us, our pair of tumblers and pitchers of iced-down spring water. E increases body temperature and heart rate and elevates blood pressure, so drinking water—not beer, not liquor—is pro forma as one rolls along. And one wishes to drink, because E causes dehydration—one of its most immediate side effects is dry mouth. (Interesting, because what it does to one's emotions is precisely the opposite. It lubricates them, emulsifies, one's feelings as gels and butters and lotions.)

With much mutually nervous, serio-comic, ceremonial chit-chat, then, we each popped our pill, swallowed, waited, and—nothing.

We locked eyes. We still were alive. I think we were only half amazed. I know we were relieved. Van was still belting as only Van can. If I was dying I knew that this was how I wanted to do it; I can think of worse voices to hear with one's dying breath than that of the Belfast Cowboy's wailing, 'It's too late to stop now!' as indeed at that moment it was. (The young are partial to other ways: techno, electronica, trance, jungle, house, hardcore, gabba, drum and bass, and they are not, I might suggest to those of another, older generation, to my generation, without their merits. Indeed, they constitute the very aural-assault, awash-in-the-sonics brand of music tailor-made to maximize the benefits of a certain kind of more, shall we say, kinetic experience. To each their own.)

Typically, it takes a while for Ecstasy to kick in. Thirty-five minutes is precipitous, that twice over dilatory. It depends—on the pill, mainly, but also on the contents of one's stomach (empty is better than full), on one's mood (up is better than down), on one's physical/mental state (alert is better than exhausted). So, that first time, you sit and wonder, precisely because you have the time to do so, if what is going to happen really is going to happen, and if it does, just when it may occur, and how you will know. And then it does, the *roll* begins—the world around you billows open like an eye—and you stop wondering those things. You stop on a dime and you go, or rather, are lifted and taken—coronaed, crowned, coroneted, spangled and lantern-lit, your smiling face flambeaued as a thousand chandeliers.

One of the most discernible early effects—it happened that first time, though often it does not, being a function of the chemical composition of the pill—is what I have heard described as 'fluttery' vision, but which I prefer to describe as 'staggered' or 'ratcheted' or 'toggled'. This phenomenon is as close to an hallucinatory quality as E produces, and it is so mild—and weirdly pleasant—that to label it as such is frankly inaccurate. When it happened to us we knew it immediately—that is, we knew something was going on, something…extra—and we looked at one another, smiled, and virtually in unison commented upon it. As I recall—we are both fifty years old, remember—we thought it 'cool'.

It is a little difficult to describe. One's vision does not blur, nor do images get darker or lighter, pulse, expand or contract, fragment or disintegrate, or change colour, but they do get a little, I suppose *choppy* is the word, choppy but not chopped up. That is, they remain intact and stationary—a lamp's a lamp, a window's a window, a fire's a fire—they just move a little, as if jagged were a verb, within the texture of their own lines. These striations. Very unthreatening, and very, well, cool. (Rad. Phat. Whatever.) There is bound to be a medical explanation for it, perhaps there is even a name, but I remain ignorant of such and so intend to remain.

And then suddenly Van was singing waaaaay over there, and then waaaaay inside here, right inside, ground zero, the very epicentre, the pith of my brain, pathing through, yet way outside and up above and down below and all around as well, vaulting in dips, convolving in loops, volplaning, vanplaning, brimming up, pouring forth, washing over and enveloping the room even as he filled and spanned and embraced in the spread of the swoon of his voice, the wings of its swanning, every corner and corridor and cubbyhole of the house inside my head. This capacious passing through of each and every note of his music, not only as sound, but as resonant space—particle, wave—and as I have learned since, time. And that also was. Cool.

What happened next was that everything and all at once, while clearly remaining itself, its old self, at the same time not became, but *was* its altered self, transfigured, transmogrified, a new self, a simultaneously deeper and higher, older and newer self, and so a better self—everything smoother and softer and rounder, every edge bull-nosed, every surface sanded. And warmer. Which was curious. Because it didn't feel warmer, it just looked warmer. But as much as the surroundings…bloomed, it was in myself that the blossoming burgeoned, surged, swelled, an harmonic wind of well-being, cognate and congruent, and in its passage, home—the world as nest, and as womb.

In any event, the world was suddenly guilt- and worry- and wrinkle-free, palpably, beautifully buoyant—visually, texturally, aurally—transcendently right and renewed, arresting and exquisite and sublime and glorious and divine (sometimes words are paltry things, such puny things), more of any and all of those things than I had ever thought possible. Or perhaps I had thought them possible, and perhaps that is part of the point: that whatever beautiful thing one can imagine or has ever imagined, it is that much more beautiful on E. I cannot prove this theory, and it would mean that those with more active or fecund or developed imaginations are likely to have better, more maximally beautiful experiences. Or perhaps it is simply that they are more acutely attuned to the beauty of those experiences. As I say, I cannot prove this, and I can conceive of no plausible way of doing so. (It is similar to the old conundrum about whether the more well-endowed man has the more intense orgasm. But how to measure such a thing? There is not, nor can there ever be a basis for comparison.) All the same, the proposition feels right to me.

And so we looked at one another and felt one another, with our fingers and our lips and our tongues, indeed with the whole of our new-found faces, this plumbing of the new map of our bodies—new softer hair, new smoother flesh, new pinker, fresher, more fragrant, shimmering, altogether fluffier genitalia (fluffier is precisely the word)—and we smelled and tasted one another—she smelled of burst peaches and tasted as the recent salts of pearls—because one's sense of smell and taste is no less augmented and intensified, honed and heightened than are the other senses. That is, we bathed in one another, each of our five senses, the ten in all, because that commingling is what had taken place, its rhapsody, and humanity, and caress. And as the world includes oneself, and as at that moment it included my lover, we looked to one another exactly as we felt and smelled and tasted: rapturous, heavenly, transcendent, numinous, aglow. She a resplendent, bejewelled goddess, I a radiant god. 'Their eyes came open into the soul of the other,' Don DeLillo once wrote of a kindred experience, the 'flow of time'. That, in so many words, is, to a very serif, how it was.

Later, if still in midstream, I got up, walked to the bathroom—walking on E is no more difficult than walking on water or floating on air—and looked in the mirror. I wanted to see what I looked like—I am just vain enough that the thought occurred to me even in the midst of the *roll*—though I already had seen reflected in my lover's eyes that I looked sufficiently, there is no other word, gorgeous. (If I looked half as gorgeous as she did to me I reckoned I was in for a treat.) And the person I saw looking back at me was, gorgeous, but gorgeous in a way that floored almost as much as it thrilled me.

As I have mentioned, I am almost fifty years old, and here, now, as I stared grinning in astonishment, I looked twenty-eight. And not some fifty-year-old version of myself at twenty-eight, but me the way I was back then, back when, when I was twenty-eight. I moved closer, peered harder. I could scarcely believe it. I had recaptured myself. Dorian Gray. Fountain of Youth. Foods of the Gods. Spontaneous regeneration. Metempsychosis. Somehow I had been restored, and I felt what I can only describe as an all-consuming nostalgia for the present.

And then, after helping each other off with our bathrobes, our old, nubby, cotton-twill bathrobes—suddenly spun of the finest cashmere and angelica, these clouds of talcum and down—we embraced, and kissed, and more, we got down, as is said, and as used to be said, to business, and she whispered in my ear: 'We've found fucking gold.'

It distinctly was not an out-of-the-body experience, as it was not a mind-expanding one.

It distinctly was a further-into-the-body experience, and a mind-clarifying one. An impenetrably penetrating experience. An excavation of the self. An exhumation of the other. Because that is how one finds gold—one exhumes it, excavates, one digs for it, deep, and deeper.

And so we did. We dug. For four hours we dug, sinking further into each other, as likewise into ourselves, and eventually, after four hours of digging, digging that was in its every decline mutually synchronized, after four hours that felt exactly like forty minutes—for on E, unlike, say, on grass, time flies, sails by, condensed, abbreviated, attenuated and tremendously foreshortened—we found it. Only it wasn't gold. It was something far better. It was sex, the very EX in sex—and the climb and climax of sex—as revelation. And as soul.

So I take it back. Maybe Ecstasy does have something to do with religion, although the word spirit seems to me a more felicitous fit, because the peace one feels, and the insights one gains—epiphanies may be a better word—are no less than oceanic. They are tidal, as they are catholic. You know, afterwards, that you contain oceans, oceans you previously had but the faintest inkling existed, and that those oceans are filled with beauty and grace and light and love—more words, bankrupt words—and that they are yours, yours to share as it may please and delight you.

And this, I might argue, is not a bad thing. Indeed it is so much the opposite of a bad thing that I believe it is worth the cost of that which one must pay to purchase it. Because there is a cost, that cost is high, it is as expensive as it is extravagant, and much like the experience itself, it is one which varies with each occasion as it fluctuates with each person who encounters that dark piper.

The simple truth is, when you eat Ecstasy, you are deliberately messing with your mind, or more accurately your brain, or more accurately still your brain chemistry. You are releasing, in a rush, as a deluge or monsoon—and that rush is unnatural, unnatural in the sense that had God intended you to experience it it would not require a flock of white-coated 'cookers' in a clandestine laboratory someplace in Holland or Israel or France to design and customize a pill for you to do so, nor would the delivery and distribution of those pills so lavishly profit the Mob—you are, as I say, triggering a veritable tsunami of serotonin, the human body's pleasure juice, that in turn floods in the most sensory, sentient way your consciousness, which in turn turns everything 'gold', or rather, golden. (Again, there is available—there always is—an exact, physiological explanation of the phenomenon and the anatomical circuitry and neural pathways involved, and again I have no interest in pursuing it. Why demystify what is in its sum, if not its parts, so mystical?) And in the wake of that rush—not the day after perhaps, when you are still basking, deliciously exhausted in its afterglow (albeit that a deep, sub-muscular, burning neck, shoulder and back discomfort often compromise it), but the day after that, or the next, or the next, what I have heard described as 'Black Tuesday'—you run the risk not only of emotionally crashing, but of feeling so rawly depleted (because your tank of serotonin is running on no more than fumes), that you are tempted to pledge, 'I have never felt this awful in my life, as empty, hollowed, flat, so soulless and lost to myself, so amputated and abscissed, so emotionally exsanguinated, and I shall never, not ever, do this again.' And also, 'Whatever was I thinking?'

My advice, for what it is worth: wait a minimum of four weeks, the time purportedly required for one's serotonin to refill its reservoir and your thoughts and feelings to sort themselves through and get up and running again, before repeating the performance. Do it more often than that, get too greedy, and the upshot is 'E-tardism'—a trimming down, clipping-off and curbing of the drug's effects, not to mention possible long-term damage to the serotonergic nerve grid of the brain, damage of the sort that may leave you so addled, you will find it not only a full-time challenge to control your own drool, but to recall that words are composed of letters and that each represents an actual sound, one intended to be pronounced aloud. So: moderation in all things, even things that are excessively restorative, for on occasion, cures do kill.

But here is the Catch-22 with which one inevitably must grapple, or at least I did, and still do: what one thinks—if one stops to think about it—is precisely this: 'What is a mind, if not something to be messed with? What is consciousness, if not a state to be altered?' I mean this quite seriously, quite literally, and if it helps to substitute for the phrase 'messed with' the word 'clarified' or 'purified' or 'alchemized' or 'beautified' or 'beatified' then perhaps my meaning is taken. A mind is a terrible thing to waste, and there is much being wasted when one deliberately chooses not to explore the ecstasy of its deeper horizons.

'Everyone is doing the best he can to keep the dark/from climbing over his back,' Charlie Smith writes in his brilliant new collection of poems, *Heroin*. 'Life should be ecstasy,' Allen Ginsberg told an interviewer before his death. They are right. In our way, we are all doing our best to dodge the dark while clearing a space where a little ecstasy might be permitted to bloom. I am only suggesting that our best can be still better, and that there exists this way of making it so, and that it is ours for the literal taking.

Perhaps there are those who feel no need to do so, to experience such ecstasy, that they are blessed with a sufficiency of it in their daily lives. Perhaps there are those who feel that such ecstasy, because it is 'unnatural', induced artificially, chemically, 'under the influence', cannot possibly be 'existentially authentic', and must therefore be false, a fraud and a lie, and that it cannot possibly be sustained. Perhaps there are those who suspect that the disparity is too great, that having experienced such ecstasy, they will find it too daunting to endure the rigours and asperities of a mundane, largely prosaic, often overwhelmingly corrupt and ugly world. Perhaps there are those who feel that such ecstasy cannot be reconciled with their religious, political, philosophical or domestic agendas, that it threatens or violates the very essence of that in which they are so wholly invested. Perhaps there are those who are reluctant to risk engaging in what our culture defines as socially unacceptable, even legally transgressive behaviour. Perhaps there are those who are afraid of footing the physical and emotional toll, or of becoming psychologically addicted. And perhaps there are those who simply, unapologetically, are flat-out scared. Scared of beauty. And of bliss.

There are such people, and they are most people, almost all people, and they have every right to their feelings and beliefs, values and convictions. They are, after all, but the sum of having lived lives that are unimaginable to any of us but those who have honourably lived them. I know, because I was, for most of my own, one of them.

I am not any more, one of them. I am not one of anything. I

am, trite as it may sound, simply me, and here lately, that is more than enough. It is plenty. And there is something else, a secret: there are times, once a month, sometimes more or less, when the truth of that makes me, well, ecstatic.

My son? He is nineteen now, and in his spare time—having some months ago kicked the Ecstasy habit himself—he spins mixes at raves, and this fall he is entering college, quite a reputable college, as a Psychology major. And he is writing poetry again. Brilliant stuff, more brilliant than ever. This righting of his ship, and the compass of its course.

Minor triumphs perhaps. Still, it does make one wonder. Would he have made it back intact without E? Would he have arrived at that which all of us deserve and so few manage to find, his chance for happiness? And it makes one wonder, too, you know, about what they say: Better living through chemistry.  □

GRANTA

# UNDER THE SURFACE

Andrew Brown

L illa Edet was so quiet a town that the first summer I lived there I learned to distinguish the smells of different trees. There were distinct scents of pine, of spruce, and of the birches whose pollen made tears run down my face.

When I cycled to the square in the centre of the town the creaking of the wheels was the loudest sound. Opposite the school buildings in which nothing seemed ever to happen there was a wide dusty verge between the asphalt road and a meadow where wild flowers grew on tall coarse stems. On this strip, magpies hopped and hoodie crows shuffled among the dust and stone chips. I never saw what they ate nor heard a songbird.

In that dry and dusty time I seemed to be cycling everywhere, either to the library, or to the lakes in the forests that surround the town. There is never enough water in my memories of southern Sweden. For three months of the year it was all frozen anyway. But even in summer, the thin soil always seemed dry; the brown pine needles that nestled in every crevice of the rocks were dry and sharp as weathered bones. So to look at the lakes, and to breathe their damp exhalations, was a kind of healing. I didn't have to catch anything; and not always even to fish. What I needed was to gaze into the surface, and, by gazing, to pass into another world, and breathe.

In town, the library was always cool, and smelled of plastic and modernity. I borrowed books about chess, which were easy to read because they were written in clichés when not in algebraic notation; comic books about a cowboy, translated from the French, which taught me more varied and idiomatic Swedish; and most of all a copy of Brian Clarke's *Pursuit of Stillwater Trout*, or *På jakt efter Stillavattens Öring*. I learned it by heart. If you had said to me any sentence in that book, I could have come up with the preceding one as well as the successor. The promise of fly-fishing was that the world I pressed against when I looked at a lake would be deeper and richer than anything I had yet imagined. I wanted to break through there. I loved the illustrations of water beasts that garnished his text. There were delicate line drawings of damselfly nymphs, which are, despite their name, incessantly voracious and shaped like rapiers with a long pointed tail and a short head like an elaborate hilt. There were veiled sedge pupae swimming towards the surface, their legs and wings all bundled up in a transparent membrane; and dangly midge larvae, feathery at each end, twisting as they wait for trout to seize them. These fabulous monsters peopled my imagination. Some have remained fabulous to this day. I still have never seen a sedge pupa that looks remotely like anything in any book.

It is a rather dogmatic book, written loudly, as if to break through to an inattentive and self-confident audience. I read it as an exercise at first, and then again and again with increasing concentration as a kind of Zen text, until the words clattered around inside my head like the blades of a helicopter that could lift me high above the valley. I had no fly rod then and there were no trout in the nearby lakes. But my course was set, even though I went on fishing for pike and perch with spinners of every shape I could afford.

The countryside round the town has been combed by glaciers from north to south. Parallel valleys ran through the granite; in the deepest and broadest of these, by the side of Lilla Edet, ran the huge Göta river which drains Lake Vänern, one of the largest in Europe; in the hills to the east, lay a chain of deep, clear lakes. They were clearer than they should have been, because of the acid rain. The furthest upstream was in fact completely dead: you could see thirty or forty feet into depths coated with white algal slime. Nothing else lived to cloud the water. But two lakes down the chain, by the bathing place for Lilla Edet, was a lake whose depths were still a deep humus colour, whose margins were full of water lilies and whose weed beds were full of pike.

Last century, in Finland, farmers were so poor they ate roach. Bream were a popular, or common, food in rural Sweden; there are poems and songs about catching them in their spawning time—they cannot at any rate taste as bad as roach. Perch were and remain a delicacy, found in the best fish restaurants. But when I was poor and hungry, I ate pike.

The hardware shop in town sold red and white plastic floats for perch fishing: sturdy, buoyant devices which even the most determined perch found hard to pull under. But I hated worms, and switched to spinning as soon as I could. Three or four days a week, I would cycle up the vicious dusty hill that led into the woods just east of Lilla Edet. I had a solid fibreglass rod around five feet long, mineral green with white streaks in it, whose brass-wire rod rings were lashed on with lumpy twine. With it came a closed-face reel from which stiff coils of twenty-pound line sprang out. The outfit cost the equivalent of twelve pounds, which meant I could afford to change the line to something limper and less frightening.

Much of the lake was inaccessible. The eastern shore fell out of the forest in a broken line of granite cliffs ten or twenty feet high and a mile long. It could only be approached by boat. At each end, it was cut off from the rest of the shore by the bogs and streamlets which linked the chain of lakes. But the accessible, western side of the lake was rounded, and scalloped with bays between seamed granite promontories. Within the seams were drifts of crunchy pine needles, but most of the granite was barren except for lichen. On hot days the beautiful desolate scent of pine clung to my fingers. There were paths through the forest for part of the way round, but they ran some distance from the water. If I wanted to fish, I stood on granite. Often I was the only person there; perhaps the only human for a mile. If I caught one fish, it was supper for all of us. Fishing was the only way I could contribute anything to the economy of my girlfriend's family. She was working in the paper mill; but I could not get a work permit. I could have left her to get on with her life. Instead I stayed with her in her father's house, and went fishing.

It was almost always a waste of time to cast straight out. The water there was four or five metres deep. The fish were in the warm shallow margins, sheltered by the lily pads. Plugs were difficult to cast and expensive, so I used spoons: the Swedish firm ABU made perhaps twenty different types of pike spoon in those days, in six or seven colourings and weights. It was enough to build a whole speculative universe around, like a fly box, except that spinning was more tactile. I could feel the different ways each lure moved in the water, and spent the hours when nothing bit working out patiently which speed seemed to bring the lure most to life. In the end, I settled on a fluttering, leaf-like motion, using an Atom spoon called 'perch-coloured', with one side copper and the other green and black dots mingled in stripes like a test for colour blindness; the larger sizes had a short red plastic tag at the rear which seemed to make a difference. Even through that terrible rod, I could feel the twittering of the lure, and could tell the difference between the knocks of a perch and the sudden irreversible haul of a pike.

Very few fish that bit at all escaped. I kept my hooks meticulously sharpened, with a hunter's instinct, and these were simple pike. There are lakes in Sweden where no other species of fish is found, and the Hobbesian war of all against all is complete. Ours was not so savage, but the pike were still overcrowded and voracious. Every lily bed held some. Except on the hottest and stillest days, there was always at least one pike that could be teased or cajoled into striking. Most were not large: they could be coiled, decapitated, into the largest saucepan in the house. Really large ones were fried in fillets.

I cooked them with as much variety as I could, but the struggle was an uphill one. In rural Sweden, potatoes marked the culinary seasons. The gradations involved were subtle: at all times of year, potatoes were eaten with every meal; and they were always boiled in their skins. But in summer you ate new potatoes peel and all; at some stage as the autumn wore in, you reverted to peeling them at the table before eating them. Mashed potatoes were available but only as a delicacy, from the hot dog stand. It took me some months to learn the knack of peeling a scalding potato on the end of a fork; my girlfriend's father concluded from this that I was almost feeble-minded.

Some days, when Anita was working the early shift at the mill, I would rise with her rather than stay in the house, and cycle at once to the lake in the hills. The last portion of the ride was downhill, through a meadow, and if I was early enough the mist would still be thick across it, so that, one day, everything above my waist was gilded in the pale sunlight, and everything below choked and muffled in white. I freewheeled, as if I were flying through clouds above the surly bonds of earth. That day was bright and still, with the forest calm as a church. I caught nothing.

As the summer wore on, I fished and bicycled with a fierce devotion. As well as the bathing lake, there were others on the western bank of the river, further away, holding the promise of novelty, but their banks were too densely forested and boggy to be fishable at all. I don't want to overestimate the wildness of these woods: they were logged regularly and broken by frequent smallholdings. Nonetheless, it would have been possible to travel from our end of Sweden to Lapland without ever leaving the forest except to cross roads; a couple of years later, a pack of six wolves was tracked from Russia, through Finland and Swedish Lapland, and then for a further thousand miles down the spine where Sweden and Norway are joined until one of them broke off, headed further south, and killed a sheep in a field just outside the town.

There were no such excitements in the pike summer. The whole world narrowed down to Lilla Edet. One day, Anita's mother took us both for a drive around the coast, which was only ten miles away. There are granite islands crumbled into the sea all down the Swedish west coast. Years later I would have a mystical experience there fishing for sea trout, going weightless in the sunset. But that day's drive, though much less dramatic, was just as overwhelming. The islands are joined by some of the longest road bridges in the world which make zooming catenary swoops across the sea. I felt drunk for a week until the new horizons faded.

From Lilla Edet, you could only look north and south to the next bends in the great Göta river. The sides of the valley rose like forested walls, cutting off the horizon, though the eastern side of the river was tamer, with a wider strip of fields. About five miles north of the town, a broad and sluggish tributary joined the Göta; and at its mouth I lost two spinners and had a tremendous tussle with a large fish which also escaped. This was playing for stakes too high. I returned to the smaller lakes in the enclosing hills.

Anita's father had few friends in the town. He and his wife had been pillars of the local Pentecostal church and temperance society until she ran off with an alcoholic they were trying to reform. Only one family would still speak to either of them after the scandal, and these good Samaritans were foreigners, half-Danish. They lent us their rowing boat, and I would use it to explore the hidden, southern arm of the bathing lake. One blazing afternoon I rowed Anita round a headland we had never passed on foot, and entered a long channel. At the end was a broad, reedy bay, a place where pike were bound to flourish. Rounded granite like a whale's flank slid into the water at the mouth of the bay. We drifted in a perfect silence until the bottom of the boat crunched gently on the rock. Once we had climbed out, silence surrounded us again. We might have been on an island: the hissing of the line as I cast, the splash of the lure, and the gentle grinding of the reel's gears as I retrieved were all sharp-edged, framed by the silence.

'We could get married,' I said. She rolled a cigarette of Norwegian tobacco and smoked it carefully. The silence held us like a mother. We returned that night with our sleeping bags and a bottle of sour Italian wine. We lit a fire of dead pine branches on the rock and ate grilled sausages for a treat. The subject was not mentioned again. We slept deeply on the uneven rock.

Mornings by the lake the whole world felt enamelled in perfection. The water would be absolutely still, and the mist would trap the metallic smell of the water and the pungency of the reeds. Slowly the mist would curl away, like sheepskin being torn from a mirror, leaving nothing but clarity. It was very cold. All the stiffness of the night would rush on to me as I awoke and struggled out of the sleeping bag to make coffee. Every sound was distinct; even the noise the water made as it swirled into the coffee kettle when I pushed it under the lake. You might find the most delicate evidences of rebirth: the shucks of dragonflies and once, lying at the edge of our rock, where the forest began, the whitish translucent skin of an adder. I suppose what Adam and Eve missed most, after they had left the garden, was a world without other people in it.

We returned and ate lunch with her father: boiled pike with dill and new potatoes. About a fortnight later, as we were digging the vegetable patch, she said, 'You're right. We could get married.'

And for many years the silence was our friend, until it became our prison, and I started to feel as dried and empty as a snakeskin: by that time, we were living in our own small house in the woods, a little beyond where the wolves had been. When I went fishing later, I would drive for hours to find lakes where I could fish for trout. In fact I don't think I have ever caught or eaten pike since, but even now, twenty years later, I still buy the grey, recycled products of the Edet paper mill, to the horror of my present wife.

# Trout

I did not catch a trout on a fly for two years after I first read Brian Clarke's book. But one September morning I crunched through the icy margins of a lake while the night was still thinning into a grey mist. By the time the bulging red sun had pulled itself above the pine forest across the water, I was balanced on a broad round boulder. The forest warmed and started to exhale distinct savours of spruce and pine: trout swirled outside a reed bed fifteen metres away.

It took about three hours to catch one, doing everything by the book. When I had landed it, I killed it with a rock and afterwards there was a puddle of cold dark blood on the lapel of my tweed jacket that I was never able to remove. I liked killing things a great deal, just as I liked walking through forests on my own and sheltering under trees when rainstorms caught me. These things made me part of the world I had escaped to. I was twenty-four. I had a job, a wife, a child and a car, and these achievements mattered; but it seemed to me that they all derived from the man I became in the woods.

I did not fly-fish any more that year. The lakes shut at the end of September; and as the month ended and the shortening of the days accelerated I would become oppressed by the idea that the earth was not spinning, but rolling like a gigantic ball, so that we on its shoulders were being rolled inexorably, day by day, towards the darkness and the frozen sludge and out of breathable air.

We had moved south from Lilla Edet to a purpose-built suburb of Göteborg: about 2,000 flats arranged in low concrete blocks the colour of dog turds on a glacial plain by the river. Nödinge was a wretched kind of prosperity. Everything was solidly built and generously equipped. Though we lived in what would in England have been a council flat, we had a freezer and two different sorts of fridge built into the kitchen. The walls of the flat were grey wallpaper on concrete: if you wanted to hang paintings or anything else to individualize them only special hooks would do. They were fixed to the wall by three thick needles set in a plastic disc, which had to be hammered in. When the time came to remove them, they had to be pulled off with pliers, leaving three neat puncture wounds that never bled at all.

Faced with all this sterile silence my hair grew ragged and my beard grew melancholy; when I walked to the shops, some of the children would call 'Jesus' after me. I thought more fiercely about fly-fishing when I heard these voices, imagining cool water. In winter

Andrew Brown

I lived still further in my imagination. The lakes would freeze over in mid-December, and seldom thawed before April. I studied magazine photographs with blinding yearning until they almost felt like real water. I read Brian Clarke again and again as if the words could helicopter me there.

Deep every winter, when the cold really squeezed, we would be pushed into a new world where everything outside became as lurid and frozen as the weather inside me. The change was announced by sudden metallic booms resounding through the house a little before midnight. This happened whenever the temperature fell to minus thirty and the concrete and girders of the flats shrank in loud convulsive shudders.

After those warnings, I would dress with special care the next morning, putting on long underpants, then jeans, and then a set of overalls when I got up at 5.30. Immediately I had struggled into all these clothes the flat was hot and itchy, but as soon as I pushed shut the door with a scrape and a click and started down the outside staircase the air felt spiky to breathe, as if it were full of pine needles that caught in my throat, and there was a numbness and tingling on the front of my thighs as I walked across the car park. Such nights were very still. The sky was black as oil: beneath it was the flare of sodium lights on snow. Noises all seemed as close as the hair on my legs. Below about minus twenty sump oil thickens suddenly and batteries grow weak. First the car must be unlocked: this meant heating the key with a lighter, and then squirting special oil into the lock. Everything was done in thick gloves. The key would fall, and have to be scooped carefully from the snow. Inside the car felt even colder and darker than the world outside and my steaming breath froze on everything. All the lights and the fan must be turned off to save precious electricity before trying to start. I learned to listen for every undertone in the hoarse thin scraping of the starter motor, and the convulsive heaving as the engine was turned over. After the engine started—if it started—I would have to wait about ten minutes while the car warmed enough to thaw the windscreen completely. Otherwise I would be blinded as soon as I started to drive, as my breath froze opaquely all over the inside of a windscreen suddenly chilled by the onrushing air outside.

The memory of those mornings is the most painful and poignant of all I have from Sweden. I don't know why. They did not make me miserable or even unhappy at the time. The cold just put up a new series of obstacles that had to be overcome, and seemed to make the chores take twice as long. But they seem to me now to have been a kind of grand theatre, as if the whole planet had been hurled into winter just to demonstrate what sadness in the bone is like. That solitary, still, inverted world where the sky was black and the ground a flaring yellow recurs to me like a nightmare.

The deep chill would not long survive daylight. By half past nine the temperature would have risen to fifteen or twenty below. Such cold demanded cloudless skies and a pale deistic sun. The curious inversion of brightness persisted: the broad flat valley would fill with half-glimpsed sparkles in the snow so that the ground seemed brighter than the sky by day just as it had at night. The smells of the world had not entirely vanished. Close up the factory still smelled of sweet and acrid sawdust; of the pale machine oil of the nail guns and of gritty diesel from the forklift trucks.

I call it a factory but it was only a large converted barn in which four or five of us made the pallets on which Volvo marine diesel motors were shipped around the world. There had been an element of deception in the way I got the job: the interview was conducted around the back of one of the forklift trucks, whose unsilenced diesel exhaust pipe rattled away between us. Both Leif, the owner and I were wearing hearing protectors. When I could hear what he was saying, I probably gave the wrong answers. When I couldn't or when I failed to understand his questions, I just nodded and grinned enthusiastically and he heard the right ones. It's a bit like catching fish on a metal lure, which is most effective when it is not a detailed model of a small fish but an almost two-dimensional abstract that wiggles with exaggerated clumsiness. You allow the pike to see what it wants and expects and he does the rest. The language the fishermen speak to their prey is wholly deceptive. Between humans, things are more complicated. Leif expected and wanted a fit young man who could speak reasonable Swedish. I was neither, but after three or four months there I had become the prey he thought he'd seized.

We worked from half past six in the morning till nine; from half past nine till half past twelve; from one till three-thirty. For the first six weeks of the job, conversation was not a problem. I would stuff my face with sandwiches for fifteen minutes, and then fall asleep, my head propped on my hand, for the remaining fifteen minutes of the breakfast break. Then I would fall asleep at lunch, and again on the bus back to Nödinge and finally lie on the concrete floor of our living room, beside the cloth-covered cardboard box that served as a coffee table, and there fall asleep again. At the end of six weeks I had expected to be sacked, but I was not. Shortly thereafter, I found that I could stay awake from morning until bedtime. Within three months the job was no longer physically impossible at all. It remained physically demanding: even on the coldest days I could work in a T-shirt after the first hour because there was so much heat coming off my body. Every movement had become a sort of dance step, though I worked in clogs: there was a quickest and least exhausting way to shoot in every nail and not a day went past without my chasing it.

The timber was delivered in two-ton bundles six or eight metres long from the sawmill. These had to be sawed down into usable lengths and stacked on ordinary pallets; some had to be further sawn into V-shaped supports for the engine's transmission. This sawing was easy work. At first it was done by a Finn who drank fourteen or fifteen cans of weak beer a day while he worked. I don't remember ever seeing him doing anything else but pissing against the outside of the barn by the far door and smoking fat crooked roll-ups. But between these breaks he sawed five tons of wood a day, beneath his sour miasma of sweat and cheap beer. He kept this up, day after day, winter and summer, for the first eighteen months I worked there, until he finally sank beneath the beer and found himself unable to get up in the mornings. Leif sacked him. The whole factory depended on the sawman.

The rest of us—three or four people for most of the two years I worked there—had to take this sawn wood and nail it together into pallets. The five types we made differed in the sort of detail that emerges only from the most grinding monotony. I remember vividly only the first I was told to make: it was the heaviest the factory built, and the one that required least skill. There were six planks in the base, held together by two thick feet; two thick pine blocks for engine supports, an inch-thick crosspiece where the transmission rested, four side-pieces nailed into a frame, and two little reinforcing bits. It was all nailed together; the noise in the barn was like continual gunfire as these nails were banged in by three different types of compressed air guns. Each gun weighed two kilos, and had to be concealed from close inspection by the health and safety people, because we had lightened the triggers on them so they could be pulled at arm's length. I only shot myself twice in two years, when the nail hit a knot in the wood I was steadying and twisted into my hand.

A fully assembled pallet weighed forty-seven kilos, or a little over a hundredweight. I had to make seventy-two of them every two days, in nine stacks of eight: the highest flung up to about head height before the whole stack was lashed together with wire tape and dragged out by a forklift truck. One day would be spent nailing the sub-assemblies together: seventy-two right-hand posts; seventy-two left-hand posts; seventy-two frames and seventy-two plank bottoms. Each had to be fixed together with a precisely specified number of nails, placed in precisely specified ways. Every day I fired around 2,000 nails into the wood, trying to place each one exactly where I had fired uncountable predecessors; every day the only break in this monotony came from trying to do everything a little faster than the day before. 'You should start at full speed, and then get steadily faster', I was advised was the trick of it.

I never really grew strong enough for the work. I was willing enough, and outlasted fifteen or twenty young Swedes whose attitude of sullen entitlement and resentment sat oddly with their enormous, well-fed bodies. One, I remember, lifted weights for a hobby, but thought it demeaning to exert himself outside the gym or for an employer. But alongside Leif and his foreman Rolf, two men in their forties who had done hard physical work every day of their lives, I would simply run out of strength. When I tried to work ten hours a day, to save for a car, I found I could make no more pallets than when I worked eight. Shifting three and a half tons of wood every day was my limit.

It was this physical incapacity that drove me back to Brian Clarke. When the demand for marine diesels grew in Australia beyond the rate at which I could build crates for them, Rolf would be transferred to that job for a few days and I would saw out for him the V-shaped cut-outs on which the transmission rested. The wood for this was thick and unplaned, with a rough splintery surface like flattened chicken skin. That observation more or less exhausted its interest. I would mark a V on 500 pieces with a pencil: the act reduced to five movements, over and over again as I shifted the stacks from a pallet to my left to one on my right. Then I would feed them into the bandsaw. Little buttocks of sawdust puffing up each side of the blade as I pushed the wood over the sleek steel table. Shrieking and screaming from the blade pressed through my hearing protectors. Pull it back. Turn it round. Press it against the blade once more until the resistance eased for a moment with a sudden clunk. Pull back smartly, and swat away the discarded triangle into a waste crate; in the same movement lift and stack the new V piece. Swivel left. Pick up another, do it again. Inside, my mind ran round in circles, screaming. This work was not particularly exhausting. It demanded about half my attention to keep up to speed. The rest was fixed on water, on a cool pewtery surface between water lilies that would stir as something rustled against their stems.

To this day, when I think of the bandsaw, I see the chipped steel housing of the motor, a thin metallic blue; and behind it the bare pale planking of the factory wall. From the ceiling hang black electric power lines to the machinery, and the air hoses for nail guns in parabolas like jungle vines. I hear the bandsaw ringing, the banging of the guns, and even the accordion music, fanged and slimy, writhing from the radio speaker above my head. But all these things seem foggy, as they were at the time, because they stood between me and the lake, which shone through them.

In the busy banging solitude of the factory I taught myself to write English. It was my language but I rarely spoke it then. I worked in Swedish, I was married in Swedish; I thought and dreamed in Swedish too: it's still the language in which I think of fishing technicalities. But I still read mostly English books, and I wanted to become an English writer. The first thing I bought when we got married was an ancient office typewriter with its base machined from solid brass, which went on an old desk borrowed from Anita's younger sister. I knew nothing about myself and very little about the world so it was hard to find a subject. But as I worked with the planks, hauling and banging, and building the boxes, phrases would appear to me. If they were good I grabbed the thick pencil used for marking wood and scribbled them on the cardboard dividers from the cases of nails. This allowed me one good fragment for every 500 nails I fired in. When I came home, the breast pocket of my overalls might have half a dozen of these bits inside it: sawdust would fall from the seams as I pulled the cardboard strips out and placed them beside the typewriter.

## Springtime

Deep winter is curiously easy to endure. The shortest days of the year in December are much better lit than the longer days to come, first by the candlelight Lucia processions, and then by Christmas and the New Year sales, which let shop windows blaze and make even the saddest towns look cosy after night falls at half past three in the afternoon. But in February the days lengthen so quickly you can feel it and you know that tomorrow will cast a clearer light on the landscape of slush and frozen, rutted mud which thaws a little every afternoon and then refreezes every night.

The thaw is never silent. Our flat in Nödinge had an aluminium railing on the walkway outside, about three feet from the kitchen window, and the measured plinking sound of water dripping on it as the snow melted from the roof was the most agonizing thing I had ever heard in my life for the six weeks that I listened to it. In later years I learned not to listen, but the first spring I could hear a whole country unfreezing, drip by drip, all day. The first few days, I thought the ringing of the balcony rail meant that spring had arrived. But every night, the snow refroze and the thaw must start again. For the next three weeks, I thought each plink must mean that spring was on its way. But every night the thaw refroze, and spring retreated further. For the last fortnight or so I believed that every plink was telling me that spring would never come. Finally came a day when all the snow had retreated, leaving patches of bare unfrozen dirt. I walked for half an hour up into the hills behind Nödinge, where the map showed a lake, carrying my spinning rod, wearing a black leather bomber jacket against the wind, burning for a fish. When I got there, the lake turned out to be little more than a pond, but very hard to miss—the only pale thing in the landscape among the bare brown hills, dirty blue and green still frozen solidly.

I went back almost every day for a week, unable to believe that it could stay frozen. I was perhaps a little mad. Most days I carried my rod and a tin of spinners. Sometimes I would tie on the heaviest spinner I owned and hurl it on to the ice in the hope of breaking through. Sometimes I would throw rock at the ice instead. One afternoon it rained for hours, solid wonderful rain after months of sleet and snow; there was a boisterous wind, and the next day the ice was a jostling crumble heaving on the waves against the lee shore. I cast for about an hour, certain the fish would greet the open water as ecstatically as I did. My fingers grew very cold. I walked home chilled and fishless, filled with a kind of grim confidence of final victory, like Churchill in the Battle of Britain.

# Cod fishing

The summer that followed was a time of extraordinary profusion. I no longer needed to fish for pike—we felt rich—but one blazing day Leif took us out on his boat into the archipelago of granite shoals and skerries that extends for miles beyond the coast. Summer in the west coast is like a carnival that goes on all the way to Norway. Everything floats in a light like mercury. The red-walled wooden houses look as buoyant and carefree as tents. The granite looks gentle as crumpled paper; it is toasty and gentle under bare feet. There aren't really any beaches. Swimming is done from rocks and boats; but owning a boat was as natural as owning a car; perhaps more so, for the people who lived near the coast. Leif's boat was magnificent, towering twice the height of a man where it rested, most of the year, swathed in tarpaulins on a trailer outside the barn. Somewhere around the end of May he would run it down to the sea behind the lorry with which he normally delivered pallets. In a fiercely egalitarian culture which hated ostentation or any sort of nonconformity, boats were the only sort of boasting that was allowed and approved. He would work more on it half the summer, then by August it would be ready for showing off.

The day he took his workers out in it for a day's fishing the others used hand lines, with heavy silvery jigs, almost the size of a fist. I had bought a spinning rod, probably Anita's, loaded with coarse line. At the little seafront supermarkets in every hamlet up and down the coast you could buy cod lures stamped from painted tinplate with a piece of lead the size of a finger welded down one side. They were extremely cheap, since they were designed to be hurled into the seaweed, where they often snagged. That's what happened to mine, anyway. But when they didn't catch the bottom, they caught fish.

Leif motored out for about an hour in his huge boat and we lounged until he had anchored by two low skerries, a few miles into the archipelago. I cast towards these rocks and let the spoon flutter back in an arc just above the seabed, sinking as it came towards the boat. It was needless craft. The fish grabbed everything and we hauled until our arms ached and our necks burned from the sun. There were cod, ling, saithe, wrasse and others whose names no one knew or cared. They were fish. All were killed, until the five blue plastic buckets on the deck were overflowing with variegated corpses, pale, dulled, and finally smelly.

Leif and Rolf had no conception of fishing for sport. They belonged to the old Sweden, where you warred with nature for everything; and when it showed weakness, you harvested until your arms ached and the light off the salt sea struck headaches from your skull. When I came home with my carrier bags, sick from killing and sunstroke, I had thirty-four fish in them, most of them ballan wrasse, which have a curious pouched stomach that makes them almost impossible to gut. Also, they taste like fermented mud, even when they are very fresh. I stood at the sink for nearly two hours, dragging my knife through the toughening flesh, and tugging out handfuls of smelly intestines with my fingers. There were two carrier bags full of guts before I gave up and threw the rest of the fish, ungutted, into the last bag. It was August: the rubbish was collected in a room at the very far end of our block of flats, and three storeys down, so the smell was still tolerable immediately outside our flat five days later, when the binmen came. I hoped very much that none of the people in the flats closer to the rubbish chute knew I was a fisherman.

For much of that summer, I was not. There were other purposes to life. We bought a car. We visited England. Even so, I remember vividly only one thing that did not happen by a lake: we were driving through a dusty forest in southern Lapland when Anita asked me to pull over. She opened the passenger door, leaned out, and was neatly and quietly sick by the side of the road. 'Drive on,' she said. I thought she had eaten a bad mushroom until a few days later she told me it was morning sickness.

# Autumn

Fishing anywhere is a form of enquiry. The patient watchful wonder of the fisherman seems to me the root of all science. In sea fishing this mapping, and bringing of order from the formless shifting waves is especially ambitious. Attention broods over the water like the spirit in Genesis, moving, casting, until suddenly all the possibilities are narrowed into one taut line. Perhaps this explains why I have always sought the sea at times of upset and disturbance in my life. The fish comes like an answer, the rod in my hand a divining instrument.

A couple of years after the expedition on Leif's boat I started cod fishing again, on my own, from the shore, in the autumn. The lakes inland would close around the middle of September and even those that did not could seem to be in the grip of a cold grey evening all through an October day. Even the berries were fading then as if the last scraps of colour were being scraped off the earth in its descent into winter. Only by the black-and-dark-green sea was there a sense of life. I had a rod well suited to the crude ferocity of my pursuit: a thick blue fibreglass pole with ugly ceramic rings that would hurl a forty gram lure into the dusk so far I could hardly see it splash into the water. I fished off rocks and round the edge of car parks; the view in front was pretty ugly too. I looked for sites with a deep current close to land and kept my eyes fixed on the water in front of me. It didn't matter if there were an oil refinery or a chemical plant across the bay. The water had for me the same kind of importance as music; and I heard music all the time, by a feat of will. I could not afford a radio or cassette for the car: to have one seemed to me as out of reach as possessing a credit card. But I learned to memorize music as I had once memorized Brian Clarke, so that as the winter night fell over the road, I would hear over and over again a fragment of a Steely Dan song, a descending piano figure and a sprightly bass: 'If I had my way, I would move/to another lifetime'.

I wasn't interested in the sporting quality of the fish. In my experience cod feed like vacuum cleaners and put up as much struggle as Hoover bags. But their skin was delicately dappled in all the colours that were disappearing in the winter on land, brown and green and silver; and they tasted delicious. This mattered because the food value of my catch had again become an important consideration in where I fished. I had stopped work at the factory after selling a couple of articles to English magazines. We lived precariously on Anita's earnings as a trainee nurse and what I could earn as a journalist and teaching English at night classes, though I spent most of my time looking after little Felix in the deep loneliness of the forest. We had left the dog-turd flats in Nödinge and moved to half a bungalow in the woods outside Lilla Edet, reasoning that if the neighbours never spoke to you there was not much point in having neighbours at all. I drove a hired transit van down the long straight road to Lilla Edet bellowing in my best Joe Strummer mockney 'This here rock is a revolution rock', as if my elated position swaying high above the front wheels would carry me through the rest of my life.

We had one neighbour in the woods, the owner of the bungalow, an ancient half-Danish and half-crooked businessman who was dying—I now understand—of congestive heart failure. He wheezed as he waddled, and he had a terrible gurgling cough, treated with regular applications of low-tar cigarettes. The dark interior of his house smelled overpoweringly of dog food, dog, cigarette smoke and old man's undershirt. This made eating with him a difficult ordeal but some social contact was unavoidable because I held a mortgage on our part of the house. It couldn't simply be rented for immensely complicated reasons which boiled down to the fact that he had no planning permission for the part in which we lived. He had hoped his married daughter would come and look after him, but until then he needed the money, he said, to finish the conversion of our part. It had started off as a caravan parked in a field as deep into the forest as the dirt road reached, about three miles from Lilla Edet on the western bank of the river. Then he had built his own bungalow, a little distance from the caravan, and standing askance from it. Finally he swathed the old caravan in wood and turned the intervening space into a crooked shack, where we lived.

It was reasonably weatherproof. There was a fireplace, which on cold nights had to be swathed in blankets to stop the draught rushing down it after the fire went out. The walls and roof were insulated. There was a bedroom for us, a little alcove for Felix, a study for me with one small desk for the typewriter and another for my fly-tying equipment, and an angled kitchen where we could eat more easily than cook: it had a boxy electric oven with two hotplates on top; you could either have two hotplates on at once, or one and the oven.

The long dirt track through the forest to the bungalow was lined with blackberries in the autumn and deeper in the woods there were chanterelles growing beside exposed pine roots. In summer I could reach out from the study window at the back of the house and almost touch the leaves of the nearest birch tree; but in front there was a cleared meadow running a hundred metres up the hill to the only other neighbour's house. Across the valley was a clear-cut jumble of stumps and bramble where sometimes we could spot elk or deer grazing but otherwise the forest closed all around. The silence among the trees was very deep; when guests came to visit from England they would get lost within a hundred metres of the house, bewildered by the endless variations on a tiny repertoire of rock and pine, spruce and birch, juniper bushes, sand and anthills.

When the autumn came, rats moved into our roof space and I began to hate the landlord. They scrabbled around the roof above our heads but he was reluctant to spend money on pest control: they're only shrews, he said. Then one morning I found a trail of crumbly plaster running down from a small hole in the wall above the cooker. The rats were trying to break into our kitchen. I grew hysterical and shouted at him. That night, when everything grew quiet, I was roused from bed by the soft noise of cascading plaster. I padded into the darkened kitchen, picked up a sharpening steel and bashed the little black nose protruding from the wall. I spent much of the night sitting on a chair and glowering at the wall with a carving knife in my hand. I might not be able to do much for my family, but I could at least try to kill any small creatures that came into the kitchen and crapped in our food stores.

There were also adders in the meadow and one that lived in the rocks at the front of the house, under the heap of sand that had been left when the landlord ran out of money for his building plans. 'It will make a wonderful place for the little one to play,' he said. Felix spent a lot of time playing there, after I had killed the adder by jabbing a crowbar into the crevice where it lived, but I still kept a pair of wellingtons by the kitchen door in case I had to rush out and kill another one. Otherwise, we lived barefoot all summer.

I practised my fly casting on the meadow for an hour every day. Only the gales that threshed the oak tree over our bedroom could stop me. Snow certainly didn't. To stand on a crisp February day with the snow halfway up my shins and a fly rod in my hand was a sort of liturgical dance, even if there were no one to observe it but a couple of elk. Fly casting is in any case a way to dance from the hips upwards. Everything depends on catching the rhythm of the line as it loops through the air and this can only be done by feel, one reason why I could often cast better in the dark than when I peered to see what was happening as dusk fell. If I could just get the movements exactly right, I felt as if I were dancing the spring a little bit closer. I had come to feel that I was only really alive when I looked at water, or when I drove towards it.

This was not a world in which women played much of a part. Anita took to spending two or three nights a week in Uddevalla, where she was training to be a nurse. It saved a lot of driving and some silences between us. I didn't notice that it was anything more than a practical arrangement. It took me ages to notice that the woman who ran my evening classes was throwing passes at me. It seemed a thing impossible. I was a married man. Evie was a slightly fluffy blonde in her thirties, divorced, with a son of about eight and a cat. She liked to talk. We would chatter for an hour on the phone some days, when I was alone in the house, and when I walked into Lilla Edet, pushing Felix's pram, I would stop at her house for coffee. Nonetheless, my first reaction when she proposed a game of strip poker was simple astonishment; my second was to flee, but three weeks later, anyway, I was weeping in the car park by an oil refinery, too weak to climb out of the car and fish. The sky was like a great grey boulder, crushing me. How could I have been so stupid? How could I face the rest of my life?

Time passed. We visited my parents, in Godalming. Surrey, the county of stockbroker Tudor and horse brasses in pubs, seems to me the place furthest on earth from Sweden. Instead of the vertiginous seasons everything is frozen at room temperature in an unchanging drizzly light. Even the soil of clay and sand is dead. Nothing looks modern or artificial; nothing is in reality old or natural. Only the trains to London were honestly disgusting: they smelled of grit and grease, and childhood misery, as if every one were carrying me off to boarding school.

My parents lived in a house with high-ceilinged rooms in which everything was tasteful and calm. It was filled with exquisite, impenetrable manners from which Anita hung as if they had been barbed wire. It all seemed part of the natural order of things. I scarcely noticed that I was shuffling round in the mud and rats of the family trench system, or that every night in our bedroom I patrolled to the other side. I talked all the time there, inexhaustibly showing off to everyone. But no one would ever say anything important out loud. Unspeakable things unsaid rang in my ears all day. I wanted to get back to the whisperings of the forest, and took my fly rod on to the Surrey lawn, where I cast again and again over the roses (the back cast flew over the gravelled drive) until after two or three hours the sweat running down my arm reacted with the black foam plastic handle of my fly rod and I developed terrible eczema. My fingers swelled and bubbled like melting plastic. Anita looked up from her book in our room. My God, she said—she had a lovely smile—they look like crayfish claws; and that is what we called them for the next five years. The claws did not stop me fishing, of course. They merely convinced me that I must spend an extra forty pounds on a fly rod with a cork handle, made in Norway.

Each time we visited my parents things were worse. After a while I no longer needed to touch a fly rod to bring my eczema out. Touching anything in Surrey would make my hands swell and itch. I rubbed my blistered fingers on the rivets of my jeans until they bled and this would stop them hurting for a while. And I went fishing. Quite close to where my parents lived, at Willingshurst, there was a lake where Brian Clarke had actually fished himself. It figured in a chapter called 'early experiences of practising what I preach'. He had caught three fish one after another, as he saw them moving along the edge of the lake towards him and deduced at once what they were eating and how to offer a deceitful imitation while hiding himself on the bank. Then he had gone to a smaller lake in the woods and caught several more by spotting the faintest glimmer in the dark water, and realizing that this meant a trout four feet under the surface had seized a single midge pupa half an inch long.

I myself never saw such things in real life, but I watched for them with such fanaticism that I must have missed innumerable fish whose signals would have been obvious to anyone who had not read the book. For some reason the easy, predatory instinct which had guided me to all those pike deserted me whenever I held a fly rod in my hands. Whatever my technical accomplishments as a fly caster and a fly tier, I was blinded, when I was trying to catch fish, by the idea that there was a right way to do it, the way that Brian Clarke would have done. So it was with very high hopes that I took little Felix to Willingshurst, when he was four and a half.

I had made him his first fly rod that summer, spreading my threads and glues and varnish bottles over the polished mahogany dining table in my parents' house. The rod was a perfect child's wand, built with as much magic as I could summon. It was only six and a half feet long and the grip was thin enough for the smallest hand. I wanted even the colours to be perfect. I had anguished for half an hour in the shop between scarlet and viridian silk to bind on the lightest rings I could find. Even with a reel and line, it weighed virtually nothing.

At one corner of the smallest lake in the woods there was a little concrete outwork; probably concealing the mechanism that kept the wild-looking water in being. The lake looked as if it had been there for as long as the woods. In fact this was Surrey, and we were fishing in a purpose-built stew pond. There we sat, with our legs dangling over, each wearing, like uniforms, waistcoats made almost entirely of pockets to hold everything that might help to charm a trout: there were fly boxes, spools of nylon in differing thickness, tubs of unguent to make the nylon sink, and of grease to make it float. None of these helped Felix to cast in the slightest, though he loved the dressing up. There were trout feeding quite close to us but in the end I laid my own rod down and cast his line out, telling him to watch.

The line lay across the dark water like a stroke from a calligraphy brush. The line's end went under, and the meaning was clear. I was almost blind with apprehension. I knew a trout was mouthing at the fly. I knocked Felix's rod into the air with my forearm so the fish was hooked. 'There! You see?' I said. 'You caught a fish!'

We killed it, of course. There is still a photograph somewhere of the two of us crouching in front of a laurel hedge in my parents' garden, Felix holding up a distended, gutted little battery trout. We are both smiling because we know it is expected of us. I can admit now, nearly twenty years later, that he has never really liked fishing. Sometimes I say he has never seen the point of fishing but in some sense he has seen the point of it all too well.

Later that summer I returned to England alone, and when Felix asked, in the car, when Daddy was coming back from this trip I could not answer.  □

# WHY NOT?

SHORT FICTION CONTEST

1ST PRIZE: $1,000

2ND PRIZE: $500

3RD PRIZE: $250

All entries must be: unpublished; 5,000 words or less; postmarked by October 1, 2001; clearly marked "Short Fiction Contest" on both the story and the outside of the envelope; accompanied by a $10 entry fee per story (checks should be made payable to AZX Publications). Please *only* include the author's name on the story's cover page. Winners will be notified by December 1, 2001 and a list of winners, including Honorable Mentions, will be published in the February 2002 issue of *Zoetrope: All-Story*. Official guidelines are on our Web site at www.zoetrope-stories.com and may also be requested via SASE to: *Zoetrope: All-Story*, 1350 Avenue of the Americas, 24th Floor, New York, NY 10019.

Zoetrope
ALL STORY

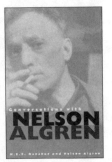

GRANTA

# THAILAND
## Haruki Murakami

TRANSLATED BY
JAY RUBIN

There was an announcement: *Lettuce angel men. We aren't countering some tah bulence. Please retahn to yah seat at thees time and fasten yah seat belt.* Satsuki had been letting her mind wander, and so it took her a while to decipher the Thai steward's shaky Japanese.

She was hot and sweating. It was like a steam bath, her whole body aflame, her nylons and bra so uncomfortable she wanted to fling everything off and set herself free. She craned her neck to see the other business class passengers. No, she was obviously the only one suffering from the heat. They were all curled up, asleep, blankets around their shoulders to counter the air conditioning. It must be another hot flush. Satsuki bit her lip and decided to concentrate on something else to forget about the heat. She opened her book and tried to read from where she had left off, but forgetting was out of the question. This was no ordinary heat. And they wouldn't be touching down in Bangkok for hours yet. She asked a passing stewardess for some water and, finding the pill case in her pocketbook, she washed down a dose of the hormones she had forgotten to take.

Menopause: it had to be the gods' ironic warning to (or just plain nasty trick on) humanity for having artificially extended the lifespan, she told herself for the nth time. A mere hundred years ago, the average life span was less than fifty, and any woman who went on living twenty or thirty years past the end of her periods was an oddity. The difficulty of continuing to live with tissues for which the ovaries or the thyroid had ceased to secrete the normal supply of hormones; the possible relationship between the post-menopausal decrease in oestrogen levels and the incidence of Alzheimer's disease: these were not questions worth troubling one's mind over. Of far more relevance to the largest part of humanity was the challenge of simply obtaining enough food to eat each day. Had the advancement of medicine, then, done nothing more than to expose, subdivide, and further complicate the problems faced by the human species?

Soon another announcement came over the PR system. In English this time. *If there is a doctor on board, please identify yourself to one of the cabin attendants.*

A passenger must have been taken sick. Satsuki thought for a moment of stepping forward, but quickly changed her mind. On the two other occasions when she had done such a thing, she had merely had run-ins with practising physicians who happened to be on the plane. Each of those men had seemed to possess both the poise of a seasoned general commanding troops on the front line and the vision to recognize at a glance that Satsuki was a professional pathologist without combat experience. 'That's all right, Doctor,' she had been told with a cool smile, 'I can handle this by myself. You just take it easy.' She had mumbled a stupid excuse and gone back to her seat to watch the rest of some ridiculous movie.

Still, she thought, I might just be the only doctor on this plane. And it might even be the case that the patient is someone with a major problem involving the thyroidal immune system. If that is the case—and the likelihood of such a situation did not seem high—then even I might be of some use. She took a breath and pressed the button for a cabin attendant.

The World Thyroid Conference was a four-day event at the Bangkok Marriott. Actually, it was more like a worldwide family reunion than a conference. All the participants were thyroid specialists, and they all knew each other or were quickly introduced. It was a small world. There would be talks and panel discussions during the day and private parties at night. Friends would get together to renew old ties, drink Australian wine, share thyroid stories, whisper gossip, exchange the latest news on their professional positions, tell dirty doctor jokes, and sing 'Surfer Girl' at karaoke bars.

In Bangkok, Satsuki stayed mainly with her Detroit friends. Those were the ones she felt most comfortable with. She had worked at the University Hospital in Detroit for close to ten years, doing research on the immune function of the thyroid gland. Eventually she had had a falling out with her securities analyst husband, whose dependency on alcohol had grown worse year by year, in addition to which he had become involved with another woman—someone Satsuki knew well. They separated, and a bitter struggle involving lawyers had gone on for a full year. 'The thing that finally did it for me,' her husband claimed, 'was that you didn't want to have children.'

They had finally concluded their divorce settlement three years ago. A few months later, someone smashed the headlights of her Honda Accord in the hospital parking lot and wrote JAP CAR on the hood in white letters. She called the police. The big, black policeman filled out the damage report and then said to her, 'Lady, this is Detroit. Next time buy a Ford Taurus.'

What with one thing and another, Satsuki became fed up with living in America and decided to go back to Japan. She found a position at a university hospital in Tokyo. 'You can't do that,' said a member of her research team from India. 'All our years of research are just about to bear fruit. We could be nominated for a Nobel Prize—it's not impossible.' He pleaded with her to stay, but Satsuki's mind was made up. Something inside her had snapped.

She stayed on alone at the hotel in Bangkok after the conference ended. 'I worked out a vacation for myself after this,' she told her friends. 'I'm going to a resort near here for a complete rest—a whole week of nothing but reading, swimming and drinking nice, cold cocktails by the pool.'

'That's great,' they said. 'Everybody needs a breather once in a while. It's good for your thyroid, too!' With handshakes and hugs and promises to get together again, Satsuki said goodbye to all her friends.

Early next morning, the limousine pulled up to the hotel entrance for her as planned. It was an old navy-blue Mercedes as perfect and polished as a jewel and far more beautiful than a new car. It looked like an object that had slipped whole from someone's other-worldly fantasy. A sparely built Thai man probably in his early sixties was to be her driver and guide. He wore a heavily starched white short-sleeved shirt, a black silk necktie and dark sunglasses. His face was tanned, his neck long and slender. Presenting himself to Satsuki, he did not shake her hand but, instead, brought his own hands together and gave a slight, rather Japanese, bow.

'Please call me Nimit. I will have the honour to be your companion for the coming week.'

It was not clear whether 'Nimit' was the man's first name or last. He was, in any case, 'Nimit', and he told her this in courteous, easy-to-understand English devoid of either American casualness or

British affectation. It had, in fact, no perceptible accent. Satsuki had heard English spoken this way before someplace, but she couldn't remember where.

'The honour is mine,' said Satsuki.

Together, Satsuki and Nimit passed through Bangkok's vulgar, noisy, pollution-ridden streets. The traffic barely moved, people cursed each other, and the sound of car horns tore through the atmosphere like an air raid signal. In addition to which, there were elephants walking down the street—and not just one or two of them. What were elephants doing in a city like this? she asked Nimit.

'Their owners bring them from the country,' he explained. 'They used to use them in logging operations, but there was not enough work for them to survive that way. They brought their animals to the city to make money doing tricks for foreign tourists. Now there are far too many elephants here, and that makes things very difficult for the city people. Sometimes an elephant will panic and run amok. Just the other day, a great many automobiles were damaged that way. The police try to put a stop to it, of course, but they cannot confiscate the elephants from their keepers. There would be no place to put them if they did, and the cost of feeding them would be enormous. All they can do is leave them alone.'

The car eventually emerged from the city, entered an expressway, and headed straight north. Nimit took a cassette from the glove compartment and slipped it into the stereo, setting the volume low. It was jazz—a tune that Satsuki recognized with some feeling.

'Do you mind turning the volume up?' she asked.

'Yes, Doctor, of course,' said Nimit, making it louder. The tune was 'I Can't Get Started', in exactly the same performance she had often heard in the old days.

'Howard McGhee on trumpet, Lester Young on tenor,' she murmured, as if to herself. 'JATP.'

Nimit looked at her in the rear-view mirror. 'Very impressive, Doctor,' he said. 'Do you like jazz?'

'My father was crazy about it,' she said. 'He played records for me when I was a little girl, the same ones over and over, and he would have me memorize the performers. If I got them right, he'd give me candy. I still remember most of them. But just the old stuff. I don't know anything about the newer jazz musicians. Lionel Hampton, Bud Powell, Earl Hines, Harry Edison, Buck Clayton...'

'The old jazz is all I ever listen to as well,' said Nimit. 'What was your father's profession?'

'He was a doctor, too,' she said. 'A paediatrician. He died just after I entered high school.'

'I am sorry to hear that,' said Nimit. 'Do you still listen to jazz?'

Satsuki shook her head. 'Not really. Not for years. My husband hated jazz. All he liked was opera. We had a great stereo in the house, but he'd give me a sour look if I ever tried putting on anything besides opera. Opera lovers may be the narrowest people in the world. I left my husband, though. I don't think I'd mind if I never heard another opera again for as long as I live.'

Nimit gave her a little nod but said nothing. Hands on the Mercedes steering wheel, he stared silently at the road ahead. His technique with the steering wheel was almost beautiful, the way he would move his hands to exactly the same points on the wheel at exactly the same angle. Now Errol Garner was playing 'I'll Remember April', which itself brought back memories for Satsuki. Garner's *Concert by the Sea* had been one of her father's favourite discs. She closed her eyes and let herself sink into old memories. Everything had gone well for her until her father died of cancer. Everything—without exception. But then the stage turned suddenly dark, and by the time she noticed that her father had vanished forever from her life, everything was headed in the wrong direction. It was as if a whole new story had started with a whole new plot. Not a month had passed after her father's death when her mother sold the big stereo along with her father's jazz collection.

'Where are you from in Japan, Doctor, if you don't mind my asking?'

'I'm from Kyoto,' answered Satsuki. 'I only lived there until I was eighteen, though, and I've hardly ever been back.'

'Isn't Kyoto right next to Kobe?'

'It's not far, but it's not "right next to" Kobe. At least the earthquake seems not to have caused too much damage there.'

Nimit switched to the overtaking lane, slipping past a number of trucks loaded with livestock, then eased back into the cruising lane.

'I'm glad to hear it,' said Nimit. 'A lot of people died in the earthquake last month. I saw it on the news. It was very sad. Tell me, Doctor, did you know anyone living in Kobe?'

'No, no one. I don't think anyone I know lives in Kobe,' she said. But this was not the truth. *He* lived in Kobe.

Nimit stayed silent for a while. Then, bending his neck slightly in her direction, he said to Satsuki, 'Strange and mysterious things, though, aren't they—earthquakes? We take it for granted that the earth beneath our feet is hard and immobile. We even talk about people being "down to earth" or having their feet firmly planted on the ground. But suddenly one day we see that it isn't true. The earth, the boulders, that are supposed to be so solid, all of a sudden turn as mushy as liquid. I heard it on the TV news: "liquefication", they called it, I think. Fortunately we hardly ever have major earthquakes here in Thailand.'

Cradled in the rear seat, Satsuki closed her eyes and concentrated on Errol Garner's playing. Yes, she thought, *he* lived in Kobe. I hope he was crushed to death by something big and heavy. Or swallowed up by the liquefied earth. *It's everything I've wanted for him all these years.*

With Nimit at the wheel, the limousine reached its destination at three o'clock in the afternoon. They had taken a break at a service station along the highway at exactly twelve o'clock. Satsuki had drunk some gritty coffee and eaten half a doughnut at the cafeteria. Her week-long rest was to be spent at an expensive resort in the mountains. The buildings overlooked a stream that surged through the valley, the slopes of which were covered in gorgeous primary-coloured flowers. Birds flew from tree to tree, emitting sharp cries. An independent cottage had been prepared for Satsuki's stay. It had a big, bright bathroom, an elegant canopied bed, and twenty-four-hour room service. Books and CDs and videos were available at the library off the lobby. The place was immaculate. Great care—and a great deal of money—had been lavished on every detail.

'You must be very tired, Doctor, after the long trip,' said Nimit. 'You can relax now. I will come to pick you up at ten o'clock tomorrow morning and take you to the pool. All you need to bring is a towel and a bathing suit.'

'Pool?' she asked. 'They must have a perfectly big pool here at the hotel, don't they? At least that is what I was told.'

'Yes, of course, but the hotel pool is very crowded. Mr Rapaport told me that you are a serious swimmer. I found a pool nearby where you can do laps. There will be a charge, of course, but a small one. I'm sure you will like it.'

John Rapaport was the American friend who had made the arrangements for Satsuki's Thai vacation. He had worked all over South-east Asia as a news correspondent ever since the Khmer Rouge had run rampant in Cambodia, and he had many connections in Thailand as well. It was he who had recommended Nimit as Satsuki's guide and driver. With a mischievous wink, he had said to her, 'You won't have to think about a thing. Just keep quiet and let Nimit make all the decisions, and everything will go perfectly. He's a very impressive guy.'

'That's fine,' she said to Nimit. 'I'll leave it up to you.'

'Well, then, I will come for you at ten o'clock tomorrow...'

Satsuki opened her bags, smoothed the wrinkles in a dress and skirt, and hung them in the closet. Then she changed into a bathing suit and went to the hotel pool. Just as Nimit had said, it was not a pool for serious swimming. Gourd-shaped, it had a lovely waterfall in the middle, and children were throwing a ball in the shallow area. Abandoning any thought of trying to swim, she stretched out under a parasol, ordered a Tio Pepe and Perrier, and picked up reading where she had left off in her new John Le Carré novel. When she grew tired of reading, she pulled her hat down over her face and napped. She had a dream about a rabbit. It was a short dream. The rabbit was in a hutch surrounded by a wire mesh fence, trembling. It seemed to be sensing the arrival of some kind of thing in the middle of the night. At first, Satsuki was observing the rabbit from outside the enclosure, but soon she herself had become the rabbit. She could just barely make out the thing in the darkness. Even after she awoke, she had a bad taste in her mouth.

Satsuki knew that *he* lived in Kobe. She knew his home address and telephone number. She had never once lost track of him. She had tried calling his house just after the earthquake, but the connection never went through. 'I hope the damn place was flattened,' she thought. 'I hope the whole family is out wandering the streets, penniless. When I think of what you did to my life, when I think of the children I should have had, it's the least you deserve.'

The pool that Nimit had found was half an hour's drive from the hotel and involved crossing a mountain. The woods near the top of the mountain were full of grey monkeys. They sat lined up along the road, eyes fixed on the passing cars as if to read the fates of the speeding vehicles.

The pool was located inside a large and somewhat enigmatic compound that was surrounded by a high wall and entered through an imposing iron gate. Nimit lowered his window and identified himself to the guard, who opened the gate without a word. Down the gravel driveway stood an old stone two-storey building, and behind that was the long, narrow pool. Its signs of age were unmistakable, but this was an authentic three-lane, twenty-five-metre lap pool. The rectangular stretch of water was beautiful, surrounded by lawn and trees, and undisturbed by swimmers. Several old wooden deckchairs were lined up beside the pool.

Silence ruled the area, and there was no hint of a human presence.

'What do you think, Doctor?' asked Nimit.

'Wonderful,' said Satsuki. 'Is this place an athletic club?'

'Something like that,' said Nimit. 'But almost no one uses it now. I have arranged for you to swim here alone as much as you like.'

'Thank you so much, Nimit. You *are* an impressive man.'

'You do me too great an honour,' said Nimit, bowing blank-faced, a man of the old school.

'The cottage over there is the changing room. It has toilets and showers. Feel free to use all the facilities. I will station myself by the automobile. Please let me know if there is anything you need.'

Satsuki had always loved swimming and she went to the gym pool whenever she had a chance. She had learned proper form from a coach. While she swam, she was able to thrust all unpleasant memories from her mind. If she swam long enough, she could reach a point where she felt utterly free, like a bird flying through the sky. Thanks to her years of regular exercise, she had never been confined to bed with an illness or become aware of any particular physical disorder. Nor had she gained any extra weight. Of course, she was not young any more; sharp trimming of the flesh was no longer an option. In particular, there was virtually no way to avoid putting on new flesh at the hips. But there was a limit to what you could ask for. She wasn't trying to become a fashion model. She probably looked five years younger than her actual age, which was pretty damn good.

At noon, Nimit served her iced tea and sandwiches on a silver tray by the pool—tiny vegetable and cheese sandwiches, cut into perfect little triangles.

Amazed, Satsuki asked, 'Did you make these?'

The question brought a momentary change to Nimit's blank face. 'Not I, Doctor. I do not prepare food. I had someone make this.'

Satsuki started to ask who the someone might be but stopped herself. John Rapaport had told her, 'Just keep quiet and let Nimit make all the decisions, and everything will go perfectly.' These were pretty good sandwiches. Satsuki rested after lunch and on her Walkman she listened to a tape of the Benny Goodman Sextet that she borrowed from Nimit, after which she continued with her book. She swam some more in the afternoon, returning to the hotel at three.

Satsuki repeated exactly the same routine for five days in a row. She swam to her heart's content, ate vegetable and cheese sandwiches, listened to music, and read. She never stepped out of the hotel except to go to the pool. What she wanted was perfect rest, a chance not to *think* about anything.

The only one swimming in the pool was Satsuki. The water was always intensely cold, as if they were drawing it from an underground stream in the hills, and the first dunk always took her breath away, but a few laps would warm her up, and then the water temperature was exactly right. When she tired of swimming the crawl, Satsuki would remove her goggles and do a backstroke. White clouds floated in the sky, and birds and dragonflies cut across them. Satsuki felt she would like to stay like this forever.

'Where did you learn your English?' Satsuki asked Nimit on the way back from the pool.

'I worked for thirty-three years as the driver for a Norwegian gem dealer in Bangkok, and I always spoke English with him.'

So that explained why his style seemed familiar. One of Satsuki's colleagues at a hospital where she had worked in Baltimore, a Dane, had spoken exactly this kind of English—precise grammar, light accent, no slang. Very clean, very easy to understand, and somewhat lacking in colour. How strange to be spoken to in Norwegian English in Thailand!

'My employer loved jazz and always had a tape playing when he was in the car. Which is why, as his driver, I naturally became familiar with it as well. When he died three years ago, he left me the car and all his tapes. The one we are listening to now is one of his.'

'So when he died, you became an independent driver/guide for foreigners, is that it?'

'Yes, exactly,' said Nimit. 'There are many driver/guides in Thailand, but I am probably the only one with his own Mercedes.'

'He must have placed a great deal of trust in you.'

Nimit stayed silent for a long moment. He seemed to be searching for the best way to respond to Satsuki's remark. 'You know, Doctor, I am a bachelor. I have never once married. I spent thirty-three years as another man's shadow. I went everywhere he went, I helped him with everything he did. I was a part of him, in a sense. When you live like that for a long time, you gradually lose track of what it is that you yourself really want out of life.'

Nimit raised the volume on the car stereo somewhat. A deep-throated tenor sax was taking a solo.

'Take this music, for example. I remember exactly what he told me about it. "Listen to this, Nimit. Follow Coleman Hawkins's improvised lines very carefully. He is using them to tell us something. Pay very close attention. He is telling us the story of the free spirit that is doing everything it can to escape from within him. That same kind of spirit is inside me, and inside you. There—you can hear it, I'm sure: the hot breath, the shiver of the heart." Hearing the same music over and over, I learned to listen closely, to hear the sound of the spirit. But still I cannot be sure if I really did hear it with my own ears. When you are with a person for a long time and following his orders, in a sense you become one with him, like husband and wife. Do you see what I am saying, Doctor?'

'I think so,' answered Satsuki.

It suddenly struck Satsuki that Nimit and his employer might have had a homosexual relationship. She had no evidence on which to base the thought, just an intuitive flash. But such a supposition would go far to explain what Nimit was now attempting to say.

'Still, Doctor, I do not have the slightest regret. If I could live my life over again, I would probably do exactly the same thing. What about you?'

'I don't know, Nimit. I really don't know.'

Nimit said nothing after that. They crossed the mountain with the grey monkeys and returned to the hotel.

On her last day before leaving for Japan, Nimit took Satsuki to a nearby village instead of driving straight back to the hotel.

'I have a favour to ask of you,' Nimit said, looking at Satsuki in the rear-view mirror. 'A personal favour.'

'What could that be?'

'Could you perhaps give me an hour of your time? I have a place that I would like to show you.'

Satsuki answered that she had no objection, nor did she ask him where he was taking her. She had decided to leave everything up to him.

The woman lived in a tiny house at the far edge of the village— a poor house in a poor village, with one tiny rice paddy after another crammed in layers up a hillside. Filthy, emaciated livestock. Muddy, pockmarked road. Air filled with the smell of water buffalo dung. A bull wandered by, genitals protruding. A 50cc motorcycle buzzed past, splashing mud to both sides. Near-naked children stood lined up along the road, staring at Nimit and Satsuki. She was shocked to think that such a miserable village could be situated so close to the high-class resort hotel in which she was staying.

The woman was old, perhaps near eighty. Her skin had the blackened look of worn leather, its deep wrinkles becoming ravines that seemed to reach all parts of her body. Her back was bent, and a flower-patterned, oversized dress hung limply from her bony frame. When he saw her, Nimit brought his hands together in greeting. She did the same.

Satsuki and the old woman sat down on opposite sides of a table, and Nimit took his place at one end. At first, only the woman and Nimit spoke. Satsuki had no idea what they were saying to each other, but she noticed how lively and powerful the woman's voice was for someone her age. The old woman seemed to have a full set of healthy teeth, too. After a while, the woman turned from Nimit to face Satsuki, looking directly into her eyes. She had a penetrating gaze, and she never blinked. Satsuki began to feel like a small animal that has been trapped in a small room with no way to escape. She realized she was sweating all over. Her face burned, and she had trouble breathing. She wanted to take a hormone pill, but she had no water. She had left her bottle of mineral water in the car.

'Please put your hands on the table,' said Nimit. Satsuki did as she was told. The old woman reached out and took Satsuki's right hand. The woman's own hands were small but powerful. For a full ten minutes (though it might just as well have been two or three), the old woman stared into Satsuki's eyes and held her hand, saying nothing. Satsuki returned the woman's strong stare with her weak one, using the handkerchief in her left hand to wipe the sweat from her forehead. Eventually, with a great sigh, the old woman released Satsuki's hand. Then she turned to Nimit and said something in Thai for a while. Nimit translated into English.

'She says that there is a stone inside your body. A hard, white stone. About the size of a child's fist. She does not know where it came from.'

'A stone?' Satsuki asked.

'There is something written on the stone, but she cannot read it because it is in Japanese: small, black characters of some kind. The stone and its inscription are old, old things. You have been living with them inside you for a very long time. You must get rid of the stone. Otherwise, after you die and are cremated, only the stone will remain.'

Now the old woman turned back to face Satsuki and spoke slowly in Thai for a long time. Her tone of voice made it clear that she was saying something important. Again Nimit translated.

'You are going to have a dream soon about a large snake. In your dream, the snake will be easing its way out of a hole in a wall— a green, scaly snake. Once it has pushed out three feet from the wall, you must grab its neck and never let go. The snake will look very frightening, but in fact it can do you no harm, and so you must not be frightened. Hold on to it with both hands. Think of it as your life, and hold on to it with all your strength. Keep holding it until you wake from your dream. The snake will swallow your stone for you. Do you understand?'

'What in the world—'

'Just say you understand,' Nimit said with the utmost gravity.

'I understand,' said Satsuki.

The old woman gave a gentle nod and turned again to Satsuki.

'The man is not dead,' translated Nimit. 'He did not receive a scratch. It may not be what you wanted, but it was actually very lucky for you that he was not hurt. You should be grateful for your good fortune.'

The woman spoke a few short syllables to Nimit.

'That is all,' said Nimit. 'We can go back to the hotel now.'

'Was that some kind of fortune-telling?' Satsuki asked when they were back in the car.

'No, Doctor. It was not fortune-telling. Just as you treat people's bodies, she treats people's spirits. She predicts their dreams, mostly.'

'I should have left her something then, as a token of thanks. The whole thing was such a surprise to me, it slipped my mind.'

Nimit negotiated a sharp curve on the mountain road, turning the wheel in that precise way of his. 'I paid her,' he said. 'A small amount. Not enough for you to trouble yourself over. Just think of it as a mark of my personal regard for you, Doctor.'

'Do you take all of your clients there?'

'No, Doctor, only you.'

'And why is that?'

'You are a beautiful person, Doctor. Clear-headed. Strong. But you seem always to be dragging your heart along the ground. From now on, little by little, you must prepare yourself to face death. If you devote all of your future energy to living, you will not be able to die well. You must begin to shift gears, a little at a time. Living and dying are, in a sense, things of equal value.'

'Tell me something, Nimit,' said Satsuki, taking off her

sunglasses and leaning over the back of the front passenger seat.

'What is that, Doctor?'

'Are *you* prepared to die?'

'I am half dead already,' said Nimit as if stating the obvious.

That night, lying in her broad, pristine bed, Satsuki wept. She recognized that she was headed toward death. She recognized that she had a hard, white stone inside herself. She recognized that a scaly green snake was lurking somewhere in the dark. She thought about the child to which she never gave birth. She had destroyed that child, flung it down a bottomless well. And then she had spent thirty years hating one man. She had hoped that he would die in agony. In order to bring that about, she had gone so far as to wish in the depths of her heart for an earthquake. 'In a sense,' she told herself, 'I am the one who caused that earthquake. *He* turned my heart into a stone; *he* turned my body to stone.' In the distant mountains, the grey monkeys were silently staring at her. *Living and dying are, in a sense, things of equal value.*

After checking her bags at the airline counter, Satsuki handed Nimit an envelope containing a hundred-dollar bill. 'Thank you for everything, Nimit. You made it possible for me to have a wonderful rest. This is a personal gift from me to you.'

'That is very thoughtful of you, Doctor,' said Nimit, accepting the envelope. 'Thank you very much.'

'Do you have time for a cup of coffee with me?'

'Yes, I would enjoy that.'

They went to a coffee shop together. Satsuki had her coffee black. Nimit gave his a heavy dose of cream. For a long time afterward, Satsuki went on turning her cup in her saucer.

'You know,' she said at last, 'I have a secret that I have never told anyone. I could never bring myself to talk about it. I've kept it locked up inside of me all this time. But I'd like to tell it to you now. Because we'll probably never meet again. That time my father died all of a sudden, my mother, without a word to me—'

Nimit held his hands up, palms facing Satsuki, and gave his head a firm shake. 'Please, Doctor. Don't tell me any more. You should have your dream, as the old woman told you to. I understand how you feel, but if you put those feelings into words, they will turn into lies.'

Satsuki swallowed her words, and then, in silence, closed her eyes.

'Have your dream, Doctor,' said Nimit as if sharing kindly advice. 'What you need now more than anything is discipline. Cast off mere words. Words turn into stone.'

He reached out and took Satsuki's hand between his. His hands were almost weirdly smooth and youthful, as if they had always been protected by first-rate leather gloves. Satsuki opened her eyes and looked at him. Nimit took his hands away and rested them on the table, fingers intertwined.

'My Norwegian employer was actually from Lapland,' said Nimit. 'You must know, of course, that Lapland is at the northernmost tip of Norway, near the North Pole. Many reindeer live there. In summer there is no night, and in winter no day. He probably came to Thailand because the cold got to be too much for him. I guess you could call the two places complete opposites. He loved Thailand, and he made up his mind to have his bones buried here. But still, to the day he died, he missed the town in Lapland where he was born. He used to tell me about it all the time. And yet, in spite of that, he never once went back to Norway in thirty-three years. There must have been some special circumstances there that kept him away. He was another person with a stone inside.'

Nimit lifted his coffee cup and took a sip, then carefully set it in its saucer again without a sound.

'He once told me about polar bears—what solitary animals they are. They mate just once a year. One time in a whole year. There is no such thing as a lasting male–female bond in their world. One male polar bear and one female polar bear meet by sheer chance somewhere in the frozen vastness, and they mate. It doesn't take them very long. And once they are finished, the male polar bear runs away from the female as if he is frightened to death: he runs from the place where they have done their mating. He never looks back—literally. The rest of the year he lives in deep solitude. Mutual communication—the touching of two hearts—does not exist for them. So, that is the story of polar bears—or, at least, it is what my employer told me about them.'

'How very strange,' said Satsuki.

'Yes,' said Nimit, 'it is strange.' He wore a grave expression. 'I remember asking my employer, "Then what do polar bears exist for?" "Yes, exactly—" he said with a big smile. "Then what do *we* exist for, Nimit?"'

The plane reached cruising altitude and the fasten seat belt sign went off. 'So,' thought Satsuki, 'I'm heading back to Japan.' She tried to think about what lay ahead, but soon gave up. 'Words turn into stone,' Nimit had told her. She settled deep into her seat and closed her eyes. All at once the image came to her of the sky she had seen when swimming on her back. And Errol Garner's 'I'll Remember April'. 'Let me sleep,' she thought. 'Just let me sleep. And wait for the dream to come.' ☐

# THE NEW APERTURE

## YOU'VE GOT THE WHOLE WORLD IN YOUR HANDS
## SHARE THE VISION

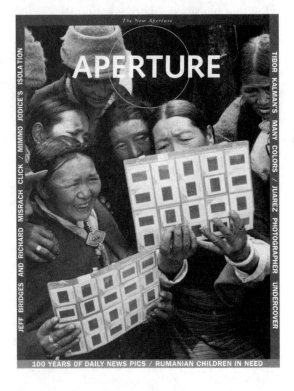

The new APERTURE evolves from nearly fifty years of publishing revelatory images from all corners of the earth, from all corners of the mind, letting us see with the power of foresight, insight, vision.

Photography sees without blinking. Every camera riots against time, grabs on to the past and the present with a single click. Dynamic photographs stop us in our tracks; the best of them have the power to change our way of thinking.

The new APERTURE teams powerful images by the photographers you know, and by photographers you should know, with the best writing of today, and lets them play off one another in dynamic counterpoint.

Four times a year, APERTURE brings you the best-quality printing and a mix of voices and visions, driven by meaning, free from thesis. Deepening the world as you know it. All of this delivered right to your door.

## SUBSCRIBE TO APERTURE NOW AND GET A FREE BOOK
### CALL 1-800-783-4903 EXT. 460 TO RESERVE YOUR FREE BOOK

**FREE GIFT**

One year of APERTURE (4 issues) is just $40, a savings of 33% off the newsstand price. If I find that APERTURE is not for me, I may cancel my subscription and receive a full refund for all unmailed issues.

Included in your subscription is PAUL STRAND, a 96-page book from the MASTERS OF PHOTOGRAPHY series. This volume features 42 of STRAND's greatest images. Yours FREE with your paid subscription.

**APERTURE Magazine / Subscriptions: 1-800-783-4903, ext. 460 / www.Aperture.org**

**GRANTA**

# THE ANDES OF
# MARTIN CHAMBI

PHOTOGRAPHS BY MARTIN CHAMBI
TEXT BY AMANDA HOPKINSON

The 'Giant of Paruro', with Chambi's assistant, Victor Mendívil, 1925

Until last year, when I made two trips to the Andes to find out more about him, what little I knew about the Peruvian photographer Martín Chambi came from seeing the few, rare exhibitions of his work (Newcastle, 1979; Toledo, 1990; Turin, 1998) and an even rarer catalogue. Generally these reproduced the same few dozen images taken from an archive said to contain over 30,000 negatives, most of them made in the 1920s and 1930s. From them it was clear that Chambi was an impressive portraitist who, unusually for his time, had photographed across the social classes and the mixture of races in his native Peru. Also unusually, rather than relying on the imitation backdrop of his studio, he had taken his camera out into the countryside and obviously delighted in making *contrejour* portraits, silhouetting his subjects against the magnificent dawns and sunsets of the high Andes and the flat plateaux of the Puno. In addition, I also owned a Chambi print. In 1999 my husband had surprised me with a birthday present of one of Chambi's most famous pictures, his portrait of the 'Giant of Paruro', with Chambi's assistant standing next to the 'giant' to demonstrate his great height. I was intrigued by this picture. Who was this man who measured over six and a half feet tall in a country where the average man's height was little over five? And who was the man who had photographed him? Given the excuse of making a radio programme in Peru, I set off in early 2000 to try to find out.

One reason why Chambi was so little known abroad was that he chose not to go there. In the course of his life (he died in 1973) he had been to Chile, to Bolivia, and once to Argentina, but he never reached the coast nor saw the Pacific Ocean. Without being in any political sense a nationalist, he supported the restoration of the rights and traditions of all Quechua-speaking peoples (Quechua is the language of the Incas, and still the language spoken by the majority of indigenous Peruvians), and his photographs embrace both the pro-Indian (*indigenista*) cultural movement, which coincided with the most fertile period of his work, and the arrival of Modernism, particularly in its more novel technical aspects. He had earned the respect of his own and the wider Latin American community without conforming to a western notion of fame, and, almost uniquely in a marketplace eager to exploit any untapped source of original prints, his massive archive, dating from the 1910s through to the 1960s, remained, largely complete, under the guardianship of his descendants. Quite how special this archive was took some time to establish.

Photography arrived in the Americas within less than five years of its invention in Europe in 1839. In South America, the rich tin, silver and gold deposits attracted foreign speculators during the nineteenth century, bringing North American and European travellers in their wake. And with them came cameras. A hundred and fifty years ago outdoor photography required as much baggage as a field expedition to the Himalayas. The local bearers employed to carry the heavy wooden box cameras with their brass lenses and glass-plate negatives, the portable studios and darkrooms were descended from the Incas. They were the ones who knew the sites of the 'hidden cities' of Sacsahuamán, Machu Picchu, Ollantaytambo and others, and the steep llama paths by which to reach them.

Many of these visiting photographers made their tour of the Andes and then went home again, leaving their unwieldy equipment behind them. Those who stayed recruited local photographic assistants. By the end of the nineteenth century there was an incipient 'Andean School' of photographers, still earning their living largely from studio portraits, but curious to document their own surroundings and customs. Their eye for what they photographed was familiar rather than foreign, and it was this native eye that I wanted to learn more about when I set off for the Andes.

We landed in Cuzco, the old Inca capital, to be greeted at the airport by a band of folkloric dancers, dressed in brilliant turquoise and fuchsia outfits, twirling scarves and skirts to the sound of *zamponas* and drum. It was not, of course, our flight the dancers were welcoming, but that of the Opposition Party candidate, Alejandro Toledo, who was hoping to contest President Alberto Fujimori's re-election for an illegitimate third term.

Teo Allain Chambi, too, turned out to be something of a local celebrity. The minibus driver taking us into town knew him, as did the couple running the little hostel on the edge of town where we were staying, as did the person in charge of the local radio station, with whom we were due to be working. Within fifteen minutes of our being installed in the hostel lobby with the cups of coca tea that are given to all guests to combat altitude sickness, Teo had arrived. A small dark-haired, quick-moving man with spectacles and a small beard, he is the son of the French painter, Teófilo Allain Alvarez, one of Chambi's close friends, and Chambi's eldest daughter, Elena.

Teo, who was once a radio presenter and a DJ, is now a colour photographer and a cultural adviser to a Swiss bank. He also manages his grandfather's estate, which can be a frustrating task. The single book in which Chambi itemized all his negatives has vanished, as have all his other notebooks. Nobody appears to have thought it worth recording an interview with Chambi during his lifetime, and only now is Andrés Garay Albujar, a postgraduate student based in Spain, engaged in the process of unravelling Chambi's 5,000 images on celluloid, taken after he switched from glass plates to film in 1950. Until Albujar began his research, it was believed that Chambi had abandoned photography altogether for the last two decades of his life.

All Chambi's work from the thirty years before 1950 has been cared for by his second youngest daughter, Julia, who is a professional studio photographer in her own right. The day I arrived in Cuzco turned out to be the day that the 'Estudio Martín Chambi' was shutting up shop on the Calle Marquez, where it had traded for the past seventy-five years, and moving to a new address on the Avenida de la Cultura, out in the suburbs. I found Julia packing her own and her father's prints into boxes which were stacked along the corridors and under the pillars of the central courtyard in the fine colonial villa, part of which had been let to the Chambi family—as its owner explained—'for far too long'. This was where Julia had lived her entire life. She said to me: 'I was born looking at photographs, I can't remember a time when I wasn't watching the pictures being either taken or developed. To me photography was two things: it was magic and it was my father.'

Though she was coy about her age, Julia was born in the 1920s and began 'playing in the darkroom' around the age of six. By ten she was working in it. One of Chambi's most popular portraits shows the entire family and servants on the roof of their villa—over which Chambi had erected a canopy to be drawn against the wet weather— hard at work tinting and retouching, the girls still in their school pinafores. At her expensive convent school, Julia was soon known as the school photographer—a post she was pleased to assume, since it got her included on every outing and helped win her a place in the basketball and tennis leagues, and she brought her camera along to take team portraits at the end of every match.

My first sight of her, huddled inside her shawl against the damp cold, was of a small frail figure surrounded by the erratically-packed boxes. She had long since abandoned the upstairs floors which her father had used and moved into a small ground-floor studio where she had continued in straitened circumstances. She perched herself on a stool at the entrance beneath a sepia self-portrait of Chambi, lovingly inscribed to her as the heiress to his vocation. Behind her the shelves were still stacked with Chambi postcards and popular artefacts, many of them religious. Like her father, Julia was deeply devout: she collected little terracotta angels, cribs and shrines. Among the photographs she gave me to sort through was a prayer card to Taytacha, the Black Christ in Cuzco Cathedral, supposedly responsible for calming the aftershocks of the major earthquakes which shook the city in 1650 and again, exactly 300 years later.

It was almost too much to take in: rarely, in all the photographic research I had ever been involved with, had it been made so easy. When I explained that I wished to look at some images with a view to doing a piece for a magazine she had never heard of in a distant country she had never visited, Julia simply handed over the nearest couple of boxes for me to rifle through.

Their contents were entirely random, but three aspects were immediately striking. All the pictures were contacted from the original plates in postcard format. The mainstay of Chambi's income did not depend, as a successful photographer's would nowadays, on a circuit of galleries, magazines and agents. He was an early popularizer of the reproducible image, selling business cards, wedding pictures, First Communion cards and postcards to a predominantly local clientele.

The variety of the images was also unexpected. Those I pulled out were not only the anticipated studio and staged outdoor portraits I had seen before, but documentation of the excavations at the Inca city of Machu Picchu in the 1940s; pictures of basketball being played in a rural village for the first time; of demonstrations during the 1930s;

a number of church altars, and the remnants of what had clearly been extensive reportages on indigenous fiestas and on the ancient cities and burial sites of the Sacred Valley along the Urubamba river. There was also a 'news picture' of the Prince of Wales, the future Edward VIII, attending an informal dinner in Cuzco in 1929. This was presumably one of many such pictures sent, not to Lima, still two weeks away by road, but by the British-built railway from Cuzco to Buenos Aires, the capital of Argentina, where Chambi was a regular contributor to the national daily, *La Nación*. Finally, in a slightly larger format, were the results of some of Chambi's technical experiments. The self-portrait above the door was the result of Chambi's use of colour dyes to tint his images. A composite portrait of a man in profile looking back at himself was an early example of his exploration of mirror effects and multiple reflections.

Julia loaned me a batch of pictures 'to go along with'. It was an instructive moment. She regarded these prints in the same way her father might have done, as items whose financial value was of little significance. She also insisted on giving me a couple of ornaments— a small vase and a pottery church—telling me her father had accepted some of these in lieu of payment. In the sense that commodities are worth only what purchasers can or will pay for them, the postcard prints and tuppeny-ha'penny ornaments were of similar value. However much dedication and attention their makers put into them, they still sold for a few *centimos* in the marketplace.

Chambi was already in his twenties when he moved to Cuzco. He was born in Coaza, a hamlet in the southern Puno, where his parents were farmers. After he left school at the age of twelve, he met an Englishman who had been commissioned by the Santo Domingo Mining Company to take photographs of shareholders' investments for the company's office in London. Chambi was fascinated by the process of photography; he hung around the Englishman, volunteered his help, and proudly took away part payment in the form of a self-portrait. Two years later he announced to his parents that he had saved enough gold from river panning in his spare time to pay his and his father's bus fares to the city of Arequipa, where the famous Peruvian photographer Max T. Vargas lived. Though he knew little more than Vargas's name, Chambi, at fourteen, was determined to become his apprentice.

Vargas appears to have welcomed Chambi into his home and treated him as one of the family, pleased to have met a young man who, unlike his own sons, wanted to follow him in his profession. (Vargas's eldest son later moved to the United States and became famous for his magazine illustrations of stylized American beauties, commonly known as 'Vargas Girls'.) At the time, photography in Peru was mainly of two kinds: studio portraiture and romantic landscapes. As in Britain and the United States, a 'Pictorialist'—or painterly—style predominated. Chambi spent the next seven years learning all he could about studio photography, experimenting at every stage, with chemical processes and the manipulation of available light, so that he achieved an extensive range of colour and tone.

By his early twenties, he was a professional photographer with a wife and two children to support (there would eventually be six children). The family moved, first to the nearby town of Sicuani then, a couple of years later, to the Andean city of Cuzco, where they settled, first in Santa Teresa, then at the first of several addresses on the Calle Marquez. Chambi had lived in the house I visited from 1923 to 1973, but had never achieved his dream of owning a home of his own. It was here, from the 1920s to the end of the 1940s, that Chambi produced the vast majority of his work.

His arrival in Cuzco coincided with the rise of what became known as the *indigenista* movement, which took the old Inca capital as its centre. It was primarily concerned with a cultural revindication of the rights of the Amerindian population and sought to rehabilitate the traditional arts which had for four centuries been sidelined (and often despised) as *lo folklórico*. Under the leadership of a group of intellectuals, Cuzco University established schools of anthropology, ethnography and sociology, and spread the message throughout the population by setting up part-time schools for workers and peasants. Chambi, with his indigenous peasant origins, his fluency in Quechua, his social ease and his talent in a relatively new art, was the ideal collaborator for such a project. Though there is no evidence that he belonged to any political party, he certainly photographed *indigenista* leaders addressing rallies and trade unions, and in return found plenty of academics who were willing to supply populist manifestos for his early books and publications.

The most important aspect of the movement was probably the cultural climate it created. (In concrete terms, the economic lot of the *indigenista* was little improved; it was the minority *mestizo* population, of partly European descent, who gained most.) Chambi covered developments from both sides. He photographed the local strolling musicians in their new role as suppliers of music (replacing the string quartet) at society weddings and parties; the weavers and embroiderers suddenly commissioned to create costumes for fashionable ladies; the revival of elaborate festivals, such as the Inti Raymi, the pageant of the Inca kings, and *Ollantay*, a sixteenth-century play in Quechua, set during the reign of the emperor Pachacutec (1438–71). He also sought out the genuine festivities of his own people, which needed no reviving because they had never lapsed, pursuing them in the Quechua and Aymara communities of Chile and Bolivia, documenting over 200 rural customs.

There is no indication that Chambi knew of the transformations of overseas photographic practice, but his shift in style paralleled that from Pictorialism to Modernism. His subject matter, too, looked to the future. He covered the arrival of every new technological device: telephones and telegraphs; a textile factory and an electricity generating station; the new chemist selling toothpaste and the offices of *El Sol*, a radical newspaper (for which he also worked). He photographed the Santa Ana railway and the city tramlines; new roads; the first cars and motorbikes; Enrico Rolandi's pioneering aeroplane flight over the Andes—and his final crash landing.

But what was Chambi like as a person? Some clues came on my second trip to Cuzco, six months after the first. His daughter Julia was by now in her new studio, where most of the cases I had seen six months earlier had been delivered but not unpacked. Once again she was happy to let me pick through unsorted boxes. Day after day I was astonished at the range and number of her father's photographs: 2,000 images of church interiors, 1,000 more documenting Machu and Huayna Picchu, a similar number of rural fiestas.

It was difficult to doubt that Chambi had been a religious man; not only a devout Catholic, but intrigued by worship in all its forms.

Amanda Hopkinson

A vision of hell carved on a lintel; a Franciscan abbot tending gladioli in his walled garden; the Last Supper with a platter of guinea pig (still a national dish in Peru) on the altar at Cuzco Cathedral; the open-air shrine at Huayna Picchu: Chambi had photographed all of them and his pictures had an extraordinary immediacy. To judge from his self-portraits, it was also difficult to doubt that he loved self-transformation. Like all studio photographers, he kept a box of costumes and props with which to dress up his subjects, and seems to have enjoyed trying them on himself.

He moved easily between his two worlds. A number of studio shots, including the one over Julia's door, show him dressed in a western suit, tie and white shirt that emphasize his dark good looks. But when he drank *chicha* (maize beer) with the mountain villagers, or joined in their pilgrimages and danced at their fiestas, he dressed as they did. As Julia said, it was his knack to dance the waltz as well as the *wayna*. Perhaps more interestingly, he liked to assume the identities of some of his subjects. After taking the portrait of a major landowner, Blas Aguilar, surveying his ranch, Chambi copied his suit and stance, put on a *hacendado*'s hat and took a self-portrait of himself as that contradiction in terms: an *indigenista* landowner. Attracted by speed and modernity, he also dressed as a racing driver and as the motorcyle champion, Mario Pérez Yañez, complete with cap, goggles and leathers. If society ladies could put on the rich fabrics which were intricately embroidered by indigenous women and still powder their faces white in the latest Paris fashion, then why shouldn't the photographer easily subvert convention by changing places with the dominant race—or with any of his subjects he chose to?

Though Chambi never overtly satirized his society clientele, it is hard for the carnival queens, the beauty parades, the imported outfits and garden-party *tableaux vivants* not to appear ridiculously affected when they are contrasted with the portraits that celebrate the dignity of labour. These have sentimental titles such as 'Inca and Llama', the 'Labourer at Sunset' or 'Andean Melancholy', the shepherds and peasants meticulously posed against the landscape to emphasize the classical profiles of men who look as if they are carved from black jade.

Chambi's photographs may not have concentrated on poverty, but he did not overlook exploitation. The situation of the *pongo* (the houseboy, the fiercely tragic subject of José Maria Arguedas's famous story *The Pongo's Dream*), was no better than that of a serf in Peru, even in the 1950s. It remained a constant reminder that the 'revindication of the rights of the Indians' rarely got more than lip service, even among its most vocal campaigners. As ancient sites became fashionable picnic spots, Chambi was invited to photograph a noted philanthropist and benefactor, Ricarda Luna, outdoors at Machu Picchu with her luncheon party. Hovering miserably in the background is the family *pongo*, barefoot, grubbily clothed, with his woollen hat pulled down over his nose against the cold. And in his portrait of the Montes family wedding, with the bride descending the palatial staircase of her home flanked by high balustrades and naked caryatids bearing candelabra, the nursemaid—who had raised the bride since infancy—can be seen huddling in an obscure corner, half-hidden under the stairwell.

Chambi's view of his countrymen can be usefully set against that of another famous photographer, who lived in Cuzco for a few months in 1948. Irving Penn found his way there after a particularly stressful series of *Vogue* fashion shoots in Lima. He found a studio on Santa Teresa and liked it so much that he dispatched its resident photographer, Flores Ochoa, to spend Christmas with distant relatives. After a week overcoming altitude sickness, he noted (in *Worlds in a Small Room)*, that in portraying 'these small closed people, three-quarter-size' how 'difficult it was to imagine the present-day inhabitants as descendants of the brilliant engineers of the Inca cities and temples'. Whenever someone arrived to be photographed, presumably from among Flores Ochoa's clientele, Penn deliberately confused their expectations by insisting on paying them for the privilege of taking their portraits rather than them paying him. With an odd kind of innocence, he declared his astonishment that there were soon lengthy queues at his door.

Perhaps he was enjoying himself too much. The lack of a common language and the clients' polite compliance allowed him to 'pose them myself, moving them around and putting them into position'. The results are his justly famous portraits of Indian families, particularly those of local children, who appear with expressions of utter bewilderment in stances worthy of actors or models. Penn's conclusion was that 'the most surprising and fascinating fact of the whole experience [was] to take people out of their natural circumstances and place them straight in front of a camera... [This] was not only to isolate but to transform them.'

Penn's approach was the antithesis to Chambi's, and though they worked only a few streets away from one another (and it was widely, if incorrectly, reported that it was Chambi's studio that Penn had hired for those few months) there is no indication that the two ever met.

Chambi's mission was to portray the dignity and traditions of his people through their lives and labours, and he was well aware of the significance of his undertaking. He spoke the same language as his subjects; his perception of who they were closely matched their own. The Argentine photographer Sara Facio believes that Chambi was 'the first great photographer not to see us through the eyes of a colonial'. And Chambi himself said, in a talk he gave on one of his rare visits to a neighbouring country, Chile: 'I feel I am a delegate on behalf of my race; this is what speaks through my photos.'

His emotional attachment to his countrymen extended to the old city that had become his home. When Cuzco was struck by an earthquake in 1950, Chambi ran around the city crying as he photographed the massive scale of the destruction. After that, he put down his large plate camera and swore he would never take it up again. We know now that although he put down his 10x15cm Inka camera forever, he continued to photograph on film during the last twenty-three years of his life.

Before Chambi died in 1973, he told Julia that he might not have money to bequeath but he had left her his wealth of photographs. He left between 17,000 and 18,000 glass plates and all his equipment to his daughter. He also left several thousand prints, almost all of them contact prints taken from the plates. And then there are the 5,000 frames of film which have yet to be sorted.

It was Julia, the only photographer among his six children, who (unlike her brothers) remained in Cuzco, unmarried, to commit herself more fully to her work in her father's studio and the care of his estate. She draws a small income from his archive, and takes considerable satisfaction in printing to order. She still makes the effort for interested tourists who find their way under the copperplate sign to the Estudio Martín Chambi on the Avenida de la Cultura, but increasingly there is an industry in prints for exhibitions overseas.

In Cuzco itself, however, neither the Bartolomé de las Casas Cultural Centre nor the Fototeca de los Andes house a Chambi archive in their collections. There is no institute dedicated to the conservation or study of his work, though the Casa Cabrera, a colonial mansion in the Plaza de las Nazarenas, houses a small reconstruction of Chambi's studio. Once inside, it was easy for me to imagine what it must have been like to be one of Chambi's subjects, sitting on the familiar armchair, facing the heavy box camera, flanked on the walls by some of Chambi's favourite landscape prints tinted in deep greens, brilliant blues and rich ochre. The only thing missing was the hefty dressing-up box of assorted costumes and the opportunity for transformation.

In the course of my visits to Cuzco I had discovered that the 'Giant of Paruro', in my birthday portrait back home, did not come from Paruro at all. His name was Juan de la Cruz Sihuana and he was from Llusco-Chumbivilcas. Apparently Chambi had found him working as a porter in the central market in Cuzco and taken him back to his studio to photograph. Even Chambi, it seemed, was not averse to a little sociological manipulation. He had tried dressing the giant in an assortment of outfits, both traditional and western, and described him as being 'gentle' and 'dignified' in his acquiescence to being posed alone or with Chambi's assistant, Victor Mendívil. Some years ago I wrote a biography of the Victorian photographer, Julia Margaret Cameron, who, oddly enough, demonstrated some of the same traits as her unlikely successor. She too had seized her subjects where she found them, terrorizing old fishermen and young schoolchildren along the cliff walk on the Isle of Wight, by dragging them into her 'glasshouse' to be photographed. She preyed on innocuous and unlikely citizens until, with a cry of 'Here's my King Arthur!' or 'You are Ophelia: kindly weep!' she would introduce them to her dressing-up trunk and her makeshift studio, to be transformed according to her personal vision. Happily, Chambi soon gave up on the idea of transforming the 'giant', having discovered, not surprisingly, that the clothes that fitted him best were his own.     □

Wayna Pichu, one of the two peaks that flank the Inca city Machu Pichu, c.1941

Martín Chambi, one of many self-portraits, this with the Andes as a backdrop, c.1940

Chambi (right) with friends, including the artist Téofilo Allain (centre), at Wayna Pichu, 1939

Tram lines at the corner of the Calle Mantas and the Plaza de Armas, Cuzco, 1927

Callejón Loreto, Cuzco, c.1930

Aftermath of the earthquake, Parque de las Arenas, Cuzco, May 1950

Popular picnic, c.1927

Lunch for the teachers of the University of San Antonio Abad, 1942

The Bocángel sisters, including Estela (left), Cuzco's first woman lawyer, date unknown

The Echave family of musicians, with their harp-guitar, the 'chavina', Cuzco, 1931

Two brothers, pupils at the La Salle Brothers' School, Cuzco, 1920s

A first communicant, posed in the School of Our Lady, Cuzco, 1920s

Bourgeois married couple, Cuzco, 1923

Chambi's housemaid and her husband, Cuzco, 1935

The Ceremony of Candles at Ayaviri Church, Puno, 1938

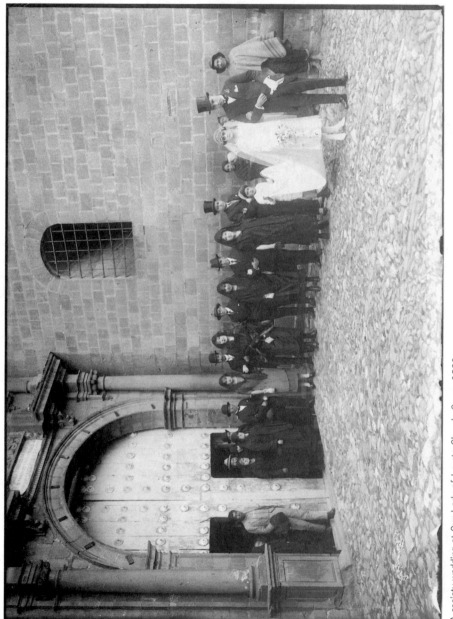

A society wedding at Our Lady of Loreto Church, Cuzco, 1930s

The organist at the chapel in Tinta, who built his own organ, 1935

Chambi and friends sliding down the 'rodadero' at Sacsayhuaman, c.1930

Dancing during carnival in the mountains above Cuzco, 1931

A football match, Cuzco, c.1950

Outdoor confessions from masked pilgrims to their priest, Q'Olloriti, c.1931

The Excelsior, Cuzco's first cinema, showing 'The Hunchback of Notre Dame', 1929

Revival of the festival of the 'Inti Raymi' (the Inca kings), showing the new car park, Cuzco, 1948

GRANTA

# THIS SIDE OF THE ODER

## Judith Hermann

TRANSLATED BY
MARGOT BETTAUER DEMBO

Koberling is standing on the hill as they arrive. The hill is a mound of soil that Koberling piled up with his own hands in the middle of the garden two years ago. Back then Constance had laughed and called it 'Field Marshal Hill'; he had countered with 'Napoleon Hill', and the name stuck. From there he has a view of the lawn, the veranda, the shady entrance to the kitchen, and the rolling meadows beyond which flows the Oder.

Koberling is standing on Napoleon Hill and smoking a cigarette; he shades his eyes with one hand and stares towards the horizon. Somewhere over there is the Oder, hidden in its river bed. Somewhere over there, too, is Constance, taking her daily walk in the afternoon heat. The child is sleeping in the kitchen, exhausted by the summer. Koberling brushes away a wasp and thinks of autumn. The sound of a car's engine comes creeping up the sandy road like an illusion. Koberling turns his head, listening, and squints; no, no car ever comes driving up the sandy road except his own. It's not an illusion though. The sound of a diesel engine, a crunch of pebbles, Koberling beside himself, his heart pounding. Out of the corner of his right eye he catches sight of an old Mercedes. Koberling remains motionless, wants to be invisible, thinks, Keep going. The Mercedes stops in front of the garden gate. Dust from the road swirls up; the door opens on the passenger side and Anna climbs out. Koberling recognizes her immediately. She looks the same as before, same as back then, only bigger, taller, a grown-up child. 'Koberling!' she shouts and stalks around the car in high-heeled shoes, stopping at the garden gate. She's wearing a red dress and is deeply tanned. The window on the driver's side is being rolled down and a young man with matted hair sticks his head out, yawning. Koberling has butterflies in his stomach and says very softly and viciously, 'Pothead.'

'Hey!' Anna shouts. 'We've just come back from Poland. We don't have any money left, and we thought we could stay with you, just for a few days. Koberling! Do you remember me?'

Koberling crushes the cigarette under his foot and comes down off the hill. 'I remember you. I can hear you. No need to shout like that.'

Anna's hand is on the handle of the garden gate, and the pothead is languidly peeling himself out of the car. Now Koberling can see that he's wearing unbelievably dirty jeans. Max calls from the kitchen in a sleepy and cracked child's voice, and Koberling knows that the light is falling on the little bed they've made for him on the window seat and that the flies are circling the lamp; suddenly he feels weak, overwhelmed. Where is Constance, he thinks, Constance who could be taking all this off my shoulders, because I don't want any visitors and especially no potheads.

He wipes the sweat from his upper lip and takes the pebbled path towards the garden gate. The crunch of the pebbles is surprisingly loud. Anna, Koberling thinks. Anna. You and your clown father, ridiculous buffoon, circus fool. When you were a child I once slapped you because you jumped on my back while I was meditating on the lawn in front of your house. When you were a child you didn't matter to me. I sat in the kitchen with your clown father and we talked and drank ourselves under the table. At worst you got on my nerves with your chocolate-smeared mouth, and you still get on my nerves now.

Koberling pushes back the bolt and pulls open the garden gate, smiling like an idiot, sweating incredibly. 'Wow, Koberling,' Anna says, grins, and follows this with a sort of, 'Oh. Wow, Koberling. It must be years since the last time we saw each other. Years!'

'Yes,' Koberling says, 'Years.'

The pothead takes two lethargic steps towards Koberling and extends a dirty hand. Koberling doesn't take it. He remains protectively near the gate as though this would make them understand, as though the mere presence of the silent and tense bastion of his body would make it clear to them that they should leave. That visitors were not welcome here. That old friendships no longer counted. But they do not understand. They stand there and stare. Koberling turns and takes the gravel path back to the veranda and, speaking into the blue, says, 'You can stay if you want to. There's a guest room in the attic.'

Towards evening Constance returns from her walk, no later than usual but for Koberling later than ever before. He's sitting on the veranda with Anna and the pothead, whose name he doesn't want to know, smoking one cigarette after the other. Max squats on the floor in front of the pothead, listening to his jumbled stories. Extraterrestrials, Druids, New Guinea, the end of the world. Max's mouth is wide open, a rope of spittle runs down his chin, his left hand rests on one of the pothead's shoes: from time to time he tugs gently and absently at the shoelaces. Koberling resents Max's unprejudiced trust in this pothead. What an idiot, Koberling thinks. Max, this guy's what I'd call an idiot.

Anna sits cross-legged in a wicker chair, staring at Koberling and lapses into childhood recollections. 'Something once happened with you, Koberling. Some funny business, I can't remember what exactly. I only know that you and my father were sitting at the kitchen table late into the night. Hey, Koberling, do you remember?'

Koberling makes no attempt to help her. He could haul out that business about the slap. He could tell her that as a child during those summers in the country she really was brown as a hazelnut. He could flatter her and remind her of all the silly children's jokes she used to tell, which her clown father proudly wrote down in an orange-coloured notebook. He could tell her that she used to be skinny and wiry, that she would disappear in the morning, taking the bridge across the river, into the woods, and not come back till evening, scratched all over, her legs covered with ticks. He could say, 'Your clown of a father left you alone. He allowed you to do whatever you wanted, so you'd simply disappear for the entire day. You weren't really there, not for any of us, and presumably that's your big childhood trauma today.'

But he doesn't feel like it. She doesn't interest him. Her clown father no longer interests him. He would like to sit here, in silence, undisturbed. Koberling lights another cigarette and realizes that he has been grinding his teeth all this time. Constance comes walking up the gravel path, a bounce in her step, dreadfully relaxed. Too late, Koberling thinks, too late, my dear, for now they're here and they won't be leaving soon.

Constance recognizes Anna immediately. She smiles a beaming and convincing smile, claps her hands softly and briefly holds them up to her face. She laughs, and plants her hands on her hips. Koberling is disgusted. He can anticipate what she's about to say: 'Anna! Little skinny Anna, and at least fifteen years older now. I can't believe it's really you sitting here!' Anna beams, looking embarrassed. She introduces the pothead, then looks over at Koberling, shy. Koberling suddenly pushes back his chair and flees into the kitchen. Little skinny Anna. What nonsense. He takes olives, cheese, salami, out of the refrigerator. Cut the bread, uncork the wine, the same as back then, the same as always. Now we'll eat supper, Koberling thinks. Now we'll eat, now we'll do something, even if it's only eating the goddamn food.

Darkness comes early because it's almost autumn. Under the plum trees at the back of the garden the light is already grey; the Oder will be pink and light blue by now. Koberling thinks it's taken him forty-seven years to find out that the wheat fields and the lakes and rivers become light again just before night falls. He needed this house to find that out. Maybe also Max, and Constance, too. If things were normal the child would already be sleeping, snoring softly, his cheeks red. He himself would be sitting on the veranda with Constance, reading or not talking. At some point he would sit down at his computer and type two or three sentences of dialogue for one of the screenplays he writes for a living. Two or three short and strange sentences, like every other evening. The light of the desk lamp would be green, because green is calming. The moths would tumble against the window screen, and he would find it both good and shitty living like this.

Now, though, the pothead is standing on Napoleon Hill rolling himself a joint. What a jerk. His absurd Zippo lighter flares up, and Koberling can smell the sweetish hashish. He thinks of Rose Martenstein. Rose Martenstein who came to a carnival party dressed as the Queen of the Night and collapsed unconscious on the kitchen floor after eating a hashish cookie, a doll in black satin. Sure, he had smoked hashish too. With Anna's clown father, for one. They'd be sitting in the garden, smoking one joint after another, and Anna's clown father would shout, 'Swazi grass!' and, 'Off to Swaziland!' till Koberling fell off his chair, laughing. Anna would be sleeping in her room under mosquito netting, talking in her sleep, and Koberling didn't know that twelve years later his own round-headed child Max would be born. How should he have known? How could he have? Back then he didn't even want to acknowledge Anna.

The pothead on top of Napoleon Hill turns around and motions to Koberling with his joint. Koberling gestures back an exaggerated refusal, and the pothead shrugs and ambles off down the hill. The glowing end of his joint disappears between the plum trees, and Koberling lingers irresolutely near the kitchen door. Constance and Anna are still sitting on the veranda, Max on Constance's lap, thumb in mouth. The child hasn't said a word to Koberling in the last four hours. He has clung to Anna or the pothead by turns, behaving as though he'd never seen another human being other than his mother and Koberling. Koberling thinks that's wrong. Max ought to be hiding behind him, ought to be asking him whether these guests are OK or not.

Anna talks about Poland. Max stares at her and from time to time breathes deeply, in and out. 'I can't understand why you still haven't been there when it's so close. They have storks there the way Berlin has pigeons. The Poles were mowing the fields, and sixty or seventy storks were walking in the furrows behind the tractors, looking for insects. And you wouldn't believe what ice-cream eaters the Poles are. *Lody* and *lody*, wherever you look they're constantly eating ice-cream.'

Max takes his thumb out of his mouth and says very clearly, 'Ice-cream.' Koberling feels tenderness creeping up his back. What a weird conversation. And the child picks out the one word he knows—ice-cream.

Anna talks, gestures with her hands, is constantly tucking her hair behind her ears. 'Constance. How are you doing here?'

Constance's voice, very deep and a little husky. Doing well. It's lonely. Koberling doesn't want a lot of visitors, a retreat after all those years in the city, a summer retreat. Anyway in the autumn it's back to Berlin. Long days. Hot days. Koberling spending a lot of time at his desk—a lie—and she herself going on walks through the Oderbruch, the Oder marshes, a most beautiful bit of nature. Good for the child too. Children belong in the country. Max is happy, she is too. And Koberling? He has trouble with being happy, but still...

Constance's hand, always arranging things. Constance, the

perpetual organizer. Four, five sentences, a life forged in one casting, one stroke of the pen and no more questions. It's that simple. In the shade by the kitchen door Koberling closes his eyes and opens them again. Anna has stopped talking. Now, in the total darkness, a sudden indignant croaking of frogs. A brief moment. Anna lights a cigarette and says, 'Yes,' begins again to tell her Poland stories, the ice-cream stories, her voice sounding somewhat remote, disconcerted. In the dark Koberling senses Constance's smile. He is surprised at how calmly she sits there listening to Anna's stories. In fact he is surprised at the interest she's showing in these guests, the obvious pleasure she takes in their visit. It doesn't matter who comes, Koberling thinks. It just doesn't matter. Anyone could be sitting here and she'd listen the same way, eagerly, glad to have a break from me for a while. It's because we've been here by ourselves the entire summer. But that's what we had agreed to do. We wanted to be by ourselves. I wanted to be alone.

Koberling goes back into the kitchen, turns out the light and sits down on Max's little daybed by the window. The contours in the garden have become sharper. Anna's red dress is dark, appears black. Koberling looks at her and feels nothing. She is young, has her father's clown face, everything round, round eyes, round mouth. A gap between her teeth that's going to make her look common ten years from now. Brown hair, very brown skin.

She's probably taking classes at the university, Koberling thinks. Journalism, and a foreign language. The pothead probably tends bar in some trendy hang-out and apart from that squanders his days. In the summertime they load their friends into old cars, drive to the Brandenburg lakes, guzzle wine till they pass out, and are convinced that the things that happen to them don't happen to anyone else. Idiotic. All of it idiotic. He rubs his eyes and feels tired. The days when he used to ask everyone, 'What do you think?' and 'What do you do?' are over. Koberling can't imagine that he ever asked these questions. Disgusting, almost embarrassing recollections of sitting around in bars all night, of swapping ideals, the destruction of illusions, carefully tended common interests. Hypocrisy, all of it, Koberling thinks. Anna's clown father was always just waiting for me to stop speaking so that he could begin with his utopias, his crazy head-in-the-clouds realities. And the same with me. I argued with him, I just wanted to out-talk him, when actually we both should have kept our mouths shut.

Max slides off Constance's lap, walks across the veranda and stands at the kitchen door. 'Why d'you sit there in the dark?' His voice is a little hoarse.

'Darkness is the friend of thieves,' Koberling says. 'Come on. Time for bed, time for the sand dragon and all that stuff.' He stands and lifts Max up; the child smells of summer and country-road dirt. 'Promise me,' Koberling feels like saying to him, 'promise me that...' But he doesn't say it.

'Are you two going to bed?' Constance asks from the veranda, her wicker chair creaking as she gets up.

'Yes,' Koberling replies, hurrying to the stairs, 'we're going to bed.' In his arms Max is already asleep. Anna calls out, 'Goodnight, Koberling!'

When he wakes up the next morning she is standing at the foot of his bed, smiling, her head cocked to one side, like a bird's. Glittering sunlight streams in through the window, and a fly bumps against the panes of glass. Koberling squints in the bright light and gropes under the covers for Constance, who is no longer lying beside him. No dreams, he thinks with relief. I didn't dream, not about her clown father nor about the past, not about smoking grass nor about sex.

Anna is shaking the bedstead so hard it sets her hair flying. 'Koberling! You sleepyhead! It's already noon, the others all drove to the city, and breakfast is ready. You're supposed to get up and show me the Oderbruch!'

'Says who?' Koberling asks. He is suddenly furious, sleep in his eyes and a bad taste in his mouth. That Anna should have dared to come in here, bursting into the intimacy of his bedroom like a child. She probably sneaked through the house first, looking into chests and drawers with her naive curiosity. Koberling sits up and pulls the covers over his chest. 'Out,' he says, 'get out now. I want to get up by myself. I want to be left in peace.'

Anna lets go of the bedstead, still smiling, and walks towards the door. 'I'll be in the garden, in case you want to know.' Koberling doesn't want to know and doesn't answer. He waits until he hears her footsteps downstairs in the kitchen and closes his eyes again. Lying there. Just lying there, in a state of exhaustion, on a see-saw between waking and dreaming. He has never felt refreshed and rested in the morning after eight hours of sleep. Always exhausted. Before, at night in his one-room apartment, Berlin and winter, he used to go to sleep dreading all the days, months, years that still awaited him. Time. Time that had to be filled up, conquered, annihilated. Then Constance came. A shared two-room apartment, Berlin and winter. In his memory always winter, warmth under the quilt, the commitment to Constance that was connected with a feeling of capitulation. Constance, behind whom Koberling hid and never emerged. Refuge and acquiescence. They used to fall asleep next to each other, saying, 'Fly slowly.' Time retreated, his dread crouched in the farthest recess of his mind. Then finally Lunow, this house, the breathing of the child, time completely dissolving. And then, again the dread—even greater than ever before—some nights when a car drove by and projected the circling shadow of the venetian blinds on the ceiling of their room. Perhaps because of this his exhaustion. Because sleep has to overcome dread, always.

Finished, Koberling thinks. Finished and done. It can't be that two little people from Berlin can walk in here and get me all mixed up. Mixed up about what? He gets up and opens the window. The fly moves out into the open in a straight line and is gone. Outside, the sky, a vast blue vault, and a newly woven spiderweb trembling in the window frame.

In the kitchen there's coffee on the table and an egg tucked into its woollen cosy. Constance has left him a note.

Dear Koberling, went shopping with Max and Tom, back some time in the afternoon, why don't you show Anna the Oderbruch, hugs and kisses.

Show Anna the Oderbruch. An imposition. Koberling looks at the little beelike squiggle that Max has put under Constance's large flowing script and places his hand on his stomach. He rolls the egg undecidedly across the wooden table top, pours coffee into a mug and sits down on the veranda. Anna, barefoot, is in the orchard picking raspberries. The noonday heat is oppressive and close, and Koberling already longs for the evening. The coffee is lukewarm and tastes bitter, leaving a furry taste on his tongue. Koberling pours it over the veranda railing into the flower bed and says softly, 'For Janis.'

Anna looks at him and picks up the berry bowl, then comes up on to the veranda. 'What did you say?'

Koberling doesn't look up but gazes into his empty coffee cup and says, 'For Janis. Your father always used to say that, long ago, when he poured leftover wine into the garden, "For Janis, for Janis Joplin."'

'Yes,' Anna says simply.

Koberling doesn't dare look up. Suddenly he feels terribly embarrassed about something. He stares at Anna's feet, at her dirty little toes.

She hides her left foot behind the right. Says, 'I thought I'd stay behind. Otherwise you would have woken up and found us all gone.'

Koberling looks up now, and acts preoccupied. Anna tilts her head and smiles at him, unsure. 'Wasn't it OK to wake you?'

What can one say to that? Nothing. And Anna doesn't seem to expect an answer. She sits down next to him, lights a cigarette, and inhales deeply. 'Tom likes it here. I do too. It's so peaceful, and besides, we are having Indian summer.'

Koberling makes a sound that could be interpreted as agreement or disapproval. Anna stares at him sideways. Koberling becomes restless and turns the empty cup in his hands; he can feel that Anna is slowly tensing up.

'Do you want to show me the Oderbruch or don't you? I mean, do you feel like going for a walk with me, or would you rather keep on sitting here?' With the last words her voice gets louder, almost stern.

Cry a little, Koberling thinks. Cry a little because you don't know how to deal with me, and also because I remind you of the time I slapped you. He too lights a cigarette, then gets up, and says, 'Yes, well. We can go for a little walk if you want.'

As Koberling closes the garden gate behind him he feels he's in unsafe territory. The house, the garden, the veranda, and above all Napoleon Hill are no longer protecting him. His back against the wall. Anna stands in the road, shifting from one foot to the other and looking almost the way she did long ago, like the child from back then, across the bridge over the river, into the woods, and away.

Koberling marches off resolutely, Anna hurries along beside him, dust whirling up between their feet. The country road becomes narrower. At the foot of the hills it becomes a small path that winds upward, through fruit trees, up into the green. Koberling, hands in his pockets, stares straight ahead. He feels a tension in his back and is already grinding his teeth again. Anna aside. Even without Anna, he has never liked the walks into the Oderbruch. Constance does. Ever since Lunow has been there for her, Constance walks off every afternoon with a happy face and comes back with an even happier face. 'The hills, Koberling. Sometimes I think it's the hills. I find them calming.'

Koberling finds the hills disturbing. For him it's all too beautiful, too enchanted, a Tarkovsky landscape, almost sinister. Once last summer he went into the Oderbruch by himself. In a tree on one of the more distant hills—he could already see the Oder—hung a piece of meat. A big piece of meat, almost the size of a man—a cow or a pig—skinned, bloody, putrid, flies buzzing around it. Koberling, panting up the hill, ready to see the Oder, to savour it, stopped and felt his heart lurch. The meat hung from one of the upper branches, the rope by which it was attached creaking and twisting. It looked like a vision, like a nightmare image, a monstrous and incomprehensible message, and Koberling turned, ran back down the hill, and screamed. Later Constance, sitting in the wicker chair on the veranda and smelling of violets, laughed and said, 'Don't be silly, Koberling. You only dreamed it.'

The next day, when they went to the Oderbruch together, the piece of meat had disappeared. Nothing was there any more. No rope, no flies, no message. They never talked about it again.

Anna kicks little pebbles, is smiling again, and whistles through the gap in her teeth. 'You don't want to talk, do you?'

'No,' Koberling says, 'I don't want to talk.' Says to himself, Talk about what, and peers through the fruit trees, straining to see. There is no vision. Nothing that he would see but Anna would not.

'That's all right,' Anna says. 'I don't want to talk either. Often I don't.' Koberling looks at her in ironic surprise, but she ignores him.

The last tall stalks of wheat still stand along the edge of the path. The trees have yellow edges, and a swarm of birds forms a triangle in the sky. In the distance the Oder gleams, a blue ribbon perforated by green river islands. The air above the meadows shimmers. Anna is breathing heavily. She twists her hair into a bun at the back of her neck.

Koberling remembers the beginning of a poem, *On the far side of the Oder, where the plain so wide,* or something like that, one of the countless poems that he used to recite to Anna's clown father on those lunatic walks at night on the moors. 'Listen to this one, and this one,' a helpless recital, a gush of words. Koberling walks along behind Anna, and his inability to describe, to express why the words sound so heart-wrenching—*On the far side of the Oder, where the plain so wide*—leaves him breathless. 'I understand,' Anna's father had said, again and again. 'I do understand.' But he couldn't have understood because Koberling himself didn't comprehend anything. He would like to grab Anna by the hair now, to shake her and slap her for the years of self-deception, for the years themselves. He wants to slap her again, to repeat himself. The Oder is dazzling, and the flat fields flow together into a green sea. Koberling calls her name and hears his voice, but as if coming from a great distance. Anna turns around, her red dress swinging into a wave. Koberling closes his eyes and thinks he is falling.

'Koberling? Are you all right?'

'Yes,' Koberling says. 'Everything's fine. I just want to go back now.'

Shortly before they reach Lunow—they can already see the country road, and behind the bend the house is about to appear—Anna touches his arm. Koberling takes a deep breath. The Oder is behind him, behind the hills, the distant unease already nearly forgotten. This will be the last time that he surrenders to it. Koberling quickens his pace. He would like to walk fast, to run, perhaps even to sing. An enormous relief spreads through him.

Anna stops and says, 'Koberling. I'd really like to know what there was between my father and you. I mean, I'd like to know why you no longer see each other, why you broke off the relationship.'

Koberling also stops and looks at her. She is smiling and looks hurt. 'There's no reason. There's no story there.' Koberling is surprised he even answered her. 'We had a few really good years together, then we saw each other less and less frequently, and at some point not at all any more. Maybe it was because he had women I didn't like. And you got older, later on he spent a lot of time taking care of you. There were minor arguments we didn't clear up, some disagreements. We lived different lives, I think. That's all. No tragedies, nothing decisive.'

Anna turns around and takes the path through the meadow down to the road. She walks very quickly. Koberling follows her and would like to call out, 'Life isn't theatre, Anna!' He doesn't know whether she can still hear him. She is running.

That evening Koberling is sitting on the veranda with Constance. Anna has gone back to the Oderbruch with the pothead. They had eaten supper together, and Koberling had three glasses of wine. He feels the alcohol in his knees and in his stomach. A cloud of mosquitoes hangs over the plum trees, and Constance is blowing smoke rings into space.

'I hope that Max will never do that. I'm not just hoping he won't, I simply won't have it,' Koberling says, not looking at Constance but at the plum trees, out into the darkness of the garden.

'What?' says Constance sleepily. 'What...will never do what?'

'What Anna did here,' says Koberling and hears a note of spite in his voice that he can't help. 'What she did by turning up here unexpectedly and under false pretences. When he grows up I don't want Max to turn up at Anna's father's place with some floozy on his arm and say—"Hey, clown father!"' Koberling raises his voice and mimics Anna. 'Hey, clown father, can we stay with you a couple of days? Only a couple of days, nothing special, just hang out, and at some point or other you can tell me why you stopped being friends with my father back then.'

Constance laughs and forms a big smoke ring with her lips. It glides away and dissolves. 'You're crazy, Koberling. Max doesn't even know Anna's father. And you probably aren't going to tell him anything either. And by the time Max grows up Anna's father may no longer be around.'

Next morning Constance and Max are singing along with the radio in the kitchen. Koberling is awakened by their voices, which mix in with that of the radio announcer. The sun is streaming through the window. No Anna in the room, no dreams during the night.

A summer day, Koberling thinks, picture perfect. He rumbles down the stairs, and pulls open the kitchen door. Max is sitting at the table, his mouth smeared with egg, looking blissful. Constance stands at the stove, her face a dark shadow against the sunlight. She doesn't look up; sings along with the radio, says, 'Good morning, Koberling.'

'Yes,' Koberling says, looking out into the garden, to the veranda, towards Napoleon Hill. Then says much too quickly, 'Where are they?'

The kettle begins to whistle. Constance turns off the gas and says, 'They left already. Anna wanted to go to some lake or other before it got really hot.'

Koberling goes over to the radio and turns it off. It becomes quiet in the kitchen. 'What? I don't understand. Why did they leave so soon?'

Constance pours hot water into the coffee filter, her expression strained. 'They didn't want to wake you again, Koberling. To abuse your hospitality. They left their address in Berlin and said they'd be happy if we visited them in the autumn.'

Koberling stares at Max. Max stares back and lets his egg spoon sink slowly on to the table. Koberling feels an ache in his stomach, like a tremendous insult. He opens the door to the veranda and pokes his left hand through a spiderweb between the doorposts. Indian summer. He says, 'By the time we go back to Berlin in the autumn I'm sure they won't be together any more,' the only pathetic put-down he can think of. Constance doesn't answer. □

GRANTA

# TEHRAN SPRING
## Christopher de Bellaigue

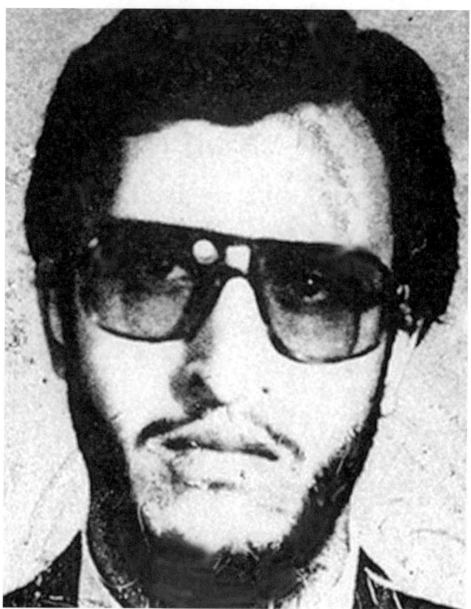

Saeed Emami, former deputy minister in Iran's Information Ministry: 'We have killed hypocrites.'  AFP

Trying to find Darioush and Parvaneh Forouhar's house for the first time, at the end of last year, I walked up Ferdowsi Street. I walked up Ferdowsi Street because I had got out of the taxi at the wrong place. Rather, the taxi driver, who was from south Tehran, and rarely ventured as far as the centre of the city, had stopped at the wrong place, in the wrong street, and I had got out without thinking. When I looked up, I saw I was way down Ferdowsi, a good twenty minutes from the Forouhars' alley, which intersects Hedayat, about a mile to the north-east. I started walking up Ferdowsi's eastern pavement, alongside the channel that runs north to south, its meltwater oily and black after flowing through half the city. I walked past the wall of the British Embassy. The shared taxis and buses kicked up a vile smoke.

It was hard to believe that this had been a sought-after area when the Forouhars, handsome and recently wed, moved in. But that, of course, was thirty or forty years ago, when it was glamorous to live in the lee of the smart European embassies, when being nice to foreigners was part of the Shah's plans to attract inward investment, and part of his cronies' plans to get rich. And the Forouhars, despite distrusting foreigners conceptually, rather liked them personally. What had been the source of Darioush Forouhar's nationalist ideas, not to mention his secular republicanism, if not the outside world?

As I turned right off Ferdowsi, heading east down Hedayat, I saw a middle-aged man with grey, clean-shaven skin, wearing a tweed jacket and tie, also turn east, and walk ahead of me. His tie, an unmistakable statement of political nonconformism, made me think of Forouhar. I was delighted that we were going in the same direction. I began to imagine that this man, like me, was going to the Forouhars' house.

In the old days, these streets must have been full of tie-wearers. There would have been the westernized Iranians and their self-conscious ties, and the foreigners and their broad loud ties; the expensive perfumes of their wives may have lain delicately over the fumes and the sweat. It was the time, in the mid-Seventies, when the five-star hotels (Hilton, Sheraton, Inter-Continental) were roaring with businessmen who had come to suggest to the Shah ways to dispose of his surplus oil revenues, and to stuff themselves with caviar poised on thinly sliced, crustless bread. (It was the time when almost all foreigners—save for a bright chap at the French Embassy, whose prescient report went unheeded—seemed not to have realized that Iran stood on a precipice.) The Shah's westward-marching kingdom, its heart pumping (how weakly, it would turn out!) in central Tehran.

That was the time when, as the rest of the city trembled with fury and anticipation, the shops in Ferdowsi and the surrounding streets did brisk business in imported booze and Swiss Army knives, and head waiters spoke a smattering of French. It was the time when the streets were full of big American sports utility vehicles, some of them bearing diplomatic wives from the large US Embassy compound a little to the north, and the wives clutched the calling card of an antique dealer who would sell them a topless Qajar beauty (reproduction) and a mildewed handwritten nineteenth-century Koran (genuine) for less than the cost of a tank of gasoline back home.

We had come 200 yards up Hedayat. The grey-faced man had slowed down, and he seemed to be looking for something, perhaps a building number. He was the only person in the street who was wearing a tie. There was not a foreigner to be seen. He paused outside an electrical shop, and looked in the window.

1979. The Islamic Revolution. The Shah's departure. Khomeini's return from exile. The students' occupation of the US Embassy compound, and the severance of bilateral relations. The banning of alcohol and the imposition of an obligatory head-covering for women. The replacement of the monarchy with the Islamic Republic. Eight years of war with Iraq. The Rushdie fervour and fatwa. Khomeini's death, and the mourners flowing around him, like lava. The Rafsanjani presidency. All the while, the Islamic authorities, the clerics who now had the power, denouncing the corrupting influence of the necktie.

The man came out of the shop, holding a length of electric cable, and carried on walking up Hedayat, only this time much faster. A minute or two later, I realized that we had overshot the Forouhars' alley; we had almost reached the far end of Hedayat. Disappointed that my hunch had been proved wrong, I retraced my steps, and found the alley. For some reason—pride? loyalty? economy?— Forouhar had carried on living in the middle of Tehran even after everyone else of his class had left. A man of the people, Forouhar, as only a patrician can be.

In the alley, most of the small brick houses with their wooden window frames had been knocked down and replaced with tiled tenements, storeys piled high. I came to a high, white gate, and rang the bell.

As I stood, waiting, I thought of Mahmoud Emami and four or five others, members of Forouhar's tiny political party, waiting at the same gate one evening in 1998, wondering why the door had gone unanswered.

Emami had asked the youngest and most athletic of his companions to climb over the gate and let the rest of them in. Parvaneh Forouhar's Renault 5 had been parked in the driveway. The outside light had been on.

My thoughts were interrupted by the sound of footsteps, and the white gate opened. The servant who had opened it gestured for me to come in. An old poodle waddled towards me to say hello. We climbed the low flight of steps that led to the front door, and went in.

We were in a gloomy hall. A woman's voice called from upstairs. The servant ambled away from me and up the stairs, leaving me alone in the hall. To my left, there was a door leading into a large room, a sitting or dining room, whose only visible wall was dominated by a large portrait of Dr Mossadegh, the old nationalist prime minister who in 1951 dared to nationalize the Anglo-Iranian Oil Company, and got toppled (by the Shah, the army and the CIA) for his impertinence two years later. Darioush Forouhar would have been twenty-five years old then.

On the right-hand side of the corridor there was another room: Forouhar's study.

That was where Emami and the others had found him, sitting in the chair nearest the door, his hands hanging by his sides, his mouth open. Later, during the rush of interrogations, leaks and rumours, they discovered that, before stabbing him twenty-five times, Forouhar's killers had orientated him towards Mecca. (This is what reliable Muslim butchers do when slitting an animal's throat—if they do not, the meat becomes *haram*, and unfit for a believer to eat.)

They had found Parvaneh's body lying on her bedroom floor.

Parastu Forouhar with a portrait of her murdered father

Then, the men had stood in the hall for a while, trembling and trying to decide what to do. That was when the telephone had rung and one of the men had gone to answer it. The line went dead when he put his ear to the receiver.

The servant came downstairs. He appeared surprised to see me in the hall, and chided me gently for not having gone into the room with the Mossadegh portrait, where I would have been able to make myself comfortable.

He led me in. It was an L-shaped room. On another wall, there was an unflattering picture of Parvaneh Forouhar, draped in an Iranian flag. The wall space next to her had been covered in black-and-white photos of her and her husband. Many of the photos had been taken when they were young. Next to a window that looked on to the courtyard were two chairs draped with Iranian flags. I sat down at a big table, in front of Parvaneh's picture.

Darioush Forouhar was seventy when he was murdered. Twenty years before, he had served briefly as a minister in the provisional government that followed the Revolution. He had to die because he made no secret of his belief that religion should be kept separate from government—a belief that makes you enemies in the Islamic Republic, which has been built on the principle of clerical sovereignty. Shortly before his death, Forouhar had declared a limited opposition to capital punishment, a declaration that some had equated with apostasy.

He had made light of all the surveillance and the harassment, mocking them with the salutation, 'Salaam to all our listeners', whenever he picked up the telephone. He had kept an elderly poodle inside his house, and dogs, as Ayatollah Mohammad Yazdi reminded his fellow countrymen not so long ago, are 'unclean'.

He had a moustache, unwaxed but rising at the tips. Like his ideas, it was a loose adaptation of western exemplar, an inadmissible expression of contempt for their bearded, Islamic way.

Parvaneh was the sort that would have raised hell to win justice for her dead husband. She had been the poet and performer in a house heavy with politics, the wife who had promised the Shah's last prime minister that she would immolate herself publicly if he didn't tell her where the secret police had detained her husband. Her adoration for Dr Mossadegh had led her to preserve the wrappers of sweets that he had sent her daughter. You might very well accuse Mrs Forouhar of *gharbzadegi*, Westoxification, and of questionable adherence to the Revolution's tenets. All good reasons for her to die.

The murdered couple's daughter, Parastu Forouhar, came down the stairs and into the room. She greeted me, and then sat down opposite me.

I felt like asking her, 'How can you bear staying in the house where your parents were murdered?'

She said, 'I hope you didn't have any trouble getting here.'

# Death to tyranny

When Darioush Forouhar was murdered, he went from being a little-known ex-minister to a martyr. Around the same time, at the end of 1998, there were four other murders and suspected murders, all of dissident writers: Pouyandeh and Mokhtari (suffocated); Davani (disappeared); Sharif (suspicious heart attack, rumoured to have been induced). But the people reacted more intensely to the Forouhar killings than they did to any of the others. The Forouhars had been killed despicably—he in his favourite chair and she in her bedroom—by men who had not bothered to take off their shoes.

Dissidents had disappeared or been killed before—at a rate of one a month, it is reckoned, since the beginning of the 1990s. But these victims were hardly discussed in public; that would have been dangerous. What the dead people had in common was a record of active or presumed political dissidence, and an abrupt, violent end. Either their deaths had not been acknowledged as murders, or judicial investigations into them had been abandoned for lack of evidence. In some cases, the families of the deceased had been quietly advised to drop their enquiries.

At the time when Forouhar and the writers were killed, however, things were different. They had become different in May 1997, when Khatami was unexpectedly elected president. Khatami was a cleric who had been close to Ayatollah Khomeini. But when he became president Khatami announced his intention to change the Islamic Republic, to make it freer and less beholden to a group of powerful clerics. His supporters called themselves reformists. His opponents were called conservatives, because the people were sick and tired of them.

Khatami had a gentle, probing touch. He was nicer to newspapermen than his predecessors had been. The previous government had tolerated ten national newspapers, only one of them wholeheartedly reformist in orientation. Khatami, on the other hand, encouraged just about everybody to start publishing news. There was an explosion of reporting and opinion—twenty-odd new dailies, weeklies and periodicals appeared—and the great majority of the new publications, faithful to the great majority of Iranians, were pro-Khatami. They printed what had never been printed before, and they goaded each other into an increasingly grave traffic of truths.

Iran became voluble again, which some people think is her natural state. The inky conservative broadsheets suffered. It was rumoured that the people at *Kayhan*, the biggest of these, were shredding a vast quantity of newspapers every day. It was a rather basic way of protecting a print run which had been computed according to machismo and nostalgia, rather than realistic sales expectations.

Before Khatami, a great many of the texts submitted by poets and novelists to the Ministry of Culture and Islamic Guidance for approval had been returned with the word BANNED written across them. After Khatami's election, however, the same authors resubmitted the same books, and they were returned with just a few corrections. A dozen publishing houses were set up to print all the un-banned books. Akbar Ganji, an investigative journalist who would do more than anyone to enlighten Iranians about the serial murders of the 1990s, called it the 'Tehran Spring'.

A lot of this washed over Forouhar. Khatami was a cleric and clerics, to his mind, were all the same. Khatami had been nurtured by the political system which had been introduced after the revolution—his presidency was a long way from the more secular regime that Forouhar had envisaged. Khatami had held ministerial office in the Islamic Republic; it was unthinkable that he would do anything to change fundamentally the regime that had so privileged him. Forouhar, on the other hand, dreamed of the day when the clerics would be removed from politics altogether.

Forouhar's killers, and those who gave their orders, were afraid that Khatami's pluralism would give heart not only to reformists, but also to outright opponents of the regime—they suspected Forouhar of being such a person. Khatami had promised to restore credibility to the Islamic Republic. The killers feared that, even if he didn't mean to, he would end up destroying it.

But killing Forouhar and the writers turned out to be a mistake, because the reformist press was ready and waiting. No matter that Forouhar was not one of them; he was surely entitled to express an opinion without being murdered. The killers found their actions denounced and picked over by Iran's new newspapers, which fell over one another in their enthusiasm to uncover the truth. 'Find the killers!' they demanded. 'What about the previous murders? Who gave the orders? This is nothing short of an attempt by Khatami's enemies to hound the president from office!'

There were more people at Forouhar's funeral than you might have expected, and lots of them shouted 'Death to tyranny!' in a way that suggested they meant it.

Khatami, who was at the peak of his political attractiveness at the time, said: 'When we don't accept someone, we make of him a counter-Revolutionary, a monarchist, corrupt, pro-western, a threat to national security and an apostate. Then, if some ignoramus says this counter-Revolutionary must be killed—well, they kill him.' With his delicate silver beard and his smile, his cream cashmere gown and careful anger, Khatami was everything the people hoped for in a *seyed*, a descendant of the Prophet.

People started to refer to the murders as Iran's biggest crisis since the Sacred Defence—the eight-year war against Iraq—back in the 1980s. It seemed as though not only the murders, but the state's very relationship with its citizens might be under review. Khatami took no chances with a conservative-minded judiciary: they might try and whitewash the affair. Instead he deputed three of his own men to investigate the murders and report back to him. The president, his busy triumvirate and the newspapers—it seemed as though they would drive all before them.

The conservatives were stirred by the cacophony. They manufactured theories: the perpetrators of Forouhar's death were friends of the family; the killers were linked to Iran's exiled opposition, counter-Revolutionary elements, and to foreign radio and television journalists; the writers were killed by people who favoured reopening relations with America; the Turkish government had had Forouhar killed to pay him back for his sponsorship of Kurdish separatism inside Turkey; the victims had been sacrificed by their paymasters, the CIA, in order to wreak havoc inside the Islamic Republic; Khatami's supporters had committed the murders, in order to discredit the conservatives.

'Even in the furthest recesses of the brain,' *Kayhan* said, 'there can be no room for the suspicion that the perpetrators of Forouhar's murder were from the forces of the Revolution! In fact, there's no logic behind the idea that the Revolutionary forces could have been behind a counter-Revolutionary action!'

On January 4, 1999, Khatami's persistence paid off. With great reluctance, the conservative-dominated Information Ministry announced 'the involvement in this affair of a handful of irresponsible, evil-thinking, deviant and obstinate figures within the Ministry. These irresponsible figures committed criminal acts as the agents of secret elements, and with the aim of fulfilling the designs of foreigners. The perpetrators of the murderers have not only betrayed the warriors of the Occulted Imam (may His return be hastened by God), but also struck a heavy blow against the prestige of the sacred regime of the Islamic Republic.' It was an unprecedented admission.

Then the case was handed over to the judiciary. The people of Iran began to hope that they might actually discover who had ordered the murders, and that these important and prominent people would be arrested. Perhaps, for the first time, the people running the Islamic Republic would become properly accountable to the people they served.

Then, one day, the judge running the case made an important announcement: 'In spite of the surveillance under which he was placed, Saeed Emami, one of the pivotal masterminds of the murders, committed suicide during bathing period on Saturday in the detention centre, by swallowing hair remover.'

Few Iranians had heard of Saeed Emami, but they understood the meaning of his death. Suddenly, it seemed unlikely that they would learn who had ordered the 1998 murders, or find out anything at all about those that had been committed before. Emami would take the information to his grave. Perhaps, the people concluded gloomily, Iran wouldn't change for the better, after all. In the offices of *This Morning*, the biggest of the reformist newspapers, Akbar Ganji smiled to himself and said: 'Over my dead body!'

# Two men

Akbar Ganji is a short, jolly man, who trims his beard rather than shaves it, in conformity with a semi-official code of the Islamic Republic, which contends that shaving is an effete Christian affectation. Soon after I arrived in Iran, he became my hero. His two books about the serial murders—made up mostly of articles he had written and interviews he had given on the subject—were the first books I read in Persian. Reading them was as close to him as I could get, since he was already in jail—although he had yet to be tried for anything. I envied those of my colleagues who had met him, before his arrest. He sounded slightly off the wall.

I saw him last November, when he appeared at Tehran's Revolutionary Court. No one was sure if he would turn up; at a previous court appearance, at the Press Court, he had refused to wear prison clothes and the judge hadn't let him in the door. Just as we started to fear this would happen a second time, from behind us we heard the sound of feet being scuffed along the linoleum, and some grunts. We turned around, and there was Ganji, being manhandled by two bewildered conscripts. He shouted: 'They tortured me! I've been tortured!'

Ganji was directing his comments at us, the members of the foreign press. As soon as we got back to our offices that afternoon, our editors rang to say they'd seen news wire headlines flashing TORTURE and MAVERICK JOURNALIST. But it was pretty obvious that Ganji hadn't really been tortured—not in the vicious, premeditated sense that our editors had in mind. It's probable that he got some fists in the face as the warders struggled to stuff him into the prison uniform they forced him to wear that day.

Ganji was determined to enjoy his day out. He harangued the judge and public prosecutor (whose roles seemed suspiciously interchangeable). He was sharper and wittier than either of them. He refused to shut up when the judge entreated him to. He grinned. He had his back to us, but every now and then he would turn around

The journalist Akbar Ganji in court

and tip his chin up, the way little people do when they want to see across a crowded room. He wanted to catch the eye of his wife and brother, and to see which Information people were there, so he could embarrass them by pointing them out publicly. He nodded at his former colleagues from the domestic press. At the end of the hearing, he announced that the state had tried to blackmail him, to try and stop him writing about the killing of dissidents. They had warned him he'd get fifteen years if he didn't shut his mouth. (And that, incidentally, is what he got, a few weeks later.) More news wire headlines. When the hearing was over, Ganji was carted back to prison, his prison jacket tucked petulantly under his arm.

Akbar Ganji, fearlessly enquiring journalist, Saeed Emami, secret plotter of murder; by the late 1990s they had inimical beliefs, and yet there was a time when they might have got along fine. Back in the days before the Revolution, they were both garrulous and devout young men, and they both loathed the Shah's rule, with its despotism and its sin. When the Revolution came, they pledged to work for the regime that took the monarchy's place. In 1979 Iran was shaking up the world's complacent polarization. In Tehran, there was a new creature, looking neither to Moscow nor Washington— nor to the vapid posturing of the non-aligned movement—but upwards, to God.

Before the Revolution, Ganji hung out a lot at the Naziabad Mosque in Tehran, where he would meet friends to pray and discuss whether or not it would be possible to replace the Shah with a government which answered people's yearnings for God and freedom. The words of an exiled ayatollah called Khomeini suggested that it might. Ganji distributed illegal tapes and transcripts of Khomeini's speeches. When the Revolution started, he and his friends took to the streets. The Shah went. Khomeini came. Grand days.

Ganji joined the Revolutionary Guard and, because he was an ideas man, they assigned him to Doctrine and Politics and sent him to Qom for training. It was from Qom that Khomeini supervised Iran after his return from exile, and from Qom that the seminary students sent their ideas on Islamic government whizzing around Iran at large. After Saddam invaded, Khomeini's strategists realized that, since they didn't have the American and European backing that Saddam did, they would have to rouse their men with the words of the Shi'a philosophers and the deeds of the Twelve Imams. After finishing his studies, Ganji returned to Tehran, where he helped instil in the officers of the Revolutionary Guard a love for the Islamic Republic that would make of them fearless warriors.

And Emami? Emami wasn't there. He had left Iran to study at Oklahoma University and watched the Revolution's vital moments on US television. But he watched them with enthusiasm. When he graduated, he went to work for what remained of Iran's diplomatic representation in Washington, and then for the mission to the UN. Already he was passing bits and bobs to the new Information Ministry in Tehran.

Then Iran recaptured the town of Khorramshahr and its refineries, and Saddam sued for terms. Iran's leaders had a choice: enjoy the fruits of victory, or fight on—until Baghdad had fallen, Saddam had been toppled, and a Shi'a theocracy installed in his place. They chose to fight and, although their objectives remained distant, they promoted a triumphal Revolutionary religiosity that took six years to fade. The young Iranians who died (while Baghdad stood firm) before the 1988 ceasefire were to become the Revolution's great moral example. But Ganji, among others, suspected that Khomeini's advisers were keeping from him the terrible casualty figures, and disguising from him the impossibility of the task Iran had set itself. His conscience troubled, Ganji got himself transferred to the Ministry of Culture and Islamic Guidance.

At the end of the 1980s, the war ended, Khomeini died, and the economy ground to a halt. The hardline conservative clerics were rampant throughout the bureaucracy and the government. The moderates were being put to flight. The war, the old justification for the harshness and repression, was over. But the harshness and repression—and the bared teeth—remained.

Rafsanjani, the new president, chose a man called Ali Fallahian to be his Information Minister. This was a controversial choice, since some people suspected that Fallahian could be rather brutal. The new minister took to Saeed Emami—who had by now returned from the United States—enormously. Before his thirtieth birthday, Emami had become one of Fallahian's deputy ministers.

It may be that Emami was ashamed of having been abroad during the Revolution, of not having witnessed at first hand the rebirth of Iran and Islam. This regret, and the desire to distinguish himself in the eyes of those who had participated—those who considered themselves to be the true Revolutionaries—may have spurred him to greater zeal, to a more unbending reading of history and correction.

Ganji, dabbling in journalism by now, was going in the opposite direction. He and people like him were concerned by the gap that had emerged between the aspirations of the ordinary Iranians who had supported the Revolution, and the stagnant lives they were being obliged to live. They had also started to examine the way the clerics had appropriated most of the plum administrative positions. Murmurs grew; people said that theological knowledge had itself been dishonoured by the clerics' thirst for power. They asked whether a more flexible approach to the interpretation of religious texts might allow Iran an escape route from its morally superior poverty. They were fed up with being hated by the rest of the world, and longed for Iran to be allowed into the family of nations. To Emami, such ideas smacked of surrender.

## Emami's lecture

There is a grainy amateur film of a speech made by Saeed Emami to a hall full of students at Hamedan University, in western Iran, which took place on or around December 23, 1996.

The cameraman has missed the first part of the speech; when the film starts, Emami is in full flow, and the camera is panning across the audience. On the left-hand side of the hall, neatly segregated, are the women, almost all of them in *chador*. When the camera pans across the men, who make up the majority of the audience, it catches a solitary cleric, sitting in his robe and a ruffled turban in the front row, coping with a winter cold. The rest of the audience are non-clerics; they wear thick coats and trousers, and different types of beard to show off their virtue, and their listless eyes attest to a Revolutionary zeal that is being pounded by doubts. Having been gloriously dynamic during Khomeini's lifetime and the Sacred Defence, the Islamic Republic is now inert. No, the situation is worse than that; Iran is being deliberately disabled from within, by liberals intent on corrupting and westernizing the regime, throwing about phrases like 'human rights' and 'representative democracy'.

Looking at the film more closely, it appears that most of the men in Emami's audience are too old and tired to fit the international stereotype of the student. Rather than attend university, many of these men spent months or years in the trenches of western Iran; they lost brothers and friends to Saddam's mines and gas, but the pain of mourning was dulled by the knowledge that these brothers and friends had at least died ecstatically, martyrs to the cause of a pristine, Shi'a Islam. Then the war came to an end and Khomeini passed away. Back home, the war veterans found themselves undefended—from poverty and unemployment and from the ingratitude of the people for whom they fought; many of these people had got fat from profiteering.

Now, hurt, the old soldiers have crowded into a lecture hall to hear Emami. They have in mind, perhaps, Khomeini's admiration for the Ministry of Information; he called its employees the 'anonymous foot soldiers of the Occulted Imam'. It's true; at least the Information boys give the impression that they haven't abandoned the struggle against vice; at least they seem willing to take the battle to the enemy, to strike pre-emptively against the hypocrites and other enemies of the state. 'Of course,' says Emami reassuringly, during the course of his talk, 'we've killed hypocrites, and we've killed members of other groups as well...what are we to do with hypocrites: sit down and play chess with them?' If anyone can provide the veterans with words of comfort, and remind them of the values of the Revolution, Emami is the man.

He wears a beard, and square-framed glasses high up his aquiline nose. When he cracks his jokes, there is a flash of teeth and a lick of tongue across voluptuous lips. The way he talks makes him at once one of the boys and way above them. His Persian is colloquial, because the Revolution was supposed to answer the call of God in a way that is intelligible to man; but he patronizes his audience, too, because he's risen fast, and he has his pride. By the time his hour and a half is up, he has conducted his listeners on a *tour d'horizon* of his prejudices, his fancies and his faith.

At the time of the Hamedan speech, Emami is in his late thirties, and no one can be appointed to a high post in the Ministry without his say-so. Fallahian has entrusted him with an astonishing degree of autonomy. Emami will use that autonomy to try unilaterally to sabotage Khatami's attempt to win next year's presidential election. He dabbles in the arts; state television ran a programme of 'confessions' of opponents of the regime, made by Emami.

He is active in foreign affairs. In 1995, Emami's boys carried out a jolly raid on a dinner party held by the German cultural attaché. At the time of the Hamedan speech, Emami's boys are trying to pin charges of spying for Germany on a dissident magazine editor whom they have tortured and plan to kill. (The plan will fail.) Later on, there will be the case of Hofer, a German businessman caught with his pants down—a capital offence in the Islamic Republic—and, later still, the ten Jewish 'spies'; their arrest, trial and conviction will upset relations between Iran and most of the rest of the world. All this, it came to be reckoned, was the work of Emami, and his boys.

# Why?

Mykonos, of course! That's the name of the restaurant in Berlin where four Iranian Kurdish dissidents were killed in 1992. At the time of the Hamedan speech, a German court is trying Iran's leaders in absentia for having ordered the crime. (The following year, Kubsch, the judge, will find them guilty of a 'flagrant violation of international law.') It's an intolerable affront to the Islamic Republic, and Emami has made it his business to come up with ways of avenging the slight.

For Emami, the man opposed to his point of view is like misshapen clay. The strength in Emami's fingers may derive in part from the close relationship he enjoys with his boss. It is possible, too, that Emami experiences a kind of joy when he breaks his subjects— once he's taken their honour and they're begging for death. But most of all, Emami is driven by love. He loves the Revolution, and he loves the memory that he cherishes of Khomeini, a love he has now transferred to Khomeini's successor as Supreme Leader. Above all, he loves his fellow-Iranians, even those he destroys. His particular brand of Islam is totalitarian, paternalistic and brash.

Emami's understanding of his own worth is apparent from his conversational style of address, from the easy way he sits on his chair, and from the audacity of his boasts and his lies.

'I want to give you the example of Saeedi Sirjani,' he says. 'The

Saeedi Sirjani that came into being after we became pals—and there's quite a story there!'

Emami's audience know about Sirjani. He was a writer, a homosexual, a drug addict. *Kayhan* revealed that Sirjani worked for SAVAK, the Shah's secret police, before the Revolution. But Sirjani was guilty of a more sinister crime; he exploited the benevolence of the Islamic Republic—which cannot, after all, be boundless!—in order to put about perverted ideas.

There was a privately circulated letter, Emami explains, in which Sirjani used diabolical cunning to fold a very august personage into a retelling of the tale of Sheikh Sanan, the diverted dervish. Everyone knows about Sheikh Sanan and his Christian girlfriend; in the noon of his obsession, she caused him to lose sight of his faith. In Sirjani's retelling, the dervish became the august personage, and the beguiling girl became political power. *Kayhan* described Sirjani as 'counter-Revolutionary, traitorous and perverted'.

But, says Emami, this is a story with a happy ending. It is impossible not to experience a surge of gratitude towards the men—Emami's men—who induced in Sirjani his eleventh-hour conversion. They put Sirjani before the TV cameras, and he apologized for the things he had been saying and writing. He announced: 'The New Sirjani is not the same as the Old Sirjani!' It was little short of miraculous. There were letters to the newspapers, and a full examination of the details of his crimes and the extent of his penitence. By the time Sirjani had had his heart attack in jail, he had been saved. (It was typical of the foreign radio stations and local gossip mongers to make out that Sirjani had been knocked about to get him chatting, and that his heart attack had been induced.)

'When he first came to us,' Emami tells his audience, 'after the boys had picked him up from the drugs combat HQ, he really thought the Information Ministry was going to thrash him, that there was going to be a set-to. To start with, he was preening: when they brought him into the detention centre at the Ministry, he said, "Go on, beat me, cut me to ribbons; I'm not telling you a thing." But the boys told him: "Listen, this is the Information Ministry. We're not into beating here. Here's a pen and paper; go and write."'

According to Emami, Sirjani wrote a poem addressed to the

Supreme Leader, asking why Iran's men of letters were being degraded by the regime. One of Emami's boys replied with a poem of his own. When Sirjani read this reply, its declaration of religious and political faith induced a dramatic transformation in him.

'Ten minutes later,' says Emami with a fond smile, 'he rapped on the door of his cell and said, "Take me out of here; I want to confess." I said, "Confess to what?" He said, "I want absolution."

'You know, we've got fifty hours of him on tape and video...he wrote 1,700 pages on why he had waged war on the clerics. On why he'd been the enemy of the Revolution. Those images we got of Saeedi Sirjani...sometimes I sit down and watch them, and I weep.'

Apparently Sirjani's penitence was so profound that he was moved to request a trip to the front. 'The boys took him off, to the section of the front where they were exhuming the corpses from the trenches...and he sat on a pile of corpses and cried his eyes out...

'At that time, he didn't know what my position was in the pecking order. I would go every now and then to the house we'd rented for him...there was a pool and some flower beds. He'd get up in the morning and pick flowers, and water the gardens—that sort of thing.

'Then one day he started to pour his heart out. He said to me, "I'll tell you something; I'm dying for some dates and ground sesame..." The following morning, I went down to south Tehran and traipsed around for God knows how long, until I'd found some ground sesame, and brought back the ground sesame along with some dates. And afterwards, when he'd realized what my post was (not that my position is anything but humble—far be it for me to contest the role I have been allocated by the Islamic Republic!) and that I'd done him this service, he said, "I can't believe you went all the way down to the south of the city and traipsed around on account of some ground sesame and dates."

'So I said, "Since I sensed that you had started to understand our values, I wanted to indulge you."'

After Emami's death, there was a lot of talk going around to the effect that he and his pals in the Information were regular sickos, that they got their kicks from inflicting mental and physical torture on their subjects. Nowadays, however, they reckon that this aspect of Emami and his pals was overplayed. It seems that trampling on people was the way Emami performed his sacred function.

Saeed Emami and his men tortured Saeedi Sirjani to extract confessions for broadcast. Then they killed him, because he was scum. In the words of Ruhollah Hosseinian, Emami's old pal from the Information: 'Saeed Emami really did believe that the enemies of the Islamic Republic should be put to the sword.'

# The cliff

The event was a symposium planned by the PEN Association of Armenia, in 1995. PEN invited all the distinguished Iranian writers they could think of.

In the days leading up to the departure, lots of the writers and journalists pulled out—a suspicious number, it is now thought. One participant said his wife had had a car accident, and it turned out later that she hadn't. Others came up with flimsy excuses.

Twenty-one of the writers were not tipped off. So there were twenty-one writers and journalists on board the tour bus when it set off for the border, after having stopped for a break in the Caspian town of Rasht.

The driver was a short, dark-skinned fellow called Barati with the liverish lips of the habitual opium user. As they headed into the mountains, and evening turned into night, some of the writers felt like another break. Barati promised to stop at a roadside cafe where they could procure bread and milk and delicious local honey.

They cleared Astar early the following morning. Most of the writers were asleep. Some of them dozed, wondering when they would get their milk and honey.

Then, suddenly, the bus lurched to the right, and came off the road. Those who were awake thought they had reached the roadside cafe which the driver had described. Then Fereshteh Sari screamed. She screamed because Barati had taken the vehicle out of gear, and leaped out. The bus was trundling towards the darkness.

Massoud Tufan, who had taken the two seats at the front on the right-hand side of the aisle, jumped to his feet and wrenched the handbrake. The bus came to a halt a few feet short of the cliff.

The only explanation for what happened next is confusion. Not all the passengers were awake. Those that were assumed that Barati had fallen asleep at the wheel, lost control, and jumped out in a panic. Therefore they made no attempt to stop him when he climbed back into the bus, turned the engine on, and reversed towards the road.

He stopped the bus, and put it back into first gear. He put his foot down on the accelerator. Once again, as the bus trundled towards the cliff, he put the bus into neutral, and leaped out.

This time, a rocky outcrop at the angle of the cliff arrested their forward motion, catching the underside of the bus and preventing it from going over the edge. The front wheels hung in the air.

The writers got out of the bus. A few of them tried to lynch Barati. The others pulled them off; killing him would compound their problems.

As they waited for the police in a nearby cafe, some of them saw a black Mercedes Benz approach, slow down near the spot where the bus had almost gone off the cliff, then speed off. The local police arrived and asked them questions. Later, Alikhani, Emami's right-hand man, arrived with some of his boys, and shooed the local police away.

Alikhani and his men took Barati away. They escorted the writers to a jail in Astar. Alikhani interrogated the writers in their cell. He asked them:

'What makes you think the driver was trying to kill you?'

'What is the purpose of your visit to Armenia?'

'What is your evaluation of the current cultural climate in Iran?'

Then he let them go.

## Ganji's campaign

Ganji is the reason we know a lot of this. He said what had only been whispered. He shouted what had been said. He gave meaning to the stuff we already knew from other sources, and didn't understand. He got Iranians to demand what they had never previously dared to demand of their seniors: an explanation. If Ganji were not Iranian and his mother tongue not Persian, but English, his journalism would have won him Pulitzers and invitations to address dinners in a dicky bow. As it is, he's just starting a ten year jail sentence and, when that finishes, he'll have five years' internal exile somewhere hot. All for saying things he shouldn't have said.

Ganji gave us Emami boasting in the company of important officials about the way his men had murdered Saeedi Sirjani. He gave us Emami cooperating with *Kayhan*'s editor to interrogate subjects, and creating the famous television confessional. He gave us Emami destroying his subjects, Emami with interesting pseudonyms (Kooshan; Mohammad Ali; Kashigar; A Senior Bureaucrat), and Emami openly advocating the murder of five or six of Khatami's close associates. He gave us Emami planning the early serial murders and guiding the latter ones. He suspected that Emami had been murdered because he knew too much. Even after Emami's death, Ganji had a use for him. Emami's brutality illustrated the brutality of which the system was capable. By following Emami, Ganji found the guys who gave the orders.

None of this is to say that Ganji could prove all, or even most, of his claims. It would have been madness for him to have revealed his sources. It may be that he had little, if any, documentary evidence for what he was writing. (The people he was writing about didn't know that, of course.) He put down what happened, quite baldly, and then hoped that he would be believed. He was.

The young journalists at *This Morning*, where he wrote his best stuff, revered him because he laughed at the threats. It buoyed them to know that he feared death no more than going to the dentist. They went out whenever he asked them to go, gathering information and conducting interviews. They were aware they were living in the golden age of Iranian journalism, and that their product sold 290,000 copies a day—a figure, already astonishing, that would have been much higher had the presses only worked faster. They were aware, too, that the golden age could come to an end at any moment, that they could be plunged into darkness and silence once more. Some people at the paper suggested that Ganji leave his articles unsigned, but he refused. His revelations were a sort of theatre, and he enjoyed taking a bow. Besides, fame gave him a kind of safety. The greater his notoriety, and the more blatantly his enemies were obliged to loathe him, the better were his chances of staying alive.

One day, in *This Morning*, he told his readers about Fatemeh Ghaem-Magham. Some of them remembered the unexplained murder of this air stewardess and mother of three from the newspapers. How could she have been a victim of the Information's scheme to murder political dissidents? It was true, Ganji said, that Ghaem-Magham had no political past. But she had been 'the witness of a regrettable event whose disclosure would cost the murderer and his ally dearly. So, there was no solution but to kill her.'

Ganji alluded to no document. His description of the way she died—shot, after a conversation with her killer that lasted an hour and a half—added nothing to the previously published newspaper reports. But the Ghaem-Magham piece was thrilling. The 'murderer' and his 'ally' knew who they were. Ganji knew who they were. Reading the piece was like eavesdropping for a few seconds on a private telephone conversation. There was Ganji, whispering down the line: 'I'm on to you...'

To help his readers remember who was who, he gave aliases to the villains. These aliases would find their way into Iran's imagination. Once upon a time, there was a Master Key, who issued orders to kill the people who used words in the wrong way—orders that Emami and his men carried out. But the Master Key, Ganji said, had a second function. It was in his power to open the door to the Dungeon of Ghosts, which was the source of all the evil. Once inside, it would be possible to make out the Eminences Grises, skulking in the shadows. The Eminences Grises were influential people who used their public standing to cast aspersions on a putative victim's character and personal mores, and to call into question his adherence to Revolutionary ideals. In some cases, the Eminences Grises invoked Islamic law to pass unofficial death sentences on the 'accused'. As Ganji's revelations progressed he produced an Eminence Rouge. 'Louis XIV,' Ganji told his readers,

> appointed Cardinal Richelieu to be his prime minister, and Richelieu gave Father Joseph a position in his administration... On the orders of Father Joseph (the Eminence Grise), dissidents were murdered, and Cardinal Richelieu stayed silent. Because Cardinal Richelieu wore red clothes, they called him the Eminence Rouge.

Ganji managed his readers. He allowed the nimbler ones, those who worked in government offices and picked up scraps of gossip, to guess the true identities of his characters early on. That knowledge made them complicit in Ganji's revelation, and even keener to find out how the story would end. For every measure of analysis and polemic, he gave them a half measure of thrill. It kept them on the edge of their seats, and receptive to his wider sermon.

> Saeed Emami...took Siamak Sanjari and a few others to a house, and he discussed matters there with him for a few hours. Then he ordered his men to stab him to death. Siamak Sanjari started to cry, and said he was due to be married in the next few days. Emami contacted the Master Key by mobile phone, and told him that Sanjari was weeping, and that his wedding ceremony was due to take place soon. 'He even has invitations addressed to you and me in his pocket.' The Master Key ordered Emami to kill him, and they stabbed him fifteen times. Then they set fire to Sanjari's Mercedes Benz in the one of the valleys around Tehran.

Put yourself in the shoes of the Master Key. To start with, you're affronted by your alias, which makes you out to be a mere facility. But, in the face of Ganji's strange and intimate knowledge, your irritation turns to apprehension. Before you know it, other journalists also interested in the serial murders pick up on your alias, and have started using it in their articles. It seems as though every paper you open contains references to the Master Key! Gossip is flowing through Tehran. What was going on between Fatemeh and the Master Key? What unorthodox relationship meant that Sanjari, the other non-political victim of the murders, had to die?

Ganji wants to see how you'll react, whether or not you'll be panicked into indiscretion. He says he's not interested in retribution, and that destroying the culture of violence is more important than destroying the perpetrators. At least on that score, you seem reasonably safe—the judge running the case has made it perfectly clear he's going to look no higher than Emami, and no further back than Darioush Forouhar. But Ganji could seriously damage you. The worst of it, of course, is that you can't sue him; he hasn't identified you. Besides, what if he has documentation to back up his claims?

Gradually, even those who hadn't guessed from the start came to realize that, when Ganji talked about the Master Key, he was referring to Ali Fallahian—Emami's boss, and Iran's Information Minister from 1989 to 1997. Ganji dribbled this into his readers' consciousness in such a way that he wouldn't get his newspaper banned. (That would come later.) He used suggestive juxtapositions, and allowed his hints to get broader and broader. He got his public used to an allegation of astonishing impudence, without making that allegation explicit. (Until the end of 2000, that is, when he named Fallahian as the Master Key, which spiced up his second appearance at the Revolutionary Court.)

Just as Emami had pointed the way to Fallahian, so Fallahian showed Ganji into the Dungeon of Ghosts. There, Ganji found (and named) the Eminences Grises, some of them senior clerics and judges—and he hinted darkly that they knew a lot more about the serial murders than they were letting on. Later he would accuse one of them of ordering one of the killings. Still Ganji didn't stop. He went a step higher, to Rafsanjani.

The audacity! Rafsanjani wasn't just a former president; he was one of the most powerful men in Iran, and reputedly the richest. He was widely tipped to cruise back into Parliament in the 2000 elections, to become the parliamentary speaker. Ganji had other ideas.

'The Eminence Rouge', the first and most notorious example of Ganji's Rafsanjani pieces, was not a very good article. It was uncharacteristically impatient; it attempted to tarnish all of the former president's brightest buttons in one go. Ganji presented his evidence hurriedly, and some of it wasn't convincing. A lot of the best stuff was submerged beneath the author's contempt. There was little, if anything, that was revelatory, little that hadn't been said a thousand times before, behind Tehran's nougat-coloured brick facades. The difference is that Ganji was addressing the whole nation, out of doors.

After 'The Eminence Rouge', Rafsanjani was no longer able to portray the Iran of his presidency as a just realm, and interpret the nation's silence as a nod of agreement. No longer could he make out that he presided over (his words) 'the cleanest period in the Information's history'.

Seventy-odd extra judicial executions; the abductions and the torture sessions; Emami's 'confessional'; the Armenian bus holiday;

these took place, Ganji reminded his readers, during 'the cleanest period in the Information's history'. Was it not Rafsanjani who had urged Fallahian on to a less than enthusiastic Parliament? Did the Rafsanjani years not coincide with Mykonos and—in the words of Ruhollah Hosseinian, Emami's old work pal—'hundreds of successful operations committed abroad by Saeed Emami'?

Ganji's piece 'The Eminence Rouge' was only incidentally about the serial murders. It was really about the abuse of power and the contempt of the ruler for the ruled. Ganji impressed on his fellow Iranians the depths to which their leaders had sunk. He questioned the miracles that young Iranians were encouraged to dream about at night.

The Friday after the piece appeared, Rafsanjani accused Ganji in the course of a sermon of 'calling into question the prestige of the Revolution'—of nothing less than a 'vast, vast betrayal'.

Rafsanjani's words did his reputation as much damage as Ganji had. People wanted him to answer the allegations, not equate his own prestige with that of the nation. In the meantime, Ganji was having the time of his life. He challenged Rafsanjani to a public debate. He entitled a subsequent article, 'I haven't even started criticizing [Rafsanjani] yet'.

Even newspapers which had previously disapproved of Ganji's presumptuousness were forced to be more dispassionate in their evaluation of Rafsanjani's record in office. They, and their readers, found it to be less glorious than they had been led to believe.

In the 2000 parliamentary elections, reformist candidates swept the field. Rafsanjani scraped into Parliament, last of the thirty deputies elected to represent Tehran. It was Ganji's finest hour, the reformists' finest hour, and it provoked the conservatives' fury.

Later that year, conservative judges banned about thirty reformist publications, including *This Morning*. They jailed more than a dozen journalists.

In January 2001 a judge sentenced to death the three Information agents who had murdered the Forouhars and two other writers. He sentenced two of Emami's boys (including Alikhani) to life imprisonment. He jailed the opium-using driver, Barati. The families of the murder victims boycotted the trial, denouncing it as a whitewash.

Some of the reformists turned against Ganji. They criticized him for having driven Rafsanjani into the arms of the conservatives, and for provoking the judges' offensive against the press. Ganji, they argued, had shown excessive disrespect to his seniors. He should have doffed his cap while he was calling them hypocrites, liars, murderers.

Many more people, however, continued to admire Ganji, and to regard his imprisonment as a tragedy. They said that Ganji represented the best and the bravest of their country. They said he had lots more information about the serial murders, and they expressed the hope that one day he would release it.

## Remembrance

Parastu Forouhar was in the hall, speaking on the telephone to a journalist in Germany. She was reading out a statement expressing her dissatisfaction with the case file that had been prepared against her parents' killers. The prosecutors and judges had forgotten to ask who had given the orders. They had left important bits out. Parastu was reading very slowly and loudly. Every now and then she would have to restart a sentence, when the line crackled from all the people listening.

Events had forced her to behave like a politician. Her parents' colleagues and friends; the young people who came on to the streets when two decent old people were murdered—their anger and righteousness had needed marshalling. Who better than the handsome daughter of the deceased, addressing the anniversary gatherings—her pride and grief against their evil? (At the funeral, her mind seeing with an adman's lucidity, she had arranged the photo that everyone remembers: a murdered nationalist lying in an open coffin, his breast overlaid with the national flag, a spade-load of Iran's soil spattered on top.)

She came back into the room, and sat down.

'Do you think your father was selfish?'

'He didn't distinguish between his children and his principles.'

Forouhar had written to her from jail, when she was very little. A serious letter, didactic, assuming intellectual responsibility, loaded up with love. While she was reading it to me, she stopped abruptly, and it looked as though she would start to cry.

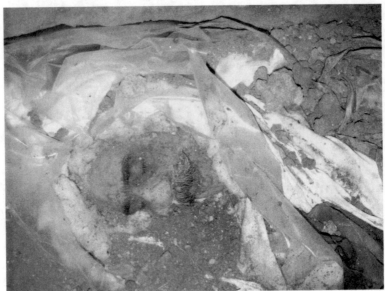

Darioush Forouhar in his grave                    BEHROUZ MEHRI/AFP

'How long are you prepared to carry on struggling for justice?'
'I don't know.'

Giving up would mean betraying. Giving up would mean hearing and uttering her parents' names a great deal less, and that might be too much for her to bear.

'What about Ganji? Have you met him?' I had Ganji's books in my briefcase, the juiciest bits underlined in pencil.

She hadn't. She spoke of him dutifully, an orphan reminded of a remote benefactor. I had expected more enthusiasm. Apart from Parastu herself, Ganji had done more than anyone to make sure that people still talked about the Forouhars. Then I thought: she distrusts him.

Ganji was a brave fighter, but for ideas—his ideas, and Khatami's ideas. Ganji thought that reforming the system would enable it to evolve and survive; Forouhar had in mind a more radical transformation. The Forouhars' deaths had spurred Ganji not because he loved the Forouhars, but because their deaths offended his politics. Ganji and his sort, the 'reformers', were using her father and his memory because it was convenient. They had press-ganged his unresponding soul into a movement for which he had had no time.

The poodle and the retainer saw me off the property, into the alley. I turned into Hedayat, hailed a cab, and told the cab driver I wanted to go to the north of the city. □

*Announcing* Boston Review's *Ninth Annual*

# SHORT STORY CONTEST

*Deadline:* September 1, 2001
*First Prize:* $1,000

**Guidelines:** The winner will receive $1,000 and have his or her work published in the December/January 2001-2002 issue of *Boston Review*. Stories should not exceed four thousand words and must be previously unpublished. The author's name, address, and phone number should be on the first page of each entry; do not send a cover letter. Manuscripts will not be returned. A $15 entry fee, payable to *Boston Review* in the form of a check or money order, must accompany all submissions. **Submissions must be postmarked no later than September 1, 2001.** Entrants will receive a one-year subscription to *Boston Review*, beginning with the December/January 2001-2002 issue. Send entries to: Short Story Contest, *Boston Review*, E53-407 MIT, Cambridge, MA 02139.

GRANTA

# LET THERE BE LIGHT!
## David Feuer

Rabbi Sternglantz showed up one day at my work place, a state-run mental facility called 'The Hill'. He was looking for a psychiatrist. Not for himself but for 'Vayehi Or', which the Rabbi translated as 'Let There Be Light!' and which he described as 'only the second mental health clinic ever to serve the Hasidic population'.

I distrusted him instantly. It was a combination of his limp handshake and his long white beard, which covered the Rabbi's entire face except for a patch of pallid skin roughly the size and shape of safety goggles. I admit, I have always distrusted those big white beards. They confer instant wisdom and spirituality upon their bearers and as such they often serve as a refuge for scoundrels. But my distrust of Rabbi Sternglantz's beard was even more intense because of the way his beard contradicted his words, which were a disconcerting mixture of Old Testament parable and New Age psychobabble. The Rabbi used words like 'cultural sensitivity' and 'empowerment' and 'underutilization', mental health buzzwords that sounded false coming out of that mystical white beard.

The Rabbi assured me that Vayehi Or was a 'highly professional' operation staffed by 'highly professional' professionals. It was reassuring to hear that it was not some amateur mental health clinic staffed by amateur professionals. Rabbi Sternglantz further assured me that by early spring Vayehi Or would be moving from its current temporary location on Grant Avenue to its new 'state-of-the-art' building on Henderson Street that had been designed by a professional architect who specialized in mental health buildings. Again, it was reassuring to know that the future home of Vayehi Or had been designed by a professional rather than an amateur architect. But in case I didn't believe him, the Rabbi produced from the pocket of his black coat a brochure on high quality glossy paper. On the front was an artist's rendering of a stately three-storey brick building sitting on a stately tree-lined street. Both the building and the street looked more likely to exist in Savannah, Georgia than in Brooklyn. The lush landscaping made it look like Paradise.

While God had commanded the Rabbi to create Vayehi Or, the New York State Office of Mental Health was now threatening to take away Vayehi Or's licence to operate unless it provided at least eight hours of psychiatric consultation per week. The Rabbi needed a consulting psychiatrist, any consulting psychiatrist, and fast.

Probably, the Rabbi would have preferred to find a Hasidic psychiatrist, but unfortunately there was no such thing. There were no Hasidic doctors of any kind since Hasidim were forbidden secular education. There were a couple of ultra-Orthodox psychiatrists in Manhattan, but they were both 'big doctors'. The Hasidim measured a doctor by the size of his fee, and these doctors were too big to work at Vayehi Or, so Rabbi Sternglantz was offering me the position. My first impulse was to say no. Not only was the Rabbi smarmy, but the Hasidim, I was convinced, wanted nothing to do with me. This conviction dated back to my childhood summers in the Catskills.

'Ah see dem!' Jeffrey Bender and I used to yell when we saw Hasidim walking along the road by White Lake, near their bungalow colony. They looked dark and scary, like vampire bats, except that we heard that unlike vampire bats the Hasidim were terrified of blood. That was why the Hasidic women soaked in hot water for ten days every month to remove all the blood. That was why the Hasidic men would not even shake the women's hands, just in case there was a speck of blood left.

We learned this fact from Jeffrey Bender's older brother Howard from whom we learned all the secrets of the Hasidim. Howard told us that the men never shaved or got haircuts and that the women shaved their heads and then covered their bald heads with wigs. He told us that the Hasidim never ever took their clothes off, not even to go swimming or to go to sleep. By far the most unbelievable thing that Howard told us about the Hasidim was that they fucked through a hole in the sheet. 'They're not allowed to look at each other.'

At the time, my image of sex—derived almost entirely from a pornographic comic book that Howard showed us—was vague enough for fucking through a hole in the sheet to make perfect sense. It seemed safer and more polite to avoid eye contact if you were engaging in something that nasty.

The secrets of the Hasidim, as revealed to us by Jeffrey Bender's older brother Howard, made the Hasidim even more mysterious to us. It was clear that the Hasidim didn't want anything to do with me and that made them the centre of my attention. What's wrong with *them*? I asked myself. But what I was feeling was, What's wrong with *me*? Why do they look at me like I'm dirt?

The more they ignored me, the more time I spent spying on them. I eavesdropped on their unintelligible conversations and I monitored the garbled announcements that came blaring over their loudspeaker. I noted what they bought at the Kosher Korner supermarket across the road and I charted each offspring and which adult it belonged to. I even gave the most interesting of the Hasidim names: there was Smelly Man, Red Beard, Little Head, Pizza Face, names like that. Between Memorial and Labor Day I gathered reams of data, but I learned very little. I was convinced that the Hasidim's juiciest secrets lay hidden from me behind the towering wooden wall that completely surrounded their bungalow colony.

Jeffrey Bender and I spent long summer afternoons scheming our way around that wall. We tried to peek between the slats, but the spaces were too narrow. We tried to peer over the wall, me standing on Bender's shoulders, but it turned out we were too short. We hatched a plan to sneak through the front gate at night but it turned out we were too chicken. We planned to drill a peephole through the wall until we realized that we didn't have a drill. We briefly considered a tunnel, which I thought was too dangerous and Jeffrey thought was too much work.

In the end, the wall surrounding the Hasidim proved impenetrable. And from that time until now, I had learned little more about them beyond what Jeffrey Bender's older brother Howard had told me.

But now, here was this Hasidic Rabbi not only inviting me to peep through the wooden wall, but actually trying to *convince* me to peep. There was, the Rabbi promised, a great and pressing need for psychiatric services among the Hasidim; a twenty-year backlog of untreated mental illnesses. Why, just recently, the Rabbi said, he had treated an elderly Hasidic hat manufacturer by the name of Goldberg who had become convinced beyond reason that the mitral valve implanted in his heart years ago was *not* the plastic valve that the doctors had promised but a pig's valve. No amount of convincing by Goldberg's doctors or his family or even the Rabbi could convince him otherwise. Not even a special blessing of the valve by Rabbi

Sternglantz himself could placate this Mad Hatter who, after demanding repeatedly that this pig part be removed from his heart, attempted to remove it himself with a penknife and a bottle of hydrogen peroxide. The resulting laceration—described to emergency room doctors by Goldberg's family as a 'shaving accident'—required more than thirty stitches to close. And this Goldberg, Rabbi Sternglantz bragged, was only the tip of the iceberg.

I was ripe for seduction. The Hill was feeling flat to me. It was time for a change, a psychiatric side-trip to somewhere exotic, and what could be more exotic than Vayehi Or; Let There Be Light!

My boss at The Hill, Chief Merkin, was surprisingly willing to lend me out to the Rabbi for eight hours per week. In fact, he almost insisted that I take the position. The Rabbi's locality fell within The Hill's catchment area and therefore Vayehi Or would be considered an 'outreach programme' of The Hill. It was a good PR move, and a potential bonanza of patients. And it was just the kind of innovative programme that might finally put Chief Merkin on the map.

'I have a good feeling about working with Doctor Feuer,' Rabbi Sternglantz told me. 'I have heard only good things about him.' Exactly what the Rabbi had heard and who he had heard it from he didn't say and I couldn't imagine, but it was obvious that the Rabbi and I had widely different opinions about my qualifications to work with Hasidic Jews. It was best, I decided, so there would be no future misunderstandings, that I lay my cards on the table right now.

'I don't know anything about Hasidic Jews,' I confessed—and, except for that business about their fear of blood and the hole in the sheet, this was true. For the Rabbi, my ignorance of the Hasidim was not a problem. In fact, he told me, it would even be an advantage. 'They will feel less judged by you,' he said.

'I'm not a practising Jew,' I revealed to Rabbi Sternglantz, and to this unsurprising news the Rabbi simply shrugged. Perhaps, I thought, if I spelled out for him exactly what my non-practising entailed he would not be so sanguine about it. Perhaps I should tell the Rabbi how I no longer went to *shul*, even on the High Holidays, and how I always enjoyed a nice piece of crisp bacon, even on Yom Kippur. Perhaps I should tell him how when I wrote out the name of God I wrote out the entire word, God, instead of G-d; that I had not laid *tefillin* since my bar mitzvah and that during the sacrilegious Sixties I had used my *tallith* bag for my pot stash and had used my *tallith* as a scarf. At last, I laid my trump card on the table. 'I don't believe in God,' I confessed to the Rabbi. He smiled. 'That,' he said, 'is between you and G-d.'

The Rabbi's unshakeable conviction that I was the only man for the job was inexplicable. (It did not occur to me then that, the Rabbi having had no luck finding any other consulting psychiatrist, I was literally the only man for the job.)

I had my doubts about the Rabbi but in the end I decided to give him the benefit of the doubt. He was probably, I decided, an honest man just trying to do the right thing by his people. I decided to accept his offer. I would begin consulting at Vayehi Or for eight hours each Wednesday starting the following week.

Despite the Rabbi's promise that he would provide guidance as necessary in Hasidic dogma, I thought it was best that I learn at least *something* about the Hasidim before I started treating them so that I did not immediately offend them, and so I did not mistake their beliefs and rituals for psychopathology.

The first thing I learned was that the Judaica Bookstore that was once on 22nd Street between Sixth and Seventh was now a Korean deli. The second thing I learned was that while the Religion Section at Barnes & Noble contained hundreds of books on Hinduism and Buddhism and Sufism, there was not one book on Hasidism.

With only a week to do my homework, I decided to consult the most Jewish person I knew. This turned out to be my accountant, who was a 'Black Hat', an ultra-Orthodox Jew who wore a broad-brimmed black fedora and was as religious as you could be and still be a Certified Public Accountant. 'Assume I know nothing,' I told him, which of course he had already assumed.

He informed me that the Hasidim were the most Orthodox of all the Jews, which I already knew. He also informed me that the particular sect of Hasidim with which I would be working were the most Orthodox of all the Hasidim, and the most insular of all the Hasidic sects. They were the most fearful and disdainful of the outside world, holding Gentiles, secular Jews and even the other

Hasidic sects in equal contempt. I should not, my accountant warned, confuse these dour Hasidim with the jumpty-jolly Lubavich (with whom I was already confusing them). The Lubavich were the friendly Hasidim who zipped around the city in Winnebagos blaring peppy Hasidic music. They called their Winnebagos 'Mitzvah Tanks' and they parked them on busy streets where friendly Lubavich asked obviously Jewish men if they were Jewish and the obviously Jewish men invariably said that they were not. It was the Lubavich who were interested in saving lost Jews. It was the Lubavich who had that public access cable TV show where, from time to time while channel-surfing in the middle of the night, I had come upon hundreds of them dancing ecstatically and elbowing their way closer to their ancient Rabbi Schneerson who was not just a Rabbi but also the Messiah.

'These people aren't like the Lubavitch,' my accountant told me. 'They look at the rest of us like we're dirt.' These words struck me like a fist in the stomach. I remembered that those Hasidim at the bungalow colony in the Catskills had also looked at me like I was dirt.

Still, there was no reason to panic. I was no longer some little pisher following the Hasidim around spying on them. Now, I was Doctor Feuer, *invited* to spy on them by their own Rabbi Sternglantz, summoned into their midst to heal their broken psyches. Now they would willingly share with me their deepest secrets. That my accountant would spend twenty minutes on the phone with me at the height of tax season was a testament to how seriously he took my decision to work with 'these people'.

In the end he offered me two pieces of concrete advice. Don't do it, and if I did, remember to save my receipts. Gas and tolls were deductible.

I drove into a part of Brooklyn I'd never seen before and immediately got lost. I had sought the Rabbi's guidance and the only guidance he had given me was to drive down Grant Avenue and look for Schwitzer's Scientific Shoes on the right. I couldn't miss it and yet somehow I did. I was in Brooklyn but these streets bore little resemblance to the Brooklyn I knew. They were bursting with activity. The contents of stores spilled out on to the sidewalks and in front of every store were dozens of baby carriages and strollers, mostly double and triple strollers. But unlike Chinatown, where you would see mostly Chinese, these streets were filled *only* with Hasidim. The men were all dressed in black. They dressed that way, my accountant had told me, to look like eighteenth-century European noblemen. The women were all dressed like Fifties Avon ladies. They dressed that way, my accountant told me, to mask their sexuality, and most of them were doing a terrific job of it.

'Excuse me,' I called out to a group of Hasidic men who were scurrying along the street. 'Can you tell me where Grant Avenue is?' Only one of them even had the courtesy to shake his head No. No, what? No he couldn't tell me or no he wouldn't?

'Excuse me,' was as far as I got with a group of Hasidic women who hurried past without even looking at me.

I found myself on Henderson Street which, I remembered from the Rabbi's brochure, was the street where the *future* highly professional home of Vayehi Or would be located by early spring. This Henderson Street looked nothing like the elegant tree-lined Henderson Street shown in the brochure. At the corner of Henderson and Burns I passed the actual site of the future home of Vayehi Or which was currently a garbage-strewn weed-infested vacant lot and bore no sign of impending construction.

Its present home, when I eventually found it, was a seven-room apartment: seven rooms of gloom. Three of these rooms were piled floor to ceiling with cardboard boxes that were taped shut. Another room seemed devoted to some sort of business activity which involved adding machines and big green ledgers. Then there was my 'Consultation Room' which was also filled with cardboard boxes. A space had been cleared just big enough to accommodate a metal desk and a single metal chair.

My 'Consultation Room' was no bigger than a broom closet. It had no windows, but its most striking feature was that it had no door. Directly across from my office was Rabbi Sternglantz's office. It had a door which was shut. The final room served as Vayehi Or's reception area and waiting room.

There was no one waiting in the waiting room, and the Hasidic girl who sat behind the reception desk made no attempt to receive me. I judged her age to be about twenty, and she was beautiful. She looked more like a beautiful young actress who was playing a beautiful young Hasidic girl than she did an actual Hasidic girl. Her skin was as white and smooth as porcelain, and on her cheeks was a burst of freckles. Her eyes were green, and her luminous red hair, the colour of root beer, spilled on to her shoulders. That's a great wig, I thought to myself.

'I'm Doctor Feuer,' I announced, extending my hand, which she made not the slightest attempt to shake. 'I'm Ruchel,' she answered without lifting her green eyes from her cluttered desk, and instantly I realized my mistake. You did not shake a Hasidic woman's hand. Nice going. I'd been here less than a minute and I'd already offended her.

Rabbi Sternglantz's office was at least five times the size of mine, or maybe it just looked that way because it was not filled with cardboard boxes. On the walls were several photographs of the Rabbi shaking hands with various politicians. Among them I recognized two former New York mayors and a US Senator. There were also dozens of letters of gratitude, all framed, and an enlarged and framed version of the artist's rendering of the future home of Vayehi Or.

The Rabbi was sitting behind an enormous wooden desk piled high with important-looking papers. He rose and greeted me with a firm handshake, the same handshake, I imagined, that he reserved for mayors and senators.

'Anything you need,' the Rabbi said, 'my door is always open.' I told the Rabbi that for starters I would need a door on my consultation room. This seemed a reasonable enough request, but Rabbi Sternglantz looked baffled. 'Why the secrecy?' his expression seemed to be asking. What was I planning to do that needed to be done behind closed doors? 'Anything else?' he asked. Yes, as a matter of fact, there was. I also needed a locked filing cabinet to keep my patients' records in, and another chair in my office for my patients to sit on. And it would be helpful if those cardboard boxes could be removed from my office; and what, I asked him, was in all those boxes anyway? 'Honey,' the Rabbi told me. He explained that Vayehi Or ran a honey business to help support certain community services. He assured me that for himself this honey business brought no personal gain.

And, as long as the Rabbi was asking, I could also use some *patients*. I had imagined that I would be greeted upon my arrival by that 'twenty-year backlog' of sick people the Rabbi had promised, and yet I couldn't help noticing that the waiting room was empty. Don't worry, the Rabbi reassured me. There were plenty of patients, but I should not expect that they would come directly to see me. Instead they would seek the Rabbi's advice, as was their custom, and the Rabbi would advise them, if he deemed it appropriate, to see me. It was a disconcerting thought that the same man who did not understand the importance of having a door on my consultation room was now going to serve as my triage officer.

After our little chat, Rabbi Sternglantz introduced me to the rest of Vayehi Or's highly professional staff. Her name was Naomi Kimil, a portly middle-aged clinical social worker who told me that she schlepped five times a week all the way from Borough Park to do 'psychotherapy' with these most insular of Hasidim, should any of the them ever decide that they wanted to do psychotherapy with her.

I was careful this time not to shake Naomi's hand but she reached out to shake mine. 'I'm Orthodox,' she smiled, 'not Hasidic.'

Naomi looked embarrassed as the Rabbi sang her praises to me—her uncommon dedication and her 'high professionalism'.

After Rabbi Sternglantz apologized for having to run off to an importing meeting at City Hall, Naomi revealed to me that she had been working at the Vayehi Or for only three weeks. During that time she had seen only two patients, one of whom did not utter a single word and another who spoke but then never returned.

Like me, Naomi had been lured to Vayehi Or by the opportunity to be part of a programme that was both new and sorely needed. Like me, she had been promised the support of a highly professional staff, but had found herself alone. As a psychotherapist at Vayehi Or, she felt both overwhelmed and underutilized. The unmedicated psychotics were too much for her and the healthier Hasidim didn't want to talk to her. She was happy that I was there now even though she was leaving at the end of the week—not because of what she had told me but because she and her husband were moving to Israel. 'Does the Rabbi know you're leaving?' I asked her. 'Of course he knows,' she said.

For the next couple of hours I sat at my metal desk surrounded by boxes of honey. Through my doorless doorway I watched a series of Hasidic men, most of them carrying briefcases or folders, enter and then exit Rabbi Sternglantz's office.

'I can still get out of this,' I reminded myself. I didn't even need to wait till the end of the week like Naomi Kimil. I could just quit and nobody except Rabbi Sternglantz would blame me. It was this thought, which I thought over and over again like a mantra, that relaxed me.

My first Hasidic patient arrived accompanied by his mother. His name was Hershel Nussbaum. He was forty-two years old and he bore the sallow complexion and the sour odour of a chronic schizophrenic. His disorganized thinking and his history, as described to me by Hershel's mother, confirmed this impression. She described Hershel as a 'sensitive' but 'normal' young man who, at the age of twenty-two, suddenly became ill. 'He began to take things too personally,' was how she understated it. 'Some days are bad, some days not so bad,' was how she summarized twenty years of continuous madness. On Hershel's 'not so bad' days he stayed in his room, where he rocked back and forth and engaged in heated arguments with invisible people. On his 'bad days' Hershel came out of his room.

Hershel heard voices. Sometimes the voices told Hershel that he was the next Messiah—and sometimes this made him feel good while at other times it made him extremely agitated. He did not want, he told his mother, all that responsibility. Did the voices ever instruct Hershel to do bad things? I asked. A couple of times, maybe three times, Hershel had set fire to his room to drive out an evil 'golem'. And once, she admitted with difficulty, he had chased his father, Rabbi Nussbaum, around the apartment with a kitchen knife. 'He doesn't mean bad,' Hershel's mother added quickly. 'It's just that he lives in his own little fantasy world.' She said this as if she were describing some dreamy teenager instead of a floridly psychotic paranoid schizophrenic.

Hershel, I thought to myself, should be in the hospital. Arson, kitchen knives; if I were seeing him on The Hill, I would probably be hospitalizing him right now. But this was not The Hill, and as far as I could tell, Hershel was no greater danger at the moment than he had been for the past twenty years.

'The Rabbi says there is medicine that can help a person like Hershel,' Hershel's mother said, and when I heard this I could barely contain my anger. It was the same anger I felt when I heard about Christian Scientists who withheld antibiotics from their children and allowed them to die of simple pneumonia.

'There is such medicine,' I told Hershel's mother. 'There has been such medicine for the last forty years.'

The 'kindling phenomenon' predicted that Hershel would not respond quickly or robustly to medication. This sick for this long, Hershel's madness should be hard-wired by now, his neuroreceptor sites welded shut. I warned Hershel's mother not to expect a miracle. If Hershel got better at all, it would be only partially and only gradually.

I started Hershel on four milligrams of Risperdal, a relatively low dose of a relatively new 'atypical' antipsychotic. Surprisingly, Hershel's mother did not ask me the name of the medication or what the side effects were or any of the other questions that a patient or his mother would normally ask. Perhaps by keeping the medicine mysterious she imbued it with magical power. Or perhaps it was simply not a Hasidic woman's place to question the actions of a man. Whichever, I told Hershel's mother the name of the medication and informed her about its possible side effects.

Less than forty-eight hours later, I found a message on my phone from Rabbi Sternglantz. It was urgent that the Rabbi speak to me. It was about Hershel Nussbaum. It could only be bad news. This was already *erev shabbos* and I knew that Rabbi Sternglantz could not answer his phone again until sundown of the following day.

I used this time to imagine the worst. I pictured Hershel suffering a severe dystonic reaction to the Risperdal that twisted his body into a spastic knot and kinked-off his windpipe. Or perhaps he had suffered a paradoxical agitation that had caused him to chase his father around the apartment with a kitchen knife. Or it could be neuroleptic malignant syndrome that caused Hershel to slip into a deep coma.

By Saturday afternoon I was convinced that I had killed my first Hasidic patient or that he had killed somebody else. How, I wondered, were the Hasidim going to deal with me? Would they let God judge me or would they haul me up before a tribunal of bearded elders? Maybe Hershel's mother and the Rabbi had already contacted some malpractice lawyer who was already telling them that they had an open and shut case?

David Feuer

I was on death row and had already exhausted my last appeal by the time Rabbi Sternglantz returned my call on Saturday night. 'Congratulations,' the Rabbi chirped into the phone. 'Hershel's mother tells me that Hershel is already a completely different person.' According to the Rabbi, Hershel had been, since two days ago, much calmer. He was now only talking to actual people and he was even beginning to make sense. He had accompanied his mother to the grocery and for once Hershel had not viciously attacked the produce. He had accompanied his father to *shul* and for once Hershel had not loudly proclaimed himself to be the *Mechiach*. In fact, he had told his father that, while he still did not like the job description of Messiah, at least he now realized that since nothing much was required of him until Judgement Day he could relax.

That Hershel's neuroreceptors cooperated so fully with a low dose of neuroleptic was just dumb pharmacological luck. But as word of Hershel's miraculous recovery sped along the sect's grapevine it conferred upon me the status of Big Psychiatrist, and it conferred upon Rabbi Sternglantz the status of Big Rabbi for finding such a Big Psychiatrist. More importantly, this Big Psychiatrist minded his own business. He didn't ask you about your dreams or your secrets or your sex life. Like a real doctor, he just gave you pills.

Over the next two or three weeks there was a steady trickle of patients. They were invariably male, invariably psychotic, and invariably I was the first psychiatrist they had ever seen.

And they, in turn, were the first insane Hasidim I had ever seen, and I confess that the very sight of these crazy Hasidim almost made me giggle. Actually, it was more like a nervous laugh than a giggle, more like the time I saw my uptight high-school science teacher Mr Schwimmer get hypnotized at the Science Fair and then cluck his way around the gym like a chicken. Here were these holier-than-thou Hasidim, these epitomes of pious self-control grinning senselessly, talking nonsense, and rubbing their genitals in public.

I dealt with my shameful secret glee by identifying it as 'negative counter-transference' and I congratulated myself for being aware of it so that I might use it in a clinically constructive way.

Soon, I felt my anger toward the Hasidim for the way they treated their mentally ill beginning to soften. There was another, a more charitable way of seeing things. Those Hasidic family members who accompanied their insane loved ones to Vayehi Or had all seemed genuinely concerned about them. That they had managed them at home for so long, and without benefit of medication, I began to see as a heroic undertaking that required great patience and diligence and self-sacrifice. They took care of their own, and while it was primitive, it was not necessarily inhumane. In fact, I decided that in many ways it was a more dignified and more respectful approach to the mentally ill than that of my own profession. And while it was true that the sect had deprived their mentally afflicted of available treatment, this treatment had probably felt no more available to them than exorcism or santeria felt to me.

It was important to remember, I kept reminding myself, that I was a secular stranger and that my view of the Hasidic community at large was distorted through the prism of my ignorance and my days as a juvenile Margaret Mead in the Catskills. I was seeing only the narrowest and sickest segment of a population that had produced remarkable traditions of religious scholarship and mysticism. One day I hoped I would meet these too. The news of my startling success with Hershel Nussbaum might spread; all kinds of sane and interesting people might knock at my door—when I eventually got one.

But after Hershel Nussbaum, I performed no further miraculous cures. A few psychotic men showed dramatic improvement, a few showed none, and the majority fell somewhere in the middle. Meanwhile, Chief Merkin was already pestering me about a possible journal article. Did I notice an unusually high incidence of any particular pathology among the sect? In what ways was their pathology specific to their belief system?—that sort of thing. The Chief was disappointed to hear, as I had been disappointed to discover, that Hasidic madness was proving no more exotic than the Hispanic, the African-American and the Anglo-Saxon madness that I saw on The Hill. The difference was only in the details—a Jewish God speaking directly to them instead of a Gentile God, a personal message received from the Talmud instead of the TV, a belief that they were the *Mechiach* instead of Jesus Christ. As far as I was concerned, a Hasidic Messiah did not trump a Hispanic Jesus, and a Mad Hatter was no more interesting than a paranoid librarian.

After several weeks, I began to notice that this steady stream of madmen was being joined by a handful of merely miserable men. The merely miserable tended to arrive at Vayehi Or unaccompanied. The vast majority of them presented physical symptoms—headaches and stomach aches, fatigue and forgetfulness, lack of appetite for food or anything else—for which their medical doctors could find no explanation. And the vast majority of these clinically depressed Hasidic men greeted the news of their clinical depression with surprise and scepticism. Why should they be depressed? No, they were not depressed, but yes, they would take the antidepressant medication if the doctor thought they should.

The rules of engagement with the Merely Miserable were simple. They were willing to talk provided that they did not have to talk about anything personal. They would talk about their symptoms but not about themselves. That depressed Hasidim couched their emotional pain in physical symptoms was not really surprising. What *was* surprising was that any of them had the courage to come see a psychiatrist at all since the consequences of being identified as a 'mental' in the community were enormous. They could slide to the bottom of the *shidduch* list.

A *shidduch* was an arranged marriage that was brokered by a professional matchmaker who rated the community's eligible marriage partners in descending order of their eligibility. A healthy Hasid from a good family who was successful in business or brilliant in *yeshiva* would be at the top of the *shidduch* list. An unmarried Mental would be at the bottom. A Merely Miserable could end up feeling a lot more miserable if he sabotaged his *shidduch* standing by admitting to his misery.

I dispensed medication from a green garbage bag full of free samples that I had lugged over from The Hill. Reaching down into my bag, I felt more like a Red Cross relief worker in the aftermath of some major disaster than I did a psychiatrist. Instead of cholera I was treating schizophrenia and depression. Instead of dispensing antibiotics I was dispensing antipsychotics and antidepressants. But if I was doing no more than a relief worker, I comforted myself in the fact that I was doing no less, either. I was providing relief.

My plan was to use my samples only for those Hasidim who had no health insurance, but as it turned out, all of the Hasidim, insured or otherwise, insisted upon getting their medication from my green garbage bag. None of this medication (even the medication like Loxitane that *sounded* kosher) was kosher. This meant that Rabbi Sternglantz was required to kosherize each medication with a special *kiddush* which became impractical as the number of patients grew, so that one day Rabbi Sternglantz popped into my office and kosherized the entire garbage bag. Shazaam! One quick prayer and just like that everything from Prozac to Prolixin became instantly kosher, except for during Passover when all the medication would have to be blessed again.

Whenever it became necessary to replenish my supply of samples, I felt the need to inform the Rabbi. But instead, I just slipped this pharmaceutical *traif* discreetly into the blessed garbage bag.

It was nearly two months into my stint at Vayehi Or and so far I had not seen a single female Hasidic patient. It was possible that the sect's women enjoyed perfect mental health, but it was far more likely that they were not being given (or were not giving themselves) permission to seek psychiatric help. The threshold of illness that they had to cross before exposing themselves to treatment was probably much higher than for the men. I imagined that if and when my first Hasidic female arrived she would already be foaming at the mouth—but I was wrong.

Her name was Rivka S. and she was, as I observed in my admission note, 'appropriate in both demeanour and attire'. The latter was not entirely accurate. Rivka was more appropriately attired for a small-town ladies' luncheon than she was for a visit to the psychiatrist. She wore a dark-blue skirt down to her ankles and a matching jacket with gold buttons up to her chin. A pillbox hat was precariously perched on top of her obviously synthetic hair. Her fashion goal seemed to be to dress attractively in a way that did not actually attract anybody.

Rivka looked considerably younger than her husband who sat solemnly and stiffly in a chair as far from Rivka as my tiny consultation room would allow. You could cut the tension between them with a knife. I knew that Rivka's husband was here not just as her chaperone but also as her censor and that if I started digging I would not see either of them ever again. It was Rivka's husband who had decided that Rivka had to get pills for her 'crazy business with the blood'.

Rivka's crazy business with the blood had begun a few months ago while she was in the *mikvah*, the monthly ritual bath that Hasidic women took to cleanse themselves of all traces of menstrual blood. The *mikvah* was the most important 'family purity' ritual in the 'eight days of cleanliness' that followed the five days of actual bleeding and involved the woman 'checking inside and out' for even one single drop of tainted blood that might contaminate her husband.

'What if...?' Rivka thought as she soaked in the *mikvah*, 'What if I'm still unclean?' What if, despite checking herself inside and out, Rivka had missed a drop of blood? A tiny speck nestled in some crevice, or maybe under a fingernail. What if, after the eight days of cleanliness, she was still violating the most important law of family purity? The horrifying consequence of this began to haunt Rivka. Everything she touched—her furniture, her dishes, her children, her husband—would be tainted.

Rivka's 'what if...' fear that she was still unclean gradually hardened into a conviction. She could soak in the *mikvah* tank until she wrinkled like a prune. She could wash her clothes, her dishes, her hands three dozen times a day and it didn't matter. She could still be unclean. The safest thing, Rivka decided, was not to touch anything, and this included her husband.

By refusing to touch her husband, Rivka was violating not only her marital obligation, to satisfy her husband, but also the Talmudic command to go forth and multiply. Already, by the age of twenty-five, she had three children but this was not nearly enough multiplying to satisfy either the Talmud or the Hasidic law, which demanded that Rivka keep multiplying as often as physiologically possible until either menopause or death, whichever came first.

Already Rivka was behind schedule. Already the neighbours were talking and the Rabbi was pressuring. It was highly unorthodox for a fertile young Hasidic woman such as Rivka not to bear fruit for nearly three years. As the Rabbi repeatedly reminded her, Rivka's youngest child was already almost three. There was not a single day left to waste with this crazy business about the blood. Rivka herself lamented the wasted time—time during which she might have given her husband two, maybe even three more children. She herself wanted once again to be the dutiful wife and the efficient childbearer that he had married.

It might be six weeks or even longer, I told Rivka and her husband, before this medication I was prescribing, Luvox, began to work. Six weeks, they told me, they were willing to wait, but six weeks the Rabbi would probably not wait unless they could get from me a doctor's note so that the Rabbi would grant them a *heter*, a special rabbinical dispensation excusing Rivka and her husband from procreating.

I had written hundreds of doctor's notes in my time, excusing patients from everything from jury duty to turnstile jumping, but this was the first doctor's note I had ever written excusing a patient from procreating. In my letter to the Rabbi I described Rivka's illness and the medication she was taking. I also stated that in my professional opinion, the stress of pregnancy at this time would be detrimental to her mental health. I thought about mentioning the fact that Rivka desperately wanted to have more children but decided that that might be gilding the lily a little too much. I thought about mentioning the possible teratogenic effects of Rivka's medication, but that would be a lie, since there was no evidence that Luvox caused any foetal abnormalities. My note, simple and factual, won Rivka a one-month reproductive reprieve.

Each week, Rabbi Sternglantz poked his head into my office to congratulate me for a job well done and to exhort me to 'hold down the fort'. Each week he promised that 'reinforcements were on the way'. Already, the Rabbi told me, he had received dozens of responses to his ad in the *New York Times* for a clinical social worker to replace Naomi Kimil. He was at this very time, he assured me, interviewing candidates in order to find the most highly professional among them.

None of the briefcase-toting men whom I observed going in and out of the Rabbi's office remotely resembled a social worker, but what went on in the Rabbi's office was none of my business. The Rabbi and I had made a deal. I would stay out of his business and he would stay out of mine, and so far Rabbi Sternglantz was keeping his promise. He was not meddling in my treatment, at least not *directly*. Whether by granting them his consent to see me or by issuing them his command to see me, the Rabbi determined which sick people I ended up seeing, and it was obvious that the Rabbi's criteria was not entirely their level of illness. A paranoid Hasid who was yelling obscenities out his window showed up at Vayehi Or long before a far catatonic Hasid who had been standing frozen for weeks in his room. A moderately depressed Hasid who refused to go to work showed up faster in my office than a more depressed Hasid who had lost twenty pounds over the last month. I was not comfortable with this arrangement, but so far, at least, the Hasids being referred to me by the Rabbi were all in genuine need of psychiatric care. So far I could live with it.

Secretly I had imagined that at some point the community would take me to its grateful bosom. I saw myself some day sitting at their *shabbos* supper tables, and dancing at the weddings of their children. But it soon became obvious that no matter how many *mitzvoth* I performed with my medicine, these Hasidim had no interest in instructing me in their ways. Even when I asked, they would simply say, 'That's what we do,' or, 'We don't do that.' Even when I ignorantly violated their laws they would simply ignore me. I could wear a big Jesus on the Cross around my neck or keep a Golden Calf on my desk and they could care less.

All of them except Ruchel the receptionist.

When I brought the patients' charts to Ruchel's desk at the end of the day, Ruchel's cheeks flushed the colour of her hair and she would begin to nervously push around the items on her desk like she was mixing mah-jong tiles. If I were a twenty-year-old Hasid I might have taken this for a crush, but as a forty-six-year-old psychiatrist, I took it simply for shyness.

One day, Ruchel began to do what no Hasidic woman had done before—she began to make direct eye contact with me. At first fleeting, then longer and—it seemed to me—deeper. Eventually, Ruchel began actually speaking to me. Not just asking me what this word or that phrase was that she could not decipher from my handwriting, but asking me questions. Personal questions.

'How long does it take to become a psychiatrist?' Ruchel asked me, and not long after that she asked me how many children I had. Ruchel found the fact that I had no children far more shocking than the fact that it took twelve years after high school to become a psychiatrist. Was the problem with my wife? she wanted to know. 'I'm not married,' I told her, 'so I guess the problem is probably with me.'

Not only did Ruchel ask me direct questions, she started answering my questions as well. She was twenty years old, she told me, she lived with her parents and she was studying in a girl's *yeshiva*. No, it was not a wig. It was her real hair. She would not have to shave her head and wear a *sheitel* until she was married, which would have been already if she did not have to wait for her next oldest sister to get married first.

I was now bringing my charts to Ruchel's desk at the end of each session instead of at the end of each day. Thus, our brief conversations were becoming more frequent. I don't know how Ruchel saw me, but I saw Ruchel as a valuable source of information about Rabbi Sternglantz. I asked her who all those men were who came and went from Rabbi Sternglantz's office. Ruchel explained that the Rabbi offered spiritual advice and religious opinion. 'Those guys with their briefcases?' I asked. Ruchel explained that they were probably coming to the Rabbi to settle disputes. For example, a man might borrow money and not want to pay it back. The Rabbi would talk to the man.

One day I asked Ruchel whether she felt like having lunch at the dairy restaurant down the block. She looked at me as if I had just asked her whether she felt like having sex on the Rabbi's desk while he was settling one of his disputes. Nowhere on earth, Ruchel's look seemed to say, could she and I ever hope to have lunch.

Until that moment I had entertained not a single impure thought about Ruchel. But now I found myself thinking not about lunch but about all those places that no man except Ruchel's future husband would ever venture. I found myself imagining what Ruchel's legs looked like above those two inches of white-stockinged ankle. I imagined the shape of those breasts—perfect peaches—and the smell of that radiant red hair that would some day be lying on some hairdressers' floor. I imagined our entire forbidden courtship. The painful pleasure of our stolen moments, the dangerous thrill of our secret liaisons, the violent response of the sect to the news of our engagement. The difficulty I would have on our wedding night negotiating that hole in the sheet.

I decided to start bringing my charts to Ruchel at the end of the day again instead of after each patient. My fantasies had frightened me. It was time to back off, which I successfully did until the day when Ruchel and I found ourselves face to face in the doorway of Vayehi Or. I was just arriving and Ruchel, I imagine, was just going out for lunch.

'*Shalom*,' I greeted her like I always did, and I stepped aside to let her pass. '*Shalom*,' Ruchel replied, and she did not make a move. Instead, with her eyes fixed boldly upon mine, Ruchel slowly pressed two fingertips against her lips and kept them there for a long seductive moment. Then, still holding my eyes, Ruchel slowly raised her fingers to touch the *mezuzah* that was nailed to the door frame.

Without hesitation and without thinking, I followed suit. It felt like hours that we stood there at that threshold, wordless. It felt like our lips were touching, like it would take the Jaws of Life to pry our eyes apart. It felt like that, and then it was over. And it never happened again.

In certain respects, Rabbi Sternglantz had proved to be a man of his word. There was now a door on my consultation room, though the flimsy plywood it was constructed from provided little in the way of privacy. In fact by some acoustical phenomenon it seemed to provide *less* privacy. There was also now a locked filing cabinet for patients' records for which I suspected Rabbi Sternglantz was holding the extra key. And the Rabbi did finally bring in 'reinforcements' in the form of an Orthodox social worker named Sam W. whose idea of psychotherapy—(from what I clearly heard through my plywood door)—was to try and scold his patients into behaving themselves. Eventually, things between the Rabbi and me began to go sour.

It started with a young Hasidic man by the name of Yitzi Namkin who was openly homosexual and who openly admitted to me that he spent at least a couple of nights each week cruising Christopher Street in full Hasidic garb picking up 'dates' whom he brought back to Brooklyn and fucked in the room just above where his parents slept. He preferred, he told me, 'farm boys'—blond, corn-fed-looking Midwestern types—who seemed to find Yitzi's Hasidic get-up a turn-on. Perhaps, Yitzi explained, they mistook him for Amish.

It was obvious that even if he lived in a gay Midwestern farming community, Yitzi Namkin would still have problems. Yitzi described periods of time during which he required no sleep and could barely keep up with his own racing thoughts. It was during these times that he felt himself to be brilliant and invincible, and it was during these times that he often ventured up to Harlem at night and ended up getting the shit kicked out of him, which explained that nasty-looking gash above his left eye. Yitzi had, quite accurately, diagnosed this behaviour as manic and he quite sensibly wanted medication to help control it—preferably medication that would not produce any sexual side effects. He seemed amenable to a trial of Depakote and he seemed amenable to seeing me again in a couple of weeks.

No sooner did Yitzi leave my office than the Rabbi stormed in. 'I don't want that sick trash in here again,' he snarled. He spat the words 'sick trash' out of his mouth like they were writhing maggots. At first, I thought the Rabbi was joking and I went along with the joke. 'You're absolutely right,' I smiled. 'We can't have any sick people at a mental *health* clinic.' But then I realized he wasn't joking. His face (what little I could see of it) glowed bright red as he explained that Yitzi Namkin was a threat to all the young Hasidic boys upon whom Yitzi preyed to satisfy his depraved appetite.

I felt my own face flush with anger. 'Don't worry,' I felt like telling the Rabbi, 'your precious little *yeshiva boochers* are not Yitzi's type. He prefers young farm boys with tight asses and uncircumcized cocks.' Instead, I calmly offered my opinion that Yitzi Namkin's homosexuality posed no danger to the Hasidic community. Homosexuality, I explained, was no longer considered a mental illness by the *DSM-IV*, the Diagnostic and Statistical Manual of Mental Disorders, Fourth Edition. Nor was it something that could just be removed by a psychiatrist as if it were a planter's wart.

I could tell that my defence of Yitzi Namkin put me in the same boat as Yitzi. We were both now, in the Rabbi's eyes, 'sick trash'. And that I would take the word of the *DSM-IV* above the word of God nearly drove Rabbi Sternglantz to the point of physical violence. By sheer force of will, he controlled his impulse to kill me and he somehow recovered his smooth self. 'It's just that we have so little of Dr Feuer's precious time,' he smiled tightly, 'and there are so many *truly* needy cases.'

One of the 'truly needy' cases that Rabbi Sternglantz soon

David Feuer

brought to my attention was a perfectly healthy young man who had
rejected a series of perfectly acceptable *shidduchim* with the totally
unacceptable explanation that these women were 'not his type'. Rabbi
Sternglantz saw this ingrate's behaviour as indicative of some severe
mental disturbance warranting psychiatric intervention. It was clear
that medication was indicated. And it was clear that Rabbi Sternglantz
did not have a clue as to what a psychiatrist was or what psychotropic
medication was for. I needed to nip this thing in the bud.

I explained to the Rabbi that the job of a psychiatrist was not
to enforce social customs and that the job of medication was not to
control transgressors. I suggested that I was in a better position than
he to determine who required psychiatric intervention. Surprisingly,
the Rabbi said he understood.

It was not by accident that the Rabbi's very next referral was a
seventeen-year-old male who had been spotted in the community
wearing a New York Yankees baseball cap. His pathology, it turned
out, was that he dreamed of becoming a major-league pitcher. By his
own account, he had developed a mean slider and an unhittable
change-up to go with his fast ball and his awesome curve. All he
wanted was a chance to some day show his stuff to the Yankees. All
Rabbi Sternglantz wanted was for me to medicate him.

Once again, I explained to the Rabbi, and once again the Rabbi
said he understood. Not long afterward he sent me a Hasidic
woman who was rumoured to be taking flamenco lessons. Then there
was an elderly gentleman who was refusing to lay *tefillin*, and a wife
who was suspected to be lesbian.

Meanwhile, Rivka's crazy business with the blood was not
budging an inch. This was not so unusual; approximately
thirty per cent of obsessive-compulsives proved refractory to
medication alone. What *was* unusual was that, despite my boosting
Rivka's medication—Luvox, and then Zoloft—to well beyond the
recommended dosage, not once did she complain of a side effect. Nor
did she complain or get any better when I augmented these drugs,
first with Lithium, then with Risperdal and finally with thyroid
hormone. 'The same,' was how Rivka responded every time every
two weeks when I asked about her symptoms. 'The same,' Rivka's

frustrated husband would echo each time, and each time he reminded me of my initial promise that by six weeks his wife would be cured of her crazy business with the blood.

Like Rivka's husband, I too was frustrated. I read everything I could get my hands on about recent developments in the pharmacological treatment of OCD, obsessive-compulsive disorder. I talked to a couple of well-known psychopharmacologists and neither of them could offer more than I was already doing.

I considered the use of behaviour modification therapy, a technique with which I had no experience. But when I described it to Rivka and her husband and suggested referring them to a behavioural therapist they wanted nothing to do with it. They would sink or swim by the psychiatrist's pills alone. Meanwhile, Rabbi Sternglantz was still granting Rivka her reproductive deferments but only on an ovulation-to-ovulation basis. I was thus required each month to write Rivka another doctor's note which essentially said this: *Dear Rabbi. Please excuse Rivka S. from conceiving this month. She is not feeling well.*

Just before Passover, another Hasidic woman showed up at Vayehi Or with OCD. Even though her symptoms were almost identical to Rivka's, even though she wanted the same medicine that was not helping Rivka, and even though she, too, wanted a doctor's note, I was not suspicious. And after Passover, another obsessional woman showed up, and then another, and I was still not suspicious. A high incidence of OCD in a highly ritualized culture like the Hasidim made perfect sense. And it made perfect sense that their obsessions would be similar to each other and would be culturally specific. It was known that a great number of Asian males obsessively believed that their penises were retracting into their abdomens, and I had heard that many Scandinavian men were convinced they were shrinking, so it did not smell fishy to me that so many Hasidic women had this 'crazy business with the blood'. It did not occur to me that Rivka S. might be malingering until the day Rivka confessed to me.

Her confession was sudden and breathless. It took her only as long to confess as it took her husband to rush out to the street, de-activate his car alarm and come back. Rivka explained that she could not bear the thought of having more children. She was worn out and desperate, and her desperation was the mother of her invention.

'You felt desperate enough to take medicine that you didn't need for six months?' I asked incredulously.

'No,' Rivka replied, and from under her stylish jacket she produced a brown paper bag filled with six months' worth of medication. 'Maybe someone else can use this,' she offered sheepishly.

'And the others?' I asked her, those other women who claimed to have the same problem as Rivka? 'They do have the same problem as me,' Rivka insisted. 'They don't want more children, either, so, we talk.'

I pictured these Hasidic women talking. Groups of them exchanging notes in furtive whispers, in bakers' shops and in fabric stores and while their children slept in their strollers and while their husbands were at work or at *shul*. I pictured Rivka as the reluctant leader of this contraceptive resistance movement. And I pictured myself, the psychiatrist, serving as their shared birth control device.

I wanted to know why Rivka chose to confess now, but Rivka said she couldn't say. Maybe it was guilt about lying to her husband and to the Rabbi. What Rivka could say for sure was that she did not want any more children and that she did not want me to mention this to either her husband or Rabbi Sternglantz. And, by the way, she needed another one of those letters for the Rabbi.

I wrestled, albeit briefly, with my conscience. What right did I have, as an ignorant outsider, to meddle in this sacred Hasidic law about procreation? What right did I have, as a Jew, to diminish the population of Jews in the world, even by one Jew, even if that one Jew was a member of this most insular sect?

There was a psychiatrist named Anita who thirty years ago wrote many of us letters for the draft board so that we would not have to go to Vietnam. 'Do you sometimes think people are staring at you on the subway?' she asked us. Yes, we told her, sometimes we did. 'Do you avoid stepping on the cracks so as not to break your mother's back?' she asked. Yes, we did, and we would get a letter the next week stating that we were too unstable to go to Vietnam. During the week between my interview and my letter, Dr Anita got busted. And even though it was not for writing letters but for distributing amphetamines that she got busted, I now used Dr Anita as my role model in this moral dilemma.

I decided that I would continue to write Rivka letters, and that I would write letters for any other worn-out desperate Hasidic woman who asked for them. It was, I decided, preventative psychiatry. By writing them bogus doctor's notes, I was preventing them from developing the very real symptoms that twenty years of continuous breeding would no doubt cause them.

By early spring, there was a growing tension on the streets of the neighbourhood. Already there had been some ugly incidents. A teenage Puerto Rican girl had been allegedly fondled by an elderly Hasid in the laundry room of her project building and charges had been pressed. A few nights later, several windows were smashed by rocks. There was already talk that things were headed for full-blown riots between races.

Rabbi Sternglantz disappeared for a couple of weeks and when he returned he was much more reclusive. He did not receive visitors in his office. And when he left his office, which he now rarely did, he was always accompanied by a couple of his Hasidic bodyguards.

The Rabbi wore a look that was neither his usual unctuous self nor his more recent contemptuous self. It was more a look of fear and suspicion.

We had not exchanged a word for perhaps three weeks until Rabbi Sternglantz summoned me to his office where he introduced me to an elderly Hasid named Schmuel R.—the man who had allegedly fondled the teenage Puerto Rican. Schmuel sat silently while the Rabbi explained that Schmuel needed a letter for the court stating that he had a mental problem and with his impulses could not help himself. 'You could not help yourself,' the Rabbi flatly stated and Schmuel shook his head No, he could not help himself. This single statement by the Rabbi was intended to be the entire mental status exam upon which I would base my letter to the court.

I refused, but Rabbi Sternglantz was in no mood to take no for an answer. He viewed my refusal as an act of wilful insubordination, tantamount to high treason during a time of war. 'You write plenty of letters already don't you?' he asked. I knew instantly that he was talking about my deferment letters for Rivka and for the others. Still, I refused. I stood my ground; and I saw in the Rabbi's face that I was now the enemy. I expected he would fire me right then and there, but he did not. I should quit, I thought, right here and now, but I could not.

I am not a quitter, and I don't mean that in any positive sense. What I mean is that for my own neurotic reasons I have trouble extricating myself from bad situations. Bad relationships, bad accountants, bad barbers, bad jobs—in twenty years I had never fired anyone nor had I ever quit.

That night I dreamed that an evil golem was living inside my mattress. I had no idea what a golem was supposed to look like but my golem was about a foot tall and looked like a cross between Rabbi Sternglantz and Dopey from the Seven Dwarves. All night I fought off this golem's attempts to inhabit me, to capture my will, and the following morning I decided to tell Chief Merkin exactly what was going on at Vayehi Or.

Like an American diplomat in some war-torn country, I expected that Chief Merkin would pluck me out of harm's way. He would land his chopper on the roof of the besieged embassy and save me. Instead, the Chief laughed. All those years I had worked in the dangerous environment of The Hill, and now I was afraid of a rabbi?

I arrived at Vayehi Or a few days later to find the door padlocked. A couple of Rabbi Sternglantz's associates were standing, arms folded, in front of it. The Rabbi was standing just behind them. I got out of my car and started walking toward the building, but the Rabbi's associates blocked my way.

'You are no longer welcome in this community,' the Rabbi called out to me. He said this as if he was pronouncing upon me a holy fatwa. 'You no longer work here,' he bellowed.

I felt relief, but I also felt shame at getting fired. I had never been fired before. I wondered what the last straw had been. Had it been that letter for the elderly Hasid that I refused to write, or was it all those other letters I had written? Was I being busted for being the ringleader of the contraceptive underground or was it those impure thoughts I had about Ruchel the receptionist? Who knew? And at this point, who cared?

'I'll need to collect my patients' charts,' I told the Rabbi. I hoped that at least a few of my Hasidic patients might follow me back to The Hill and I would need their charts.

'They are not any more your patients,' the Rabbi hissed.

'Well, they certainly aren't your patients,' I whined.

I sidestepped the Rabbi and was headed for the door when the bigger of his two men snagged me by the upper arm. He held me with the firm painless pressure of a blood pressure cuff. 'Get your hands off me,' I demanded, not because I could make him get his hands off me, but because that was what I knew I was supposed to say in a situation like this. The Rabbi spat out some words in Hebrew. I did not understand them but they did not sound like 'have a nice day.' Then, like two tugboats, the Rabbi's men began nudging me toward my car.

I can take the Rabbi one on one, I calculated to myself. He is fat, he has thick glasses and he is, after all, a Rabbi.

The man with my arm seemed to sense what was in my mind. 'It's better you should go,' he advised. There was no particular malice in his voice. It was for him just settling another dispute. □

GRANTA

# THE CHINESE
# LESSON

## A. M. Homes

I am walking, holding a small screen, watching the green dot move like the blip of a plane, the blink of a ship's radar. Searching, I am on the lookout for submarines. I am an air traffic controller trying to keep everything at the right distance. I am lost.

A man steps out of the darkness on to the sidewalk. 'Plane gone down?' he asks.

It is nearly night; the sky is still blue at the top, but it is dark down here.

'I was just walking the dog,' he says.

I nod. The dog is nowhere to be seen.

'You're not from around here are you?'

'Not originally,' I say. 'But we're over on Maple now.'

'Tierney,' the man says. 'John Tierney.'

'Harris,' I say. 'Geordie Harris.'

'Welcome to the neighbourhood. Welcome to town.'

He points to my screen; the dot seems to have stopped travelling.

'I was hoping to hell that was a toy—a remote control,' he says. 'I was hoping to have some fun. Are you driving a car or floating a boat somewhere around here?'

'It's a chip,' I say, cutting him off. 'A global positioning screen. I'm looking for my mother-in-law.'

There is a scratching sound from inside a nearby privet, and the unmistakable scent of dog shit rises like smoke.

'Good boy,' Tierney says. 'He doesn't like to do his business in public. Can't blame him, if they had me shifting outside, I'd hide in the bushes too.'

Tierney, I hear it like *tyranny*. Tyrant, teaser, taunting me about my tracking system, my lost mother-in-law.

'It's not a game,' I say, looking down at the blinking green dot.

A yellow Lab pushes out of the bushes and Tierney clips the lead back on to his collar. 'Let's go, boy,' Tierney says, slapping the side of his leg. 'Good luck,' he calls, pulling the dog down the road.

The cellphone clipped to my belt rings. 'Who was that?' Susan asks. 'Was that someone you know?'

'It was a stranger, a total stranger, looking for a playmate.' I glance down at the screen. 'She doesn't seem to be moving now.'

'Is your antenna up?' Susan asks.

There is a pause. I hear her talking to Kate. 'See Daddy. See Daddy across the street, wave to Daddy. Kate's waving,' she tells me. I stare across the road at the black Volvo idling by the kerb. With my free hand I wave back.

'That's Daddy,' Susan says, handing Kate the phone.

'What are you doing, Daddy?' Kate asks. Her intonation, her annoyance, oddly accusatory for a three-year-old.

'I'm looking for Grandma.'

'Me too,' Kate giggles.

'Give the phone to Mommy.'

'I don't think so,' Kate says.

'Bye, Kate.'

'What's new?' Kate says—it's her latest phrase.

'Bye-bye,' I say, hanging up on her.

I step off the sidewalk and dart between the houses, through the grass alley that separates one man's yard from another's. A sneak, a thief, a prowling trespasser, I pull my flashlight out of my jacket and flick it on. The narrow Ever-Ready beam catches patios and planters and picnic tables by surprise. I am afraid to call out, to attract undue attention. Ahead of me there is a basketball court, a slide, a sandbox, and there she is, sailing through my beam like an apparition. Her black hair blowing, her hands smoothly clutching the chain-link ropes as though they were reins. I catch her in mid-flight. Legs swinging in and out. I hold the light on her—there and gone.

'I'm flying,' she says, sailing through the night.

I step in close so that she has to stop swinging. 'Did you have a pleasant flight, Mrs Ha?'

'It was nice.'

'Was there a movie?'

She eases herself off the swing and looks at me like I'm crazy. She looks down at the tracking device. 'It's no game,' Mrs Ha says, putting her arm through mine. I lead her back through the woods. 'What's for dinner, Georgie?' she says. And I hear the invisible echo of Susan's voice correcting—it's not Georgie, it's Geordie.

'What would you like, Mrs Ha?'

In the distance, a fat man presses against a sliding glass door, looking out at us, his breath fogging the pane.

S usan is at the computer, drawing. She is making a map, a grid of the neighbourhood. She is giving us something to go on in the future—coordinates.

She is an architect, everything is line, everything is order. Our house is G4. The blue light of the screen pours over her, pressing the flat planes of her face flatter still—illuminating. She hovers in an eerie blue glow.

'I called Ken,' I say.

Ken is the one who had the chip put in. He is Susan's brother. When Mrs Ha was sedated for a colonoscopy Ken had the chip implanted at the bottom of her neck, above her shoulder blades. The chip company specialist came and stood by while a plastic surgeon inserted it just under the skin. Before they let her go home, they tested it by wheeling her gurney all over the hospital while Ken sat in the waiting room tracking her on the small screen.

'Why?'

'I called him about her memory. I was wondering if we should increase her medication.'

Ken is a psychopharmacologist, a specialist in the containment of feeling. He used to be a stoner and now he is a shrink. He has no affect, no emotions.

'And?' she says.

'He asked if she seemed agitated.'

'She seems perfectly happy,' Susan says.

'I know,' I say, not telling Susan what I told Ken—Susan is the one who's agitated.

'Does she know where she is?' Ken had asked. There had been a pause, a moment where I wondered if he was asking about Susan or his mother. 'I'm not always sure,' I'd said, failing to differentiate.

'Well, what did he say?' Susan wants to know.

'He said we could try upping the dose—no harm in trying. He said it's not unusual for old people to wander off at twilight, to forget where they are. He said there are all kinds of phenomena that no one really understands.'

'You haven't ever called my brother before, have you?' Susan asks.

'I have not, no.'

Mrs Ha has only been with us for three weeks. Before that, she was in her own apartment in California, slowly evaporating. It was a fall that brought her to the hospital, a phone call to Ken, a series of tests, the chip implant and then Ken put her on a plane to us—with a pair of tracking devices packed in her suitcase. When she arrived I drove her around the neighbourhood, I showed her where the stores were, the library, post office and the train station. I don't tell Susan that now I live in fear Mrs Ha will find the station herself, that she'll hop on a train—and the mother hunt will become an FBI investigation. We have only been here ourselves for five months, before that we were on 106th and Riverside, and most mornings when I wake up I still have no idea where I am.

'I don't like coming home any more,' Susan says, turning to face me, the light from the computer an iMac aura around her head. 'It scares me. I never know what to expect.' She pauses, 'I can't do it.'

'You can do it,' I say, plucking a fragment from my childhood, the memory of Shari Lewis telling Lamp Chop, 'You can do anything.'

There is nothing Susan likes less than to fail. She will do anything not to fail, she will not try so as not to fail.

Susan is reading. She turns the pages of her book, neatly, tightly, they almost click as they flip. 'Listen to this,' she says, quoting a passage from *In Cold Blood*. '"Isn't it wonderful, Kansas is so American."'

When I told my family about Susan, they said, 'She doesn't sound Chinese.'

'An architect named Susan from Yale who grew up in LaJolla, that's not Chinese,' my mother said.

'But she is Chinese,' I repeated.

And later when I told Susan the story she said angrily, 'I'm not Chinese, I'm American.'

Susan is minimal, flat, like Kansas. She is physically non-existent, a plank of wood, planed, smooth. There is nothing to curl around, nothing to hold on to. Her design signature is a thin ledge, floating on a wall, a small trough wide enough to want to rest something on, too narrow to hold anything.

I drape my arm over her, it lies across her body like dead weight. Her exhalations blow the little hairs on my arm like a warm wind.

'You're squishing me,' she says, pushing my arm away. She turns the page—click.

'When she dies do they take the chip out?' Susan asks, hooking me with her leg, pulling me back.

'I assume they just deactivate it and you give them back the tracker—it's leased.'

'Should we have one put in Kate?'

'Let's see how it goes with your mother. No one knows if there are side effects, weird electromagnetic pulls towards outer space from being tracked, traced as you walk along the earth.'

'Where did you find her tonight?' she asks as we are falling asleep. We sleep like plywood, pressed together—two straight lines.

'On a swing. How can you be angry with an old woman on a swing?'

'She's my mother.'

In the morning Mrs Ha is in the front yard. She is playing a Jimi Hendrix tape she brought with her on our boom box: she is a tree, a rock, a cloud. She is shifting slowly between poses, holding them, and then morphing into the next.

'T'ai chi,' Susan says.

'I didn't know people really did that.'

'They all do it,' Susan says, glaring at me. 'Even I can do it.' She takes a couple of poses; the first like a vulture about to attack, her fingers suddenly talons and then she is a dragon, hissing.

When Susan and I met there was a gap between us, a neutral space. I saw it as an acknowledgement of the unbridgeable gap; not just male and female, but unfamiliar worlds—we couldn't pretend to understand each other.

I look back out the window. Kate is there now, standing next to Mrs Ha, doing her kung fu imitation chop-chops. Kate punches the air, she kicks. She has nothing on under her dress.

'Kate needs underpants,' I tell Susan, who runs, horrified, down the stairs, shooing the two of them into the backyard. For a moment the boom box is alone on the grass—Jimi Hendrix wailing, 'And the wind cries Mary,' at 8.28 a.m.

I see Sherika, the nanny, coming up the sidewalk. Sherika takes the train from Queens every morning. 'I could never live here,' she told us, the day we moved in. 'I have to be around people.' Sherika is a single ebony stick almost six feet tall. She moves like a gazelle, like she is gliding towards the house. In Uganda, where she grew up, her family is part of the royal family—she may even be a princess of some sort.

I go downstairs and open the door for her. My top half is dressed in shirt and tie, my bottom half still pyjamaed.

'How are you doing this morning?' she asks, her intonation so melodious, each word so evenly enunciated that just the sound of her voice is a comfort.

'I'm fine, and you?'

'Good. Very good,' she says. 'Where are my ladies?'

'In the backyard, warming up.' I am still standing in the hall. 'What does the name Sherika mean?' I'm thinking it's something tribal, something mystical. I picture a tall bird, with thin legs and an unusual sound.

'I have no idea,' she says. 'It's just what my auntie in Brooklyn calls me. My true name is Christine.' She smiles. 'Today, I am going to take my ladies to the library and then maybe I'll take my ladies out to lunch.'

I find my wallet on the table and hand Christine forty dollars. 'Take them to lunch,' I say. 'That would be nice.'

'Thank you,' she says, putting the money in her pocket.

Susan and I walk ourselves to the train, leaving the car for Sherika–Christine.

'Fall is coming, clocks go back tomorrow, we can rake leaves this weekend,' I say as we head down the sidewalk. It is my fantasy to spend Saturday in the yard, raking. 'We have to give it a year.'

'And then what—put her in a home?

'I'm talking about the house, we have to give ourselves a year to get used to the house.' There is a pause, a giant black crow takes flight in front of us. 'We need shades in the bedroom, the upstairs bathroom needs to be re-grouted, it's all starting to annoy me.'

'It can't be perfect.'

'Why not?'

Sitting next to Susan on the train, I feel like I'm a foreigner, not just a person from another country, but a person from another planet, a person without customs, ways of being, a person who has blank spots, rather than bad habits. I am thinking about Susan, about what it means to be married to someone I know nothing about.

'It's exhausting,' I say, 'all this back and forth.'

'It's eighteen minutes longer than coming down from 106th Street.'

'It feels further.'

'It is further,' she says, 'but you're moving faster.' She turns the page.

'Do you ever wonder what I'm thinking?'

'I know what you're thinking, you confess every thought.'

'Not every thought.'

'Ninety-nine per cent,' she says.

'Does that bother you?'

'No,' she says. 'Everything is not so important, everything is not earth-shattering, despite what you think.'

I am silenced.

We arrive at Grand Central. Susan puts her book in her bag and is off the train. 'Call me,' I say. Every morning when we separate there is a moment when I think I will never see her again. She disappears into the crowd, and I think that's it, it's over, that's all there was.

Twenty minutes later, I call her at the office—'Just making sure you got there OK.'

'I'm here,' she says.

'I want something,' I confess.

'What do you want?'

'I don't know,' I say. 'More. I want more of something.'

Connection, I am thinking. I want connection.

'You want something I don't have,' she says.

I am at my desk, drifting, remembering the summer my parents divorced and my bar mitzvah was cancelled due to lack of interest on all sides.

'I just can't imagine doing it,' my mother said. 'I can't imagine doing anything with your father, can you? I think it would be very uncomfortable.'

My father gave me $5,000 to 'make up the difference' then asked, 'Is that enough?' I spent my thirteenth birthday with him in a New York hotel room, eating ice-cream cake from 31 Flavors with a woman whose name my father couldn't remember. 'Tell my friend about school, tell my friend what you do for fun, tell my friend all about yourself,' he kept saying, and all I wanted to do was scream— what the fuck is your friend's name?

On Memorial Day weekend, my mother married her 'friend' Howard and took off on an eight-week second honeymoon and I was sent to my father's new town-house condo in Philadelphia.

There was a small room for me, made out of what had been a walk-in closet. My father was taking cooking lessons, learning a thousand and one things to do with a wok. On different days, different women would come for dinner. 'I'm living the good life,' my father would tell me. 'I'm getting all I want.' I would eat dinner with my father and his date and then excuse myself and hide in my closet.

I spent my summer at the pool, living entirely in the water, with goggles, with fins. I fell in love with the bottom of the pool, a silky sky blue, a slippery second skin. I spent days walking up and down, trying to figure the exact point where I could still have my feet on the ground and my head above water.

'It's vinyl,' I heard the lifeguard tell someone.

The extreme stillness of the sky, the hot oxygenless air, the water strong like bleach, was blinding, sterile, intoxicating, perfect.

The only other person who came to the pool regularly was a girl who had just gotten out of the nut house for not eating. Deformedly thin, she would slather herself with lotion and lay out and bake. She was only allowed to swim one hour a day and at noon her mother would carry out a tray and she had to eat everything on it—'or else I'm taking you back,' her mother would say.

'Don't stand over me. Don't treat me like a baby.'

'Don't act like a baby.'

And then the mother would look at me. 'Would you like half a sandwich?'

I'd nod and she'd give me half a sandwich, which I'd eat still standing in the water, goggles on, feet touching the bottom.

'See,' the mother would say, 'He eats. And not only does he eat, he doesn't make crumbs.'

'He's in the water,' the girl would say.

In the evening I would crawl into my cave and read postcards from my mother—*Venice is everything I thought it would be, France is stunning, London theatre is so much better than Broadway. Thinking of you, hoping you're having a fantastic summer. I am imagining you swimming across America. Love Mom.*

'We're still your parents, we're just not together,' became the new refrain.

Later, when I started to date, when I would go to girls' houses and their mothers and fathers would ask, 'What do your parents do?' I'd say, 'They're divorced,' as though it were a full-time job.

And they'd look at me, instantly dismissive, as though I too was doomed to divorce, as though domestic instability was genetically passed down.

And then, later still, there were families I fell in love with. I remember sitting at the Segals' dining room table, happily slurping chicken soup, looking up at Cindy Segal, who stood above me, bread basket in hand, glaring at me in disgust. 'You're just another one of them,' she said, dropping the bread, unceremoniously dumping me. Too stunned to swallow, soup dribbled down my chin.

'Don't go,' Mrs Segal said, as Cindy slammed upstairs to her room. After that, the Segals would sometimes call me. 'Cindy's not going to be here,' they'd say, 'come visit.' I went a couple of times and then Cindy joined a cult and never spoke to any of us again.

My mother used to say, marry someone familiar, marry someone you have something in common with. The flatness, the hollow, the absence of some unnameable something—was familiar. The sensation that Susan was on the outside, waiting to be invited in was something we had in common.

Never did Susan ask for an accounting of my past, never did she pull back and say—'You're not going to hurt me, are you? You don't have any weird diseases, do you? You're not married, right?'

Susan looked at me once, squarely, evenly and said, 'Nice tie,' and that was it.

In the morning, after our first night together, she rearranged my furniture. Everything immediately looked better.

It is late in the afternoon, I have spent the day lost in thought. There are contracts spread across my desk waiting for my review. Outside, it is getting dark. I leave and instinctively walk uptown. All day I have been thinking about the house, about Mrs Ha, etc., and now I am heading towards our old apartment as though it was all a dream. I am walking, looking forward to seeing the grocer on the corner, to riding up in the elevator with Willy, the elevator man, to smelling the neighbours' dinner cooking. I am thinking that once these things happen, I will feel better, returned to myself. I go three blocks before I catch myself and realize that I am moving in the wrong direction. I belong in Larchmont—Larchmont like Loch Ness. I hurry towards the station. Stepping on to the train, I have the feeling I am leaving something behind. I check my messages— Susan has left word, something about a client, something about something falling, something about it all being her fault, something about staying late. 'I don't know when,' she says, and then we are in a tunnel and the signal is lost.

I am going home. I imagine arriving at the house and having Sherika tell me Mrs Ha is gone again. I picture changing into hunting clothes, a red-and-black wool jacket, an orange vest, a special hat and going in search of her carrying some kind of wooden whistle I have carved myself—a mother-in-law call. I imagine Mrs Ha hearing the rolling rattle of my call *Mrs Haa...Mrs Haaa Haa...Mrs Ha Ha Ha...Mrs Haaaaaahhhh*—it ends in an upswing. She is roused from her dream state, her head tilts towards the sound of my whistle and she is summoned home as mystically as she was called away.

I phone Sherika and ask—can she stay late, can she keep an extra eye on Mrs Ha. I take a taxi from the train—there is the odd suburban phenomenon of the shared cab, strangers piling in, stuffing themselves into the back of the sedan, briefcases held on laps like shields and then each calls out his address and we are off on a madcap ride, the driver tearing down the streets, whipping around corners, depositing us at our doorsteps for seven dollars a head.

Home. The sky is five minutes from dark, the floodlights are already on in the backyard. Kate and Mrs Ha are down in the dirt, squatting in a primal pose, elbows resting on thighs, buttocks dropped down, positioned as if about to shit.

'Mrs Ha, what are you doing?'

'I am thinking, Georgie. And I am resting.'

There is something frightening about it—Kate imitating Mrs Ha, grotesque in her gestures, rubber-limbed like a circus clown, contorting herself for attention, more alive than I will ever be. Her freedom, her full expression terrifying me—I am torn between interrupting and simply watching her be.

'We are planting a garden,' Sherika says, straightening up, extending to her full six feet. 'After lunch I took them to the nursery. We are putting in bulbs for spring.'

'Tulips,' Kate says.

Sherika drops sixty-nine cents of change into my hand and somehow I feel guilty, like I should have left her a hundred dollars or my credit card.

'What a good idea,' I say.

'We are just finishing up. Come on, ladies, let's go inside and wash our hands.'

I follow them into the kitchen. They wash their hands and then look at me, as though I should have something in mind, a plan for what happens next.

'Let's go for a ride,' I say, unable to bear the anxiety of staying home. Not knowing where else to go, I drive them to the supermarket. Sherika takes Mrs Ha and I have Kate and we go up and down the aisles, filling the cart.

'Are you the apple of your daddy's eye?' A clerk in the produce section pulls Kate's hair and then looks at me. 'There's lots of these Chinese babies now, nobody wants them so they give them away. My wife's sister adopted one—otherwise they drown 'em like kittens. You don't want to be drowned, do you, sweetheart,' he says, looking at Kate again.

'She's not adopted. She's mine.'

'Oh sorry,' the guy says, flustered as though he's said something even more insulting than what he actually said. 'I'm really sorry.' He backs away.

Sorry about what? I look at Kate. Her head is too big. Her skin is an odd jaundicy yellow and now she's playing some weird game with the cantaloupes, banging them against the floor. It occurs to me that the guy thought there was something wrong with her.

'Did you find everything you were looking for?' Sherika asks as we're wheeling up the frozen foods towards the checkout.

'I'm finished.'

In a strip mall across the street, I notice an Asian grocery store. When the light changes, I pull in.

'Ah,' Sherika says, 'look at that.'

It is small, dingy and a little other-worldly. There are wire racks for shelves and things floating in tubs filled with melting ice—none of it incredibly clean. Mrs Ha scurries around collecting tins of spices, bottles of vinegar. She seems happy, like she has recovered herself, she is chatting with the man behind the counter.

She shows me fresh vegetables; water chestnuts, shanghai cabbage, *'Bau dau gok,'* she says, 'snake bean.' Lotus leaves, brown slab sugar, and now she is in the freezer case—handing me a bag that says, FROZEN FISH BALLS. She hands me others with writing in Chinese. *'Fatt choy?'* she asks the man behind the counter and he points towards it.

'What is it?' I ask.

'Black moss,' she says.

'What is it really?' I ask.

She shrugs.

I want Mrs Ha to feel comfortable. If pressed seaweed is to her what mashed potatoes are to me, I want her to have ten packages. Why not? I start picking things off the shelf and offering them to her.

She shakes her head and continues shopping.

The man behind the counter says something and she laughs, I am sure it is about me. I hear something about three Georges, about water and then a lot of clucking from Mrs Ha. He talks quickly, flipping back and forth from Chinese to broken English. She answers—her speech, suddenly rhythmic, her accent shifting into the pure diphthong, the *oo* long, an ancient incantation.

The man takes a small beautiful box out from a shelf below the counter. Mrs Ha makes a soft cooing sound before he opens it. 'Bird's nest,' he says. 'Very good quality.'

'What is bird's nest?'

The man blows spit bubbles at me. He drools intentionally and then sucks his saliva back in. 'The spit of a swift,' he says, flapping his arms.

Mrs Ha checks her pockets for money, finds nothing and looks at me as if to ask, can we get it?

'Sure, why not?'

'I have never had so much home in a long time,' she says.

'Come again soon,' the man says, as we are leaving. 'Play bingo.'

I carry two shopping bags out to the car, imagining Mrs Ha is going to start dating this man—I picture tracking twin positioning chips, two dots, one on top of the other. I make a mental note to ask Susan—is Mrs Ha allowed to date?

In the car on the way home Mrs Ha asks, 'Do you like Sony? Mr Sony make the tape recorder and Mr Nixon make friends with the Chinese. Then Mr Nixon erase and now Mr Sony die, I read in your *New York Times*.' She laughs. 'Stupid old men.'

Kate is on the floor in front of the television. Mrs Ha is in the kitchen making soup. Sherika takes the car to the train station, she will drop it off and go home to Queens, Susan will pick it up and come home to us.

'What's that smell?' Susan says, when she comes in the door.

'Your mother is making soup.'

'It's so weirdly familiar, I thought I was hallucinating.'

'Everything OK?' I am looking at her, trying to tell if she is lying, if there's more to the story or not.

'It's fine,' she says. 'It's fine. The client got hysterical, a little piece of the wall came down—it wasn't my fault. I was so upset. I thought I had done something wrong.'

I don't tell Susan that I was worried she might not come back. I don't tell her that I took everyone to the supermarket because the idea of staying alone in the house with the three of them inexplicably terrified me.

'Dinner is ready,' Mrs Ha says.

'It looks delicious.' I stare into my bowl. There are white things and black things floating in the soup—nothing recognizable. I am starving. I assume it is mushrooms.

'Hot,' Kate says, her face over the bowl, blowing steam like a dragon.

Susan stares speechless at her bowl.

The broth is rich, succulent. I slurp. It is skin, skin and bones, small bones, soft, like little fingers, melting in the mouth.

I look at Susan. 'Feet?' I ask in Latin. Susan nods.

I don't want to say anything more. I don't want to throw Kate off—she is eating, not noticing. And Mrs Ha is clearly enjoying herself.

'Georgie took me shopping,' Mrs Ha says.

'I had a late lunch.' Susan carries her bowl into the kitchen.

Later, I overhear her on the phone with her brother, whispering. 'She tried to poison me, she made chicken-feet soup.'

I pick up the extension in the kitchen and hope neither of them notice the click.

'Where did she get the feet?'

'I think he's helping her.'

'Who?'

'Geordie.'

'Why?'

'He hates me.'

I hang up.

When I was young my mother made cupcakes for my birthday and brought them to school. The teacher had us all write her thank-you notes in thick pencil on wide-lined paper. *Dear Mrs Harris, thank you for the delicious cupcakes. We enjoyed them very much. Sincerely, Geordie.*

'Dear Mrs Harris, Sincerely Geordie, what kind of letter is that to send a mother?' She still talks about how funny it was. When she telephones and I answer she says, 'It's Mrs Harris, your mother.'

We are in bed. Susan is reading. I look over her shoulder, page 297 of *In Cold Blood*, a description of Perry Smith, one of the murderers. 'He seems to have grown up without direction, without love.'

'I'm lonely,' I tell her.

'Read something,' she says, turning the page.

I go downstairs and fix a bowl of ice cream for Susan.

'I'm not your enemy,' I tell her when the ice cream is gone, when I have helped her finish it, when I am licking the bowl.

'I don't know that,' she says, taking the bowl away from me and putting it on the floor. 'You act like you're on her side.'

'And what side is that?'

'The side of the dead, of things past.'

'Oh, please,' I say, and yet there is something in what Susan is saying; I am on the side of things lost, I am in the past, remembering. 'You're scaring me,' I say. 'You're turning into some weird minimalist monster from hell.'

'This is me. This is my life,' Susan says. 'You're intruding.'

'This is our family,' I say, horrified.

'I can't be Chinese,' Susan tells me. 'I've spent my whole life trying not to be Chinese.'

'Kate is half Chinese and she likes it,' I say, trying to make Susan feel better.

'I don't like that half of Kate,' Susan says.

Something summons me from my sleep. I listen—on alert, heart racing. The extreme silence of night is blasting full volume. Moon pours into the room like a gigantic night light. Outside, the trees, thick with leaves, are still—it is haunting, romantic, deeply autumnal. Night.

And there it is, far away, catching me, a kind of bleating, a baleful wail.

I go down the hall, each step amplified, the quieter I try to go the louder I become.

I check Kate—she is fast asleep.

It becomes more of a moan—deep, inconsolable, hollow. There is no echo, each beatified bellow is here and then gone, evaporating into the night.

Downstairs, Mrs Ha is crouched in the corner of the living room, like a new end table. She is next to the sofa, squatting, her hands at her ears, crying. She is naked.

'Mrs Ha?'

She doesn't answer.

Her cry, heartbreaking, definitive, filled with horror, with grief, with fear, comes from someplace far away, from somewhere long ago.

I touch her shoulder. 'It's Geordie. Is there something I can do? Are you all right?'

I step on the foot switch for the lamp; the halogen torch floods the room. Susan's Corbusier chairs sit bolt upright—tight black leather boxes, a Prouve table from France lies flat, waiting, the modernist edge, dissonant, vibrating against the Tudor, the stone, the old casement windows, and Mrs Ha, my Chinese mother-in-law, sobbing at my feet. I turn the light off.

'Mrs Ha?' I lift her up, I put my hands under her arms and pull. She is compact like a panda, she is made of heavy metal, her skin is at once papery thin and thick like hide. She clings to me, digging in.

I carry her back to her bed. She cries. I find her nightgown and slip it over her head. When she cries, her mouth drops open, her lips roll back, her chin tilts up and her teeth and jaws flash, like a horse's head. It is as though someone has just told her the most horrible thing; her face contorts. Her expression is like an anthropological find—at eighty-nine she is a living skeleton.

I touch her hair.

'I want to go home,' she wails.

'You are home.'

'I want to go home,' she repeats.

I sit on the edge of her bed, I put my arms around her. 'Maybe it was the soup, maybe the dinner didn't agree with you.'

'No,' she says, 'I always have the soup. It is not the soup that does not agree with me, it is me that does not agree with me.' She stops crying. 'They are going to flood my home, I read it in the *New York Times*, they build the three Georges, the dam, and everything goes underwater.'

'I don't know who they are,' I say.

'You are who they are,' she says. I don't know what she is talking about.

Mrs Ha reaches to scratch her back, between her shoulder blades. 'There is something there,' she says, 'I just can't reach it.'

I imagine the little green blip on the tracking device, wobbling. 'It's OK. Everything is all right now.'

'You have no idea,' she tells me as she is drifting off. 'I am an old woman but I am not stupid.'

And when she is asleep, I go back to bed. I am drenched in sweat. Susan turns towards me. 'Everything all right?'

'Mrs Ha was crying.'

'Don't call her Mrs Ha.'

I take off my shirt, thinking I must smell like Mrs Ha. I smell like Mrs Ha and sweat and fear. 'What would you like me to call her—Ma Ha?'

'She has a name,' Susan says angrily. 'Call her Lillian.'

I cannot sleep. I am thinking we have to take Mrs Ha home. I am imagining a family trip reuniting Mrs Ha with her country, Susan with her roots, Kate with her ancestry. I am thinking that I need to know more. I once read a story in a travel magazine about a man who went on a bike ride in China. I pictured a long open road, a rural landscape. In the story the man falls off his bike, breaks his hip and lies on the side of the road until he realizes no help is going to come and then he fashions his broken bike into a cane, raises himself up and hobbles back to town. □

GRANTA

# KEMP AND POTTER
## Nicholas Shakespeare

Nicholas and Max George Tasman Shakespeare, Tasmania, 2000

Early in 1999 I flew from London to Sydney and then, on Valentine's Day, to Tasmania. I'd just finished writing a long biography, seven years work on one man, the writer and traveller Bruce Chatwin, and I was burnt out. One of Tasmania's attractions was its remoteness; another was that Chatwin, who specialized in the remote, had never been there. The island would be terra incognita, unevoked in my mind by his writing and my research into his life. Tasmania's freshness—its wind and its light (friends in mainland Australia remarked on the light especially)—might empty me of the biographer's condition: that dull, unfriendly abstraction brought on by too many months in the shade of old documents. I was, I suppose, sick of a life already lived. I hoped never to read another old letter again.

My girlfriend came with me. Our idea was to walk for a week through Tasmania's western highlands before returning to Sydney, but the landscape—a mixture of low-growing rainforest and fragile alpine heath—cast a spell on us and we delayed our departure. We hired a car and drove south to Port Arthur and then to the East Coast. One afternoon, outside a town called Swansea, we saw a beach house for sale on a nine-mile shelf of coastal dunes. It was a single-storey building made from cedar and glass.

We knocked at the door. It was answered by a middle-aged woman in a lavender sarong. Her name was Helen and she told us that she had built the house with her husband, a retired radio executive who was now ill and needed to be closer to a hospital. She was an artist and photographer—the house was hung with her vast red moodscapes—and as she led us on an impromptu tour of the rooms, she spoke of 'destiny' and 'serendipitous unions'.

Inside the house, the glass intensified the sunlight, dissolving her chatter. Strangely suspended by the light, I followed Helen into rooms she'd christened 'the solarium' and 'the veranda cafe' and then through clumps of boobyalla to the deserted beach and her 'bliss spot', a small clearing in the spinifex where, she said, she liked to sunbathe naked. There was a fenced-off garden below the house, planted with apple trees, and a small tin shed where I pictured myself at a desk. Less than an hour later we were bidding her an emotional farewell on 'the grand staircase'.

We were oddly subdued as we drove away. We had no family connections, no friends, no reason to linger, but I couldn't stop thinking of the view from the windows of the house on to the peninsula. I started to wonder if Helen's house might be somewhere we could live. By the time we arrived at our accommodation for that evening, a bed and breakfast on the road to Hobart, I was seriously considering the possibility of the house—and therefore Tasmania—becoming a destination as well as an escape.

I thought of what I knew about Tasmania—not very much. I knew that it was the smallest Australian state, an island the size of Ireland but populated by only 450,000 people and separated from the mainland by 170 miles of the treacherous pitch and toss of Bass Strait; that it was poor and that people were leaving; that while it was beautiful it was also palpably melancholy; that it had once been known as Van Diemen's Land—a synonym for all kinds of terror and dread—in its days as a colony of British convicts; that, some time during the nineteenth century, its original Aboriginal population had been ruthlessly wiped out.

As soon as we arrived at the convict-built bed and breakfast we found a message from Helen, asking us to call her. It turned out that she just wanted to say that she saw herself in us and how rare it was to feel such a connection to strangers and that there were no accidents in life. Oh, and incidentally, did we like the house?

We went home to England and plotted our return. We could both get away; the major obstacles were residency visas and money. We could just afford the beach house, although buying it would mean spending every penny I'd earned from the biography. The commitment would seem less enormous if we could rent the place first, so I phoned Helen and proposed that we take a six-month lease. Whether impressed by our karmic connection or by a lack of offers (the house, like many in Tasmania, had been on the market a long time), she agreed. At the end of six months we could decide whether to buy or not.

I sent off my residency application. The same week I took a trip to see my father in Wiltshire. Halfway through the visit he produced a yellowing plastic bag filled with letters which he'd unearthed from the basement of my grandmother's house in Worcestershire. Her father had left them to her and she had never got round to reading them. My grandmother was ninety-six, but my father thought that the letters were probably older than that.

'I think,' my father said, 'we may have relatives in Tasmania.' He'd glanced at the contents of the bag and discovered that an ancestor of ours had left London at the end of the eighteenth century to become a merchant in Hobart.

This was the first I'd heard of any Tasmanian relatives, and I didn't really take it in. I chucked the bag in the back of the car where it remained, unopened, for several months. I was finished with old letters. And there were more important things to think about. In July, I got married in Wiltshire and took my wife to Saxony, to an artists' residence in Wiepersdorf. It wasn't until we were there that, in a moment of idle curiosity, I finally opened the bag and started to go through its contents.

My time in the archives had taught me the frustration of going through the letters of the dead. We want the dead to reveal to us what they did not reveal in life, some confessional strain they kept hidden from the world. But more often what we exhume is the random detritus of their everyday lives: barely legible wishes for good health, polite hellos, how are yous, thank yous, numbing résumés of the day got through—and scattered among them faded receipts and photos without dates, without names.

The contents of the plastic bag smelled like rotten vegetables. The first thing I pulled out was a loose slip of paper, a cheque made out, in 1815, to 'Kemp & Potter, brandy and tobacco merchants'. Potter was my grandmother's name and I remembered that our family had, long ago, been involved in the drinks trade. But the name Kemp meant nothing to me.

Next came a bundle of about thirty letters written on stiff paper in the days before stamps. They were folded away in chronological order: the first letter dated 1791, the last 1825. Occasionally they were signed with a woman's name: Amy, Susannah, Elizabeth. But most of the correspondence appeared to have taken place between two men, William Potter and Anthony Fenn Kemp.

Kemp's letters to Potter were sent from all over the world: Brazil, Cape Town, Sydney, Hobart. The ink had faded to sepia but the handwriting remained distinctively slanted, the words scratched aggressively on to the page, with exaggerated tails to certain letters. By contrast Potter's responses—all sent from an address in Aldgate— were written in a neat, upright hand, and he had made copies of his own replies, so providing both sides of their correspondence.

I opened a red marbled business ledger dated March 25, 1789, the year of the French revolution. The ageing paper had the scent of damp nutmeg. On the first page, under the heading *I Anthony Kemp being of Age have this day rec'd of Coll John Arnott my guardian* there was a long list. It included properties in Surrey and central London, stocks and cash. Together it amounted to a fortune today worth several million pounds. I wondered what had happened to it.

Kemp was evidently a very rich young man, but as I read more of the ledger it became clear that, despite his wealth, he had worked as an apprentice in his father's brandy and tobacco business, Kemp & Son, based at 87 Aldgate. He appeared to have had a pretty free hand in its affairs, though. While the ledger recorded Kemp the father tramping with his samples to Biggleswade and Newport Pagnell, Kemp the son was ordering hogsheads of rum from Antigua, pipes of port from Lisbon and fine shag from plantations in Maryland. Nor, I discovered, did he restrict himself to buying only tobacco and rum. As I turned the pages the purchases mounted until they culminated in the outfitting of an entire boat, the *Neptune Galley*, to bring a lavish cargo of cinnamon, cochineal, sugar and silk from Jamaica. Then suddenly the ledger stopped. One of the last entries was in the younger Kemp's handwriting: 'June 14, 1789: Lost by betting at an horse race £15.10.' It seemed to me to have an ominous note, and I turned to the letters, hoping to piece together more of the story.

It transpired that Kemp had run through his entire inheritance in two years. By 1791, he couldn't even repay twelve crowns to a man called Page, instead organizing for a 'very shabby insolent low-bred woman' to march into Page's favourite London coffee house and 'utter impertinencies' about him at the top of her voice. Page reported this incident in a letter to Kemp's father. Kemp's father's reaction was furious: he wrote to his son, who had, it appeared—

undoubtedly wisely—absented himself from Aldgate, threatening to sue him unless he reflected upon the situation '[his] early vice and infamy had placed [him] in'. Only if Kemp admitted to his 'evil conduct' and confessed his faults would he be welcome to return home to his father and mother. 'If this overture is rejected expect that I shall take speedy and effective public measures to prevent further injury.'

One week later, a letter was brought to Aldgate by an attorney of Clement's Inn. Its delivery had been delayed by order of Anthony Fenn Kemp until its author was safe across the Channel. 'Hon Sir and Madam,' he addressed his parents. 'Behold my reply. At present I am not sensible of what distress is nor pray to God I ever shall and as to returning with compunction I hope when I do come I may.'

On the outside of the envelope, an unknown hand had scribbled the enticing phrase, 'First elopement'. Apparently Kemp's story was just beginning.

I was hooked. I rifled through the batch of letters, anxious to find out what Kemp got up to in France, but there was a gap of several years in the correspondence. The next letter I unfolded was dated March 1816, and the address was not France, but Sydney, Australia.

In October 1999, one month before I was due to fly back there, I learned that my application to live in Tasmania had been successful. We moved into the house. Helen had sprinkled handfuls of rosemary into our pillows, which my wife mistook for spiders' eggs, and she exhorted us by telephone and fax to maintain what she had begun in the garden.

The house was more beautiful even than I remembered, all wood and glass and views of Oyster Bay. On our first afternoon, we walked two hundred yards to the deserted beach. There was a southern equinox cooling the sea and a clear sky over the hills above Swansea. We took off our clothes and jumped into the surf, and afterwards ran back to the house, startling a young wallaby on the path. It stared at us, then bounded off through the boobyalla, its feet thumping the warm sand with a sound like a heavy fruit dropping.

For the first time in my life I started gardening. I planted seeds, bought trees, learned about mulching. I was bemused when I found myself, out of the garden, still wanting to dig.

Sitting at my desk in my new study one day with the bag of letters in front of me, I held up my hands and counted out the relationships that I'd discovered. Potter, my great-great-great-great grandfather; Kemp, my great-great-great-great uncle. Their letters had revealed that they were closer than business partners: they were brothers-in-law. To me, their unfolding story seemed to be about nothing so much as two ways of being in the world. On one hand there was Kemp, roistering, opportunistic, corrupt. On the other was the sedentary and abstemious Potter.

I was still going through their letters. In 1791, the eighteen-year-old Kemp was being groomed to take over the family firm. But after he left England, his father turned to William Potter, the man who had married Kemp's elder sister Amy. He invited Potter to move into the Aldgate premises and granted him a third share of the business. On the death of Kemp's father, a reluctant Potter took over the running of the firm. It was now called 'Kemp & Potter'.

There are those who go to New South Wales and there are those who mind the store. Potter inched off the page—in his handwriting and in his character—as the opposite of his brother-in-law: a cautious, fussy, meticulous man, forever advising his family how to behave. The following pieces of advice all appeared in letters to his son: 'Never play cards in Grantham *or in any other place with strangers*'; 'Remember one above sees and knows all and will reward or punish as we deserve'; 'Be careful at Brighton. It's a rotten place'. And—oddly (or perhaps not) for a man in the liquor business—there were various admonitions about drink. 'Drink no more than you can help' he counselled; on the same theme, in a letter warning his son about which public houses in Ware were 'safe' or not, 'We must be very careful what we are about…the owner of the Little White Lion likes you to spend an hour with him in the evening which calls for a bottle of wine which you may mix with water.'

By contrast, out in Australia, his absentee partner was peddling family connections with the rum trade for all they were worth; or not worth, for Kemp's letters—despite their considerable charm—had already revealed to me that he was a feckless businessman. He borrowed a vast sum from Potter, which he never repaid. He wrote out several cheques in the name of 'Kemp & Potter' which were never redeemed. His letters took up to fourteen months to reach London and each contained an excuse.

I found it painful to observe Potter's struggles to cope with Kemp's escalating debts. 'For eighteen months I have had weekly applications from one or another of your creditors for the amount of bills made payable at our house'—and yet, from Kemp, 'not a farthing has arrived, which I am much astonished at.' The etiquette of the early nineteenth century fails to check his frustration: 'I am now completely sick of shipping goods to you.'

Yet Potter could not cut off his feckless brother-in-law. I could see him sitting at night at his double mahogany desk, wearing a calico nightcap. I could feel his sense of responsibility, born of duty, blood, grudging envy and just enough imagination to believe in his brother-in-law's schemes.

One morning, my wife woke up with a toothache. It refused to get better, so I drove her to the dentist in Hobart in Helen's ancient green Peugeot. The two-hour drive along the coast took us through the counties of Glamorgan, Pembroke and Buckingham, through countryside eerily similar to where we'd lived in Wiltshire: Georgian sandstone houses with deep windows—fingertip to ankle; rose gardens and wicket fences; names like Annandale and Clarendon and Bust-Me-Gall Hill. 'Everything in Tasmania is more English than is England herself,' noted Trollope who was tempted to 'pitch [his] staff' in the country permanently (he liked the mulberry jams in particular). And yet we were most certainly not in England. It looked like an English nobleman's park, but beyond the bourgeois topiaries there was sadness—and not just because of the haunting absence of the native population. Anyone with ambition, I'd been told, followed the example of Errol Flynn, who—born in Tasmania—got out as soon as he could. Young Tasmanians took their leaving as a rite of passage. The old and the very young were left behind, perhaps to study the blackboards we passed at the side of the road chalked with advertisements for 'horse-poo', 'chook-poo', and kilos of flies.

Tasmania's capital is a clean, unselfconscious port whose water throws back smooth reflections of white sails, bright facades and a dramatic mountain. ('My predominant recollection is of its apples, its jams, its rose-cheeked girls,' wrote Errol Flynn in his autobiography, *My Wicked, Wicked Life.*). Once the last port of call for Arctic explorers, modern Hobart feels like an English market town. 'Last, loneliest, loveliest,' said Mark Twain, who thought it 'the neatest town that the sun shines on'. It was still true: I couldn't stop marvelling at the clarity of the sunlight. Mainlanders put the transparency down to the frazzled ozone layer, but whatever the cause, the light was so clear that there seemed to be no gauze between it and the first settlers.

In a place as obsessed with history as Tasmania the present quickly leads back to the past. I dropped off my wife at the dentist's and went for a walk round the town. Passing Kemp Street I found myself wondering about the name—if it was connected in some way with my distant uncle. I dismissed the thought as ridiculous, but then, in Murray Street, realizing that my route was taking me past the Hobart archives, I couldn't resist going in. Habit, I suppose: a biographer's reflex action. I told myself, as I climbed the stairs, that I was being led less by an investigating spirit than an extinguishing one. I'll just quickly check him out and then I can be done with him, I thought.

The archivist was a friendly woman of about sixty-five. I told her what I knew about Kemp and asked her whether she had heard of him, and where she thought I should start my researches. At this, she smiled and calmly told me that Anthony Fenn Kemp was commonly known as 'The Father of Tasmania'.

*The Father of Tasmania*. The man who up until now I had been thinking of as some dodgy character in the rum and tobacco trade. Nothing in the letters I had read so far had prefigured this fame.

'He also wished to be known as the "George Washington of Van Diemen's Land" and the "Father of the People"' she told me, adding, however, that there was some debate over whether this sobriquet saluted Kemp's role in Tasmania's history, his sublime egoism or his eighteen children.

Still trying to digest this unexpected piece of information, I asked her for more background. It turned out that Kemp had been one of the very first colonists to set foot in the territory. He had helped to establish the first permanent settlement in the north and for seven months had been left in command of half the island. Nor was his influence limited to Van Diemen's Land. He was witness to many crises in the early history of Australia and responsible for several more. He fomented one mutiny, saw off two Governors of New South Wales, two more Lieutenant Governors of Tasmania and risked war with the French. He was also the great-grandfather of the Victorian novelist Mrs Humphrey Ward and the great-great-grandfather of Aldous Huxley.

I felt rather pleased. I told the archivist, with a hint of pride, that he was a distant relative of mine.

'If I were you, I would not go round divulging that information.' She pressed her yellow pencil to her chin. 'He's a man of whom I've heard not one word of good.'

So I began to sift in earnest through the vast, messy junk drawer of Anthony Fenn Kemp's life: to do, in fact, the very thing I had come to Tasmania not to do. But how could I not?

It was as if, having arrived in this place to escape Chatwin, I'd found myself caught up with the kind of characters he adored and would have delighted to count among his ancestors.

I hoped I would be able to fill in the gaps quickly. The so-called Father of Tasmania would surely have inspired a biography. But no. Despite his credentials, it seemed that little had been written about Kemp; and although he began to pop up everywhere, he resisted any move to pin him down, to fix him.

I began to track him down: in libraries in Sydney, London and Hobart; in leather-backed books the archivist brought to my desk; in interviews with his descendants. Step by step, I chivvied him out of the undergrowth until what emerged was not the indigent remittance man I'd expected, but an important and extraordinary figure—one of the founding sires of Australia, who led like a lightning rod back to the island's past, giving me a thumbnail sketch of the whole bizarre and brutal early history of Tasmania and New South Wales.

And as I followed Kemp to Australia, I felt like Potter's accidental auditor, crossing the world as Potter never could to bring Kemp to account. It was the opposite of everything I intended. I had come here, like Kemp, to begin afresh in the way of Van Diemen's Land when it was renamed Tasmania. But you can't just shed yourself like that, not even if you go and live on the rim of the world. Too often the Potter and rarely the Kemp, I was back at my desk, a clerk again.

Anthony Fenn Kemp stepped ashore at Calais and headed south on foot. He walked through a country in mid-revolution, a penniless outcast driven by the need to escape his family's censure.

Back in Aldgate concern about his safety had confined his mother to her bed. Susannah Kemp was a highly-strung woman who rode for her health and was addicted to a tincture of valerian and castor known as 'Bevan's nervous drops'. When she died, six months after he left, her only son was in Liège, dancing the 'Marseilleise' around the cap of Liberty.

His resentment of his father had slowly transmuted into contempt for all authority. He sympathized with the revolutionaries, who egged him on—he was able to communicate his feelings expansively in their language. He had learned his French at Dr Knox's school in Greenwich (where, according to his obituary which I looked up in an old copy of the *Tasmanian Times*, he also acquired a fondness for quoting Latin 'which afforded frequent amusement to his intimate friends'). He was apparently never happy 'unless talking'.

In fact, he talked himself out of most friendships, being prone, when piqued, to address his listeners in rather an abrupt manner. One of few to take him at face value was James Calder, an amateur surveyor and writer of the *Times* obituary. As an old man in his nineties, Kemp spoke at length to Calder from his wheelchair in 'Mount Vernon', his estate outside Hobart. (The house is still there: tall, three-storeyed, Georgian, with a facade the colour of dried orange peel.) He talked about his anarchic experiences in Liège, the wild excesses he had witnessed, and revealed how, after gaining a taste for republicanism, he spent the next year in America 'as a pleasure-seeking traveller'. It was there, at his farm in South Carolina, that he had a brief, if unlikely meeting with the only man he ever admired. He loved George Washington, he told Calder—with a power for self-deception that remained undimmed at ninety-five—for strengthening his 'inherent aversion to despotism'.

But not even America was far enough from Aldgate.

Why else did Kemp go to Australia? From the books in Hobart library I got the impression that the first people who went to Australia were either felons who didn't want to go; those sent to guard them, who also didn't want to go; and a handful of free settlers who were making a huge gamble, comparable, at that time, to settling on the moon. No one came with the high ideals of the Founding Fathers. It was, in fact, a very odd place for someone like Kemp to choose. It must simply have suited him to be 13,950 miles away from home. Distance is a great aid to a rascal.

Aged twenty, he bought himself a commission in the 102 Regiment of Foot (later called the New South Wales Corps), raised to manage convicts in a new penal colony at Sydney Cove, a wild, empty, desperate place at the other end of the world. He was one of only eighteen officers, but his red and white sash was never a coveted uniform. Kemp himself calculated that two hundred of the 460 soldiers under him were ex-convicts, recruited from the ranks of those they were supposed to garrison. Kemp and the Governor of New South Wales travelled to Australia on the same decrepit ship, along with the town clock, a windmill and a returning Aborigine suffering from flu.

On the evening of September 7, 1795, Kemp sailed between the Sydney Heads into slack water. He had spent six months ricocheting between the walls of a cabin with no head space and poor ventilation, breathing in the stench of sanitary buckets. In Sydney it was late spring, the air hot and scented. A crew of bluejackets rowed him ashore. He saw a town settled on spurs of sandstone covered with immense grey trees. Flights of strange birds jabbered at him and the sinking sun gave to everything it touched a ghost-like quality. It was a mesmerizing setting, though not altogether foreign (one settler called it, in a magnificently potty description: 'A Wapping or St Giles in the beauties of a Richmond'). It was also a microcosm of all that was riotous in Georgian society.

The town was only seven years old and spread back from the harbour in a shabby crescent. The population of five thousand lived in tents and bush-timber huts covered in rammed earth. Rationing was in force and there was not much to eat 'except rats'. Few knew anything about agriculture or how to grow food. In this strange banished place they found relief in alcohol. On his way to Barrack Square, Kemp passed men and women slumped beside buckets of pure alcohol—they drank it from quart mugs until they passed out. Historians unite in describing early colonial Sydney as a drunken society from top to bottom. Thanks to Kemp, it soon became even drunker.

In Sydney Cove the twenty-two-year-old Kemp proved adept at swindling his way to the top. It was his good luck to find himself at large in a society that thrived on the commodities he knew most about: tobacco, which the convicts prized above food and sex, and rum (a term used to describe any spirit) which they prized even more. Kemp exploited their craving with an unexpected ace: the good name and credit of 'Kemp & Potter'.

Born into the trade, Kemp knew the shippers and agents in Mauritius, the Caribbean, India. (By far his most profitable liquor, he told a government commission, was Bengal rum: 'There is a particular flavour in it which the lower orders prefer.') His contacts and education quickly secured him the post of the Corp's acting paymaster. He knew Latin, and his father, he reassured everyone in one of his rare honest statements, was 'one of the most respectable men in the City of London'. First up the ropes when a ship entered harbour, he purchased the cargo using a combination of promissory notes to 'Kemp & Potter' and the Treasury Bills with which he was supposed to pay the regiment. He then sold the cargo to his captive clientele, through his store the 'Golden Corner', at grossly inflated prices.

Kemp was not alone in his racketeering, but by most accounts, he was the most energetic and unscrupulous of the officer-traders. His special racket was rum. He and a ring of army cronies bought every incoming barrel for as little as seven shillings and sixpence a gallon and resold it for up to eight pounds, a mark-up of more than two thousand per cent. Soon rum was the currency of the colony. For half a pint of 'Bengal', a desperate settler gave three bushels of wheat, a convict chopped a hundred feet of timber, a woman offered her body. And Kemp was chief supplier. His commerce earned the regiment its nickname: the Rum Corps.

In the same month that he opened his emporium, Kemp got Judith Simpson, a twenty-five-year-old convict woman, pregnant. She had eighteen months of her sentence left to serve when she gave birth to Kemp's daughter. Emily's arrival on June 4, 1800 stirred unusual emotions in Kemp. He put pressure on the Governor who, the same day, granted Emily's mother an absolute pardon.

Five months later, Kemp sailed home on leave with his 'concubine'—as Judith is called in the Female Muster—and his illegitimate daughter. They occupied a rare berth as a family unit. On board the *Buffalo*, Judith conceived again.

Back in London, Kemp moved to patch things up with his father, but his homecoming was less impressive than he might have hoped. Only one communication survived the eleven-year silence between them, a letter describing how Kemp has decided to marry the woman he decorously calls Miss Crawford. Too ashamed to introduce his pregnant 'Moll' to Aldgate, he took lodgings at 15 Baker Street, from where he wrote to his father: 'I feel my Happiness entirely depending on your acquiescence to accomplish my union with her, having Mr & Mrs Crawford's consent.' He was confident that his marriage to Miss Crawford would 'add much to my prosperity in New South Wales'.

But Kemp's father sent a cousin around with a blunt message: his son was free to do what he liked. Three weeks later Kemp did exactly that—abandoned Judith in London, dumped his eighteen-month-old daughter Emily on the Potters and eloped for a second time to the Antipodes.

Tasmania—alone of all the former penal colonies—has a tendency to sit on its family secrets. We had been living in our new house for some time before I discovered that Emily's descendents owned a vineyard just ten miles from where I lived. When I found out, I decided to go and visit.

The farmhouse was at Coombend, at the end of a small valley. It once served as the district post office and belonged to a family from what I later learned was Tasmania's landed gentry. While buying a bottle of Cabernet Sauvignon, I fell into conversation with the proprietor, an agile man of sixty with stubborn blue eyes. Twenty minutes later I was sitting in his drawing-room examining Anthony Fenn Kemp's 'christening mug'—a pint-sized silver tankard which his wife had been using as a vase. They were clearly interested in my research, although their curiosity was hedged with anxiety about what I might have discovered in this new hoard of letters. With a markedly casual air, the winemaker said: 'It's very fashionable to be descended from convicts?'

I picked the flowers out of the tankard—it was more drinking bucket than christening mug. Stamped on the side there was a crest: a long-necked vulture standing on a wheatsheaf, and the words: *Sic copia campis.*

'Let there be plenty in the fields,' translated the winemaker's wife.

Her husband started to laugh. 'The only thing I know, he was a bastard. It's stressful being a philanderer, but they live to a great age.' He shot me a look: 'The genes, they come down.'

A fortnight later, I was buying some sausages in a Hobart delicatessen when a woman who introduced herself as the winemaker's sister darted round the counter and gripped my shoulder: 'Welcome to the family.' She had red hair and direct eyes and gave me a discount. She glanced at my wife, conspiratorial: 'Are you going to call him Fenn?'

We knew it was a boy thanks to a midwife in Launceston. I had asked in a general way if it was possible to tell a child's sex at fourteen weeks, whereupon she pointed at the ultrasound image: 'Oh yes.' The fact of a son had overwhelmed me. Like his sex, which was already formed, his character was presumably out of my hands. I'd started thinking that it was a good thing that there was no technology to tell you whether you were going to get a Potter or a Kemp; whether this child would lean towards the ledger or the rum.

In 1801, while in London with Judith, Kemp had his portrait painted. The original had been lost, but I learned of a man in the north of Tasmania—another descendant of Kemp—who apparently had a copy.

When I arrived at the weatherboard cottage in Hawley Beach where Paul Edwards lived, he showed me the picture straight away, with few preliminaries. It depicted Kemp in the scarlet tunic of a Rum

Corps lieutenant. He had the features of a determined sensualist: large dark eyes, powdered white hair, a prominent nose.

'He's a very devious, interesting gentleman with a cruel mouth,' Paul said. 'My children wonder how I can sit here with him looking at me.'

Paul, an amateur genealogist and retired papermaker, was a descendant of Kemp via his marriage to a sixteen-year-old girl called Elizabeth Riley. He met her in Sydney soon after he sailed back from London; they had known each other, at most, for a month before they married, but they remained so for sixty-three years and she gave him sixteen children. As Paul Edwards said, gruffly, 'Fancy siring sixteen children on a woman. I reckon that's disgusting.'

And Judith? According to Edwards, she ran a series of pubs and boarding houses, was gaoled for debt and died in Sydney in 1836 aged sixty-one. I assumed that Kemp never gave her another thought, but then later I came across a poem he had published in a Hobart newspaper twenty-two years after abandoning her with their second child. Titled 'The Contrast', it was a shockingly sentimental tribute to a distraught young woman who had relied on a man's promise:

> She had given
> Life's hope to a most fragile bark—to love!
> Twas wreck'd—wreck'd by love's treachery.

As Kemp expanded the Potter in me contracted. A monster and a blaggard he may have been, and yet there was something satisfying about the repeating pattern of his life—one minute facing catastrophe, the next getting off scot-free. And the next chapter in Kemp's story turned out to begin in the same way as the last: with him striking out at a father figure.

On his return to Sydney, Kemp found himself at loggerheads with the new Governor. Philip King was a pious, gout-afflicted anti-Republican, with a mission to tidy up Kemp's cartel of army racketeers. He cut both the price and consumption of spirits and when the supply ship *Atlas* sailed into port with a cargo of rum, he refused her permission to unload. Kemp started to hate King 'abominably'. While the *Atlas* lay uselessly at anchor, he began to plot against him.

In June 1802, a French ship appeared off the Heads with no one at the tiller. The British tars who climbed aboard *Le Géographe* found the crew sick with scurvy; even the animals were affected. The ship was part of a French scientific force which had been mapping Van Diemen's Land and in the days ahead it alarmed Governor King to discover that the French commander, Nicolas Baudin, had baptized the coast after members of his expedition. At the far end of the bay— just visible from our new house—Cape Péron commemorated a one-eyed zoologist from the ship who used a contraption known as Régnier's Dynamometer to measure the hand clap of Tasmanian Aborigines (he concluded they had a weak one); while the Freycinet Peninsula opposite our home was named after Baudin's cartographer.

At the time, relations between Britain and France were delicate. Lieutenant Freycinet's unrolling of a chart marking regions of Australia 'Terre Napoléon' unsurprisingly filled King with panic. Nonetheless, he gave the sailors safe passage ashore to get their blackened gums treated. And he allowed them to buy eight hundred gallons of rum from the *Atlas*—on Baudin's strict promise that the spirits would be consumed on his ship.

King's kindness outraged Kemp. Smarting over the loss of potential profits, he started a rumour that Freycinet and another officer had secretly rowed the rum ashore and sold it. King summoned the accused in order to investigate this 'inflaming report'. They swore that the charge was false. Not one pint had reached land. French officers demanded a duel. Baudin pointed his finger at the man responsible: 'Monsieur Kemp.' The crisis was eventually averted— anticlimatically—after Kemp sent a written apology to both officers.

In November, Baudin's expedition left port. No one knew his destination, but that didn't prevent Kemp from starting another rumour just hours after the topsails had vanished over the horizon. He implied that the French officers had been overheard declaring their intention to establish a settlement on Van Diemen's Land. Indeed, he'd heard that one of them had even indicated the proposed site on a map.

Governor King had come to trust Baudin, but the whispers alarmed him. What if the Frenchman's ambition extended beyond hand claps? Van Diemen's Land, as yet unsettled by either power, offered vital access to southern waters. Alarmed by the spectre of a hostile French colony, King fitted out a schooner with seventeen marines and launched them after Baudin 'to make the French commander acquainted with my intention of settling Van Diemen's Land'. They found the French scientists peacefully netting insects on an island in Bass Strait. The marines hastily tied a Union Jack to a tree, fired a volley over the tents and gave three aggressive hurrahs. Insulted once again, Baudin complained to Governor King about this 'childish ceremony'. (The flag, he noted, was hoisted upside down and resembled a dish rag hung out to dry). He assured King he had no intention of claiming the territory and once again identified the culprit. 'The story you have heard, of which I suspect Mr Kemp, captain in the NSW Corps, to be the author, is without foundation.'

By now, King's gout had advanced into his chest, and he had been forced to take to his bed with breathing difficultires. But Kemp's vendetta continued. Somehow a tightly rolled piece of paper found its way to the bed-bound Governer. On it were 'seditious drawings' of King and two short poems: 'Extempore Allegro', a brisk assault on the Governor's character ('for infamous acts from my birth I'd an itch'), and 'Epitaph', which cheerfully anticipated his demise ('A wretch to whom all pity is bereft').

King's discovery of this anonymous doggerel enraged him. He arrested Kemp and prosecuted him. The trial was a farce. King had to draw the court martial from Kemp's cronies, such as the Rum Corps commander, Lieutenant Colonel 'Phlegmatic' Paterson, an inebriate botanist with failing eyesight who had witnessed Kemp's marriage; and Major Johnston, Paterson's no less alcoholic second-in-command, who had been the first officer to step ashore at Sydney Cove. This was a tribunal that protected its interests.

On February 25, 1803, the trial was suspended and Kemp acquitted. A startling despatch from the Colonial Office advised King to forget the whole business and 'consign to oblivion' all that had passed. He was urged to colonize Van Diemen's Land.

In October 1804, King left his sickbed to wave off an occupying force led by Paterson, with Kemp as second-in-command. The three vessels, led by the *Buffalo*, a leaky armed supply ship, carried 181 soldiers, convicts and settlers, including Kemp's wife Elizabeth and her brother, Alexander Riley, who was to act as storekeeper.

The Governor's relief at seeing Kemp go must have cheered him at least a little; at any rate, he provided an eleven-gun salute for the expedition's departure.

One cloudless morning I drove the old Peugeot to Georgetown and parked above the beach where Kemp landed. The river mouth was sprinkled with caravan parks and bungalows called 'Ups-n-downs', but the shoreline was pristine, the sand empty and the sea an outlandish ultramarine. This was not the ruined coastline of most countries and I thought it would probably have looked much the same on the day Kemp's ship slammed into an unexpected sandbank off Lagoon Beach.

I doubted the future Father of Tasmania would have been happy to be on board. He would have been separated from his grog store. He wouldn't have shared my love of the sea: for him it would have been something for convicts to wash in. He would have avoided the sun so as to preserve his complexion and distinguish himself from the Aborigines who watched the bungled landing of the *Buffalo* in puzzled silence.

I walked along the beach, trying to make sense of Kemp's appearance in my life in this place at this time. The discovery of his letters had thrown up questions about everything from British history to personal identity. I couldn't get over the strangeness of his actions— just setting sail and pitching up in a country about which he effectually knew nothing. But wasn't that exactly what I had done? And while I didn't share Kemp's sense of entitlement, was I not somehow in his debt? Whatever brutal means he had employed, he had made me, I realized, complicit. Because of people like him, people like me were gardening, and writing, in far-flung places like Tasmania.

Kemp and the crew hurried to unload the stores on east shore of the river. The wind blew in heavy squalls and was still blowing four days later when Paterson, the Rum Corps commander, took formal possession of the colony and swore in Kemp and his brother-in-law Riley as its magistrates.

It didn't seem like an especially good place for a settlement, with its brackish water and stony soil. Leaving Kemp to oversee the erection of a church and gaol, Paterson crossed the River Tamar and decided to establish a permanent residence on the edge of a shallow rivulet. 'It is my opinion,' he wrote in his diary, 'that the Country will turn out to be Superior to any yet discovered.'

The settlement of Patersonia is recollected today by a brass relief map in a deserted picnic spot beside a garden supplier. Pyramids of wood-chips and 'chook-poo' are all that remain of what, on the map, is 'Major Kemp's garden'. The original garden was, in fact, Paterson's creation. His horizons reduced by ophthalmia, Paterson concentrated on his plants and was soon able to treat Kemp to a corned beef dinner served with eight different vegetables and an impressive cucumber. But his optimism had already started to ebb.

Kemp watched his commander go steadily barmy. The site had indeed been a disastrous choice. The closest a ship could anchor was six miles away. After rain, the place became 'a complete swamp'. The climate was colder than in Sydney and as winter set in the animals started to die. Within six months half of the six hundred cattle they had bought with them on the initial voyage had perished. And there was trouble in the garden. Nettles had grown whose sting was so violent that it killed four dogs and gave several officers a terrible fever. In February, Kemp discovered a small white insect, 'the most destructive in the world of its size', had devoured his coat and was now advancing through the vegetables. Paterson surrounded his garden with soap suds in a forlorn attempt at defence. Then one morning Paterson woke to find that unidentified predators had devoured all of his ducks and chickens: only their feathers were left.

In August Paterson sailed for Sydney. He left behind Kemp as acting Lieutenant Governor.

Years later, as a bankrupt in London, Kemp argued in a petition to the government to restore his land grant that he had spared neither trouble nor expense 'converting a howling wilderness into a cultivated plain'. But he was not a natural leader and under his command the settlement almost starved to death. Floods destroyed the crops. The settlers survived on seaweed and pigs which they'd fed on whale scraps and which tasted of lamp oil. In February, Kemp sent five men in the long boat to row and sail seven hundred miles to seek help on the Australian mainland. They were never heard from again.

In the following April Paterson sailed back up the Tamar to find the settlement in a state of anarchy. Kemp had distributed guns to the convicts so that they could hunt kangaroo and many had stayed out in the bush, harassing the settlers. He himself wanted to get out. Complaining of 'extreme ill health' he requested permission to take his wife and nine-month-old son George to Sydney. The placid Paterson agreed, but warned Kemp that the new Governor, William Bligh, was a different kind of man to the Governor who'd preceded him.

This was Bligh of the *Bounty*, the man who seventeen years earlier had set Mr Christian and his fellow mutineers adrift in a boat. Now he had arrived in Sydney with the express intention of stamping out the rum trade. He wasn't favourably disposed towards Kemp's return—he considered Rum Corps officers to be 'tremendous buggers'—and was suspicious of his reasons. As it turned out, he had excellent cause. On a scorching evening five months later, the Rum Corps mutinied and it no longer surprised me to discover who marched up the drive at their head, sword drawn, into Government House.

I wondered briefly if this was Kemp finally exercising his republican ardour; but it transpired—of course—that the rebellion had been prompted by liquor and corruption. Major Johnson, acting Rum Corps Commander in Paterson's absence, conceived—if that isn't too fine a word for it—a desire to unseat Bligh, a plan that was largely formulated when Johnson and Kemp were drunk. And so it was that the mutineers barged into the Governor's residence around supper time and after a couple of hours stumbling around the house, frightening Bligh's recently-widowed daughter and an Irish parson who was there to comfort her, discovered Bligh hiding in a neglected upstairs room. One of Kemp's soldiers noticed a bedcover twitching, prodded it with his musket, and struck a boot. There was the Governor, covered in spiderwebs and with his shirt hanging out.

As a reward for his part in the mutiny, Johnson gave Kemp twenty-four cows, four thousand acres of land, and appointed him Judge Advocate.

For the next seven months Kemp ruled as the supreme legal officer in an area the size of Western Europe, a position of extraordinary power. For seven months there was no court of appeal after Kemp—except to God. With tremendous relish, he transported former adversaries like William Gore, chief of the constabulary, to seven years on the Coal River. 'Take him away, take him off; take him away, take him away.'

Kemp's duties also expanded to performing all the marriages in the colony. I discovered from a copy of the *Tasmanian Times* dated November 4, 1868 a terrible story. One morning, with eleven services to conduct and through a combination of impatience and drink, Kemp married the wrong couples. 'The Parson-Captain, when subsequently applied to, bade them "settle it amongst them, for he could interfere no further!"'

One day in 1810 there was a knock at Potter's door in Aldgate. Kemp had come home from Sydney to give evidence at Major Johnson's court martial. Bligh had singled out Kemp as the person he particularly wished to see prosecuted for the mutiny, but—of course—Kemp managed to avoid punishment. Commended for his candour in the witness box, he forfeited only his four thousand acres and his twenty-four cows, rather than his freedom.

Nevertheless his return was hardly triumphal. A letter from his sister Susannah described him as 'a strange man', often silent—and a bankrupt, the same state he'd left England in twenty years before. I could only find out bits and pieces about his next five years. From the letters I gathered he'd tried his hand at various ventures, but the same practices that allowed him to prosper in Sydney took him quickly into the bankruptcy court in London. He was briefly a shipping agent, a pawnbroker, and a wine merchant, but 'lost much on Bordeaux wine speculation'. At one point he bet £150—vainly— against the capture or death of Napoleon.

By 1815, he had exhausted his options. The world regarded him, he complained, as 'an uncertificated bankrupt, alias an outlaw'. There was nowhere to go but back to the Antipodes. He prepared to flee the country for a third time. Pursued by 'clamorous' creditors, he went cap in hand to see Potter in the house where he grew up and with staggering optimism requested his biggest loan to date: an amount equivalent to the entire annual turnover of 'Kemp & Potter'.

Kemp asked Potter to guarantee two shiploads of goods worth

'upwards of five thousand pounds'. He assured Potter that he would be able to sell the goods at considerable profit in Van Diemen's Land, thanks to the exceptional contacts of his other brother-in-law, Alexander Riley, who had recently built Sydney's new hospital and made thirty thousand pounds from the contract. A similar 'most splendid fortune', he promised Potter, would be realized by 'Kemp & Potter' from the cargoes of tobacco, brandy and seedlings. Kemp required the money only for nine months and would pay full interest.

Unbelievably, Potter agreed.

The first sign of trouble came in a letter dated several months later from Paraiba (now Jão Pessoa) in Brazil. Kemp's ship was detained after losing her anchor. Her captain 'appeared a little deranged'. And Kemp has run out of money. 'I have been under the necessity of drawing on you for sixty pounds.'

Potter heard nothing else for the next two years. He wrote letter after letter appealing to 'our agreement with your good self', but they remained unanswered. By now Kemp's father had died and Potter was having to steer the firm from the rocks on which Kemp's negligence threatened to pitch it. At Aldgate, his desk piled up with demands for Kemp's five thousand pounds (more than four hundred thousand pounds today). Kemp's sisters wrung their hands uselessly. Susannah wrote to Amy: 'It's complete swindling to fly one's country for speculation.'

At last, in August 1817, a letter arrived from Hobart. It begins breezily: 'I arrived here about six weeks ago and have commenced my mercantile pursuits.' But due to 'the severe trials' lately experienced, combined with 'unprecedented mercantile circumstance', Kemp fears he will not be able to make his remittances 'so punctual as I would wish'. He details his sales to date:

Tobacco: 'I am sorry to say there is no market for that now'—although he has sold some sacks of Prince's Mixture in Cape Town ('You was either rob'd or cheated,' Potter replies).

Brandy: 'The market is completely glutted with spirits and all other goods, such that to force sales would be ruinous.'

The seedlings: 'They are unsaleable and good for nothing.'

But Kemp was encouraging. 'What is possible for man to do

shall be done. You may rely on it, there is no cause for alarm.'

The family's distress is summarized in one of Susannah's letters: 'There are characters in life who care very little for each other, self-consideration their first and justice their last.' She united with the Potters in wishing never to see her brother again.

Kemp was only too delighted to be separated from Aldgate 'by the circumference of the globe'. On January 12, 1816, he was rowed ashore in Hobart. The town consisted of a thousand people living in wattle and daub huts, more like a campsite than a capital. That night, he dined in Government House (actually a barn) as a guest of the volatile Lieutenant Governor, Thomas Davey. He informed Davey of his 'valuable cargo' and of his wish to become a free settler. He was then my age: forty-three.

Davey, who liked to entertain in shirtsleeves, was a jovial incompetent known as 'Mad Tom'. He was also the most alcoholic of Kemp's superiors. His favourite tipple was 'Blow-my-skull', a cocktail he served in half-pint glasses consisting of rum, brandy, gin, port, Madeira, sherry and claret.

Davey and Kemp had plenty to discuss over dinner. Davey was engaged in a desperate struggle with kangaroo hunters, convicts who remained out in the bush and terrorized the island. Kemp was familiar with the problem: the bushrangers were, after all, a legacy of his administration nine years before.

Anxious to encourage the right sort of settler who might bring security to the interior, Davey greeted his predecessor with open arms. Tucked inside a letter to Potter from Hobart, I find a faded copy of the Governor's grant which gives the bankrupt Kemp eight hundred acres and four convict workers and appoints him a magistrate.

Kemp's land lay forty miles north of Hobart. Kemp decided to use Potter's wealth to create, in effect, a parody of Potter's world. He mortgaged the land against a building in Hobart where he opened a ramshackle store in partnership with a former convict transported for stealing an eyeglass. In a letter he assured Potter: 'I have given a person a share in the concern who is a complete man of business.' In July 1816, the *Hobart Gazette* carried adverts for Potter's hogsheads of tobacco, Potter's brandy, Potter's souchong teas—'to be sold on a liberal Credit'. Potter never saw a bean.

By 1820, Kemp controlled eighty per cent of the spirits landed in Hobart and 'nearly all the Rum in the colony'. He guarded the monopoly with a mixture of greed and flammability. He overcharged customers. He boarded ships without permission. The only magistrate to own a pub, he invoked the law to protect his interests. When a rival merchant accused him of acting 'like a peddlar', he sent him to prison.

Truculent, intolerant, inconsistent, Kemp exemplified the transition from rollicking empire-founding to the humbug of empire-ruling. In May 1817, sitting as magistrate, he had the 'high satisfaction' of announcing the arrest of the last bushrangers. He rounded on his creditors with the same spleen. While in Aldgate Potter wrote yet another despairing letter (referring his brother-in-law 'to my letters No 1, 2 & 3'), Kemp placed announcements in the *Hobart Gazette* warning he would sue his debtors unless they settled instantly. Astonishingly, Kemp brought one action to recover twelve pounds. Given his less than reflective nature, I guessed he wouldn't have noticed the symmetry: it was the same sum that he had fled England for as an eighteen-year-old.

His antagonism to his father never flagged. He treated anyone who exerted authority over him with hysterical vehemence. When the Governor rode past him in the street, Kemp refused to take off his hat and laughed at him. His attitude to successive Governors was that they were all 'equally bad'.

Genealogy is considered the domain of the elderly, but the impulse to look back at the tracks in the sand can be triggered by having a child, especially when that event occurs for the first time, as in my case, later in life.

In the uproar of my unborn son's ancestry I saw some pretty disappointed expectations, but like any incipient parent I was prone to self-deception and wishful thinking: I wanted his life to be perfect.

*The genes, they come down.* If I had a say, whose genes would I wish my son to inherit: the sensible Potter's or the adventurous Kemp's?

Parenting, by definition, is about Pottering. Every parent says hopefully to their child, 'Go and get a qualification and a job.' But was I a Potter secretly longing to be a Kemp—and wasn't this the case for all writers? From our secure beach-houses we look out on a chaotic world and shape a pattern from it. By coming to Tasmania, I'd repeated the pattern of an ancient, unknown relative and the discovery pleased me in a profound and mysterious way. However tenuous, it linked me to this place. It suggested that life was not a series of arbitrary events. That there were, if you like, no accidents.

On December 4, 1819, Potter wrote his last letter to Kemp. 'In every letter I have requested to know if you receiv'd a Copy of your Father's will, mourning ring, etc etc... to these repeated questions I have not as yet got an answer.'

He directed his son up a ladder to erect a new sign: WILLIAM POTTER & SON.

I can see him hesitate as he begins to clear Kemp's papers from his desk. Endings are always difficult. The end of a failed business, like the end of a failed love affair, is charged with the same nostalgia and sadness. Perhaps unrequited love is not so far from the unrequited loan.

He stores the letters away.

Potter without Kemp eventually peters out. As Potter muses to his son: 'An Englishman fails because he fears he shall and is continually stumbling over the shadow his fancy raises.' Potter's son lives faithfully by his maxims and rises to become Master of the Vintners Company, where I find an entry in the minutes book commending him for 'his able and zealous discharge of the duties of his office and for his kindness and courtesy on all occasions'. But these qualities, on their own, are not enough to save the business and the family moves to Birmingham, where my grandmother—the last of the Potters—was born.

And Kemp without Potter? When he died, in 1868, he had lived long enough to be known to a man who was still alive in 1936 (who called him 'a Jewish type'). But despite his eighteen children he left behind no descendants called Kemp in Tasmania. Today his warehouse is occupied by Madame Korner's beauty college and a hearing-aid retailer. Even his gravestone has disappeared. All that is left of his person are some letters in a yellow plastic bag.

Kemp was a baby once, some mother's darling. So was Potter, for that matter. Their letters make me think that what holds both men back is that each is not more like the other. If Kemp had hurried a little more slowly, if Potter had had left his desk and lived a little more.

Perhaps every affair of business, of love, of writing itself, calls for a necessary balance between the Potters and the Kemps, between the Apollonian and the Dionysiac, between the ledger and the rum. And I suppose I wish this balance for my son.                              □

GRANTA

# OUR LIVES ARE ONLY LENT TO US

## Penelope Fitzgerald

Penelope Fitzgerald with her daughters in Venice, 1965

In the winter of 1953, Penelope Fitzgerald sailed from England on the Queen Mary with her five-year-old son, Valpy, on a long and quixotic voyage to Mexico. She had two purposes in mind: one was the nebulous prospect of a legacy from distant relations which never in fact came to anything; the other was to research one of the long essays on painting and sculpture that she was then writing for *World Review*, the cultural monthly she had been editing with her husband since 1950. The first result of her trip, 'From the Golden Land', was published in the magazine's April/May 1953 issue, which turned out to be its last. This story was probably written twelve years later, for submission to a short-story competition in *Blackwood's* magazine, now also long defunct, and is her first known, and only unpublished, fiction. Her novels later won the Booker and the American National Book Critics Circle Award. Penelope Fitzgerald died last year.                      T. D.

None of the native inhabitants of San Tomas de las Ollas saved any money and this was a moral imperative, although it worked differently from ours. We would think it a sign of respectability to 'put by' now so as not to be an encumbrance to our relatives later. We wouldn't wish to be a burden to our folks. Mrs Clancy put it this way at the get-together, the chicken-fry, which she, as the wife of the representative of the local manager of Providence Williams Marketing (Central American Division) gave from time to time to the American and European community; and in this she showed herself a sympathetic hostess because all the community were much occupied with assurance and its twin sister death, but the native inhabitants, although they too thought about death, had little interest in either saving or assurance. If they accumulated a little money by chance they used it to employ a less fortunate member of their family to do something they found disagreeable and did not wish to do themselves. The benefit to their relatives came earlier but was not less welcome for that.

All this serves as an explanation of a visit Mrs Sheridan paid one morning in October to her chauffeur Pantaleon—or rather to his wife—for it was a visit of congratulation on the birth of a new baby. Mrs Sheridan was the widow of a banker who had invested in silver mines (but the mines were nationalized now); her house, with faded shutters and faded pepper trees, was pointed out to strangers on the corner of the main square.

Pantaleon did not 'live in' and was not required to work on saints' days, so that, as Mrs Sheridan did not drive a car, it had taken some organization for her to make the call at all since in Santo Tomas it was not possible to travel in a car some days and walk on others; you were either a walker or a driver and it would not have done to come to the *vivienda* in Calle Lopez Mateos on foot. She had had to ask Señor Azuela, an engineering executive with Mr Clancy's firm, to call for her.

'Thank you, Don Salvador,' she said as they arrived opposite the crumbling, well-like entrance.

'I'll stop by for you in ten minutes,' said Mr Azuela, always available, clever but difficult to like with his gold teeth and blue suit, opening wide the car door.

Mrs Sheridan walked steadily, not picking her way, out of the entrance shadow across the brilliant sun of the courtyard. Pantaleon's wife was not at the communal stone wash-tub and Pantaleon himself was not to be seen. Directed by enthusiastic neighbours, Mrs Sheridan found him in the tiny inner patio, sunk in a basket chair, his face covered with soap; an elderly man was shaving him with a cut-throat razor.

'Don't get up, Pantaleon,' she said, but he had done so already, knocking over the chair. His gentle Indian face under the mask of white suds creased with distress. Mrs Sheridan shook hands with the elderly man, who wiped his hands on the seat of his trousers for the purpose—'my uncle'; and with two other quarter cousins, not at all young, who had been cleaning respectively his right and left shoe.

'I am temporarily employing these people so that they can share in a little good fortune I have had,' Pantaleon explained in his grave majestic voice. 'It is not a matter of charity, of course. They are people of substance in their way; my uncle has a stall in the market.'

Mrs Sheridan knew that Pantaleon's wages were adequate and suppressed the thought that perhaps they were too generous.

'It was Rosario I really wanted to see, and your new son,' she said.

'My wife is out shopping,' Pantaleon replied.

'At the mercado, carrying a heavy basket! It's only ten days since the baby was born,' protested Mrs Sheridan.

'She is not at the mercado—she is at the supermercado and my brother-in-law's niece is accompanying her to push the wire basket.'

'And baby?'

'The baby is indoors with my little cousin—the great-niece of the señor uncle who is shaving me.'

Mrs Sheridan was used to the impact of the living room which, with its gleaming chromium bed, Virgin of Guadalupe framed in plastic lace, tall earthenware pitcher of water, sewing machine and worn stone grinder showed the Indian genius for accepting from an overriding culture only what suited it best. In the rocker with its cushion of embroidered electric-blue silk sat a girl of perhaps eight years old holding in her arms a baby wrapped in a shawl.

The Victorian novelists were right to make such children die; symbolically they were right since beauty of that kind is impossible in human beings beyond nine or ten. The girl's face had a golden waxy pallor and the modelling was so slight that there were hardly any shadows on it—even the lower eyelids made almost none. The round head was set with doll-like precision on the tiny neck that seemed ready to snap and as it turned towards Mrs Sheridan the pale and golden lights changed on the perfectly circular cheek. The child's golden stud earrings flashed and the very long eyelashes, which had a dusty or mealy look, opened slowly to contemplate the visitor.

'What is your name?' asked Mrs Sheridan.

'Esperanza, señora.'

'And you're Pantaleon's cousin? You're a relation of his?'

The child stood absolutely transfixed, turning on her a dark bright stare from the huge eyes of the undernourished. It was not an Indian stare—not blank, not withdrawn. Mrs Sheridan, who had lived thirty-six years in Santo Tomas and was not a fool, recognized that she was treading on delicate ground, that of legitimacy.

'And where do you live?'

'In the mercado.'

'But where do you sleep?'

'Under the stall: my great-uncle is from Chiapas—from the mountains: he doesn't like houses.'

Esperanza traced something on the floor with her slender dirty foot—whitish, not blackish, with the eternal white dust of the mesa.

'But we are going to live here now, with cousin Pantaleon. He is paying to have mattresses made for us; they are being sewn now by his sister-in-law's great-aunt.'

Mrs Sheridan again felt surprised, and ashamed of her surprise.

'Will you like living here?' she asked.

'Yes, I shall like living with the baby. His life is my life.'

She lifted a corner of the shawl and Mrs Sheridan looked at the red-brown miniature face, still as an idol's. Now she was closer to the exquisite little girl she noticed too an odour of fish and guessed what stall it was the great-uncle kept. The baby winked suddenly and blew a solitary shining bubble which broke without a sound.

'I do hope he's strong and healthy,' said Mrs Sheridan.

The little girl carefully replaced the shawl.

'*Venimos prestados*,' she said. 'Our lives are only lent to us.'

Colonel Terence Kvoa lived at the Quinta Maria de los Desamparados, way above the town in its thick shelter of vines, choyotes, climbing pink geranium and organ-pipe cactus. The road out to it was a stony and featureless thirty kilometres and many of Mrs Clancy's friends had said to her that it reminded them of the Holy Land, but once you were out there the Quinta, with its sounds of deeply moving foliage and falling water, was beautiful. It had seemed sad that all this might be largely wasted when the Colonel departed stateside for an operation for cancer of the throat, but now he was home again and, although he had not yet recovered his voice, he lay stretched out on the white wicker chaise longue well assured and insured, gentle, hospitable and long-suffering.

'There isn't any skill a man can't master, once he's learned to discipline,' said the new, youngish doctor. 'That's where your Army experience can't help but come in handy, Colonel. Now, this question of speaking without actually allowing the passage of air through the mouth—well, a lot of people might think that'd rule a lot of the vowels and consonants out altogether; but that's because they've never orientated themselves to the idea of using the resonance inside the mouth and chest. You take that talking bird, Colonel.'

The Colonel, caged in the white painted chair, looked up to where his tame starling hung among the high flowers and leaves of the first-floor balcony. The guests, Mr and Mrs Clancy, Mr Azuela, several of the business community, gazed up as he did to the lightly swinging cage.

'Salud, Salud, Salud,' raved the high-hung starling; the whole cage shook at the stream of pure liquid bubbling sound, 'Pretty Georgie Porgie, pretty *pajarito*, pretty boy. My God I can't bear it. My God I must get out. My God I must go home. Pretty boy, *Salud, Salud, Salud.* Estraight home, *Salud.*'

'Plenty of people will tell you that a bird can't pronounce those "s" sounds,' continued the doctor, 'but there's proof positive that it can be done and you don't see that bird's beak open a crack. The "st" sound it can't quite manage—not one Spanish native speaker in a hundred can say that sound and not make it "est", and you can't expect a bird raised here to do any better.'

They all watched and they did not see the bird's beak open a crack. The doctor explained further and told them—it was a semi-formal gathering—that the Colonel needed constant practice if his voice was to return at all.

'Georgie Porgie. Get out you bitch,' trilled the starling.

'I think I represent the feelings of the Colonel's circle of friends pretty closely,' said Mr Clancy at last, 'when I say we are determined to see him through this thing and that we confidently expect that by Christmas he'll be a hundred per cent talking member of the community. We confidently expect that.'

They faced the doctor with their good, unanimous eyes fastened on him and flashing through spectacles and contact lenses while above them the ragged mutterings of the starling died out in a long whirring trill, a clicking and whispering to itself and then silence. There was never quite silence though in the Quinta Terence where there were so many movements in the spiked and creeping plants, servants shuffling across to throw water and sweep the patio five times a day, not bothering to pretend not to listen to what was said.

It was difficult to avoid the sensation of lecturing over the Colonel as if he were a lay figure. 'It's a great relief to feel you're taking a hand in the treatment,' the doctor said. 'I want you always to let him take the initiative in a conversation: don't start the talking—let him search for the words.' The servants brought tequila, lime, salt and Montezuma beer, and the lay figure got up at last and poured and chinked the ice.

'It's certainly hard being called in at this late stage,' added the doctor as they bumped away in his station wagon down the dry hillside. 'Not that my predecessor didn't leave everything in order. I've formed the definite impression that the Colonel came here to escape from something. He's unfailingly kind and courteous but there's a difficulty getting through...when I asked him to sign the forms before the operation...we simply ask routinely that all patients understand where our responsibility ends and theirs begins...'

'You mean if they die, their responsibility would begin there,' said Mr Azuela.

'You're certainly wrong about the Colonel escaping,' said Mrs Clancy. 'He was married when he came here and very proud to bring his bride to the Quinta; I mean she was quite young...and you have to consider that life can seem limited here...people can be homesick and say they feel trapped.'

'I'm just wondering how much more my tyres will take,' said the doctor. 'This road's a killer; do you know, it reminds me of the Holy Land.'

'We can't get close to them,' said Mrs Sheridan. 'I've been living here thirty-six years and I feel I can't get in touch with them.'

Since Mrs Clancy was out, Mrs Sheridan was received in the cool, double height drawing-room by her niece, a serious sweet-faced girl who had been training for a field trip with the Regional Centre for Fundamental Education.

'They told us at the Centre that responsibility for contact rested entirely with us, as we're guests in this country,' the niece said. 'You know we have six months' theory and workshop practice before we go out to the mountain villages and they impressed on us that you could fail just as easily as you could succeed. You can go too fast speeding things up, like when one of our groups tried to get them to slap their tortillas twice with each hand instead of three times, but they didn't take into account that this three-time rhythm had a definite soothing effect. Or you can react and go the other way and feel that there's nothing to beat that cradle-to-the-grave pattern of peasant life and then you can't help them at all—you just get to be a cradle-to-graver yourself. Truly, although I'm not presuming to advise *you*, Mrs Sheridan, it's just a question of study—you have to study the Indian mentality so you can understand where they can't be moved and where they're prepared to stretch a point.'

'So you'll be going soon...to Oazaca, is it?' said Mrs Sheridan. 'You must meet Colonel Terence first...' She was truly interested in what Mrs Clancy's niece was saying but her mind seemed to drift across the high shadowy ceiling, circling back always to its first point: I have been here thirty-six years and I am still no more than a guest.

'Pantaleon's father and mother came down from a mountain village,' she added suddenly. 'He's pure Indian, one supposes, but his little cousin didn't look like him at all. She reminded me of a wax doll or a golden doll.'

As she left the house Mrs Sheridan met Mr Clancy rounding the corner of the *huerta*; he apologized for missing her in the usual half-shout which he kept for the open air. The garden was beautifully kept, with thick tropical grass in which the paths seemed like partings and among the figs and bananas there were papery late roses, never quite fresh, never quite withered.

'You want to watch that Pantaleon of yours,' said Mr Clancy while they were still at a distance from the waiting car. 'You may have noticed he's treating all his relatives lately; he's been shutting off the irrigation channels in your garden and diverting the water into his own patch; he's raising pumpkins and I daresay he reckons to make a killing on flowers for the Day of the Dead. No harm I'd say in having a word with him; the truth is, he's studied your mentality; he'd never take money but water's different; he knows where you can't be moved and where you're prepared to stretch a bit.'

The mercado of Santo Tomas was not particularly old, neither was it picturesque. It was not visited by tourists nor by visiting experts from the Craft Section of the National Institute of Fine Arts. It had been erected, together with the little-used bullring, by a benefactor, a successful banderillero who had retired and died in his native town. It was a crazy structure of wood, a forest of rotting planks and struts, patched up with old doors from nearby building sites. The centre, where the meat and fish were sold, was to be avoided by all but the strongest minded; the butchers hewed the carcasses as Samuel did Agag; they threw the entrails and the reproachful eyes behind the stall; a piece of meat, in any shape, was meat to the poorer customers. It was here that Esperanza and her great-uncle sold (when they could get them) fish and eels from the lake. Then came a wooden maze where fruit and sugar cane, aphrodisiacs, charms, spices and penicillin tablets were arranged in heaps on green leaves, and often sold by pinches or handfuls. The sweet stall was hopelessly outmoded, with a dusty showpiece of a hospital operation table, patient and surgeon all executed in sugar; there was a section for clothes and household goods and shoes soled with pieces of Dunlop tyre—you could buy one shoe at a time in the mercado, or half a cigarette; and the whole thing petered out into a circumference of hopelessly ruined structures where old women offered oranges freshly cut and sprinkled with red pepper, or bootlaces and matches. Only the breadth of a street away glittered the supermercado, where everyone with the least pretensions to status or to spending money went to see and be seen. And yet the old mercado provided a precarious livelihood for perhaps a hundred people and gave many others a chance to scramble through on the right side of starvation.

Rosario, Pantaleon's wife, kept (sporadically, when she had the leisure) a toy stall with a stock-in-trade of pottery figures mixed up with plastic trash and objects filched from cornflake packets, while behind hung a selection of religious pictures; the guardian angel leading two children in buttoned boots past a precipice, the Virgin of Guadalupe, the Sacred Heart, all illuminated with gold and silver paper. Only the pottery figures, however, showed the native Mexican genius, the philosophy of the Toby jug, the gentle teasing of the world, bringing it down to the scale of pitchers and cups and household objects. There were whistles with ears, pink horses and purple angels with stripes and flowers made into jugs with rough dabs of glaze. In the dark recesses behind the shop were the obscene figures, combinations of men and animals which were bought by out-of-towners on a spree.

'They're artists' work,' said the sweet-faced niece who, unlike most visitors, had penetrated, escorted by Mr Azuela, into the dingy mercado. 'It's delightful to think they make them with such a sense of form and colour for children to play with.'

'It is the children who make them here. Not the children who play with them,' replied Mr Azuela. 'Their fingers are small and they learn early. Rosario's cousin, Esperanza, makes these when she isn't selling fish or minding the baby.'

Rosario sat smiling broadly and peacefully.

'Let me purchase you something,' said Mr Azuela politely. 'A *cochinito*—a piggy bank. Perhaps this one with purple roses.'

'It doesn't seem economic only to have one opening,' said the sweet-faced girl, turning the rough pottery pig over and over. 'How would you get your money out again?'

'Only by breaking it, señorita,' said Rosario decisively. 'That is the *gracia* of the little pig; when you have saved you must break everything and spend everything; then you can begin again.'

The Colonel sat alone with the starling. He had had them lift its cage down and put it on the broad stone coping that ran round the patio. The bird was capricious. If anyone spoke to it, or if there was any noise about the place, it would listen intently, only moving slightly from one leg to another. Its favourite sounds were intermittent ones—hammering or sneezing, or the slapping of tortillas, or a pig being killed. Then, after about a quarter of an hour's silence it would wheeze like a mechanism about to strike and begin to talk, but the speech, as the doctor had said, was not outward-going but inward; its cheeks filled with air, its chest swelled, but its beak remained shut.

'I'm not going to be licked by a darned bird,' thought Colonel Terence and, uncertainly and rustily at first, he began to follow it word by word...

'Salud, Salud...pretty Joey—I want to get out of this place—estraight home...estraight home...'

Then he sank down sweating in the dark green shade of the vines. 'I'll take a rest when the bird does,' he thought.

Mrs Sheridan did not really find it awkward to 'speak' to Pantaleon; indeed, like an old married couple they could express many things without words, in a way which satisfied them both.

'Every man's obligation is to do what he can for his family,' said Pantaleon with spacious gestures. 'Nature and religion both demand this. The señora is aware that failure of the family hearth is the cause of many evils in this world. If men and women act without scruple it is because they have forgotten what God has made due to the family.'

'All the same, I think you should cancel the order for the two extra mattresses: you might not find it possible to earn quite as much extra money in the future as you have done in the past.'

It was just before Christmas when the old mercado caught fire; earlier in the year, when the whole population was seated outside till late at night catching the cool air, someone would have noticed at once; that night, however, the first indication was the ruinous sound of cracking and snapping as the outer supports went. The actual smell of burning went unnoticed at first; few nights went by in Santo Tomas when someone did not let off firecrackers to celebrate something, even if it was only a win in the football pools, and the firecrackers were nearly always followed by scorching of some kind. But the bitter stench of burning wood grew stronger and then smoke rolled down some of the tiny narrow streets which radiated from the market towards the Plaza Mayor; almost in a moment it was mixed with a still more pungent smell of burning meat and fish.

San Tomas had no fire engine of its own; the only fire engine had been adapted from a crop sprayer by Providence Williams; it was kept in the Clancys' carport along with the Clancy cars and Mrs Clancy's runabout. The provision of this public service helped to promote good relations between the Mexicans and Providence Williams, and it demonstrated the benefits of efficiency since Mr Clancy's 'team' of ambitious juniors kept it in good running order, thinking it was the old man's hobby. The crew were volunteers from the town, but two of the Company's staff had to be on board to drive and to direct operations; and Mr Clancy himself kept the ignition key.

'*El Señor Clancy no está*. This is Chela, the cook, speaking. The family are out.'

'I must have him, woman, we need him; we need the fire engine.'

Chela could hear the sound of voices and the radio in the background and knew that the *jefe* of police was speaking from the Cafe Central. The *jefe* was, in any case, her cousin on her mother's side, Mrs Clancy having been shrewd enough to see the advantage of having a cook related to the police.

'It's you, Salvador, *Madre de Dios*, what's burning?'

'Where is he?'

'At the Quinta Terence. Ring him at the Colonel's.'

Like wild animals from a cut cornfield, the stallholders whose only home was their upturned stalls staggered out of the burning market. They made gestures to show that others were still left inside. The patiently accumulated goods, the savings of a lifetime, were devoured one by one; the serapes, woven of raw sheep's wool with the oil still left in it, blazed up with a suffocating smell of ancient sacrifice. The owner, weeping, dragged at the burning fragments; meanwhile, people came running round corners and up the *callejuelas*, as if blown from nowhere; Pantaleon was there among others, his mouth moving and his arms sweeping grandly, but anything he had to say was quite inaudible in that din. He was like one of the masked jumping figures in a fiesta, still in the white coat in which he had driven Mrs Sheridan out to dinner. He was trying to explain about the question of the mattresses and about the relatives to whom, after all, he had not been able to offer the hospitality of his house. Someone handed him a bucket; they were filling them one by one at the single cold tap in the patio of one of the *viviendas*; people were colliding with each other; the children darted between their legs and burned their fingers in the stream of brilliantly coloured melted sweets.

'It's nice to see a wood fire,' said the guests at Colonel Terence's. 'If they stick to the new government regulations...if we're not allowed to cut down a single tree for firewood...'

'That's a problem I'm hoping to study at first hand,' said the serious and sweet-faced girl. 'Up in the mountain villages, in spite of all that the commissions could do, I understand that currently they're still burning down trees to plant themselves another little patch of maize...'

'You will never go up to the mountain villages, señorita,' said Mr Azuela, flickering at her his gold teeth, his lizard's eyes.

'Why ever not, what makes you say this?'

'You undertook this training for the best possible motive— because you have a pitiful heart; you pity those who need help and, in consequence, you help those who need pity. You will find enough material here, I think, without making the journey to the mountains.'

The telephone rang. It rang from the table beside the Colonel's chair and Mr Clancy with quiet deliberation leaned forward and held up his hand.

'No one will answer this telephone call for the Colonel,' he said. 'It can wait; we can all wait until such time as the Colonel can find words to answer it. I think we're all in danger of forgetting, in the enjoyment of our host's very good food and wine—I wish Chela could fix *huevos rancheros* like your cook does, Colonel—we're in danger of forgetting Doctor Smith's very explicit instructions about the recovery of your voice. I've noticed that you've spoken less than usual this evening; now's your opportunity—don't force it, simply take your time while you search for the words.'

But the Colonel must have been tired that evening or perhaps it wasn't one of his 'nights' for his new-found skill seemed to have deserted him; although he made a visible struggle, glancing out into the lighted patio where the bird cage hung, the telephone rang on and on unanswered.

The new mercado at Santo Tomas de las Ollas was built as a spontaneous gesture by Providence Williams Marketing (Central American Division). It is designed by a modern architect with a German name from Mexico City, is made of reinforced concrete with murals of glass mosaic and is accepted, even by reactionaries, as a very real improvement. The funeral of Esperanza and her great-uncle was paid for by Mrs Sheridan, who spared herself nothing, not even (under the firm guidance of Rosario) the most distressing details; there was no photograph available to put in the lace-framed holder on the white coffin, so the undertaker obligingly produced one from his reserve stock; it was of a blonde, simpering little girl. 'It is cute,' said the undertaker. Thus even the image of Esperanza perished completely from the earth. The new fire station is at this moment under construction; the money is being raised by members of the American and European communities, a very large donation having been given by Colonel Terence and the serious sweet-voiced Mrs Terence.

Before the site was cleared, however, the old mercado rose for a short time a little way from its ashes; the poorest of the stallholders, to whom the loss of their tiny stock (nothing was insured) meant ruin, set up improvised fit-ups among the charred heaps of rubbish and tried to make enough to tide them over Christmas.

Mrs Sheridan went down honour bound to spend what she could; she was escorted—since Pantaleon's duties in the garden seemed to be more absorbing than ever—by Mr Azuela.

'This question of the interaction of two cultures is not well understood,' said Mr Azuela, slowing down competently for the school crossing. 'Some think that one will destroy the other, some think that the two will unite and create something new, as the Spanish civilization did with that of the Indian and the Jew. In my view, both are wrong. The two cultures are complementary but in the way that death is to life. The two cannot exist together but just as surely they cannot exist without each other.'

Rosario was squatting broadly behind her stall, her head wrapped in her *tapaboca* against the morning air, which she thought it unhealthy to breathe. There was in fact a streaming white mist that morning which mingled with the smell of frying doughnuts and condensed on everything it touched. Rosario was offering for sale the clay figure of the *Nacimiento*—the Christmas crib. Whoever had made them, they were all there—angels, kings, peasants and knife grinders, shepherds and their strange-looking dogs, the Holy Innocents terribly streaked with bright red paint. Mrs Sheridan smiled at Rosario, chose about a dozen figures and then hesitated.

'And the señora will buy the Holy Child,' Rosario asked with calm confidence. 'Certainly you will want the Jesucristo.'

'But it's so big, Rosario,' cried Mrs Sheridan, for the infant Jesus had clearly been salvaged from another 'set' and was over a foot long. Made of rough earthenware, he towered over the delicate miniatures.

'What does it matter if He is big,' said Rosario, wrapping up the figure swiftly in a piece of greyish-white paper. 'After all, He is the King of the whole world.'

Mrs Sheridan looked round at the mercado, at the ruined black stumps of wood which seemed bewildered and the silent black stumps of old men and women.

'Oh, Rosario, I'm so sorry—so very sorry about everything.'

'You mustn't worry so much,' said Rosario. 'That is a fault...*venimos prestados*—our lives are only lent to us.'  □

# NOTES ON CONTRIBUTORS

**Anonymous** is anonymous, but not the Anonymous who wrote *Primary Colors*, who is no longer anonymous.

**Christopher de Bellaigue** is a reporter who has worked in India and Turkey and now lives in Tehran. He is writing a book about Iran since the Islamic Revolution for HarperCollins.

**Andrew Brown** writes for the London *Guardian* and *Independent*. His latest book, *The Darwin Wars*, is published by Simon & Schuster in the UK and US. He is researching a book on the nematode worm *C. elegans*, the first animal to have its genome sequenced. He lives in Essex.

**David Feuer** is a practising psychiatrist in New York. He is working on a book drawn from his professional experience, to be published by Riverhead in New York. He lives on Long Island.

**Penelope Fitzgerald** was born in 1916 and died in 2000. Her newly discovered short story will be published in an expanded paperback edition of her short-story collection, *The Means of Escape*, to be published this autumn by Flamingo in the UK and Mariner Books in the US. She won the Booker Prize in 1979 for her third novel, *Offshore*, and the American National Book Critics Circle Award in 1997 for *The Blue Flower*.

**Judith Hermann** was born in 1970 in Berlin where she lives and works as a writer. 'This Side of the Oder' is taken from her first collection of short stories, *The Summerhouse, Later*, which will be published by Flamingo in the UK and Ecco Press in the US.

**A. M. Homes**'s books include *The End of Alice* (Scribner), *The Safety of Objects* (Anchor Books/Quill) and most recently *Music for Torching* (Anchor/HarperPerennial). She teaches creative writing at Columbia University and lives in New York.

**Amanda Hopkinson**'s short book on Martín Chambi will be published by the Phaidon Press in October this year and she is in the process of researching an extended biography. She is a senior research fellow at Cardiff University.

**Haruki Murakami**'s novels include *The Wind-Up Bird Chronicle* and *Norwegian Wood* (Harvill/Vintage). His most recent book, *Sputnik Sweetheart*, is published by Harvill in the UK and Knopf in the US.

**Nicholas Shakespeare**'s biography of Bruce Chatwin is published by Vintage in the UK and Anchor in the US. In 1993 he was one of *Granta*'s Best of Young British Novelists. John Malkovich has directed a film based on his novel, *The Dancer Upstairs*, which is awaiting release. He is currently at work on a novel set in Leipzig.

---

Unfeasibly large: in Ian McEwan's piece 'Dunkirk' (*Granta* 73) the weight in the sentence 'A Stuka carried a single 1,000-ton bomb' should have read '1,000-lb'. We apologize.

# Global
# Transformation
# and
# the
# Third
# World

*edited by*
## Robert O. Slater
## Barry M. Schutz
## Steven R. Dorr

Lynne Rienner Publishers • Boulder
Adamantine Press • London

Published in the United States of America in 1993 by
Lynne Rienner Publishers, Inc.
1800 30th Street, Boulder, Colorado 80301

Published in the United Kingdom by
Adamantine Press, Ltd.
3 Henrietta Street, Covent Garden, London WC2E 8LU

**Library of Congress Cataloging-in-Publication Data**
Global transformation and the Third World / edited by Robert O.
Slater, Barry M. Schutz, Steven R. Dorr.
    Includes bibliographical references and index.
    ISBN 1-55587-289-1 (alk. paper)
        1-55587-383-9 (pbk.: alk. paper)
    1. Democracy—Developing countries. 2. Developing countries—
Politics and government. 3. Developing countries—Economic
conditions. 4. World politics—1989–  5. Economic history—1990–
I. Slater, Robert O. (Robert Owen), 1950–  . II. Schutz, Barry M.
(Barry Mayer) III. Dorr, Steven R.
JF60.G58    1992
321.8'091724—dc20                                        92-26100
                                                            CIP

**British Cataloguing in Publication Data**
A Cataloguing in Publication record for this book
is available from the British Library.
ISBN  0-7449-0085-9
        0-7449-0086-7 (pbk.)

Printed and bound in the United States of America

The paper used in this publication meets the requirements
of the American National Standard for Permanence of
Paper for Printed Library Materials Z39.48-1984.

*To*

*Lt Gen Eugene F. Tighe, Jr., USAF (Ret)*

# Contents

PART 4   CONFLICT AND ITS RESOLUTION

PART 5   CONCLUSIONS

# Preface

In December 1990, the editors of this volume were privileged to bring together a group of internationally distinguished scholars to discuss the dramatic changes in global politics and their effect on what we euphemistically label the "Third World." Papers were commissioned to direct attention to three major focuses of global change: the move toward more democratic political systems, the impact of increased global economic interdependence and competition, and the control—or mitigation—of conflict. During the months that ensued between the presentation of conference papers and the completion of the manuscript for this book, the contributors made extensive revisions to their essays.

As this book goes to press, new challenges to global order continue to present themselves. The promising ideals of a "new world order" are harshly contrasted with the horrors of a fragmented Yugoslavia and the death and destruction in Somalia. States that comprised the Soviet Union struggle to survive economically, socially, and politically. Never in the past century has the global system manifest so much promise, yet so many complex and vexing dilemmas. It is to the credit of the contributors to this book that they have been able to capture the major issues and challenges of global change and avoid being handcuffed by current events.

The editors are indebted to General Eugene Tighe, for his support and encouragement of honest intellectual debate. We owe a debt to the authors for their willingness to undertake major and timely revisions of their essays. We would also like to acknowledge the endless energies of the staff at the Defense Intelligence College, particularly Pat Lanzara, who somehow manages to do the work of three. Among the others we would like to acknowledge are Lt. Neysa Slater, USN, and Ed Collier from the staff and Max Gross and Mark Kauppi, two stimulating faculty members from the college.

*Robert O. Slater*
*Barry M. Schutz*
*Steven R. Dorr*

# PART 1

## THE RESTRUCTURING OF WORLD POLITICS

# Introduction:
# Toward a Better Understanding
# of Global Transformation
# and the Third World

*Robert O. Slater*
*Barry M. Schutz*
*Steven R. Dorr*

The dramatic transformation in international politics that has occurred since the late 1980s has created an imperative for critical re-examination. We are not interested in querying the fact of this transformation—it is obvious. Rather, we are concerned with the question of how this transformation has affected the relative strength and capabilities of the states that comprise what we have heretofore labeled the "Third World."

At first glance, the substance of the transformation is played out on an East-West field. The three main issues highlighted by this perspective are: (1) the meaning of the fragmentation of the Soviet Union and Eastern Europe for the international system; (2) the emergence of new centers of economic hegemony in the West (namely, Japan, a unified European Community, and a North American economic regime); and (3) the advent of a political hegemony based on a Euro-American centered world. This focus, though self-evident in its importance, detracts from the issues that are challenging, impinging upon, and reshaping the political economy of the mass of the weaker states.

Given the complexities in comprehending global transformation, our very definition of the "Third World" must be revisited and re-examined, if not revised. The Third World, as a concept, derives from the past international system. The concept both reflected the objective reality of a bipolar world and also served as a vehicle for political expression and action by a multiplicity of states attempting to enhance their own status and influence within that bipolar context. The transformation of that context has led to a Third World that is less coherent and increasingly marginalized with respect to the emerging international system. Indeed, we cannot even speak about a Third World in the same way to which we had become accustomed.[1]

1

Although the Third World was never a monolithic entity or concept, the structure of the emerging global system renders it even less meaningful. For example, the term "Second World," formerly used in relation to the Marxist-Leninist bloc, emerges as a socio-economically transformed complex of states that previously belonged either to the now-defunct Marxist-Leninist bloc or to the Third World. Examples of the first type of Second World state might be Hungary or Czechoslovakia; those of the second type might be Malaysia or Mexico. Those states remaining as part of the Third World continue to face more severe problems of development and dependence than those now classified as Second World. Such Third World states might include Egypt, Peru, and Nigeria. Moreover, this category might grow with the addition of some of the more desperate socioeconomic cases from the old Second World. One could identify here states such as Albania, Romania, and the emerging republics or entities of the former Soviet Union and Yugoslavia. But what had been only a tendency in the previous international system has now become a reality: the increasing identification by the international community of states that are so totally unproductive, so increasingly dependent, and devoid of any capacity for development that they exist as no more than internationally recognized political entities. Such states might include Somalia, Haiti, and Bangladesh.

In the transformed world of the 1990s, the Third World, in its largest sense, will be the laboratory for developing new political and economic responses to the requirements of the reordered international system. This volume is introduced by Ken Jowitt's interpretation of the meaning of the "Leninist Extinction" for the international system and for the Third World. The chapter sets the stage for understanding many of the implications of the end of the Cold War. Following this introductory essay, three critical dimensions of the global transformation that are of central concern to the Third World will be examined: (1) the expanding range of choices of political systems; (2) the changing political economies of the developed and developing worlds and their interrelationships; and (3) the evolving nature of conflict and its mitigation and resolution. The chapters in this volume are designed to approach these three dimensions from both theoretical and case study approaches.

## Political Systems: The Trend Toward Democratization?

Diamond, Linz, and Lipset, in *Democracy in Developing Countries*, their major effort analyzing democratic experiences in the Third World, point to the unprecedented growth of democratic systems throughout the world. The fundamental changes in world politics, particularly the breakdown of Marxism-Leninism and the significant advances toward democracy made by many regimes during the 1980s, have tended to result in an overly optimistic and sometimes even euphoric view of democracy in the Third World. However, relationships between democratic consolidation and global restructuring remain tenuous. What manifestations do we find of the spread of democratic systems spurred by changing global politics? In Africa, only Zambia has concretely moved from one-party rule toward democratization since the beginning of 1991. What evidence suggests that democratic systems will be able to cope with the severe economic pressures that are sure to exist during the 1990s and beyond? On the other hand, is there evidence that supports the more successful performance of authoritarian regimes? Remmer argues in *World Politics* that the "conventional wisdom about democracy and economic crisis not only exaggerates the relationships between political regime characteristics and policy choice; it also fundamentally misconstrues the strengths and weaknesses of democratic forms of governance."[2]

The objective of the essays in Part 2 of this volume is not only to describe and explain the phenomenon of democratization in the Third World but also to examine whether or not it is likely to extend its influence both horizontally and vertically. While clearly this process is rooted in indigenous factors—legitimacy, political culture, social structure, socioeconomic development—foreign influence cannot be excluded from consideration. Yet foreign influence takes on new meanings in the restructured world of the 1990s. Our frame of reference when considering past foreign influence on the democratization process is often one of colonial legacies and imposed political structures. As we consider the decade ahead, this frame of reference is likely to undergo substantial alteration. Certainly international economic influence will be paramount in testing a system's effectiveness. A specific regime or political system will be less likely to win support by playing off superpowers against each other in the fashion of Cold War politics. In a sense, the type of system may become less important than the success of that system in coping with the demands of the 1990s.

Larry Diamond's essay surveys the global status of democratization and extends from a view that the world is in the midst of the "third wave" of democratic expansion.[3] Diamond assesses and analyzes this recent phenomenon, first by reviewing the major democratic developments in the late 1980s and early 1990s, and then by offering quantitative measures to support his contention. He weighs the relative value of international and domestic factors causing this new wave of democratic expansion and estimates that the prospects for the further expansion of democracy in the coming decade are positive.

Claude Welch examines civil-military relations within the new context of global transformation, of rising democratization, and of a reduced political role for the armed forces, especially in the Third World. He describes and explores the multiple meanings of "civil" and "military" and then analyzes three classic models of civil-military relations: Western professional, Communist penetration, and Third World praetorian. Turning to the process of liberalization and democratization, Welch identifies many of the obstacles to the re-establishment of civil governments in developing countries. He underscores the view that recent global changes have served to hasten, but not initiate, the armed forces' "retreat to the barracks" in many Third World countries.

Following the Diamond and Welch essays are three important case studies that consider the democratization process in very distinct environments: Karen Remmer examines the process in Latin America, where there is considerable history of democracy; Thomas Bernstein analyzes China, where an apparent process of democratization was initiated and quickly curtailed; and Steve Dorr investigates the Middle East, where little history of democratization is in evidence.

Karen Remmer reminds us that Latin America has experienced several waves of democratization that were often followed by retrenchment into authoritarianism. She argues, however, that the wave of the 1980s is different; it has already lasted longer and influenced societies more deeply than previous waves. For evidence of this she points to the growing levels of popular support for democratic institutions throughout most of Latin America. Yet she also notes the failure of theory to explain this phenomenon in regional terms. While emphasizing that the process began a decade before the fall of the Berlin Wall, Remmer nevertheless finds that the end of the Cold War has undercut political forces at both extreme ends of the political spectrum.

Thomas Bernstein examines the reform era of the 1980s in China, culminating in the Tiananmen demonstrations of 1989. Although Tiananmen has come to signify a "democracy movement," Bernstein sees these demonstrations more as demands for liberalization, not democracy. Bernstein traces this process of liberalization in the 1980s through several examples of changing relations between the party-state and society—changes encouraged by a leadership that had become aware of the alienation caused in part by an insensitive bureaucracy.

The Middle East case examined by Steve Dorr falls somewhere between the new wave of democratization in Latin America and the retreat to repression in China. Dorr sees evidence of nascent democratization, which may be characterized as political liberalization, stirring in many Middle Eastern countries; but these developments are still vulnerable and could be overwhelmed by all too familiar patterns of authoritarian rule. Possible explanations for the tentative movement toward democratization are discovered in global, regional, and internal factors. Nevertheless, the process is too new for Dorr to be more than "hopeful" about its future prospects.

## Global Economic Interdependence

There is significant consensus that the world economy of the post–Cold War period will present the greatest challenges to both the developed and developing worlds. As we continue to move toward a more competitive world market economy with the entrance of newly transformed Leninist economic systems, the interdependencies become even more significant. Gilpin raises three issues central to the impact on international relations of the rise of a world market economy: (1) the economic and political causes and effects of the rise of a market economy; (2) the relationship between economic and political change; and (3) the significance of a world market economy for domestic economies.[4] The questions these three issues generate are particularly applicable to the Third World setting. For example, what types of harmony and conflict are created by a more interdependent world economy which, while it creates significant opportunities, also creates serious vulnerabilities? What impact will the transformation of Eastern European Leninist economies have on the Third World? How successful can such an interdependent world economy be without a major hegemonic power? What international role will Japan take on in the 1990s? How does the world market economy affect the economic development of the LDCs and the economic decline of advanced economies? How stable will a potential tripolar (United States, Europe, Japan) world economy be, particularly in light of what we already know about the unstable tendencies of tripolarity?

All of these questions, and more, need to be answered in order to understand the very complex relationship between the evolving global economic interdependence and the capability and effectiveness of Third World states to successfully compete in the world arena. The essays in Part 3 define the critical relationship between economic interdependence and Third World economies. Both Tom Callaghy and Michael Dolan look in depth at the critical relationship between a transforming international political economy and the dilemmas of the Third World. Dan Unger's essay provides an important analysis of the role of Japan—a major international economic power—as a global actor, particularly vis-à-vis the Third World.

Tom Callaghy, in a landmark effort, compares and contrasts the political economies of the primary Third World regions, addressing the state of economic transformation in each and delineating those factors that distinguish each region. Callaghy's effort, which raises important questions about the "brilliant vision of global transformation," focuses primarily on the capacity of the *state* to effect economic transformation, the real and potential clash between economic and political reform, and the importance of global, "contextual" factors in transforming Third World economies.

Michael Dolan also examines the impact of global transformation on the economies of the Third World, but he focuses primarily on the degree of ability that Third World states have to accommodate change, most specifically the structural changes associated with post-Fordism. Dolan begins by examining these changes in the economies of the North, where post-Fordism has brought about specialization in production and inhibited and potentially exacerbated their economic plight.

Dan Unger's essay takes a necessary and serious look at the potential role of Japan in the transformed international system. Unger analyzes the opportunities and imperatives facing Japan, within a framework that questions that country's comfort with exercising a greater degree of foreign *economic* influence.

## Changing Patterns of Conflict and Conflict Mitigation

The ongoing disengagement of East and West from the bipolar Cold War politics characteristic of the past forty-five years has magnified changes in international conflict and its mitigation. The multipolarity that is emerging will not necessarily engender a more stable and less violent international regime. Many argue that the dramatic change in the international system will result in considerably less stability, both in Europe and throughout the world. Mearsheimer argues, for example, in the case of Europe, that the Cold War was "principally responsible for transforming a historically violent region into a very peaceful place."[5] While the concern for major nuclear exchange between superpowers has ebbed, and Europe is less likely to become a stage for major superpower confrontation, international politics is likely to continue to be characterized by regional conflicts. Conflicts have already erupted in the Balkans that resemble the challenges to the legitimacy of state boundaries and governmental authority that broke out in many Third World states at the end of the colonial era. Such conflicts may emerge elsewhere in Eastern Europe as well and even between the new states of the former Soviet Union. They signal an international environment of the 1990s that could easily be characterized by a high degree of regional and ethnic tension, unbridled by the relative stability created by the Cold War. New regional conflicts that may result will present the greatest challenges to international peace and stability.

Conflict will also take different forms as we continue to move toward a more interdependent world market economic system, with multiple centers of power. It is quite possible that a considerable amount of conflict will be generated as states are forced to operate in a more competitive international political economic environment.

At the same time that we consider the potential for considerable increase in the level of international political or economic conflict, we must also evaluate the significant possibilities arising for conflict *mitigation* in an increasingly interdependent world.[6] We use the concept of mitigation to differentiate the process from what is commonly called resolution. Mitigation refers to efforts for channeling conflict productively in order to lessen its potential to (1) create or sustain domestic upheaval, (2) extinguish ethnic minorities at risk, and (3) disrupt regional stability. In the transformed global system of the 1990s, it will not be possible to resolve all conflicts nor will they all be seen as directly threatening the international system. Some conflicts may be candidates for mitigation through the efforts of international actors such as states or regional and international organizations. Yugoslavia, the Kurdish problem, and Sri Lanka might be good candidates for mitigation, for example, since these are situations where resolution seems to be unattainable but where continuation of the conflict would either further destabilize a region or be unacceptable to international norms. Other conflicts may present opportunities for resolution by addressing their root causes. There are, however, very few cases on record of successful resolution of conflict; perhaps Nicaragua and Angola might be considered under the rubric of conflict resolution.

Robert Slater's essay focuses on the implications for conflict of a globally transformed international system. He examines the evolving challenges to the *state*, suggesting that the 1990s will emphasize a more nonideological and more "traditionally" based system of confrontations *within* the state. He disagrees with many in international relations who argue that the state system is eroding. Instead, along the lines argued by Jowitt, Slater sees a return to a pre–Cold War era of domestic and territorial challenges, modified by the transformed context of a highly competitive international political economic system. Slater sees ethnonationalism and challenges to legitimacy based on "nonperformance" as presenting the greatest conflict potential.

William Zartman addresses the distinction between conflict resolution and conflict mitigation in post–Cold War terms. His conceptual multilevel panorama of conflict mitigation comes to rest on the evolving role of the United States as The Superpower. Recognizing its solitary international paramountcy, Zartman stresses that "the United States is left custodian of multilateral as well as bilateral economic assistance, wearing a reputation for successful conflict management, condemned to play the role in the future." Zartman sees an ounce of "conflict mitigation" as worth a pound of conflict resolution through the democratization of Third World regimes. Only popular participation can route such conflicts into constructive political channels. Through its mediatory role as superpower, the United States could midwife such domestic transitions to democratic governance.

Barry Schutz swings the conceptual focus away from the "Lone Superpower" back to the level of regional action. Expositing the three cases of Nicaragua in relation to Central America, Cambodia in relation to East/ Southeast Asia, and Mozambique in relation to Southern Africa, Schutz illustrates the predominant role of regional actors in each case. Indeed, the passing of the Cold War has only accentuated the roles of regional actors in mitigating these three conflicts. Moreover, the post–Cold War domestic transformation of these regional actors serves to enhance their interest in regional conflict mitigation.

Our focus on global transformation is deliberate and distinct from an analysis of "new world orders." In discussing the Third World, the issues involve sorting out the evolving global and regional political and economic forces that are challenging the efficacy and potentially the survival of many states. Global transformation has brought about the most significant shift in international politics since 1945. While it will take years to define and characterize the dominant factors that may define a new world order, the impact on the Third World demands more immediate attention and thoughtful analysis. The aim of the essays that follow is to provide such analysis and to provoke further debate on the major issues confronting the Third World: the choice of political systems, the adaptation to a global and highly competitive economic system, and the control of conflict.

## Notes

1. There are other conventional approaches to defining the Third World's relationship to the international system. These include a North-South delineation and reference to a nonaligned movement situated between the East and West blocs of the Cold War.

2. Karen L. Remmer, "Democracy and Economic Crisis: The Latin American Experience," *World Politics* 42, no. 3 (April 1990): 315–335.

3. Samuel P. Huntington, *The Third Wave* (Norman, OK: University of Oklahoma Press, 1992).

4. Robert Gilpin, *The Political Economy of International Relations* (Princeton, NJ: Princeton University Press, 1987).

5. John Mearsheimer, "Back to the Future: Instability in Europe After the Cold War," *International Security* 15, no. 1 (Summer 1992): 33.

6. The emphasis in our discussion of conflict will be on political, not economic, variables. This does not suggest a diminution of the importance of economic conflict; in fact, we agree with others that economic conflict may be rife in the 1990s. Economic aspects of global transformation are addressed in essays in this volume by Callaghy, Dolan, and Unger.

# 2

# A World Without Leninism

## Kenneth Jowitt

### From Joshua to Genesis

For nearly a half century the boundaries of international politics and the identities of its national participants have been directly shaped by the presence of a Leninist world regime centered in the Soviet Union.[1] The Leninist Extinction of 1989 poses a fundamental challenge to that set of related boundaries and identities.

Boundaries are an essential component of a recognizable and coherent identity. Whether territorial, ideological, religious, economic, social, cultural, or amalgams thereof, the attenuation of or dissolution of boundaries is more often than not a traumatic event—all the more so when boundaries have been organized and understood in highly categorical terms.

By the end of the 1940s, world politics was largely anti-politics. The Cold War provides a striking instance of a stereotyped political division of labor. In each of the parallel worlds (West and East), one country patriarchally monopolized political decisions. For the most part, the behavior of any member of either world (Liberal or Leninist) could be predicted by knowing the camp to which it belonged. Mutual fear of ideological contamination manifested itself as murderous hysteria in the Soviet Union and gratuitous hysteria in the United States, and this mutual fear was exacerbated by efforts to disrupt each other's camp. Ideally, the members of each world, camp, or bloc were one-dimensional entities who defined themselves exclusively in terms of membership in their respective political and military organizations; they had one dominant referent, the leader of their respective camps, and one identity, the ideology that formally distinguished one camp from the other. Thus, entities as different as Albania and East Germany were viewed almost exclusively as communist, while Turkey and Norway were viewed one-dimensionally as free world countries.[2] Exceptions to this view did occur, but they constituted rare and, more significantly, indecisive challenges to the rigid boundaries and identities that defined world politics for forty years. Yugoslavia's defection from the Soviet bloc in 1948; France and England's invasion of Egypt in

9

1956; Romania and France's assertion of national military autonomy; U.S. and Soviet recognition of a "Third World"; and the substitution of "peaceful coexistence" and Détente for the Frigid War that followed World War II were substantial developments. But neither alone nor together did they break through the categoric political and ideological boundaries or the correspondingly rigid political identities of the postwar period.

The Cold War was a "Joshua" period, one of dogmatically centralized boundaries and identities. In contrast to the Biblical sequence, the Leninist Extinction of 1989 has moved the world from a Joshua period to a Genesis environment: from a world centrally organized, rigidly bounded, and hysterically concerned with impenetrable boundaries to one in which territorial, ideological, and issue boundaries are attenuated, unclear, and confusing. We now inhabit a world that, while not "without form and void," is one in which the major imperatives are the same as those in Genesis, "naming and bounding."[3]

In one important respect 1989 resembles 1066. In that year England did not move a geographical inch, but the "conceptual geography" of all Europe changed decisively. As Douglas has lucidly argued:

> Beyond doubt, the latter half of the eleventh century witnessed a turning point in the history of western Christendom. By the conquest of a great kingdom [the Normans] effected a political regrouping of north-western Europe with lasting consequences both to France and England . . . [The Normans] contributed also to a radical modification of the relations between eastern and western Europe with results that still survive.

A reconfigured, differently named and bounded world emerged, one "centered upon France [including] not only . . . England . . . but the Italy which the Normans helped to transform."[4]

In the mid–eleventh century the political tectonic plates radically shifted. In the late twentieth century it has happened again. There is, however, a radical difference between 1066 and 1989: today it is hard to find the "Normans." That is, we can identify neither a self-confident elite nor institutions with the power both to break up existing boundaries and identities *and* to effectively export or impose a viable substitute. If we take Kristof's distinction between frontiers and boundaries, the political, economic, and ideological collapse of Leninist regimes in Europe (and their inertial persistence in parts of Asia and in Cuba) has destroyed existing political/ideological boundaries and created a nebulous frontier condition in international politics. According to Kristof,

> The nature of frontiers differs greatly from the nature of boundaries. Frontiers are a characteristic of rudimentary socio-political relations and/or absence of laws. The presence of boundaries is a sign that the political community has reached a relative degree of maturity and orderliness. . . . [Frontiers] are the result of rather spontaneous, or at least ad

hoc solutions and movements, [boundaries] are fixed and enforced through a more rational and centrally coordinated effort after a conscious choice is made among the several preferences and opportunities at hand.[5]

In the aftermath of the Leninist Extinction, frontiers are likely to replace boundaries in a number of settings.

In light of this contention, it is interesting to see how quickly some academics and political figures have discovered a "normal reality" able both to stave off the threatening turbulence associated with the Leninist Extinction and to create new and more desirable boundaries and identities. Both Fukuyama's "end of history" thesis and the "transition to democracy" school either explicitly or implicitly see the liberal democratic West as constructive Normans—ready and able to take advantage of the "clearing away" of boundaries and identities in the wake of the Leninist Extinction and to shape the world in its own image.[6] This prevalent optimism rests on several assumptions. First, it assumes that the Leninist legacy— the cultural, social, political, and economic inheritance left to successor regimes in Eastern Europe (and what was the Soviet Union)—though not negligible, is not debilitating enough to overwhelm indigenous efforts at democratization. Second, it assumes that the Leninist Extinction is a self-contained event that will not significantly disrupt the boundaries and identities of the Western and Third worlds. Third, it assumes that the strength of the Western world is characterized by ideological, institutional, and national self-confidence and promise—not simply by power and wealth. I question all these assumptions.

## The Leninist Extinction

I have argued elsewhere that one can identify at least two rare historical events: (1) the emergence of an authoritatively standardized and centered institutional format dominating a highly diverse set of cultures—examples being Roman Christianity, Arabic Islam, British Liberalism, *and* Soviet Leninism; and (2) the "mass extinction" of a species—precisely what happened to Leninism in 1989.[7] Mass extinction refers to the abrupt and accelerated termination of species that are distributed globally or nearly so. What separates it from other forms of extinction is its speed and comprehensiveness. Developments in the Leninist world in 1989 can be understood as a mass extinction. Leninism's "genetic" or identity-defining features, those that provided Leninist regimes with a continuously recognizable identity over time and across space, were destroyed. Class war, the Correct Line, the Party as a superior and exclusive locus of political leadership and membership, and the Soviet Union as the incarnation of revolutionary socialism, have all been rejected in the Soviet Union, and the support of the Soviet Union has been withdrawn from Leninist replica regimes in Eastern Europe. The momentous result has been the collapse of these regimes and the emergence of successor governments aspiring to democracy and capitalism but faced with a distinct and unfavorable Leninist legacy.

That legacy includes a "ghetto" political culture that views government and the political realm suspiciously, as a source of trouble and even danger. It includes societies marked by distrust; filled with Hobbesian competition; and habituated to hoarding—and sharing only with intimates—information, goods, and goodwill. The Leninist legacy also includes rumor as a mode of discourse that works against the sober public discussion of issues; a segmentary rather than complementary socioeconomic division of labor, in which the semiautarchic workplace favors social insulation; a political leadership whose charismatic and storming approach to problems did very little culturally or psychologically to familiarize these societies with "methodically rational" action; and Soviet-enforced isolation among the nations of Eastern Europe, something that reinforced and added to their mutual ignorance, distrust, and disdain. All in all these features do not constitute a legacy that favors liberal capitalist democracy.[8]

The Leninist Extinction's impact, however, will not be limited to the former Leninist world. Any argument that the collapse of Leninist regimes is some sort of historical surgical strike leaving the rest of the world largely unaffected should qualify as a striking example of political and intellectual denial. The Leninist Extinction should be likened to a catastrophic volcanic eruption, one that initially and immediately affects only the surrounding political "biota" (i.e., other Leninist regimes) but whose effects most likely will also have a *global impact* on political "biota," in other words, altering the boundaries and identities that for half a century have politically, economically, and militarily defined and ordered the world.

Like the Norman victory, the Leninist defeat will lead to a reconfigured world. But the Leninist extinction differs fundamentally from the Norman conquest. Extinctions create turbulent rather than pacific environments characterized by shifting and contested boundaries of all types—territorial, ideological, cultural, economic, and political—and by insecure identities. Such environments can predictably give rise to political assertions and intellectual schemes whose explicit or implicit intent is to alleviate the anxiety inevitably accompanying the unexpected and dramatic removal of existing boundaries. Attempts to maintain beneficial and familiar boundaries and identities are also predictable. The fear of chaos seems to be a culturally and historically shared human instinct. Political and intellectual efforts at reassurance are an amalgam of rational, superstitious, denying, and inertial behavior (with greater weight assigned to each succeeding element). A good example is the fetishistic emphasis the Bush administration places on the institutional and political boundaries that constitute NATO identity. But reassurance and optimism are not substitutes for examining what is in its nature difficult to examine: in this case the potential maelstrom emerging in the aftermath of the Leninist Extinction.

## Where to Draw the Line

In an important article on "Borders, Boundaries, Taxes and States in the Medieval Islamic World," Ellis Goldberg has contrasted the bounded territorial closure typical of medieval Europe to its absence in medieval Islam. Goldberg's point is that bounded economic and cultural communities did exist in the medieval Islamic world but did not require the existence of a politically predominant territorial state.[9] Be that as it may, since the nineteenth century, territorial boundaries have become a more salient concern in the Arab world. In fact, with the ascendance of the Western nation-state as the internationally dominant mode of political loyalty and economic organization, the nation-state as reality, fiction, and aspiration has become the obligatory mode of political organization and loyalty in the world. And territorial boundaries are intimate and crucial components of nation-state identity.[10] The Leninist Extinction threatens some and will challenge many other existing territorial boundaries.

An immediate and obvious challenge to territorial boundaries has already been seen within the Soviet Union and parts of Eastern Europe. The establishment of sovereign republics within the former Soviet Union has created a turbulent, tense, unresolved situation in one of the world's two thermonuclear superpowers.[11] In Eastern Europe, Yugoslavia has collapsed, and efforts to save Czechoslovak unity with a hyphen (Czecho-Slovak) emphasize how widespread the potential is within the former Leninist world for territorial boundary change and corresponding changes in political identity. In fact, it may turn out that it was a great deal easier to contain a well-bounded and -identified Soviet bloc than to prevent the current boundary and identity breakdown in the same area from spilling over into adjacent areas.

*Like Central Asia.* "Central Asia is an old idea taking on new life not only in Pakistan but also in the Asian Muslim world beyond the Middle East— as far east as China's Xinjiang region."[12] Crossette is certainly right when she says that

> no one expects a new Central Asian empire to stir the ghost of Tamer-lane, certainly not in an age when nationalisms are fragmenting rather than enlarging geographical domains. But a process, however tenuous and exploratory, of rediscovering old cultural, historical, religious, and

commercial bonds is under way, perhaps most of all in Pakistan, the nation in the middle.

Equally important, continues Crosette, is the fact that "not all the interest in Central Asia is benign or cultural. William Maley of the Australian Defense Force Academy . . . says . . . thoughts of a new community of interests unsettle India, which fears it may one day confront a bloc of conservative Islamic lands from its western borders to the horizons of Europe."

*Like Eastern Europe.* In the former Soviet republic now known as Moldova, there are clear signs that the majority Romanian population want an integral political relationship with Romania. Similarly, the Hungarian president, Arpad Goncz, was the first head of state to visit Ukraine after it declared sovereignty.[13] The significance of Ukraine becoming a sovereign state includes its potential emergence as a major regional actor in a set of complementary and conflicting coalitions with Hungary, Czechoslovakia, Romania, and Poland.[14] For example, the Hungarian president's visit has obvious significance for the ethnic and territorial dispute between Romania and Hungary over Transylvania.

*Like the Balkans.* The potential disintegration of Yugoslavia should alert us to the possibility of a new boundary and identity configuration in Southeast Europe. The Macedonian issue is latent, not extinct, and will involve Serbia, Bulgaria, Greece, and most likely Turkey. In fact, given the situation in Iraq, the crisis in Central Asia, and the crises in both Bulgaria and Yugoslavia, Turkey may emerge as a pivotal rather than peripheral nation in a radically reconfigured political region that partially blurs, overlaps, and displaces the boundaries between the Middle East, Balkans, and Central Asia. The disintegration of territorial boundaries and political/ideological identities in the former Leninist world is likely to extend to territorially proximate boundaries and identities.

*Like Western Europe.* Developments in Czechoslovakia, particularly the bitter relations between its two ethnic components, heighten the prospect of a political/territorial revision of boundaries and identities in favor of confederation. Add to that Slovenia's desire to be free of "backward" Yugoslavia, and the existence of an "increasingly potent regional party [in North Italy] called the Lombard League [demanding] full autonomy to Lombardy and other regions in [Italy's] affluent North,"[15] and you have yet another potential for a reconfiguration of Europe's territorial, commercial, and political boundaries. Such a reconfiguration is likely to favor what Mazowieczki, the former Polish prime minister, bemoaned as the tendency to split Eastern Europe and all of Europe into an A and B category —a division I have described as the "Orange County–Watts" split.[16]

Nor should we exclude the Asian Leninist world from our consideration of potential territorial boundary and political identity changes. The
persistence of Leninist rule in China rests on the longevity and continued
presence of its founding cadres, the Old Bolsheviks, leaders who have the
one thing that East European Leninist rulers lacked in 1989, self-confidence in their political and ideological purpose. But even the Chinese,
North Korean, and Vietnamese regimes find it impossible to define that
purpose in practical "combat" terms. They suffer from the same combination of revolutionary ritualization and ad hoc modernization that characterized Leninist neotraditionalism in Europe.[17] In the absence of even an
ambivalently viewed Soviet Center, and given their ideological acceptance
of the politically benign—not equal—nature of their societies, these
regimes are on an inertial path to extinction. In North Korea, the death of
Kim Il-sung will immediately and threateningly raise the issue of unification with South Korea—of territorial boundary and political identity
change. In China, the eventual physical demise of its leadership strata will
immediately raise the threat of regionalism. It is true that "one of the Chinese Party's proudest accomplishments is that it reunited a nation torn
apart by warlords and recreated a central government that could lead the
country." Nonetheless, while

> that achievement stands . . . in these days of economic slowdown, it is
> somewhat undermined by provinces that are quietly carving up the vast
> national market into protectionist fiefs . . . The new restrictions on [in-
> ternal] trade . . . underscore the strength of the centrifugal forces that
> some Chinese fear could lead eventually to the fragmentation of their
> motherland.[18]

Regionalism in China is no more likely to be self-contained than bound-
ary/identity changes in the former Soviet Union or Eastern Europe. Peaceful, violent, decisive, or indecisive reconfiguration within China will necessarily involve both Taiwan and Hong Kong.

If we can identify potentials for territorial boundary and political identity changes in the former Leninist world *and* potentials for direct spillover
into neighboring areas in Asia, the Middle East, and Western Europe, then
the collapse of Leninism as an internationally identified and bounded entity will also affect boundaries and identities in the rest of the world, particularly the Third World.

Just as the British navy gave substance to the Monroe Doctrine
boundary declaration, the compelling reality of the Soviet-U.S. conflict
gave substance and stability to the formal declaration of territorial boundaries in the Third World. The influence exercised by superpower patrons
on Third World clients in their role as models, warehouses, and armories,
when added to each superpower's fear that a change in boundaries could
add to their rival's power, helped stabilize Third World territorial bound-

aries.[19] The Leninist Extinction and U.S. declaration that the Cold War is over[20] have altered those environmental constraints.[21] Furthermore, the fact that those constraints were largely coercive meant that they repressed rather than removed a number of underlying historical issues and frames of reference that continue to have a latent claim on many Third World elites. Consequently, many of those issues and frames of reference should now begin to re-emerge. In this connection, Kenneth Stein's comments about the Middle East are quite apt. "For the last 200 years, Middle Eastern peoples and their leaders have been reacting to outsiders' notions of political organization—nationalism, modernization, secularization—and to the evolving rules of international behavior. But now they have greater control over their own affairs."[22] The fact that Hafez al-Assad had a mural in his office depicting the Battle of Hittin in 1187, where Saladin won a crucial victory over the Crusaders, and the fact that he values it because it was "where the Arabs defeated the West,"[23] speaks to one frame of reference that may become more salient and consequential in a world without Leninism.

Finally, there are developments in the West itself with territorial boundary and identity implications. Those developments are neither a direct nor indirect response to the Leninist Extinction, but their course will be affected by the turbulent environments, the boundary/identity instability, created by that event. I have in mind two Western developments: the Chunnel and Quebec. It is remarkable that, as William Grimes has noted, "British workers will meet their French counterparts somewhere under the middle of the Channel—La Manche, to the French—and for the first time in 8,000 years England will again be linked to the Continent." Grimes goes on to point out that "as the most dramatic example of shrinking European frontiers, [the Chunnel is] already carrying heavy symbolic freight." More than that, when combined with the evolving transportation infrastructure in Western Europe, and the moves toward a common currency, the Chunnel has quite understandably led some to "fear it will blur their national identities." In this Chunnel era, boundaries and identities in Western Europe will differ radically from that day in 1930 when a headline appeared in the British press saying: "Fog in Channel: Continent [not Britain] Cut Off."[24]

Ironically enough, the British-French connection plays a major role in another instance of potential boundary/identity change in the West, in Quebec. "After the collapse of a constitutional accord that would have granted protection to Quebec's distinct culture, the province's Government made it clear that it will no longer deal with the national Government as a superior entity, but as an equal partner in managing common interests."[25] The possibility that Quebec might secede from Canada is real. Should that occur, one can assume that several other Canadian provinces will reconsider their existing relation to Canada *and* to the United States.

## "Many Are Called But Few Are Chosen"

Simply outlining these potential changes will irritate many social scientists and will make policymakers apprehensive, because if I am right, policymakers had better hire political cartographers to draw new maps that more accurately reflect changing territorial boundaries and political identities. Even more unsettling, the policymaker will have to entertain the real possibility that national, regional, and international boundaries and identities will be contested for a long time to come. As for social scientists, some would say I have indulged in sheer speculation. Not so.

I have deductively concluded that the extinction of a defining and bounding element of the international order is likely to create disorder both within its own boundaries and in adjacent areas. I have inductively argued that one can identify *potential* spillover effects of the Leninist Extinction in Central Asia, the Balkans, Asia, and Western Europe in the form of new political orientations, concerns, and aspirations. I have also argued that one should be alert to the possibility of specific loci for new political coalitions, e.g., Ukraine and Turkey; and equally alert to the possibility of new territorial entities, e.g., an independent Quebec, a confederal Czecho-Slovakia, an expanding Pakistan, a united Korea, and conflict in China between center and region, involving Taiwan and Hong Kong as well.

However, when I say, "many are called but few are chosen," I also recognize that potentials may not—in fact some are highly unlikely to—materialize, and even if they do, they may be defeated by opposing developments or realities. For example, regionalism may become a genuine threat to China's integrity and be contained or defeated by a national Chinese army. Similarly, Pakistan may try to expand at the expense of a disintegrating Soviet Union and may be defeated by a Russian (not Soviet) army. One has to be either dull or lazy not to try and identify potential boundary/identity changes in a world struck by the extinction of one of its defining components; one has to be foolish to assume that all potential boundary/identity revisions have equal chances to succeed. In any case, my primary concern is not the success or failure of potential boundary/identity changes; *that* would be sheer speculation—in fact, indulgence in a claim to prophecy. My point is that the Leninist Extinction poses a dramatic and worldwide challenge to existing territorial boundaries and political identities. The outcomes will vary from the possible creation of a Goldberg-like trade community in Central Europe to a change in Korean political geography, a proliferation of military boundary conflicts in the Third World as in Iraq and Kuwait, and the emergence of what David Calleo has so suggestively termed a "multinational continental system" in Western Europe, which would be better able to "regulate centralized national structures of the earlier continental systems, the United States and the Soviet Union."[26] I suggested earlier that analyzing a maelstrom is intrinsically difficult. It is not impossible. I suggest we begin with challenges and threats to territorial boundaries and identities within the former Leninist world; with the effects of the disintegration of established territorial boundaries and identities in the Leninist world upon adjacent areas; and with discovering the location of new territorially bounded political entities, i.e., locating and analyzing new pivotal nations or core areas around which reconfigured political regions and coalitions may form.

## Civic vs. Ethnic: Boundaries and Identities

The Leninist Extinction's direct, indirect, and reinforcing impact on global, regional, and national boundaries and identities will *not* be limited to territorial boundaries. Its influence on the redefinition of *issue* boundaries and its consequent reshaping of political identities will be as, perhaps more, profound. The civil/ethnic identity issue is a defining one for all the Soviet empire's successor states. This cleavage expresses itself in three ways: First, it can be seen in the form of ongoing discussions about, declarations of, and possible efforts to secede. Second, it is expressed as possible irredentas. The previously mentioned visit of the Hungarian president to Ukraine focused largely on the Transcarpathian Oblast in western Ukraine with its nearly 200,000 ethnic Hungarians. It is a fair assumption that this visit was noted in Slovakia, with its half million Hungarians, and in Romania, with its nearly two million Hungarians. No "logic" inexorably leads Hungary to reclaim its ethnic kin in Slovakia, Yugoslavia, the Ukraine, and Romania. In fact, as Horowitz argues, "the decision to embark upon an irredentist course is freighted with elements that counsel restraint. Unlike aid to secessionists, it probably means direct involvement in actual warfare."[27] But turbulent and fragmented East European and Soviet environments[28] do support the appearance of groups and programs favoring a predominantly ethnic and territorial definition of political identity.

The third expression of the civil/ethnic issue is internal conflict over the predominant definition of national identity. *The national state is a partially antagonistic amalgam of state, civic, and ethnic orientations and organization.* Metaphorically, these national components can be matched with the French Revolution's slogan: Liberty (the civic), Equality (the state), and Fraternity (the ethnic). In a nation-state the impersonal secular state creates a domain in which, ideally, all are treated equally. However, the state's emphasis on impersonalism and standardization jars with the "gemeinschaft" qualities of ethnic affective identifications; and while supportive of civic equality, the state's ethos and structure is at odds with the critical scrutiny that is the civic or public realm's distinctive feature. In a related manner, the civic and ethnic components of national identification and organization are partially antagonistic. The civic component emphasizes the individual, while the ethnic component emphasizes the group; the civic orientation is critical, while the ethnic evokes solidarity. At issue, then, in every nation-state is how the "three persons" of the state, civic, and ethnic trinity are weighted and defined.

If under Leninist rule *kto kovo?* asked whether or not the party was dominant, the question today in the nations of the extinct Soviet bloc is whether civic or ethnic forces dominate their political life.[29] In 1989 the civic orientation predominated. The year 1990 saw the forceful emergence of ethnic political forces in Croatia, Serbia, Slovakia, Hungary, Romania, Ukraine, and Poland. The boundary between those representing one or the other identity—civic or ethnic—tends to be stark and the psychological, cultural, and political confrontation intense. Far from being complementary, these groups, programs and orientations are competing for dominance in a fashion that threatens to divide their societies and destabilize their governments. Should ethnic political forces prevail, as they already have in Serbia, Croatia, and Romania, the potential for violence in and between countries in Eastern Europe, and for the involvement of Western Europe and Russia, will increase.

The civic/ethnic issue has not only replaced the party/society issue in Eastern Europe, but it is increasingly salient in Western Europe as well. In part, this is due to the Leninist Extinction of 1989 and resulting immigration. The recent electoral success in Austria of a nativist party can be directly attributed to fear of Balkan immigrants. The prospect of some two million refugees from the Soviet Union and Eastern Europe in 1991 led to political apprehension and ethnic rejection of "foreigners." The combined fear of migrants from North Africa and refugees from the "East" has made the civic/ethnic issue in Western Europe a source of divisive instability in a region that presently appears more confident and purposive than any in the world.[30]

The civic/ethnic divide is not limited to the former Leninist world or Western Europe. The conflict between Afrikaners and Blacks in South Africa, and between the civic ANC and the more ethnic Inkhata in the same country; the conflict in Canada between British and French descendants; and the growing conflict over the status of the English language in India all speak to the increasing international salience of this particular identity cleavage. Ethnicity and race are also making growing claims on citizens in the United States. Expressions of these claims vary: affirmative action, multicultural education, the Rainbow Coalition, Spike Lee's movies, Farrakhan's Muslims, David Duke's Klan politics, and Bush's flag mania are all examples. They all contribute to the ethnically bound polarization of a civic polity.

Civic/ethnic identity issues inside, adjacent to, and distant from the former Leninist world will interact with one another in a more or less direct and consequential way. The language and reality of this conflict is becoming universal regardless of existing boundaries and identities.

In the aftermath of the Leninist Extinction, the world is becoming more permeable. One can detect a number of issues, more loosely related to the civic/ethnic divide, that don't "match up well" with existing territorial and ideological boundaries and identities. For example, the status of women is such an issue.

*Gender.* Antifeminism is palpable throughout Eastern Europe. The Roman Catholic church's antiabortion stance is a striking but not solitary example, as the literature in Hungary blaming women for the social disorder in that country testifies.[31] The presence of U.S. troops in Saudi Arabia helped trigger renewed demonstrations there against the categoric, gendered division of labor. In South America, the phenomenal growth of evangelical Protestantism has at its core the disproportionate role of women as members and leaders.[32] This is not to say the gender issue means the same thing in each of these settings. Nor should that cautionary note prevent one from grasping the emergence of a new issue with potential national, regional, and international boundary and identity implications.

*Religion.* Since the Iranian revolution, radical Islam has been recognized as a resurgent boundary-making and identity-claiming force. Fundamentalist Muslims in Tunisia, Algeria, *and* Saudi Arabia are serious and influential political players who, if they come to power, particularly in Saudi Arabia, will have a crucial impact on relations between the West and the Middle East. When a figure such as Dr. Safar al-Hawali, the dean of Islamic Studies at Umm al-Qura University of Mecca, interprets the Iraqi situation not as "the world against Iraq" but as the "West against Islam" one should take note. According to Mamoun Fandy, "Dr. Hawali is one of Islam's most respected theologians and the primary spokesman for the Wahabi sect." The House of Saud adheres to the Wahabi sect. Fandy notes that while stopping "short of calling for the overthrow of the Saud family [Hawali does emphasize that it is] contrary to the laws of Islam . . . to join with non-Moslems in a battle against Moslems." Dr. Hawai reminded his listeners of the Prophet's warning: "Rome will attack you in many forms." He went on to point out that "the Crusaders, the British and French colonialists, and now the Americans are all forms of Rome."[33] The Islamic factor didn't disappear with Khomeini; nor is the religious factor limited to Islam.

Roman Catholicism is on the political offensive in Eastern Europe, the former Soviet Union, and Western Europe; on the political defensive in Latin and North America; and politically active everywhere. Whether calling for obligatory religious education in Hungarian or Polish schools, opposing abortion in Poland and the United States, or sponsoring "base communities" in Latin America, the church with its pope has re-emerged as a newly invigorated global political actor.[34] The Orthodox church could emerge as a regional actor in Russia and the Balkans through offering support to the army and ethnic nationalists in their possible efforts to create a stable authoritarian order. The psychological, cultural, economic, and cultural dislocation resulting from the Leninist Extinction in the former Soviet Union and Eastern Europe favors the growth of the Catholic and Orthodox churches. In a related manner, the collapse of the dominant East-West boundary offers greater scope for the identity claiming power of Islam.

*Urban divisions.* Cities have become gathering places of pollution and poverty—sites of invidious contrasts between cosmopolitan and lumpen life styles, religious conflict, and ungovernability. Cities as different as Detroit, Cairo, Lagos, Mexico City, and Bucharest may become the sites of urban jacqueries.

*AIDS.* The spread of the HIV virus is another example of a new national and international issue, one that directly affects political alignments and conflicts. In the United States, AIDS is a medical, sexual, and racial issue, bounding and defining issues and actors in new ways, while reinforcing existing racial and sexual polarities. In Africa, AIDS is a medical epidemic that threatens the lives of millions; in Uganda maybe a third of the population is infected. In Romania, the incidence of the HIV virus among infant orphans in hospitals and the latent hysteria among the population are both high. China, "which as recently as last spring was blaming AIDS on the rotten mentality and lifestyle of capitalist society . . . is seeking Western help." China's Minister of Public Health, Chen Minzhang, has recently said, "We have an AIDS problem that has a very dangerous potential to expand."[35]

All of these issues—gender, religion, cities, and AIDS—are linked to the civic/ethnic divide. In the United States, a *New York Times*/CBS-TV news poll found that "10 percent of blacks said the AIDS virus was deliberately created in a laboratory in order to infect black people." "Another 19 percent said that theory might possibly be true, and 63 percent said it was almost certainly not true." "Of the whites polled 4 percent said it was true, 12 percent said it was possibly true, and 75 percent said it was almost certainly not true."[36] AIDS has become a medical and sociocultural base for potential hysteria in the United States, and a powerful issue reinforcing polarized racial identities and boundaries.

Religious identity claims challenge civic and secular identities in the Middle East and the former Leninist world in the former Soviet Union and

Eastern Europe. The decay of cities pits the more affluent, educated, cosmopolitan, civic (and often culturally invidious) dwellers against the poorer, less educated, more parochial (and often more violent) residents.

The Leninist Extinction destroyed the dominant East-West international boundary and identity distinction. In the turbulent environments emerging today, the civic/ethnic distinction (while not centrally organized as in the case of the East-West conflict) operates as a boundary/identity distinction in two respects: it can serve as a conceptual base for making sense of a disordered world, and it does serve as an increasingly powerful political base for national and international conflicts.

## "Intermestic" Issues

While no boundary or identity is absolute, at least the one between domestic and international issues has been clear. Developments in the last two decades have challenged that clarity; so will the Leninist Extinction.

In the 1970s, the proliferation of multinational corporations led many to question the clarity of the distinction between national and international boundaries. The point was dulled for many U.S. academics by the observation that most multinationals were U.S. companies operating in other nations. In the 1990s, however, the likelihood that an important number of the most pressing problems in the United States will *simultaneously be national and international* should make it increasingly difficult to maintain this boundary distinction. There is nothing unique or new about international and national issues overlapping. In fact, with the exception of nuclear weapons, there is precedent for practically everything. However, only the sun isn't new; there are new things under it. If in the First and Second World Wars, a number of German, Italian, Irish, and Japanese-Americans were ambivalent toward or opposed to U.S. policy, one could still *readily* distinguish the international issue and the domestic responses. That task is more difficult in an "intermestic" situation.[38] The ideal type of intermestic relation is one in which nations simultaneously adhere to their respective sovereignties, while elites and publics from each nation regularly and reciprocally involve themselves, "mix," in the other's domestic affairs. Intermestic conflict superimposes conflicts between nations and conflicts within nations.

To date, Israel has been the United States' sole intermestic issue. In order of likelihood, South Africa, Mexico, Canada, and Japan may very possibly join Israel. In the case of South Africa, for example, domestic/international boundaries are blurred by a number of factors. These include the crystallization of an African-American middle class and a college generation of U.S. blacks for whom the status of black South Africans, affirmative action, and multicultural education are all domestic issues. The emergence of an intermestic relation with South Africa has also been fostered by the visits of Nelson Mandela, specifically his political adoption by liberal whites and African-Americans, his brilliant identification of race relations in the United States and South Africa in the course of his speech before the U.S. (*not* African National) Congress, and his support of Native Americans.

Economic ties between Canada and the United States, Quebec's possible secession, and the influence of U.S. culture in Canada have created a unique relation between two sovereign neighboring countries. And then there is Japan. U.S. sponsorship of the postwar Japanese polity and economy, Japanese investment in and ownership of properties in the United States, and its continuing economic strength and decreasing need for U.S. military support—all combined with increasing envy and irritation at Japan's success on the part of U.S. citizens—have created a situation very different from past national military, ideological, and economic rivalries.

Relations between the United States and Mexico offer a particularly striking example of an intermestic situation. The pertinent issues here include immigration from Mexico (and resulting ethnic turmoil and tension in cities such as San Diego), potential political disorder in Mexico,[39] the explosive growth of "maquiladoras"[40]—factories owned by U.S. companies along the Arizona-Mexican border (approximately 1,800 such factories employing approximately 500,000 Mexican workers), and a growing politically articulate and organized Chicano population in the United States.

War in the Middle East with Israel and Saudi Arabia on opposite sides, a civil war in South Africa and/or in Mexico, Quebec seceding from Canada, or a decision by Japan to curtail investing in and operating plants in the United States are all events that would shape U.S. national debate and internal conflicts in a novel way; and our inertial definition of international boundaries and national identity would leave us ill-prepared to deal effectively with them.[41]

## Jeremiah or Hananiah

The Leninist Extinction is a "world historical event." It challenges and threatens the currently existing boundaries that shape and reflect political identity. The thrust of my argument has been threefold: (1) to argue the "universal" rather than self-contained quality of the Leninist Extinction; (2) to do so in terms of its impact on existing boundaries and identities; and (3) to use the framework of boundaries and identities to underscore the changing issues and anxiety that are likely to shape our political future. Analyzing the probable consequences of the Leninist Extinction leads me to conclude that we face a period of global, regional, and national turmoil over boundaries and identities. In this regard I am more of a Jeremiah than a Hananiah.[42] Lest anyone worry, there is no shortage of academics who are optimistic about developments in a world without Leninism: "Hananiah" Hough's work on Gorbachev's "controlled chaos" in the Soviet Union, Juan Linz's and Giuseppe DiPalma's prognosis for Eastern Europe, Fukuyama's belief in Liberalism's historically definitive triumph and Ben Wattenberg's view of developments in the United States are all characterized by a degree of optimism I don't share.[43]

## The United States and the Leninist Extinction

Should the current U.S. leadership continue its *inertial* conception of and relation to both international and national developments, the United States will become a variant of the "Kling-On empire" (a meaningful term for Star Trek fans!)—that is, an economically rusty, ambivalently viewed military protector for Western Europe and an overextended border patrol.

The response of the United States to Iraq's aggression was a classic example of denial of changes that have taken place. In this case it was 1990 not 1950; it was Iraq and Kuwait, not North and South Korea; it was North vs. South, not West vs. East. In the aftermath of the Leninist Extinction any number of Iraq-Kuwait situations may arise and there is no criterion upon which to decide when and how to intervene. For example, had U.S. intervention in the Middle East been explicitly and largely based on the supposed threat to Saudi oil, there would have been no need to demand Iraq's complete evacuation of Kuwait. Had our intervention been designed primarily to free our hostages, our actions would also have been very different. In fact, though, the premise of U.S. intervention was to deter a "Hitler-like aggression," thereby preventing regional chaos and maintaining global order.

For fifty years the United States has defined every international issue as *the* issue. U.S. foreign policy has been absolutist, not imperialist. It is ironic that a nation so adept domestically at compromise and bargaining should be so resistant to and unwilling to develop those talents in international relations. Obviously, some conflicts are not amenable to compromise; it should be equally obvious that some are and that the United States cannot sustain its absolutist position, if for no other reason than it can't afford it. As David Calleo notes:

> America is today in no position to return to its hegemonic dreams of 1945. Financially the U.S. has grown dependent on the inflow of foreign capital and can reduce its dependency only by reducing its fiscal debt— a difficult course quite incompatible with sustaining its present military establishment, let alone transforming it into a world police force.[44]

## Notes

1. See my "Moscow 'Centre'" in *East European Politics and Societies* no. 1 (Fall 1987): 296–349.

2. See my *Images of Detente and the Soviet Political Order* (Berkeley: Institute of International Studies, University of California, 1977), pp. 1–26.

3. On Joshua and Genesis "environments" see *The New English Bible with the Apocrypha* (New York: Oxford University Press and Cambridge University Press, 1970), pp. 1–60, 241–269.

4. See David C. Douglas, *William the Conqueror* (Berkeley: University of California Press, 1964), pp. 6–7.

5. Ladis D. Kristof, "The Nature of Frontiers and Boundaries," *Annals of the Association of American Geographers* 49, no. 3 (1959): 269–282.

6. See Francis Fukuyama, "The End of History?" *The National Interest,* no. 16 (Summer 1989): 3–18. See also Guillermo O'Donnell, Philippe Schmitter, and Laurence Whitehead, eds., *Transitions from Authoritarian Rule* (Baltimore: Johns Hopkins Press, 1986).

7. Ken Jowitt, "The Leninist Extinction," in *The Revolutions of 1989,* ed. Daniel Chirot (Seattle: University of Washington Press, 1991).

8. On this legacy see Ken Jowitt, "The Leninist Legacy," in *Revolution in Eastern Europe*, ed. Ivo Banac (Ithaca, NY: Cornell University Press, 1992).

9. Ellis Goldberg, "Border, Boundaries, Taxes and States in the Medieval Islamic World" (Paper presented at SSRC Conference, University of Washington, Seattle, April 1990).

10. On the relationship between the two in very different historical settings, see Peter Sahlins, *Boundaries: The Making of France and Spain in the Pyrenees* (Berkeley: University of California Press, 1989); and W. D. Davies, *The Territorial Dimension of Judaism* (Berkeley: University of California Press, 1982).

11. On the current status (as of December 1990) of claims to sovereignty, see Ann Sheehy, "Fact Sheet on Declarations of Sovereignty," *Report on the USSR,* Radio Liberty, pp. 23–25.

12. Barbara Crossette, "Central Asia Rediscovers Its Identity," *New York Times,* 24 June 1990, E3.

13. See Alfred Reisch's "Hungary and Ukraine Agree to Upgrade Bilateral Relations," *Report on Eastern Europe* 1, no. 44 (2 November 1990): 6–13.

14. For a most insightful and provocative suggestion concerning Poland's geopolitical orientation, see Roman Szporluk, "The Burden of History—Made Lighter by Geography?" *Problems in Communism* 5, no. 39 (July–August 1990): 45–58.

15. Clyde Haberman, "Rising Party in Italy's North Wants to Get Rome and the South Off Its Back," *New York Times,* 24 June 1990.

16. See Ken Jowitt, "A Research Agenda for Eastern Europe," *East European Politics and Societies* 4, no. 2 (Spring 1990): 193–197.

17. Ken Jowitt, "Soviet Neotraditionalism: The Political Corruption of a Leninist Regime," *Soviet Studies* 35, no. 3 (July 1983): 275–297.

18. Nicholas D. Kristof "In China, Too, Centrifugal Forces Are Growing Stronger," *New York Times,* 26 August 1990.

19. The relatively weak transportation infrastructure and state power of many Third World regimes also play a major role in the passive integrity of their territorial boundaries. For the African case, see Immanuel Wallerstein, "The Range of Choice: Constraints on the Policies of Governments of Contemporary African Independent States," in *The State of Africa* ed. Michael Lofchie (Berkeley:

University of California Press, 1971), pp. 19–37; and I. William Zartman, *Ripe for Resolution: Conflict and Intervention in Africa* (New York: Oxford University Press, 1989), pp. 19–20.

20. Made most recently by President Bush at the signing of the Charter of Paris. See R. W. Apple Jr.'s column, *New York Times,* 22 November 1990.

21. The massive U.S. presence in Saudi Arabia contradicts this statement. I will discuss the Bush administration's response to the end of the Cold War shortly.

22. Kenneth W. Stein, "A Tradition of Intrusion Collides with Western Rule," *New York Times*, 16 September 1990.

23. Stein, "A Tradition of Intrusion,"

24. William Grimes, "Chunnel," *New York Times Magazine*, 16 September 1990.

25. John F. Burns, "Ottawa and Quebec Search for a New Relationship," *New York Times,* 26 June 1990.

26. David P. Calleo, "American National Interest and the New Europe: Some Early Thoughts," in Chirot, *The Revolutions of 1989.*

27. Donald L. Horowitz, *Ethnic Groups in Conflict* (Berkeley: University of California Press, 1985), p. 282. See all of Chapter 6, "The Logic of Secessions and Irredentas."

28. Jowitt, "The Leninist Legacy."

29. The Russian phrase *kto kovo?,* literally *who whom?,* idiomatically conveys "one top dog and one bottom dog."

30. See Alan Riding, "Four European Nations Planning a New Focus on North Africa," *New York Times,* 30 September 1990.

31. See Joann Goven, "On the Men's Mutiny" (typed manuscript), 1990. See also Celestine Bohlen, "East Europe's Women Struggle with New Rules, and Old Ones," *New York Times: This Week in Review,* 25 November 1990.

32. On this movement see the following: John Marcum, Jr., "The Fire Down South," *Forbes,* 15 October 1990; David Stoll, *Is Latin America Turning Protestant?* (Berkeley: University of California Press, 1990); and David Martin, *Tongues of Fire: The Explosion of Protestantism in Latin America* (Cambridge, MA: Basil Blackwell, 1990). To Marcum's observation that "Brazil as elsewhere the media have tended to ignore the religious revival," one can add: so has academia.

33. Mamoun Fandy, "The Hawali Tapes," *New York Times,* 24 November 1990.

34. In this connection see Malachi Martin's *The Keys of This Blood: The Struggle for World Dominion Between Pope John Paul II, Mikhail Gorbachev and the Capitalist West* (New York: Simon and Schuster, 1990).

35. *Oakland Tribune,* 21 November 1990.

36. Jason DeParle, "Talk Grows of Government Being Out to Get Blacks," *New York Times,* 29 October 1990.

37. See Dirk Johnson, "Seeking New Harmony, But Finding a Racial Rift," *New York Times*, 25 November 1990.

38. I take the term "intermestic" from Bayless Manning, "The Congress, the Executive, and Intermestic Affairs: Three Proposals," *Foreign Affairs* 35, no. 2 (January 1977): 306–324. Manning refers to international issues that become national ones. I refer to issues where that distinction loses a good deal of its meaning.

39. See Mark A. Uhlig's "Mexico's Salinas Rains on His Own Parade," *New York Times,* 25 November 1990.

40. See the article by Sandy Tolan, "The Border Boom: Hope and Heartbreak," *New York Times Magazine,* 1 July 1990.

41. It should be clear that the U.S.-Japanese relation has fewer intermestic features than any of the other cases.

42. On Jeremiah's pessimism and Hananiah's optimism, see *The New English Bible,* "The Book of the Prophet Jeremiah," p. 950. At a recent conference at Yale, Juan Linz, in the course of his optimistic evaluation of democracy's chances in Eastern Europe, characterized my analysis of the Leninist legacy as Jeremiah-like. I am in his debt. It led me to rediscover Jeremiah and discover Hananiah.

43. In 1987, Professor Hough claimed that Western observers were "exaggerating the difficulty of reform [in the Soviet Union]" and had "exaggerated Gorbachev's problems at home." In 1989, Hough spoke of Gorbachev's "controlled chaos [which was] not simply directed at strengthening his political control for the sake of power. It is to maintain his control while he transforms Russia." That's optimism. According to Professor Hough, his predictions about Soviet developments have been consistently accurate for ten years. Which ten years? See Jerry Hough, "The End of Russia's 'Khomeini' Period," *World Policy Journal* 4, no. 4 (Fall 1987): 583–605; "Gorbachev's Politics," *Foreign Affairs* 68, no. 5 (Winter 1989–1990): 26–42; and "Gorbachev's Endgame," *World Policy Journal* 7, no. 4 (Fall 1990). See note 29 in that article for the claim to "ten years of successful prediction." Giuseppe DiPalma's optimist arguments can be found in *To Craft Democracies: Reflections on Democratic Transitions and Beyond* (Berkeley: University of California Press, 1990).

44. Calleo, "American National Interest."

# PART 2

---

## DEMOCRATIZATION
## AND THE THIRD WORLD

# 3

# The Globalization
of Democracy

## Larry Diamond

The 1980s, and particularly the final stunning years of that decade, recorded extraordinary progress for democracy around the world. It could even be argued that the decade saw the most widespread diffusion of democratic forms of governance since the inception of the nation-state. By the end of 1990, more independent countries could be rated democratic or "free"—65, by the count of Freedom House—than at any time in the history of the modern world. Using the same annual data from Freedom House, one could claim that more people, and a higher proportion of the world's people, were living under democratic forms of government by the end of the decade than ever before. Freedom House counted over two billion for the first time in 1989.[1]

With some important exceptions and reversals, this progress has continued into the 1990s. Freedom House rated 75 countries (including the three newly independent Baltic states) "free" at the end of 1991—an increase of 10 in one year. And by a more generous standard for classifying "democracies," it counted 89 at that time, well over half the 171 independent countries it rated, and twice the number 20 years ago. Considering as well "another thirty-two countries in some form of democratic transition," 70 percent of the world's countries had democracy or were moving toward it by the end of 1991.[2]

In his book, *The Third Wave*, Samuel Huntington argues that we are now in the midst of a "third wave" of democratic expansion in the world. "A wave of democratization is a group of transitions from nondemocratic to democratic regimes that occur within a specified period of time and that significantly outnumber transitions in the opposite direction."[3] He dates the first "long" wave of democratization back to 1828, with the expansion of democratic suffrage in the United States. It began to expire in the early 1920s with the coming to power of Mussolini in Italy, giving rise to a "first reverse wave." A second, shorter, democratic wave began with the Allied victory in World War II and continued until around 1962, incorporating a number of Latin American and newly independent (primarily former British) colonies. But by then a second reverse wave had begun, bringing widespread military and one-party rule and leaving only two states in South America democratic. The third wave, which began with the overthrow of the Caetano dictatorship in Portugal in April 1974, became a truly global phenomenon during the 1980s, doubling by 1990 the number of democracies in countries with populations exceeding one million.[4]

Democrats around the world have been exhilarated by this widespread democratic progress—what could be called the "globalization of democracy"—in terms of the nearly universal diffusion of popular demands for political freedom, representation, participation, and accountability. However, the gross numbers and almost miraculous developments disguise a much more complex and variegated picture. An important element in that complexity has been the more subtle erosion of democratic institutions and norms in many developing countries in recent years. Another is the vexing economic and social problems, including the resurgence of virulent nationalist passions, that stand in the way of democratic consolidation in Eastern Europe and the republics of the former Soviet Union, as well as in the Third World.[5]

This chapter assesses and analyzes the global trend toward democracy in recent years. It begins with a brief accounting, by regions and countries, of the major democratic developments of the late 1980s and early 1990s. A brief quantitative assessment is then offered. The principal section analyzes the relative weight of international vs. domestic factors in this most recent wave of democratic expansion. In conclusion, I explore the prospects for democracy in the coming decade, and how international and domestic factors interact to condition those prospects.

## The Global Democratic Revolution

The global democratic revolution transformed the face of Communist Eastern and Central Europe during 1989 and 1990. By early 1991, Poland had elected its first democratic head of state in more than 60 years; Hungary and Czechoslovakia were struggling with the challenges of restructuring and consolidating formally democratic institutions; Bulgaria was moving toward radical economic reform and full democratization under a minority non-Communist parliamentary government; and large demonstrations in Belgrade were demanding the ouster of a Serbian government that remained communist in everything but name. In multiparty elections during 1990, Communists lost power in four of the six Yugoslavian republics. However, intense nationalist mobilization brought violent conflict between Serbia and Croatia during 1991, and then between Serbia and Bosnia-Herzegovina. These bloody ethnic battles, on the same soil where World War I began, were a chilling portent of the possible negative consequences of the end of the Cold War. As Kenneth Jowitt has argued, the extinction of Leninism has left in its wake a multipolar, fluid, and volatile world, in which political regimes, ideologies, identities, and boundaries will experience vigorous contestation and change.[6]

In the Soviet Union, the most artificial and most ethnically complex of the former Communist states, nationalist mobilization merged with democratic sentiment to undermine the power of the Communist central government. More than a year before the spectacular demise of Communist rule following the failed coup attempt of Communist hardliners in August 1991, power was rapidly shifting to governments in the republics, many of them elected through a competitive, at least quasi-democratic process that granted some significant popular legitimacy (most significantly to Boris Yeltsin's government in Russia). The sudden collapse of Communist authority at the center left a daunting triple challenge for the Soviet Union: (1) hastening the transition from state socialism to a market economy, (2) crafting and institutionalizing new democratic structures in each of the republics, and (3) working out a new system of economic and political interaction among the republics. Those challenges are likely to preoccupy most of the republics for perhaps the rest of this century. Only the three Baltic states—which have some previous democratic history and a greater prospect of economic integration with Europe—seem poised to achieve relatively rapid democratic institutionalization.

The stunning changes in Eastern Europe and the Soviet Union reverberated visibly throughout the Third World, particularly dramatically in Africa, where authoritarian rule has been nearly pervasive. Ignited by President De Klerk's bold decision in February 1990 to release Nelson Mandela and legalize the anti-apartheid opposition, South Africa began a process of dialogue and reconciliation that signaled the effective initiation of a transition to a nonracial democracy, though the transition process has proved to be protracted and intensely conflictual.[7] Inspired by the changes in both Eastern Europe and South Africa, and disgusted with the oppression, corruption, and economic and moral bankruptcy of one-party rule, the rest of the continent was swept by a wave of regime openings and popular demands for multiparty democracy. By the end of 1991, roughly 26 African countries, or about half of all the states in the continent, could be "classified as either democratic or moderately or strongly committed to democratic change."[8]

During 1990, dictators who had ruled without challenge for 20 to 30 years, such as Felix Houphouet-Boigny in the Ivory Coast, Omar Bongo in Gabon, and Kenneth Kaunda in Zambia, found themselves forced by popular mobilization and international pressure to accept multiparty electoral competition.[9] Kaunda's landslide electoral defeat in October 1991 and his graceful exit from office marked an important turning point in Africa's postindependence politics. The start of this "second African independence" may be traced to Benin, where President Mathieu Kerekou, in power since 1972, was toppled from effective control in early 1990, when a constitutional conference he had called was used by angry participants to strip him of his authority and initiate a transition to democracy. Subsequently, authoritarian regimes in the Congo, Togo, Niger, and Madagascar were forced (after considerable resistance) to accept this same formula of a sovereign national conference. In early 1991, the island nations of Cape Verde and Sao Tome y Principe voted out long-ruling single-party regimes in competitive elections that marked transitions to democracy. Zimbabwean prime minister Robert Mugabe was forced by widespread popular opposition to abandon his dream of a one-party state (even as his regime continued to harass the only opposition party), and President Abdou Diouf of Senegal "refurbished the democratic image of the country's political system by broadening his government to include some of the opposition parties."[10] Even Africa's Marxist regimes were shaken by the rapid breakdown of Communist rule abroad as well as by their own abysmal economic failures at home. Ethiopia's regime finally collapsed after many years of civil war, while Mozambique and Angola moved to negotiate an end to their civil wars, to dismantle socialism, and to open up their economic and political systems. Denouncing democratic demands as inspired by foreigners, stubborn opponents of political pluralism and liberty—for example, Kenya's President Daniel Arap Moi, Cameroon's Paul Biya, and Malawi's Hastings Banda—appeared increasingly isolated from domestic and international opinion in their corrupt autocracies.[11] The Moi regime, heavily dependent on international aid, did in fact feel itself compelled to legalize competing parties in 1992 and jettison some of its most corrupt ministers.

No region experienced more thorough political change during the late 1970s and 1980s than Latin America and the Caribbean. Until the military coup in Haiti of 29 September 1991, which displaced Haiti's first truly democratically elected president, Jean-Bertrand Aristide, after only eight months in office, Cuba had been the only authoritarian holdout in the region. Beleaguered Peru joined the retreat from democracy in 1992 with President Alberto Fujimori's executive coup. Like Yugoslavia for the postcommunist states of Eurasia, Peru could prove to be a harbinger of democratic reversals, even a "third reverse wave," among debt-ridden, violence-wracked countries of Latin America. Still, by mid-1992 the region was composed mainly of democratic or at least semidemocratic regimes, and the extraordinary peaceful settlement of the civil war in El Salvador, concluded in January 1992, showed that the way remained open to democratic progress even in the most bitterly polarized and war-torn circumstances.

A crucial turning point for democratization in Latin America came with the peaceful resolution of the Nicaragua conflict in 1990 through an electoral transition to multiparty democracy, though the country was besieged by economic collapse and social polarization.[12] The February 1990 elections in Nicaragua were preceded and followed by several other landmark developments for democracy in the region: the decisive victory of the democratic coalition in Chile's December 1989 presidential elections; the inauguration in Panama of the democratically elected government of Guillermo Endara, following the ouster of Noriega's dictatorship by U.S. troops in December 1989; the peaceful succession of democratic administrations in economically troubled Brazil, Peru, and the Dominican Republic, following tense presidential elections in December 1989 and May 1990; the progress toward a liberal and authentic democracy in Paraguay, following the overthrow of Alfredo Stroessner's 35-year-old dictatorship in February 1989 and the opening up of free (if not fair) electoral competition;[13] and the growing signs that Fidel Castro's 31-year-old communist dictatorship, increasingly bereft of its international props and regional allies, was entering a "terminal crisis."[14] The authoritarian hegemony of Latin America's most durable ruling party, the PRI (Partido Revolucionario Institucional) of Mexico, also came under intense challenge from both the left and the right, producing in 1988 its narrowest margin of victory in a presidential election since it came to power in the 1920s, and escalating pressure for full democratization.[15]

Some of the most dramatic instances of democratic progress during the 1980s came in Asia, beginning with the massive demonstration of "people power" in the Philippines that toppled Ferdinand Marcos from power after he attempted to steal the February 1986 "snap" presidential election. This democratic revolution, involving more than a million Filipinos, was witnessed live by millions of television viewers around the world, and word of it spread far and wide. Its demonstration effects appear to have been particularly strong in other East Asian countries, especially in South Korea, Taiwan, and among elites in China. Soon after the ouster of Marcos, South Korea's own transition to democracy began in earnest. However, a year later, on 13 April 1987, President Chun Doo Hwan suspended all consideration of constitutional reforms necessary for meaningful democratization. This unleashed the tidal wave of protest by enraged students and by a nearly universally disapproving public that was only stemmed when Chun's designated successor, Roh Tae Woo, split with him and conceded entirely to opposition demands, paving the way for the direct presidential elections won by Roh on 16 December 1987.[16]

During the late 1980s, far-reaching, though more incremental, democratic transitions also took place in Taiwan and Thailand. Taiwan's democratic breakthrough came in October 1986, shortly after opposition leaders formed a new political party, the Democratic Progressive Party (DPP). Rather than respond with repression, President Chiang Ching-kuo and the top leaders of the ruling KMT announced the termination of martial law and of the prohibition on other political parties. Throughout the past decade, democratic change in Taiwan has involved this combination of initiatives from above and pressures from below, a process of strategic interaction between government and opposition.[17]

Thailand's breakthrough from a military-dominated, parliamentary semidemocracy to an increasingly authentic and autonomous democratic system can be dated from the accession to the prime ministership of Chatichai Choonhavan, leader of the largest party in Parliament, on 9 August 1988. Under Choonhavan—the first elected member of Parliament to become prime minister since the breakdown of Thailand's previous democratic experiment in 1976—the locus of political power gradually shifted from the military and bureaucracy to political parties and Parliament.[18] However, in another indication of the fragility of democratic progress in the Third Wave, Prime Minister Chatichai's effort to assert greater civilian political control over the military triggered a coup on 23 February 1991.[19] Although the military restored a constitutional electoral regime one year later, its domination by military-backed parties and an unelected prime minister (who led the 1991 coup) brought massive popular demonstrations in May 1992 that led to constitutional changes and new elections. For many observers, these demonstrations were evidence that the movement for real democracy in Thailand, based (as elsewhere in East Asia) among a burgeoning middle class, was coming of age.

The trajectory of development in Korea, Taiwan, and Thailand (though not yet Singapore) suggests that the combination of "liberal economics and illiberal politics" is sustainable only to a certain point, after which a society energized and transformed by liberal economic growth demands and requires liberal politics as well. Three decades of quantitative research and historical change give strong support to the thesis of a positive causal relationship between economic development and democracy.[20] From the experience of Thailand and of many other countries, we know that this relationship is not linear. Nevertheless, over time, it can be powerful.

Though its per capita GNP is only half Thailand's $1,000, Indonesia has experienced continuous and often vigorous economic growth over the past two decades that has "laid the foundations for 'sustained and relatively rapid growth' over the next decade," even possibly the "economic miracle . . . that doubles real incomes in ten years and lifts whole countries out of poverty in two generations."[21] Ironically, this steady and impressive performance is making the military a victim of its own success. Its corporatist-authoritarian domination of political and social life is beginning to wear thin. The combination of obvious accomplishment by its ruling elite—in eliminating the threats that brought it to power—with aging leadership and growing divisions within that elite is generating the political conditions for a democratic opening, "an opportunity for democratization." And the growth in sophistication, resources, and autonomy of organized groups in civil society is generating democratic pressure and mobilization from below.[22]

Opportunity does not guarantee a successful transition, however. China's brutal suppression of prodemocracy demonstrations in Tiananmen Square in June 1989 "left in its wake a regime that is the weakest in PRC history," although the underlying trends—including the continuing shift of economic power to private enterprises and the growth in independent media—suggest the likelihood of renewed democratic progress when the current aging leadership dies off.[23] Burma's transition out of a disastrous three decades of one-party military rule was completely aborted when the military junta refused to honor the results of the People's Assembly elections it called on 28 May 1990, in which the opposition National League for Democracy won 80 percent of the seats despite massive official harassment and arrest of its leaders.[24] The subsequent arrest and torture of numerous democratic leaders and detention under house arrest of the leader of the democratic movement, Daw Aung San Suu Kyi (winner of the 1991 Nobel Peace Prize), indicated an indefinite prolongation of authoritarian rule.[25]

Elsewhere in Asia, some longstanding or emergent democracies have visibly eroded in recent years. Sri Lanka has been plagued by ethnic hatred, terrorist violence, state repression, and virtual civil war. India's democracy has been so seriously marred by rising electoral and terrorist violence, deteriorating human rights, escalating religious, caste, and ethnic conflict, political corruption and opportunism, and decay of the party system that Freedom House downgraded its status in 1992 to "partly free." Belying notions of monolithic democratic progress in the world, this one change caused the sharpest decline in the proportion of the world's population living in "free states" since Indira Gandhi's declaration of emergency in 1975.[26] Barely recovered from its pangs of birth (completed only after the violent death of the military president, Zia ul Haq), Pakistan's new democracy deteriorated significantly in August 1990 when the 20–month-old government of Benazir Bhutto was toppled in irregular fashion, on the apparent urging of the military, amidst charges and evidence of massive corruption.[27]

Like China, Vietnam has been experiencing significant pressure for democratization from intellectuals, journalists, students, and ordinary peasants and laborers, who have staged numerous protest demonstrations and riots since 1988, despite a pervasive totalitarian machinery of surveillance and control capable of brutal repression. Like China, Vietnam embarked some years ago (in 1986) on a political opening. But like China, Vietnam's aging leadership prefers the "road of economic liberalization coupled with political intransigence," and when the press and public began to use the more liberal climate of "renovation" to question Communist rule itself, the party cracked down with a vengeance in 1988. However, like Cuba, Vietnam seems likely to be caught increasingly in the whipsaw of changes at the core of global communism: the demonstration effects of democratization in Eastern Europe and the Soviet Union and the drying up of aid from the latter. Both of these render it more vulnerable to democratic pressure from the West.[28] In addition, the success of the VCP's current drive to modernize the economy figures to generate a "multisectoral economy" and a more pluralistic society that will make a more pluralistic and liberal political system inevitable.[29]

That the Communist regimes of Southeast Asia will not be able to resist the global democratic tide was indicated dramatically in October 1991, when the Communist party in Cambodia declared a formal end to a decade and a half of Communist rule and embraced the principles of multiparty democracy and a free market economy. In conjunction with the signing of an internationally mediated peace accord ending the 12-year civil war and providing for U.N.-supervised democratic elections, this metamorphosis opened the way for the emergence of at least semidemocratic government in one of the poorest and most brutalized countries in the world. At roughly the same time, Laos also abandoned Marxism-Leninism, though it did not legalize opposition parties.

The Middle East, and more particularly the Islamic and largely Arab world stretching from Morocco to Iran, has remained one of the least democratic regions of the world today and, many believe, the one with the bleakest prospects for democracy. This is suggested partly because of the endemic violent conflicts of the region but more substantially because of the deeply authoritarian tendency in Arab cultures and in Islam itself. Such judgments are too sweeping, however. While it is true that, philosophically, Islam "rejects any distinction between the religious community and the political community," and that, empirically, "only two of the 37 countries in the world with Muslim majorities were ever rated 'free' by Freedom House" between 1981 and 1990, so it is also true that "great cultural traditions like Islam and Confucianism are highly complex bodies of ideas, beliefs, . . . and behavior patterns."[30] Moreover, Islam has coexisted with democratization in Turkey and has shown signs of doing so in Pakistan.[31] The determining factor is which interpretation of Islam becomes dominant, and, consequently, the degree to which Islam becomes explicitly mobilized as a political force and a political philosophy of government.

In the Islamic Middle East there is now, more than ever in modern history, some democratic momentum, as a number of longstanding authoritarian regimes—especially in Tunisia, Egypt, Jordan, and Algeria—have found it necessary to liberalize and to search for what Daniel Brumberg terms "a new ruling bargain." Fueling democratic change in the region has been the breakdown of the old ruling bargain that stood for three decades, under which "the ruled traded their rights to independent political activity in return for the rulers' guarantee of social welfare and job security." As that bargain has proven economically unsustainable, the rulers have had to propose a new compact, in which political pluralism and limited if not full democracy are to be exchanged "for popular acquiescence to painful economic reforms."[32]

Algeria's transition to democracy collapsed in 1991 amidst Islamic mobilization and political repression. However, Tunisia, Egypt, and Jordan have moved more gingerly toward semidemocratic structures and liberties. If these do not yield fully open and competitive democracies, in which elections of uncertain outcome fully determine the control of government, neither are they likely to revert back to the much more closed and authoritarian systems of the past.

## Measuring the Global Democratic Trend

Before we can measure the spread of democracy we need a precise and non-ethnocentric definition of the term. Following (and just slightly reformulating) the lead of Robert Dahl in his seminal contribution, *Polyarchy,*[33] Diamond, Linz, and Lipset have defined democracy as

> a system of government that meets three essential conditions: meaningful and extensive *competition* among individuals and groups (especially political parties) for all effective positions of government power, at regular intervals and excluding the use of force; a highly inclusive level of *political participation* in the selection of leaders and policies, at least through regular and fair elections, such that no major (adult) social group is excluded; and a level of *civil and political liberties*—freedom of expression, freedom of the press, freedom to form and join organizations—sufficient to ensure the integrity of political competition and participation.[34]

Implicit in this definition also are the notions that rulers will be held accountable for their actions in the public realm by citizens and their representatives; and that there exist multiple channels for representation of citizen interests beyond the formal political frameworks of parties, parliaments, and elections.[35]

These features of democracy are closely (though not perfectly) captured by Freedom House's annual ratings of political rights and civil liberties in every country of the world. Each country is rated from one to seven on each of these two measures, with one signifying most free and seven most authoritarian.[36] The two ratings (which actually summarize a more detailed "raw point score" of 0 to 44) are then aggregated into three broad categories: "free," "partly free," and "not free."[37] These categories do not entirely overlap with other groupings of countries into, for example, democracies, semidemocracies, and authoritarian/totalitarian regimes. Elsewhere, I have proposed a typology of seven regime types, moving in step fashion from the most highly closed and authoritarian to the stable and fully liberal and institutionalized democracies.[38] Tracing the movements between these seven categories over the past decade shows even more dramatic progress than is revealed by the movement between the categories of free, partly free, and not free. The two most extremely authoritarian regime types, which I call "state hegemonic" regimes, remained stable in number between 1980 and 1989 but declined sharply between 1989 and 1991 (from 41 percent to 30 percent of all states). There are also significantly fewer moderately authoritarian regimes and more semidemocracies. Most encouragingly, in the three most democratic categories, the biggest increase has come in the most democratic regime type ("stable, liberal democracies"), an increase from 18 to 29 between 1980 and 1991. Democracy, it appears, is becoming not only more common in the world but more rooted.

The broad trends may be seen in Table 3.1, which shows the numbers of states rated free, partly free, and not free for 1972 (the first year of the Freedom House survey), 1980, and 1991. The number of democracies (or "free" states) in the world has grown steadily over the past 20 years, increasing by 10 states from 1972 to 1980 and by another 23 states from 1980 to 1991. Part of the increase during the 1970s was due to the growth in the number of independent states, with the final phase of European decolonization producing fairly stable new democratic states in such countries as Papua New Guinea, Belize, and a number of island ministates in the Caribbean and South Pacific. However, the percentage of countries rated "free" also increased slightly during the 1970s, and there was a much more substantial decline—from 46 to 36 percent—in the proportion of states that were solidly authoritarian, or "not free." The period 1980–1991 witnessed even more significant democratic progress, with "free" states increasing from about 32 to an unprecedented 44 percent of all the world's states, and the proportion of "not free" states continuing to decline to 24 percent.[39] Part of this progress reflected substantial change during 1990 and 1991, with 16 more states moving into the democratic category and four falling from it (see Table 3.2 for specific states).[40] Perhaps just as significantly, the number of "not free" states declined by 18 from 1989 to 1991, reflecting widespread movement in Africa in particular.[41]

**Table 3.1  Freedom Status[a] of Independent States**

|  | 1972 | | 1980 | | 1991 | |
|---|---|---|---|---|---|---|
|  | Number | Percentage | Number | Percentage | Number | Percentage |
| Free | 42 | 29.0 | 52 | 31.9 | 75 | 43.8 |
|  |  | (32.0)[b] |  | (35.9) |  | (25.3) |
| Partly Free | 36 | 24.8 | 52 | 31.9 | 55 | 32.2 |
|  |  | (21.0) |  | (21.6) |  | (43.0) |
| Not Free | 67 | 46.2 | 59 | 36.2 | 41 | 24.0 |
|  |  | (47.0) |  | (42.5) |  | (31.8) |
| Total | 145[c] | 100 | 163[d] | 100 | 171[e] | 100 |

*Source: Freedom in the World 1990–91* (New York: Freedom House, 1991), and *Freedom Review* 23, no. 1 (1992).

[a]States designated as "free" are rated at least 2 on political rights and at least 3 on civil liberties; "partly free" states are rated from 3 to 6 on political rights and on civil liberties, but with a combined freedom score not exceeding 11; and "not free" states are rated 5 to 7 on both political rights and civil liberties, with a combined score of at least 11. (Countries scoring a total of 11 are rated "partly free" or "not free" by the judgment of Freedom House.)

[b]Figures in parentheses represent percentages of world population living in countries in each category.

[c]Vietnam is listed as two states. I have counted South Africa as one (not free) state, though the Freedom House survey presented separate ratings that year for White and Black South Africa.

[d]Divided Cyprus was counted as a single country.

[e]Includes a number of newly independent states and lists Cyprus as two states, but lists the newly reunited Germany and Yemen each as single states.

**Table 3.2 Changes in Democratic Status 1974–1991**

| States which suffered democratic breakdowns or erosion between 1974 and 1991[a] | States which experienced democratic transitions between 1974 and 1990[b] | States which became democratic during 1991 |
|---|---|---|
| Antigua & Bermuda[c] (1991) | Argentina (1984) | Bangladesh |
| Burkina Faso (1980) | Bolivia (1982) | Benin |
| Colombia[c] (1989) | Brazil (1985) | Bulgaria |
| Cyprus[c] (1974) | Burkina Faso (1977–1980) | Cape Verde |
| Djibouti (1979) | Chile (1990) | Estonia |
| Dominican Republic[c] (1974) | Cyprus (1987) | Latvia |
| Fiji[c] (1987) | Czechoslovakia (1990) | Lithuania |
| Ghana (1981) | Dominican Republic (1978) | Mongolia |
| Grenada (1980) | Ecuador (1979) | Nepal |
| Haiti (1991) | Ghana (1978–1981) | Sao Tome & Principe |
| India[c] (1975, 1991) | Greece (1974) | Zambia |
| Lebanon[c] (1974) | Grenada (1985) | |
| Nigeria (1983) | Honduras (1984) | |
| Pakistan[e] (1990) | Hungary (1980) | |
| Peru[c] (1989) | Namibia (1990) | |
| Philippines[c] (1990) | Nicaragua[d] (1990) | |
| Seychelles (1977) | Nigeria (1979–1983) | |
| Sri Lanka[c] (1983) | Pakistan[d] (1988–1990) | |
| Sudan (1989) | Panama[d] (1990) | |
| Suriname (1980) | Peru (1980–1989) | |
| Thailand (1991) | Philippines (1987–1990) | |
| Turkey (1980) | Poland (1990) | |
| | Portugal (1974) | |
| | South Korea (1987) | |
| | Spain (1977) | |
| | Sudan (1986–1989) | |
| | Thailand (1989–1991) | |
| | Turkey[d] (1983) | |
| | Uruguay (1985) | |

*Source: Freedom in the World 1990–91* (New York: Freedom House, 1991), and *Freedom Review* 23, no. 1 (1992).

[a]Excludes El Salvador, Guatemala, and Vanuatu, which qualify technically but where the changes have been slight and subtle.

[b]Excludes Gambia, Malta, and Mauritius, which declined to "partly free" status only temporarily and by a small degree, and Guatemala and El Salvador, because of continuing military dominance of those polities. The first date in parentheses marks the first year a country was rated democratic, or "free"; a second date indicates the year of a breakdown or erosion of democracy.

[c]Indicates movement from free to partly free (semidemocratic).

[d]Included even though it is (or was) classified as "partly free" by Freedom House.

[e]Counted as a democratic erosion with the downfall of the Benazir Bhutto government in 1990, even though it had never been rated as "free" by Freedom House.

As indicated in Table 3.2, roughly 29 countries could be said to have experienced transitions to democracy between 1974 (the beginning of the "third wave") and the end of 1990, and during 1991, 11 more countries joined that list.[42] Before 1990, however, all four of the African transitions (Burkina Faso, Ghana, Nigeria, and Sudan) ended in military coups, while the new democratic states of Africa have yet to be tested. Moreover, many of the democratic transitions have yet to be completed, much less consolidated, as indicated by the relatively low scores on civil liberties (and even political rights) of such new or renewed multiparty regimes as those in Turkey, Pakistan, South Korea, and the Philippines. In fact, more than 20 countries that have had democratic government at some point during the "third wave" are no longer fully democratic today; we may note here the deterioration in recent years of Pakistan, the Philippines, and Peru, all "third wave" democracies, as well as the decline of longstanding democracies in Colombia and, more disputably, India. A number of countries have gone from authoritarianism to democracy (or near-democracy) and back to fully authoritarian rule during the third wave. Clearly, one important feature of the third wave is not simply movement toward democracy but more general political fragility and instability.

Before proceeding to analyze the global trend toward democracy, one other point about the "free" or democratic states is worth noting. They are much more likely to be found among the world's "microstates"—those with less than one million people. Such states were much more likely (57 percent) to be democratic in 1990 than states with more than one million people (34 percent). Microstates are also much less likely to have the most extreme form of authoritarian rule; only one of 37 rated a 13 or 14 on the Freedom House scale for 1990. This correlation may in turn be related to another curious fact, the extraordinarily high levels of democracy among the world's island states (mainly microstates but including such larger states as Japan, the Philippines, and Sri Lanka). More than half are democracies; four in five have at least a semidemocratic form of government. Almost all enjoy at least some degree of political pluralism and openness. Why this is so may constitute one of the more interesting and neglected questions in the study of democracy. Certainly it is salient that most of these were colonized at one point or another by Britain, which has left a legacy of political institutions and culture much more conducive to democratic success than that of any other major European colonizer.[43] Island countries may also benefit from the relative security of not having a landed border that must be defended, permitting the maintenance of a much smaller army.[44] They are also more open to and involved in international trade.

## Causes of the Democratic Trend

It is well beyond the scope (and space constraints) of this chapter to survey in any comprehensive way the multiple factors that have helped to foster and sustain the growth of democracy in the world.[45] Rather, the focus will be on the key factors that have been propelling the global democratic trend, and particular attention will be paid to the relative weight and interplay of domestic and international factors. Before coming to the latter, let us consider two types of domestic factors: (1) divisions within and failures of the departing authoritarian regimes; and (2) changes in the development, organization, consciousness, and mobilization of civil society.

## Authoritarian Divisions and Failures

In their important study of transitions from authoritarian rule, O'Donnell and Schmitter flatly assert "that there is no transition whose beginning is not the consequence—direct or indirect—of important divisions within the authoritarian regime itself, principally along the fluctuating cleavage between hard-liners and soft-liners."[46] Their compelling analysis, based on cumulative evidence from their case studies of democratic transitions in southern Europe and Latin America, shows that the central dynamic of the transition process is constituted by the strategic divisions and interactions among contending regime factions and between the regime and the opposition. Looking to Asia and Africa as well, one would be hard pressed to find cases where divisions within the leadership, or at least in the support base of the authoritarian regime, did not constitute a central factor pressing for or permitting transition. Certainly in all cases of democratic transition (as O'Donnell and Schmitter also emphasize, along with Dankwart Rustow, Juan Linz, and others), the choices, behaviors, and strategies of a relatively small number of leaders in regime and opposition—including the conflicts they wage, the understandings they reach, and the agreements they negotiate—are critical in determining whether, how, and at what pace a democratic transition will be effected.[47]

Everywhere, then, democratic transitions come about because of shrewd and inept actions and judgments on the part of key elites. In all instances of democratic transition (save those by foreign conquest or revolutionary upheaval), the dictatorship loses its will, its cohesion, and/or its base before it loses its power. But while these dynamics may be nearly universal in the movement toward democracy, their causal primacy is often overrated. The more compelling question is why the split occurs, why some leaders and supporters of the authoritarian regime come to believe that it must liberalize and then ultimately democratize.

In answer to this prior question, two factors emerge as decisive: Pressure for liberalization builds because of (1) a decline in the regime's political legitimacy and/or (2) a decline in its access to material or coercive resources.

First, the authoritarian regime loses legitimacy—or at least what legitimacy it had—either because it has succeeded in solving the problems that ushered it into power (economic crisis, social polarization, political violence, or insurgency), or because it has failed to realize its self-proclaimed mission. It may also lose legitimacy in part, as we shall see, because societal values have changed to become less tolerant of authoritarian rule. Spain,

Chile, and South Korea are three classic instances of authoritarian regimes that became victims of their own success, producing economic growth and social change that generated new interests and coalitions in society demanding democratic change. The repressiveness of the Chilean and South Korean regimes early on and periodically thereafter also served to narrow their support bases. Although their democratic transitions have been more incremental, evolutionary, and ambiguous (and now in the case of Thailand, clearly reversible), Thailand and Taiwan also saw a narrowing of support for authoritarian rule and defections from authoritarian commitment at the very top because of the economic success and social change effected by their respective regimes. By contrast, democratic transitions were more or less forced upon the authoritarian regimes in Greece, Argentina, Uruguay, the Philippines, and Eastern Europe precisely because they had proven themselves such miserable failures economically and politically. The Greek, Argentine, and Portuguese transitions were also ignited or hastened by stunning military setbacks (in the cases of Argentina and Greece, in wars recklessly initiated by the regime).[48] By the late 1980s, even the Communist party elites no longer believed in the efficacy of the systems in Eastern Europe. The staggering failures of authoritarian regimes in Africa are also a crucial reason why their legitimacy and viability have been rapidly crumbling; the average economic growth rate for the continent (south of the Sahara) in the past decade has been minus 2.2 percent, not to mention the pervasive corruption and human rights abuses.[49] In these cases of regime failure, too, one can locate divisions in the authoritarian coalition that have opened the way for transition, but the origin of change lies in their failures rather than their divisions.

Of course, authoritarian regimes are capable of surviving with much less legitimacy than democratic ones. In fact, the Communist regimes of Eastern Europe persisted for four decades amidst manifest signs of an extremely narrow and largely superficial and cynical base of "legitimacy." A number of personalistic, or what Linz terms "sultanistic,"[50] regimes in the less developed countries persist not because of any belief in their moral entitlement to rule, but because they are able to mobilize and manipulate the material resources necessary to buy support and the coercive resources adequate to repress opposition. Where civil society is weakly organized and extremely poor in resources and information, it may not take much in the way of bribes and force to sustain a dictatorship for a long time.

A *shrinkage* in resources, however—often occurring rather abruptly—is the second factor that brings down dictatorships. Such a decline—in material, symbolic, and coercive resources—is often due to changes in the international environment. The Eastern European Communist regimes fell, as most of them would have thirty years ago, when the essential prop of Soviet coercive backing was withdrawn by Mikhail Gorbachev. In addition to negating the Brezhnev doctrine, Gorbachev made a number of decisions and interventions during the fateful months of 1988 and 1989 that undermined the Communist regimes in Poland, East Germany, Czechoslovakia, and Bulgaria (especially the hard-liners who controlled the latter three).[51] Communist regimes in Angola, Mozambique, Ethiopia, Cuba, and Vietnam are unraveling, or have collapsed, partly because the Soviet financial, commodity, and military aid on which they have been massively dependent has dried up. The current wave of authoritarian crises in Africa has been partly generated by the critical resource scarcities they face at both the societal and regime levels. This has a deeply wounding double edge: On the one hand, popular support or even tolerance for the regime evaporates, because living conditions decline severely, often deteriorating further with the imposition of harsh adjustment measures. On the other hand, the regime's active support coalition dissolves as well, because it can no longer find the money to pay off strategic elites. Western governments and multilateral institutions finally tire of throwing away money to subsidize the larceny and repression of these despots.

Thus, steep or sudden declines in either political legitimacy or material or coercive resources—or very often, both of these—can split an authoritarian regime and induce it to vacate power. But this gives us only a very partial view, from the top of the regime down. Often, the real locus of change lies in what is either percolating from the bottom up or raining down on the regime and society from outside.

## Changes in Civil Society

While their theory of democratic transition is heavily elite-centered, Schmitter and O'Donnell do recognize the importance of ferment and mobilization in civil society. However, their argument is inadequate to comprehend the democratic trend throughout the world for two reasons. First, the image of civil society they present, which is largely accurate for their European and Latin American cases, is one of resurrection, resurgence, restructuring: the return to open expression and activity of pre-existing structures. Missing is the process of development and change that transforms many societies, creating organizations and capacities that never existed before. Second, they locate the critical contribution of civil society exclusively during the period after the authoritarian regime has split and after the "soft-liners," now in the ascendancy, have begun to open and liberalize the regime. At this point, an "upsurge" of popular mobilization pushes the transition forward, keeping it on track through its now-demonstrated potential for eruption.

To begin with, we need to examine again what causes the split in the regime, or in this model, the emergence of the soft-liners. O'Donnell and Schmitter advance early on (but do not develop) this crucial point: that what turns some hard-liners into soft-liners "is their increasing recognition that the regime they helped to implant . . . will have to make use, in the foreseeable future, of some degree or some form of electoral legitimation," and thus will have to begin by introducing certain freedoms.[52] Most such "visionary" regime liberalizers undertake democratic reform not out of any intrinsic commitment or conversion to democratic norms, but for hardheaded, calculating, strategic reasons. They foresee or recognize that they cannot hold on indefinitely to absolute power. The reason they cannot is often the real origin of democratic transitions: the changes and mobilization in civil society.

While some limited authoritarian regimes (e.g., recent military regimes in Turkey and Nigeria) get out in due time because they never intended to remain indefinitely in power, most authoritarian rulers abandon power because they see they cannot hold it indefinitely, at least not without costs they do not wish to pay. And they cannot hold it because society will not let them.

Any one of several changes may explain why society will no longer condone the continuation of authoritarian rule. The predominant values and norms in the society may have altered over time to reduce tolerance for repression and concentration of power and to stimulate demands for freedom. In much of Latin America during the 1970s and early 1980s, this value change among influential groups in society came about partly as a result of the experience of brutal repression, which brought in its wake a "revalorization" of democracy, especially on the left.[53] As people come to place a higher value on political freedom and civil liberties—in and for themselves—they also become more inclined to speak out, demonstrate, and organize for democratization, beginning with the denunciation of human rights abuses.

In addition to changing norms and values, the alignment of interests in society may shift. As O'Donnell and Schmitter note, an important turning point in the transition to democracy comes when privileged elements of society—landowners, industrialists, merchants, and bankers—who had been part of the regime's support base "come to the conclusion that the authoritarian regime is dispensable" (again, either because it has succeeded or because it has failed) and that its continuation might damage their long-term interests.[54] Such large-scale shifts in strategic elite interests were crucial in bringing about the democratic transition in the Philippines and have also been visible more incrementally in Thailand, Taiwan, and, perhaps now embryonically, in Indonesia. They constitute a major element among the forces pressing for democratic transition in South Africa, where the major white industrial and banking interests have been among the leading critics of apartheid, because they see it as inconsistent with the long-term security of a capitalist system increasingly dependent on skilled black labor.

A third change in society that may undermine authoritarian rule derives from the growth of formal and informal organizations in civil society, and from their expanding resources, autonomy, and self-confidence. This profound development can radically alter the balance of power in the country, as an authoritarian regime that could once easily dominate and control the society is thrown on the defensive. It is this phenomenon that underlies the "upsurge" of popular mobilization that O'Donnell and Schmitter describe. Students march in the streets demanding change. Workers paralyze key industries. Lawyers refuse to cooperate any longer in legal charades. Alternative sources of information pierce and then shatter the veil of secrecy and disinformation. Local development groups break the dependence of peasants on landlords or the state and generate alternative sources of power and activity. Informal networks of production and exchange emerge that deny the state resources and control. Not all of these developments are necessarily positive in their implications for the development of democracy, but they all contribute in a cumulative way to the erosion and destruction of authoritarian control.

What is striking about the process of socioeconomic development is that it tends, in the long run, to generate all three of these changes. At the individual level, increasing education, income, and social/occupational status foster more democratic norms, values, and behaviors. People become more tolerant of differences and opposition, more valuing of freedom, more interested and better informed about politics, more inclined to participate in politics and to join organizations, more politically effective, and thus, more politically confident and assertive.[55] Changes in the class structure associated with more advanced stages of economic development may also foster norms and attitudes favoring democratization. While early stages of economic development often aggravate inequality (Taiwan being a notable exception), after a certain middling point development tends to reduce inequality and mitigate feelings of relative deprivation and injustice in the lower class, thus reducing the likelihood of extremist politics polarized around class divisions.[56] Even where inequality in money income is not much reduced, development broad enough to improve the living standards and opportunities of all classes of people may profoundly strengthen the democratic prospect by reducing the mass poverty that is a breeding ground for religious and ethnic, if not class-conscious, extremism.[57] (Alternatively, uneven development, too, can generate democratic pressure, in the form of a new threat to social and political stability that the dictatorship is ill-equipped to resolve.)

Socioeconomic development may also alter interest coalitions. Shrewder and more visionary economic and political elites are likely to see that the defeat or withering away of extremist threats renders authoritarianism obsolete, or that the political system must open and enlarge its boundaries to incorporate newly assertive social groups, or that the contradictions engendered by uneven development under authoritarian rule—as in Brazil and South Africa—must be mitigated if stability is to be preserved. The perspective of these elites will be altered in conjunction with changes in the nature and interests of the bourgeoisie, as a country moves into higher stages of industrial development that increase the size of the middle class and reduce the power of populist labor and peasant organizations. "The potential threats to democracy thus declined, and those (middle class) groups became increasingly confident of their ability to advance their interests through electoral politics."[58]

Finally, socioeconomic development pluralizes and empowers civil society, for development involves not just growth in overall economic output but a vast array of interrelated transformations. Society becomes more differentiated as people move into a much more complicated and specialized array of occupations and functions. Urbanization fosters wider and more numerous overlapping circles of communication and interaction. Communication expands, as does intellectual life in general. The sheer quantity of information available to citizens increases, as well as the intellectual resources that enable them to make sense of it. Control over information becomes less, not more, centralized as telephones, photocopiers, fax machines, computers, modems, satellite television dishes, and other modern technologies become physically and financially accessible to a much wider range of people. All these developments promote a more pluralistic civil society, creating a citizenry more inclined to organize through structures and for goals independent of those sanctioned by the state.

In much of the world, it is this secular increase in independent organizational capacity and density that represents the real indigenous origin of the democratic trend. And this is not a new development; it was a crucial dimension in the spread and invigoration of democracy in the United States almost two centuries ago,[59] and in the mobilization for and subsequent success of democracy in India before and after independence.[60] In Eastern Europe, the Soviet Union, and China, the growth of autonomous organizational, cultural, and intellectual life, surreptitious at first, has formed the cutting edge of movements for democracy.[61] Democratic change in Taiwan during the 1980s has been stimulated and advanced by a host of social movements—of consumers, workers, women, aborigines, farmers, students, teachers, and the environmentally concerned—breaking free of traditional deference or of state intimidation and control to seek both specific demands and long-range goals.[62] Similar developments have been deepening the democratization process in Thailand in recent years and perhaps inaugurating it in Indonesia, where the rapid proliferation of private development organizations has increased awareness and autonomous activity in the countryside, while diminishing the hegemony of the state.[63]

In the Philippines under Marcos, Nigeria under the military, Kenya under Moi, and before that Latin America under various military regimes, associations of all kinds—often initially of students, intellectuals, lawyers, and human rights workers, and then of trade unions, business associations, manufacturers, women, doctors, teachers, and peasants—have been crucial in keeping democratic aspirations alive, protesting authoritarian abuses, and then pressuring for democratization.[64] Particularly in Africa, the widespread growth of informal organizations and movements, and of political participation in them, has come to constitute the chief pressure and hope for democratization in much of the continent.[65] Religious institutions, especially the Catholic Church, have been prominent in the movements of a great many countries—notably, Brazil, Chile, El Salvador, Nicaragua, the Philippines, South Korea, Poland, Haiti, South Africa, and most recently Kenya—to oppose, denounce, frustrate, and remove authoritarian regimes.[66] Specialized political but nonpartisan organizations, such as the Philippine poll-watching organization, NAMFREL, have also played crucial roles at sensitive moments in the transition process.[67] Finally—as we see, for example, in the Philippines, South Africa, and Nigeria—in countries where the press has been allowed some autonomy, or where an alternative, underground press has emerged, its exposure of abuses and airing of liberal viewpoints has made an important contribution to the momentum for democracy.[68]

## International Factors

International influences and pressures have interacted with and often quickened all of the above processes of authoritarian breakdown. Specific responses to human rights violations and democratic pressures from powerful established democracies, especially the United States, have sometimes served to narrow the domestic support of authoritarian regimes and to aggravate the divisions within them. The pressure exerted by the Carter administration on Uruguay and especially Argentina, through sanctions such as cutoffs in military and economic aid, had this kind of effect, while bringing significant improvement in those human rights situations.[69] Carter administration human rights policies, along with specific diplomatic initiatives, also supported democratic transition in Peru, "prevented an authoritarian relapse" in Ecuador in 1978, and, in that same year deterred electoral fraud in the Dominican Republic's presidential balloting.[70] Reagan administration diplomatic and economic pressure on the authoritarian regimes in Chile and South Korea significantly contributed to democratic transitions in those two countries, while preventing planned military coups in El Salvador, Honduras, and Bolivia in the early 1980s and in Peru in January 1989.[71] Increasing, and increasingly open, dissatisfaction with Ferdinand Marcos in the U.S. Congress and administration, and in U.S. public opinion, undermined his support base in Manila and led him toward the ultimately disastrous step of calling a presidential "snap election."[72] U.S. military intervention (in the form of overflights by U.S. planes based near Manila) helped defeat the 1989 coup attempt in the Philippines, while U.S. invasions restored constitutional democracies in Grenada in 1983 and Panama in 1989. U.S. pressure, both coercive and diplomatic, also figured prominently in the decision of the

Sandinistas to hold early and free elections, as did a mix of other domestic and international factors (the desperate state of the Nicaraguan economy, the uncertainty of continued Eastern bloc aid, the promise of new Western aid after free elections).[73]

Overall, as Huntington concludes, "U.S. support was critical to democratization in the Dominican Republic, Grenada, El Salvador, Guatemala, Honduras, Uruguay, Peru, Ecuador, Panama, and the Philippines," and "it was a contributing factor to democratization in Portugal, Chile, Poland, Korea, Bolivia and Taiwan."[74] Sikkink, however, points out that U.S. human rights pressure has not been particularly effective in Guatemala. He cautions that even superpower pressure for democratization may be ineffective unless it is applied in a comprehensive and forceful manner—clearly conveyed through multiple channels and utilizing a wide range of policy instruments— and unless there exists a moderate faction within the authoritarian regime prepared to be receptive to such pressure.[75]

Both governments and societies do respond to international sanctions, as well as to anticipated rewards. In Taiwan, "the political reform movement was initially triggered" in the early 1970s, when the "forced severance of its formal ties with many Western countries and its loss of membership in the United Nations" catalyzed a wave of new intellectual concern with domestic politics.[76] Sophisticated Taiwanese began to realize that democratization was the only way their country could become politically reintegrated into the world and ultimately accepted as a full partner among the advanced industrial nations. In fact, this is a lesson that is increasingly discerned by East Asian business and professional elites, whose countries are so dependent on international trade. It played an important, if intangible, role in the transition to democracy in South Korea, as Sung-joo Han has noted:

> For a country such as South Korea, which has placed the utmost importance in the promotion of exports, expansion of external relations is an inevitable consequence as well as a requirement of economic growth. In due course the government and the people realize that democratization is the necessary ticket for membership in the club of advanced nations. This provides a strong incentive for political, as well as economic, liberalization at home.[77]

Of course, such conditionality will be more effective the more explicit it is and the more tangible are the rewards at stake. The fact that "democratic practices and respect for fundamental rights and freedoms" are explicitly a requirement for membership in the European Community has been "an important incentive for the consolidation of democratic processes in the Iberian Peninsula," Greece, and now Turkey.[78]

Specific sanctions can also work, especially when reinforced by international demonstration effects and domestic factors. Years of stiffening international sanctions and opprobrium, along with other dramatic changes in the international environment, have been instrumental in inducing key elites in

South Africa's business establishment and ruling National Party to abandon apartheid and opt for a negotiated transition to democracy. Economic sanctions and disinvestment by the Western powers—"as much a psychological as a financial blow"—merged with the decline in global gold prices and domestically generated debt and inflation to produce "protracted recession, capital flight, and a profound sense of isolation. . . . Whites began to realize that unless they came to terms with the political demands of the black population, the economic noose would not loosen." At the same time, the collapse of communism in the Soviet Union and Eastern Europe "removed a perceived external threat, undermining hardliners in the security establishment," while raising concerns among state officials "about South Africa's long-term vulnerability to popular upheaval."[79] That a political system so different from communism would draw such a direct lesson underscores the potency of international demonstration effects, especially in the contemporary world of instant and highly visual communications.

One should also not discount the capacity for authoritarian leaders to read the international environment and learn from comparative experience, however cynically they may be motivated by the sheer instinct for survival. The movement toward a more democratic and constitutional monarchy in Nepal has been facilitated not only by mass pressure from below (stimulated by international demonstration effects) but by the realization of King Birendra that massive repression would ruin the international standing he needs in his aid-dependent country.

*Demonstration and Diffusion Effects.* The pressure for democratic change in South Africa has also been stimulated by political changes in the region, which have added both to the reduction in security threats (with the withdrawal of Cuban troops from Angola) and to the sense of isolation on the part of the administration (with the passage of Namibia to independence under Black majority rule). Yet Black Africa as a whole has in turn been affected by developments in South Africa in the past decade. Since the late 1980s, Africans themselves have been exposing the hypocrisy of demanding political liberties in South Africa that are routinely trampled elsewhere in Black Africa. In condemning the authoritarian abuses and intransigence of the Doe regime in Liberia, for example, a prominent Nigerian newspaper editorialized, "The very same reprehensible practices, which the world has persistently condemned in South Africa, are being daily replicated by the government of an independent African country."[80] Declared Roger Chongwe, chairman of the African Bar Association, "All Africa demands: if South Africa is to have one man, one vote, why not us?"[81] African leaders themselves finally began to concede, as they put it in a statement at their Organization of African Unity summit meeting in July 1990, that they would need "to democratise further our societies and consolidate democratic institutions."[82]

Significantly, that OAU statement on the need for human rights, political accountability, and the rule of law was titled, "The Political and Socio-

Economic Situation in Africa *and the Fundamental Changes Taking Place in the World.*"[83] Africans have shown an acute responsiveness to the democratic wave sweeping through Eastern Europe and across the globe. International diffusion effects have contributed heavily to the eruption of pressures in virtually every country on the continent for more liberal, accountable, responsive, popularly based forms of government. As Nigeria's U.N. ambassador Ibrahim Gambari (who is also an astute political scientist) observed, Africans "listen to the BBC, the Voice of America, Radio Moscow, sometimes in their local language. They're fully aware [of what's been happening in Eastern Europe] and they ask, 'Why not here?'"[84] Indeed, "Many young African protesters, inspired by television images showing Eastern European crowds demonstrating against communism, are seeking to emulate the success of Poles, Hungarians, East Germans, Czechoslovakians, Bulgarians and Romanians in throwing off unpopular one-party governments and demanding multiparty democracy."[85] Even one of the architects of the African one-party state, Tanzania's Julius Nyerere, conceded that his country could learn a "lesson or two" from Eastern Europe.[86]

Of course, the East European democracy demonstrations themselves spread like a wave from one country to the next. What Huntington calls the "snowballing" effect—the phenomenon of earlier transitions "stimulating and providing models for subsequent efforts at democratization"[87]—was clearly evident in 1990 in Bulgaria, Romania, Yugoslavia, Albania, Mongolia, Nepal, much of Africa, and several Arab countries, such as Egypt, Jordan, Tunisia, and Algeria, where the Eastern European upheavals "prompted leaders . . . to open up more political space for the expression of discontent."[88]

As Huntington observes, demonstration effects "remain strongest among countries that [are] geographically proximate and culturally similar."[44] Thus, the impact of Poland's democratic transition spread most rapidly and intensely to its neighbors in Eastern Europe, and their collective transformation has probably had the greatest impact on the countries of the former Soviet Union. As noted earlier, the strongest and most immediate impact of the "people power" democratic revolution in the Philippines was in South Korea. "A month after Cardinal Sin played a central role in the regime change in the Philippines, Cardinal Kim for the first time called for constitutional change and democracy in Korea," and a month after that (in April 1986), Korean democratic opposition leader Kim Dae Jung declared (with specific reference to the Philippines), "This is the time of people's power in the developing countries of Asia. We have never been so sure before."[90]

Diffusion effects also resonate deeply from history; the fact that virtually all of the democratic countries in Asia, Africa, and the Caribbean are former British colonies is striking testimony to the potency of cultural and institutional diffusion, and the current mobilizations against authoritarian regimes in Africa draw in part from this same reservoir of values and institutions that took (fragile) root during colonial rule.

Finally, diffusion effects are typically, by their nature, widespread and long-term. They involve the spread not only of specific models, strategies, and tactics for democratization, but more profoundly, of generic preferences for personal liberty, pluralism, political voice, and market competition. In Taiwan, most of the leaders of the democratic movement that emerged in the 1970s were educated abroad, in law and the social sciences. They returned "ready to apply at home" the "ideas and institutions of a reference society" in the West. "They adopted Western democratic ideals as well as democratic procedures, institutional design, political techniques, and legal frameworks."[91] Through overseas study, economic exchange, and especially the international communications revolution, democratic and antiauthoritarian values, norms, and ways of life have slowly been seeping into the cultures of many undemocratically ruled countries. While the points of contact and influence are initially through elites, the broader diffusion of Western culture, ideas, and information—not only news and opinion but music and entertainment—has had a big impact on mass thinking in many countries.[92]

Technological progress has sharply accelerated the speed and widened the spread of this diffusion.[93] Large proportions of many Third World populations now have access to television, and even more have access to radio. By 1985 there were about 14 radios per 100 people, on average, in Asia and Africa.[94] Given the size of the typical family in many poorer developing countries and the communal character of radio listening in village and urban slum settings, such proportions can translate into some access for over half the adult population. Satellite television and telephone linkages convey news with stunning speed; CNN is now watched routinely by elites in every region of the world. All of these increasingly dense international communication linkages feed a global democratic "zeitgeist" of unprecedented scope and intensity.

The diffusion of democratic values, models, and ideologies is also heightened by the relative absence of alternative visions. This is not just linked to the waxing and waning of intellectual fashions but is grounded in objective realities. Communism, state socialism, and one-party mobilizational regimes have shown themselves to be miserable failures at even the rapid material progress they promised, not to mention the nourishing of the human spirit. As news has spread of these developmental failures, and of the nearly universal corruption and cynicism of party elites and nomenklaturas, peoples living in these countries have been able to place their own national experiences in a wider context. They "could and did ask the relevance for themselves of political events in far-off countries."[95] The failures of individual regimes now appear as systemic flaws in principle and design, not the perversion of an individual experiment gone wrong. State socialism as a system has now been discredited as thoroughly as was fascism in World War II. The only systemic alternative to democracy that remains viable in world politics is the still largely untested Islamic State, but its record of accomplishment in Iran hardly inspires confidence. This does not mean that the demo-cratic alternative can and will succeed everywhere; it does mean that it is the only *systemic* alternative that is empirically and normatively attractive to a broad range of peoples today.

All of these types of diffusion and demonstration effects have helped to divide authoritarian regimes, undermine their legitimacy, erode their support bases, disillusion and embolden their populations, and thus foster transitions to democracy. As indicated above, however, even more forceful and deliber-ate forms of international pressure have also been at work.

*Democratic Assistance.* For the past two years, talk has been escalating among international aid donors of the need for greater political accountabil-ity, participation, and consensus building if recipient countries are to use aid effectively for development. The United States has moved explicitly to es-tablish political democratization as a third condition for assistance (in addi-tion to human rights and economic reforms), and Britain and France have also begun to signal that their aid may favor countries moving toward democracy.[96] Just as political conditionality is likely to induce political openings (however superficial at first), sanctions can undermine dictators, and indeed did so in Benin in 1989–1990.[97] Because of their economic desti-tution and political fragility, most African regimes are heavily dependent on international support. During the past two years, even such longstanding dic-tators as Mobutu Sese Seko in Zaire have been losing economic and security assistance and the external legitimacy they need to sustain their rule.

Of course, while economic, political, and military dependence does ren-der developing countries more susceptible to pressure from abroad, this does not necessarily have democratic consequences. To the extent that powerful external actors pursue economic and strategic goals compatible with, or even requiring, repressive regimes abroad, external intervention may prop up dic-tators and undermine popular struggles for democracy, as it often did during the Cold War.[98]

In recent years, international assistance has increasingly interacted with and strengthened democratizing changes in civil society. Although they are primarily indigenous phenomena, the proliferations of autonomous and largely democratic associations around the world have been aided and abetted by for-eign influence and assistance. Organizational models have spread across bor-ders, including alternatives to the styles and strategies used by Western civic and interest groups. The women's civic movement, *Conciencia*, founded in 1982 by 20 Argentine women "to transform a passive citizenry accustomed to authoritarian governments," now has affiliated movements in 14 other Latin American countries, forming a cooperative network to educate for democracy and to motivate and train women to organize for democracy.[99] And as democrats around the world establish communications and face-to-face links with one another, such models spread across even regional boundaries (inspir-ing, for example, a similar effort in the Philippines).

Financial and technical assistance from the industrialized democracies has played an important and sometimes critical role in the expansion of autonomous democratic organizations and media. For some three decades the four (West) German party foundations (*Stiftungen*) have channeled large amounts of aid and exchange activity to democratic organizations and parties abroad; they continue to spend more money for this purpose than any other network of nongovernmental organizations from the industrialized democracies.[100] A more recent example is the U.S. National Endowment for Democracy (NED), which has had a significant impact since its establishment in 1983.[101] Its extensive efforts in Poland, Chile, and Nicaragua provided critical support to the democratic movements that brought down those dictatorships. Throughout Eastern Europe it helped to build the independent civic infrastructure that undermined communism in the late 1980s, and it is now doing the same in Russia and other post-Soviet states, through more than 20 projects aiding democratic movements, independent publications and research institutes, modern information systems, and (through the Free Trade Union Institute) democratic trade unions. NED efforts were also credited with a major role in facilitating the transitions to democracy in Namibia and Haiti, in part, as we shall discuss later in this chapter, through international projects to observe elections there. NED programs also help to strengthen new and troubled democracies. They provide support to civic education efforts such as that of *Conciencia*; to new democratic political parties, legislatures, judicial systems, electoral systems, and local governments; and to independent trade unions, business associations, and human rights groups. They also advance innovative efforts in many countries to demonstrate the need for economic reform, advise legislatures on economic issues, and promote the teaching of private enterprise principles and techniques.

The globalization of the resource bases of democratic movements is a significant dimension of the global democratic trend. NED's annual budget increased from $17 million to $25 million in fiscal year 1991 and to $27.5 million the following year, despite an unprecedented budget crisis in the United States. If one considers the efforts of the U.S. Agency for International Development, current U.S. spending for democracy promotion is probably about $200 million (or twice that if the relevant programs of the U.S. Information Agency are included).[102] In proportional terms, the German party foundations spend considerably more of their budgets than do U.S. institutions and agencies to promote democratic civic and political life in new, prospective, and struggling democracies (about $100 million on such overseas projects in 1988).[103] There is also a growing network of foundations, both governmental and nongovernmental, in the other established democracies to support democratic initiatives and institutions abroad; Britain established in 1992 a Westminster Foundation for Democracy modeled on NED, and now the Japanese too are showing interest in developing a similar type of political assistance program. By providing resources and technical assistance to nascent democratic institutions, and to democratic groups in civil society, the established democracies are playing an increasingly aggressive, sophisticated, and long-term role in helping to initiate and consolidate democratic transitions.

As we have seen, international factors influencing democratizing movements can be identified in a wide range of forms, styles, and processes. Sometimes these factors can be elusive; often, they may overlap with and amplify each other. In Nicaragua, the democratic opposition triumphed only because it was able to unite almost completely in the broad front of the National Opposition Union (UNO) and its single presidential candidate, Violeta Chamorro. We will probably never know to what extent official and unofficial U.S. actors encouraged those forces to coalesce and remain united, but pressures and inducements were probably considerable. In the Philippines, the challenge of defeating Ferdinand Marcos was similarly threatened by intense factionalism among the opposition, especially between supporters of Corazon Aquino and Salvador Laurel. Although Cardinal Sin appears to have been the decisive force in producing unity around the Aquino candidacy, the "U.S. embassy also played a part by ensuring that the two sides kept talking to one another,"[104] and some U.S. citizens, acting privately, also became involved in mediation between the two camps.

Yet another dimension of the internationalization of the democratic struggle is also reflected in Nicaragua's democratic transition: the role of international election monitoring. In circumstances where democracy is just beginning to emerge after years of oppression or violent conflict, both international observation and international mediation of the electoral process have made a critical contribution to its credibility and hence success. At a minimum, a well-organized team of international observers can help to verify the election results so as to enhance the credibility and legitimacy of the declared victor in a polarized contest, as in South Korea in 1987 and Bulgaria in 1990. In some countries, the presence of observers has deterred an authoritarian or incumbent government from rigging the election or forging or canceling the result, as with the 1988 plebiscite that ended Pinochet's rule in Chile. Where fraud does occur, as in Panama under Noriega and the Philippines under Marcos, observers can demonstrate it and deny it domestic and international acceptance. In all of these cases, international election observers bolster participation and confidence in the electoral process, "by ensuring that the election will either be free or denounced as fraudulent." At times, observers can also go much further, helping bitterly opposed sides to negotiate mutually acceptable terms of the electoral game, and even mediating the implementation of "a collectively guaranteed process of national reconciliation and democratization." This was the formula that ended the civil war in Nicaragua and appears likely to do so in Angola, El Salvador, and Cambodia as well. Official diplomacy—particularly within the context of multilateral organizations such as the OAS and the U.N.—may also help to bring hostile parties to the bargaining table and guarantee an agreement. Many times, the international role is truly indispensable, since mediation and observation of elections requires impartial arbiters whom all sides can trust.[105]

Two other dimensions of the international variable in democratization require mention. First, democratic movements in some countries have drawn significant financial assistance, international political support, and intellectual and strategic counsel from their compatriots working, studying, or living in exile overseas. Taiwanese democratic opposition leaders made an important breakthrough in a 1982 trip to the United States when they discovered not only the salience of U.S. congressional concern for democracy and human rights in Taiwan but a whole network of "overseas Taiwanese organizations, several of whom were already active in the lawful lobbying business." With Taiwan dependent on U.S. trade and security assistance, this discovery helped to establish democratic publics abroad, and especially the U.S. Congress, as an important arena of bargaining and maneuver for Taiwan's democratic activists (an arena where they held the upper hand).[106] Exile communities from countries as diverse as Poland, Nicaragua, Haiti, and Zaire have played important roles in generating U.S. and European pressure for democratization and in aiding democratic movements with their own financial resources. A single Hungarian emigre, Wall Street financier George Soros, contributed more than $15 million in 1990 alone to democratic dissidents and organizations throughout Eastern Europe. He has been assisting such groups for years.[107]

Finally, transnational organizations have strengthened civil society and thereby fostered democratization, wittingly and unwittingly. The most powerful force here has been the Catholic church, which underwent a striking shift in doctrine, "manifested in the Second Vatican Council of 1963–1965," that transformed "national Catholic churches from defenders of the status quo to opponents of authoritarianism."[108] The international democratizing role of the Catholic church gathered momentum with the accession of Pope John Paul II, who spoke out eloquently for human rights, and whose papal visits lent powerful symbolic support at strategic moments to movements for democracy in Poland, Brazil, the Philippines, Argentina, Central America, South Korea, Chile, and Paraguay.[109] Other types of international nongovernmental organizations—for example, the Asia Foundation, the African-American Institute, and Freedom House—have played a more subtle role by supporting the long-term development of independent organizations and think-tanks in civil society.

## Conclusion: Ripe for Diffusion

The world is shrinking rapidly in many respects. With every year, national borders are rendered increasingly porous, as goods, services, people, values, news, symbols, ideas, and technologies pour across them with increasing density and speed. This "global trend of intensifying communication and economic integration" itself constitutes one of the most powerful long-term impulses for the opening and democratization of political regimes.[110] But it also makes the interaction between domestic and international factors increasingly difficult to untangle. In such circumstances, it may eventually become fruitless to try to untangle them or to parcel out the relative weights of their causal contributions. When a women's movement for democracy, indigenous in its conception, staff, and programs but assisted financially from abroad, spreads to a dozen other countries in its region, is that an international or domestic phenomenon? When East Asian elites concede to democratic pressures from their own masses in part because of concern not to isolate themselves and their country internationally, how do we partial out the domestic from the international pressure?

Still, however, the nation-state persists, stubbornly and sometimes with a vengeance. This raises an important caveat in the way we view the diffusion of democracy and the intermingling of domestic and global factors. Domestic factors structure and limit how global influences will be received and acted upon. Images bounce off communications satellites, but different countries receive them in vastly different quantities, with different values and mindsets, and with different propensities for democratic change.

Plainly, the likelihood that a country will effect a transition to democracy during this period of global turbulence and of democratic pressure depends on the degree to which it is "ripe" for democratic diffusion. This is not to say that it must possess certain "preconditions" for democracy; certainly the experiences of India and Costa Rica show that democracy can develop and endure without the kind of wealth that is often assumed to be necessary. Nonetheless, the higher the level of socioeconomic development, the larger the middle class, the more educated the population, the more organized and informed the society, the "riper" it will be for diffusion.

The only absolute requirement for transition (short of foreign conquest and imposition) is a commitment to democratization on the part of strategic elites. But this need not stem from any profound moral conviction or conversion; often in the past elites have embraced democracy as a tactical and instrumental choice, because there was no other good way to resolve their internal divisions or to secure their substantive goals.[111] In such circumstances, democratization may precede the deep changes in political culture and institutions that permit it to endure; these may follow in a "habituation phase" when "both politicians and citizens" come to accept and internalize the new rules and to forge "effective links of party organization."[112]

The importance—and highly contingent nature—of this process of democratic consolidation raises the issue of "ripeness" in a second sense. It is one thing to get to democracy. It is quite another—and often much more difficult—thing to keep it, to consolidate it, to breathe real life and meaning into it, to make it endure. Many of the countries that have made transitions to democracy in the past decade are in grave political crises now because democracy is simply not working to deliver the broad developmental progress, honest and decent government, protection for human rights, and political and social tranquility that people want. Peru has already experienced a suspension of democracy that is due in large measure to this failure, and many other recently established democracies remain vulnerable to either complete overthrow or gradual descent into an illiberal semidemocracy. Indeed, as I have noted repeatedly in this chapter, many of the recently established democracies either have not yet achieved or have not been able to maintain a level of civil liberties and political freedom sufficient to qualify as "free" (and thus, I would argue, as substantively democratic) in the judgment of Freedom House. And those that have made the descent to "partly free" may also be the most vulnerable to complete breakdown. A prime example would be the Philippines, where the democratic regime proved unable, in its first six-year presidential term, to relieve the urgent problems of rural landlessness, communist and Muslim insurgency, nearly pervasive political corruption, and military insubordination.[113] And even before the Fujimori coup in Peru, democratic institutions had been severely hollowed out by economic destitution, raging guerrilla and drug-related violence, and human rights abuses by the military.[114]

Given such conditions, it is difficult to assert that "democracy" has diffused to the Philippines, Pakistan, or Peru, or to Guatemala and El Salvador (at least until the 1992 settlement), where "the military virtually define the extent of civilian authority and influence most aspects of government policy."[115] At best, international democratic pressures, together with domestic democratic aspirations and actors, are locked in a profound contest with antidemocratic forces in these and many other countries that have acquired the formal institutions of democracy during the third wave.

The third wave of democratization has encompassed not only numerous transitions to democracy but, as shown in Table 3.2, about 22 reversals of democracy as well. Half of these were complete breakdowns of democracy. Nine of these reversals have occurred in the three years between 1989 and 1992, raising the question of whether a "third reverse wave" might not already be gathering. One of the most striking features of the global democratic trend as documented by Freedom House is not only the shift toward greater democracy but the intense fluctuation in the level of political and civil liberty as countries attempt this transition. During 1990, Freedom House judged that fully 56 countries—about a third of all the world's independent countries—merited a change in their freedom status (of at least one point on the combined 13–point scale). Thirty-six became more free but 18 became *less* free. (Two showed offsetting changes in political and civil liberties.)[116] In short, we are living in a tremendously turbulent and volatile period in global political history, not only in reference to the relations between nations but to the political conditions within them. Movement, both positive and negative, is likely to be a dominant feature of the coming years.

Does this mean, as Samuel Huntington asks, that we will soon experience a third reverse wave, like the reverse waves of the interwar period and of the 1960s and early 1970s? As Huntington notes, many of the generic causes of those first two reverse waves are still with us, in the form of shallow value commitments to democracy, intense economic problems and social conflicts, dangers of political polarization, resistance of conservative forces to redistribution of power and wealth, terrorism and insurgency. If the difficulties of Peru, the Philippines, and Brazil are characteristic of the new democracies of the third wave, we are likely to see a reverse wave at some time in the next decade. Although there is no coherent contending formula for political legitimacy in the world today, "sustained inability to provide welfare, prosperity, equity, justice, domestic order, or external security could over time undermine the legitimacy even of democratic governments." And the breakdown of even one or two high-profile or regionally powerful democracies—such as Brazil's—"could trigger reverse snowballing."[117] This likelihood would particularly intensify if the nascent and very fragile democratic trend in Russia were to implode into a right-wing authoritarian or fascist dictatorship.

Nor should we be sanguine about the current absence of alternative formulas for political legitimacy. Liberal democracy has its own normative weaknesses that have been exploited historically by

> a heterogeneous set of opponents: Romantic poets, Persian ayatollahs, aristocrats, the Roman Catholic Church, and fascists. For all the real and massive differences that separate these diverse oppositions, one can detect a shared critique. Liberal capitalist democracy is scorned for an inordinate emphasis on individualism, materialism, technical achievement, and rationality; . . . for undervaluing the essential collective dimension of human existence.[118]

The alternative to liberal democracy in some countries may be an Islamic fundamentalist state, or some coherent new revolutionary vision as yet unarticulated. Alternatively, it may be a series of neofascist movements that fall back on the historic passions of ultranationalism or ethnic prejudice. Perhaps many challengers will take the form of the nihilistic "movements of rage" (such as Sendero Luminoso, the Khmer Rouge, or new millenarian sects) that Jowitt believes will be increasingly advanced as a response to chaos and despair in the Third World. Or the alternative may come in the familiar uniforms of a praetorian guard pledged to restore national order and honor. Whatever the form, there will always be an alternative to democracy.

If this third global wave of democracy is to sustain its momentum, the democracies it has brought into being, as well as those, such as India's, that emerged previously—but that have become embattled during the third wave—must actively cultivate the conditions that make democracy not only ripe for diffusion but ripe for persistence; and the wealthy and established democracies must help them to do so. Strong social and economic foundations and strong political foundations are necessary if democracies are to endure. Their economies must be vigorous engines of self-sustaining growth, based on open, market-oriented economic structures. Their societies must be increasingly just and inclusive; a democratic polity that endures will have at its foundation a densely organized, democratically concerned, and informed civil society. Its political foundations will be comprised of effective governance and a well-articulated and reliable rule of law, and durable, coherent political parties with effective ties to major interest groups and internal structures that make them democratically responsive and accountable. These political foundations, in turn, require constitutional formulas that are appropriate for the particular social conditions, cleavages, and culture of the country. This means that the West must be careful to assist the organic development of these institutions in the particular "soil" of each country, without imposing its own particular vision of *how* democracy should work.

The new democracies will also need economic assistance, access to Western markets, and debt relief if they are to show that democracy can work to solve the staggering economic and social problems they face. The international system can play a crucial role in creating the economic space for struggling democracies to undertake badly needed economic transformations with a social safety net and a human face, thereby making them politically sustainable.[119] At the same time, these fragile, unconsolidated, or embattled democracies must show that they can function politically to produce coherent policies and stable, settled political alternatives within the spectrum of democratic norms and values. This will primarily be determined by the degree of vision of the democratic leadership, its ability to choose the right policies and to build political constituencies around them, and to conduct the business of government and politics with probity, respect, and restraint. This is the point at which we confront the limits of the international variable and the considerable weight of domestic political choice.

For the near term, democracy is likely to continue to expand and to manifest itself as a global phenomenon; nevertheless, in most of the world throughout the 1990s, democracy will remain insecure and embattled. During this period there will be new democratic breakdowns as well as many badly functioning, illiberal, and unstable democratic regimes. Whether that will mean the onset of a reverse wave or continuing turbulence within a sustained *long* wave of democratic expansion will depend on the political skill, vision, and judgment of leaders and citizens—both in the new democracies *and* in the established ones that can lend a strategic helping hand.

# Notes

1. R. Bruce McColm, "The Comparative Survey of Freedom: 1990," *Freedom at Issue*, no. 112 (January–February 1990): 6–7.

2. *Freedom Review* 23, no. 1 (January–February 1992): 5.

3. Samuel P. Huntington, *The Third Wave: Democratization in the Late Twentieth Century* (Norman: University of Oklahoma Press, 1991), p. 15.

4. Both Huntington and Freedom House accept a looser standard for classifying a country "democratic" than the one I will use in this paper. I will count as democratic a country that not only has a formally democratic constitutional system but that rates at least a "2" in political rights and "3" in civil liberties on the Freedom House scale, i.e., a country that is rated as "free." That is no small distinction; as noted above, the looser standard yields an estimated 89 democracies in 1991; the more rigorous one, 75. For Huntington's data, through 1990, see *The Third Wave*, Table 1.1, p. 26.

5. See for example, Ken Jowitt, "After Leninism: The New World Disorder," *Journal of Democracy* 2, no. 1 (Winter 1991): 11–20.

6. See his essay, Chapter 2 in this volume, and also "After Leninism."

7. Pauline Baker, "South Africa's Future: A Turbulent Transition," *Journal of Democracy* 1, no. 4 (Fall 1990): 8–24.

8. Richard Joseph, "Africa: The Rebirth of Political Freedom," *Journal of Democracy* 2, no. 4 (Fall 1991): 11–24.

9. For a summary of these and other recent democratic developments in Africa, see *Africa Demos* 1, no. 1 (November 1990) (Publication of the Carter Center of Emory University).

10. Joseph, "Africa: The Rebirth of Political Freedom," p. 15.

11. Kenya's crackdown on the movement for democracy and human rights is detailed in Todd Shields, "Kenya: Lawyers vs. the Law," *Africa Report* (September–October 1990): 13–16; and Gibson Kamau Kuria, "Confronting Dictatorship in Kenya," *Journal of Democracy* 2, no. 4 (October 1991): 115–126.

12. See the articles by Robert A. Pastor, Robert S. Leiken, and Pablo Antonio Cuadra in *Journal of Democracy* 1, no. 3 (Summer 1990): 13–47.

13. Charles Guy Gillespie, "Paraguay After Stroessner: Democratizing a One-Party State," and Humberto Rubin, "Paraguay After Stroessner: One Step Away from Democracy," *Journal of Democracy* 1, no. 4 (Fall 1990): 49–61.

14. Carlos Alberto Montaner, "Castro's Last Stand," *Journal of Democracy* 1, no. 3 (Summer 1990): 71–80; Susan Kaufman Purcell, "Cuba's Cloudy Future," *Foreign Affairs* 69, no. 3 (Summer 1989): 113–130.

15. Wayne Cornelius, "Mexico: Salinas and the PRI at the Crossroads," *Journal of Democracy* 1, no. 3 (Summer 1990): 61–70.

16. Sung-joo Han, "South Korea: Politics in Transition," in *Democracy in Developing Countries, Vol. 3: Asia*, ed. Larry Diamond, Juan J. Linz, and Seymour Martin Lipset (Boulder, CO: Lynne Rienner, 1989), pp. 284–292.

17. Tun-jen Cheng, "Democratizing the Quasi-Leninist Regime in Taiwan," *World Politics* 41, no. 4 (July 1989): 471–499; Tun-jen Cheng and Stephan Haggard, "Taiwan in Transition," *Journal of Democracy* 1, no. 2 (Spring 1990): 62–74.

18. Clark D. Neher, "Change in Thailand," *Current History* 89, no. 545 (March 1990): 101–104, 127–130; Scott Christensen, "Thailand after the Coup," *Journal of Democracy* 2, no. 3 (Summer 1991): 94–106. For useful background on developments through 1987, see Chai-Anan Samudavanija, "Thailand: A Stable Semi-Democracy," in Diamond, Linz, and Lipset, *Democracy in Developing Countries: Asia*, pp. 305–346.

19. *New York Times*, 24 February 1991, p. 6; Christensen, "Thailand after the Coup," pp. 99–100. The military also cited political corruption to justify its take-over domestically and internationally, but its primary motives appear to have been personal and institutional power, rather than "saving" the country.

20. Larry Diamond, "Economic Development and Democracy Reconsidered," *American Behavioral Scientist* 35, nos. 4–5 (March–June 1992): 450–499.

21. *The Economist*, 17 November 1990, pp. 37–38.

22. R. William Liddle, "Regime in Crisis? Presidential Succession, the East Timor Massacre, and Prospects for Democratization in Indonesia" (Paper presented to the Forty-fourth Annual Meeting of the Association for Asian Studies, 2–5 April 1992), p. 26; and "Indonesia's Democratic Past and Future," *Comparative Politics* 24, no. 4 (July 1992): 443–462.

23. Andrew Nathan, "Is China Ready for Democracy?" *Journal of Democracy* 1, no. 2 (Spring 1990): 56; see Minxin Pei, "Societal Takeover in China and the USSR," *Journal of Democracy* 3, no. 1 (January 1992): 108–118.

24. Robert H. Taylor, "Burma's Ambiguous Breakthrough," *Journal of Democracy* 1, no. 4 (Fall 1990): 62–72.

25. *The Economist*, 20 October 1990, p. 37, 17 November 1990, p. 43; *New York Times*, 26 October 1990.

26. *Freedom Review* 23, no. 1 (1992): 6. On India's recent democratic woes, see Atul Kohli, "Indian Democracy: Stress and Resilience," *Journal of Democracy* 3, no. 1 (January 1992): 52–64; Atul Kohli, ed., *India's Democracy: An Analysis of Changing State-Society Relations* (Princeton, NJ: Princeton University Press, 1988); Paul Brass, *The Politics of India since Independence* (Cambridge: Cambridge University Press, 1990); James Manor, "India after the Dynasty," *Journal of Democracy* 1, no. 3 (Summer 1990): 102–113; Atul Kohli, "From Majority to Minority Rule: Making Sense of the 'New' Indian Politics," in *India Briefing, 1990*, ed. Marshall M. Bouton and Philip Oldenburg (Boulder, CO: Westview, 1990), pp. 1–24; *The Economist*, "India Survey," 4 May 1991, pp. 15–28; Barbara Crossette, "India's Descent," *New York Times Magazine*, pp. 27–31, 57, 60, 67.

27. *Washington Post*, 9 August 1990; *The Economist*, 8 September 1990, p. 36. Ms. Bhutto's subsequent shattering defeat at the polls was not judged by outside election observers to have been the work of massive rigging; but the military-backed interim government's control of the media, which was used relentlessly to discredit her, as well as violence and intimidation against members of her Pakistan People's Party, suggest that the election was anything but "free and fair." See *The Economist*, 27 October 1990, p. 35; and Kiren A. Chaudry, "In Pakistan, A Candidate Flees," *New York Times*, 26 October 1990.

28. Vo Van Ai, "Reform Runs Aground in Vietnam," *Journal of Democracy* 1, no. 3 (Summer 1990): 81–91.

29. *Washington Post*, 13 October 1990.

30. Huntington, *The Third Wave*, pp. 307–310. This discussion also appears in Samuel P. Huntington, "Democracy's Third Wave," *Journal of Democracy* 2, no. 2 (Spring 1991): 16–18.

31. See the respective case studies on Turkey and Pakistan by Ergun Ozbudun and Leo Rose in Diamond, Linz, and Lipset, *Democracy in Developing Countries: Asia*.

32. Daniel Brumberg, "Islam, Elections, and Reform in Algeria," *Journal of Democracy* 2, no. 1 (Winter 1991): 58–71.

33. Robert A. Dahl, *Polyarchy: Participation and Opposition* (New Haven, CT: Yale University Press, 1971).

34. Larry Diamond, Juan J. Linz, and Seymour Martin Lipset, eds., *Democracy in Developing Countries,* 4 vols. (Boulder, CO: Lynne Rienner, 1988 and 1989), p. xvi.

35. Philippe C. Schmitter and Terry Lynn Karl, "What Democracy Is . . . and Is Not," *Journal of Democracy* 2, no. 3 (Summer 1991): 75–88.

36. For a concise explanation of the meaning of each of these scores, see the explanation in any of the annual Freedom House volumes; for example, Raymond D. Gastil, ed., *Freedom in the World: Political Rights and Civil Liberties 1988–1989* (New York: Freedom House, 1989), pp. 31 and 38–39, or *Freedom in the World . . . 1990–1991*, pp. 53–54.

37. Countries are rated "free" if their combined score on civil liberties and political rights is 5 or lower; "partly free" if their combined score is between 6 and 11; and "not free" if their combined score is from 11 to 14. For countries with combined scores of 11, the raw point scores are consulted to determine their category: 0–14, not free; 15–29, partly free. See *Freedom in the World, 1990–1991*, p. 51. The current classification involves a slight change from the procedure used when the survey was under the direction of Gastil.

38. Larry Diamond, "Ripe for Diffusion: International and Domestic Factors in the Global Trend toward Democracy" (Paper presented to the annual meeting of the International Studies Association, Vancouver, 20–23 March 1991). This chapter represents an updated and condensed version of that paper. The seven regime types (and their corresponding range of freedom scores) were: state hegemonic, closed (13–14); state hegemonic, partially open (11–12); noncompetitive, partially pluralist (10); semicompetitive, partially pluralist (7–9); competitive, partially illiberal (5–6); competitive, pluralist, partially institutionalized (3–4); and stable, liberal democracy (20).

39. Although comparable ratings for political rights and civil liberties do not exist prior to 1972, it is a reasonable conjecture that this proportion of "not free" states is the lowest since the bulk of the world's nation-states came into being after World War II. It is also likely that the percentage of the world's population (31.77) living in "not free" political circumstances in 1991 is the lowest ever in modern history.

40. Two countries that joined the Freedom House list of independent democratic states in 1991, Micronesia and the Marshall Islands, are not listed in Table 3.2 as democratic transitions, because they had long been democratic when they were grouped among the related territories of the United States in previous years of the survey.

41. Such quantitative assessments are bound to vary from one to another depending on the data source and rating criteria. In *The Third Wave* (p. 26), Huntington counts 58 democratic states in 1990, out of a total of 129 with over one million population—or 45 percent. However, in 1990, only 44 states with one million population were rated as "free" by Freedom House, representing 34 percent of the total. Huntington's larger count resulted from the fact that he included as "democratic" a number of countries—such as Turkey, Peru, the Philippines, Colombia, Guatemala, El Salvador, Bulgaria, and Romania—that were rated only partly free by Freedom House in 1990. While the line between democracy and semidemocracy inevitably involves difficult judgments, I believe the classifications of Bulgaria and Romania as democratic in 1990 were premature, and those for Guatemala and El Salvador were incorrect because of military dominance and human rights problems. At the conceptual level, it is a serious fallacy to accept as "democratic" countries that have civilian, constitutional, electoral systems but lack other important attributes of democracy, as virtually all of the above countries do. This is precisely why Diamond, Linz, and Lipset, in *Democracy in Developing Countries* (p. xvii), reserved the term *semidemocratic* for

those countries where effective power of elected officials is so limited, or political party competition is so restricted, or the freedom and fairness of

elections so compromised that electoral outcomes, while competitive, still deviate significantly from popular preferences; and/or where civil and political liberties are so limited that some political orientations and interests are unable to organize and express themselves.

42. These countries are also listed in Table 3.2, along with a 12th, Haiti, which entered and exited the list the same year (and which probably would not have qualified as fully "free" by Freedom House's rating even if the military had not overthrown Aristide). Some countries with more subtle and temporary shifts are omitted from this list of transitions, as indicated in the footnotes to Table 3.2.

43. One of the best analyses of this legacy will be found in Myron Weiner, "Empirical Democratic Theory," in *Comparative Elections in Developing Countries*, ed. Weiner and Ergun Ozbudun (Washington, D.C.: American Enterprise Institute, 1987), pp. 18–22. As Weiner observes, "Every country with a population of at least 1 million (and almost all the smaller countries as well) that has emerged from colonial rule since World War II and has had a continuous democratic experience is a former British colony."

44. Those sharing an island are excluded from this group.

45. For a more comprehensive survey of these factors, see Larry Diamond, Juan J. Linz, and Seymour Martin Lipset, "Introduction: Comparing Experiences with Democracy," in *Politics in Developing Countries: Comparing Experiences with Democracy*, ed. Diamond, Linz, and Lipset (Boulder, CO: Lynne Rienner, 1990), pp. 1–37; and their forthcoming *Democracy in Developing Countries: Persistence, Failure and Renewal*. Among the most important surveys of the sources of democratic sustenance and breakdown are Robert A. Dahl, *Polyarchy: Participation and Opposition* (New Haven, CT: Yale University Press, 1971); Juan J. Linz, *The Breakdown of Democratic Regimes* (Baltimore, MD: Johns Hopkins University Press, 1978); and G. Bingham Powell, *Contemporary Democracies: Participation, Stability, and Violence* (Cambridge, MA: Harvard University Press, 1982). Prominent recent works on the expansion of democracy include Huntington, *The Third Wave*; Guillermo O'Donnell, Philippe C. Schmitter, and Laurence Whitehead, eds., *Transitions from Authoritarian Rule: Comparative Perspectives* (Baltimore: Johns Hopkins University Press, 1986); and James A. Malloy and Mitchell Seligson, eds., *Authoritarians and Democrats: Regime Transition in Latin America* (Pittsburgh: University of Pittsburgh Press, 1987).

46. Guillermo O'Donnell and Philippe C. Schmitter, *Transitions from Authoritarian Rule: Tentative Conclusions about Uncertain Democracies* (Baltimore: Johns Hopkins University Press, 1986), p. 19.

47. See for example, Dankwart A. Rustow, "Transitions to Democracy: Toward a Dynamic Model," *Comparative Politics* 2, no. 3 (April 1970): 337–363; Juan J. Linz, "Innovative Leadership in the Transition to Democracy and a New Democracy: The Case of Spain" (Paper presented to the conference on "Innovative Leadership and International Politics," Hebrew University, Jerusalem, 8–10 June 1987), and "Transitions to Democracy," *The Washington Quarterly* 13, no. 3 (Summer 1990): 143–162. For a perspective focusing more on elite structure, see Michael Burton and John Higley, "Elite Settlements," *American Sociological Review* 52, no. 3 (June 1987): 295–307; and John Higley and Michael Burton, "The Elite Variable in Democratic Transitions and Breakdowns," *American Sociological Review* 54, no. 1 (February 1989): 17–32.

48. For a survey of how such legitimacy crises undermined these regimes, see Huntington, *The Third Wave*, pp. 49–57.

49. Claude Ake, "Democratizing Africa," *Journal of Democracy* 2, no. 1 (Winter 1991): 32–44.

50. Linz, "Transitions to Democracy," pp. 145–146.

51. Huntington, *The Third Wave*, pp. 99–100.

52. O'Donnell and Schmitter, *Transitions from Authoritarian Rule*, p. 16.

53. Robert Barros, "The Left and Democracy: Recent Debates in Latin America," *Telos* 68 (1986): 49–70; Juan Linz and Alfred Stepan, "Political Crafting of Democratic Consolidation or Destruction: European and South American Comparisons," in *Democracy in the Americas: Stopping the Pendulum*, ed. Robert A. Pastor (New York: Holmes and Meier, 1989), p. 47.

54. O'Donnell and Schmitter, *Transitions from Authoritarian Rule*, p. 50.

55. Gabriel Almond and Sidney Verba, *The Civic Culture* (Princeton, NJ: Princeton University Press, 1963); Alex Inkeles, "Participant Citizenship in Six Developing Countries," *American Political Science Review* 63, no. 4 (1969). There also appears to be an independent contextual effect on attitudes and values of living in a more developed country. See Alex Inkeles and Larry J. Diamond, "Personal Development and National Development: A Cross-National Perspective," in *The Quality of Life: Comparative Studies*, ed. Alexander Szalai and Frank M. Andrews (London: Sage, 1980), pp. 73–109.

56. Seymour Martin Lipset, *Political Man* (Baltimore, MD: Johns Hopkins University Press, 1981 (first published in 1960), p. 45.

57. In fact, recent quantitative analysis shows that indicators of physical well-being and absolute poverty reduction—such as the Physical Quality of Life Index or the U.N.'s Human Development Index—are even more closely associated with democracy than is per capita GNP. Diamond, "Economic Development and Democracy Reconsidered," pp. 458–461, 465–468.

58. Huntington, *The Third Wave*, p. 67. This was not simply the result of economic development, however. In much of Latin America, the power of populist groups often decreased precisely because of repression under authoritarian rule.

59. Alexis de Tocqueville, *Democracy in America* (New York: Random House, 1945) (first published in 1835).

60. Jyotirindra Das Gupta, "India: Democratic Becoming and Combined Development," in Diamond, Linz, and Lipset, *Democracy in Developing Countries: Asia*, pp. 53–104; Richard Sisson, "Culture and Democratization in India," in *Political Culture and Democracy in Developing Countries*, ed. Larry Diamond (Boulder, CO: Lynne Rienner, forthcoming).

61. Christine M. Sadowski, "Autonomous Groups as Agents of Change in Communist and Post-Communist Eastern Europe," report prepared for the National Council for Soviet and East European Research, July 1990; S. Frederick Starr, "Soviet Union: A Civil Society," *Foreign Policy* no. 70 (Spring 1988): 26–41; Gail Lapidus, "State and Society: Toward the Emergence of Civil Society in the Soviet Union," in *Politics, Society and Nationality: Inside Gorbachev's Russia*, ed. Seweryn Bialer (Boulder, CO: Westview, 1989), pp. 121–147; Pei, "Societal Takeover"; and Nathan, "Is China Ready for Democracy?"

62. Thomas Gold, "Civil Society and Taiwan's Quest for Identity" (Paper presented to the Eighty-Sixth Annual Meeting of the American Political Science Association, San Francisco, 30 August–2 September 1990).

63. Liddle, "Indonesia's Democratic Past and Future."

64. O'Donnell and Schmitter, *Transitions from Authoritarian Rule*, pp. 48–56; Larry Diamond, "Introduction: Civil Society and the Struggle for Democracy," in *The Democratic Revolution: Struggles for Freedom and Pluralism in the Developing World*, ed. Diamond (New York: Freedom House, 1991), pp. 6–18; Clement Nwankwo, "The Civil Liberties Organization and the Struggle for Human Rights and Democracy in Nigeria," in Diamond, *The Democratic Revolution*, pp. 105–123;

Larry Diamond, "Nigeria's Search for a New Political Order," *Journal of Democracy* 2, no. 2 (Spring 1991): 54–69; and Kuria, "Confronting Dictatorship in Kenya."

65. Naomi Chazan, "The New Politics of Participation in Tropical Africa," *Comparative Politics* 14, no. 2 (January 1982): 169–189; and "Civil Society in Africa," typed manuscript, 1990.

66. Huntington, *The Third Wave*, pp. 73–85. On the Philippines, see also Carl H. Lande, "The Political Crisis," in *Crisis in the Philippines: The Marcos Era and Beyond*, ed. John Bresnan (Princeton, NJ: Princeton University Press, 1986), pp. 118–122. In Kenya, politically outspoken Protestant and Catholic clergy have taken courageous stands—both individually and through ecumenical bodies such as the National Council of Christian Churches (NCCK) and the Peace and Justice Commission—on behalf of democracy and human rights. As a result, they have suffered severe intimidation and also violent attacks by agents of the ruling party. See Africa Watch, *Kenya: Taking Liberties* (New York: Human Rights Watch, 1991), pp. 217–236.

67. Dette Pascual, "Building a Democratic Culture in the Philippines," in Diamond, *The Democratic Revolution*, pp. 53–56; Lande, "The Political Crisis," pp. 140–143.

68. Felix B. Bautista, "The Philippine Alternative Press and the Toppling of a Dictator," pp. 145–166; Anthony Hazlitt Heard, "The Struggle for Free Expression in South Africa," pp. 167–179; and Ray Ekpu, "Nigeria's Embattled Fourth Estate," pp. 181–200; all in Diamond, *The Democratic Revolution*.

69. Kathryn Sikkink, "The Effectiveness of U.S. Human Rights Policy: Argentina, Guatemala, and Uruguay" (Paper presented to the World Congress of the International Political Science Association, Buenos Aires, 21–25 July 1991). Uruguay's first posttransition democratic president, Julio Sanguinetti, declared shortly after taking office in 1984, "The vigorous policies of the Carter administration were the most important outside influence on Uruguay's democratization process." Quoted in Huntington, *The Third Wave*, p. 96.

70. Huntington, *The Third Wave*, pp. 96–97.

71. Huntington, *The Third Wave*, p. 95.

72. Karl D. Jackson, "The Philippines: The Search for a Suitable Democratic Solution, 1946–1986," in Diamond, Linz, and Lipset, *Democracy in Developing Countries: Asia*, p. 254.

73. Robert A. Pastor, "Nicaragua's Choice: The Making of a Free Election," *Journal of Democracy* 1, no. 3 (Summer 1990): 15.

74. Huntington, *The Third Wave*, p. 98.

75. Sikkink, "U.S. Human Rights Policy," pp. 32–38.

76. Cheng, "Democratizing the Quasi-Leninist Regime in Taiwan," p. 484.

77. Sung-joo Han, "South Korea: Politics in Transition," p. 294.

78. Laurence Whitehead, "International Aspects of Democratization," in *Transitions from Authoritarian Rule: Comparative Perspectives*, ed. Guillermo O'Donnell, Philippe C. Schmitter, and Laurence Whitehead pp. 21–23. See also Huntington, *The Third Wave*, pp. 87–89.

79. All quotes from Pauline H. Baker, "South Africa's Future," pp. 8–9.

80. *Sunday Concord* (Lagos, Nigeria), 25 March 1990.

81. "The New Wind of Change," *Guardian Weekly* (London), 23 September 1990, p. 25.

82. "New Wind of Change," p. 25.

83. Ake, "Rethinking African Democracy," p. 36; emphasis mine.

84. Quoted in Robert M. Press, "Africans Join Protests for Multiparty Rule," *Christian Science Monitor*, 11 April 1990, p. 2.

85. Jonathan C. Randal, "In Africa, Unrest in One-Party States," *International Herald Tribune*, 27 March 1990, p. 1.

86. Quoted in Huntington, *The Third Wave*, p. 288.

87. Huntington, "Democracy's Third Wave," p. 2.

88. Huntington, *The Third Wave*, p. 287.

89. Huntington, *The Third Wave*, p. 102.

90. Huntington, *The Third Wave*, p. 103

91. Cheng, "Democratizing the Quasi-Leninist Regime in Taiwan," p. 483.

92. James Lee Ray, "The Global Origins of Transitions to (and From?) Democracy" (Paper presented to the annual meeting of the International Studies Association, Vancouver, 20–23 March 1991), pp. 13–15.

93. See, for example, Ray, "The Global Origins of Transitions," p. 14, on the spread of television.

94. James N. Rosenau, *Turbulence in World Politics* (Princeton, NJ: Princeton University Press, 1990), p. 342.

95. Huntington, *The Third Wave*, p. 102.

96. Ake, "Rethinking African Democracy," p. 39.

97. Ake, "Rethinking African Democracy," p. 40.

98. This lone reference to the possible *negative* influences of the international environment on democratization is not meant to trivialize their significance. U.S. and European armed interventions, military assistance, and economic aid or sanctions often contradicted democratic principles and possibilities in the 1950s, 1960s, and early 1970s. See, for example, Edward N. Muller, "Dependent Economic Development, Aid Dependence on the United States and Democratic Breakdown in the Third World," *International Studies Quarterly* 29 (December 1985): 445–461. This history lies beyond the scope of our focus here on explaining the *current* global democratic trend. Nevertheless, one should not dismiss the possibility of renewed Western resistance to, or even sabotage of, some democratic developments abroad (e.g., electoral triumphs of leftist or Islamic forces) that appear hostile to Western interests. Even in the current era, democracy promotion remains for the Western democracies only one of several foreign policy goals. Unless the Western democracies (especially the United States) support global democratization with more coherence and consistency than they have done in the past, their efforts are unlikely to be effective. See Larry Diamond, "Promoting Democracy," *Foreign Policy* 87 (Summer 1992): 25–46.

99. Maria Rosa de Martini, "Civic Participation in the Argentine Democratic Process," in Diamond, *The Democratic Revolution*.

100. Michael Pinto-Duschinsky, "Foreign Political Aid: The German Political Foundations and their U.S. Counterparts," *International Affairs* 67, no. 1 (January 1991): 33–63.

101. NED is an independent, nongovernmental organization but is almost entirely funded by an annual appropriation from the U.S. Congress. It programs assistance directly as well as through its four "core" institutes: the National Democratic Institute for International Affairs (NDI), the National Republican Institute for International Affairs (NRIIA), the Free Trade Union Institute (FTUI), and the Center for International Private Enterprise (CIPE). My general discussion here refers to this entire family of organizations.

102. Diamond, "Promoting Democracy," p. 46.

103. Pinto-Duschinsky, "Foreign Political Aid," p. 35.

104. Jackson, "The Philippines," p. 254.

105. This paragraph summarizes the arguments of Jennifer L. McCoy, Larry Garber, and Robert A. Pastor, "Making Peace by Observing and Mediating Elections," *Journal of Democracy* 2, no. 4 (Fall 1991): 102–114. See also Joshua Mu-

ravchik, *Exporting Democracy: Fulfilling America's Destiny* (Washington, D.C.: AEI Press, 1991), pp. 208–210.

106. Cheng, "Democratizing the Quasi-Leninist Regime in Taiwan," pp. 487, 491–93.

107. *New York Times*, 15 October 1990. Soros' personal fortune is estimated at over $500 million.

108. Huntington, "Democracy's Third Wave," p. 2. See also his *The Third Wave*, pp. 75–83; and George Weigel, "Catholicism and Democracy: The Other Twentieth Century Revolution," in *The New Democracies: Global Change and U.S. Policy*, ed. Brad Roberts (Cambridge, MA: MIT Press, 1990), pp. 25–27.

109. Huntington, *The Third Wave*, p. 83.

110. Dankwart A. Rustow, "Democracy: A Global Revolution?" *Foreign Affairs* 69, no. 4 (Fall 1990): 79–80.

111. The classic presentation of this thesis is Rustow, "Transitions to Democracy," but further evidence is presented in Burton and Higley, "Elite Settlements," and Higley and Burton, "The Elite Variable."

112. Rustow, "Transitions to Democracy," p. 360.

113. Carl Lande, "Manila's Malaise," *Journal of Democracy* 2, no. 1 (Winter 1991): 45–57.

114. Inter-American Dialogue, "The Americas in a New World" (Washington, D.C.: Inter-American Dialogue, 1990; and Queenstown, MD: Aspen Institute, 1990), pp. 47–48; see also Peter Hakim and Abraham F. Lowenthal, "Latin America's Fragile Democracies," *Journal of Democracy* 2, no. 3 (Summer 1991): 16–29.

115. Hakim and Lowenthal, "Latin America's Fragile Democracies," p. 49.

116..A similar pattern characterized movement during 1991. In its end-of-the-year ratings, Freedom House judged 34 countries as more free but 16 as having declined at least one point on the freedom scale.

117. Huntington, "Democracy's Third Wave," p. 8. See also his *The Third Wave*, pp. 290–294.

118. Jowitt, "The New World Disorder," pp. 16–17.

119. These arguments are elaborated in Diamond, "Promoting Democracy."

# 4

## Changing
## Civil-Military Relations

### *Claude E. Welch*

The rule of the "man on horseback" is declining, as a consequence of the global political and ideological changes to which this book is devoted. Civil-military relations are changing dramatically with the spread of the call for democracy around the world. Although armed forces remain primary political actors in most states, their direct political roles have been reduced in recent years. The result, to overstate the case, is fundamental transformation—and nowhere is it more marked than in developing countries. The Third World is now witnessing the slow, difficult, but significant consolidation of civilian governments after, in many cases, several decades of military rule.

Societies throughout history have been plagued with the fickle loyalties of armed forces. To whom will their armed forces give allegiance and support? To a narrow, self-serving group within society, be it class, ethnic group, religious sect, or dominant political party? To an image of the "national interest," as the military might define it? To the government, however it may be constituted? To their own individual and corporate interests? If the armed forces are the supreme guarantors of political independence from external attack and internal collapse, who will guard the guards themselves? In short, what patterns of civil-military relations will prevail? For most Third World countries, the simple answer was, "clubs are trumps." In the early decades following independence, the fastest route to power came through the barrel of a gun, not the ballot box.

This chapter is divided into the following sections: an introduction, briefly exploring the multiple meanings of "civil" and "military"; a second part, analyzing three classic models of civil-military relations and their respective strengths and weaknesses; a third, summarizing findings of major scholars on regime changes under conditions of endemic military involvement in politics; and a more speculative final section, linking recent dramatic global changes (including, but certainly not confined to, the late 1989 transformation of Eastern Europe) with internal alterations (primarily, but not exclusively, the moves in Third World countries toward liberalization and democratization). I conclude that scholars have given insufficient attention to external factors in recent "retreats to the barracks" but also suggest that dramatic political changes in the Second World, especially democratization in Eastern Europe, hastened rather than initiated a process in the Third World that was already underway.

## What Is "Civil"? What "Military"?

Several months ago, I traveled to Nigeria, and attended a conference at the University of Lagos on the transition to "civil rule." The wording struck me. The word "civil" has three important, relevant connotations.

First, "civil" indicates "civilian." One speaks, for example, of the military providing "aid to the civil." Clearly, this was the major intention of the conference in Nigeria. Civil servants of Lagos state were to prepare themselves for the intended 1992 handover of control from the federal military government. Learning to work with "civilian" leaders would impose new concerns on all. A "civilian" government would presumably be a democratic one, based on open, peaceful competition among political parties representing different points of view. Their claim to rule would be based on ideas, and ideals, of popular sovereignty. Ultimately, the interests of the people would provide the ultimate guide to governmental actions; elected civilians would make political decisions, not self-appointed military officers.

Second, "civil" connotes "polite." A "civil" society is not a Hobbesian state in nature, in which life is nasty, solitary, brutish, and short; it is marked by codes of behavior, both explicit and implicit in the culture itself. In such a society, though differences among individuals exist, these differences should not negate the right of each person to correct behavior on the part of others—and particularly on the part of "civil" servants.

Third, "civil" suggests "civic." A "civic" political order is one in which regular, institutionalized, and valued procedures exist to resolve conflicts. Specified, constitutional means of problem solving are utilized. In general terms, a written constitution, supplemented by appropriate laws and regulations, sets forth broad policy guidelines and establishes entities for specific responsibilities.

The problem with many, and perhaps most, military governments is that they are not "civil" in any of the three senses just noted. First, policymaking is vested in the hands of military officers, who are recruited into the armed forces and promoted within them on the basis of expertise, seniority, and other relevant factors. Officers are schooled in the "management of violence." Their professional formation involves lengthy education—of a sort different in many respects from that enjoyed by "civilian" leaders. Although a national administration based on the armed forces may claim popular support, it does not necessarily rely upon popular sovereignty. Even though almost all so-called "military regimes" rely heavily on civilian advisers and administrators, the key policy decisions remain in the hands of the ruling junta. The system of government is thus not "civilian."

Nor is it necessarily "polite," the second connotation of "civil." An efficient, effective military operates on the basis of immediate, unswerving obedience to commands. The ideal armed forces organization is based on hierarchy, not upon equality; an order, once given, is to be carried out; persuasion is rarely part of officers' training. Hence, the brusqueness with which military men move into political positions follows directly from the requirements of the type of organization in which they have spent their professional careers.

Nor, finally, are military governments "civic," particularly in their initial assumption of power. A coup d'état, by definition, overturns a government the members of the armed forces had pledged to support. Newly installed juntas customarily suspend national constitutions; they legislate by decree rather than through popularly chosen representative bodies; they set aside procedures for selecting new leaders until the problems that justified their intervention are solved. That power was taken by nonconstitutional means does not, to be certain, mean that coup leaders lack immediate popular support or legitimacy, nor does it mean that they cannot establish procedures that create a "civic" order. They must take steps to foster public acceptance and keep grievances internal to the military from spilling over into domestic violence or countercoups. Nonetheless, they are not necessarily "civic" in taking and exercising political control.

The noun/adjective "military" is, like the term "civil," liable to different interpretations. In the Third World, "military" means far more than the uniformed armed services of the state housed within its ministry of defense. Many Third World countries have heavily armed police, gendarmeries, border guards, railway troops, and other groups responsible to a ministry of the interior. Quite likely an elite presidential guard reports directly to the office of the president. The dominant political party may sponsor some form of militia. In federalized countries such as Brazil or India, provincial or state governors may have detachments under local control. And, certainly not least important, indigenous groups may sponsor armed units for protection in ethnically riven situations (witness, for example, the Eelam Tigers, an especially militant Tamil group in Sri Lanka). Given the relatively "light" arming of several national militaries in the Third World, these other types of forces constitute formidable factors in domestic politics.

Further complications arise when the term "military" is used in the phrase "military regimes."[1] A large number of Third World governments have been so characterized. This term is inaccurate if one assumes that military officers hold untrammeled control—for they do not. These governments are, in reality, civil-military coalitions, almost invariably installed by force, but responding in varying degrees to the grievances of significant social sectors. As one well-informed African specialist has written,

> [To] classify regimes as military since their origins lie in a *coup d'état*
> serves to obscure the multitude of differences between "military regimes"
> on such characteristics as civil-military relations, ideology, political organi-
> zation, etcetera . . . Military rule should be viewed as one manifestation of
> military intervention and influence on the political process . . . The ideal-
> typical dichotomy drawn between civilian and military regimes has not
> been fruitful for theoretical analysis; in contemporary Africa it serves only
> to obfuscate the heterogeneity of political processes and regime types.[2]

In response to the question, Who governs in a military government?
Finer distinguishes among four types of regimes: military-supported, inter-
mittently indirect-military, indirect-military, and military regimes proper (29
of which, by his count, existed in late 1979). Noting that analysts must examine both supreme policy-making authority and penetration of the bureaucracy, he arrived at four subsets of the latter: military juntas, in which political parties and legislatures were suppressed; military juntas with parties or
legislatures as simple ancillaries or appurtenances; personalist-presidential
regimes; and authoritarian regimes.[3] The complexity of Finer's scheme
shows that the term "military" is as fraught with ambiguity as the word
"civilian."

In my view, the source of much cloudy thinking about civil-military relations lies in overemphasizing two extremes: on the one hand, violent over-
throws of governments by militaries, and on the other hand, unquestioned
acceptance of governmental dominance by armed forces. This simple dichotomization leaves aside the great bulk of civil-military interactions, especially in developing countries. It would be better, I believe, to term military
"intervention" in politics military "involvement" or "participation" in politics. There are levels and types of participation; different balances exist between "civil" and "military" elements. Perhaps this becomes clearest with a
spectrum, marked at one pole by unquestioned dominance of military officers over all political decisions, and at the other pole by untrammeled control by governmental officials; one end is thus "civilian control of the military,"[4] the other "military control of the government."[5]

An alternative, attractive perspective on civil-military relations comes
from Colton.[6] His thought-provoking matrix includes on one axis the scope
of issues and on the other axis, the means employed. The scope of issues
ranges from minor matters appropriately within the internal control of the
military to fundamental questions of national strategy. Means also vary.
Coups d'état are the most extreme. Military officers can also utilize political
bargaining, proffer expert advice, or stand on their official prerogatives.
Spectra and matrices should be prepared for other countries, to assess the
balance among contending political groups and the most important means of
civil-military interaction.

In the spectrum of civil-military relations sketched in Table 4.1, or in
Colton's matrix, changes can occur as a result of domestic pressures, international pressures, or various combinations of both. Dynamism is not readily

Table 4.1 Spectrum of Civil-Military Relations

| Military Influence in Politics | | Military Participation in Politics | Military Control of Government | |
|---|---|---|---|---|
| Civilian Control | Military Veto of Policy | Mixed Civilian- Military Government | With Subordinate Partners | Without Subordinate Partners |

represented in such spectra or matrices; indeed, both my spectrum and Colton's matrix express the balance of governmental and military decision-making powers at particular times. How changes come about must be explicitly incorporated into the study of civil-military relations. In reference particularly to the subject of this volume, the impact of shifts in Eastern Europe on Third World civil-military relations must be examined.

In the 1980s, well before the dramatic loosening of single-party rule in the Socialist bloc, the twin processes of liberalization and democratization[7] had started to make a substantial impact on the juntas that had governed throughout large parts of Latin America. In addition, the number of successful coups d'état dropped markedly in sub-Saharan Africa, the Middle East, and South and Southeast Asia. Reduced direct political roles for the armed forces often occurred in bleak economic settings, with mountainous debts, for example, burdening many emerging democracies in Africa and Latin America. Paradoxically, many observers presumed economic decline would enhance the likelihood of military intervention; in reality, economic decline undercut the legitimacy of whatever government was ruling. Governing military juntas as well as single-party Eastern European regimes fell victim to worsening economic performance. Patterns of civil-military relations in the Third World were in major flux as Communist regimes collapsed at the end of the 1980s, calling into question the classic models.

## Classic Models of Civil-Military Relations

As Caesar divided Gaul into three parts and Freud the unconscious into the same number, so scholars of civil-military relations customarily trichotomize into three P's. The classic models can be termed Western professional, Communist penetration, and Third World praetorian. First, Second, and Third Worlds alike gave birth, so the theories run, to distinctive patterns. Though misleading in some key respects, as I shall illustrate shortly, the three-fold division has dominated literature from the late 1950s to the present.

### Professionalism

The historic roots of Western professionalism lie in Prussia early in the eighteenth century[8] (or perhaps even earlier in the Dutch army late in the sixteenth and early in the seventeenth centuries)[9] and in the dramatic social, economic, and political transformations of the Industrial Revolution. Professionalism interacted with other changes to produce armed forces that, in Mosca's words, represented a "most fortunate exception" to the behavior of armed forces generally in history.[10] Although the military exercised unprecedented might, it remained politically quiescent in European domestic politics. The establishment of military academies open to talented young men irrespective of social rank enhanced the professional caliber of the officer corps. The nineteenth century witnessed the growth of staff work and planning. Commanders benefited from the ability to equip, mobilize, and move hundreds of thousands of soldiers through new transportation networks. Mass armies, motivated by nationalist sentiments, equipped by products of mass production factories, and commanded by men chosen and promoted on military merit rather than class of birth, could be mobilized. The conquest—or "pacification," in the value-laden term of the time—of large parts of Africa and Asia further enhanced national pride and military experience.

In organizational terms, professionalism involves two linked processes affecting the ethos and cohesiveness of the armed services. The classic distinction by Abrahamsson between historical and sociological processes (respectively, professionalization stage 1 and professionalization stage 2) merits mention. A historic transformation took place, from an officer corps that was ascriptively recruited, usually temporarily employed, and generally poorly educated to a well-trained group of experts that was recruited on the basis of achievement and permanently hired. Officership shifted from an exclusive club of the landed gentry or Junker class, in which social pedigree and wealth were of paramount importance, to a more widely open institution. Like practitioners of medicine or the law, military officers claimed specialization through extensive training, cohesiveness and solidarity, and social responsibility. A strong corporate sense complemented the specialization of the officer corps. Rather than serving the interests of a segment of society, the military as an organization became able to act in a cohesive, coherent fashion to protect its own institutional interests. "Professionalization stage 1 refers to processes which have led to the establishment of the military as a *pressure* group, whereas professionalization stage 2 turns it into a pressure *group*."[11]

One paramount contrast with other professions must be noted, however. While doctors or lawyers could practice their professions under license from the state, military officers were subject to far closer governmental control—for the armed forces were the servants of the state, symbols of national sovereignty. The loyalty of the professional military officer, Huntington argued in his highly influential book *The Soldier and the State*, lay to his employer, the state; more sociologically inclined scholars argued that the soldier was loyal to his comrades in arms.[12] While Huntington asserted that

**Table 4.2  Stepan's Contrasting Paradigms of "Old" and "New" Military Professionalism**

| | Old Professionalism | New Professionalism |
|---|---|---|
| Function of military | External security | Internal security |
| Civilian attitudes toward government | Civilians accept legitimacy of government | Segments of society challenge government legitimacy |
| Military skills required | Highly specialized skills incompatible with political skills | Highly interrelated political and military skills |
| Scope of military professional action | Restricted | Unrestricted |
| Impact of professional socialization | Renders the military politically neutral | Politicizes the military |
| Impact on civil-military relations | Contributes to apolitical military and civilian control | Contributes to military-political managerialism and role expansion |

Source: Alfred Stepan: *Authoritarian Brazil: Origins, Policies and Future* (New Haven, CT: Yale University Press, 1973).

properly regulated training could render the officer corps "politically sterile and neutral,"[13] other scholars pointed to the prominence of highly professional officers in coups d'état. In reality, the context of Third World politics made professionalism an incentive in many respects for military "intervention" in politics—not only "participation" as suggested in the earlier spectrum. The nineteenth-century European setting encouraged clear differentiation between governmental and military roles, whereas the "new professionalism of national security," ably delineated by Stepan,[14] blurs the distinction. I reproduce as Table 4.2 his table of the contrasting paradigms: the "old professionalism of external defense" versus the "new professionalism of internal security and national development."

A further obstacle to the purportedly nonpolitical nature of professionalism arose in this century in the racially charged atmosphere of decolonization. Maintenance of "standards" was seen as a code word in some African states for retaining expatriate officers following independence, meaning that while indigenous politicians controlled policy formulation and indigenous civil servants policy execution, foreign military personnel directed the armed forces. Racial tensions resulted in the mutiny of the Zairois Force Publique barely a week after the former Belgian Congo's independence; the rebellions of army units in Tanzania, Kenya, and Uganda early in 1964 resulted to a large extent from a sense that promotions were blocked because of expatriates' continuing role. "Localization" of military personnel was a key demand, once independence had been won. Where "nonpolitical," "professional," and "foreign" coincided, tensions in civil-military relations resulted. Boundaries became fragmented between the armed forces—once relatively self-contained entities—and the societies in which they were embedded. The introduction of societal tensions *within* the officer corps and the rank and file marked the third model, praetorianism, which will be discussed later in this chapter.

To summarize the lessons and implications of the preceding paragraphs: the paradigm of professionalism was rooted in Western European experience and was transplanted only partially and with great difficulty to Third World, postcolonial states. Rather than encouraging deference to politicians and acceptance of governmental control, high levels of officer training appeared to enhance the propensity to become politically involved.

## Penetration

The model of Communist penetration rested to a substantial extent upon civil war and revolutionary restructuring of armed forces. It was characterized by direct surveillance by the dominant political party over military officers, lest they seek to usurp power. Though identified with the Soviet Union, China, and other self-proclaimed Marxist-Leninist states, the penetration model resulted more broadly from (1) revolution achieved primarily through a civil war won by party-led indigenous guerrilla troops (e.g., Yugoslavia), or (2) revolution imposed through the occupation of Soviet troops (e.g., Czechoslovakia).

The Communist model was held by some scholars to be antithetical to values of military professionalism. Most notably, Kolkowicz[15] posited the following divergences between "natural" military traits and attributes favored by the party:

| "Natural" military traits | Traits favored by the party |
| --- | --- |
| Elitism | Egalitarianism |
| Professional autonomy | Subordination to ideology |
| Nationalism | Proletarian internationalism |
| Detachment from society | Involvement with society |
| Heroic symbolism | Anonymity |

In reality, with the exception of periods of restructuring that occurred late in World War I, in the Civil War, and during the Stalinist purges, a modus vivendi was reached between penetration and professional autonomy. The militarily disastrous effects of Stalin's ravaging of the officer corps (1936–1939)[16] graphically manifested the consequences of dictatorial paranoia. The reckless adventurism of Khrushchev in the Cuban missile crisis illustrated the weakness of Soviet military strategy. Untrammeled party control, by means of political officers countersigning orders or of extensive interference in promotions, is a matter of historical record. A symbiotic rather than competitive relationship between the CPSU and the Soviet armed forces has been carefully documented by Colton, Jones, Rice, and Herspring.[17] In Rice's summary, "The party and the military have made the system work by being responsive to each other . . . The military is confined to advising the party of the best options for constructing the strongest and most advanced armed forces possible. It is not a perfect system of military management, but it has worked pretty well."[18] Perhaps one could say that the Leninist Extinction, discussed by Jowitt earlier in this book, reached the armed forces of the Soviet Union earlier than it did other parts of Soviet society.

An important subset should be noted. Revolutionary transformation through guerrilla warfare did not always give birth to hegemonic parties. The ideal of a "nation in arms" manifested in Israel, as documented by Peri,[19] has provided a distinctive model of civil-military relations. Other scholars have noted the importance of the Yugoslav military, an indigenous Communist army much like the PLA.[20]

Third World efforts to emulate Communist penetration were, almost without exception, dismal failures. By focusing on direct control rather than what Rice calls "loosely coupled" control, national leaders occasionally hastened their own political demise. One of the most telling examples comes from Ghana, where the president, Osagyefo ("Redeemer") Kwame Nkrumah, moved rapidly from a model of government characterized by nonpolitical professionalism to a version of apparat control. In September 1961, early in the regime, he told the cadets of the Ghana Military Academy at their passing-out parade, in a speech entitled "Politics is not for Soldiers":

> You must at all times have confidence in your superior officers in the army, in your Commander-in-Chief, and in the political leaders in the Government. You must have confidence that the Government is doing what is best for the country and support it without question or criticism. It is not the duty of a soldier to criticize or endeavor to interfere in any way with the political affairs; he must leave that to the politicians, whose business it is.[21]

Echoing thus the sentiments of British officers and their preferred model of civil-military relations, he sought to insulate the nascent Ghanaian military from any hint of politicization.[22] This situation was not to last. A few months later, affected perhaps by his travels in Eastern Europe and China, Nkrumah scrapped the nonpolitical army that British officers on contract had been helping to craft, firing them abruptly. Misled by the lack of effective formal opposition to his dominant Convention People's Party, confident in the party's ability to recast Ghanaian society in a new format, and willing to adopt "emergency measures of a totalitarian kind,"[24] he consciously jettisoned the inherited British model of disengaged professionalism, in which nonpolitical expatriate officers held major command and training positions, and adopted aspects of the penetration model. Nkrumah further threatened the military's internal autonomy by creating President's Own Guard Regiment with extensive Soviet equipment. He ordered officers to attend courses at the Kwame Nkrumah Ideological Institute. This forced politicization was deeply resented by many officers, who nostalgically recalled the values of the mess and who idealized British and professional values.[24] In response to this situation, and to significantly worsening economic and political conditions, such that military and police action seemed the only way out, Ghanaian officers overturned Nkrumah's government in February 1966. The attempt to impose the model of party/apparat control had become a dismal failure.

The case of Ghana was not unique. Communist models of civil-military relations have almost uniformly failed in Third World states. Notably, most of these states have not experienced the kind of sweeping revolution that leads to a restructuring of the armed forces and to their subordination to the dominant political ideology. Nor, following independence, have many of them experienced external occupation. In the absence of Soviet military occupation, which marked, for example, the experience of Eastern and Central Europe, the only major incentive to adopt party control came from presidential predilection and pressure by Communist advisers. Only a few states, generally dependent to a substantial extent on close political ties with the U.S.S.R. and its satellite states, made the attempt to move toward party hegemony over the armed forces. And, as in the case of Ghana, the ouster of political leaders with whom these policies were identified generally spelled the demise of such attempts at controlling the military. In my judgment, the underlying sociopolitical conditions of most Third World states doomed in advance the model of civil-military relations characterized by party control. (One might even speculate that analogous factors applied to many Eastern European countries with the collapse of apparat control.) I would include, among the most significant reasons for the failure of this model, the absence of a real revolutionary heritage, boundary fragmentation between segments of the military and groups within the society, and a lack of tightly disciplined parties. African one-party systems were in reality hollow shells, as had been recognized by astute observers by the mid-1960s.[25] Efforts to cement presidential or party control backfired, encouraging endemic involvement in politics by the armed forces.

## *Praetorianism*

The third classic model of civil-military relations we must examine is the "praetorian" one. It took its name from the Roman praetorian guard—elite bodyguards to the emperor who drew three times the normal pay, served only 16-year terms, and, not infrequently, made and unmade rulers.[26] "Praetorianism" became a synonym for widespread interference by the military in political change, resulting in short-lived governments installed by force. In praetorian systems, military intervention in politics is by far the most common form of removing regimes.

For many years, a dominant academic industry among scholars of the Third World was analyzing the causes and consequences of coups d'état. With bullets far more significant than ballots in changing government leadership, the stress on military restiveness was quite understandable. To cite some typical counts: in the 1946–1970 period, 274 coups or coup attempts, spread over 59 countries;[27] in the 1958–1982 period, 195 coups and coup attempts, 124 of them successful, almost exclusively in the Third World.[28] In the early 1980s, only on the isolated island state of Mauritius had an African opposition won political control by electoral means and been allowed to take office; by contrast, on the rest of the continent, over 70 successful military seizures of power had occurred following independence.[29]

Praetorianism, as a type of civil-military relationship, involves numerous aspects of a society. It reflects a complex mixture of political and social factors. The absence of strong political institutions—of established, valued, recurrent patterns of decisionmaking and implementation—and the extensive mobilization of social forces together result in political decay. In the influential, provocative terms of Huntington, "In a praetorian society, social forces confront each other nakedly . . . Each group employs means which reflect its peculiar nature and capabilities. The wealthy bribe; students riot; workers strike; mobs demonstrate; and the military coup [sic]."[30] Coups and countercoups come in recurrent cycles. Within the armed forces, praetorian conditions fragment the officer corps on lines of personal ambition, ethnic, regional, or religious affiliation, and/or rank. Military discipline is shattered.

The checkered postindependence history of Benin (né Dahomey) testifies to the divisive effects of social division and intramilitary rivalries: a brief intervention in 1963 eased tensions between rival civilians but did not eliminate democratic trappings; in 1965 General Soglo intervened twice, first in October to hand power to another civilian, then in December to set up a regime dominated by the military; in December 1967, Colonel Kouandété tried unsuccessfully to organize a presidential election and then appointed a civilian head of state; in December 1969, yet another coup occurred, with the new military directorate pressing for a three-member Presidential Council; in October 1972, Major Kérékou imposed a seemingly relatively stable system that experienced strong stirrings of multipartyism early in 1990.[31] Benin's floundering for much of its history illustrated regionalism and personalism run rampant.

Analysts of the praetorianism of recent decades could more easily describe its consequences than predict its future in any given place. No ready escape from the cycle of division seems to exist. Nonetheless, to understand better the changes of the late 1980s that facilitated liberalization and democratization, we must explore whether praetorianism carries the seeds of its own demise. Few scholars foresaw successful transitions—yet change has occurred. Why?

## Liberalization and Democratization in the Third World

In this section, I shall briefly discuss obstacles to the establishment or re-establishment of "civil" governments in developing countries—using "civil" in the three senses suggested at the start of this paper.

It should first be noted that, despite widespread praetorian conditions, some Third World countries have maintained governmental control over their military forces, a sine qua non for successful liberalization and democratization.[32] What common elements have been found? If a cycle of coups and countercoups exists, is there any likelihood of transitions to effective "civil" institutions?

In 1976, Nordlinger pointed out that when governing officers lack political skills, they can achieve only shallow or temporary change and fail therefore to uproot the conditions that perpetuate praetorianism.[33] The average lifespan of governments installed by military intervention is five years. Returns to the barracks are usually promised and often achieved, but they are rarely maintained over extended periods. Voluntary disengagement is the most common form of returns to barracks; less frequently, strong civilian pressure returns control to civilians, or intramilitary revolt against governing officers results in rapid recivilianization. Because of the absence of fundamental alterations in sociopolitical conditions, Nordlinger argued, "the most common aftermath of military government is military government."[34]

Finer was equally pessimistic. In *The Man on Horseback: The Role of the Military in Politics*—still a classic nearly 30 years after its initial publication—he held little hope for successful transition in countries of "low" or "minimal" political culture, in short, under "praetorian" conditions.[35] Updating his book in the mid-1970s, Finer suggested four conditions necessary for establishment of a new civilian government under military auspices: (1) the leader of the junta must want the armed forces to quit politics; (2) he must establish a regime able to function without direct military support; (3) the military itself must support the new government; and (4) the armed forces must have confidence in the new government leader.[36] He cited France, Turkey, Mexico, and South Korea as cases in point.

*Political Order in Changing Societies* presents a similar perspective. According to Huntington, as already noted, major contrasts exist between praetorian and civic societies. "Intermittent military intervention" in politics is, to Huntington, the "essence" of praetorianism. The armed forces in post-colonial societies might play a "gatekeeper" function for the middle class, bringing about reform in toppling the landed oligarchy but retarding change when the lower classes are politically mobilized. Only by means of "sustained military participation" in politics can new institutions be built and a civic order encompassing all segments of society thereby be established. However, since officers follow a "nonpolitical" model of nation building, their efforts may be doomed. Huntington pointed to Turkey, Mexico, and

South Korea as societies where armed forces have brought about fundamental transformations in political institutions.[37]

Although their cases were drawn from southern Europe and Latin America, the authors of *Transitions from Authoritarian Rule* make a distinction useful for all analyses of civil-military relations. O'Donnell and his colleagues note that governments based on the armed forces may well initiate programs of liberalization. Rarely, however, do they complete programs of democratization. Liberalization seeks modest reform within the system, with the armed forces potentially continuing a degree of political involvement; democratization opens the field of political contestation and introduces significant uncertainties.

In the most widely ranging comparative study of armed forces' disengagement from direct political roles, the Bangladeshi scholar Maniruzzaman surveys 71 removals (voluntary or coerced) of governing military juntas.[38] As should be expected, almost all of these took place in Third World countries. The great majority of these would-be returns to the barracks ended unsuccessfully. Civilian control was rarely re-established, unless revolutionary change occurred. In other words, Maniruzzaman suggested, without sweeping transformations in the overall political, economic, and social structures, the praetorian conditions that facilitate military involvement in politics will persist.

In my own analyses of military disengagement from politics in praetorian societies, I have sketched short- and long-term strategies.[39] Re-establishment of civilian control can be achieved within a brief period by mutual restraint on the part of the government and of the officers departing from power and by avoidance of major budgetary and staffing cuts in the military. Such forbearance does not guarantee long-term political neutrality for the armed forces; only enhanced governmental legitimacy and effectiveness can guarantee this. My most recent major book on the topic compared paths to liberalization and democratization in six Third World countries, three from Andean Latin America (Bolivia, Colombia, and Peru) and three from West Africa (Côte d'Ivoire, Ghana, and Nigeria).[40] I set forth six hypotheses about planned returns to the barracks. These hypotheses involved factors internal to the military (role perceptions, funding and internal management, and military mission and deployment) and factors characterizing the sociopolitical system as a whole (levels of internal strife, economic trends, and political conditions). My conclusion was pessimistic—or, as I would prefer to say, sober and realistic: "For several decades to come . . . armed forces will continue to play central roles in the politics of African states, and to a lesser extent in Latin American countries. Since there can be no farewell to arms for many years to come in large parts of the world, the real question is then how the excesses and problems can be kept to the irreducible minimum."[41]

Huntington and Rustow suggested conditions necessary for implanting and nurturing democracy. Huntington saw a three-step process: establishment of national unity; establishment of political authority; and achievement of equality.[42] He also differentiates between reform from within, and "transformation," which involves substantial "replacement," which occurs "when an authoritarian regime collapses or is overthrown as a result of military defeat, economic disaster, or the withdrawal of support from it by substantial groups in the population. Huntington found the prospects for democratization highest in Brazil and other South American bureaucratic-authoritarian regimes; less likely in newly industrializing East Asian states; low in Islamic and most of tropical Africa "unless more fundamental changes occur in their economic and social infrastructure"; and "virtually nil" in Eastern Europe.[43] So much for prognostication! Rustow found four successive phases: national unity, as a background condition; preparation (in which polarization, not pluralism, will be prominent); decision (political leaders accept the existence of diversity in unity); and habituation. His prognosis for religiously or ethnically complex societies was gloomy, given the tension between the centralizing claims of the state and the decentralizing demands of the group. "The vast majority of citizens in a democracy-to-be must have no doubt or mental reservations as to which political community they belong to . . . In order that rulers and policies may freely change, the boundaries must endure, the composition of the citizenry be continuous."[44]

What role might external actors play? The international aspects of democratization merit attention as well. Perhaps the most suggestive schema has come from Stepan,[45] distinguishing between changes induced by warfare and conquest and those induced by internal alterations. The former category of changes includes (1) internal restoration after external conquest, (2) internal reformulation, and (3) externally monitored installation of democratic regimes; the latter category includes (4) redemocratization from within (led by the military as government, by the military as an institution against the military as government, or by civilianized political leaders), (5) society-led regime termination, (6) a pact among parties, (7) organized violent revolt coordinated by democratic reformist parties, and (8) Marxist-led revolutionary war. Does this classificatory scheme adequately account for the tumultuous changes of Eastern Europe in the latter half of 1989, given the importance not of warfare and conquest but of withdrawal of military forces? Since removal rather than imposition of Soviet forces appears to have been crucial, Stepan's schema appears to require expansion.

In summary, military disengagement from politics usually involves a planned series of steps emanating from within the ruling junta and its allies, during which process pressures mount for more rapid, fuller change. "Liberalization" is more readily undertaken than "democratization." With open contestation between political parties, a new, stronger dynamic emerges. The initial steps toward change can be undertaken by the armed forces. They can initiate liberalization—but find it difficult to achieve democratization. Subsequent steps involve negotiation, for which officers may be poorly prepared. The success of democratization does not depend solely, or perhaps even primarily, on the officer corps. It requires sensitivity to the military's needs during the process of disengagement/democratization. It further requires the development of popular attitudes supporting compromise, protection of human rights, and efforts to achieve equitable distribution among major regions and groups.

## 1989: Watershed, Culmination, or Self-contained Events?

Logically, the major transformations that swept through the regions of eastern and central Europe in late 1989 can be viewed in three ways. As a watershed, they can be understood as the source of subsequent major changes elsewhere in the world. As a culmination, they represent the climax of changes outside the area, finally brought to bear on Warsaw Pact countries. As self-contained events, they can be viewed as the result of internal dynamics, with few ripples outside their own borders. A case could be made for each, if time and space permitted. As a watershed influencing the course of Third World events, for example, the rapid, unexpected collapse of Communist party rule might have affected formerly self-proclaimed Marxist-Leninist states such as Benin and Congo, both of which dropped their rhetorical identification and single-party formats early in 1990. As culmination, the apparent trend toward democratization in Eastern Europe might have several sources. The dramatic consequences of perestroika and glasnost in the Soviet Union can be viewed as initiating changes for the entire Socialist bloc, with the democratization of late 1989 as culmination; alternatively, the initial stress of President Carter on human rights and the "evil empire" rhetoric of President Reagan might have eventuated in the Berlin-to-Bucharest shifts; or, to take a third plausible scenario of culmination, the demonstrated stagnation of Comecon and the obvious prosperity of the European Economic Community—readily viewed on television—might have made market and political reform inevitable. Finally, were the sweeping, exciting events of the "Revolution of 1989" viewed as self-contained, the crackdown in China would be viewed as unrelated to the liberalization of Eastern Europe; the dramatic decline of bureaucratic-authoritarian regimes in Latin America would be seen as a response to hemispheric and domestic changes; the political unrest and continued prominence of the military in much of South Asia and tropical Africa would be understood as consequences of praetorianism and severe economic vicissitudes; and the stirrings of religious animosities in the Islamic world and the regional rivalries fueled by petrodollars would be seen as unconnected with the political fates of either Nicolae Ceauşescu or Egon Krenz. Such speculations may be fascinating—what, however, do they tell us about civil-military relations?

First, the collapse of Communist party control undermined further the already questionable model of apparat control. Party surveillance over the

Soviet military, as I suggested earlier, was essential in the tumultuous period between the October revolution and the end of the Civil War. Essentially personalized control of the officer corps carried out in the name of the party (exemplified by Stalin's decimation of his most senior commanders and Ceauşescu's direct interference)[46] dealt a serious blow to the idea that the CPSU as an institution, not a projection of its general secretary, controlled the armed forces. Significantly, though, the passage of time muted the antagonism between line officers and *zampolits*—the political officers who immediately after the revolution had the power to countersign orders, but who found common cause with other officers in maintaining troop morale. The unusual political juggling act of General/President/Party Secretary Jaruzelski in Poland in the 1980s rendered the civil-military relationship even more anomalous. The importance of professional, nationally oriented armed forces in curbing ethnic separatism was further underscored by rumblings of discontent among Eastern European minorities long silenced under Communist rule.

But it is important to note that much of Eastern Europe had not been characterized by the praetorian conditions described earlier in this paper. The combination of Soviet occupation troops, stress on party loyalty and Socialist solidarity, the "old professionalism" of external defense, and other means of quieting or deflecting potential military distaste with domestic conditions, seems to have precluded military intervention in politics—the ultimate "means" available to officers, according to Colton's scheme. It is difficult to say whether the assumption of power by Jaruzelski and the imposition of martial law constituted a coup d'état through the corporate involvement of the armed forces, an imposition of an unusual individual, or a reassertion of party power under trying circumstances. In any case, with this single exception, Communist governments have avoided military seizures of power. As noted earlier, this fact heightened the attractiveness of apparat control to leaders such as Nkrumah and to officers such as Kouandété (Benin), Mengistu (Ethiopia), or Sassou-Ngesso (Congo), all of whom drafted Marxist-Leninist terminology and party organization to combat internal praetorian tendencies. Party organization and terminology, however, were not sufficient to eliminate their respective heritages of regional particularism and ethnic animosity.

My conclusion is that the 1989 liberalization/democratization of Eastern Europe was simultaneously watershed, culmination, and self-contained set of events. It initiated a major redefinition with Europe of continental security. Civil-military relations throughout Europe will shift; they are likely to move increasingly toward a modified combination of "old professionalism" and "constabulary" concepts under the umbrella of the Helsinki accords. This watershed will indirectly affect the Third World through diminished military aid and greater emphasis on peacekeeping, possibly through the sponsorship of troops by the U.N. As culmination (be it from differential rates of economic growth within Europe, perestroika and glasnost penetrating the entire former Socialist bloc, or the pressure of U.S. ideas), the changes in Eastern Europe have called into question the already discredited model of party control of the military. And, as a self-contained set of events, the liberalization of Eastern Europe followed rather than preceded analogous changes in much of the Third World, notably Latin America: Brazil had quietly scrapped most aspects of its once vaunted military administration; the *distensão* (decompression) and *abertura* (opening) of the 1970s eventuated in the 1985 presidential election.[47] Argentina had dismissed the leaders of the Malvinas (Falklands) invasion and restored civilian rule. Other Latin American states had civilianized their leadership as well. The 1980s was, in essence, a coup-free decade south of the Rio Grande—one of the first in the continent's history.

What, then, are the consequences for civil-military relations in the Third World of the Budapest/Prague/Sofia autumn? Whereas ensuring governmental control through the dominant party had by and large been a successful recipe for curbing the military's appetite for direct political power, democratization, paradoxically, simultaneously eliminated this curb and unleashed the possibility of growing domestic unrest through economic restructuring and greater opportunities for individual and group expression. Democratization introduced a host of uncertainties into the once fixed constellation of linkages between government and armed forces. But, if anything, the shifts in Central and Eastern Europe became possible through fundamental relaxation in Moscow under Gorbachev, under the impetus of global pressures for democracy. In certain respects, Latin America preceded the Warsaw Pact in adjusting, while Africa has followed.

The diminishing relevance of the apparat model reflected, as well, the decline in foreign assistance from the Second World. Soviet and Eastern European military aid to Third World countries dropped off dramatically in the late 1980s. Much of this assistance had been concentrated on a few states (notably Angola and Ethiopia) that were combatting strong, externally assisted, and regionally based independence movements, as well as on some Middle East states (notably Iraq and Syria) in order to counter U.S. and Israeli presence in the region. Although the reduction in Warsaw Pact aid reduced the military resources of Angola and Ethiopia, it did not necessarily cut the antagonisms that brought about civil war in the first place. It could even be argued that the pressures for self-determination unleashed by democratization have enhanced the likelihood of conflict. Might there be another paradoxical effect here, in that domestic unrest may continue, threatening precisely those central governments that now lack resources to respond adequately?

Ultimately, changes in praetorian conditions rest upon efforts initiated within individual countries, *assisted* by shifts in the international arena. The much heralded "end of the cold war" has significantly reduced East-West tensions, made possible greater cooperation among the Great Powers in North-South matters, and diminished the opportunity for Third World states to play off contending aid givers. The dramatic internal alterations in Eastern Europe have encouraged partisans of democracy, such as the Sierra Leone Bar Association, which, in its summer 1990 conference, adopted the theme, "The Effect of Contemporary Constitutional and Political Changes in Eastern Europe in Africa: Sierra Leone, A Case Study."[48] There is no proof that democratization in the former Socialist bloc has directly ushered in liberalization and democratization in the Third World. Nonetheless, the "revolution of 1989" has encouraged fundamental rethinking of civil-military relations. The "man on horseback" has considerably less scope for independent political activity than he did less than a decade ago.

## Notes

1. For an example of (in my opinion) misleading dichotomizations between "military" and "nonmilitary" systems, see R. D. McKinlay and A. S. Cohan, "Performance and Instability in Military and Nonmilitary Regime Systems," *American Political Science Review* 70, no. 3 (September 1976): 850–864.

2. John Ravenhill, "Comparing Regime Performance in Africa: The Limitations of Cross-National Aggregate Analysis," *Journal of Modern African Studies* 18, no. 1 (March 1980): 124–125.

3. S. E. Finer, "The Morphology of Military Regimes," in *Soldiers, Peasants, and Bureaucrats: Civil-Military Relations in Communist and Modernizing Societies*, ed. Roman Kolkowicz and Andrzej Korbonski (London: George Allen & Unwin, 1982), pp. 281–309.

4. As Huntington accurately observed, "civilian control" is in reality "governmental control." Samuel P. Huntington, *The Soldier and the State: The Theory and Politics of Civil-Military Relations* (Cambridge, MA: Harvard University Press, 1957), p. 380.

5. I first utilized this spectrum in Claude E. Welch, Jr., ed., *Civilian Control of the Military: Theory and Cases from Developing Countries* (Albany, NY: State University New Press, 1976), p. 3. The version produced in this chapter appears in Claude E. Welch, Jr., *No Farewell to Arms? Military Disengagement from Politics in Africa and Latin America* (Boulder, CO: Westview, 1987), p. 13.

6. Timothy Colton, *Commissars, Commanders, and Civilian Authority: The Structure of Soviet Military Politics* (Cambridge, MA: Harvard University Press, 1979), p. 243.

7. Guillermo O'Donnell and Philip Schmitter, eds., *Transitions from Authoritarian Rule: Tentative Conclusions from Uncertain Democracies* (Baltimore, MD: Johns Hopkins University Press, 1986), pp. 7–10.

8. Huntington, *The Soldier and the State,* p. 19.

9. M. D. Feld, "Middle Class Society and the Rise of Military Professionalism: The Dutch Army 1589–1640," *Armed Forces and Society* 1, no. 4 (Fall 1975): 419–442.

10. Gaetano Mosca, *The Ruling Class* (New York: McGraw-Hill, 1939) (first published in Italian in 1884), p. 235.

11. Bengt Abrahamsson, *Military Professionalization and Political Power* (Beverly Hills, CA: Sage, 1972), p. 55.

12. Abrahamsson, *Military Professionalization*; S. E. Finer, *The Man on Horseback: The Role of the Military in Politics* (London: Pall Mall, 1962); Morris Janowitz, *The Professional Soldier* (Glencoe, IL: Free Press, 1960).

13. Huntington, *The Soldier and the State*, p. 381.

14. Alfred Stepan, ed., *Authoritarian Brazil: Origins, Policies and Future* (New Haven, CT: Yale University Press, 1973).

15. Roman Kolkowicz, *The Soviet Military and the Communist Party* (Princeton, NJ: Princeton University Press, 1957), p. 21.

16. Note the following dismal death rates as a result of execution during the purges: 13 of 15 army commanders; 57 of 85 corps commanders; 110 of 195 divisional commanders; 186 of 406 brigade commanders. John Erickson, *The Soviet High Command: A Military-Political History 1918–1941* (New York: St. Martin's, 1962), p. 505.

17. Colton, *Commissars, Commanders*; Ellen Jones, *Red Army and Society: A Sociology of the Soviet Military* (Boston, MA: Allen and Unwin, 1985); Condoleezza Rice, "The Party, the Military, and Decision Authority in the Soviet Union," *World Politics* 40, no. 1 (October 1987): 55–81; Dale R. Herspring, *The Soviet High Command: Personalities and Politics* (Princeton, NJ: Princeton University Press, 1990).

18. Rice, "The Party, the Military," pp. 80–81.

19. Yoram Peri, *Between Battles and Ballots: The Israeli Military in Politics* (Cambridge: Cambridge University Press, 1983).

20. Anton Bebler, "Civil-Military Relations in Communist Systems," typed manuscript, 1990.

21. Kwame Nkrumah, "Politics is Not for Soldiers" (Accra, Government Printer, 1961), pp. 1–2.

22. Claude E. Welch, Jr., "Civil-Military Relations in New Commonwealth Nations: The Transfer and Transformation of British Models," *Journal of Developing Areas* 12, no. 2 (January 1978): 153–170.

23. Kwame Nkrumah, *Ghana: The Autobiography of Kwame Nkrumah* (Edinburgh: Nelson, 1957), p. x.

24. As Akwasi Afrifa, key leader in the 1966 coup d'état that deposed Nkrumah, glowingly wrote about the Royal Military Academy Sandhurst: "I entered Sandhurst as a boy and left a soldier . . . Now I look back on Sandhurst with nostalgia. It is one of the greatest institutions in the world . . . Sandhurst deepened my understanding of the world and also opened me to the new world of adventure and tolerance." A. A. Afrifa, *The Ghana Coup, 24th February 1966* (New York: Humanities, 1966), pp. 50–52.

25. Aristide R. Zolberg, *Creating Political Order: The Party States of West Africa* (Chicago, IL: Rand McNally, 1966) and "The Structure of Political Conflict in the New States of Tropical Africa," *American Political Science Review* 62, no. 1 (March 1968): 70–85.

26. As in the year 193, when the guard murdered Emperor Publius Helvius Pertinax and sold the position to Marcus Didius Severus Julianus.

27. William R. Thompson, *The Grievances of Military Coup-Makers* (Beverly Hills, CA: Sage, 1978), p. 7.

28. Samuel E. Finer, "The Military and Politics in the Third World," in *The Third World: Premises of U.S. Policy*, ed. W. Scott Thompson, rev. ed. (San Francisco, CA: Institute for Contemporary Studies, 1983), pp. 75–114.

29. Claude E. Welch, Jr., "The Military Factor in West Africa: Leadership and Regional Development," in *West African Regional Cooperation and Development*, ed. Julius Emeka Okolo and Stephen Wright (Boulder, CO: Westview, 1990), pp. 176–178.

30. Samuel P. Huntington, *Political Order in Changing Societies* (New Haven, CT: Yale University Press, 1968), p. 196.

31. Samuel Decalo, *Coups and Army Rule in Africa: Studies in Military Style* (New Haven, CT: Yale University Press, 1976), pp. 39–85; Claude E. Welch, Jr., "Obstacles to Disengagement and Democratization: Military Regimes in Benin and Burkina Faso," in *The Decline of Military Regimes: The Civilian Influence*, ed. Constantine Danopoulos (Boulder, CO: Westview, 1988), pp. 25–44.

32. David Goldsworthy, "Civilian Control of the Military in Black Africa," *African Affairs* 80, no. 314 (January 1980): 49–74, and "Armies and Politics in Civilian Systems," in *Military Politics and Power in Black Africa*, ed. Simon Baynham (London: Croom Helm, 1986), pp. 97–128; Samuel Decalo, "Modalities of Civil-Military Stability in Africa," *Journal of Modern African Studies* 27, no. 4 (December 1980): 547–578.

33. Eric A. Nordlinger, *The Military in Politics* (Englewood Cliffs, NJ: Prentice Hall, 1976), pp. 139–147.

34. Nordlinger, *Military in Politics*, p. 210.

35. Finer, *The Man on Horseback*.

36. S. E. Finer, "The Man on Horseback—1974," *Armed Forces and Society* 1, no. 1 (Fall 1974): 17–18.

37. Huntington, *Political Order*, pp. 194–262.

38. Talukdar Maniruzzaman, *Military Withdrawal from Politics: A Comparative Perspective* (Cambridge, MA: Ballinger, 1987).

39. Welch, *Civilian Control*, pp. 313–327.

40. Welch, *No Farewell to Arms?*

41. Welch, *No Farewell to Arms?* p. 204.

42. Huntington, *Political Order*, p. 348.

43. Samuel P. Huntington, "Will More Countries Become Democratic?" *Political Science Quarterly* 99, no. 2 (Summer 1984): 193–218.

44. Dankwart Rustow, "Transitions to Democracy: Toward a Dynamic Model," *Comparative Politics* 2, no. 3 (April 1970): 401.

45. Alfred Stepan, "Paths toward Redemocratization: Theoretical and Comparative Perspectives," in ed. Guillermo O'Donnell, Philip Schmitter, and Laurence Whitehead *Transitions from Authoritarian Rule: Comparative Perspectives* (Baltimore, MD: Johns Hopkins University Press, 1986), pp. 64–84.

46. William Crowther, "'Ceaușescuism' and Civil-Military Relations in Romania," *Armed Forces and Society* 15, no. 2 (Winter 1989): 207–226.

47. Thomas Skidmore, *The Politics of Military Rule in Brazil, 1964–1985* (New York: Oxford University Press, 1988).

48. *West Africa,* 13–19 August 1990, p. 2279.

# 5

# Democratization in Latin America

*Karen L. Remmer*

During the 1980s Latin America experienced the longest and deepest wave of democratization in its history. Paradoxically, the process began at precisely the point when scholarly consensus had been achieved on the improbability of democratic development in the region. Thus the second edition of Guillermo O'Donnell's seminal book, *Modernization and Bureaucratic-Authoritarianism,*[1] the English translation of Fernando Henrique Cardoso and Enzo Faletto's influential work on dependency,[2] and the important collaborative effort entitled *The New Authoritarianism in Latin America*[3] all appeared in 1979—the same year the Ecuadoran military inaugurated an unhearalded series of regional transitions to political democracy.

The process of political transformation continued for more than a decade, progressively eliminating military rule in Ecuador, Peru, Bolivia, Argentina, Uruguay, Brazil, and Chile. Among the South American nations, only Paraguay failed to undergo a democratic transition, and even there significant political liberalization occurred as a result of the toppling of the long-standing Stroessner dictatorship. The Caribbean Basin experienced a diluted version of the same process. Although in some countries the transition from military to civilian rule was more nominal than real, in the mid-1980s for the first time in history all five of the Central American republics were headed simultaneously by an elected civilian president. Even Mexico, long renowned for the resilience of its one-party regime, was seen to be moving in the direction of greater political competitiveness.

Waves of democratization are not a new phenomenon in Latin America. In the immediate aftermath of World War II, dictatorships crumbled throughout the hemisphere, establishing a new, albeit often ephemeral, basis for competitive rule in Bolivia, Brazil, Cuba, Ecuador, Guatemala, Peru, and Venezuela. In 1958, when the military ceded power to elected leaders in Argentina, Colombia, and Venezuela, regional observers began celebrating another "twilight of the tyrants." Like its predecessor, however, this wave of regime change was promptly reversed. In 1962, military coups displaced elected governments in Argentina and Peru. Two years later the Brazilian

91

military seized power and proceeded to institutionalize a regime that was to endure for more than two decades. A long series of other authoritarian reversals followed. By the mid-1970s, even the well-established Chilean and Uruguayan democracies had been swept away by authoritarian currents, placing two-thirds of the region's total population under the domination of the military.

Given this history, regional specialists have been reluctant to herald the recent cycle of democratization as representing anything very new or profound. The lesson that has been drawn from the past is that liberalizing trends are inherently temporary phases that occur within the framework of a broader pattern of authoritarian development. As this essay will argue, however, the current wave of democratization differs from its predecessors in ways that pose major theoretical challenges to established scholarly interpretations of Latin American politics. For the purposes of this discussion, political democracy may be briefly defined in accordance with prevailing conventions as a form of regime characterized by electoral competition and oppositional rights.[4]

## Latin Democracy in the 1980s

The recent process of political transformation in Latin America stands out historically on several related dimensions. First, no previous wave of democratization in the region lasted as long or affected as many countries. The process of regime change did not always proceed smoothly or necessarily result in a full or permanent transition to political democracy; yet no country reverted from democratic to military rule during the 1980s. The same cannot be said of any other decade in twentieth-century Latin American history. The recent process of democratization is equally unprecedented in terms of its scope. With the exception of Cuba, during the 1980s all of the 20 countries conventionally counted as part of Latin America either were governed by a democratic regime or experienced major political changes involving expanded political competition and oppositional rights. The military still retained considerable power in many countries; but for a brief period in the early 1990s, for the first time since the beginning of the century, no purely military regime held power on the continent.

New political records were also established in individual countries. In 1985 for the first time in Bolivian history, presidential power was transferred from one political party to another on the basis of competitive elections. Subsequent to the 1983 breakdown of military rule in Argentina, Raúl Alfonsín became the first elected president in more than 60 years to weather the threat of a military coup and cede power to an elected successor. The Peruvian election of 1985 represented an even more path-breaking occasion: it established the basis for the first transfer of power from one democratically elected leader to another in the country's history. The same is true of the Nicaraguan election of 1990. Other nations, such as El Salvador and Mexico, held the most competitive elections in their history. Even established democracies participated in the shift toward more competitive and participatory forms. As a result of democratic reform, the political duopoly of the Conservative and Liberal parties in Colombia was broken in favor of expanded competition. Colombian voters also gained the right to elect local officials for the first time in 1988. Venezuela extended the scope of its electoral system the following year, when citizens participated in the first direct elections of provincial governors, mayors, and local councillors.

Another key contrast with the past concerns the depth of the democratization process. The generation of competitive regimes that emerged from the process of political transformation in the 1980s was not only larger and more durable than any of its predecessors but also far more inclusionary. In the past the modal form of democracy in Latin America was exclusionary or oligarchical; i.e., competitive institutions were based on the electoral participation of less than one-third of the population.[5] Due to the elimination of literacy requirements, reductions in the voting age, and the removal of restrictions on competition, the situation changed rapidly in favor of inclusionary rule during the 1980s. Between the presidential elections of 1980 and 1985, for example, the Peruvian electorate increased from 25.7 percent of the population to 39.4 percent: a figure exceeding that of the 1984 U.S. presidential election.[6] Likewise, the Ecuadoran electorate expanded by one-third between the presidential elections of 1979 and 1984.[7] Noteworthy gains were also achieved in Brazil, El Salvador, and Honduras, where participation topped the 33 percent mark for the first time during the 1980s.[8] The mobilization of popular forces through the organization and expansion of social movements, including feminism, buttressed these trends by drawing new social elements into the political system.[9]

A third key contrast with the past is that democratization in the 1980s was characterized by unprecedented attempts to build consensus around competitive institutions. Among the most notable of these efforts was the 1985 Bolivian Pact for Democracy, which united the government and leading opposition party behind a series of drastic reforms designed to address a rapidly mounting economic crisis. The pact represented the first time in Bolivian history that government and opposition forces attempted to agree on a common set of policy proposals.[10] The process of consensus formation was continued after the presidential election of 1989, when the right-wing Acción Democrática Nacionalista and left-wing Movimiento Izquierda Revolucionaria agreed to form a national unity government.[11] Similar attempts at building elite consensus around democratic institutions were made successfully in Chile, where in 1988 a broad coalition of 16 political parties united behind the "Campaign for the No" and defeated the Pinochet regime in a plebiscite designed to perpetuate military rule into the 1990s. This effort established the basis for a transition to democratic rule under the leadership of a broad coalition government headed by Patricio Aylwin. Parallel developments may be traced in countries such as Nicaragua, where the government of Violetta Chamorro sought to reach an accommodation with the Sandinistas; Argentina, where the Peronist government of Carlos Menem entered into an improbable alliance with the former head of the conservative Unión del Central Democrático; Uruguay, where the "Coincidencia Nacional" formally incorporated opposition forces into a coalition government after the 1989 election; and Colombia, where peacemaking efforts paved the way for the participation of former guerrilla groups in the democratic process. Elites in country after country also turned to *concertación social* or pact making among labor organizations, business groups, and state elites as a means of building consensus.[12]

Whatever the long-term success of these efforts, the political experience of the stable democracies in Latin America emphasizes their potential importance.[13] Political pacts between rival sets of elites, which were incorporated into the constitution by means of a plebiscite, paved the way for the reestablishment of a stable competitive political system in Colombia in the late 1950s.[14] The process of political pact formation was equally critical to the establishment of modern Venezuelan democracy, which also dates back to the late 1950s.[15] The interwar history of Western Europe is no less suggestive. Confronted with a combination of economic crisis and extremist political challenges, only a minority of European democracies weathered the 1930s. According to recent research, those that did were distinguished less by economic conditions or policy performance than by processes of national consensus formation among elites.[16]

Reflecting the efforts at elite consensus formation, Latin America during the 1980s also stands out relative to the past in terms of the comparatively high levels of popular support for democratic institutions. For example, whereas 25.9 percent of Chileans favored military rule in 1973, by the mid-1980s the percentage favoring authoritarian political options had fallen to 6.3 percent.[17] Democratic attachments grew even more significantly in Brazil between the early 1970s and the 1980s.[18] As a result of such changes, levels of support for democratic institutions in Latin America have come to resemble those expressed by citizens in Southern Europe. In the 1985–1989 period, for example, support for democracy in Spain fluctuated within the 68 to 75 percentage range.[19] A national survey of Peruvians taken in 1988 produced nearly identical results: 75 of the respondents preferred an elected democracy to any other form of government.[20] Similarly, Argentine survey results for the 1983–1988 period consistently showed 79 to 84 percent of the population agreeing that the best political system is one based on elections.[21] Such figures also compare favorably with indicators of support for democratic governance in Venezuela and Costa Rica, which are widely regarded as the best-established democracies in the region.[22]

Public opinion surveys also document shifts in the direction of political moderation. In the Chilean case, for example, where severe polarization undercut democratic institutions in the early 1970s, data for the 1980s indicate that residents of greater Santiago identified more strongly with the political center than at any point in the preceding 30 years. When democratic institutions were overthrown by the military in 1973, the percentage opting for the center was only 26.8; the figure registered in 1986 was 41.2.[23] In a similar vein, Juan Rial has commented with reference to the Uruguayan election of 1984, "The 1984 vote was a vote for moderation, pacification, and democracy. . . . Many of those who in 1973 had an extreme left position supporting different types of radical actions now defended moderate positions. Many who had espoused an extreme right view abandoned it for a centrist one."[24] Electoral outcomes evince the same tendency. With the exception of Peru, which experienced a significant growth in the relative strength of the left, during the 1980s extremist parties lost ground to centrist political options.[25]

The legacy of the 1980s was thus a set of competitive regimes that was larger, more durable, more inclusionary, and more consensually based than any in the past. Pendulum theories establish no basis for understanding this change. The democratization process of the 1980s involved more than the restoration of the status quo ante: the strengths and weaknesses of the new generation of competitive regimes differed fundamentally from those of their predecessors. The theoretical paradigms that have dominated the study of Latin American politics for the past two decades also fail to provide a framework for understanding the political transformation of the region. Nearly all of them, including corporatism, bureaucratic authoritarianism, political culture, and dependency, were constructed around the problem of explaining authoritarianism, not democracy. None left room for, much less predicted, a major reversal in the pre-existing pattern of authoritarian development. The political events of the 1980s thus outpaced scholarly efforts to grapple with changing political realities, engendering widespread theoretical confusion that parallels that created by the breakdown of Communism in Eastern Europe.

The process of theoretical recovery has been slow. More than a decade after the process of democratization began, the study of Latin America remains in a state of paradigmatic crisis. Some scholars have simply dismissed recent trends as epiphenomenal and emphasized the continuing fragility of democracy in Latin America. Others have responded to theoretical failure by focusing upon the uncertainty of social reality and attempting to understand democratization in terms of *virtù* and *fortuna*. Still others have sought inspiration in discarded theories of modernization or have abandoned the realm of theory altogether. Whatever insights may have been derived from such responses, a major task of theoretical reorientation still confronts regional specialists. While the short-term horizons and case-study approach of most recent research have provided no lack of plausible explanations for recent events, the problem we face is an absence of general explanations. What we have instead are many complex and often competing sets of propositions about the politics of individual countries that fail to account for regional developments as a whole.[26]

## The International Origins of Political Crisis

To address the causes and consequences of the recent wave of democratization, theories of regime change need to incorporate several levels of analysis. Given the nearly simultaneous establishment of democracy in countries throughout Latin America, the international system is an obvious starting point. The challenge, however, is to mesh the analysis of the role of international factors with the study of social change at the national and subnational levels in a way that will make it possible to explain not merely the onset of the process of democratization but also significant cross-regional variations in the timing, pace, and impact of that process. In view of the variety of forces that have been identified as buttressing authoritarianism in the region, the key issues are: How and why were shifts in the international system translated into democratization? How and why did this process vary across the region? As Adam Przeworski has emphasized in discussing recent events in Eastern Europe, underlying causes need to be distinguished from precipitating conditions.[27] The process of regime change may have been set off by external developments, but variations in the speed and relative ease with which authoritarianism was demolished and replaced by competitive institutions underline the important role of domestic conditions.

In terms of the international system, the critical changes affecting Latin America were economic rather than political or ideological in origin. When the process of democratization began, the breakdown of the Berlin Wall was more than a decade away. Indeed, Cold War tensions in the region were mounting rather than waning in response to the Sandinista victory in Nicaragua, the growth of revolutionary violence in El Salvador, the election of Ronald Reagan, and the related increase in Cuban, Soviet, and U.S. involvement in Central America. Likewise, it is hardly possible to account for the origins of the democratization process in Latin America in terms of the disappearance of alternative regime models or the globalization of democracy. For Latin America, the restoration of democracy in Spain specifically was significant. Intraregional effects may also be noted: e.g., the process of regime transition in powerful neighboring countries helped undercut military rule in Uruguay. Nevertheless, in the immediate wake of the Nicaraguan revolution, alternative political models and ideologies remained very much alive in the hemisphere. The Sandinista victory gave impetus to revolutionary movements in Guatemala and El Salvador and inspired the Chilean Communist party to abandon its long-established commitment to peaceful, democratic struggle.[28]

For those who have portrayed the process of democratization in Latin America as a reflection of broader international political currents, it may also be noted that patterns of regime change in Latin America have not necessarily followed international trends, either historically or in the 1980s. The recent wave of democratic transitions began earlier in Latin America than in the rest of the world. This relative independence is not unprecedented. Latin political realities in the past several decades have failed rather consistently to conform to the broader pattern of international political change. The hazards of ascribing predictive importance to changing external political fashions are emphasized by the events of the 1970s. Right-wing authoritarianism achieved its pinnacle of success in the region three decades after it had ceased to represent an internationally respectable political alternative.

The reorientation of U.S. foreign policy provides an even less persuasive explanation for the political transformation of the region. The process of democratization began to develop momentum at precisely the moment when U.S. support for human rights was waning. Throughout most of the 1980s, the U.S. subordinated the goal of democratization to other foreign policy objectives. As a result, its foreign policy represented more of an obstacle to the process of political transformation than an asset. As Thomas Carothers has pointed out, "In the early 1980s, when most of the democratic transitions in South America took place, the Reagan administration was trying to support the military governments that were on the way out."[29] Likewise, in Central America, U.S. policy was not pro-democratic but anti-Sandinista and thereby served to buttress military forces at the expense of civilian political actors. Although the Reagan administration readily took credit for the demise of authoritarian rule in Latin America, the process was well underway before U.S. foreign policy shifted in directions favorable to democratic development.[30]

No less problematic are explanations that attribute causal significance to global processes of socioeconomic modernization. The course of political events in modern Latin America is not consistent with the notion that modernization fosters democracy. At the individual level, the propensity to support military coups has not declined with education, income, or social status; if anything, as José Nun emphasized in his now classic essay, "The Middle Class Military Coup Revisited,"[31] the reverse has been true. Similarly, at the societal level neither cross-sectional nor diachronic data offer support for the proposition that democratization reflects socioeconomic development. The most modernized countries in Latin America have not necessarily been the most democratic, nor have gains in literacy, per capita income, or popular organizational capacity been predictably translated through time into democratization. As emphasized in the literature on bureaucratic authoritarianism,[32] the opposite pattern was observed during the 1970s, when two decades of unusually rapid socioeconomic development culminated in the emergence of repressive military rule throughout the Southern Cone. The reversal of this trend offers no basis for returning to the formulas of the early

1960s, particularly since the democratic advances of the 1980s were associated with economic decline, deindustrialization, and precipitous drops in regional standards of living rather than with socioeconomic development.

Structural changes in the international economy offer a far more plausible explanation for the onset of the process of democratization. The OPEC price increases and growth of the Eurodollar market in the 1973–1974 period, in particular, provoked changes in economic expectations, performance, and policy that were to prove unsustainable and destabilizing throughout the region. For most Latin countries, the key shift was increased access to international lending. As long as exports continued to grow faster than debt payments, no major problems developed, but following the second oil shock of 1979 the situation changed dramatically. World interest rates soared, international trade declined, commodity prices plummeted, and capital flight accelerated. Instead of curbing large budget deficits or adopting more realistic exchange rates, Latin America responded to these global shifts by increased international borrowing. Between 1979 and 1981 the major regional debtors doubled their net liabilities to international banks, paving the way for the outbreak of acute financial crisis following the cutoff in new lending to the region in mid-1982.[33] The process of recovery was to prove slow and uneven. As the decade drew to a close, average per capita income in the region was 8 percent lower than at its outset. Argentina, Bolivia, Nicaragua, and Peru, which entered the crisis in unusually fragile economic condition, experienced declines of more than 20 percent.[34]

The timing and magnitude of the difficulties provoked by international economic change varied across the region. The petroleum producers began to run into difficulties in the mid-1970s, largely because of a combination of nationalist policies and excessive economic optimism. In 1975–1976 Mexico experienced a run on the peso that was rapidly translated into a severe economic crisis.[35] The Ecuadoran economy also foundered in 1975, when multinational opposition to statist oil policies disrupted petroleum income and contributed to the mobilization of business opposition to military rule.[36] Peru experienced similar difficulties. In 1975 a severe balance-of-payments crisis forced the military government to abandon statist policies, launch a stabilization program, and turn to the IMF. The Peruvian crisis continued through the late 1970s, producing negative rates of economic growth in both 1977 and 1978.[37] Although Bolivia managed to maintain its economic momentum, between 1974 and 1977 the external public debt doubled, growth declined, and balance-of-payments problems began to develop in response to the Banzer regime's program of state-funded development, which presupposed petroleum exports that never materialized.[38]

Significantly, the earliest transitions to competitive rule in Latin America took place in the petroleum producing countries of the Andes. The nationalist Rodríguez Lara government in Ecuador was ousted in January 1976, paving the way for a phased military retreat from power that culminated in the inauguration of President Jaime Roldós in mid-1979. The breakdown of Peruvian authoritarianism began a year earlier in 1975, when the reformist government of General Juan Velasco Alvarado was ousted from power. Faced with progressively deepening economic difficulties, the military convened a constituent assembly in 1978 and transferred power to an elected civilian successor in 1980. The Bolivian transition, which began as a directed program of political liberalization, was more protracted. After the Banzer regime was overthrown in mid-1978, inconclusive elections led to the installation of a transitional civilian government that was almost immediately ousted by the military. A second set of competitive elections was held in 1980, but again the military intervened. The formal process of democratization was thus not completed until 1982, by which time the Bolivian economy was verging on collapse.[39]

The process of authoritarian breakdown also began in Central America during the 1970s in response to shifts in the world economy. The acceleration of world inflation, rapid increases in oil prices, and the collapse of the Central American Common Market interacted to produce a variety of destabilizing results for the relatively open economies of the region, including declining growth, rising inflation, falling real wages, balance-of-payments problems, fiscal imbalances, the concentration of industrial production in larger units, and increased landlessness.[40] These changes contributed to growing peasant and worker unrest and helped to undermine authoritarian rule throughout the region. After a brief period of recovery, the economies of the region suffered a second set of shocks in 1979 as a result of another major round of oil price increases and mounting regional conflict. Indeed, 1979 marks a major watershed in the economic history of Central America. Macroeconomic performance declined severely, the stability in exchange rates established over a period of 60 years collapsed, and the existing export-led model of economic growth underwent major revisions in response to changing external realities and the pressures of international lenders.[41] Although democratization was limited, even in the narrow, institutional sense of the term, significant political shifts followed. Honduras returned to civilian rule in 1982, Nicaragua and El Salvador held elections in 1984, and the Guatemalan military ceded power to an elected government in 1986.

The last wave of regime transitions occurred in Brazil and the Southern Cone. In Argentina, the process began in late 1981 with a military coup that set the stage for the outbreak of conflict in the South Atlantic, military defeat, and the transfer of power to an elected government in late 1983. The Uruguayan transition followed in 1985, the Brazilian in 1986, and the Chilean in 1989. The difference in timing relative to the Andean region reflects economic as well as political conditions. Boosted by the high level of international borrowing, the economies of Brazil and the Southern Cone grew comparatively rapidly in the 1976–1980 period by both cross-sectional and historical standards. In 1979, for example, the Argentine economy registered a growth rate of 11.1 percent. The figures for Brazil, Chile, and Uruguay, respectively, were 7.2, 8.3, and 6.2 percent, as contrasted with an average figure of 3.3 for the Andean nations that made transitions from military to civilian rule in the 1979–1982 period.[42] By 1981, however, signs of mounting economic instability were also becoming evident in the Southern Cone, undercutting claims that neoliberal economic policies had fostered "economic miracles." The collapse began in Argentina, where pressures on the peso forced the military government to abandon a fixed exchange rate in early 1981. The result was an effective devaluation of nearly 400 percent, severe recession, and a financial crisis that threatened the solvency of most of the private sector. The Uruguayan and Chilean economies followed suit in 1982. For Brazil the second oil price shock of 1979 marked a critical economic turning point, but as a result of the relatively favorable structure of its external debt and its relatively low ratio to GDP, the country was comparatively slow to feel the full impact of the debt crisis.

## The Role of Domestic Factors

As indicated by the political history of the Great Depression, economic crises are not automatically translated into political crises. Their outcome depends on the way in which they work their way through social and institutional structures and exacerbate the fragilities of established regimes. Legitimacy is not a useful way of conceptualizing this issue. The concept not only pushes the analysis of regime change in the direction of tautology, but directs attention away from important questions of political agency, resources, and self-interest. In any case, few of the military regimes governing Latin America in the 1970s ever enjoyed much in the way of legitimacy, if by that concept we mean measurable public support and acceptance. The Somoza dynasty was infamous for corruption and thuggery but nevertheless retained power for 40 years. Its undoing was not a sudden loss of legitimacy but a breakdown in coercive capability. Central to any understanding of this issue is the way in which economic setbacks affected the state and its relationship to civil society.

Although recent literature on Latin America has emphasized the accidental and indeterminate character of democratic transitions, major similarities and differences among countries can be traced back to structural and institutional forces. The timing, pace, and impact of the breakdown of authoritarianism in Latin America have varied not only with the magnitude of the adjustments demanded by external shifts, but also with the social foundations and institutional structure of military rule. Particularly important is the nature of the relationship that developed between the government and the business community, whose growing opposition to authoritarianism played a key role in the process of political change throughout the region.[43]

In the Andes, where the earliest and least traumatic authoritarian break-downs occurred, the statist orientation of the military had alienated business elites even before economic clouds appeared on the horizon. The economic setbacks of the 1970s, which were comparatively minor by the standards of the 1980s, were thus rapidly converted into mobilization of business opposi-tion to authoritarianism. The political might of private capital was felt first in Ecuador, where the cohesion of the dominant class was most pronounced. Business groups had begun to coalesce in opposition to military reformism during General Guillermo Rodríguez Lara's first year in office.[44] His ouster four years later and the military's subsequent phased retreat from power re-flected the fragility of a regime that had attempted to confront solid private sector opposition without any independent political base of support.[45] Hence, although Ecuador sustained quite positive rates of economic growth through the end of the 1970s, the 1975 slump in petroleum income was rapidly converted into a regime crisis. It should be emphasized that popular mobilization played no significant role in the process. As Catherine Conaghan has put it, "The irony of the return to democracy in Ecuador is that it reflected not the strength and pervasive demands of popular-class or-ganizations and political parties, but was contingent on their weakness."[46]

Business interests were slower to mobilize against military rule in the other Andean nations. The Peruvian bourgeoisie was initially divided in its response to authoritarianism. It was only after the economy began its steady descent into economic crisis in the mid-1970s that the private sector began to unite, thereby altering the pre-existing correlation of forces in favor of the restoration of civilian rule.[47] The Bolivian bourgeoisie was even more am-bivalent. From 1974 to 1978 the Banzer regime ruled with the support of pri-vate sector interests, notably agro-industrialists of eastern Bolivia who de-rived major economic benefits from the regime's development policies. Bolstered as well by international borrowing, the Bolivian economy re-mained on an expansionary trajectory until the late 1970s. Private sector op-position to military rule therefore emerged comparatively late and was fu-eled less by reformist policies than by the uncertainties and instability associated with the constant rotation of governments in the 1978–1982 period.[48]

Outside of the Andean region, military rule was more exclusionary in nature and built around the support of the private sector. It thus required far deeper economic crises to rupture the relationship between military officers and business elites. The exception is Nicaragua, where bourgeois coopera-tion with the Somoza regime ended in the mid-1970s in response to a variety of threats to established interests, including mounting social unrest and the expansion of the Somoza family's business domain in the wake of the 1972 earthquake.[49] In other parts of Central America, however, the alignment of elite and military interests survived the 1970s largely unscathed. The same is true in the Southern Cone, where it was not until most of the private sector was facing the prospect of bankruptcy that business groups joined other sectors of society in criticizing military rule and pressuring for a transition to political democracy. Economic reversals were not the only motive; after the outbreak of revolution in Central America, the perpetuation of military rule came to be seen elsewhere in Latin America less as a guarantor of capitalism than as a potential source of instability, particularly in countries such as Chile where the left had reoriented its political strategy in favor of revolutionary violence. Popular mobilization fed into this process by accentuating the fear of instability.

The second factor influencing the timing, pace, and impact of regime change in Latin America was the structure of military rule. Military regimes vary along two key institutional dimensions. One is the level of military involvement in the day-to-day process of governance; the other is the relative concentration of political power.[50] The two dimensions interact and influence regime resilience such that regimes armed with similar ideologies and class allies may evince very different patterns of breakdown in response to comparable external challenges. *Ceteris paribus,* authoritarian rule has broken down most readily where the roles of military as institution and military as government have not been separated *and* where political power has been dispersed. The Argentine military regime of the post-1976 period provides a pivotal example of this institutional pattern, which may be described as feudal. As indicated by appointments to the cabinet and other key posts, military and governmental roles were not separated in Argentina. Military officers participated actively in the government at all levels; all major policy decisions involved the military; and the most powerful active-duty officer in the armed forces held the position of chief of state. This fusion of military and governmental roles was combined with the dispersion of political power among the three services of the armed forces. As a result, the work of the government was poorly coordinated, policy formation erratic and incoherent, and the vulnerability of the regime to internal fragmentation extreme. Due to the lack of centralized control, every crisis of government was converted into a crisis of regime.

Argentina represents an extreme combination of role fusion and power dispersal, but military rule in Bolivia, Ecuador, and Peru approximated in varying degrees the Argentine pattern. Accordingly, these regimes proved unusually susceptible to internal breakdown. The high level of institutional involvement in the process of governance and the absence of centralized control capable of imposing military unity meant that political divisions emerging in the broader society were rapidly replicated within the state, undercutting regime cohesion. The importance of this issue has been appropriately emphasized by Guillermo O'Donnell and Philippe C. Schmitter:

"No transition can be forced purely by opponents against a regime which maintains the cohesion, capacity, and disposition to apply repression."[51] Significantly, all four of the Latin regimes that conformed to a feudal institutional pattern began to break down prior to the official onset of the debt crisis, including Argentina. Although conventional wisdom attributes the demise of Argentine authoritarianism to military defeat, the process of regime breakdown began with the coup against General Viola in late 1981.

Far greater challenges had to be mounted to destroy the cohesion of regimes that conformed to other patterns of organization that might be described as oligarchic and sultanistic. In the former, political power is diffused collegially, but the stability of the regime is protected by limited military involvement in the process of governance. In the latter, the military participates actively in the government, but the principal basis for regime stability is protected by a high concentration of political power. Brazil and Uruguay, where relatively collegial structures of military rule were combined with limited military involvement in the day-to-day process of governance, provide examples of the oligarchic pattern. The process of transition in these cases was controlled, late, and protracted. The Central American cases might be discussed under the same general rubric, although, to date, the transition from military to elected civilian rule has remained provisional.

Chile provides a key illustration of the sultanistic pattern: high levels of military participation in the process of governance were combined with the extreme centralization of political power in the hands of General Augusto Pinochet, whose list of official titles came to include President of the Republic, Generalissimo of the Chilean Armed Forces, Captain General, and Commander-in-Chief of the Chilean Army. This concentration of personal power protected the internal unity of the regime in the face of drastic economic setbacks, mounting business opposition, external pressures, and mass protests. Hence whereas Argentine authoritarianism, whose origins, ideology, social base, and policies were similar to those of the Pinochet regime, had begun to disintegrate after only five years in power, the cohesion of the Chilean military remained largely unbroken into the late 1980s. The process of transition was accordingly late, slow, and in many respects incomplete. As of early 1992, Pinochet still retained control of the most powerful armed service, and he was but one of many authoritarian vestiges constraining his elected successor.[52]

The impact of international economic change on politics in Latin America was thus mediated by the alignment of dominant economic interests and regime structure. The two factors may be seen as interacting but not covariant; e.g., feudal patterns of military rule have been associated with both inclusionary (or reformist) and exclusionary (or conservative) authoritarianism. The same is true of highly personalistic military regimes. Because reformist military projects characteristically alienate dominant economic forces, the least resilient combination has been that of feudal regime struc-

tures and inclusionary rule. At the other end of the spectrum are exclusionary authoritarian regimes with sultanistic institutional patterns. The process
of political transformation in Latin America began with the first set of
regimes and as the regional economic crisis deepened, gradually encompassed the latter.

## Democratic Transitions and Political Outcomes

As suggested above, the outcome of the process of political democratization
in Latin America was as unanticipated as its onset. Instead of yielding a set
of fragile and short-lived democracies, as in previous decades, the political
retreat of the military in the 1980s paved the way for the emergence of a relatively durable, inclusionary, and consensually based set of competitive
regimes. The fragilities of authoritarianism per se do not account for this
outcome, nor do changes in the international economic system and related
domestic political realignments. The conditions associated with the breakdown of authoritarianism have not necessarily favored the consolidation of
competitive rule, much less fostered the creation of inclusionary and consensually based regimes. Indeed, since 1982 regional observers have repeatedly
warned that the international debt crisis, which played such an important
role in the breakdown of authoritarianism, also threatens democratic political stability. Thus in many respects the key puzzle is not why the process of
democratization began but rather why it persisted and deepened through
time in the face of intractable economic problems. This outcome reflects a
combination of structural and conjunctural forces that are of fundamental
importance for assessing the future of competitive institutions in the region.
Several key sets of factors may be identified.

First, although external political forces played a limited and rather
mixed role in terms of the etiology of regime change, by the mid-1980s the
international political environment had shifted in directions favorable to the
consolidation of competitive rule. Arguably the key factor accounting for
this difference was not enhanced international support for democracy but diminished threat.[53] The Cold War environment not only fostered the expansion of Latin American military institutions but offered a national security
rationale for external and internal actors to collaborate in jettisoning democratic institutions. With the waning of East-West tensions, popular pressures
are less readily defined as Communist threats; the incentives for the regional
hegemon to promote the overthrow of elected governments have diminished;
and the rationale for the maintenance of large military establishments or aid
programs within the region has largely disappeared, helping to shift the balance of power in favor of civilian actors.

In terms of U.S. policy, a major consequence of these changes is that
support for elected governments in Latin America has become less vac-

illating than at any time in the past several decades. The closest parallel is probably the early 1960s, when the United States launched the Alliance for Progress. The reformist momentum of that era, however, was rapidly dissipated in the face of perceived challenges to regional security associated with the Cuban revolution. In the context of the Cold War, the tension between democratic ideals and national security was routinely resolved in favor of the latter. The relaxation of international rivalries thus has enhanced the prospects for democracy in the hemisphere, as emphasized by the recent history of Nicaragua, where the end of the Cold War paved the way for the end of the contra war and the participation of a full spectrum of opposition elements in the 1990 election.[54]

The international climate of the 1980s and early 1990s has also differed from that of the past in the sense that alternative political models of the extreme left and right have been discredited along with their international sponsors. This change has had important domestic repercussions. With the notable exception of Peru, it has disoriented, divided, and otherwise helped to weaken the political left and removed a principal rallying point for the organization of authoritarian political projects. The left may represent a continuing threat to General Pinochet, but his vision is one that others find increasingly unpersuasive and removed from political reality. The end of the Cold War has thus undercut political forces at both ends of the political spectrum, reducing challenges to democratic stability and altering the preexisting political dynamic in favor of moderation, pragmatism, and the construction of political consensus.

A pattern of broadening external linkages between Latin America and the rest of the world has buttressed these changes. During the 1980s, social groups within Latin America began to reach out to build transnational coalitions around such concerns as human rights and the environment. European governments, political parties, and other actors also began to play a more active role in hemispheric affairs during the 1980s, creating conditions for democratic development in Latin America that are increasingly analogous to those existing in southern Europe during the 1970s.[55]

Global economic forces created a second set of conditions working in favor of the persistence of democracy. The internationalization of capital markets coupled with the post-1982 reversal of historic patterns of capital flow to Latin America have restricted the options of policymakers across the region, minimized the margin for policy error, and forced a wholesale abandonment of pre-existing patterns of state-led import-substitution development. The contemporary development orthodoxy or "Washington consensus" prescribes fiscal discipline, privatization, trade liberalization, deregulation, and, in general, increased reliance upon market mechanisms.[56] The perceived alternatives to this agenda are virtually nonexistent, given the limited bargaining position of Latin nations, the increasingly strict conditions of International Monetary Fund and World Bank lending programs, and the important role played by these multilateral institutions in regulating international financial flows. Also relevant, as Miles Kahler has emphasized, is the absence of competing intellectual models.[57] The economic collapse of the Eastern bloc, the related loss of alternative founts of economic advice, education, and financial support, the success of the Asian NICs, the perceived failures of the past, and the disastrous results of efforts to formulate autochthonous responses to the international economic crisis have all contributed to the sense that Latin nations have little choice but to pursue policies whose short-term impact has proved both politically and economically painful, if not positively disastrous.

In response to these developments, governments throughout the region have turned to political pacts, coalitions, and other modes of elite consensus formation to reduce political risks and create the political space necessary for the adoption of drastic economic reforms. Popular participation in policy formation processes has thus been carefully circumscribed at the same time that the international banking community has gained enormous influence over domestic policy choice. Concomitantly, forces that might challenge elite interests, including trade unions and parties of the left, have been weakened by international political developments, deindustrialization, prolonged economic crisis, and, especially in the Southern Cone, past political repression. As a result of this combination of developments, domestic elites have received unprecedented guarantees that party competition will not lead to populist destruction of the prevailing economic order. Such reassurance was often lacking in the past, which created incentives for privileged groups to knock on the doors of the barracks and subvert democracy in search of less risky forms of governance.

The policy constraints faced by Latin governments have also limited the attractiveness of authoritarian rule for the military institutions themselves. Under conditions demanding strict fiscal austerity, the gains to be achieved through control of the state are more limited than in the past and the difficulties of maintaining any base of civilian support behind military rule much larger. The incentives and opportunities for the creation of alliances between the forces that have historically posed the greatest challenges to Latin American democracy have accordingly declined rather dramatically.

The net result has been a major increase in the potential viability of political democracy in a region perennially characterized by extreme social inequalities, intense redistributive pressures, and a related propensity toward political polarization. Since the 1970s, the perceived costs of political defeat have declined along with the benefits of victory. This change has reduced the stakes of the political game and facilitated the search for consensual solutions to outstanding social problems. The importance of these developments is emphasized by Adam Przeworski's recent work on democratization[58]—although, in a fashion contrary to his analysis, negative rather than positive economic conditions have enhanced the sustainability of democratic institutions in the Latin American context.

Considerable political learning has also occurred in Latin American societies as a result of the authoritarian experiences of the past two decades, further reducing the attractions of the traditional alternatives to political democracy. Business elites have learned that the military is not necessarily a reliable ally; the military has paid a heavy professional and institutional price for political intervention; the church has felt the pressure of political repression and rallied behind democratic political alternatives; and the populace has gained a new appreciation of democratic forms, particularly in countries where the political experience of the past decade has been characterized by unusually high levels of political violence. The reorientation of political values that has been documented in country after country is a reflection of this process.

Last, but not least important, modernization processes over the past two decades have significantly broadened the base for democratic institutions and fostered higher levels of citizen participation in political affairs. Although the commercialization of agriculture, urbanization, increased literacy, access to mass communications, and other sets of related changes have not necessarily promoted democracy in Latin America, as the early literature on political development suggested; such changes have nonetheless meant that democratic institutions in the 1980s are far more inclusionary and participatory than in the past.

For the future of Latin American democracy a key question is the relative permanence of the changes that have been outlined above. Some are obviously susceptible to reversal. Strong citizen preferences for democratic rule, for example, may wane along with the memories of authoritarian political violence and policy failure. Similarly, economic recuperation may expand the menu of policy choices in ways that may threaten powerful economic actors and undermine elite consensus. And so on. Such reversals in the existing political dynamic will take time, however, and in the interim institutional changes are occurring that strengthen the probabilities of consensual political solutions and raise the costs of authoritarian reversals. The growth in the political capacity of civilian actors relative to the military, which reflects the restoration of organizational freedom, economic austerity, and the new international context, is a particularly significant development.

## Conclusion

This review of the last decade of democratization suggests that Latin America is not merely experiencing another episode in a cycle of democratic and authoritarian alterations, but has instead entered a distinctive historical phase in which broad electoral participation and respect for oppositional rights have become widespread and relatively durable features of the political landscape. The origins of this transformation are to be found in the interaction between domestic and international forces. At the international level, the most influential developments were the oil shocks of the 1970s, the related expansion of international lending, and the subsequent debt crisis. The speed with which and extent to which these changes in the international political economy were translated into democratization were conditioned by the political alignments of the private sector and by the structural fragilities of authoritarianism at the national level.

The process of regime transformation in Latin America continued through the early 1990s, yielding a set of political democracies that has proved unexpectedly resilient. This outcome reflects a combination of structural and conjunctural conditions that have converged at the domestic level to reduce the incentives and opportunities for authoritarian reversals. Global political change, the receding threat from the revolutionary left, the internationalization of capital markets, the triumph of free-market paradigms, political learning, constraints on domestic policy choice, and the related elimination of perceived regime alternatives have all contributed to the sustainability of political democracy in the 1980s. Particularly notable at the national level in Latin America are the efforts that have been made to mobilize elite consensus around competitive institutions. That such efforts should have emerged in what was once despairingly called "conflict societies" reflects the magnitude of the changes that have occurred in the region.

Not all of the elements underlying the transition to relatively consensual and inclusionary political democracy are to be found in every country in the region, leaving space for authoritarian regression, as in Haiti and Peru. Yet as suggested by the experience of the northern European democracies, or more recently, those of southern Europe, once the international and domestic incentives are in place for continued participation by key political forces in the agreements and institutions that characterize democratic regimes, such regimes may develop a self-sustaining character missing from authoritarian alternatives.

## Notes

1. Guillermo O'Donnell, *Modernization and Bureaucratic-Authoritarianism: Studies in South American Politics,* 2d ed., (Berkeley: Institute of International Studies, University of California at Berkeley, 1979).

2. *Dependency and Development in Latin America,* trans. Marjory Mattingly Urquidi (Berkeley: University of California Press, 1979).

3. David Collier, ed., *The New Authoritarianism in Latin America* (Princeton: Princeton University Press, 1979).

4. For additional definitional specification and discussion of the institutional concept of democracy, see Terry Lynn Karl, "Dilemmas of Democratization in Latin America," *Comparative Politics,* 23, no. 1 (October 1990): 1–2. See also Guillermo O'Donnell and Philippe C. Schmitter, *Transitions from Authoritarian Rule: Tentative Conclusions about Uncertain Democracies* (Baltimore: Johns Hopkins, 1986), pp. 7–8; Samuel P. Huntington, "The Modest Meaning of Democracy," in ed. Robert A.

Pastor, *Democracy in the Americas: Stopping the Pendulum* (New York: Holmes and Meier, 1989), pp. 11–28.

5. Karen L. Remmer, "Exclusionary Democracy," *Studies in Comparative International Development* 20, no. 1 (Winter 1985–1986): 64–85.

6. Enrique C. Ochoa, "The Rapid Expansion of Voter Participation in Latin America: Presidential Elections, 1845–1986," in *Statistical Abstract of Latin America,* vol. 25, James W. Wilkie and David Lorey, eds. (Los Angeles: UCLA Latin American Center Publications, University of California, 1987), pp. 894, 900.

7. Ochoa, "The Rapid Expansion of Voter Participation," p. 880.

8. Ochoa, "The Rapid Expansion of Voter Participation," pp. 872, 882, 886.

9. See, for example, Jane Jaquette, ed., *The Women's Movement in Latin America* (Boston: Unwin Hyman, 1989); Sonia E. Alvarez, *Engendering Democracy in Brazil: Women's Movements in Transition Politics* (Princeton, NJ: Princeton University Press, 1991); Susan Eckstein, ed., *Power and Social Protest: Latin American Social Movements* (Berkeley: University of California Press, 1989).

10. Eduardo A. Gamarra, "Mass Politics and Elite Arrangements: Elections and Democracy in Bolivia" (Paper presented at the Fifteenth International Congress of the Latin American Studies Association, Miami, December 1989), p. 4. See also Catherine M. Conaghan, James M. Malloy, and Luis A. Abugattas, "Business and the 'Boys': The Politics of Neoliberalism in the Central Andes," *Latin American Research Review* 25, no. 2 (1990): 3–30.

11. *Latin American Regional Reports,* no. 7 (31 August 1989): 1–2.

12. See Mario R. dos Santos, ed., *Concertación político-social y democratización* (Buenos Aires: Consejo Latinamericano de Ciencias Sociales, 1987).

13. See, in particular, Guillermo O'Donnell, Philippe C. Schmitter, and Laurence Whitehead, eds., *Transitions from Authoritarian Rule: Tentative Conclusions about Uncertain Democracies* (Baltimore: Johns Hopkins, 1986), pp. 37–47.

14. See Jonathan Hartlyn, "Colombia: The Politics of Violence and Accommodation," in *Democracy in Developing Countries,* Vol. 4: *Latin America,* eds. Larry Diamond, Juan J. Linz, and Seymour Martin Lipset (Boulder: Lynne Rienner, 1989), pp. 306–308.

15. Terry Lynn Karl, "Petroleum and Political Pacts: The Transition to Democracy in Venezuela," in O'Donnell and Schmitter, *Transitions from Authoritarian Rule: Tentative Conclusions,* pp. 196–219; Daniel Levine, "Venezuela since 1958: The Consolidation of Democratic Politics," in *The Breakdown of Democratic Regimes: Latin America,* Juan Linz and Alfred Stepan, eds. (Baltimore: Johns Hopkins, 1978).

16. Ekkart Zimmermann and Thomas Saalfeld, "Economic and Political Reactions to the World Economic Crisis of the 1930s in Six European Countries," *International Studies Quarterly* 32 (1988): 305.

17. Carlos Huneeus, *Los chilenos y la política* (Santiago: Instituto Chileno de Estudios Humanisticos, 1987), pp. 58, 128.

18. Thomas R. Rochon and Michael J. Mitchell, "Social Bases of the Transition to Democracy in Brazil," *Comparative Politics* 21, no. 3 (April 1989): 307–322.

19. Centro de Estudios de la Realidad Contemporánea, "Evaluación del primer año de gobierno democrático" (Santiago, 1991), p. 5.

20. Cynthia McClintock, "Peru: Precarious Regimes, Authoritarian and Democratic," in Diamond, Linz, and Lipset, *Democracy in Developing Countries: Latin America,* p. 359.

21. Edgardo Catterberg, *Los argentinos frente a la política* (Buenos Aires: Planeta, 1989), p. 64.

22. McClintock, "Peru," p. 359; Mitchell A. Seligson and Edward N. Muller, "Democratic Stability and Economic Crisis: Costa Rica, 1978–1983," *International Studies Quarterly* 31, no. 3 (1987): 312.

23. Huneuus, *Los chilenos,* p. 163.

24. Juan Rial, "Political Parties and Elections in the Process of Transition in Uruguay," in *Comparing New Democracies: Transition and Consolidation in Mediterranean Europe and the Southern Cone,* ed. Enrique A. Baloyra (Boulder: Westview, 1987), p. 258.

25. Karen L. Remmer, "The Political Impact of Economic Crisis in Latin America in the 1980s," *American Political Science Review* 85 (September 1991): 777–800.

26. See Karen L. Remmer, "New Wine or Old Bottlenecks? The Study of Latin American Democracy," *Comparative Politics* 23, no. 4 (July 1991): 479–495.

27. Adam Przeworski, "The 'East' Becomes the 'South'? The 'Autumn of the People' and the Future of Eastern Europe," *PS: Political Science and Politics,* 24, no. 4 (March 1991): 20–24.

28. See Augusto Varas, ed., *El partido comunista en Chile* (Santiago: Facultad Latinamericana de Ciencias Sociales and Centro de Estudios Sociales, 1988).

29. Thomas Carothers, "The Reagan Years: The 1980s," in *Exporting Democracy: The United States and Latin America,* ed. Abraham F. Lowenthal (Baltimore: Johns Hopkins, 1991), p. 108.

30. Carothers, "The Reagan Years," pp. 90–122.

31. José Nun, "The Middle-Class Military Coup Revisited," in *Armies and Politics in Latin America,* ed. Abraham F. Lowenthal (New York: Holmes & Meier, 1976), pp. 49–86.

32. O'Donnell, *Modernization and Bureaucratic-Authoritarianism;* and "Reflections on the Patterns of Change in the Bureaucratic-Authoritarian State," *Latin American Research Review,* 13 (1978):3038; Collier, ed., *The New Authoritarianism.*

33. See Jeffrey D. Sachs, ed., *Developing Country Debt and Economic Performance,* Vol. I: *The International Financial System* (Chicago: University of Chicago Press, 1989).

34. Comisión Económica para América Latina y el Caribe, *Notas sobre la economía y el desarrollo* (December 1990), p. 26.

35. For an overview of the responses of the Mexican economy to shifting external conditions, see Robert Kaufman, "Economic Orthodoxy and Political Change in Mexico: The Stabilization and Adjustment Policies of the de la Madrid Administration," in *Debt and Democracy in Latin America,* ed. Barbara Stallings and Robert Kaufman (Boulder: Westview, 1989), pp. 109–126.

36. See John D. Martz, *Politics and Petroleum in Ecuador* (New Brunswick, NJ: Transaction Books, 1987).

37. International Monetary Fund, *International Financial Statistics* (Washington, DC: International Monetary Fund, 1987), p. 161.

38. International Monetary Fund, *International Financial Supplement on Economic Indicators* (Washington, DC: IMF, 1975); Jeffrey Sachs and Juan Antonio Morales, *Bolivia: 1952–1986* (San Francisco: International Center for Economic Growth, 1988), p. 21.

39. For a detailed account of this period, see James Dunkerley, *Rebellion in the Veins: Political Struggle in Bolivia, 1952–1982* (London: Verso, 1984). See also Laurence Whitehead, "Bolivia's Failed Democratization, 1977–1980," in O'Donnell, Schmitter, and Whitehead, *Transitions from Authoritarian Rule: Latin America,* pp. 49–71.

40. Victor Bulmer-Thomas, *The Political Economy of Central America since 1920* (New York: Cambridge University Press, 1987), pp. 200–229. On the relation-

ship between these changes and challenges to the social order, see John Booth, "Socioeconomic and Political Roots of National Revolts in Central America," *Latin American Research Review* 26, no. 1 (1991): 33–73.

41. Bulmer-Thomas, "Political Economy of Central America," pp. 291–294.

42. International Monetary Fund, *IMF Yearbook* (Washington, DC: IMF, 1988), n.p.

43. For an overview of this issue, see Sylvia Maxfield, "National Business, Debt-Led Growth, and the Political Transition in Latin America," in Stallings and Kaufman, *Debt and Democracy in Latin America,* pp. 75–90.

44. Conaghan, Malloy, and Abugattas, "Business and the 'Boys,'" p. 7.

45. Catherine M. Conaghan, *Restructuring Domination: Industrialists and the State in Ecuador* (Pittsburgh: University of Pittsburgh Press, 1988). See also Martz, *Politics and Petroleum in Ecuador.*

46. Conaghan, *Restructuring Domination,* p. 141.

47. See Peter S. Cleaves and Henry Pease Garcia, "State Autonomy and Military Policy Making," in *The Peruvian Experiment Reconsidered,* ed. Cynthia McClintock and Abraham F. Lowenthal (Princeton, NJ: Princeton University Press, 1983), pp. 209–244; David Booth and Bernardo Sorj, *Military Reformism and Social Classes: The Peruvian Experience, 1968–1980* (New York: St. Martin's, 1983).

48. Conaghan, Malloy, and Abugattas, "Business and the 'Boys,'" p. 8.

49. See John A. Booth, *The End and the Beginning: The Nicaraguan Revolution* (Boulder, CO: Westview, 1985).

50. For an elaboration of these issues, see Karen Remmer, *Military Rule in Latin America* (Boulder, CO: Westview, 1991).

51. O'Donnell and Schmitter, *Transitions from Authoritarian Rule,* p. 21.

52. Brian Loveman, "Misión Cumplida? Civil Military Relations and the Chilean Political Transition" (Paper prepared for the meeting of the Latin American Studies Association, Washington, DC, April 1991).

53. On this point, see John Markoff and Silvio R. Duncan Baretta, "Economic Crisis and Regime Change in Brazil: The 1960s and the 1980s," *Comparative Politics,* 22, no. 4 (July 1990): 435.

54. See Joseph S. Tulchin and Knut Walter, "Nicaragua: The Limits of Intervention," in *Exporting Democracy: The United States and Latin America,* ed. Abraham F. Lowenthal (Baltimore: Johns Hopkins, 1991), pp. 233–262.

55. See Laurence Whitehead, "International Aspects of Democratization," in *Transitions from Authoritarian Rule: Comparative Perspectives,* ed. Guillermo O'Donnell, Philippe C. Schmitter, and Laurence Whitehead (Baltimore: Johns Hopkins, 1986), pp. 3–46.

56. See John Williamson, ed., *Latin American Adjustment: How Much Has Happened?* (Washington, DC: Institute for International Relations, 1990).

57. Miles Kahler, "Orthodoxy and Its Alternatives: Explaining Approaches to Stabilization and Adjustment," in Joan M. Nelson, ed., *Economic Crisis and Policy Choice: The Politics of Adjustment in the Third World* (Princeton: Princeton University Press, 1990), pp. 33–61.

58. Adam Przeworski, *Democracy and the Market: Political and Economic Reforms in Eastern Europe and Latin America* (New York: Cambridge University Press, 1991).

# 6

## Democratization in China

### *Thomas Bernstein*

With respect to democratization in the 1990s, China remains "odd man out." In East Asia, Taiwan and South Korea have been making a democratic transition, while liberalizing and democratizing changes have been underway with varying degrees of success in Eastern Europe and the former republics of the Soviet Union. In sharp contrast, the rulers of the People's Republic of China have stuck resolutely to the "Four Principles"—the leading role of the Communist party, the thought of Mao Zedong, the socialist road, and the proletarian dictatorship. Yet, only a short time ago, in May 1989, millions of demonstrators in Beijing's Tiananmen Square and in many other cities and towns vigorously voiced demands for political change in the most extraordinary popular upsurge in the PRC's history. China's conservative rulers felt so threatened by this upsurge that they resorted to armed force to suppress it. They repressed the protests and sought to insulate themselves from the winds of political change, domestic and foreign.

The Tiananmen demonstrations suggested that people in China wanted political change; just what kind of change they wanted was not as clear. The demonstrations, while universally labelled a "Democracy Movement," exhibited few demands for the essential core of a democratic system, i.e., for free and competitive elections and freedom to form parties. Most of the demands were for better rulers, for a dialogue with the party-state leaders, for recognition of autonomous organizations, and for a freer press. Had these demands been granted, the Chinese Communist system would have begun a profoundly important process of liberalization, but not necessarily democratization. Liberalizing changes might in the future have led to full democratization. The question that remains is whether the suppression of the 1989 movement was only a temporary setback for liberalizing forces in China or whether the crushing of the movement in 1989 signified deeper obstacles to political change.

### The Reform Era of the 1980s: Socioeconomic Change and Political Ferment

Most striking about May 1989 was the immense number of demonstrators and the obvious sympathy shown by much of the urban population. Previous episodes of public dissent during the Communist period had been small, consisting mainly of students and intellectuals. Tiananmen, however, must be seen against the background of years of rapid social and economic change, social mobilization, and political ferment.

In 1978, Deng Xiaoping broke with radical Maoism and inaugurated economic reforms designed to speed up the pace of modernization and to raise living standards. Agriculture was to a significant extent decollectivized, a private entrepreneurial sector was allowed to develop, the country "opened up" in relation to the outside world, and efforts, not very successful, were made to loosen controls over state industry so as to increase efficiency. Politically, the reform era saw substantial relaxation (*fangsong*) and increased permissiveness. The tight social, political, and economic controls over individual lives that had been a hallmark of the previous era were loosened. Mass political campaigns largely disappeared and the regime sanctioned greater tolerance. But considerable conflict persisted among top leaders, and periodic crackdowns, especially on daring writers and artists, demonstrated that power relations had not been significantly altered.[1]

The policy of opening to the outside world exposed many Chinese to foreign ideas, breaking with the isolationism of the Cultural Revolution decade. More than 40,000 students studied abroad, most in science and technology, but some in social sciences as well. Foreign students studied in China's higher schools and foreigners came to teach English. Foreign scholars, including political scientists, lectured or taught in China and many Western books were translated. Major cities saw a substantial foreign presence of businesspeople, tourists, scholars, students, and journalists. Much informal contact developed.

Social mobility increased substantially as small private businesses flourished, and as peasants, who had previously been tied to the land, went to work in small towns and temporarily in large cities. Career choices expanded. Young people could decide whether to compete for entrance to higher schools or to go into business and make money, while peasants had new opportunities to go into business and enter markets. Efforts to reform the lifetime tenure system in the bureaucracy and the "iron rice bowl" system in the enterprises were evidence of official intent to promote further mobility. Overall, the capacity of the state to control the lives of people diminished.

The new era brought new opportunities for enrichment but also inequality and new insecurities. Private entrepreneurs made more money than those working for the state. Workers in the state sector began to worry about unemployment and the consequent loss of state welfare benefits.[2] Intellectuals, however, benefited least in material terms. They, along with the vast cadre force, continued to live on fixed incomes that created feelings of deprivation and resentment. Sayings such as "the experts who make missiles earn less than the peddlers who sell eggs" expressed this resentment.[3] Differential opportunities to benefit from the mixed economy caused a good many people to feel disadvantaged and to complain about the fairness of the existing system.[4] Rising inflation in the second half of the 1980s severely compounded feelings of insecurity, particularly of those on fixed incomes.

The reform era also saw a major increase in corruption, particularly in the public's perception. The reforms created numerous opportunities for party and government officials to use power for personal gain (yi quan mou si). Party leaders used influence to give their children opportunities to study abroad or to establish lucrative businesses in Beijing or Hong Kong.[5] Many students bitterly resented such advantages. The state was intent on abolishing the job assignment system for college graduates, meaning that students had to rely on personal connections to get good jobs.[6] Partial economic reform gave rise to numerous new official and unofficial economic relationships and interests. The creation of opportunities for illicit deals between officials and entrepreneurs was often a necessity if anything was to be accomplished.

The puritanical revolutionary ethos so noticeable among cadres in the 1950s had long since eroded, but the process was exacerbated by privatizing reforms. Legal norms did not replace revolutionary values, and legal sanctions appeared to be ineffectual; the government thus resorted to periodic political campaigns against corruption. Popular disaffection with the commercialization of power became a central problem for the Chinese party and hence for the authority of the state. Suspicion of corruption affected the personal authority of leaders all the way to Deng Xiaoping.

Within this changing context, a number of factors significantly altered the political relations between the party-state and society. First, the rapid spread of radio and television enabled large numbers of Chinese to listen not only to their own stations but also to the Voice of America and other foreign radio stations.[7] Second, some observers believe that a nascent civil society began to arise, characterized by a proliferation of autonomous social groups and activities, uncontrolled by the state. This was a consequence of the appearance of private business and of greater permissiveness in the conduct of social and other organized activities.[8] Estimates of nongovernmental associations in China ran to a thousand national associations (xiehui) and an estimated hundred thousand local ones, including literary societies, poetry groups, business associations, etc. Most of these were not political in purpose. Political ones included the so-called "democratic salons" organized by older intellectuals and students prior to Tiananmen. Formally organized associations had to register with the Ministry of the Interior and required a "legal counterpart," usually in the government.[9] Linkage with a government unit whose leaders were tolerant made possible the establishment of some private social science institutes and in turn some remarkably unfettered policy studies and survey research. On the other hand, while there was an enormous proliferation of groups that could be characterized as private to varying degrees, the term "civil society," implying autonomy from or institutional separateness from the state, does not seem fully appropriate when one compares the Chinese case to the richer and more diverse range of organized activities in Latin America, in Poland in the 1980s, or even in the pre-Gorbachev Soviet Union.[10] Nonetheless, a striking increase in social activities and organizations did alter the relationship between state and society.

Third, critical attitudes toward the political system among Chinese largely precipitated the decline in prestige of the Chinese Communist party. By the late 1980s, the party was tainted by corruption and many of its members were held in disrepute. Students were particularly disaffected. Asked what they thought of cadres, 41.9 percent of one sample described them as "contemptible, hateful and detestable." Only 2.5 percent thought them "worthy of respect and approachable."[11] Rosen reports that survey data show that students' former unquestioning obedience to the Communist party was replaced by independence of thought and judgment, respect for talent, and privatistic concerns.[12]

Fourth, high-ranking establishment intellectuals spoke out more vigorously than they previously had on behalf of liberalization. Su Shaozhi, director of an ideological institute of the Chinese Academy of Science, proposed that the party should be placed under the rule of law and that legislative and judicial organs should be independent. Mass organizations should not be treated as "conveyor belts" but "should represent the interest of the masses." Various social strata, groups, and organizations should have an opportunity to express their interests in the political realm. Su suggested that "democratic centralism" had been invented by Lenin, not Marx, to suit the specific needs of the Russian revolution and that Stalin later distorted it. "'Democracy' under centralized guidance means that the people are not the masters, but the ruled." The feudal tradition of trust in wise leaders was perpetuated by this Leninist concept, he asserted, and must be repudiated.[13]

Some of the arguments for liberalization were clearly wedded to elitist views. Intellectual elitism was not only a reaction to the persecution and lowly status of the educated under Mao; it was also based on China's ancient heritage of rule by an educated elite and on skepticism about the qualifications of the peasants to participate in democratic government. Both the Chinese rulers and many Chinese intellectuals believed that peasant parochialism, backwardness, ignorance, and "feudal" mentality meant that they were likely to rely on a great patriarchal ruler rather than to value their democratic rights. Many Chinese intellectuals who wanted democracy believed that peasants were a tragic drag on the goal of democratization. Students interviewed by foreign scholars said they were horrified at the suggestion that truly popular elections would have to include peasants, who would certainly outvote educated people like themselves.[14] An exception to this view, Fang

Lizhi argued in his writings on democracy that peasant participation was essential for China.[15]

## The View from the Top: Deng Xiaoping and Zhao Ziyang

Chinese Communist leaders, beginning with Mao, had been aware of the alienation resulting from unfettered bureaucratic rule and sought a remedy in the form of popular participation. Mao Zedong encouraged popular criticism in 1957 in order to defuse the kind of dissatisfaction that, in his view, had resulted in the Hungarian revolution and the Polish October of 1956. But when students, intellectuals, and members of tightly controlled small parties criticized the "one-party empire," Mao massively repressed dissent.

Deng too was critical of insensitive bureaucracy. He recognized the need for new channels between state and society in order to accommodate demands from below, check arbitrary exercise of power, and promote initiative. Deng attacked the unlimited power of "patriarchal" party secretaries to whom everyone "has to be absolutely obedient" and even "personally attached." He argued that without political reform, "our party will be in a position antagonistic to the masses. Such a situation has already emerged in some localities and units."[16] Yet, even while advocating changes that would loosen the party's grip, Deng also saw the party as the key to the country's unity and stability; in his view, the goal of curtailing the excesses of party dominance was to "maintain and further strengthen Party leadership and discipline, and not to weaken or relax them."[17] This stance served his interest in retaining power but also reflected fears of chaos (*luan*) deeply rooted in Chinese political culture, in relation particularly to the pre-1949 period and more recently the Cultural Revolution.[18] Deng believed that it was his achievement to have brought the country out of the chaos of the Cultural Revolution. He believed that a strong party-led authoritarian regime was essential to hold China together. During the reform years, Deng sought to reduce controls, but he proved ready to tighten them whenever he thought that various social or political forces were getting out of control. In 1986, he called for political reform, but when the ensuing relaxation led to student demonstrations, he clamped down.

In 1987, at the 13th party congress, General Secretary Zhao Ziyang sought to reconcile the perceived need for a more liberal political system with party dominance. Zhao stated that China would stick to party leadership and to democratic centralism: "we shall never abandon them and introduce a Western system of separation of the three powers and of different parties ruling the country in turn." He stressed the need for stability and proper management of the "relationship between democracy and stability and between democracy and efficiency." Zhao suggested that the goal of leadership should be coordination of interests rather than transformation of society. He acknowledged that modernization was giving rise to "complicated social contradictions" as groups develop "different interests and views" and spoke of the task of reconciling differing interests, which required a system of "consultation and dialogue."[19]

Proposals for political liberalization ran into increasing hostility from the remaining first-generation revolutionary leaders, who wielded power despite their nominal retirement. They saw in Zhao Ziyang an inadequate defender of Marxist-Leninist orthodoxy. Zhao was therefore constrained, as he remained dependent on Deng Xiaoping, who shared the other senior leaders' determination to maintain the primacy of the party. As Zhao indicated in his speech to the 13th congress, he wanted at best very limited political liberalization. Indeed, he sympathized with the concept of the "New Authoritarianism," which was debated in China in the late 1980s and which proposed that China required a stage of rule by an enlightened strongman who would force economic reform and development.[20] Democracy would come afterwards, more or less according to the pattern of development in South Korea. In sum, if a democratic transition required top-level leaders who, whether for reasons of self-interest or of principle, favored a breakthrough to liberalization and democratization, they were not yet in evidence in China.

## The Tiananmen Demonstrations

In 1988 and early 1989 public disgust with the country's situation escalated under the impact of inflation and corruption. The protest demonstrations that broke out in April 1989 were a product of this popular anger. They represented a watershed in China's political development, lasting for almost six weeks and bringing a million and more participants to Tiananmen Square. They spread into a hundred cities. Literally millions of urban residents rallied to the students, cheering them on as they marched, providing food and drink, and, in the end, seeking to restrain the military as it moved on the square.

Students played the core role but involvement cut across many strata. Older intellectuals played an important role in precipitating the demonstrations. They led discussions and debates throughout 1988–1989 in "democratic salons" organized by students at Beijing University. Well-known intellectuals such as Fang Lizhi discussed the need for political pluralism, the institution of checks and balances, free speech, and independent social organizations. One salon met from May 1988 to May 1989. Following the Tiananmen protests, the "salons" were condemned as breeding grounds for "bourgeois liberalization" and as having prepared for a "second revolution."[21] Intellectuals also became petitioners in the winter of 1988–1989. Forty-four leading scientists and scholars wrote a "Letter of Opinion" sent to the Standing Committee of the National People's Congress asking for structural political reform. Fang Lizhi petitioned Deng to release political prisoners, especially Wei Jingshen, an uncompromising activist of the 1979 Democracy Wall movement.

The immediate precipitating cause of student demonstrations was the death in mid-April of the former secretary-general of the party, Hu Yaobang, who had been purged in 1986 for excessive sympathy for student demonstrations. Students marched to have his reputation restored. The impending 70th anniversary of the historic May 4 Movement of 1919 also impelled students to march, as did fortuitous international events, especially the visit of Gorbachev. These events conspired to inhibit suppression both for symbolic reasons (the CCP's origins lay in the May 4 Movement) and to avoid a display of massive repression in front of the foreign journalists accompanying Gorbachev. Student leaders quickly learned to manipulate the Western media.

While demonstrations initially consisted of students from such elite schools as Beijing University, they were quickly joined by their confreres from the many other higher schools in Beijing. As news of the demonstrations was disseminated by the students, through China's own media and then through the China programs of the BBC and VOA, students from the provinces travelled to Beijing, though most marched at home. As the movement escalated, nonstudents joined in. By mid-May, the *New York Times* listed an impressive range of participants in the demonstrations: teachers, professors, museum and factory workers, writers, artists, scholars, entrepreneurs, low-level officials, middle school students, journalists from the official party paper.[22] Some peasants also participated, but the May events were mainly an urban affair. Peasants also had major grievances, but an urban-rural linkage was not established during the May movement.

The lack of a decisive regime response undoubtedly played a major role in enlarging participation. The regime repeatedly prohibited demonstrations but failed to enforce its injunctions. On 26 April, a People's Daily editorial written on Deng Xiaoping's instructions labeled the demonstrations as "an organized conspiracy to sow chaos led by people with ulterior motives." The response was that 150,000 marched. When General Secretary Zhao Ziyang pleaded with students to disperse before the Gorbachev visit to avoid humiliation, no one paid heed. Premier Le Peng's proclamation of martial law on 20 May was disregarded as well. A cycle of injunctions and defiance without penalty made the party-state look weak and impotent and increased defiance.[23]

The mushrooming movement was thus fueled by an "exhilarating sense of popular power" and of liberation from the stifling control system.[24] Some participants felt a sense of moral liberation akin to that articulated by Vaclav Havel. Thus, some journalists, five hundred of whom demonstrated on 4 May for press freedom, spoke of their disgust with having had to tell lies all through their careers. The movement was characterized in part by the recovery of civic courage and by willingness to speak out, also spurred by safety in numbers and by the fact that some high-level leaders, including Secretary Zhao Ziyang, took a conciliatory attitude toward the demonstrators. Ziyang encouraged freer press reporting, resulting in extensive and sympathetic coverage of the protests.

What began as the "Beijing University Student Solidarity Preparatory Committee," set up on 19 April, was quickly transformed into the "Federation of Autonomous Student Unions in Beijing Colleges and Universities," which played a central role in mobilizing thousands of students to occupy Tiananmen on 22 April. Subsidiary groups were formed, such as the "Dialogue Delegation," whose purpose was to talk to party and state officials, and the "Hunger Strike Delegation." A core of student leaders emerged. Some—among them, Wan Dan—had been organizers of "democracy salons"; others emerged as the movement progressed. The Beijing students established liaison with their provincial counterparts, and in the second half of May, a "Self-Government Union of Students of Colleges Outside Beijing" was organized to represent non-Beijing students in Tiananmen Square.

Nonstudent organizations were formed in Beijing as well as in many other cities. These included autonomous workers' associations, among them a city-wide one established in Beijing on 19 May. In the provinces, examples of workers' organizations included the "Xi'an Workers' Democratic United Autonomous Association," the "Zhejiang United National Salvation Association," and the "Hangzhou Citizens' Spontaneous Support Group." It is not yet completely clear to what extent workers participated spontaneously. Preliminary research reported by Andrew Walder suggests that Beijing workers did not manifest a strong independent capacity either for participation or organization. Independent unions were formed as a consequence of the demonstrations, not as a cause. Although workers demonstrated, they often did so as organized delegations from their enterprise work units, apparently under the leadership of their cadres. Thus, the units, or *danwei*, may have turned from units of control to units of protest.[25] There apparently was little student-worker cooperation.

Most of the demands that characterized the demonstrations did not initially imply a break with the system. But as the movement escalated, "it tended towards a fundamental critique of the state itself."[26] First, the students appealed to the stated norms and ideals of the Chinese political system and pleaded for their realization, thus taking seriously the professed democratic commitments of the CCP and state constitutions. They disavowed any intent to overthrow the Communist party, a point well-made by their theme song, the Internationale. They wanted to be viewed as a legitimate, patriotic movement, whose purpose was to help the system improve itself.[27] "The mainstream democratic movement has always maintained hope that the authorities would initiate the changes for which it was calling."[28]

Students and their older supporters charged that absolute power corrupts and that the people must supervise the government. They seem to have believed that the existing party and state constitutions permitted this if properly enforced. It was not only students who appealed to the existing constitutions. After the declaration of martial law, high-level supporters circulated petitions for a meeting of the Standing Committee of the National People's Congress to dismiss Premier Le Peng for having unconstitutionally invoked martial law. Similarly, after General Secretary Zhao Ziyang had been fired, calls were voiced for a meeting of the party's national congress to undo this illegal act.[29]

Students also asked that the existing leaders be replaced by good and capable men, not tainted by corruption—a traditional theme emphasizing the moral quality of officials rather than legal restraint. They criticized the leaders' corrupt behavior, in promoting, for example, their children's personal careers. Students wanted a truthful press that would expose corruption and special privileges. They launched personal attacks on Deng Xiaoping, both because his children had benefited from their father's position and because of his age. Nasty cartoons and verses lampooning Deng's senility were circulated, while Li Peng was depicted as a fascist. The fact that the highest leader of the land was denounced represented an important milestone in mass assertiveness.[30] The cost was that it inflamed the leader's anger.

The demand for a student-government dialogue also posed a challenge to the political system. After an initial meeting between student leaders and second-rank officials failed to produce results, the student demand for a dialogue was backed by a widely publicized hunger strike, which earned students wide public sympathy. Li Peng did meet with student leaders but defended the government and urged them to return to class. The students wanted negotiations on an equal footing. They demanded that the student representatives be elected by the autonomous student organizations rather than the official transmission belt organizations. As Nathan puts it: "Here was the Trojan horse that the regime could not accept. Had it been granted, the students would have achieved the legalization of the first completely independent political organization in PRC history and the effective negation of Deng Xiaoping's four basic principles, as Deng understood them."[31]

Without the massacre of 4 June the May demonstrations might have grown into a movement that unambiguously demanded pluralization and democratization. A few senior intellectuals, particularly those now in exile, moved in this direction in May. Nevertheless, "for every Yan Jiaqi who moved from tolerance of the Party's leading role (i.e., absolute domination) to rejection, there were scores who stayed on the fence or on the safe side of it."[32] Had the movement not been crushed, some senior intellectuals might perhaps have provided the kind of leadership that a Vaclav Havel represented in Czechoslovakia, but such leadership was largely absent in China in 1989. Conversely, the movement might well have splintered had the army not acted. During May, it was weakened by disagreements over strategy and tactics. Factions and cleavages developed between the Beijing students and all those who were not students, and a lack of cooperation emerged between workers and students. Student romanticism, including professed readiness to die, made realistic decisionmaking difficult. The most experienced student leaders, for instance, proposed to vacate the Square on 27 May and declare victory, but others, especially from outside Beijing, dissented.

The hard-liners used force because they feared that things were getting out of control and that the demonstrations were escalating into a Leninist "who-whom," or challenge, giving rise to the possibility of intellectual-worker coalescence à la Polish Solidarity. Deng Xiaoping claimed to have feared that progressive erosion of party authority would lead to counter-revolution.[33] Undoubtedly, these leaders wished to demonstrate visibly that they still had the physical means of maintaining state power.

## The Quest for Stability

In the years since the Tiananmen demonstrations, the Chinese regime has sought to preserve itself in power under the slogan that "stability must prevail over everything."[34] In the quest for stability, three factors have emerged as most important: repression, education, and economic progress.

Rulers have first chosen to rely on repression. Arrests, sentences of variable length, and executions of a number of workers (but not of students) followed the crushing of the demonstrations. However, China's rulers did not return to the terror of the Maoist era, which had victimized some of them during the Cultural Revolution. Overall, a mosaic of intimidation was established. The ruling group appeared ready to use violence against the population once more if necessary, according to an interview given by Premier Li Peng in the spring of 1991.[35]

The commitment to control was bolstered further after Tiananmen by the fall of communism in Eastern Europe and the Soviet Union, which demonstrated that Marxist-Leninist states could in fact collapse if they let down their guard. In the hard-liners' view, the Eastern European parties had made the mistake of tolerating the "mischief of bourgeois liberalization for a long time." Having failed to take preventive measures, those parties had no defense when a major change in the international climate occurred. According to Deng Xiaoping, Eastern Europe showed that "our guiding principle of quelling the rebellion was completely correct." "But some comrades inside the party simply turn a deaf ear to it, saying that we are talking nonsense. Now everything is clear." The lesson for survival was, "Never show mercy" to bourgeois liberalization.[36]

Specifically, control over the army had to be strengthened. In Romania, the military had turned on China's old friend Ceauşescu, suggesting that military loyalty was the key to survival. Controls in the Chinese PLA had to be strengthened so as to teach resistance to bourgeois liberalization. Those who had advocated that the army ought to be separate from the party and become a politically neutral organ of the state had to be silenced. The party had to continue to exercise absolute leadership over the PLA, a point of great significance, since some in the PLA had been reluctant to use force against the demonstrators.[37] The new leaders did in fact expend much effort after June 1989 to tighten political education in the military and to reshuffle military personnel.

The second lesson Deng Xiaoping learned from the May events was that the biggest mistake of the 1980s had been neglect of "political work and education."[38] Hence, major efforts were made to step up the ideological indoctrination of the population, especially the students. Marxist-Leninist study in the universities was intensified and Western-oriented social science courses were cut. Old models of Maoist rectitude and devotion, such as Lei Feng, were once more trotted out for emulation. Work requirements for the students were once again instituted. At Beijing University, entering students had to undergo military training before beginning their academic work. Newspapers that had been excessively liberal were closed down. Some journalists were arrested or fired. The publication of books and magazines was curtailed and stricter censorship imposed.

Part of this education effort utilized the theme of foreign subversion, thereby seeking to mobilize China's powerful, grievance-laden nationalism against the democracy movement. The West, it was charged, had consciously sought to subvert China. This theme was not new—it had been used earlier in the 1983 campaign against "spiritual pollution," but it was now propagated more intensively. In particular, China was said to be threatened by the strategy of "peaceful evolution," which John Foster Dulles had invented. According to General Secretary Jiang Zemin, peaceful evolution posed a "major danger" for socialist states as demonstrated by the events in Eastern Europe and of 4 June: "It revealed their viciously plotted scheme to overthrow the Chinese communist leadership and socialist system." Bourgeois liberalization created an atmosphere in which peaceful evolution could succeed. International reactionary forces, declared the central committee, were targeting China after the socialist defeats in Europe. China had to be prepared to wage acute struggles against these forces.[39]

Alleged ties between domestic bourgeois democrats and foreign supporters were a major focus of attack. Some bourgeois liberals "colluded with external hostile forces." They spread chaos and violence, hoping to establish a "capitalist republic appended to the West."[40] Western human rights pressures, for instance, constituted not only "wanton interference" in China's internal affairs, but were part of this conspiracy. U.S. human rights policy was aimed at mobilizing a democratic upsurge in communist states. The United States sought contact with "democratic elements," supporting independent publications, trade unions, and enterprise, in efforts to "break through" the monopoly of the ruling party and government. By using the pretext of human rights, it was argued, the United States was attempting to force China to recognize illegal organizations, such as the various autonomous groups established in May 1989, in pursuit of the "sinister aim" of overthrowing the party and socialism.[41]

The Chinese dissident "elite" that advocated bourgeois liberalization betrayed the country by its advocacy of "wholesale westernization." This elite viewed the Chinese as an "inferior race" who should be governed as a colony for three hundred years in order to escape backwardness. A "foreigner should be welcomed to serve as China's premier," they believed, thus causing loss of independence. This "scum of the nation" fled abroad after 4 June and has been trying to subvert the people's government since then.[42]

The "subversive" activities of "hostile international forces" are portrayed as an outgrowth of a process that began with the Opium War of 1839–1842. Since then, "Western capitalism has never stopped its aggression against China and its plundering of China." Now that the PRC has been established, the U.S. embargo, the advance of the United States into North Korea, and its "peaceful evolution strategy" have all been aimed at "triumph without fighting a war." Western capitalism seeks to impose pluralist ideology. The economic sanctions imposed after 4 June were designed to create confusion and disrupt stability and unity. Young people who have not had the painful experience of losing independence have to be taught the realities of Western attempts to reduce China to the status of a dependent state.[43]

The effort to smear the democracy movement by linking it to foreign subversion has historical roots. Xenophobic, isolationist, and nativist currents of thought have long existed in China, together with deep ambivalence about relations with the West.[44] Democratic ideas had in fact come to China in the wake of Western aggression and under the protection of Western gunboats. Many intellectuals rejected Western democracy for this reason and turned instead to Marxism-Leninism, also a Western import, but anti-Western in spirit.[45] The association between imperialism and democracy did not prevent the rise of democratic movements, but it did give those opposed to democracy a stick with which to beat them. That it retained potency in China is shown by the demand of student demonstrators in May 1989 for official recognition as "patriotic" (*siguo*). Despite these historical roots and legacies, it appears that the regime has not gained much credibility with its messages, especially among students and intellectuals.

Finally, in addition to utilizing repression and education, the regime sought to secure performance legitimacy by promoting *economic stability*— fostering slower and less destabilizing growth and, above all, stable prices. It scored a big success, for example, in reducing the rate of inflation. But urban and rural unemployment and other consequences of austerity did not significantly improve the regime's standing with the populace.[46] Fundamental structural economic reforms designed to tackle the costly inefficiency of state enterprises have not progressed further. Moreover, because of inadequate macroeconomic controls, a new policy of stimulating rapid growth will probably run once more into destabilizing inflation.


## Prospects

In this volume, the essays by Diamond and Jowitt represent the optimistic and pessimistic assessments of the future possibilities for democratic transition. The Chinese case suggests that a pessimistic view is warranted; at the least, democratization would be a highly protracted, contested, and difficult process. Even if the regime were to pursue appropriate stabilizing strategies, it is not likely to succeed. This is due both to the fragility of the regime itself and to the volatility of Chinese society, which continues to undergo rapid change. Not only has the regime lost legitimacy in the eyes of key groups such as the intellectuals, but it doesn't even hold power. Ultimate power is exercised by a group of first-generation revolutionary gerontocrats now in their mid-80s, including Deng. They control the younger leaders formally in power. Once they die, the younger leaders will have to rely on their own political bases of support. Whether these bases exist is highly questionable, as illustrated by the case of the party's secretary-general, Jiang Zemin, who as the top party leader also heads the highest military decision-making organ—the Military Affairs Commission—but who lacks significant ties to the military. The fundamental question of which civilian leader will command the loyalty of the military will be a key factor in the coming struggle for succession. Furthermore, the 1989 crackdown undid attempts made in the 1980s, inadequate as they may have been, to institutionalize the regime and establish binding rules on how leaders should be chosen or dismissed.

In the coming elite conflicts, it is possible that some contenders for power will calculate that it is in their interest to turn to social forces, such as intellectuals, students, or workers, among whom there are no doubt many who are ready to respond to a total call for action. The result could be an opening for liberalization or even democratization. One of the noteworthy aspects of May 1989 was the participation of cadres from the central committee and government departments, suggesting that desire for change has penetrated into the higher bureaucracies of party and state. Chinese democrats have always believed that change within the CCP was the key to change in China. This belief conflicts with the assumption of dissidents that the only way out is through the collapse of the party, as in Eastern Europe. It is highly unlikely that the elites favoring democratization can carry with them the entire party, a situation that will necessarily lead to increased intraparty conflict rather than the conversion of the party to a new political system.

The social changes inaugurated by the reform era that contributed to May 1989 continue, because the reforms were not reversed but only halted or slowed down. Family farm contracting essentially remains, as does private enterprise. The combination of public ownership with private gain, the hallmark of partial reform in communist systems, continues to give rise to privatization of official power and, hence, to further degeneration of the nominally Marxist-Leninist party. Some hard-liners would like to restore an orthodox mobilization system but cannot do so because the economic costs of reverting to a fully planned economy are too high. Shutting down private and semiprivate enterprise would, for instance, greatly increase unemployment and, consequently, discontent.

The necessity for reform undermines the hard-liners' dreams of returning to orthodoxy and compels pursuit of contradictory social and economic policies. The suspicion of foreign subversion, for example, goes hand in hand with the maintenance of the Open Door, as insisted upon by Deng. Despite its vehement denunciations of the West, China did not turn to isolationism after Tiananmen, as it had in the era that followed the break with the Soviet Union. The reason lies in the new realities of China's international interdependence. The reform era brought about a revolution in Chinese foreign trade, with an unprecedentedly high proportion of the country's GNP dependent on foreign markets. External markets, foreign investment, importation of foreign technology, and education of Chinese abroad had by the late 1980s become essential components of China's economic survival. China cannot retreat into the isolation of Kim Il-sung's socialism of self-reliance (*juche*). Consequently, foreign ideas, including those of democracy, are bound to continue to infiltrate into the Chinese ideological fortress. The social conditions that generate demands for political change thus continue to exist. Widespread participation in political movements can, then, be the result of political opportunities combined with economic crisis.

How this political and socioeconomic potential for change will work itself out is impossible to predict. The list of variables is long and dauntingly complex. Even a summary view can only begin to highlight the obstacles to movement in a pluralist and democratic direction.

First, the forces for pluralization and democratization are weak. Elements of civil society are present, but they are interwoven with the state rather than being autonomous. In a future process of liberalization, which would parallel to some degree developments in 1988 and early 1989, multitudinous political and social organizations would no doubt spring up, while many of the current party-state-dominated organizations might come under the members' control. This process, however, of building a civil society with a strong foundation of autonomous organizations would have to occur during a liberalizing and democratizing transition; it would not pre-exist as a facilitating condition for transition, as in Latin America. An immense task of organization building would lie ahead, including the building of organizations that could reach into and integrate the vast peasantry.

Given the weakness of liberalizing forces, reliance on internal changes in the Communist party seems inevitable and is likely to constitute a major factor limiting possibilities for democratization. To be sure, keen observers such as Orville Schell discern a new independence of mind among intellectuals, a new attitude toward authority, which draws them toward "overthrowing the psychological and intellectual tyranny" that in the past bound them to the party.[47] But even if intellectuals will, in the future, pose a challenge to the party, the CCP (an immense organization of 47 million members) will not easily be displaced. While elements of the CCP may well be sympathetic to pluralism, others will not, whether for reasons of self-interest or because of residual commitment to doctrine or to modes of rule.

As a third obstacle in the path toward democratization, an opening to political change may well involve conflict between the center and provinces or coalitions of provinces. Reform has exacerbated regional divisions. Coastal provinces in the dynamic southern region close to Hong Kong and Taiwan, for example, favor market-based growth and resist their Beijing bosses, who emphasize planning and centralization of financial control. However, conflicts between the center and the provinces—with the possible exception of Tibet and Central Asia (where ethnic strife is a major issue)—will not resemble the bitter ethnic conflicts over secession we have been seeing in the Soviet Union and Eastern Europe. Conflicts in China's provinces have been about resources and economic strategy, not about the nature of China. Perhaps as regional conflicts become more sharply defined, they will generate demands for autonomy or political liberalization. Provinces with a stake in faster reform and with more liberal attitudes could, at some point, provide a base for agitation. Should this occur, China's powerful nationalist sentiments would probably also assert themselves, leading to an effort to crush divisive forces.[48]

Fourth, as the preceding discussion indicates, fear of chaos and disorder, deeply rooted in Chinese culture, may result in the emergence of a new dictatorship devoted to order. In fact, order as a value would probably be reflected in a democratic outcome as well, leading to a statist democracy. Historically, because of China's weakness, proponents of democracy were attracted more to its potential to strengthen the state than to its promise of defending individual rights. With some significant exceptions, the various democracy activists in the PRC from 1978 to 1989 accepted such statist and unitary approaches to democracy, which suggests that democratic outcomes may turn out to be more authoritarian than the term democracy implies.[49]

Fifth, there is reason to doubt whether China's cultural traditions offer adequate soil for democracy. China has an immensely rich and complex tradition, which can no doubt accommodate a range of political choices. But the dominant political traditions are authoritarian, elitist, and centrist. As Lucian Pye has often pointed out, the culture does not see the "selfish" articulation of interests as legitimate; and while this may now be changing under the impact of modernization, it cannot be assumed that organizations articulating partial interests will readily find acceptance.[50] Instead, what may emerge are organizations outwardly devoted to the national interest but actually pursuing their narrow interests, thereby reinforcing the suspicion of motives that, as Jowitt notes in this volume, is already deeply rooted in Leninist systems. Given time, tolerance for interest conflicts, for opposition parties, and for appropriate rules of the game may well develop. But tolerance for differing interests as a normal aspect of the political system will depend crucially on the extent to which fundamental issues of governance—including the division of power between center and provinces and the nature and definition of property rights—will have been resolved. Issues that cannot be compromised because they will be viewed as matters of life and death may arise, exacerbating conflict.

In short, the coming crises over China's future government may well yield rather bleak outcomes. Renewed dictatorship, the emergence of a nationalistic movement regime, military rule, civil strife, and perhaps even civil war, cannot be ruled out. Neither, to be sure, can liberalization. But China's transition to democracy is not likely to be easy.

## Notes

1. For an overview of the reforms, see Harry Harding, *China's Second Revolution* (Washington, DC: Brookings, 1987).

2. Xinhua News Agency, Beijing, 5 September 1988, in *Daily Report—China, Foreign Broadcast Information Service* (henceforth abbreviated as FBIS), no. 174 (Washington, DC: U.S. Government, 1988), p. 50.

3. *China Daily*, 5 November 1988.

4. See Martin King Whyte, "Social Trends in China: The Triumph of Inequality?" in *Modernizing China: Post-Mao Reform and Development*, ed. A. Doak Barnett and Ralph N. Clough (Boulder, CO: Westview, 1986), pp. 103–124.

5. *Far Eastern Economic Review*, 18 September 1986.

6. See Tinjian Shi, "The Democracy Movement in China in 1989: Dynamics and Failure," *Asian Survey* 30, no. 12 (December 1990): 1186–1205.

7. For statistics from recent surveys see Min Qi et al., *Zhonguozhengzhi wenhua: Minzhu zhengzhi nanchan de shehui xinli yinsi* (China's political culture: social psychological factors which make it difficult for democratic politics to appear) (Kunming: Yunnan Renmin Chubanshe, 1988), p. 226.

8. See Martin King Whyte, "Urban China: A Civil Society in the Making?" (Paper presented at the conference on "State and Society in China: The Consequences of Reform, 1978–1990," Claremont McKenna College, 16–17 February 1990.

9. Susan Whiting, "The Nongovernmental Sector in China: A Preliminary Report," *The Ford Foundation* (July 1989).

10. See Frederick Staar, "Soviet Union: A Civil Society," *Foreign Policy* no. 70 (Spring 1988): 26–41.

11. Stanley Rosen, "The Impact of Reform Policies on Youth Attitudes," in *Chinese Society on the Eve of Tiananmen*, ed. Deborah Davies and Ezra F. Vogel (Cambridge, MA: Harvard University Press, 1990), pp. 292–293.

12. Rosen, "The Impact of Reform Policies," p. 289.

13. "Su Shaozi discusses political structural reform," *Dushu*, no. 9, 10 September 1986; translated in *Joint Publications Research Service*, Washington, DC: US Government, no. CPS-20, 8 April 1987, pp. 25–30.

14. Mary C. Erbaugh and Richard Curt Kraus, "The 1989 Democracy Movement in Funjian and Its Aftermath," *Australian Journal of Chinese Studies* no. 23 (January 1990): 153.

15. Fang Lizhi, op cit., chapter entitled "The Democrat," pp. 85–188.

16. "Confidential Document: A Speech of Deng Xiaoping for Restricted Use Only," *Pai Hsing*, Hong Kong, no. 122, 16 June 1986, in *FBIS*, no. 117, pp. W 1–2.

17. *Selected Works of Deng Xiaoping, 1975–1982* (Beijing: Foreign Language Press, 1984), pp. 302–325.

18. On the cultural significance of chaos and disorder, see Richard Solomon, *Mao's Revolution and the Chinese Political Culture* (Berkeley: University of California Press, 1971).

19. Zhao Ziyang, "Advance along the Road of Socialism with Chinese Characteristics," *Beijing Review* 30, no. 45 (9–15 November 1987): 1–27.

20. See Mark P. Petracca and Meng Xiong, "The Concept of Chinese Neo-Authoritarianism," *Asian Survey* 30, no. 11 (November 1990): 1099–1117.

21. *Wen Hui Bao*, Shanghai, 2 December 1989, in *FBIS*, no. 237, pp. 18–23; *Renmin Ribao*, Beijing, 22 July 1989, in *FBIS,* no. 143, pp. 21–22; *Guangming Ribao*, Beijing, 22 July 1989, in *FBIS*, no. 151, pp. 30–33.

22. *New York Times*, 16 May 1989.

23. For a chronicle of the events and documentation, see Yi Mu and Mark V. Thompson, *Crisis at Tiananmen: Reform and Reality in Modern China* (San Francisco: China Books and Periodicals, 1989), pp. 271–278.

24. Andrew Walder, "The Political Sociology of the Beijing Upheaval of 1989," *Problems in Communism* 38, no. 5 (September–October 1989): 89.

25. Andrew Walder, "Urban Industrial Workers" (Paper presented at conference on "State and Society in China: The Consequences of Reform, 1978–1990," Claremont McKenna College, 16–17 February 1990).

26. Tony Saich, "The Rise and Fall of the Beijing People's Movement," *Australian Journal of Chinese Affairs* no. 24, (June 1990): 191.

27. Dorothy Solinger, "Democracy with Chinese Characteristics," *World Policy Journal* (Fall 1989): 621–632.

28. Andrew J. Nathan, *China's Crisis: Dilemmas of Reform and Prospects for Democracy* (New York: Columbia University Press, 1990), p. 172.

29. For documentation, see Han Minzhu, ed., *Crises for Democracy: Writings and Speeches from the 1989 Democracy Movement* (Princeton, NJ: Princeton University Press, 1990), pp. 249–251.

30. Interview in *Der Spiegel*, 10 July 1989, pp. 124–127.

31. Nathan, *China's Crisis*, p. 185.

32. David Kelley, "Chinese Intellectuals in the 1989 Democracy Movement," in *The Broken Mirror: China After Tiananmen*, ed. George Hicks (Chicago: St. James Press, 1990), p. 45.

33. "Deng's Talks on Quelling Rebellion in Beijing," 9 June 1989, in *Fourth Plenary Session of the CCP 13th Central Committee* (Beijing: New Star Publishers, 1989), pp. 12–20.

34. "Wending yadao yiqie" (Stability must prevail over everything else), *Renmin Ribao*, editorial, 4 June 1990.

35. *New York Times*, 10 April 1991.

36. *Cheng Ming*, Hong Kong, no. 147, 1 January 1990, pp. 6–8, in *FBIS*, no. 250, pp. 20–21.

37. *Tang Tai*, Hong Kong, no. 6, 30 December 1989, in *FBIS*, no. 2, p. 9.

38. "Deng's Talks," p. 16.

39. *Nanfang Ribao*, Guangzhou, 10 January 1990, in *FBIS*, no. 35, pp. 1–2; and *Cheng Ming*, Hong Kong, February 1990, in *FBIS*, no. 151, pp. 8–10.

40. *Nanfang Ribao*, Guangzhou, 10 January 1990, in *FBIS*, no. 35, pp. 1–2.

41. *Renmin Ribao*, Beijing, 7 July 1989, in *FBIS*, no. 131, pp. 2–4.

42. *Renmin Ribao*, in *FBIS*, no. 131, pp. 2–4.

43. *Ban Yue Tan*, Beijing, 5 June 1990, in *FBIS*, no. 131, pp. 34–36; and *Nanfang Ribao*, 10 January 1990, in *FBIS*, no. 35, pp. 1–2.

44. Kenneth Lieberthal, "Domestic Politics and Foreign Policy," in *China's Foreign Relations in the 1980s,* ed. Harry Harding, (New Haven, CT: Yale University Press, 1984), pp. 43–70.

45. See Joseph R. Levenson, *Liang Ch'i-ch'ao and the Mind of Modern China* (Cambridge, MA: Harvard University Press, 1953).

46. See David Shambaugh, "China in 1990: The Year of Damage Control," *Asian Survey* 31, no. 1 (January 1991): 40–46.

47. Orville Schell, "The Silence of Intellectuals in China," *The Yale-China Association China Update* 11, no. 1 (Spring 1991): 9.

48. See *Far Eastern Economic Review* (4 April 1991): 21–30 for an assessment of current center-provincial conflicts.

49. The distinctive Chinese approach is analyzed in Andrew J. Nathan, *Chinese Democracy* (New York: Alfred Knopf, 1985), esp. p. 41 ff.

50. See Lucian Pye, *Asian Power and Politics: The Cultural Dimensions of Authority* (Cambridge, MA: Harvard University Press, 1985), Chapter 7.

# 7

# Democratization in the Middle East

## Steven R. Dorr

The conventional American wisdom relies on the to-be-hoped-for spread of democracy to solve the problems of international order. But the struggles for democracy are likely to be as protracted as the conceptions of democracy are different in the various cultures.

*—Henry Kissinger[1]*

We believe in a united Arab world. But not unless it is a democratic Arab world. We will never accept unity under a dictatorship. The most important thing is not unity but is bringing democracy and human rights to the Arab world. America can help do that now.

*—Hamed Juwan[2]*

The crumbling of the Eastern bloc and the demise of the Marxist-Leninist experiment in Eastern Europe and the Soviet Union seemed to promise the rise of new democracies in the 1990s where authoritarian regimes once ruled. If some of the most rigid and ideologically pure Communist authoritarian regimes could be swept away, might not other variants on this authoritarian model (some long viewed as close Soviet allies and even clients) also be vulnerable to a similar fate? During the 1980s, democracies emerged in virtually all the Latin American states where military and authoritarian regimes had existed. Numerous persistent conflicts within and between African states came to an end, and new, potentially democratic, regimes were coming into being. In Asia democratic experiments that had been subverted by entrenched authoritarians—such as the experiments in the Philippines and South Korea—were being revitalized. But what of the Middle East?

How can one speak of democratization in a region where authoritarianism has flourished for so long and even appeared to be impenetrable? Larry Diamond, in Chapter 3 of this volume, pessimistically describes the Middle East as "one of the least democratic regions of the world today and, many believe, the one with the bleakest prospect for the future."[3] Even among those Middle East analysts who are the most optimistic, such as Michael

Hudson, optimism remains guarded, as they search for "signs of democrati-zation and liberalization" and not "full fledged democracy itself." [4]

With authoritarian rule seemingly entrenched in the Middle East, often the only debate is over explanations as to why democracy is unlikely to de-velop in the near future.[5] The range of explanations is broad. Many oriental-ists, as well as some Islamic fundamentalists, argue that Islam is incompati-ble with democracy.[6] Some political analysts assert that Middle Eastern society and political culture are patriarchal or patrimonial, where loyalties to religious sects, clans, or ethnic groups tend to vitiate any incentive toward the individual initiative and choice necessary to the democratic process.[7] Others point to the growth of authoritarian-bureaucratic states, which are often virtual police (*mukhabarat*) states whose "legitimacy" is more likely to be based on fear than on popular acceptance.[8] Dependency theory highlights the role of external political and financial powers, who manipulate local pol-itics through local collaborators who in turn block the growth of democracy or any political liberalization.[9]

This essay will review these and other aspects of the debate over de-mocratization in the Middle East. The first section sketches the current sta-tus of democratization in the region with an emphasis on the nature and sig-nificance of the electoral process. The second section examines the global, regional, and internal factors that have contributed to the current status of democracy in the Middle East. The concluding section assesses the future prospects for democracy in the Middle East.

## The Status of Democracy in the Middle East

Latin America has experienced several waves of democratization that were often followed by retrenchment into authoritarian patterns of rule. Karen Remmer argues in Chapter 5 of this volume that the current wave in Latin America is notable in that it has already lasted longer and influenced these societies more deeply than previous "waves." In December 1991 Algeria was in the midst of what many were characterizing as the freest elections ever held in the Middle East, certainly in the Arab world. But on 12 January 1992, the process was stopped to prevent the Islamic Salvation Front (FIS), the party expected to win, from taking control of the National People's As-sembly, Algeria's parliament. Just the week before, *The Economist* had asked: "What is the point of an experiment in democracy if the first people it delivers to power are intent on dismantling it?"[10] The Algerian army appar-ently gave its answer.

If the conventional definition of political democracy used by Remmer in this volume—"a form of regime characterized by electoral competition and oppositional rights"—were applied to the Arab world, no state would fit that description.[11] In 1987, when Michael C. Hudson was searching for a definition that might fit the less than ideal situation of the Middle East, he defined democratization for his purposes as "a process through which the exercise of political power by regime and state becomes less arbitrary, exclusive, and authoritarian."[12] If the decade of the 1980s was the decade of democratization in Latin America, then for the Middle East, the decade of the 1990s might mark the beginning of its democratizing process. And, like the earlier pattern in Latin America, that beginning may lead only to retrenchment, and then to another experiment with democracy.

This brief survey of the status of democratization in the Middle East will be organized around a somewhat arbitrary classification of the states of the region as more or less democratic, in which states classified as democracies may actually only be moving in a more liberalizing direction. We shall proceed from the most democratic to the least.[13]

## Democracies and Near Democracies with Multiparty Systems

The political institutions in Israel, Turkey, Egypt, and Lebanon most nearly resemble a more conventional conception of democratic institutions and operations. In essence, in each state, competitive political parties representing divergent views on public policy vie for power within a system of agreed rules of political behavior. Israel and Turkey freely chose this system and have long accepted its Western roots. Israel has been the most successful in implementing it, while Turkey has been the most persistent, despite setbacks, in pursuing democracy. The Egyptian and Lebanese experiences with democratic institutions have been colored by their colonial roots. Each country has endured systems tainted by foreign manipulation, and both are attempting, without assurance of success, to reinvigorate their political institutions.

The only country that can be described as a democracy in the Middle East is Israel. The country has a relatively free press—although military censorship, while controversial, exists—open and free elections, and a parliamentary system of government. Its exceptionalism lies not only in its democratic system but in its European rather than Middle Eastern origins. Because of these unique circumstances, Israel might be characterized as an "enclave democracy," safe as long as it is insulated from the regional political environment. When questions arise on occasion about the future of democracy in Israel, their context is likely to be a concern about Israel becoming more Middle Eastern and less European. In this regard, some fear that Israel's democracy might be undermined by a substantial population shift from Jews of European origin to Jews of Middle Eastern origin who may not have the same regard for democracy as Europeans. Recent immigrants from Russia also have little experience with democracy.[14] Others argue, from a different perspective, that Israel's continued rule over a vast number of Arabs in the occupied territories, who do not enjoy full civil rights, creates a circumstance that undermines the moral fiber and democratic institutions of Israel. These concerns arise more frequently among Labor party supporters and others on the political left. These groups identify with the socialist origins of the Zionist movement and are cautious about any deviations from that ideal. Having been in opposition from 1977 to 1992 substantially heightened their anxiety about Israel's future. The political right has been dominated by the Likud party, whose origins lie in the revisionist Zionist movement established by Vladimir Z. Jabotinsky in the 1920s.[15] Likud supporters and their allies tend to place their nationalist agenda ahead of democratic political ideals. Nevertheless, even when these concerns are taken into account, Israel remains the only democracy in the area at present.

Political institutions and social features resembling those found in democratic societies can be found elsewhere in the Middle East. Unfortunately, they do not usually indicate the existence of a healthy democracy. For example, many Middle Eastern states have multiparty political systems. They are often manipulated by the regime in power, however, or dominated by a single party. Turkey's multiparty political system has persisted despite military interventions in 1960, 1971, and 1980. Military involvement usually was precipitated by the inability of civilian political leaders to insure civil order. In each case, the military was reluctant to take over political power and did in fact return political power to civilian control as soon as possible.

The most recent case of military intervention in Turkish politics, in 1980, occurred because political violence had become so intense and the civilian political leadership so paralyzed, that the military felt compelled to take control to restore order and to reform the political system. Political parties were disbanded and about one hundred political leaders associated with those parties were prevented from seeking office for 10 years. Tens of thousands of people were arrested and questioned by the military. Over one hundred were sentenced to death and thousands were sentenced to prison terms. A new constitution was written, new political parties were formed, and new leaders were elected in 1983. However, in 1991, when the previously barred politicians were allowed to run again for office, Suleiman Demirel, prime minister when the military intervened in 1980, was re-elected as prime minister. The legacy the military intervention left behind was a newly vibrant but somewhat tarnished Turkish democracy—with corruption surrounding the president's family, continued reports of political prisoners and abuses of human rights, and continued clashes with the Kurds. Nevertheless, after Israel, Turkey comes closest to the ideal of democracy in the Middle East.

Egypt, like Turkey, experienced periods of multiparty politics that gave the appearance of democracy. The first period, from 1923 to 1953, was based on Western liberal traditions, but final power was left in the hands of

an unelected monarch and his British colonial supervisors. The revolution of
23 July 1952, which ultimately brought Gamal 'Abd al-Nasir to power,
overturned the old system. During the Nasir "interregnum" in the multiparty
system, a single-party system was established to mobilize the populace to
carry out the policy goals of Nasir. The second multiparty period began in
1977, the seventh year of President Anwar el-Sadat's regime. It was an outgrowth of Sadat's 1974 economic opening (*infitah*) or liberalization program, and it was intended to begin the process of political liberalization.
This process continues up to the present, but it remains an imperfect attempt
at parliamentary democracy. The parliament has little impact on or control
over most areas of national policy. The electoral law makes it very difficult
for opposition parties to gain seats, and the president faces no genuine electoral opposition. However, other signs of liberalization are present. The judiciary has begun to act with increasing independence; for example, in May
1991 the courts declared the election law unconstitutional, thus overturning
the 1987 parliamentary election results and requiring new elections. Moreover, the continuing development of a civil society—a process Robert Bianchi
describes as the growing "unruliness of associational life"[16]—is enabling a
variety of groups to become more active participants in domestic political
and economic debates. Furthermore, the variety of political parties and
Islamic groups has grown, and though they are often constrained, they are
becoming a more active and vocal part of Egypt's political life.[17] Again, we
are looking at an imperfect democracy, but one in which movement in a positive direction continues.

The most spectacular failure of democracy in the Middle East might be
Lebanon. Until the Lebanese civil war broke out in 1975, Lebanon was often
cited as the only example of a functioning democracy in the Arab world. The
Lebanese had crafted a system that reflected the religious and ethnic mosaic
that was their society. Interests were articulated through the political elites
of Lebanon's religious sects. These leaders struck bargains among themselves and then ensured that their followers kept the agreements. Lebanon
was a prime example of a functioning "consociational" democracy. The civil
war brought that to an end. Only in 1989 was a political agreement signed to
reform the political system by more equitably distributing political power
among the various Christian and Muslim religious sects. With this agreement, the al-Taif accord, the Lebanese began trying to put the remnants of
their political life back together under the close supervision of Syria.[18] New
parliamentary elections, the first since 1972, were held in September 1992.
Even so, the outcome for restored democracy in Lebanon is still uncertain.

## Semicompetitive Multiparty Systems

Jordan, Algeria, Yemen, Tunisia, and Morocco have legislative bodies of
varying degrees of independence that are selected through a competitive

electoral system. The head of state, however, is above this competition and often manipulates it. These countries are facing growing economic difficulties—including rising expectations and increasing unemployment—especially among the young, who constitute the vast majority of the population. Various Islamic movements and tendencies have developed, in the estimation of the disaffected, into credible alternatives to the ruling elites. Opening the political system has become a useful tool in the hands of current regimes to attempt to channel the disaffections of the population. None of these experiments has been in existence long enough, or developed sufficiently, to ensure a further move toward a fully democratic system.

Since the breaking up of the Soviet bloc and the emergence of new democracies in Eastern Europe, the countries of the Arab world that have been followed most closely for new signs of democratization and liberalization are Jordan, Algeria, and Kuwait. Kuwait, which will be discussed in the next section of this chapter, attracted attention because of its occupation by Iraq and the subsequent war of liberation led by the United States under United Nations auspices. Yemen, on the other hand, has attracted little attention, but it deserves more in light of its new experiment with parliamentary democracy.

Jordan did not open up its political system until 1989, when it was faced with the precipitous economic downturn begun in 1988 and with the popular protests in April 1989 that accompanied efforts to implement austerity measures required by the International Monetary Fund (IMF). King Hussein changed prime ministers and called for parliamentary elections. The November 1989 elections produced a victory for Islamists in 34 out of the 80 seats in parliament. Even so, the king decided to pursue political liberalization further by creating a royal commission to draft a new "National Charter." Issued in December 1990, the charter calls for democracy and grants Jordanians the right to form political parties. The international repercussions of the Gulf crisis formed the context for these events. By 1990 Jordan's already declining economy was reeling even further from the embargo on Iraq that cut transit fees along with all other trade with Iraq. Jordan was also inundated with refugees from the Gulf region, particularly Palestinians. By supporting the new National Charter, the king hoped to draw more people into the process of governing and share with them the responsibilities for the tough economic choices Jordan had to make.

Jordan had experimented with political liberalization in 1955, but the experiment was cut short in the wake of the April 1957 coup attempt. In 1958 political parties were banned. The attempt to create a National Consultative Council in the 1970s ultimately failed and the parliament was recalled in 1984. Even if this new effort through the 1990 National Charter to offer broader political participation succeeds, it will still be only a move in the direction of greater political participation and liberalization; it will not create a full democracy. King Hussein, the center of political power in Jordan, is not up for election.[19]

Algeria, from October 1988 until January 1992, was moving more rapidly than any other Arab state in the direction of full democratic reform. As in Jordan, the impetus for Algeria's political liberalization policies flowed from economic grievances. Violent riots erupted in Algiers and several other cities in October 1988 in response to severe economic conditions. In 1986 rising unemployment and Algeria's three-year-old austerity program had already escalated public dissatisfaction with government policies; riots in Constantine in that year alerted the government to the growing discontent. Even so, no specific government action precipitated the October 1988 riots, and the government was surprised and ill-prepared to respond.[20] President Chadli Bendjedid seized this opportunity and decided to tie his economic reforms to new political reforms. The constitution was revised to allow political pluralism, thus threatening the monopoly the National Liberation Front had held for the previous 26 years. The media were also allowed a greater degree of openness. New parties, once established, would have the right to publish papers.

By 1989 many new parties were forming. Some were purely secular, such as the Socialist Vanguard Party (PAGS); others combined secular goals with ethnic solidarity, such as the Rally for Culture and Democracy (RCD), a reincarnation of a long-clandestine Berber movement; and still others were religious in orientation, such as the Islamic Safeguard Front (FIS), headed by Abbas Madani.

The FIS, better organized than its rivals, used the mosques and neighborhood programs to provide much needed social services and even emergency aid, especially after the 1989 earthquake. It thereby gained a reputation for effectiveness and valuable organizational and networking advantages over its secular political rivals.[21] In the municipal and provincial elections of June 12, 1990, the FIS scored a stunning victory, winning 67 percent of the provinces (as opposed to 14 percent for the FLN) and 55 percent of the municipalities (versus 32 percent for the FLN). Although this election was a great blow to the FLN—interpreted by some as a vote against the FLN rather than a vote for the FIS—the FLN still had time to regroup before the legislative elections scheduled for June 1991. Although those elections were actually postponed until December 1991, the extra time helped the FLN little; the FIS swept to a second victory that was even more impressive than its first. The Islamic Front won 188 of the 231 seats decided in the first round of the elections, just 28 short of a majority needed in the 430-member parliament. A run-off election was scheduled for 16 January 1992, and in early January the FIS candidates were estimated to be leading in 150 of the 199 still-contested seats. If this lead held, it would have given the FIS well over the two-thirds majority needed to change the constitution; they could have called for early presidential elections and introduced their Islamic program quickly. The expected outcome was clear, but President Bendjedid thought he could still use the considerable powers of the presidency to steer the process toward democracy. The army, however, decided otherwise. Bendjedid resigned on 11 January, and the newly formed ruling State Security Council, reconstituted within days as the Supreme State Council, canceled the elections and installed Muhammad Boudiaf, a former National Liberation Front dissident who had been in exile for 27 years, as head of the presidential council. The security forces arrested several thousand Islamists and sent them to detention camps, deposed many local officials elected in 1990, and dissolved local assemblies. The FIS itself was officially dissolved by a court ruling in March 1992. On 29 June 1992, Boudiaf was assassinated. Algeria's move toward democracy has been interrupted. Some observers believe the Islamists will recover and ultimately gain power in Algeria.[22] If so, it will be instructive to see if their commitment to democracy will have been enhanced or undermined by their success at the ballot box and the consequences of that success.

The Republic of Yemen was created by the unification of North and South Yemen on 22 May 1990. One year later the republic's new constitution was ratified. Among other things, it calls for the establishment of a multiparty political system, guarantees for women to vote, freedom of political expression and association, and a popularly elected House of Representatives. The house can call a "no confidence" vote on the Council of Ministers, approve the budget and other laws, and override vetoes of the Presidential Council.[23] Already parliamentary proceedings have been broadcast on television.[24] The success of these new political developments remains to be seen, but certainly Yemen has produced an experiment worth watching.

Tunisia might now be considered an example of a semicompetitive multiparty system. For many years, however, Tunisia was considered a prime example of a modernizing single-party state, one that might serve as a model for other Third World countries. The theory was that developing countries could ill afford the luxury of protracted political debate between competing political parties. What competition existed could be managed best within the single party. Once the state had evolved sufficiently, a multiparty system would emerge. Unfortunately, the founding father of the party and the independent state in Tunisia, Habib Bourguiba, could not solve all of Tunisia's mounting economic, social, and political problems. Nevertheless, he made himself president for life and was unwilling to loosen the reigns of power. In 1981 Bourguiba allowed multiparty elections, but he was unhappy with the outcome, and the true results were not released. The economic difficulties of the 1980s led to bread riots as well as to growing competition between the government's increasingly erratic program and that of the more and more influential Islamic Tendency Movement (MTI). After a series of rapid reshuffles of government officials following a demand by Bourguiba for a retrial of several previously convicted members of MTI, the prime minister, Zine al-Abidine Ben Ali, staged a "constitutional coup." He had several doctors declare Bourguiba's absolute incapacity to govern and then assumed the presidency. Since that time Ben Ali has attempted to open up the political system, but he remains extremely wary of the MTI, which has formed the Renaissance party (*Hizb al-Nahdah*). The Nahdah party leader, Rashid al-Ghannoushi, has repeatedly proclaimed his support for multiparty democracy but has failed to convince Ben Ali's government to recognize al-Nahdah.[25] The political parties that do exist, besides the Constitutional Democratic Rally (RCD) that runs the government, are mainly small left-wing parties. They were allowed to run in the April 1989 National Assembly elections, but all the seats were won by the RCD. The president also ran un-opposed in a plebiscite, gaining over 99 percent of the vote. Ben Ali has moved Tunisia closer to a multiparty democracy, but his main achievement has been to revive the ruling party. The main drawback is his unwillingness to tolerate the Islamic party, al-Nahdah, which would undoubtedly gain sub-stantial electoral support from the many Tunisians who are dissatisfied with the old order.[26] Keeping them out, in the long run, may be more dangerous than letting them in.[27]

In Morocco, a multiparty system has been in place since independence; indeed, some of the parties, most notably the Istiqlal (Independence) party, were instrumental in the independence movement. Since independence in March 1956, a number of new parties have appeared and disappeared, often giving the impression of a dynamic political environment. In reality, the king is the center of all power in Morocco, and the parties have relatively lit-tle impact on the policies of the king's government. Systems of consultation exist, but the king is not obliged to take advice. The king appoints all impor-tant officials, including all regional governors. He also has the power to dis-solve the House of Representatives. Since his accession to the throne in 1961, King Hassan II has gained a well-deserved reputation as being skilled at playing one party off against another while encouraging the pervasive in-fighting that exists within most parties. The competition among the parties is all too often for the king's patronage rather than to promote particular poli-cies. The controversial effort by King Hassan to annex the former Spanish Sahara has, in fact, gained the king support in the country, since the issue takes on larger nationalist overtones in Moroccan domestic politics. It seems unlikely that the king would willingly open up a system he has so skillfully manipulated for so many years. Nevertheless, economic and political discon-tent do exist, and Moroccan concern over the recent rise of the Islamic movement in neighboring Algeria will continue to test the political skills of the king. Although Hassan II may not have to open up the Moroccan politi-cal system, the same may not be true for his successor.[28]

## Modernizing Oligarchies

The states that make up the Gulf Cooperation Council—Saudi Arabia, Kuwait, Bahrain, Qatar, the United Arab Emirates (UAE), and Oman—have no tradition of liberal democracy of the type discussed by Larry Diamond. These states have always been highly paternalistic; the accountability of the rulers was greater, however, before the advent of oil wealth, because wealthy merchants as well as rivals within the ruling family were more likely to be credible claimants to rule. Since the rise of oil wealth, the ruling families have had access to wealth that far exceeds that of any rival family or individual. They can use their wealth and the new state institutions to ensure that supporters are rewarded. A loss of that wealth, however, or the emergence of outside threats that cannot be contained, might undermine such traditional arrangements. The drop in oil prices in the 1980s led to some open expressions of discontent, and the Gulf war undermined the prerequisite that a paternalistic ruler be able to protect his people. Kuwait, traumatized by the 1990 Iraqi occupation and subsequent war, is hesitantly reintroducing a measure of participation, through an elected assembly, into an otherwise traditional patrimonial system. Expressions of desires for greater political participation are rising elsewhere in the Gulf.

The war in 1991 to liberate Kuwait provided an opportunity for some intellectuals in these states to raise the issue of political participation more forthrightly. Unfortunately, their sentiments were often expressed as a hope that the United States would put pressure on its regional allies to open up their political systems further. Since the United States had come and saved these regimes, it would be unthinkable, these intellectuals felt, for it to leave without attaching political strings to all its military aid.[29] Later, many realized that the United States had acted to reimpose the status quo ante, not to overturn it.

Stirrings for increased political participation in these patrimonial systems have been limited; Kuwait has been the most promising prospect. Many expected that Kuwait, once the Iraqi occupation was reversed, would be a prime candidate for a new experiment in political liberalization. At the "Popular Kuwaiti Conference" in Jiddah, Saudi Arabia, on 13 October 1990, Kuwaitis from the ruling al-Sabah family and from other significant sectors of society met to discuss Kuwait's future. The promise of greater political participation seemed to be a distinct possibility.[30] A major goal of the opposition was the reinstitution of the 1962 Kuwaiti constitution and a return of the National Assembly. The Amir was inclined to create a new national council that would have no fiscal oversight or legislative powers but that would offer advice to the Amir on the future consultative role of a new parliament. This plan appears to be an attempt to turn Kuwait's former National Assembly into an advisory council or *majlis al-shura*. Elections scheduled for the fall of 1992 should reveal more about the prospects for democratization in Kuwait. It seems inevitable that the full restoration of the National Assembly will not be among the goals achieved. Some signs of political opening allow, however, for tentative optimism: Kuwait's first political party, the Kuwaiti Democratic Forum,[31] was formed in December 1991, and prepublication press censorship was lifted on January 12, 1992.[32]

Saudi Arabia, inundated by Western military personnel during the Gulf war, was able to revert to familiar patterns of behavior once the majority of Westerners left. Though King Fahd promised to establish a consultative council for the kingdom, he has made this promise during a number of crises in the last 30 years and never acted on it. Nevertheless, despite the skepticism of many observers,[33] on 1 March 1992, King Fahd issued new decrees establishing a "Basic Law of Government" and an advisory council of 60 members appointed by the king.[34] Elections are not part of the new law.

Several of the smaller Gulf states have experimented with various forms of advisory councils or national assemblies, but these have seldom lasted, nor have they been particularly effective. Kuwait in 1921 and 1938, Bahrain in 1938, and Dubai (one of the seven members of the UAE) in 1938 all experienced political reform movements of varying degrees of effectiveness. Merchants were usually behind these efforts; their interest was in gaining more power for themselves vis-à-vis the ruling shaykh. All of these efforts collapsed.

When these states gained full independence from Great Britain, some of them began to experiment with national assemblies—Kuwait in 1962 and Bahrain in 1972—and with consultative councils—Qatar in 1972 and Oman in 1981. (In preindependence Qatar in 1964, a council was appointed but never convened.) The national assemblies of Kuwait and Bahrain, most of whose members were elected, have been suspended, but the consultative councils in Qatar and Oman, whose members were appointed, remain active. With assembly elections, both Kuwait and Bahrain had gone the furthest down the road toward some form of institutionalized political participation. In Bahrain, in particular, there seems little likelihood that the assembly will be restored anytime soon. Nor is it likely that the two consultative councils in Qatar and Oman will be transformed into elected bodies.[35] These two assemblies have simply institutionalized a form of consultation that is very much within the traditions of the Gulf Arab societies. They allow the ruler to appoint notables from outside his family to positions of some visibility, if not real power. It would be misleading to read more into these institutions. The *majlis* system that operates informally in these societies allows the rulers and other members of the ruling family to receive petitions and requests for assistance from ordinary members of society. This is a normal mechanism in Arab patrimonial society, and although it is sometimes referred to as "desert democracy," it is not a real sign of incipient democratization. Seldom are critiques of the particular shaykh or ruler raised directly with him during such sessions. Although a petition calling for greater democratization and an elected advisory council was recently presented to the Amir of Qatar by 50 notables, no action in this direction has been taken.[36] These states are still far from the current wave of democratization.[37]

## One-Party (or No-Party) Dominant Authoritarian Systems

Iraq, Syria, Libya, and Iran do not share the same political system. They do share, however, the experience of having overthrown or dismantled an old order that was tainted by colonial or foreign domination. The subsequent struggle to establish new institutions has succeeded in creating new personalistic systems rather than institutionalized bases of legitimacy. Assad in Syria, Saddam Hussein in Iraq, Qaddafi in Libya, and first Khomeini and now, presumably, Rafsanjani in Iran are the loci of political power in each of these countries. Broader political participation is constrained in different ways in each case.

Even though Iraq and Syria are ruled by separate branches of the Baath party, they are implacable enemies whose national outlooks and goals for the Baath party differ dramatically. Libya and Iran do not even have political parties. What these four countries share is a political system designed to mobilize support or impose a revolution from above, even as it limits political debate within specified boundaries and stifles opposition viewpoints arising from outside those boundaries. The legislative bodies that exist go through the formalities of popular elections, but their roles in political debate are severely circumscribed, usually limited to local administrative issues and almost never addressing national policies, except to endorse the programs of the ruler or ruling party. Of these four, Syria and Iraq are the most similar institutionally. They both have legislatures with multiparty systems for contesting elections. Efforts are made to include (or co-opt) representatives of significant groups, both socioeconomic and ethnic, into the political process. Little effort is ever made to create a more open political system. Since the Iraqi occupation of and subsequent expulsion from Kuwait, prospects for opening up the Iraqi system under Saddam Hussein are more remote than ever.[38]

Libya under Muammar Qaddafi has introduced a unique political system, which he calls a *jamahiriya*, a "state run by the people without a government."[39] This system allows for a kind of "direct democracy," where grievances are aired at the annual meeting of the General People's Congress (GPC). Many of the complaints are about economic issues and the inefficiency of economic arrangements. Even though this system is an effort at mobilizing the people to support Qaddafi's plans for Libya, the congresses, composed of approximately one thousand delegates elected by the 45 district-level Popular Congresses, often suffer from 30 to 50 percent absenteeism.[40] Islamic groups such as al-Takfir wal-Hijra, al-Dawa wal-Jihad, and others are beginning to attract support, especially among the youth in urban areas. Opposition is also still active outside the country. Inside, the political system allows for no real opportunity to criticize or replace the national leadership. Even though Qaddafi has freed political prisoners on occasion and made other gestures to his opponents, he has no intention of liberalizing the political system. The establishment of political parties or organizations independent of the state is strictly forbidden.[41]

Elections for Iran's legislative assembly, or *majlis*, are also organized without parties. Even though a variety of viewpoints are expressed, and although disagreements within the regime are evident, these disputes do not allow for any opposition to clerical rule. Opposition parties and movements either went into exile or were eliminated during the early years of the revolution.

The political contest in Iran is centered on the clerical establishment. Clerical factions exist, but they do not always follow constant political lines. Supporters may cluster around particular personalities, and clashes may arise between junior- and senior-level politicians. Competition also develops between clerics with responsibilities within the government and those outside the government.[42]

The clerically dominated system, however, leaves many outside the political life of Iran. Secular Iranians can become indifferent or alienated and the lower classes disillusioned. A number of members of the Assembly of Experts have called for greater political tolerance, but any move in this direction will undoubtedly be opposed by the regime's religious ideologues.[43] Prospects for democratization in Iran are therefore still weak.

This cursory review of the status of democratization in the Middle East, while generally pessimistic, and focused somewhat narrowly on parties and the electoral process, nevertheless confirms the view that some hints of liberalization are discernible.

## Democratization: Global, Regional, and Internal Factors

After the First World War, attempts at parliamentary democracy in the Arab East were initiated in several countries, but they were undermined by the corruption of the landlords and merchants who controlled the parliaments.[44] In the wake of the disillusionment caused by these failures, nationalist, populist, socialist, and statist ideologies swept across the region and fueled the establishment of authoritarian alternatives. The failure of these new visions to achieve Arab advancement and dignity has brought disappointment again and a search for another path. The Islamic impulse behind some of the more successful new experiments with democracy in the Middle East has both excited and horrified large segments of the populace. To the extent that the new democratic tendency derives from an indigenous inspiration, it offers a greater promise of success than previous democratizing efforts, since it avoids the opprobrium of being labeled "foreign." To the extent that it fails to find solutions to the mounting economic, social, and political grievances of the people, however, it is likely to suffer defeat, as have so many earlier political experiments. As noted in a book by Muhammad Jabir al-Ansari, published ten years ago in Kuwait:

> Every new [Arab] generation becomes disappointed with the convictions and beliefs of prior generations and therefore is forced to demolish these convictions and begin all over again. It does not take long, however, for the new generation to become tormented by its own convictions leaving nothing for coming generations but its bitter experience.[45]

Paul E. Salem of the Lebanese Center for Policy Studies, in a paper titled, "Theoretical Perspectives on Prospects for Democratization in the Arab World,"[46] proposed two theoretical paths to democracy. The first path is an ideological commitment to democracy, a belief in the system for its own sake. The best examples are the United States, France, Mexico, and Eastern Europe. The second path he labels "non-ideology," or the path selected by default, after the failure of another system. Russia in the 1990s is but the latest example; after the Second World War, Germany, Italy, and Japan also followed this path. In these latter cases democracy was chosen in the belief that it would lead to prosperity. In the current "wave" of democratization in the Arab world, it appears that the Arab experience conforms more to the second path.

The belief that democracy will bring prosperity develops as the society evolves from tradition to modernity and as individuals suffer loss of identity and become vulnerable to new ideologies. During the period extending from the First World War to the 1950s, the Arab world experienced an age of ideology that transformed Arab economies, institutions, and classes. Cities grew, and the mass media, among other factors, challenged the political culture. Ideology was used to explain and derive strength from the shocks of World War I, World War II, and the Arab-Israeli wars of 1948 and 1967.

Salem argues that the age of ideology in the Arab world is ending and that the cyclone of modernity has hit. The ebb in ideology has led to interest in democracy, as kings, *Faqih*, and parties search for new bases of legitimacy. If they fail in their search, they can opt for coercion. Politically, the Middle East area is still in a pre-Gorbachev stage, characterized predominantly by authoritarianism. It is like China in that some economic liberalization is allowed. Moves toward democracy in Jordan, Egypt, and Algeria, however, are like those in the Soviet Union were in that they are dictated by necessity or political convenience. Paul Salem cannot imagine Arab rulers being thrown out, and he concludes that these democratizing moves will not take Arabs to real democracy.

Who will initiate real breakthroughs toward democracy? Paul Salem sees several paths. One possibility would be *the rulers or the ruling elites*, as was the case in the Soviet Union with Gorbachev or Yeltsin. He sees no such leader now in the Arab world. The second possibility would be *outsiders* who force the issue, as was the case after World War II in Germany,

Italy, Japan, and even the Philippines, where the United States was the outside force. Some Arabs hoped that the United States would give its Arab friends a similar push toward democracy after the war to liberate Kuwait. The *youth* are the third path Salem identifies. One could argue that they played a significant role not only in China and Korea but also in Algeria, where over 70 percent of the population is under 25 years of age.[47] Youth may easily attach themselves to an ideological challenge to the old order; Salem argues that in the Arab world, passage from liberalism to nationalism to Islamic fundamentalism is a natural dialectic of generations. A fourth path derives from a *socioeconomic class*, such as the middle class, as was the case in the revolutions of England, France, and the United States. In Egypt after the First World War, it was the landowning class that saw democracy as useful for maintaining its power. The middle class dissented since they had a stake in the status quo, and they only gave their support to change when it was to their benefit.

The signs that give promise of democratization are not necessarily directly linked to obvious democratic institutions and practices. These signs, and the theories designed to explain how they help lead to democracy, involve factors that are global, regional, and internal. Exploration of these factors should give some indication of the future direction of democratization in the Middle East.

## Global Factors

Political and economic linkages certainly exist between the international environment and the Middle East. The question is, how significant are these linkages in either promoting or hindering democracy? Between 1988 and 1992, Jordan and Algeria provided the best examples in the Arab world of movement toward greater political participation. In both cases, economic issues pushed the governments in the direction of political reform. Falling global prices for gas and oil cut revenues to both countries, further straining their weakened economies and adding to their already high unemployment rates. In addition, large numbers of Palestinians and Jordanians lost jobs in the Gulf, first because of lower oil prices and the consequent contraction of the Gulf economies, and then because of the Kuwait-Iraq war, which added still more refugees to the unemployed in Jordan and severely cut remittances to Jordan from the Gulf. These international economic forces were beyond the control of either Jordan or Algeria. Nevertheless, they contributed to the move toward democratization, since both Algeria and Jordan hoped that the public would participate in the difficult economic choices the government had to make.

The demise of Marxism-Leninism, the collapse of the Soviet bloc, and the ultimate dissolution of the Soviet Union have also had an impact on democratization in the Middle East. When a state's principal international patron disappears, such as the Soviet Union for Syria, political adjustments have to be made. A move toward democracy may or may not result. The impact on Syria seems to have been greatest in terms of its willingness to participate in the U.S.-led effort to oust Iraq from Kuwait and in the U.S.-sponsored Middle East peace talks that followed the war against Iraq. The impact on Syria's domestic political institutions, however, has been minimal. Some observers took note when the Romanian dictator, Nicolae Ceauşescu, was overthrown and killed, and his regime replaced by a government that appeared to be more democratic. It was thought that other authoritarian leaders, such as Saddam Hussein of Iraq, might respond by making moves toward accommodation with their opponents. Saddam Hussein announced some intentions toward greater political participation; in reality, though, he only offered palliatives to some opponents while crafting new techniques (or refining old ones) for maintaining himself in power. Since the Kuwait crisis, the possibility of any move toward democracy under Saddam Hussein has become even more remote.

The emergence of democracies in Eastern Europe and the former Soviet Union may not necessarily be replicated in the Arab world. The limitations of the "demonstration effect" on the Middle East are drawn by those who argue that democracy is an alien concept to Arab and Muslim societies.[48] This perspective can be propounded by adherents of the Islamic trend and by some Arab nationalists. A young Algerian graduate of the Islamic Science Institute of Algiers commented, "The modern world is going through a major moral crisis which can be very confusing to young people. Just look at what is happening in Russia. Personally I have found many of the answers and the solutions in Islam."[49] In this case one might argue that the "demonstration effect" consists of the moral vacuum left by the collapse of the Soviet empire, representing a kind of bewilderment or emptiness for which Islam is the answer. Even so, Abdelqader Hashani, a leader of the Islamic Salvation Front (FIS) in Algeria, argues that FIS will

> guarantee freedom of opinion in Algeria. Our purpose is to persuade, not to oblige people into doing what we say. I challenge anyone to prove that so far we have repressed any other political tendencies. You must remember we have won control of some 800 municipalities in elections more than a year ago. We have a record of tolerance that no one can deny. This is the essence of Islam.[50]

Westernized elites in the Arab world are often the core promoters of greater democracy, but many of these secularized elites have also held power or have benefited from the policies of the ruling elites who are now discredited. In some cases they have been discredited for being linked to (or being virtual instruments of) foreign—particularly Western—commercial and financial interests. This dependency undermines their credibility; it is inevitable that their ideologies should also be discredited. The perception is reinforced when Western governments express fear over the prospect of

Islamic governments, even freely elected ones, coming to power. To the extent that democracy is tied either to failed elites or suspect Western ideologies, it is in danger. Yet, if democratic means can bring Islamic or other legitimate political forces and voices to power, democracy may, in the eyes of Arabs and others in the Middle East, be vindicated as authentic and acceptable. It may be some years, though, before this occurs.

The absence of the Cold War presents another possible indirect impetus to democratization. During the Cold War, the United States and the Soviet Union spent large sums of money supporting their regional allies, often to prevent them from becoming the allies of the other side. Such behavior flowed directly from the concept that the global superpower competition was a zero-sum game, in which any loss of an ally on one side was interpreted as a gain for the other. Consequently, allies extracted (or extorted) aid from the superpowers in order to prevent them from going to the other side for a better deal—a perverse sort of international political free-market mechanism. Without superpower rivalries the incentives are gone for the United States and Russia to continue to compete this way. The loss of aid means greater economic difficulties globally, and especially in "command" economies, or their Middle Eastern prototypes. In these countries more pressure will be brought to bear on political elites to accept political change, with the possibility that such change will include moves toward democracy.

These global factors have their regional corollaries, some of which have greater significance for Middle Eastern events than the international factors themselves.

### Regional Factors

The end of the Cold War has opened up new possibilities for democratization in some parts of the world. Throughout Latin America, for example, except possibly in Peru, the charge that political opponents and critics are communists or tools of the Soviet Union is no longer a credible excuse for delaying democratization. In the political vocabulary of the Middle East, however, Arab rulers during the Cold War characterized Israel as the major threat to the Arab world and argued that its first priority—certainly ahead of democracy—was the need to liberate occupied Arab land. Such excuses were often used to avoid opening up the political system. The threat from "godless communists," whether local or international, was also exploited, especially in the Arabian peninsula (most notably during the reign of King Faisal of Saudi Arabia), but it was not the only, nor necessarily the most salient, rationale used against political pluralism and wider participation in the political system.

Communist parties have existed in the Middle East for years, whether or not they were tools of Soviet foreign policy. In Iran the Soviet Union gave support to a revolt by Kuchik Khan in Gilan province after the First World War; after the Second World War, it aided the Tudeh party's effort to establish a separate communist state in Iranian Azerbaijan. Both efforts, ostensibly intended to promote communism in Iran, failed.[51] The Communist party was very strong in the Sudan in the 1960s. It was influential in Syria before the Baath party consolidated its position and also significant in Egypt, where it was suppressed. The party is still legal in Tunisia and Morocco. Yet, whenever local governments cracked down on communists, the Soviet government seldom did more than issue pro forma protests, since ties to the existing governments were regarded as more useful than the activities of local, usually ineffective, communist parties. Hence, a number of countries still have a communist presence, though it has generally been well under control and not posed much of a threat. What they *have* lost is support from the Soviet Union in inter-Arab and Middle Eastern regional disputes. In a geopolitical sense, the elimination of the Cold War has had only an indirect, but potentially significant, impact on domestic political processes in the region: renewed efforts by the United States and by a now somewhat more united international community to find a solution to the Arab-Israeli conflict may eliminate the regional issue that has been utilized most often to impede democratization or broadened political participation.

Since the 1979 Iranian revolution, the Middle East has witnessed the rising involvement and influence of Islamic political movements in regional and domestic politics. This Islamic political phenomenon is a manifestation of discontent with the political and economic status quo. The overthrow, by popular revolution, of the Shah, who represented the archetypal example of Western influence in a Muslim country, attracted many to the power that could be drawn from Islam to achieve political objectives previously deemed impossible. Whether the objectives were economic, social, or political justice, or the mitigation of injustice, the Islamic success in Iran reawakened interest in the Islamic model among many groups in the Middle East. Despite the widespread use of Islamic symbols by most Middle Eastern governments, these ruling elites remained vulnerable to the Islamic critique of contemporary politics and society. The call of Islamic groups for reform and for justice, through a return to a purer Islam, has a long tradition in the Muslim world. That some are now making the link between Islam and democracy could be a hopeful sign.[52] Paradoxically, substantial financial support for Islamic movements comes from Saudi Arabia, a country not known to be anxious to support democratization!

The usual response to the Islamic challenge to the privilege of the ruling elites has been to attempt to undermine these Islamic groups. Such attempts have met with varying success. In Egypt, Anwar el-Sadat attempted to clamp down on the Islamic opposition and paid for it with his life in October 1981. His successor, Husni Mubarak, has made tentative moves to open up Egypt's political system, while maintaining institutions such as the parliament as collaborators in state power. Hafez al-Assad dealt with the 1976–

1982 Muslim Brotherhood revolt against his regime by leveling, in 1982, parts of the town of Hama, their political power center. Since 1989, Assad has attempted to remobilize support for his regime through greater emphasis on the links between the state and popular organizations within civil society. However, for Assad, order takes precedence over freedom, since freedom can tend dangerously toward anarchy.[53] The Palestine Liberation Organization (PLO) has tried by turns either to stifle or to co-opt their Islamic rival organization, HAMAS (the Islamic Resistance Movement). This Islamic organization has been among the most hostile to democratization and to any accommodation with Israel, since both the political concept of democracy and the State of Israel are considered to be alien imports into the region that must be expelled.

In contrast, as noted above, in the early 1990s Jordan and Algeria decided to allow Islamic groups or parties to participate in local and national legislative elections. In Jordan, Islamic groups made substantial gains in the national assembly, but not enough to challenge the ruling order. In Algeria, the process led to the real possibility that the Islamic Salvation Front (FIS) would take over the government. The military decided that it had seen enough democratization and canceled the January 1992 run-off elections, thus aborting a dramatic and nearly successful shift to Islamic government there. The involvement of Islamic movements in the drive for greater political participation brought Algeria closer than any other Arab country to democracy. It might still succeed.

Other regional factors have indirectly influenced the growing efforts at democratization in the Middle East, usually by exacerbating already difficult domestic problems. The war over Kuwait, 1990–1991, not only produced hope among some intellectuals in the Gulf that the United States might exert some pressure on its allies to allow greater political participation, but it also pushed still more refugees into Jordan, thus contributing to the local economic crisis. The Saudi expulsion of Yemeni workers poisoned relations even further between those two states; it also heightened domestic strains in the new Yemeni nation-state, which was attempting to reconcile the Imamate and republican political experience of North Yemen with South Yemen's Marxist legacy, in order to create a united country.

Intellectuals throughout the Middle East, from North Africa and Egypt to the Fertile Crescent and the Arabian peninsula, have discussed and debated the prospects for democratization and greater political participation in their countries.[54] A 1983 conference of Arab intellectuals in Hammamet, Tunisia, issued a declaration critical of Arab governments for curtailing political and civil rights in the Arab world, complaining that "the last thirty years have witnessed the complete disappearance of democratic freedoms in the Arab world. . . . Authority in the Arab countries is today based on intimidation, subjugation and cooptation."[55] Also in 1983 the Arab Organization for Human Rights (AOHR) was organized and began to monitor and document human rights abuses throughout the region. These are modest regional initiatives, but they are essential ingredients in the democratization process.

## Internal Factors

The fall of Marxism-Leninism and the end of the Cold War may have had only limited and indirect impact on the Middle East, but the "demonstration effect" of the fall of authoritarian regimes and the rise of democracy in Eastern Europe has nonetheless become a part of the political consciousness of the region. Throughout this period, Islamic movements have achieved the most significant political gains of all the groups that have attempted to take advantage of those political openings that have appeared. In many cases, however, internal political and economic factors may have been more important in affecting political consciousness than all the other factors discussed so far.

Pressure for change has appeared most strongly in the countries with the fewest available resources to counter these pressures: Jordan, Yemen, Algeria and the other North African states, and Egypt. Unemployment, national debt, and the population have increased to such an extent that they have outstripped the economic capabilities of these states to deliver even minimal improvements in the living standard, or even, in most cases, to prevent its decline. Furthermore, advances in civil society, which are important prerequisites for democratization, are slowly beginning to emerge in the region. Based on the studies available to date, it appears that Egypt and Turkey may have made longer strides in this direction than most other Middle Eastern states.[56] Even so, economic liberalization in the region has not led to any significant dismantling of the public sector.[57]

In addition, groups similar to the Arab Organization for Human Rights (AOHR) have formed at the state level. Implementing policies long advocated by the *Ligue tunisienne des droits de l'homme* (LTDH),[58] Ben Ali, after becoming president in 1987, abolished Tunisia's infamous state security court and cut back on the practice of pretrial incommunicado detention. (Recently, because of internal disputes over the war to liberate Kuwait, he has become less inclined to listen to the group.)[59] Even in Morocco, the *Ligue marocaine de défense des droits de l'homme* (OMDH) has had some success in "putting human rights on the [political] agenda constructed and otherwise controlled by the King."[60]

The crisis of legitimacy in many Middle Eastern states—coupled with and abetted by corruption among many of the ruling elites—may be the leading domestic factor legitimizing the discussion of democracy in the region. Whether that discussion is couched in an Islamic framework or in a more secular-positivistic one, it nevertheless is addressing topics long thought to be beyond acceptable discourse. This may be a sign for optimism in a region thought to be virtually immune to democratization.

## Prospects for Democratization

Robert Bianchi has pointed to four factors to support his optimism about the future of democratization in the Middle East: "the strengthening of Islamic movements, the growing unruliness of associational life, the unavoidable task of confronting economic hardship, and the pervasive fear of popular revolt."[61] He believes that these factors are pressing authoritarian and oligarchic regimes to move toward greater liberalization. How far these regimes will have to move is debatable, but, judging from the foregoing survey, movement is apparent in almost all Middle Eastern countries. It is certainly not the kind of rapid change that has occurred in Eastern Europe, but it may be the beginning of a process that could produce the kind of sustained improvements that have been underway in Latin America since the 1980s.

Leonard Binder, a cautious optimist in regard to possibilities for democratization in the Middle East, sees a growing middle class there as a sign of movement toward more liberal regimes, but he concludes that the time is not yet right for liberal democratic regimes to emerge. Indeed, they may not appear until what Binder calls Islamic liberalism develops vigorously enough in the region to counter the fundamentalist trend.[62] To many, including Binder, this development seems to be a long way off.

Whether Islam is a potential source of positive pressure for democratization or a menace to be feared remains the subject of much debate.[63] Serif Mardin, in a recent paper,[64] argues that Islam can be viewed not as the false originator of democracy but as containing elements that support the concept of democracy. He believes that an historic dialectic in the Middle East between inchoate populism and modernization has resulted in an incremental process toward democratization. Nineteenth-century Western liberalism, followed by secular-positivistic nationalism that focused on nation creation or class division, denied the cultural reality of the Middle East: Islam. Examining the "project of Islam"—which Mardin says is the establishment of a just society—and its interaction with the "project of democracy" will yield the most productive results.

Since the birth of Islam, Mardin argues, groups of pious Muslims have risen from time to time in opposition to what they have seen as unjust rule. Today, he argues, the "fundamentalists" have cast themselves in the role of the "just." The tension between the "just" and the "unjust," in its promotion of social change throughout Islamic history, may be compared to the tension in Western history between the "state" and "civil society."[65] In Islam the idealized goal of the "just," in its classic formulation, was "direct democracy," where the ruler settled the problems brought to him in person by his loyal subjects. The Islamic concept of *shura*, or consultation, is not, according to some Muslim scholars, popular sovereignty, since sovereignty belongs to God. Rather, it is a means for obtaining unanimity from the community of believers, which allows for no legitimate minority position. The goal of the "just" is an Islamically based society.

Liberty in the West has its parallel in equality and justice in Islam. Mardin admits that there are seemingly unbridgeable differences between the Islamic notion of justice and democracy, but he insists that any discussion of democracy in the Middle East that fails to address these Islamic concepts will lead to a misunderstanding of current democratization efforts. With the Islamic movements taking the lead in the latest Arab experiments in democracy, Serif Mardin's advice is worth heeding.

## Notes

1. Henry Kissinger, "What Kind of New World Order?" *The Washington Post*, 3 December 1991, p. A21.

2. Hamed Juwan, "Democracy, Not Dictatorship," *Washington Post*, 10 April 1991, p. A23. Juwan, a prominent Kuwaiti lawyer, was shot and paralyzed within hours of the liberation of Kuwait.

3. Chapter 3 in this volume, p. 60.

4. See especially Michael C. Hudson, "Democratization and the Problem of Legitimacy in Middle East Politics," *Middle East Studies Association Bulletin* 22, no. 2 (December 1988): 157–171; Hudson, "The Democratization Process in the Arab World: An Assessment" (Paper presented at the 1990 Annual Meeting of the American Political Science Association, San Francisco, 2 September 1990) and Hudson, "After the Gulf War: Prospects for Democratization in the Arab World," *Middle East Journal* 45, no. 3 (Summer 1991): 407–426.

5. Michael C. Hudson, "The Possibilities for Pluralism," *American-Arab Affairs* 36 (Spring 1991): 3.

6. The contradictory views that Islam is or is not compatible with democracy are discussed in some detail by John L. Esposito and James P. Piscatori in "Democratization and Islam," *Middle East Journal* 45, no. 3 (Summer 1991): 427–440. See also James J. Coyle, "Islamic Movements in the Maghreb" (Paper presented at the 1991 Annual Meeting of the Middle East Studies Association, Washington D.C., 1991, pp. 5–7, where he cites contradictory attitudes toward democracy among Islamic leaders. For example, Dr. Abdeslam Harras of Fez, Morocco, leader of the *Jama'at al-Da'wa al-Islamiyah*, said he opposed democracy because the concept is a Western import, but he also asserted that the ruler of the country should be elected by a majority of the people. See also Bryan Turner, "Orientalism and the Problem of Civil Society in Islam," in *Orientalism, Islam and Islamists*, ed. Asaf Hussain, Robert W. Olson, and Jamie Qureshi (Brattleboro, VT: Amana Books, 1984), pp. 26 and 39, on the absence of civil society, a building block of democratization, in the Oriental world, cited in Ghassan Salamé, "Introduction," in *The Foundations of the Arab State*, ed. Salamé (London, 1987), pp. 9–10.

7. Hudson, "Pluralism," p. 4.

8. Hudson, "Democratization Process." See also Jean-Claude Vatin, "Les partis (pris) démocratiques. Perceptions occidentales de la démocratisation dans le monde arabe," *Egypte/Monde arabe* 4, no. 4 (1990): 9–24.

9. Samih K. Farsoun and Lisa Hajjar, "The Contemporary Sociology of the Middle East: An Assessment," in *Theory, Politics and the Arab World: Critical Responses*, ed. Hisham Sharabi (New York: Routledge, 1990), pp. 180–186.

10. 4 January 1992, p. 10.

11. Larry Diamond, Juan J. Linz, and Seymour Martin Lipset, *Politics in Developing Countries: Comparing Experiences with Democracy* (Boulder, CO: Lynne Rienner, 1990), pp. 6–7, offer a useful definition of democracy (or "polyarchy" in Robert Dahl's terms):

> a system of government that meets three essential conditions: meaningful and extensive competition among individuals and organized groups (especially political parties) for all effective positions of government power, at regular intervals and excluding the use of force; a 'highly inclusive' level of *political participation* in the selection of leaders and policies, at least through regular and fair elections, such that no major (adult) social group is excluded; and a level of *civil* and *political liberties*—freedom of expression, freedom of the press, freedom to form and join organizations—sufficient to ensure the integrity of political competition and participation.

12. Hudson, "Democratization and Legitimacy," pp. 157–158:

> a process through which the exercise of political power by a regime and state becomes less arbitrary, exclusive, and authoritarian. Bargaining, as opposed to command, takes on increasing importance in power relationships. Alternative centers of power, or influence, begin to appear. Public political debate, and the expression of criticism and opposing views, becomes increasingly evident. Powerholders increasingly recognize the costs of governance by coercion and threat as opposed to persuasion and reward. They increasingly realize that policy goals, such as economic growth and even political stability, may be enhanced by allowing, or acquiescing in, greater autonomy for societal elements in politics. Increased participation, they may come to feel, enhances their (and the system's) political legitimacy; and political legitimacy comes to be seen not as an abstract (and perhaps dispensable) value but as an important political commodity or resource. For their part, aspirants to power begin to perceive the realistic possibility of achieving power, or sharing it, through conventional, legal procedures rather than by irregular and violent means. I am not talking about plebiscitory [sic] democracy, guided democracy, tutelary democracy, or regime-manufactured, "facade" democracy. My conception . . . is clearly liberal, instrumental, pluralistic and "polyarchic"—very much in the tradition of American political science as represented by Robert Dahl and other scholars.

13. See Muhammad Muslih, "Arab Systems of Government and the Prospects for Democratization," in a forthcoming volume coauthored with Augustus Richard Norton. The typology here is a variation on that offered by Muslih, who gives three classifications of the seven Arab governments he surveys: (1) single-party authoritarian, (2) oil oligarchies, and (3) semicompetitive multiparty systems.

14. Bernard Reich, Noah Dropkin, and Meyrav Wurmser, "The Impact of Soviet Jewish Immigration on Israeli Politics and Policy," Paper prepared for the Defense Academic Research Support Program, November 1991, 64 pages.

15. See Lenni Brenner, *The Iron Wall: Zionist Revisionism from Jabotinsky to Shamir* (London: Zed Books, 1984).

16. Robert Bianchi, "Democratization in the Middle East: Four Reasons for Optimism," *American-Arab Affairs* 36 (Spring 1991): 5.

17. On the issue of democracy and the political opposition, see Kirk J. Beattie, "Prospects for Democratization in Egypt," *American-Arab Affairs* 36 (Spring 1991):

31–47; Mona Makram-Ebeid, "Political Opposition in Egypt: Democratic Myth or Reality?" *Middle East Journal* 43, no. 3 (Summer 1989): 423–436; and Robert Springborg, *Mubarak's Egypt: Fragmentation of the Political Order* (Boulder, CO: Westview, 1989), especially Chapter 5, "The System of Political Control," pp. 135–181, and Chapter 6, "Secular and Islamicist Opposition," pp. 183–253.

18. Augustus Richard Norton, "Lebanon after Ta'if: Is the Civil War Over?" *Middle East Journal* 45, no. 3 (Summer 1991): 457–473.

19. Philip Robins, "Jordan's Election: A New Era?" *Middle East Report* nos. 164–165 (May–August 1990): 55–57; Donald Kirk, "Counting on the Center: Jordan Inches Toward Democracy," *The New Leader* 74, no. 6 (6 May 1991): 5–7; Laurie A. Brand, "Democratization in Jordan," *American-Arab Affairs* 36 (Spring 1991): 21–23; Hudson, "After the Gulf War," pp. 418–420; and John M. Roberts, "Prospects for Democracy in Jordan," *Arab Studies Quarterly* 13, nos. 3–4 (Summer–Fall 1991): 119–138.

20. For a description of the background to the riots and their aftermath, see Robert A. Mortimer, "Algeria after the Explosion," *Current History* 89, no. 546 (April 1990): 161–164, 180–182. Other articles on democratization in Algeria: Mortimer, "Islam and Multiparty Politics in Algeria," *Middle East Journal* 45, no. 4 (Autumn 1991): 575–593; Daniel Brumberg, "The Prospects for a 'Democratic Bargain' in Contemporary Algeria," *American-Arab Affairs* 36 (Spring 1991): 23–26; Hudson, "After the Gulf War," pp. 414–418 and Hudson, "The Democratization Process," pp. 12–18.

21. For the reform period prior to the 1990 elections, see Mortimer, "Algeria after the Explosion," pp. 161–164 and 180–182.

22. Robin Wright, "Islam, Democracy and the West," *Foreign Affairs* 71, no. 3 (Summer 1992): 131–145.

23. Hudson, "After the Gulf War," pp. 420–424.

24. Jonathan Addleton, "Economic Prospects in a United Yemen," *Journal of South Asian and Middle Eastern Studies* 14, no. 4 (Summer 1991): 4.

25. Ghannoushi remarked in an interview, "The key problem that we have to solve, otherwise we will achieve nothing, is political freedom and multiparty democracy. Without this, there is no chance of improving the economy." See "We Don't Have a Religious Problem," *The Middle East* no. 203 (September 1991): 19–20.

26. Mark Tessler, "Tunisia's New Beginning," *Current History* 89, no. 546 (April 1990): 169–172, 182–184 and I. William Zartman, "The Conduct of Political Reform: The Path Toward Democracy," in *Tunisia: The Political Economy of Reform*, ed. I. W. Zartman (Boulder: Lynne Rienner, 1991), pp. 9–28.

27. Jonathan C. Randal, "Tunisia Faces Renewed Threat from Islamic Fundamentalists," *Washington Post,* 11 January 1992, pp. A14, A20; and Graham E. Fuller, "Islamic Fundamentalism: No Long-Term Threat," *Washington Post* 13 January 1992, p. A17.

28. Mark A. Tessler, "Morocco: Institutional Pluralism and Monarchical Dominance," in *Political Elites in Arab North Africa*, ed. I. William Zartman (New York, 1982); John P. Entelis, *Culture and Counterculture in Moroccan Politics* (Boulder, CO: Westview, 1989); Mark A. Tessler and John P. Entelis, "Kingdom of Morocco," in *The Government and Politics of the Middle East and North Africa*, ed. David E. Long and Bernard Reich, 2d ed. (Boulder, CO: Westview, 1986), pp. 398–402; and Youssef M. Ibrahim, "Tunis Chief Calls for Arab Repression of Militants," *New York Times*, 5 January 1992, p. 10.

29. See Hamed Juwan, "Democracy, Not Dictatorship."

30. After the liberation of Kuwait, the government of Kuwait asked the National Republican Institute for International Affairs to sponsor a conference on "Political Participation and Constitutional Democracy in Kuwait," which was held in Washing-

ton, 29 April 1991. The institute issued the proceedings of that conference in August 1991, stating that "democracy is a force which can no longer be ignored in Kuwait." Participants included, among others, Jill Crystal, Shafiq Ghabra, and Michael Hudson. See also Mary Ann Tétreault, "Kuwait: The Morning After," *Current History* (January 1992): 6–10. See also the Kuwaiti Government's "The Final Communique of the Kuwaiti People's Conference held from 24–26 Rabi'Awwal 1411H (13–15 October 1990) in the City of Jeddah, the Kingdom of Saudi Arabia."

31. "Kuwait Political Party," *Washington Post*, 11 December 1991, p. A29.

32. "Government in Kuwait Ends Censorship of Newspapers," *New York Times*, 13 January 1992), p. A10.

33. David B. Ottaway, "Saudi Liberals See Reforms Unlikely," *Washington Post*, 16 April 1991, pp. A1, A14; Youssef M. Ibrahim, "Saudi Clergy and Scholars Petition for Change," *New York Times*, 26 May 1991; Caryle Murphy, "Islamic Right Petitions for Role in Saudi Rule," *Washington Post*, 10 June 1991, p. A13.

34. For English translations of these laws see: *Foreign Broadcast Information Service Daily Report: Near East and South Asia* (FBIS-NES-92–041), 2 March 1992, pp. 24–36.

35. In Oman, a newly appointed advisory council (*majlis al-shura*) was established in November 1991. It has 57 members, one for each province (*wilaya*). Each province proposes three names to the government and one is selected. Meetings are held in the provinces where the three are selected. Provincial leaders gather to make their suggestions, and local citizens are allowed to comment on the candidates. The local leaders make the final selection. Its predecessor, the "government's advisory council" (*majlis al-istishari al-dawlah*) has been disbanded in favor of this new people's advisory council. The former council included members of the government; the new one does not. Information from an interview with J. E. Peterson, 20 January 1992. See also Caryle Murphy, "Oman's Ruler To Broaden Citizen Panel," *Washington Post*, 19 November 1990, p. A22.

36. "Qatar: une pétition pour la démocratie addressée à l'émir," *Le Monde*, 21 January 1992, p. 28; "54 Qatar Citizens Petition Emir for Free Elections," *New York Times*, 13 May 1992, p. A15.

37. J. E. Peterson, *The Arab Gulf States: Steps Toward Political Participation* (New York: Praeger, 1988).

38. Ahmed Hashim, "Iraq, the Pariah State," *Current History* (January 1992): 11–16. On Iraq, see also Phebe Marr, *The Modern History of Iraq* (Boulder, CO: Westview, 1985); Amazia Baram, "The Ruling Elite in Bathi Iraq 1968–1986: The Changing Features of a Collective Profile," *International Journal of Middle Eastern Studies* 19, no. 4 (November 1988); and Pierre-Jean Luizard, "L'improbable democratie en Irak: le piege de l'Etat-nation," *Egypte/Monde Arabe* 4, no. 4 (1990): 47–85. On Syria, see Raymond A. Hinnebusch, "Political Parties in the Arab State: Libya, Syria, Egypt," in *Beyond Coercion: The Durability of the Arab State*, ed. Adeed Dawisha and I. William Zartman (London: Croom Helm 1985), pp. 43–50; Hinnebusch, "Party and Peasant," *Cairo Papers in Social Science*, 3, no. 1 (November 1979); Hinnebusch, "Rural Politics in Ba'athist Syria," *Review of Politics* 44, no. 1 (January 1982): 110–130.

39. Mary-Jane Deeb, "New Thinking in Libya," *Current History* 89, no. 546 (April 1990): 149.

40. Hinnebusch, "Political Parties in the Arab State," pp. 36–43, see especially p. 38 for explanation of the People's Congresses; see also Dirk Vandewalle, "Qadhafi's *'Perestroika'*: Economic and Political Liberalization in Libya," *Middle East Journal* 45, no. 2 (Spring 1991): 216–231, who argues that Qadhafi's reforms are generally designed to allow Libyans to vent their grievances, not to truly open the system.

41. Vandewalle, "Qadhafi's 'Perestroika,'" pp. 149–152, 177–178. See also Lisa Anderson, "Tribe and State: Libyan Anomalies," in *Tribe and State Formation in the Middle East*, ed. Philip S. Khoury and Joseph Kostiner (Berkeley: University of California Press, 1990), pp. 288–302.

42. Nikola B. Schahgaldian, "Iran after Khomeini," *Current History* 89, no. 544 (February 1990): 61–64, 82–84; and Fred Halliday, "The Revolution's First Decade," *Middle East Report* no. 156 (January–February 1989): 19–21.

43. Eric Hooglund, "The Islamic Republic at War and Peace," *Middle East Report* no. 156 (January–February 1989): 12.

44. Khaldoun Hasan al-Naqeeb, "Social Origins of the Authoritarian State in the Arab East," in *Statecraft in the Middle East: Oil, Historical Memory, and Popular Culture*, ed. Eric Davis and Nicolas Gavrielides (Miami: Florida International University Press, 1991), pp. 36–70.

45. Muhammad Jabir al-Ansari, *tahawwulat al-fikr wa-l-siyasa fi-l-mashriq al-'arabi, 1930–1970* (Intellectual and political transformations in the Arab East, 1930–1970) (Kuwait, 1980), p. 91, quoted and translated by al-Naqeeb, "Social Origins," p. 37.

46. This discussion is a summary of the essence of Paul E. Salem's paper, originally entitled, "Ideological Change and Democratization in the Arab World" (Paper presented on a panel on "Democratization: The Arab World," at the 25th Annual Meeting of the Middle East Studies Association, Washington, D.C., 23–26 November 1991).

47. Kim Murphy, "Islamic Party Wins in Algerian Elections," *Washington Post*, 28 December 1991, pp. A1 & 22.

48. Samuel P. Huntington, "Will More Countries Become Democratic?" *Political Science Quarterly* 99, no. 2 (September 1984): 216–217, cited in Beattie, "Prospects for Democratization in Egypt," p. 31. Elie Kedourie, in *Democracy and Arab Political Culture* (Washington, D.C.: The Washington Institute for Near East Policy, 1992), pp. 1–11 and 83–105, details the failures of parliamentary democracy in the Arab world, primarily in the first half of the twentieth century.

49. Quoted in Youssef M. Ibrahim, "Islamic Plan for Algeria is on Display," *New York Times,* 7 January 1992, p. A3.

50. Quoted in Ibrahim, "Islamic Plans."

51. Sepher Zabih, *The Communist Movement in Iran* (Berkeley: University of California Press, 1966).

52. A theoretical exposition of this perspective can be found in Serif Mardin, "The 'Venture' of Democracy in the Middle East" (Paper presented to the Euro-Arab Seminar on Euro-Arab Understanding and Cultural Exchange, organized by the Secretary General of the Council of Europe, Strasbourg, 14–15 November 1991).

53. Steven Heydemann, "Can We Get There from Here? Lessons from the Syrian Case," *American-Arab Affairs* 36 (Spring 1991): 27–30.

54. See Hudson, "Democratization Process," pp. 4–6. See also essays in the following books: *azmah al-dimuqratiyah fil-watan al-'arabi* (The crisis of democracy in the Arab nation) (Beirut: markaz dirasat al-wahdah al-arabiyah, 1984); Sa'd al-Din Ibrahim, ed., *al-ta'addudiyah al-siyasiyah wal-dimuqratiyah fil-watan al-'arabi* (Political pluralism and democracy in the Arab nation) (Amman: Arab Thought Forum, 1989); *al-dimuqratiyah wa huquq al-insan fil-watan al-'arabi* (Democracy and human rights in the Arab nation) (Beirut: markaz dirasat al-wahdah al-'arabiyah, 1986); and Fu'ad Bitar, *azmah al-dimuqratiyah fil-'alam al-'arabi* (The crisis of democracy in the Arab world) (Beirut: Editions Beryte, 1984).

55. Quoted by Jill Crystal, "The Human Rights Movement in the Arab World," *American-Arab Affairs* 36 (Spring 1991): 14.

56. Augustus Richard Norton, "Rulers under Siege," *American-Arab Affairs* 36 (Spring 1991): 12–14; Shafeeq Ghabra, "Voluntary Associations in Kuwait: The Foundation of a New System?" *Middle East Journal* 45, no. 2 (Spring 1991): 199–215; and Michel Camu, "Trois questions à propos de la démocratisation dans le monde arabe," *Egypte/Monde Arabe* 4, no. 4 (1990): 25–46. In Camu, see especially pp. 29–39.

57. Alan Richards and John Waterbury, *A Political Economy of the Middle East* (Boulder, CO: Westview, 1990), pp. 238–261.

58. Susan Waltz, "Making Waves: The Political Impact of Human Rights Groups in North Africa," *The Journal of Modern African Studies* 29, no. 3 (1991): 482.

59. Waltz, "Making Waves," p. 504.

60. Waltz, "Making Waves," p. 498.

61. Bianchi, "Four Reasons for Optimism," p. 5.

62. Leonard Binder, *Islamic Liberalism: A Critique of Development Ideologies* (Chicago, IL: University of Chicago Press, 1990). See especially Chapter 4, "'Ali 'Abd al-Raziq and Islamic Liberalism: The Rejected Alternative," pp. 128–69; and Chapter 9, "Conclusion: The Prospects for Liberal Government in the Middle East," pp. 336–359.

63. For a recent example of this debate, see Fuller, "No Long-Term Threat"; and Amos Perlmutter, "Wishful Thinking About Islamic Fundamentalism," *Washington Post*, 19 January 1992, p. C7.

64. Mardin, "The 'Venture' of Democracy in the Middle East."

65. Mardin, "The 'Venture' of Democracy in the Middle East," pp. 2–3.

# PART 3

## EMERGING GLOBAL ECONOMIC INTERDEPENDENCE

# 8

## Vision and Politics in the Transformation of the Global Political Economy: Lessons from the Second and Third Worlds

*Thomas R. Callaghy*

Since 1989 Western leaders have shared a brilliant vision of global transformation. This vision has its roots in the Third World with the debt crisis that began in Mexico in August 1982, but it was greatly intensified in the Second World by the "collapse of communism" in Eastern Europe and the Soviet Union that unfolded with stunning speed in 1989. By late 1990, a "new world order" had apparently arrived, only to be further certified by the Russian revolution of August 1991. This vision of the transformation that is supposedly sweeping the world is based on an alleged new consensus that has twin economic and political aspects.

The economic aspect of the vision is as follows: liberal, neoclassical economic reform—with its stress on markets, competition, strong linkages to a world capitalist economy, and a minimal role for the state—will, with the help of the International Monetary Fund and the World Bank, transform policy and bring development and prosperity to the Third and Second Worlds, which have pursued misguided strategies of transformation for so long. These economic changes will be undergirded by new globalized capital markets and a reborn world trading order, so that the gap between the world's rich and poor will not continue to widen. On the political side, the rapid spread of democratic political structures will bring freedom and dignity to formerly oppressed peoples around the world. These political changes will be supported by a reborn United Nations system, which will settle international disputes in a peaceful and orderly manner.

This vision asserts a positive and reinforcing synergy between its economic and political aspects such that economic liberalization and democratization are to take place simultaneously—indeed, the vision can only be truly fulfilled if they do. A single world community of prosperity and democracy will thus emerge—truly a new world order. A powerful aspect of this vision is its almost euphoric expectation that these changes, if they take place simultaneously, can blossom relatively quickly and easily, that the magic of the market and the ballot box can bring about dramatic global transformation.

How in tune with reality is this vision? How in touch is it with the economic and political realities of the world today? Can the Second and Third Worlds be so easily "saved"? Might the state, in fact, have to play a more central role in economic transformation? Might economic reform have more to do with authoritarian and semiauthoritarian forms of politics? Have the difficulties and the costs of economic and political reform been grossly underestimated, especially those relating to the creation of new institutions? Are the regions and countries of the world becoming more differentiated in their wealth and prosperity rather than less? Do strong countries and regions get stronger while weak ones get weaker? Is the world trading order characterized more by economic mercantilism and regionalism than this vision acknowledges, and are the world's credit markets characterized more by skewed flows of capital and technology?

A striking thing about this new, or actually reborn, vision is how apolitical it is. It is a vision propelled by the competition of autonomous economic markets and rational, autonomous citizens working their will on minimalist state structures that are now democratic, as both economic and political arrangements adjust to changing conditions. Does this transcendent vision collide with the political realities of everyday life? Are vision and politics at odds? This chapter will seek some answers to these questions by looking at the record of economic and political reform in the Third and Second Worlds over the last several decades and at current prospects.

## Embedded Liberalism and Economic Transformation: A Balanced Tension Between Economics and Politics

Another striking thing about this vision is that it is not the accurate reflection or representation of Western economic and political realities that it is alleged to be. Western industrial democracies have been preaching the vision and doing something else all along, especially on the economic side. Contrary to popular assumption and official rhetoric, orthodox liberalism, especially its free-market core, has not been the dominant form of political economy in the industrial West since World War II. Instead, the dominant political economy has been a form of compromise called "embedded liberalism," which involves the use of quite extensive state power, simultaneously in the interests of domestic stability and well-being on the one hand and international economic adjustment on the other.[1] At the international level, market forces have been permitted to move, if haltingly, toward comparative advantage and adjustment. As trade, finance, production, and technology have evolved within industrial countries, state power has been employed to varying degrees to restructure the economy, while minimizing and buffering the disruptive domestic political and social consequences of liberal economics at the international level. As a result, modified international economic liberalism and domestic political stability and prosperity via state intervention coexist in a strained and uneasy balance, mediated by the pressures of democratic politics. This is not the autonomous interplay of free markets and minimalist states.

The compromises of the postwar political economy are sometimes viewed as liberalism with lots of cheating. But the "cheating" (protectionism, for example) as a form of political buffering and economic adjustment is, in fact, an inherent and defining characteristic of the system. In other words, international economic liberalism is real, but "compromised" by being "embedded" in the political and economic realities of domestic state-society relations. International economic efficiency is not sacrificed to domestic political stability, nor vice versa; a modus vivendi is established through embedded liberalism by uniting the entanglements of domestic and international politics and economics.

Embedded liberalism is an inherently unstable equilibrium, based on a delicately balanced tension between state and market and between economic and political logics, which can easily tip into unbalanced and unproductive statism—a form of malign mercantilism—on the one hand or the instabilities of unbridled market forces on the other. Maintaining this balanced tension, and getting economic and political logics to reinforce rather than contradict each other, requires special state capabilities and sophisticated political and statecraft skills.

The compromise of embedded liberalism has not been extended by the major powers to the Third World since the onslaught of the debt crisis in 1982. Nor has it been extended now, with the collapse of communism, to what used to be the Second World.[2] I will argue, however, that it is more likely to be extended for the old Second World countries of Eastern Europe and the former Soviet Union, because more central, and threatening, interests are at stake there. Until now, developed countries have attempted to force Third and Second World countries to adjust to full orthodox liberalism without embedding it in the realities of their domestic state-society relations. In their efforts to cope with the Third World debt crisis, Western states and actors have attempted to apply the "monoeconomics" of the dominant neoclassical orthodoxy about development to countries dependent on the International Monetary Fund and the World Bank. The two central tenets of this view are export-led growth and a minimalist state, and its major instrument of reform is the market. The new orthodoxy views the state itself as a key obstacle to development, whereas older structuralist views found key obstacles in internal and external socio-economic structures and in the political relations produced by them.[3]

Yet there is a paradox in the new orthodoxy: external actors have found themselves using what they view as the key obstacle to development—the state—as a primary weapon in their struggle to implement economic liberalization. In short, it takes a relatively competent and extensive state to achieve a liberal political economy. In addition, how do you convince governments to change policies and institutions that neoclassical orthodoxy believes to be economically damaging or irrational, yet which these governments see as politically rational and deeply rooted in local political economy and history? Is serious economic crisis enough? The recent answer, the one of the vision, is that political liberalization via full-fledged democracy is necessary at the same time. Western neoclassical orthodoxy, however, does not have a theory of state reform—other than trying to remove the state from the economy and, in an amazing leap of faith, advocating concomitant political liberalization. The neoclassicists are finding it very difficult to develop a substantive theory.

There is thus also an irony to the orthodox paradox: the IMF and the World Bank do not always practice what they preach. Much of their activity actually reinforces the role of the state—attempts to improve monitoring, data gathering, and analytic and planning capabilities; the provision of technical assistance and training missions; the reform of parastatal sectors; and even the privatization of state-owned enterprises, which, if done effectively, requires a capable state apparatus. The simple fact that the fund, the bank, and Western countries funnel resources through the state leads to a concern with policy formulation, implementation, assessment, and other state-related factors. In practice, these external agencies have begun to recognize a central role for the state and for the need to balance state and market forces and economic and political logics. But rhetoric and policy design often fail to reflect these insights.

Historically, the state has played an integral role in successful economic development, as the pioneering work of Weber, Polanyi, and Gerschenkron demonstrated. More recent work by Douglass North, Albert Hirschman, and others has further punctured the liberal myth that the original rise of capitalism in Europe was purely, or even predominantly, a private matter of the market and the development of technology. In reality the process required a properly balanced tension between emerging bureaucratic states and consolidating capitalist markets and structures of production, set in a larger context of changing institutional, social, and attitudinal factors.[4]

The impressive economic development of East Asian countries such as Korea and Taiwan has more recently underscored this point, despite the efforts of the fund and the bank to use these cases to illustrate the liberal myth about the marginal role of the state. These cases, in fact, demonstrate that economic liberalization and export-oriented development demand at least semistrong and capable states. Recent research on Latin American newly industrializing countries (NICs) points in the same direction. While in some of the East Asian and Latin American cases proper liberal incentive structures (especially foreign exchange, interest, and credit policies), trade liberalization, and conservative fiscal and monetary policies have played a significant role, these successful exporters have at times also maintained high levels of protection against imports of competing goods, parastatal sectors including import-substitution activities, and a very interventionist role for the state, especially in the allocation of credit and bargaining with a host of external actors. This has entailed decreasing the level of corruption and other forms of rent-seeking behavior, displacing or superseding old political networks, and creating quite centralized and autonomous decision-making structures in which technocrats play a crucial role and with which domestic business groups and international actors communicate regularly and in a detailed way.[5] The main task, then, is not "getting the state out" but finding the state's appropriate roles for fostering economic growth and development via *both* state and private sectors. It is maintaining a balanced tension between state and market. As shall be discussed later in the chapter, in a 1991 report the World Bank finally began to adjust its official rhetoric by talking about "market-friendly" state intervention.

Thus, partly as a result of these internal contradictions in the Western neoclassical orthodoxy, the number of successful cases of economic adjustment has been quite small so far and is not likely to grow rapidly. Increasing realism, as the 1980s progressed, about the difficulties of economic reform in the Third World was reinforced by the stunning yet sobering events in Eastern Europe and the Soviet Union; Northern actors most involved in the process—the fund, the bank, and major Western aid agencies—slowly began to realize that economic liberalization without attention to domestic political stability, to political and social buffering, is likely to prevent successful economic and political adjustment, thereby threatening crucial Western interests both at the systemic level and at the level of individual countries. A number of leaders in the Third and now Second Worlds are also beginning to see the wisdom of some form of embedded liberal compromise, for, without some degree of economic liberalization, their countries have no maneuvering room in the current international political economy, and, without some form of political and social buffering, their regimes, especially the fledgling democracies, may not survive. Many Western governments and legislatures, however, have been slower to perceive this reality and to act upon it. They have underestimated the need for state bureaucratic and technical capabilities to carry out reforms and have usually assumed that political capabilities boil down to a matter of sufficient will on the part of political leaders, or, more recently, to full-blown democratization.

A balance between state and market roles in economic change depends, therefore, in part on state and bureaucratic capabilities to formulate and implement the necessary policies—to carry out state functions efficiently and to support and promote private functions effectively. Yet a sustainable balance between economic logics (measures needed to pursue economic efficiency in both international and domestic arenas) and political logics (measures needed to ensure domestic political stability) also depends on political capabilities both to permit adjustment and to buffer its costs. Third and former Second World states pursuing economic adjustment must have both types of state capabilities—the bureaucratic and the political. These in turn may not be fostered by simultaneous economic and political liberalization unless significant and very costly political buffering takes place—in short, a form of embedded liberalism for all, not just for the First World.

## Economic Transformation and the
## Political Economy of Delegation

How, then, do we explain the varying ability of Third and Second World governments, caught as they are between strong and often contradictory internal and external pressures, to engage in sustained economic reform? The degree to which a government can adjust appears to be determined in large part by its ability to insulate or buffer itself from the political logics and social pressures characteristic of the inward-oriented, antimarket statist syndrome that has dominated so much of the Third and Second Worlds, while adopting new externally directed, market-oriented policies, largely through a process of technocratic delegation. These efforts can involve quite varied levels of economic statism, however, ranging from those of Korea to Chile.

The ability to insulate, delegate, and buffer is affected primarily by five sets of variables: (1) the manner in which the economic crisis is perceived by state elites and social groups—particularly whether it is perceived to be caused by external or internal factors and whether it is seen as temporary or systemic; (2) the degree to which decisionmaking is influenced by technocratic and economic concerns rather than countervailing political considerations (such as patron-client politics and rent-seeking); (3) the degree of governmental autonomy in relation to powerful sociopolitical forces and groups—particularly in relation to their distributional demands—with techniques ranging from outright repression to selective forms of policy buffering that do not jeopardize economic restructuring; (4) the administrative capabilities of the state apparatus—a factor referred to here as the level of *stateness*; combined with the overall level of economic development; and with *cosmopolitanism*, defined as the degree of sophisticated knowledge about how the international political economy works; and (5) the international conjuncture characterized by the degree of dependence on and nature and extent of external influence and resource flows (political and strategic as well as economic), including market forces of the world political economy such as the openness of trading markets and levels of international lending and foreign direct investment (FDI). All of these factors are influenced by political regime type, quality of leadership, coherence of national sociopolitical structure (from relatively homogenous and unified to heterogenous and fragmented), and, particularly, by the sequencing of change. The optimal sequence appears to be quite substantial economic transformation followed by staged but increasingly open political liberalization.

This argument maintains a balance between agency and structure, between voluntarist perspectives that stress "political will," so common to external actors, and more pessimistic perspectives that stress structural constraints, so common to academics and to hesitant and fearful domestic political actors. Proper policies and adequate levels of cosmopolitanism, commitment, and statecraft skill (plus luck—a greatly underestimated variable) are necessary but not sufficient; stateness, sociopolitical insulation, and adequate external resources are also necessary but not sufficient. Some combination of both sets of factors is required. Delegation to economic technocrats without some degree of state autonomy from societal forces is not sufficient; neither is state autonomy without delegation of the right type and substance. Both are required. Leaders need to rely on, insulate, and protect the technocratic staff while keeping it informed of the political and social effects of its adjustment policies on both domestic and external actors. This places the technocratic team at the heart of complex two-level policy-making and implementation "games"—economic and political games played simultaneously at domestic and international levels for very high stakes. Given this argument, and the nature of most Third and Second World political economies, it is not surprising that there have been few examples of sustained economic transformation.

In many ways delegation is a statecraft strategy that attempts to create or reassert key Weberian bureaucratic attributes in a small but intense manner under conditions of stress. These attributes may not have existed previously, or they may have been greatly diluted by "politics as usual" and by the long-term effects of older strategies and policies. Using insulated but informed delegation is an attempt to expand the arena of discretion and maneuver in order to diminish the constraints of the everyday "rules of the game"—legal, political, administrative, and social.

Given the effort to reassert these attributes in a small but powerful "core" of officials and institutions, the strategy is, at least in the short run, an additive rather than a transformatory one in regard to overall state capabilities. As an additive variable in statecraft, however, it exists and operates in a larger and much less malleable historically defined political, administrative, social, and international context, which greatly affects the likelihood that such a strategy can become institutionalized and histori- cally rooted. As we shall see, these larger contextual variables are not to be underestimated. The IMF and the World Bank are increasingly, if grudgingly, giving them more analytic and policy weight.

These technocratic and bureaucratic capabilities and contextual fac- tors vary considerably from region to region and country to country, re- flecting different levels of overall development and political structure, dif- ferent historical legacies. But successful cases of delegation and economic reform cut across both political regime type and level of economic and ad- ministrative development. In addition, they pose a significant challenge, at least in the medium run, to societalist views of social and economic change that assert that successful economic reform requires the existence of supporting societal coalitions. Clearly in some cases, viable economic reform can come without major coalitional support in the short to medium run, as part of a statecraft strategy that is heavily institutional, and often authoritarian, in its thrust. How such a strategy can become institutional- ized and relinked to society in the longer run is a larger and more complex question, one that now confronts Korea, Taiwan, Mexico, Chile, and Turkey in a very stark fashion.

A relatively common set of characteristics appears to make insulation, economic delegation, and political buffering possible. These characteris- tics are more commonly found in authoritarian regimes (Korea, Chile under Pinochet, Ghana) but are not restricted to them. Under certain con- ditions, formally or partially democratic regimes can manifest functional variants which allow them to operate effectively, at least for a while (Mex- ico, Turkey, Argentina). They can also exist in regimes of very different levels of socioeconomic development (Turkey and Bolivia,[6] Chile and Ghana).

The most important of these characteristics is the ability to insulate the economic teams from pressure, opposition, and requests for particular- istic exceptions—from major social and political groups, from elements of the state bureaucracy, *and* from the top leadership itself. This insulation can be provided by repressing or fragmenting opposition groups via direct coercion, states of emergency, internal or external exile of opponents (Chile, Ghana, Nigeria), corporatist control and buffering mechanisms in military or single-party regimes (Mexico), formal and informal political pacts (Bolivia), co-optation via selective and controlled patronage (Turkey, Bolivia), and the disempowerment of legislative bodies (Ja- maica,[7] Bolivia). The formal structure of executive authority may also be important, such as the constitutional power to rule by decree or the strong executive power provided to a prime minister by a Westminster parlia- mentary system (Seaga in Jamaica, Menem in Argentina).

Less tangible sources of executive authority may also be important—the personal popularity of a ruler, at least initially (Rawlings in Ghana, Collor in Brazil, Menem), a positive international reputation for the ruler, increasing the probability of external support (Seaga, Alfonsin in Argentina), an electoral mandate (Seaga, Ozal in Turkey, Collor), the chaos and decline left by previous governments (Ghana, Bolivia, Argentina), and even classic obfuscation efforts.

Just as executive authority and protection are key bases for delegation, they can also be its worst enemy. Often the major threat to the productive insulation of a technocratic team comes from the executive itself. Deviations from technocratic considerations can be productive or unproductive for the viability of economic reform. Political buffering, via side payments, for example, that facilitates the continuation of a reform program without unduly undermining it may well be very sensible (Chile, Turkey). Much executive meddling is driven by the clash of economic and political logics related to the need to stay in power, especially in democracies (Ozal, Paz in Bolivia). Such executive intervention can quite easily cross the fine line into the unproductive (Kaunda in Zambia, Sarney in Brazil, Babangida in Nigeria). A good deal of meddling, however, is, often quite intentionally, of a less facilitative, more predatory variety (Belaunde in Peru, Marcos in the Philippines, Mobutu in Zaire).

Unity of views and continuity of personnel—both indicators of coherence—are central to the effective performance of insulated economic teams in the short to medium run (Korea, Mexico, Ghana, Turkey). Several other factors are important, however, to the longer-run coherence and eventual institutionalization of these processes and forms of statecraft. Two of the most important of these "nonbureaucratic elements of bureaucracy" are: (1) intrabureaucratic and extrabureaucratic informal networks of cohesion, and (2) the development of a bureaucratic political culture, esprit de corps or ideology. Both of these elements have been very important in the emergence of the role of the state in the development of the Japanese political economy, for example. The former element has two parts. The first is the development of informal recruitment and performance networks that are based on competence and role definition. It is not a question of competence versus connection, as in the distinction between bureaucratic and patrimonial administration, but rather of the *fusion* of connection and competence in the service of bureaucratic coherence and effectiveness. The second set of informal networks are extrabureaucratic, linking the bureaucracy with social groups, mostly business, in a way that facilitates economic transformation rather than retards it—an approach that Peter Evans calls "embedded autonomy."[8]

The difficult task is to institutionalize such a technocratic political culture while finding ways to relink it to society in a productive balance between insulation and social connectedness. These are challenges that remain of central importance to the ongoing development of Korea, for example. They can be affected both positively and negatively by political liberalization depending on how various forms of "democracy" are institutionalized. The development of both informal networks and a bureaucratic political culture helps to make possible the emergence of a distinctive outlook among state officials, one that focuses on a more broadly defined "general interest" rather than on particularistic interests. This is one of the key characteristics that separates developmental from predatory states. Although the long-run institutionalization of delegation requires some form of "embedded autonomy"—usually democratic or semidemocratic of one sort or another—the line between productive relinking with society and succumbing to particularistic rent-seeking behavior by state and societal groups, especially business, is very fine indeed.

## Current Conjuncture and Regional and Country Differentiation: International Conjuncture

The prospects for economic transformation by Third and former Second World states are significantly affected by the international conjuncture in which such efforts take place. Four factors are central: (1) access to markets, (2) access to credit, (3) the role of the major powers, the IMF, and the World Bank in monitoring the condition of the world economy, coordinating macroeconomic policy, and managing economic reform efforts in a growing number of countries, and (4) regional and international political/strategic conditions.

### Access to Markets

Economic reform and transformation, especially integration into the world economy, hinges centrally on access to markets, on the ability to engage in external trade. Such access directly affects growth levels, the ability to attract credit and investment, and the capacity to use and control debt. Both the emergence of regional trading blocs in Europe, Asia, and the Americas and the stalled Uruguay Round negotiations of the General Agreement on Tariffs and Trade (GATT) pose the specter of increasing protectionism. International trade appears to be increasingly mercantilist—that is, based on state-to-state bargaining—but without being necessarily narrowly protectionist or leading to a complete breakdown of the "liberal" or open trading order erected after World War II. In fact, the liberal trading order has been quite statist all along—a manifestation of the "cheating" inherent in embedded liberalism. It has been only selectively open to the Third World, however, while the Second World largely opted out. The dangers of both trends—economic regionalism and the death of GATT—are probably overstated. They are certainly not fully zero-sum; increasing economic regionalism and at least a semiopen liberal trading order can continue to co-exist uneasily. Whether such a system is sufficiently open to Third and former Second World states is more problematic.[9]

Clearly though, the ability of Third and former Second World countries to engage in international trade hinges increasingly on the ability of the individual state to bargain for trade agreements and to manage "open" trade to the degree that it exists. The trading order is increasingly based on complex, multiple, overlapping, and nearly continuous trade negotiations in multiple arenas simultaneously. Hence, stateness and cosmopolitanism are central factors.

GATT is in serious trouble. The Uruguay Round negotiations stalled in December 1990, primarily over the European Community's unwillingness to reform its Common Agricultural Policy (CAP) and allow increased imports of agricultural goods. There were more than a dozen other issues yet to be resolved, but their resolution hinged on the outcome of the agricultural dispute. The impasse is a classic example of the tensions inherent in embedded liberalism and of the powerful domestic roots of the international political economy. CAP exists primarily to protect powerful domestic constituencies in each European country; these interests have been placated through quite costly buffering mechanisms. While the Europeans readily admitted the need to reform CAP in order to adjust to changing international needs and conditions, finding a politically satisfactory way of achieving reform proved very difficult.

The dispute pitted the European Community against the United States and fourteen agricultural exporting countries (referred to collectively as the Cairns group and headed by Australia), but it had serious implications for the Third and former Second Worlds as well. The gap between rhetoric and reality was enormous. At each of the recent Group of Seven (G-7) annual summits, the quick completion of the Uruguay Round was given the highest importance. In July 1991 the G-7 countries meeting in London pledged yet again to complete the round by the end of the year, noting that no issue had more far-reaching implications for the future prospects of the world economy.

A GATT "Draft Final Act" was presented just before Christmas 1991, but it was eventually rejected. Easter 1992 was set as the new "deadline"; it too passed. Finally, at the end of May, the EC, with great fanfare, announced a major reform of CAP. Although French and German farmers protested vigorously—French farmers even blockading EuroDisney—the United States and other countries felt that the reforms made progress in only one of three key areas, domestic price supports, leaving export subsidies and import barriers unresolved. In fact, even domestic price supports were lowered only because European governments shifted the type of buffering mechanism to direct income support. Embedded liberalism was far from dead; it had just changed its face somewhat. Hence the tensions between the EC and the United States continued, complicated greatly by domestic political concerns on both sides of the Atlantic, and GATT remained deadlocked. In addition, the CAP reforms had yet to be tested electorally in Europe, and by mid-1992 they became intertwined with the ratification of the Maastricht treaty on European integration.

Thus, despite the fine rhetoric, very little was resolved. One chief negotiator observed that, "It's as if they were sending messages from another planet, it's spooky," while GATT's director-general asserted that one should not count on "magic or good luck." As one leading observer put it, "Developing countries, many of which have spent the last decade liberalising their own economies at the self-righteous behest of the industrial world, have a right to feel cruelly deceived by the EC's grudging attitude." In April 1992, Alejandro Foxley, Chile's finance minister, found it very "disturbing" that the Uruguay Round was stalled because the teachers of reform in the wealthy countries did not have enough courage to obey the rules they gave to their students in the developing countries. The former Second World countries of Eastern Europe and the Soviet Union were also distressed as they tried to establish links with the EC. Poland discovered this all too vividly in the second half of 1991, when its beef exports became a major stumbling block in negotiations over association with the EC. Is embedded liberalism only for the already powerful and developed?[10]

The Uruguay Round remains stalled. Beyond agriculture have lurked other disputes, especially over services. Here the United States has been the major culprit, again for domestic political reasons related to its own version of embedded liberalism. Other countries have been waiting to make compromises on remaining issues until the agriculture dispute is resolved. If major concessions are eventually made by the EC and ratified politically, others might be more willing to change as well. If not, very little is likely to change. A major fear, and more likely outcome, is that the Uruguay Round will ultimately be completed, but only via fudged formulas and papered-over disputes that would render "success" a very hollow victory, leading not to full-scale world trade warfare, but rather to guerrilla warfare.

If the unwieldy GATT process breaks down, there will be more calls for the OECD to take up trade reform and for the creation of a new International Trade Organization as envisioned in the original Bretton Woods proposals. A more likely prospect is the increased importance of emerging regional trading blocs. Such a bloc has been developing in Europe for several decades, reaching a new milestone in late 1991. With much celebration and self-congratulation, the governments of the European Community signed the Maastricht Treaty on European Union in early December, but were stunned when the Danish public narrowly rejected it in early June 1992, in the first ratification election. Two weeks later, the Irish voted two-to-one to ratify the treaty, but the issue was now joined. In the process, ratification became linked with other contentious issues, such as CAP reform. The other 11 members of the EC decided to continue with the ratification process, which was to last until the end of 1992. Speaking of senior government officials and Eurotechnocrats, the Bank for International Settlements (BIS) noted, "Having managed to spring the programme on a largely unprepared public they are now faced with debate and dissension very late in the day."[11] In the context of long-established democracies, the dangers of too much technocratic insulation, especially when it is not politically sensitive or tested, were now crystal clear.

The definition of Europe had become much more complex by 1992. Should the states of Eastern Europe become full members of the EC, as countries in northern Europe are still expected to do? Or should membership be restricted to the more developed ones such as Poland and Hungary? What about the Baltic states and other parts of the former Soviet Union? If so, when and under what status—as full members, as associate members? Tensions already existed in the EC, fueled by the reunification of Germany, fears of immigrant waves from the east, the civil wars in Yugoslavia, and the breakup of Czechoslovakia. The British were proposing "widening" the community while the French were for "deepening" it. These positions were influenced strongly by domestic politics in each country and by perceptions of its eventual role in a European regional bloc in "the new world order." The relationship of this new Europe to Africa, which has been linked to it via the Lome Convention, remains very unclear, as does its effect on the rest of the Third World.

In the Americas, the United States and Canada have formed a free trade area and have extended it as well to include Mexico. In East Asia the preponderance of Japanese trading might has led to an informal "co-prosperity sphere," with some countries proposing regional trading organizations of various types. Some of these proposals include Japan; others do not. Levels of stateness and cosmopolitanism, as well as overall economic strength, will be important factors in the progress of these efforts.

## Access to Credit

Assuming some access to markets, economic growth and trade also require credit—private and public loans and debt relief, foreign investment, and multilateral and bilateral assistance. Since the early 1980s an implicit bargain, or what Michel Camdessus, the managing director of the IMF, has called an "unwritten contract,"[12] has existed between the IMF, the World Bank, and the major Western governments on the one hand and Third World and more recently former Second World governments on the other. The unspoken agreement stipulates that if these latter countries successfully reform their economies in a neoclassical manner with the direction and help of the fund and the bank, then new voluntary international bank loans and foreign investment will be available to underpin and sustain the reform efforts. This implicit bargain has failed in most places. As one seasoned observer noted, "Free flowing funds will not be available from the banking system to finance all the needs of the global economy in the 1990s. Only top quality borrowers will attract finance and the strong, whether they be countries or companies, will have an even bigger advantage over the weak."[13] The same holds for foreign investment, putting in jeopardy one of the major planks of IMF and World Bank reforms—privatization.

In real terms, financial flows to the developing world in 1990 were a little more than half their level at the start of the 1980s, and most of this finance was going only to the stronger countries. Despite some claims to the contrary, the debt crisis is far from over.[14] For example, even if the net flow of capital to developing countries grows by about 10 percent a year until 1995 (which is a very big "if"), aggregate net financial transfers will still be only slightly positive, owing to the large stock of debt and high real interest rates. Furthermore, new claimants are now making additional demands on an already fragile international financial system, one with a quite low level of overall savings. In July 1991, the IMF announced that the world economy would need to generate additional savings of about $100 billion in the short run to cope with the new demands of German unification, reform in Eastern Europe and the Soviet Union, and recovery from the damage of the Gulf war. The fund pointed out that this goal could be met by a 20 percent reduction in military spending—not a likely prospect.

In addition to low levels of savings, there has been little interest by the private sector in lending or investing in many areas of the Second and Third Worlds. For example, in August 1991, U.S. banks refused to join in government-guaranteed loans for grain sales to the Soviet Union unless the loans were completely guaranteed. By 1992 the enormity of the reform task in Eastern Europe and the Soviet "black hole" was finally sinking in, while voluntary lending and foreign investment in many parts of the Third World were at historically low levels.

The fragility of the international financial system has been striking, with huge budget deficits and interlocking banking crises in the United States; a stock market crash, plunging property values, and financial scandal puncturing the "bubble economy" in Japan; and compelling regional preoccupations in Europe and in the oil-rich states of the Middle East concerned with their own reconstruction. Moreover, major weaknesses in international financial regulation have been made painfully manifest by the nearly worldwide Bank of Credit and Commerce International (BCCI) scandal and, in 1992, by the trauma of Olympia and York's desperate efforts to restructure the $12 billion it owed to over one hundred banks. This situation has been aggravated by the Basle accord of the Bank for

International Settlements, aimed at raising the capital adequacy levels of the world's major banks by 1993. The Basle accord has been a particular problem for Japanese banks. In 1991 indications already existed that Japan was slowing its provision of capital to the world economy. Although it had become the largest provider of official development assistance, Japan's outflow of long-term capital in 1990 fell to $43.5 billion from $89.2 billion the previous year. In addition, financial "globalization," one of the much ballyhooed trends of the 1980s, looked distinctly battered and bruised by the early 1990s.

The clear implication of these trends is that many countries attempting the difficult reforms urged by the World Bank and IMF might not have the capital they need to make them work well. Reduced levels of credit mean lower levels of imports, stagnated structural reforms, and increased social unrest resulting from slow economic growth—a real threat to fragile political liberalization efforts.

These trends have led to an increasing "officialization" and politicization of credit flows to Third and former Second World countries. The debt of developing countries rose to $1,306 billion in 1990, accompanied by a net overall debt service flow to the creditor banks, governments, and international financial institutions. With the hesitance of private capital markets to respond to growing needs, this officialization of credit flows has put increasing burdens on Western budgets and placed more emphasis on rescheduling public and publicly guaranteed debt via the Paris Club mechanism. At the same time, rescheduling has become more politicized as debt pressures mount and resistance to generalized debt relief continues.

These two trends were vividly illustrated in the spring of 1991 by spectacular Paris Club reschedulings for Poland and Egypt, largely because of U.S. insistence. Both countries received an unprecedented 50 percent reduction in their Paris Club debt in return for, and contingent upon, new IMF agreements. The United States tried to argue that these two cases were unique and thus would not set new precedents. Brazil, ironically a creditor in the Polish case, argued, however, that it deserved equal treatment. The size of the reductions reflected private market hesitation to lend and invest, and the political nature of the agreements reflected the powerful domestic and foreign policy roots of U.S. insistence. A number of major powers objected, including Japan. Japan took an increasingly hard line on debt rescheduling, arguing that significant debt rescheduling would preclude its own ability to lend. Hungary was greatly angered by the deal for Poland for "moral hazard" reasons. It had continued to service its Paris Club debt; Poland had not. Preoccupation with Second rather than Third World debt has intensified because it strikes at more crucial national interests and domestic constituencies.

Some of the major powers have also resisted extending more generous terms to the least-developed countries of the Third World under the proposed "Trinidad terms," which would replace the current menu of options under the so-called "Toronto terms" for debt rescheduling. In a particularly impassioned plea at the 1991 IMF–World Bank annual meeting in Bangkok, Michel Camdessus called for extending the Paris Club terms for Poland and Egypt to other lower- to middle-income countries such as India, Nigeria, and the Philippines. He also supported adoption of the Trinidad terms for the poorest countries, and, with intentional irony, noted that 45 developing countries have unilaterally liberalized their trade structures without corresponding action by the industrialized countries.

Credit flow issues have thus clearly been becoming increasingly politicized. Powerful members of the U.S. Congress have linked discussion of new credit authorizations or quotas for the IMF, the World Bank, and the recently created European Bank for Reconstruction and Development (EBRD), to support for Poland and to other particularistic interests that have strong domestic roots, while generalized rules for debt relief have been resisted because of their budgetary implications. Western governments have also insisted on forms of political and even security conditionality in the form of political liberalization and reductions in military spending.

A final example of the complex interaction between credit flows, domestic and international politics, and the functioning of the world economy is in order. The German government greatly underestimated the cost and political trauma of reunification. West Germans became increasingly unhappy about having to pay for it. This was manifested by a bitter 11-day strike by public sector workers in late April and early May 1992. Such pressures made maintaining stable macroeconomic policy even more difficult, while increasing tension among the G-7 countries.

As a result, the German government decided that interest rates needed to be raised in order to encourage domestic saving, to control inflation, and to strengthen the mark. This meant resisting U.S. and other pressure to stimulate world economic growth by holding interest rates down. The decision has also added considerable new tension to the ongoing development of European monetary union, affecting in turn the overall move toward European integration. In addition, raising interest rates affects Third and Second World debt pegged to floating rates, thereby increasing the cost of debt service and reducing the credit available to support economic reform. Unlike the late 1940s, the world of the early 1990s no longer has a hegemon that can both design and pay the costs of implementing a new world order, despite the nearly complete collapse of its major rival of 50 years. The current era is much more complex and much more uncertain.

## Management of the World Economy

Throughout the 1980s the major industrial democracies groped toward new cooperative structures to monitor and manage the world economy.

This trend was intensified by the end of the Cold War, the liberation of Eastern Europe, the outcome of the Gulf war, and the implosion of the old Soviet empire. But the reality of this new world order has rarely matched its rhetoric; states that each possess their own version of embedded liberalism have encountered increasingly obvious difficulties in coordinating macroeconomic policy. At the heart of their efforts have been the policy consultation and coordination efforts of the G-7 countries, the broadening and deepening of the roles of the IMF and the World Bank, and the emergence of the Organization for Economic Cooperation and Development and the Bank for International Settlements (BIS) as research and debating fora for this new structure. These recent institutional developments have their roots in complex and interrelated changes in both the international state system and the world economy over the last several decades. Despite obstacles to coordination, these institutions are, however, undergirded by a relatively coherent consensus among the powerful about the basic norms and principles, the economic and political mantras, of this new world order.

Because any serious disruption or decline of the world economy would have had devastating effects for the major industrial democracies, they moved in the 1980s to coordinate macroeconomic policies, especially to control inflation and manage industrial recessions. The policy coordination efforts of the G-7, including the annual economic summits, were also a mechanism for integrating Japan more centrally into international governance structures. Japan's inclusion was paralleled by its slow emergence as a force in the IMF and the World Bank.[15]

These two institutions have been central to the incremental but increasingly coherent processes of global economic governance, as manifested by two major trends: (1) increasingly sophisticated and intensive monitoring and analysis of the world economy, and (2) intensified efforts to manage the world economy by offering advice to the major powers and by intervening directly and quite pervasively in the political economies of Third and former Second World countries, via "voluntary" programs of economic stabilization and structural adjustment. Michel Camdessus described these roles in very explicit terms:

> More and more we are going to monitor a very diversified world. We will have the major pillars, the US, EC, and Japan. But we'll also have what was so far a kind of black hole in the system—eastern countries and the Soviet Union. There will be a diversified universe, not unified by the dollar or a tripolar system. And the centre is the IMF. The work of the institution at the centre will grow in importance. . . . We have a permanent dialogue with the major countries on their economic policies. . . . And we put in motion the system of peer pressure among themselves. . . . [This] is also a way of establishing a bridge between the G7 and our global surveillance. The G7 work on co-ordination of policies is a significant

contribution to the evolution of the international monetary system. . . .
What we are looking at with the eastern countries is not a 19th century–
like *laissez faire* but a new and better governance. The modern economy
cannot work without government but it needs a new form of government.
. . . [The IMF] will remain a small institution dealing with crises, with
structural adjustment growth, centering its action on the balance of payments, providing countries with sensible catalysing elements for medium-
and short-term financing. The World Bank would continue having its
formidable longer-term sectoral responsibilities.[16]

While it may remain a relatively small institution, the reach and membership of the IMF—like that of its much larger cousin, the World Bank—
has grown significantly. Recent entrants include Namibia, Angola,
Mozambique, Switzerland, Bulgaria, Czechoslovakia, and the Baltic states.
The Soviet Union wanted to join the IMF as a full member but, at the insistence of the United States, it was forced in October 1991 to settle for a
special association status that did not give it the right to borrow from the
fund. After the United States changed its mind, Russia became a member
in June 1992. With these institutions approaching 160 members, their
reach is now nearly global.

As of April 1992, the IMF had active economic reform programs with
46 Third World and five former Second World countries; a number of additional programs were about to be approved or were being renegotiated.
The role of the IMF and the World Bank in stabilization and structural
adjustment programs is very intrusive; the process of developing these
programs is laden with conditionality. It involves these institutions in the
formulation and management of national economic policies in a quite
detailed way—a process that some are calling the "new neocolonialism." The effectiveness of these attempts at economic "management" at
the national level will be discussed in greater detail later in the chapter.
Initial indications are that the results have been relatively modest because the task is enormous and little understood, and because resources
are scarce.

These two international financial institutions and the major industrial
democracies have asserted that there is a new global consensus about the
nature of these reforms. While a basic consensus does exist among Western states about what reforming countries should do, their prescription
does not resemble the embedded liberalism characteristic of the industrial
democracies; nor do former Second World governments fully accept the
content of the "consensus." It is a consensus only to the extent that a viable and coherent countervailing strategy no longer exists. Grudging acceptance does not necessarily reflect agreement, but rather sheer necessity
and a desperate need for credit. The tenor of this situation is captured by
an encounter between an African and a beleaguered Soviet diplomat at a
public forum in Harare, Zimbabwe, in early 1991:

> "It's your fault!" shouted an angry African, his finger wagging at the diplomat, as he accused the Soviet Union of forsaking its traditional support for Middle Eastern and Third World causes and its role as adversary of the West. "You turned tail and ran away! You left everything for the Americans! Now, they are free to work whatever mischief they want."[17]

Contrary to this attitude, the most successful Third World countries have been those that have taken a tack succinctly described by a former World Bank chief economist: "The key is moving away from saying that the world is unfair to saying however unfair it is, we want to make the best use of it."[18] In large part, it is a self-help world, but one with an external rather than an internal orientation. And, as we shall see, this orientation does not mean having to bend fully to the economic mantras of the new consensus or to the conditionality dictates of the IMF and the World Bank. Nonetheless, in the early 1990s, these Western mantras broadened from the pervasive economic conditionalities of the 1980s to political and security-related conditions that call for better governance, political liberalization, and reductions in military spending. Such new mantras, even if they could be fully implemented, might well end up impeding transformation rather than facilitating it.

Finally, an additional institution needs to be mentioned. The OECD has quietly developed into an influential research and debating forum, a "think-tank" for analyzing and monitoring the world economy on behalf of a "club" of 24 developed industrial states. With the collapse of the North-South dialogue of the New International Economic Order, the OECD took on an intermediary role between developed and developing countries much more effectively than was possible for the unwieldy United Nations bureaucracies. In addition, new countries lined up to become members—South Korea and Mexico, for example—while Poland, Hungary, and Czechoslovakia became part of a "Partners in Transition" program in mid-1991. The OECD will now also assist the IMF, the World Bank, and the EBRD in monitoring economic events in the former Soviet Union.

### International and Regional Political/Strategic Conditions

With the end of the Cold War and the collapse of the Soviet empire, the world has become unipolar without having a hegemon that can both impose its grand design *and* pay to have it implemented. Unipolarity without hegemony does not equal multipolarity, but the emergence of Europe and Japan as major players makes for a much more complex world from the perspective of Third and former Second World countries. The East-West struggle is gone, allowing "traditional quarrels" and "traditional arenas" to take on new vigor, all the while merging with new processes and arenas in complex ways.

Regional wars, civil wars, arms races, and disasters both natural and made by humans now make attempts at economic transformation and integration into the world economy much more difficult than previously, if not impossible. Yugoslavia devours itself, Czechoslovakia breaks up, and Hungarians demand autonomy in any new Slovakia, while disputes on the periphery of the Soviet empire have similar potential. Traditional invasion in the Gulf led the world into multilateral regional war and a mini–oil crisis, with negative effects for much of the Third and former Second Worlds. The Horn of Africa is in turmoil as Ethiopia and Somalia do ritual dances of fragmentation; the Sudan continues its own rituals of self-devastation; West Africa is reeling from an unexpected and nasty outburst of regional and civil war; and Mozambique continues to plummet into a social hell difficult to comprehend. Vicious internal wars also continue in the Philippines, Peru, and elsewhere.

The United States and Europe, and to a lesser degree Japan, have become increasingly preoccupied by internal affairs and by events in Eastern Europe and the former Soviet Union precisely because they threaten very central interests. If the former Soviet Union were to really implode into a series of interlocked civil conflicts similar to those in Yugoslavia, in the context of uncertain control of nuclear weapons, the outcome could be quite devastating. Preoccupation will lead to increasing concentration of resource flows, despite rhetorical protestations about continued concern for Third World needs, and to delayed work on other areas and problems. Though not widespread in the early 1990s, revived forms of isolationism, especially in the United States and Japan, could also have quite negative consequences for the Third and former Second Worlds.

In such an international context, the weakest will suffer the most. Africa, for example, is rapidly being marginalized both economically and in political/strategic terms. With the end of the Cold War, Africa is simply of much less interest to the major powers and the principal actors in the world economy. Africa used to pit "internationalists" concerned about big power rivalry against "regionalists" concerned about African issues. Ironically, the internationalists have now voluntarily ceded the field to the regionalists. The latter used to call for the major powers not to turn Africa into an international battlefield, but rather to let Africans solve their own problems, to leave Africa alone. Now the internationalists have declared the game over, packed their bags, and gone home, while the regionalists search desperately for a rationale to keep external interest—and re-sources—focused on Africa. Even the French have begun to reassess their "special relationship" with Africa. A senior African diplomat notes that "we are an old tattered lady. People are tired of Africa. So many countries, so many wars."[19]

This situation has led major powers, international organizations, and private voluntary organizations to seek ways to better coordinate their humanitarian efforts to cope with famines and civil wars, with the intent of making scarce resources go further. These efforts at coordination are not seen as efforts to solve Third World political/strategic problems but rather to create an international safety net, an international form of triage, for the victims of them. The major thrust of these efforts has been organizational, particularly the call for a coordinating U.N. "supremo" or, at the least, for the recreation of such U.N. agencies as the 1985–1986 Office for Emergency Operations in Africa (OEOA). Based on experience in the Horn of Africa and the Gulf, these ideas have also included consideration of direct but not intensive military intervention to establish internationally controlled relief beachheads in troubled areas, such as the intervention in Bosnia in mid-1992.

Finally, with the collapse of Leninist versions of Marxism and continued dissatisfaction with the negative underbelly of industrial capitalism, new or reinvigorated efforts to find alternative ideas, different ideological thrusts, are underway in the First, Third, and remaining corners of the Second Worlds. Among these efforts, the most interesting and realistic focus on giving capitalism a more human face; they range from reworked visions of democratic socialism to the Catholic Church's 1991 encyclical "Centesimus Annus" ("The Hundredth Year") on the moral and economic lessons of the collapse of communism.

## Regional Differentiation

As the World Bank correctly points out, "the 1980s saw a sharp divergence in economic performance across developing regions," and these "regional disparities in growth will continue."[20] An enormous chasm exists between East Asia and Africa. In between lie South Asia, the Middle East, Eastern Europe, and Latin America. The disparities among these regions preceded the 1980s, however, and they were seriously aggravated by "the lost decade." (See Tables 8.1 and 8.2 below for data on the period 1965–1989.) In developing countries generally, the average annual aggregate real GNP per capita increased 2.5 percent between 1965 and 1989, but in East Asia it grew 5.2 percent a year, while in Africa it "increased" at only 0.4 percent a year. Thus, some regions have performed better than others, and some countries in each region have outperformed others in the same area.

Despite the diversity of these regions and countries, the key seems to be linkages to the world economy, "a recognition of the importance of international trade and finance for improving growth and per capita incomes . . . Economies that chose to limit their links with the world economy have not fared as well." Countries that stressed linkages also "tended to do better during the turbulent 1980s than did others."[21] This held particularly for

East Asia, including Korea, Taiwan, Thailand, and Malaysia; for several countries in Latin America, especially Mexico and Chile; and even for Ghana and Botswana in Africa. As we shall see, however, outward orientation did not have to be of the "liberal," minimal-state variety recommended by the IMF and the World Bank. In fact, explaining differentiation and its speed requires taking into account much more than externally oriented policies and the international economic environment. Stateness, cosmopolitanism, regime type, political-strategic linkages, overall level of development, and historical context all play a key role.

Developments in the early 1990s were not encouraging, but need to be disaggregated by region and country. The overall developing country GDP growth rate for 1989 was 2.9 percent; it fell to 1.9 in 1990 and fell again in 1991. In both 1990 and 1991 per capita incomes declined; this was the first time this had happened in two consecutive years since the World Bank started collecting data in 1965. In East Asia, however, GDP growth rose from 5.5 percent in 1989 to 6.7 in 1990 and 7.1 in 1991. In Latin America, without Brazil, it rose from -0.2 percent in 1989 to 2.0 percent in 1990, and to 2.6 percent in 1991. In the Middle East it increased from 2.6 in 1989 to 3.2 percent in 1990, then fell to -1.9 percent in 1991. Significant drops were also recorded in Brazil, Eastern Europe (-14.2 percent in 1991), much of Africa, and, above all, in what used to be the Soviet Union, with a 4 percent drop in net material product (NMP) in 1990 and 14 percent in 1991.[22]

While the World Bank correctly expects these disparities to grow, its assessments often seem overly optimistic. This has long been the case for the weakest region—sub-Saharan Africa. The bank is now carefully hedging its assessments for this region as a whole. In 1991 it saw "the first tentative signs of economic recovery," but expected a "fragile" recovery, with many economies remaining in "precarious" conditions. But, for the countries that it saw as reforming, it was much more optimistic. They were "expected to grow relatively fast in the 1990s and to show significant improvement in performance over the 1980s." The "ifs" were quite substantial, however:

> Such sustained growth could be achieved *if* these countries maintain steady progress in implementing structural reforms, *if* their terms of trade do not deteriorate significantly, and *if* gross disbursements of official development assistance increase by about 4 percent a year in real terms. Much depends on the supply response induced by these conditions. So far, supply has responded hesitantly because of inadequate infrastructure and little confidence in the permanence of the reforms.[23]

The bank's assessment for Africa's nonreformers is more likely to hold for the continent as a whole, precisely because reform is so very difficult:

"These economies can expect significant deterioration in coming years. . . . They have become estranged from the world economy, and their isolation is expected to grow in the coming decade unless their domestic political and economic policy situations turn around significantly *and* international efforts to support growth in these economies are renewed." Unfortunately then, "the composition of Africa's sources of external finance reinforces the composition of its production, exports, and debt in limiting Africa's opportunities in the medium term."[24]

For Latin America the World Bank expected some overall improvement in growth from the 1.7 percent average of the 1980s to 3.8 percent in the 1990s, and a significantly stronger showing if Argentina, Brazil, and Mexico "manage to stay the course of reform." This is a big "if" for Brazil, however. Increased resource flows to heavily indebted Latin American countries will be central. The Middle East too will need considerable capital to recover from the effects of the Gulf war. Prospects for Eastern Europe were "expected to brighten in the second half of the decade," but, yet again, substantial external credit would be required "for substantial investments in social and physical infrastructure." The bank admitted that most of this credit will have to be in the form of official credits, until the confidence and liquidity of the private sector increases. The bank is only now beginning to publish even vaguely systematic data on the economies of the former Soviet Union. The performance of South Asia hinges greatly on the outcome of attempted reforms in India and the politics surrounding them, although the region as a whole was "not expected to do as well in the 1990s as it did in the 1980s," when its progress was slow but steady. East Asian economies were "expected to continue to grow at rates significantly above the average for developing countries" except for China and the Philippines.[25]

The enormous chasm between East Asia and sub-Saharan Africa, especially in regard to the existence of effective linkages to the world economy, is growing, not shrinking. This can be illustrated vividly by noting the response in the endpoint regions of the continuum to a rise of one percentage point a year in OECD growth. For the developing countries as a whole, it would bring a 0.7 percent increase in growth, but for Africa it would only be 0.5 percent, while for East Asia it would be 1.0 percent.

In 1991 the World Bank presented four scenarios—low case, downside, baseline, and high case—of future performance by region, which took into account trade, credit/debt, energy costs, and "policy." The latter refers to the "management dimension" or reform variable—the character of policies adopted and the degree to which they are effectively implemented at both the international level (G-3 macroeconomic coordination) and the national level (stabilization and structural adjustment). The results are presented in Tables 8.1 and 8.2.

The World Bank candidly admitted for the first time in its 1991 *World Development Report* that many of its past projections, even the low-case ones, had been overly optimistic. The bank forthrightly declared that it was "generally too hopeful about growth in the 1980s." Except for East Asia, the high cases were too favorable, with the low cases being "much closer to the mark." For Latin America, however, "even the low-case projections were too optimistic." For Africa, both the high and low cases "were revised downward" over time to a "fairly significant" degree as a result of "sharp economic deterioration." Why did the bank have such undue optimism? Projections of world trade levels and inflows of capital were much too high; real interest rates did not come down as expected; and the "potential severity of the debt crisis" was underestimated, especially "the large negative transfer of resources from developing countries after the mid-1980s." Finally, and "perhaps most important," was the fact that "domestic policy weakness" was underestimated.[26]

Despite dealing more with the "policy" or "management dimension," current scenarios are still too optimistic, in large part because they do not adequately take into account larger contextual variables that not only affect the policies formulated but go far beyond them in determining regional capabilities for economic transformation. These variables include stateness, cosmopolitanism, regime type, political stability, external political/strategic linkages, overall level of development, and historical dynamics. As a result, in taking these factors into account, I have indicated which scenario I believe is the most likely for each region and for several key countries likely to be outside the regional norm. Note that the bank's probability percentage for each scenario is as follows: low case (15 percent), downside (30 percent), baseline (40 percent), and high case (15 percent).

These modified projections reinforce the argument that the disparity in economic performance results from the effect of regional economic and contextual differentiation upon the flow of private and official resources and in turn upon prospects for the realization of the Western liberal vision. Each of these regions needs to be disaggregated, however.

## Disaggregated Regions

We have now seen the wide regional variations in performance and capabilities from East Asia to Africa. Yet such regional distinctions tend to hide as well as to reveal. It is thus important to disaggregate these regions in order to understand better key processes and dynamics. We will examine some of the more interesting cases of attempted economic transformation as a way of illustrating general points made in the preceding sections.

Table 8.1 Growth of Real GDP Per Capita, 1965–2000 (average annual percentage change, unless noted)

| Group | Population 1989 (millions) | 1965–1973 | 1973–1980 | 1980–1989 | Projection for 1990s[a] |
|---|---|---|---|---|---|
| *Industrial countries* | 773 | 3.7 | 2.3 | 2.3 | 1.8–2.5 |
| *Developed countries* | 4,053 | 3.9 | 2.5 | 1.6 | 2.2–2.9 |
| Sub-Saharan Africa | 480 | 2.1 | 0.4 | -1.2 | 0.3–0.5 |
| East Asia | 1,552 | 5.3 | 4.9 | 6.2 | 4.2–5.3 |
| South Asia | 1,131 | 1.2 | 1.7 | 3.0 | 2.1–2.6 |
| Europe, Middle East, and North Africa | 433 | 5.8 | 1.9 | 0.4 | 1.4–1.8 |
| Latin America and the Caribbean | 421 | 3.8 | 2.5 | -0.4 | 1.3–2.0 |
| *Developing countries weighted by population*[b] | 4,053 | 3.0 | 2.4 | 2.9 | 2.7–3.2 |

*Source:* World Bank, *World Development Report 1991* (New York: Oxford University Press, 1991), p. 3.

[a]Projected on the basis of the two main scenarios (baseline and downside)

[b]Using population shares as weights when aggregating GDP growth across countries.

## East and South Asia

*Korea.* In 1950 Korea had a per capita income of $146 (in 1974 U.S. dollars), while the figures for Nigeria and Kenya were $150 and $129 respectively. Forty years later, Korea had become an impressive economic and industrial power—a transformation of quite startling speed and scope. Nigeria and Kenya, on the other hand, while stronger African cases, had not witnessed significant transformation, despite, in the Nigerian case, considerable oil wealth. The GNP per capita figures (in 1989 U.S. dollars) and their respective average annual growth rates for 1965–1989 were: Korea, $4,400 and 7.0 percent; Nigeria, $250 and 0.2 percent; and Kenya, $360 and 2.0 percent.

Korea is almost the paradigmatic case of economic transformation in the Cold War era. It is also a case around which swirls considerable debate, in large part because it does not match the neoclassical liberal prescriptions of the IMF and the World Bank. These two institutions have now finally begun to confront the implications of this interesting case, a point we shall return to in the conclusion.

Although market- and export-oriented, the Korean transformation was heavily statist in its thrust. A quite typical predatory state became an effective, yet heavily authoritarian, developmental one. Following essentially a Japanese model, a series of military governments centralized economic decisionmaking in the hands of technocrats who were delegated

**Table 8.2  Growth in Developing Countries, by Region and Analytical Group, 1965–1989 and the 1990s (average annual percentage change)**

| Region or group | 1965–1989 | 1980–1989 | Scenarios for the 1990s | | | |
|---|---|---|---|---|---|---|
| | | | Low | Downside | Baseline | High |
| All developing countries | 4.7 | 3.7 | 2.9 | 4.1 | 4.9 | 6.5 |
| *Geographic regions* | | | | | | |
| Sub-Saharan Africa | 3.2 | 2.0 | 2.8[a]* | 3.5 | 3.6 | 4.4 |
| East Asia | 7.2 | 7.9 | 3.9[b]* | 5.6[c]* | 6.7* | 8.8 |
| South Asia | 4.2 | 5.4 | 3.3 | 4.2* | 4.7 | 6.5 |
| E. Europe, Middle East | 4.2 | 2.5 | 2.5 | 3.2* | 3.6 | 4.7 |
| Latin America | 4.3 | 1.7 | 1.9 | 3.1* | 3.8[d]* | 5.3 |
| *Analytical groups* | | | | | | |
| IDA-only adjusting Africa | 2.3 | 2.5 | 3.2[a]* | 4.0 | 4.5 | 5.6 |
| Severely indebted middle-income countries | 4.4 | 1.9 | 1.9 | 3.1* | 3.8 | 5.4 |
| Exporters of fuels | 3.2 | 1.8 | 3.5 | 4.5 | 4.1[e]* | 3.5 |

*Source:* World Bank, *Global Economic Prospects and the Developing Countries 1991* (Washington, D.C.: World Bank, May 1991), p. 48.

*Author's selection of most likely scenario

[a]May be too high
[b]Philippines
[c]China
[d]Mexico and Chile
[e]Depends on region and context

considerable economic powers; created considerable state autonomy from key social groups, especially labor; established a controlled yet close tacit alliance with large business groups, the *chaebol*; and restructured the bureaucracy, bringing about considerable institutional transformation. This new developmental apparatus reversed a relatively short experiment with import-substitution industrialization and set about aggressively to further export-oriented industrialization. The government provided the *chaebol* with credit, subsidies, information, logistical assistance, protection, and controlled labor, yet forced them to follow world market signals and to cope with international competition and some domestic competition. In the process, corruption was controlled but never eliminated, and political participation was heavily constricted.

Korea was assisted by a Japanese colonial legacy of bureaucratization, centralization, and the beginnings of an entrepreneurial class; by postwar land reform imposed by the United States; and by the presence of a major security threat and of a big power patron that wanted an anticommunist bastion. This patron was willing to provided considerable financial, economic, and technical assistance, while acquiescing grumpily in a heavily statist political economy. With good timing, Korea also gained from relatively open world markets and overall economic growth. Compared to major Latin American countries, Korea relied more on aid and borrowing from the international capital markets and less on foreign direct investment, while having far less initial presence by foreign capital. As a result, the United States, as primary external patron, was not trying to protect existing foreign assets but rather helping to build a regional bastion against communism. Drawing on substantial societal and cultural integration and on relatively high levels of educational achievement, the Koreans managed to attain higher levels of both stateness and cosmopolitanism than did Latin America—factors which became central ingredients in their success. They aggressively sought to build links to the world economy; they ventured out to acquire and master new technologies, knowledge, and institutions to build up their local capacities; and they learned to understand, use, and manipulate the world economy—in other words, to manage and transform their dependence.

By the late 1980s, however, after a 25-year sprint, Korea was forced to confront the dilemmas of its success. At home the government faced considerable pressure for political liberalization, and abroad it confronted significant competition and substantial demands for economic liberalization. After considerable unrest, the military government extended partial political liberalization and began several forms of economic liberalization. Both processes brought challenges that spelled difficulty for the developmental model of the preceding two and one-half decades. Above all, it was time to begin paying back some of the costs of the economic transformation and to come to terms with the threats of external actors.

More limitations on authoritarian rule brought considerable labor activity in 1987–1989 and substantial pressure for higher wages and more equitable distribution of the benefits of the economic miracle. By early 1991 the number of labor disputes had begun to level off, in the wake of important concessions and the emergence of a labor relations learning curve.

Halting yet progressive trade liberalization brought outcries from farmers and other formerly protected groups and resulted in initial caution in the Uruguay Round of GATT trade negotiations. As a member of the powerful Economic Planning Board noted, "It is a big problem for us. Korea needs an open international trading system and has to make progress in GATT. But our agricultural sector is weak while the farmers are becoming an ever more powerful lobby" because of political liberalization. Trade liberalization also brought a seriously weakened trade balance. As one major newspaper put it, "Imports are killing us. We're floating in foreign goods of all description."[27] Yet the government remains committed to some trade liberalization, and many consumers seem to like the increased availability of foreign goods. Financial liberalization, on the other hand, progresses more slowly, to considerable external displeasure. A limited opening of the stock exchange will come in 1992; yet foreign actors grumble loudly about significant exchange and capital controls and about weak reform in the banking sector.

Despite the fact that the spring of 1991 brought the most threatening political unrest since 1987, the ruling Democratic Liberal party made major gains in local elections in June. In March 1992, however, legislative elections cut its control of the National Assembly to a bare majority and badly split the party, as a struggle raged over who was to be the party's presidential candidate in December. That all the candidates were likely to be civilians was a sign that democracy was continuing to develop in Korea. Democratic life was further invigorated by the entry of Chung Ju Yung, the head of Hyundai, into politics.

The country has to retool economically to maintain its international competitive edge. As part of this process, the government has launched a major infrastructure rehabilitation program. In addition, Korean firms are investing elsewhere in East and South Asia and in Europe, including Eastern Europe, despite tensions with the government about how competitiveness will be maintained at home and abroad. A sign of Korea's new international vigor is its willingness to extend $3 billion in loans and credits to the former Soviet Union.

Despite all its dilemmas, the Korean "miracle" appears to remain robust. In 1989 the growth rate was "only" 6.8 percent and was described as a recession, but in 1990 the rate was 8.8 percent. It fell to 8.4 percent in 1991 and a projected 7.3 for 1992. Despite these uncertainties and the tensions resulting from incomplete but important political and economic liberalization, Korea seems far enough along to be able to confront its problems successfully. As it haltingly moves away from its political and economic statism, economic policy will be harder to formulate and implement, but the country may well be moving toward its own versions of embedded liberalism and embedded autonomy. Its sequencing of economic transformation followed by incremental political and economic liberalization may prove to be a powerful and sustainable formula.

*China.* In the 1980s China engaged in impressive—but, given the country's needs, ultimately limited—economic reform, and it did so without any major change in political structure. When I visited China in June 1988, Chinese officials repeatedly told me that the Soviets were making a major mistake by attempting both perestroika and glasnost—that is, both economic and political reform. Subsequent events in the Soviet Union have confirmed the validity of their fear. A year later the aging Chinese leadership made it very clear that, while economic reform was important, it would not be allowed to challenge the dominance of the Communist party. The government demonstrated this in Tiananmen Square via bloody repression in full view of the world press. Two years later Chinese leaders still faced the same dilemma—the need for continued and deepened economic reform but unwillingness to make political changes. In July 1991, Jiang Zemin, party general secretary, asserted both that socialism was good and that it was alive and well in China. He maintained that class struggle would continue for a long time and warned against hostile foreign forces trying to subvert socialism by fostering "peaceful evolution" to capitalism. China would build a "great wall of iron and steel to hold back these forces."[28]

At the same time, however, the Chinese economy continued to suffer from the effects of partial reform: declining industrial productivity; huge budget deficits as vast subsidies for inefficient industries, food, social services, and energy continued to be required; uncontrolled monetary expansion; rising inflation; increasing unemployment; declining tax revenue; uneven foreign direct investment; debt difficulties; trade tensions with the United States; and domestic center-periphery tensions over the nature, impact, and uneven spread of existing reforms. Political fear and technical uncertainty about what to do and how to do it meant that continued reform was limited to ineffective tinkering. For example, no major price reform, privatization of existing state enterprise, or trade liberalization was attempted.

In an effort to control the impact of reform, real experimentation was still restricted to the multiplying special economic zones, especially Shenzu in Guangdong province and the much discussed Pudong New Area in Shanghai. These areas are of particular interest to Hong Kong, Taiwanese, and, to a lesser extent, Japanese and Korean investors. China still courts foreign investment and wants some integration into world markets, despite continued fear of them, as witnessed by its renewed attempts to enter GATT. Foreign investors, however, need both long-term stability and major economic reform; in the absence of the latter, they continue to find it difficult to do business in China. Trade tensions with major external actors would, according to one experienced observer, have a "deadly impact" on the "China of reform"—that is, the open coastal provinces and cities.[29] Other analysts argue that the changes in these special zones will not be controlled, especially in the southern region, and that creeping economic reform from the bottom will eventually overtake the aging communist leadership, providing the basis for dramatic changes by a new generation of Chinese modernizers.

Thus, by early 1991, despite considerable progress in the 1980s and growth rates of 5 and 7 percent in 1990 and 1991, China appeared to be stuck with the dilemmas of what might be called "embedded socialism," rather than to be moving toward some form of embedded liberalism. The Chinese leadership perceived an immediate economic crisis and had considerable authoritarian insulation from social forces, but did not use its power to make major changes. China's level of statehood was considerable but was not of the correct type to orchestrate economic reform. China was swamped by its overwhelmingly antimarket statism. Moreover, its modest level of cosmopolitanism was stunted by political fear and technical caution. The key to China's dilemma was not, as commonly portrayed, the unwillingness of its aged Leninist leadership to engage in political liberalization, but rather its unwillingness to make the right economic policy choices for fear of their political consequences. Those choices could still be quite statist, as Korea shows. The fear was that a shift from authoritarian Leninist communism to authoritarian state capitalism would bring the regime down. While China was not likely to disintegrate as the Soviet Union had, neither did it seem likely to engage in successful economic reform.

This situation appeared to change dramatically in 1992. After a startling trip in January to East Asia's "fifth dragon," the Shenzu special economic zone in southern China, 87-year-old Deng Xiaoping, still China's most powerful elder statesman, issued a personal statement calling for renewed economic reform. The press lauded Deng's "Gold Coast" strategy, called for one hundred years of market-oriented change, and exhorted everybody to "be bolder in reforms." After an intense internal battle, Li Peng and other hard-liners were put on the defensive, and, at least for the time being, fell into step with the new line. The fourteenth Congress of the Communist Party late in the year would determine whether the new rhetoric had any substance. Sustained macroeconomic stability and major structural changes were still required, especially price and banking-sector reform.

The process could easily reverse direction again. The most interesting question, however, was the degree to which the ability of the communist government to halt ongoing economic changes would diminish with each turn of the wheel in China's vivid form of disjointed incrementalism. Marxism faded in and out in Beijing as markets developed unevenly in the provinces, but political Leninism at the center remained. Would economic prosperity, as Deng seemed to hope, save the Leninist regime and the new political generation that it had created?

*Vietnam.* Even Vietnam has finally begun modest efforts at economic reform. Unlike another small bastion of the Second World, Cuba, Vietnam now admits the need to change its economic orientation. The roots of reform there date back to 1986, but change was undertaken afresh in the summer of 1991, spurred by major cuts in Soviet assistance and prospects of better relations with the United States. In June a top party official pleaded for international help to end his country's long years as a "poor and backward nation," to escape from years of economic stagnation. The IMF and other external actors have provided advice, and a new prime minister and reform-oriented cabinet were appointed in August 1991. The outcome of these efforts will hinge greatly on resolving existing tensions with major powers, particularly the United States. In October 1991 the Bush administration announced that it was willing to begin talks on normalizing relations, provided progress was made on the MIA issue. In April 1992, the national assembly approved a new constitution that enshrined market-oriented economic reform *and* gave the Communist party the responsibility of guiding the state and the workers "according to Marxist-Leninism and the thought of Ho Chi Minh"![30] If substantial reform does begin to take place, the Vietnamese leadership will eventually confront the same dilemmas with which China now wrestles.

*Indonesia.* Indonesia emerged from the political and economic chaos of the 1960s into President Suharto's "New Order." After 25 years of his quite personalized and authoritarian "Pancasila Democracy," Indonesia's rapidly diversifying economy now displays impressive economic development, with 20 years of more than 6 percent growth behind it. Relatively effective economic liberalization and reform, led by Western-trained technocrats, have led to a stable economic environment, including usually sensible macroeconomic policy. Both domestic and foreign investment have soared in recent years—including substantial investment by Japan and the major East Asian newly industrializing countries—which has allowed the country to decrease its dependence on oil and gas.

Many Third World countries have complained that they are prevented from developing by their status as primary product producers, which renders them susceptible to fluctuating prices and related protectionist barriers. One of the interesting aspects of the Indonesian case has been its quite conscious effort to engage in primary commodity export competition with other Third World countries, particularly exports of cocoa, rubber, copper, and coal. It has systematically improved the quantity, quality, and production efficiency of these exports, thereby taking market share away from other producers. In the cocoa trade, this strategy has produced enormous difficulties for Ghana and Côte d'Ivoire and even for aggressive producers such as Malaysia and Brazil. In copper, the strategy has been vindicated by the Freeport copper mine in the rugged mountains of Irian Jaya province. In rubber exports, Indonesia is aggressively challenging Malaysia, and its success with coal is beginning to worry Australia and South Africa. From this base Indonesia has moved steadily into export-oriented manufacturing.

All of these efforts rest on a foundation of long-term political stability provided by the de facto single-party state and by fragile social peace despite the country's great heterogeneity. This relative calm has been attained largely because of the personalized authoritarianism of President Suharto and the military. Such a structure has produced considerable corruption as well as family and crony forms of capitalism, but it has also allowed effective change to occur despite the corruption and cronyism—a development worth noting, since change of this kind never emerged in the Philippines under the Marcos version of personalized authoritarianism. In June 1992 Indonesia's ruling party won legislative elections with 67.5 percent of the vote, down from 73 percent in 1987. Indonesia is witnessing early signs of possible political change, something made more likely by aging leadership. Much will hinge on Suharto's decision whether or not to run for a sixth term in the March 1993 presidential elections. More open forms of politics could threaten the economic dynamism of the last several decades. Continued economic growth and sequenced, incremental political liberalization might, however, make possible the consolidation and extension of recent gains.[31]

*Philippines.* The personalistic authoritarianism of the Marcos era did not leave a positive economic legacy for the Philippines, and political liberalization has not brought dramatic economic reform or accelerated development. The case of the Philippines thus demonstrates vividly that authoritarian rule is not enough. Crony capitalism and ritual games of economic reform with the IMF and World Bank left the Philippines in very weak shape after Marcos. The initially popular but fragile democratic government of President Corazon Aquino was buffeted by a series of problems, including periodic attempts at military overthrow, an ongoing insurgency movement, considerable political factionalism, vocal societal demands for further change, external shocks such as the Gulf war and its effect on oil prices, and a striking series of natural disasters—drought, earthquakes, typhoons, and volcanic eruptions.[32]

Under these conditions, it proved very difficult to engage systematically in economic reform, despite the efforts of external actors to ease the debt burden and provide bilateral and multilateral assistance. Macroeconomic policy was unstable and ineffective; legislative resistance prevented the government from increasing tax revenue significantly while budgetary discipline was hard to maintain; and new foreign direct investment was quite modest; Taiwanese investors, for example, showed signs of moving to more propitious countries in the region. The investment climate was also badly affected by serious infrastructure disintegration.

The Philippines is a classic example of the "hollowing out" phenomenon. Economic reform programs, whether imposed or voluntary, are rarely ever repudiated or terminated formally. President Kenneth Kaunda's dramatic expulsion of the IMF from Zambia in 1987 is one of the few such instances. Most programs have died more unobtrusively. They are rarely repudiated formally because the governments are very dependent on external actors for funds and rescheduling. Both authoritarian and new democratic regimes will instead—whether by design, by default, or in response to strong political and social pressure—let a reform effort be quietly "hollowed out" of real substance. This process eventually leads the IMF and the World Bank to suspend programs, as happened repeatedly in the Philippines, and then to attempt to renegotiate and restart them. Under Marcos these hollowing out cycles went on for nearly two decades, mostly by design on the part of the government and by partial acquiescence on the part of external actors. Under Aquino a similar process unfolded, but more by default and opposition than by design. Hollowing out is particularly common in new democracies because of populist political logics and heavy dependence on external goodwill and resources. As we shall see, other prime examples include Turkey, Nigeria, Brazil, and Argentina under Alfonsin; while Poland, Russia, and India are possible future candidates.

Special efforts to cope with the Philippines' debt crisis under Aquino, including a Brady Plan program and relatively generous Paris Club reschedulings, had modest results, and domestic pressure to limit debt payments increased. A three-year economic reform program with the IMF collapsed during the Gulf crisis in part because of rising oil costs—merely the latest, though, in a long line of ineffective programs. It was replaced with new agreements with IMF and the World Bank in February 1991, accompanied by new pledges of bilateral assistance, and capped off with a new Paris Club rescheduling in June. The IMF program collapsed again, however, in July. Just before the end of the year, the Philippine Senate blocked tax enhancements demanded by the IMF to cut the budget deficit and passed a debt service ceiling of 10 percent of export earnings. Aquino vetoed the debt service cap and forced the tax enhancements through the Senate in February 1992, at which point a new IMF program went into effect.

By the time of the presidential elections in May, the economy was restabilized, but it was neither healthy (1991 "growth" was -0.5) nor transformed. After a bruising seven-way battle, Fidel Ramos, the former general who had protected the Aquino democracy from seven coup attempts, was elected president with only 23.5 percent of the vote. It was the smallest percentage in Philippine history. When he was inaugurated in late June, in the first peaceful transfer of power in more than a quarter-century, Ramos challenged his people: "Let us begin by telling ourselves the truth. Our nation is in trouble and there are no easy answers, no easy fixes for our basic ills."[33] The preoccupation of major countries with changes in Eastern Europe and the former Soviet Union, compounded by the departure of the United States from its military bases in the Philippines, may mean diminished external support for the country in the future.

The Aquino government had little capacity to insulate economic policy or buffer societal resistance; it continued to suffer from relatively low levels of technocratic capabilities, statehood, and cosmopolitanism; and it was buffeted by negative domestic and international contexts. Above all, economic transformation proved extremely difficult under fragile democratic conditions. Despite his tough rhetoric, it was far from clear whether Ramos would be able to transform the Philippine political economy or whether his efforts, like those of his democratic predecessor, would merely reflect it.

*India.* Political factors are also having a major impact in what is probably the most interesting Third World case of the last half-decade—India's efforts finally to engage in serious economic reform. India is a huge and extremely heterogeneous, but amazingly persistent democracy, with a very inward-looking, heavily statist economy that is justified and defended by a powerful ideological blend of socialism, self-reliance, nationalism, and Third World pride. Interestingly, the reform effort came at a moment of great political crisis and fragility.[34]

The immediate trigger of the reforms was a debt crisis, but larger economic pressures had been building for some time. Economic growth in the 1980s averaged 5.4 percent a year, the highest since independence, but this rate was still considerably below that of the major East Asian economies. As leading Indian officials noted, Korea and India had the same per capita income in 1956, but Korea had surged ahead, with a per capita figure 10 times that of India. Since exports accounted for less than 5 percent of GDP, India's economy needed to be relinked to the world economy if it were to grow substantially and develop. But recent years have seen a serious breakdown of macroeconomic, especially fiscal, policy induced primarily by increasingly weak governments unable to maintain discipline. In India, both the balance of payments and inflation moved beyond control; foreign exchange reserves dropped; a debt crisis loomed; and pervasive statism and bureaucratic controls were having increasingly negative consequences that were unmitigated by weak liberalization efforts between 1985 and 1987. All of these problems were aggravated by the Gulf crisis, as India initially resisted going to the IMF for help.

By the middle of 1991, with its foreign reserves almost depleted, India was about to default on its $72 billion debt, third to that of Brazil and Mexico. One senior government official asserted that without dramatic action "we face a Latin American situation."[35] The government had never faced such a serious financial crisis in 44 years of independence. For reasons of pride, it ruled out rescheduling, and it could not turn to the Soviet Union, which had long been a major supporter. It even quietly sold confiscated gold contraband to generate foreign exchange, a move that proved very embarrassing when it became public. By early July the government was due to make about $600 million in payments, funds it simply did not have. There were no other soft options; so the government turned to the IMF.

From a less immediate vantage point, the broader political context of the move was the progressive decline of the Congress party. The immediate political opening was brought about by major political crisis: rising political violence and increasing social tensions; fragile governments and repeated elections, with four finance ministers in two years; the assassination of Rajiv Gandhi in the midst of an electoral campaign; the victory of his party in the subsequent elections but its return to power as a weak minority coalition government under P. V. Narasimha Rao.

Prime Minister Rao seized a political honeymoon resulting from trauma and political exhaustion to launch a major economic reform effort. In June he selected Dr. Manmohan Singh, a respected technocrat, as finance minister. With the assistance of the IMF, Dr. Singh introduced a program of economic liberalization that was bold by Indian standards but relatively limited by international ones, even if fully implemented—an outcome without a high probability. Its goal was to end India's isolation and to relink it to the world economy. Though not sweeping, the reforms sought to challenge deeply rooted Indian attitudes and perspectives. In many ways they were a direct attack on the legacy of Jawaharlal Nehru, in that they rejected Fabian socialism, self-reliance, and fear of the world economy.

Dr. Singh proclaimed, "Let the world hear it loud and clear. India is now awake." The country must forget its "ideological hangovers" and "wake up to the harsh realities of this new world." He used East Asian referents, noting that "we have fallen way behind while South Korea has emerged as an economic giant." He asserted that India must no longer see foreign investment as "dangerous and immoral." It is not at all clear, however, that old perspectives can be changed easily or quickly. One experienced and respected analyst of India noted, "Intellectual conviction is almost always the mother of a radical economic reform. But crisis has usually been its midwife."[36] While that may be true for technocrats such as Dr. Singh, for the country as a whole the reverse is more apt—crisis is almost always the mother of a radical economic reform, but intellectual conviction is its midwife. The crisis needs to be deep and the midwife highly skilled—and lucky.

Although the obstacles confronting this reform effort were enormous, it did have some supporting elements, most significantly the willingness of external actors to help—especially the IMF, the World Bank, the British, and the Japanese. In October 1991 the IMF indicated that it was willing to greatly expand its support for India. Unlike the Soviet Union, Eastern Europe, and weaker parts of the Third World such as Africa, India has a strong and vibrant private sector and, relatively speaking, fairly high levels of stateness and cosmopolitanism. The barriers to success, however, were substantial: a fragile minority coalition government in a much larger, complex, and equally fragile political context. This context was marked by weakening national cohesion; autonomy movements fanned by the example of the collapse of the Soviet Union; Hindu and other revivalist movements; caste, regional, linguistic, and religious tensions; rising political violence; and an increasingly fragmented structure of political parties. All of these factors existed in a huge and very heterogenous country and in a parliamentary political system that increasingly reflects, and often intensifies, these tensions.

Much of the bureaucracy was opposed to various elements of the reforms, and the business community was ambivalent—wanting the reforms but fearing competition. There was substantial opposition to cuts in subsidies, the closing of public sector firms, increased levels of foreign investment, and trade liberalization—policies that were all susceptible to the highly emotional charge of selling out to the IMF. A weak democratic government possessing few insulation or buffering capabilities was not likely, then, despite the existence of a fine economic team, to be able to implement an effective and sustained program of reform. It was also somewhat doubtful whether the scope of the reform effort would be broad enough and whether its benefits would arrive soon enough to really make a difference.

In February 1992, the opposition, playing on fears of external dictation and the destruction of the socialist legacy, forced the Rao government to reveal letters with the World Bank, but the government survived an informal vote of no confidence in March, in large part because it stood its ground and because the divided opposition feared immediate elections. Nonetheless, this political fragility bred caution in the government's economic reform efforts. Its difficulties were then compounded by the emergence of a major stock market and financial scandal in Bombay, with accusations that senior officials were involved. The opposition planned to use the scandal to seek the resignation of key members of the economic team when parliament reopened in July. In addition, a major drought clouded the economic horizon. Left-wing unions organized a one-day strike in mid-June by 15 million workers to protest the economic reforms.

The government's hesitance to confront major groups meant that it backed away from reducing fertilizer subsidies, cutting the size of the civil service, ending inflation-indexed wage increases, moving aggressively on privatization, and continuing to lower tariffs. As one external observer put it, "Between knowing where he wants to go and getting there, the prime minister has lost his nerve."[37] A hollowing out of the reforms was thus a real possibility. Nevertheless, in late June 1992, while expressing growing concern, Western actors committed an additional $6.7 billion in aid, plus $3 billion in balance-of-payments support, provided that the reforms continued.

## Latin America

*Mexico.*  Under the Institutional Revolutionary Party (PRI), a stable, de facto single-party regime has existed in Mexico for decades. It has long maintained a delicate balancing act between contending social forces and political and economic logics. By Third World standards, Mexico has had quite high levels of technocratic and bureaucratic capability, cosmopolitanism, and insulation provided by the semiauthoritarian and corporatist thrust of the PRI; in addition, the government has pursued strategies of economic delegation through various cycles of intensity and looseness. Beginning in the 1950s, the Mexican state quietly developed and sustained an impressive core of financially orthodox technocrats, located primarily in the central bank and the treasury. This system provided growth and stability in Mexico from the mid-1950s through the 1960s.

In the early 1970s, however, strains over distributive issues began to appear in reaction to policies of the previous 15 years that constituted a gradual moving away from the PRI's populist and reformist roots. As a result, Mexico moved once again in a more populist direction—especially with regard to land, labor, and social policy—first under Luis Echeverria from 1970 to 1976, and then under Jose Lopez Portillo from 1976 to 1982, both well within the authoritarian structure of PRI dominance. This reformist and expansionary tendency produced fiscal pressures in response to growth of the state enterprise sector and increased social expenditure. These pressures were temporarily relieved by the oil boom and by external borrowing.

By the end of 1982, however, Mexico was in a major economic crisis, touching off the Third World "debt bomb" in the process. It also had a new president, Miguel de la Madrid, and an IMF agreement. The crisis—

and the very powerful external pressures that it produced—led this new Mexican government to strengthen its already orthodox leanings and to reinvigorate a strategy of intense delegation in the direction of orthodox economic liberalization.

Under de la Madrid, a technocratic "countercoup" took place, albeit well within the PRI control structure. A technocrat himself, de la Madrid appointed fellow technocrats to all key policy positions and consistently stuck to a neoclassical line while attempting to juggle very delicate negotiations with domestic and external actors. This delegation strategy was reinforced by a number of factors: the insulation built into the PRI system, the tradition of strong executive authority, the personal commitment of the "technocrat as ruler," the increased power of northern Mexican business interests, and strong external pressure accompanied by important resource support and some policy leeway. The result was important economic change.

Yet, as the July 1988 presidential elections and resulting political crisis demonstrated, even with these strong bases for delegation and accompanying facilitating factors, the political costs of delegation were very high indeed. The PRI nearly lost the election and was very badly shaken. Without extensive election fraud it might, in fact, have lost. Orthodox liberal trends had gone too far to be politically sustainable and had threatened the very existence of the PRI system. Mexico thus had a new president, Carlos Salinas de Gortari, another U.S.-trained technocrat, who promised political reform and intensified economic liberalization. The results were modest for the former, and impressive for the latter.

Economic growth continued, with a respectable 3.9 percent growth rate in 1990 and approximately the same rate for 1991. Inflation, which had been at 160 percent in 1987, was under 20 percent by 1992. Exports were growing at nearly East Asian rates, wage levels remained stable, and a surprising level of privatization was taking place, including the reprivatization of the banks. The debt crisis had been brought under control via a variety of mechanisms. They included a Brady Plan program, a major agreement with the international banks in 1990 that cut the overall size of existing debt and extended new credits, and rescheduling. As one senior official put it, "Now there is life after debt,"[38] though "life with debt" would have been more accurate. Although a current account deficit remained, it was financed by capital repatriation, continuing inflows of foreign investment, the proceeds of privatization, improved tax collection, and a return to international credit markets via major bond offerings. Mexico and Chile were the first Latin American countries to return to those markets after the "lost decade" of the 1980s. The implicit bargain held here because existing strength built confidence and brought results. The increase in oil revenue from the Gulf crisis also helped, of course. Finally, the Salinas government moved vigorously to begin negotiations with the

United States about establishing an expanded North American free trade area.

Salinas believed that Gorbachev's policy of glasnost in the Soviet Union made it impossible to implement perestroika effectively. "Salinas-troika" thus received priority attention in the beginning, but the political side was not to be neglected.[39] Opposition parties initially appeared to gain strength, and the political reforms promised by the new government were slow to materialize. Based on lessons he learned while doing his Harvard doctoral research about the political benefits of public works, President Salinas developed a buffering strategy that would allow the continued dominance of the PRI under conditions of more electoral openness. Called the National Program for Solidarity, it targeted public works spending to projects that had real benefit and visibility, primarily to carefully chosen local communities. Although expensive, with about $3.5 billion spent, the program was financed within a context of continued macroeconomic stability, growth, and ongoing liberalization using the increased revenue flows listed above. Opinion polls showed considerably renewed strength for the PRI. In one poll, a 70 percent majority indicated that they expected to be better off in 1994 than they were at the time.

Solidarity worked even better than the government dared to hope. In the August 1991 midterm legislative elections, the PRI, despite fraud charges, reversed the setback of 1988 and dealt opposition parties on both the left and right a stunning blow. President Salinas declared the results a victory for his economic liberalization program, while he coped skillfully with the most serious and justified fraud charges. Based on this new strength, President Salinas announced that the economic reform program would be intensified, in part by modifying constitutional restrictions of foreign investment. In short, a semiauthoritarian regime managed to use its insulation and strategies of delegation and buffering to engage in successful economic liberalization long enough to bring visible benefits, which were in turn translated into a formula for survival in a more open, but not fully democratic, political environment.

*Chile.* Chile under General Augusto Pinochet had a regime with relatively high levels of technocratic and bureaucratic capabilities, cosmopolitanism, and substantial insulation via an extremely repressive form of military domination. The government was heavily influenced by a very pure, almost extreme, form of neoorthodoxy as represented by the composition of its early technocratic team, referred to as the "Chicago Boys." The statecraft strategy of delegation, insulation, and economic restructuring produced impressive economic results, but with very high sociopolitical costs.[40]

Despite its high levels of delegation and insulation and significant technocratic and bureaucratic capabilities, the Pinochet government nonetheless had to deviate from its strict orthodox liberalism of the 1970s to buffer sociopolitical tensions created by market forces that threatened sustained adjustment. Beginning in 1982, growing political pressure increasingly constrained technocratic discretion. In the context of an economic slowdown, the effects of unrestricted market forces—including insolvent businesses, failed banks, and collapsing farms—threatened the unity and very survival of the regime. Confronting the political limits of "automatic adjustment" in 1983 and 1984, the government reluctantly increased state intervention to protect key elements of the ruling coalition, maintain the unity of the military regime, and dampen persistent political protests. Measures included selective reflation, increased protectionism (including higher tariffs), huge subsidies to banks and large corporations, loan bail-outs, and special treatment for the construction and agricultural sectors.

The economy responded, and the political protests temporarily died down. In 1985, a new minister of finance, Hernan Buchi, sought to balance the tensions between the earlier technocratic laissez-faire model and the more recent state interventions. Buchi appeared to be a more pragmatic and flexible version of the Chicago Boys, advocating a small state and open economy, in the long run but a more interventionist model in the interim. This activist economic approach, combined with a more open personal style, allowed Buchi successfully to conduct two-level negotiations with key coalition partners: both external actors who provided resources and policy leeway and domestic business groups that provided badly needed support. Contending factions of the military were reunited in the process.

While this was a relatively successful delegation strategy economically, one that brought the state back in, it was made possible by the tight social control exercised by the military regime and by the high level of technocratic and bureaucratic state capability. Sustained political protest finally forced Pinochet into elections in 1988 and 1989 that he lost, leading to substantial but not complete political liberalization. In March 1990, with the more participatory, hybrid democratic regime—Patricio Aylwin was elected president, but General Pinochet remained head of the military—continued economic adjustment was in some doubt. President Aylwin and Alejandro Foxley, his new finance minister, clearly accepted some of the economic lessons of the Pinochet strategy.[41] It was not evident at first, however, whether these lessons would be sustained. The creation of an autonomous central bank in November 1989, the first in a developing country, was an interesting early move. The intent was to increase the chances of maintaining stable and effective macroeconomic policies that would be free of undue political meddling, a frequent problem under democratic conditions.

Economic success has been maintained since March 1990, and achieved with innovative vigor. GATT now considers Chile to be a trade superstar. Between 1973 and the early 1990s, Chile's range of exports widened from about 140 to nearly 1,500 items. Copper dropped from 70 percent of exports to roughly 50 percent. Strong trade performance has allowed steady debt service. A major bank rescheduling in September 1990 may be the last one Chile needs. In fact, the post of chief debt negotiator was abolished. Chile pioneered a number of new instruments for coping with debt; it was, for example, an early innovator of debt for equity swaps. In early 1991, remaining Chilean debt was selling at 85 cents to the U.S. dollar on the secondary debt market. Chile's high levels of stateness and cosmopolitanism are evident in its increasing use of "derivative markets"—futures, options, swaps—to manage financial risk, particularly to protect against adverse movements of interest rates.[42] Here again the role of the central bank is key. Chile is also pioneering in the creation of an oil stabilization fund financed from copper revenues, again to hedge risk.

Countries such as Chile that have stable relations with the world's financial markets are best equipped to take advantage of such mechanisms. Because of its overall economic and debt performance, Chile was the first Latin American country to return to voluntary sovereign lending in international financial markets since the beginning of the debt crisis in 1982. As noted earlier in this chapter, it was followed quickly by Mexico. Chile started with a $320 million Eurobond issue in early 1991. Foreign capital continued to flow into Chile after the change in regime, $1.2 billion in 1990 alone, and joint ventures with foreign firms are on the rise. Chile's private firms have also begun to approach private international capital markets, and the domestic credit markets remain robust. Because of skepticism about GATT progress, Chile has worked toward both bilateral and regional trading agreements with the United States and Mexico. Again, the implicit bargain held because strength bred confidence, and success was capped by political liberalization.

This positive economic performance greatly facilitated the transition to democratic politics, despite the fact that the transition was incomplete. Pinochet was to remain head of the army until 1997. Moreover, the military dominated the National Security Council, was shielded from prosecution for acts committed during the Pinochet government, was protected from any budget cuts by the legislature, and was guaranteed 10 percent of gross copper earnings. The outgoing regime packed the judiciary with conservatives and picked eight of 47 senators, each of whom were to serve for life. The incomplete political liberalization, and its implication that the military might seize power again, bred caution in the Aylwin government and helped to nurture bargaining norms by the conservative opposition because it was not pushed completely out of the political arena.

Another, more positive, legacy of the Pinochet era was that Buchi and other Chilean technocrats were kept busy consulting with other governments about economic reform, including Brazil, Mexico, Czechoslovakia, Poland, and Russia.

The Aylwin government also benefited from an initial honeymoon period with major social groups, particularly organized labor. The honeymoon came to an end in the summer of 1991, however, with a series of interlocking copper mine strikes. Strikes were illegal between 1973 and 1990, so considerable social pressure had built up. Copper miners wanted significant wage increases, salaries indexed to inflation, and a purge of managers appointed during the Pinochet era. The new government resisted major concessions, and the disputes were eventually settled peacefully. It was hoped that a new pattern of labor relations had been established.

Copper remains central to the Chilean economy. World demand is likely to remain strong—especially with difficulties in Peru, Zaire, and Zambia—but many of Chile's mines are overstaffed and aging. Codeleco, the copper parastatal, badly needed new investment in 1991. With the opening of the world's third largest copper mine in that year, however, Chile remains the world's largest producer.

Despite economic and social progress, considerable tension continued to exist between the new democratic government and the military, especially over investigation of human rights abuses after 1973. The delicate moderation on both sides generated by this incomplete liberalization was tested in municipal elections in late June 1992, the first since 1971. Aylwin's supporters won 53 percent of the vote, compared to 30 percent for Pinochet supporters. Given these results, the Aylwin government may very well attempt to rewrite the constitution imposed on it as a condition for free elections. Although this move toward full political liberalization would be risky, skillful statecraft might allow Chile to consolidate its new democratic status and return to its earlier nineteenth- and twentieth-century reputation as a democratic stronghold in Latin America. If this is achieved, economic transformation prior to renewed political liberalization should get its due share of the credit.

*Brazil and Argentina.* These two major Latin American countries serve to illustrate the difficulties of economic reform under fully democratic conditions without prior economic transformation, particularly the difficulty of insulating economic policy from sociopolitical pressures.[43] In the middle and late 1980s, Brazil under José Sarney and Argentina under Raúl Alfonsín, two countries with high levels of technocratic and bureaucratic capabilities, pursued heterodox economic adjustment strategies, in an attempt to reconcile economic and political logics through policies distinctly different from those recommended by the IMF and World Bank. Drawing on well-developed technocratic skills outside the state sector and then incorporating them into state capabilities, Brazil and Argentina announced heterodox shock reform programs designed to contain raging inflation.

Heterodox proposals were very attractive to new democratic political rulers because they appeared to avoid key political dilemmas of orthodox contraction. The Brazilian heterodox strategy collapsed because, despite the pleas of the heterodox technocrats, the second-stage orthodox fiscal and monetary brakes required to make such a strategy work over time were never implemented—the government could not risk their political cost. The heterodox economic adjustment strategy was sabotaged by the very political logics that made it so attractive in the first place. Ironically, the Argentine program worked better at first because Argentina was more dependent on the IMF, which insisted that more orthodox brakes be built into the program from the outset. The Argentine effort ultimately collapsed too, however.

In the early 1990s both countries elected presidents willing to attempt more orthodox economic reform strategies. At first both President Fernando Collor de Mello in Brazil and President Carlos Menem in Argentina found it very difficult to control inflation, dampen corruption, increase tax revenue, stem capital flight, attract foreign investment and voluntary international bank lending, respond to the demands of organized labor, maintain stable macroeconomic policies, engage in consistent debt management policies, or privatize and reform state enterprises.

By June 1992, President Collor's effort in Brazil was near total collapse, in large part because he was unable to restructure state institutions so that economic policy could be insulated from powerful political forces, and also because his presidency became tarnished by Brazil's worst corruption scandal since 1954. As the economy continued to decline, his efforts to change significant elements of the constitution via an "Emendao" or Very Big Amendment also failed, to a great extent because he was a young political outsider who lacked a solid base of support in the legislature. Collor admitted that what the Brazilians had been calling his "Indiana Jones" approach to reform had not been effective. He also confessed that his early economic team was not very capable: "It was a team of young idealists without experience. I've learnt through time that I needed people with more experience and thus I have now brought into my cabinet older people with professional qualifications and sound ethics."

By midyear growth was stagnant with the economy in its third year of recession, inflation was running at 23 percent a month—more than Mexico's annual rate—and external actors were unhappy. By late June, as a result of "Collorgate," the disclosure of the existence of a "parallel scheme of government,"[44] the president was faced with persistent calls for his impeachment. Unlike Argentina, the underlying strength of the Brazilian economy had thwarted the development of a sense of crisis profound enough to change attitudes toward reform.

In Argentina, a country that appeared to be in an unstoppable downward spiral, President Menem's government initiated another round of attempted reform in mid-1991 under the aggressive and creative direction of Domingo Cavallo, the economy minister. Against enormous odds, and most expectations, the reform effort appeared finally to take root, at least for the time being. The key seemed to be the synergy between the flamboyant politician as actor and the tough Harvard-trained technocrat.

After winning provincial and legislative elections in September 1991, Menem acquired enhanced powers to rule by decree, something that only a Peronist was likely to achieve. The charismatic populist, who was not a political upstart and outsider like Collor, used his knowledge of the political arena to give Cavallo the insulation he needed to make real progress. Menem ran for president as a Peronist populist who had doubts about Alfonsín's reform efforts, and then became a reformer once in power. He then used his enhanced executive authority, acquired while he was still popular, and skillful patronage to bypass Congress and the judiciary and to weaken the unions. These reforms included a law forbidding the central bank to print money that was not backed by foreign currency.

As one experienced observer has noted, the Menem-Cavallo relationship "is a marriage made in hell." They could "never survive for long without each other. Equally, their relationship is racked with fear, jealousy and suspicion. Little wonder then that they are regularly said to be on the verge of splitting up." The key was the fusion of political and economic logics in the context of insulation, an admitted crisis, and external support. Menem observed that, "There are two forces: the force of his [Cavallo's] capacity, talent, honesty. And there is political force, which is more important, which the president gives him." Cavallo was well aware of this fact of life: "To carry out change like this requires power, and power is essentially a political question."[45]

These central elements, however, were facilitated by a pervasive sense that Argentina's crises needed finally to be tackled in a serious manner. Another unusual dimension of this case is that the military regime simply collapsed after its defeat in the Falklands war. It was for this reason that political liberalization preceded attempts at economic liberalization. By mid-1992 Argentina had reversed a decade of capital flight, had a three-year, $3 billion agreement with the IMF, and had achieved a major London Club debt rescheduling. Economic growth, which was -0.7 percent in 1990, rose to 4.5 percent in 1991 and was expected to rise to 6 percent in 1992.

This successful "muddling through" process, however, remained a fragile phenomenon. As in Brazil, corruption stalked the Menem government. It was still not clear how the personalized power Menem used to break the logjam could be translated into an ongoing, institutionalized political and economic process. This was made more uncertain by Menem's desire to serve another term, something forbidden by the constitution. The fear was that in order to get the support he needed to change the constitution, he would bargain away key elements of the reform effort. In addition, the tense jealous partnership between Menem and Cavallo could also break down, especially as Menem feared that Cavallo also wanted to be president. It was thus far from clear, despite these early successes, that Menem would accomplish his passionate desire to bring Argentina back into the First World, or whether, instead of breaking the country's cycle of sterile reform efforts, his programs would merely echo their futility.

*Peru.* Peru is a Latin American country in a downward spiral from which it might not recover. From 1985 to 1990, the country was ruled by a democratically elected populist government headed by President Alan Garcia.[46] Prompted by the democratic context, he tried to cope with Peru's enormous problems with a weak, ill-conceived, and badly implemented heterodox economic adjustment strategy, plus a debt moratorium and generalized hostility to external actors, all with disastrous consequences. By the time a new government was elected in 1990, the country was at the edge of an abyss. Peru's problems have long been exacerbated by a series of interlocking contextual factors—the existence of the Shining Path revolutionary movement, a weak and ineffective state apparatus, political factionalism and corruption, rapidly disintegrating infrastructure, massive and growing poverty reflected in the pervasive informal economy, drug production and distribution, and eventually a cholera epidemic.

Alberto Fujimori was swept into office in 1990 by bold but vague promises to turn the economic situation around. By this time inflation had reached 3,000 percent a year, foreign exchange reserves were almost completely gone, and the country's real GDP had dropped 20 percent in just two years. In August 1990 President Fujimori instituted a harsh economic austerity program and attempted to end Peru's international financial isolation, its pariah status caused by its substantial arrears on a $22 billion debt. Peru had interest arrears to the IMF, World Bank, and Inter-American Development Bank alone amounting to $2.1 billion by the end of 1990. Such arrears prevented these institutions from assisting the new government. Fujimori had been counting on substantial international assistance, which was not immediately forthcoming.

The harsh social effects, or "Fujishock," of the austerity program, especially massive price increases on basic items, combined with the effort to repay debt arrears to the international financial institutions and banks, greatly increased domestic tensions, the number of demonstrations and strikes, and the level of violence. The dilapidated and decapitalized state had been unable to increase its income. Tax revenue as a percentage of GDP fell from almost 20 percent in 1979 to 4 percent in 1990.

By early 1991 external assistance began to materialize. Bilateral assistance started to increase, and, most importantly, a way was found to allow the IMF, World Bank, and Inter-American Development Bank to help Peru. This was accomplished by using a procedure called "rights accumulation," developed originally to get Zambia out of a similar dilemma of totally unmanageable debt service arrears. By late summer 1991, the IMF had endorsed Peru's economic reform plan and pledged assistance, paving the way for more bilateral assistance and rescheduling from the Paris Club. Despite the eventual emergence of this international assistance, Fujimori's domestic popularity dropped dramatically. Unlike Menem, he was a complete political outsider. But like Menem, Fujimori ran as a populist who promised to end the economic crisis without bringing on a depression but who was very vague as to how this was to be achieved. After achieving power, he, like Menem, turned to tough neoclassical economic surgery.

Having little knowledge of the political arena and an intense dislike for the political elite and its parties, Fujimori soon clashed with Congress and the judiciary. He charged them with corruption and obstruction of the reform efforts. Then in dramatic fashion, on 5 April 1992, he staged, with the help of the military, an *autogolpe*, a "self-coup." He dissolved Congress, suspended the constitution, and harassed the judiciary, announcing that he would launch a war against terrorism and corruption, continue the economic reforms, and return the country to democracy in two years.

The coup generated 70 percent popular support. Even before the *autogolpe*, the people were calling him "the Emperor." But the domestic political elite and foreign governments, institutions, and observers roundly condemned this destruction of democracy. Mario Vargas Llosa, the novelist Fujimori defeated for the presidency, called it "the Road to Barbarism," while Argentina's Raúl Alfonsín identified "the main factor that determined the demise of democracy in Peru: Fujimori's frankly authoritarian personality."[47] Fujimori's belligerent style certainly encouraged such views.

Western institutions and governments, including Japan, suspended all but humanitarian assistance. This included $1.3 billion that would have gone far to pay off the arrears to the IMF, the World Bank, and the Inter-American Development Bank, making possible new support from them as well as Paris and London Club reschedulings.

These governments and institutions were caught in their own rhetoric; Fujimori has violated the vision even though he was committed to economic liberalization. The vision demanded simultaneous political and economic liberalization. U.S. Secretary of State James Baker asserted, "All of us recognize that democracy can be inefficient, all of us recognize that democracy can be slow, and all of us recognize that democracy can be frustrating. But there is no alternative." In an editorial, *The New York Times* declared that "Peru's problems won't be conjured away by strong-armed rule or political stunts."[48] There clearly was an alternative, however; it just did not square with the Western vision. Western officials asserted in public that Fujimori had to tackle Peru's enormous problems via democracy, while in private many of them admitted that they did not know how he would be able to do it with democracy.

In response to international pressure, and in an effort to head off economic sanctions, Fujimori promised the Organization of American States in mid May that he would return Peru to democracy within five months. In June, however, he postponed two sets of elections, while claiming that he was going to build "a new democracy."

It is a sad and ironic tale. Ironic because Garcia had the wrong economic policies but the right type of political system, and international actors isolated him, fostering further social and economic decline; while Fujimori had the correct economic policies but the wrong type of political system and international actors isolated him, fostering even deeper social and economic decline. Sad because Fujimori clearly miscalculated by believing that he would continue to receive international support for his tough economic reform effort; he misread the vision and the intentions of major Western actors. Lacking the will, skill, and luck necessary to create democratic functional equivalents of insulation inside a formally democratic system, as Menem had done in Argentina, Fujimori went outside the system. Could he have chosen instead a strategy resembling de Gaulle's, creating insulation via referenda and forcing current political players to voluntarily accept major institutional change? Possibly, but this strategy seems to require a level of historical political stature, both domestic and international, that Fujimori, despite his arrogance, certainly lacked. Unfortunately, Peru's terrible travail was likely to continue.

### Middle East

*Turkey.* Turkey represents a successful economic reform strategy of delegation and buffering that has cut across several regime changes and types, but which was ultimately weakened by the political logics of redemocratization.[49] In early 1980, in the midst of societal crisis and economic decline, Suleyman Demirel's Justice party launched a new economic reform strategy based on delegation of considerable decision-making and implementation power to a team of high-level technocrats focused around Turgut Ozal. A former head of the State Planning Organization, Ozal had worked for the World Bank in the mid-1970s.

The military assumed power in September 1980, but it continued the delegation reform strategy. Ozal became deputy prime minister in charge of economic policy. The military reinforced the insulation of the technocratic team, particularly by controlling labor. The strategy was supported by considerable external resources, especially from the IMF and the World Bank. These resources provided the technocrats with considerable financial slack and incentive. The result was substantial economic progress in the early part of the 1980s.

Although Ozal left the government in 1982 as the result of a crisis, he was elected prime minister in November 1983 as head of the new right-of-center Motherland party. Drawing on his electoral legitimacy, which derived in large part from the earlier economic success, he launched a reinvigorated delegation strategy of economic liberalization. In the process, the powers of the central government and of the prime minister were considerably extended and consolidated, at the expense of both the legislature and the cabinet. The aim was to weaken traditional patrimonial interests inside the state apparatus by delegation and by the creation of new institutions that would weaken existing ones. The result of the delegation strategy, however, was clearly additive, not transformatory. The state was not in retreat; it was being partially reconstituted.

But the need to consolidate political support around a new and divided party began to threaten the insulation upon which the delegation strategy was based—even though, or rather because, the technocrat had become the democratic ruler. The political business cycle swung in favor of state and fiscal expansion, facilitated by favorable external conditions, especially large resource flows from the IMF and the World Bank. In addition, there was no attempt to relink the delegation strategy to society via any productive form of embedded autonomy based on *generalized* rules and norms. Rather, as part of the political logic dictated by the redemocratization process, individual business firms reattached themselves to the state via *particularistic* and politically determined rent-seeking linkages; the only difference was that these ties were now more export-oriented than inward-oriented.

Although it weakened the delegation thrust of the economic restructuring effort, this political strategy led to a major success in the November 1987 general elections. These were followed, however, by worsening economic conditions and by the softening of popular support in local elections. The maintenance of the reform effort was now in doubt.

By the early 1990s, Turkey was struggling to consolidate the considerable gains of the 1980s, especially in export performance, while suffering disarray in economic policy caused by the familiar problems of inflation, large budget deficits, slow privatization, and protests from labor and farmers. Ozal believed that continued transformation and growth required integration into the European Community. Already a member of OECD, Turkey applied for admission in 1987, but had its application shelved in December 1989, ostensibly because of the community's preoccupation with changes in Eastern Europe. Apparently fears existed that Turkey was not yet developed enough economically or politically; concern was expressed particularly about the solidity of its democracy and about Islamic tensions. Ozal therefore believed that political as well as economic consolidation was important, but the former posed challenges for the latter. His Motherland party was weakening, economic policy was in poor shape, and elections loomed.

Then along came the Gulf crisis, in which Turkey played a major role. Strengthened by the gains of the 1980s, Turkey's economy was able to weather the negative consequences of the crisis, while Ozal skillfully used his strategic position to increase external resource flows and apply pressure for more open markets for Turkey's exports. The World Bank, for example, finally released a major loan that had long been delayed because of poor performance in financial sector reform. In the short run, these resources took the squeeze out of the country's debt crisis. In the longer run, having won the 1987 elections through major spending, Ozal apparently planned to use the extra resource flows to consolidate his position; he called for elections in mid-October 1991.

As in 1987, however, such political buffering further weakened economic policy and reform efforts. By the time of the elections, Turkey had 70 percent inflation, a spiraling budget deficit, and surging domestic debt. Ozal's party came in second to Demirel's True Path party, and other parties also did well. Ozal was particularly hurt by the widespread corruption and nepotism of his government. The election result was a weak coalition government, with negative consequences for economic policy despite the fact that economic views had converged somewhat in the preceding years. Ozal's presidential term runs until 1996. His "cohabitation" with Demirel has been marked by simmering feuds; above all, Ozal has charged that the new coalition undermines the reforms he fought so hard for in the 1980s. In fact, the hollowing out process began under Ozal as he struggled to operate and then survive in a democratic context. The election seriously weakened financial discipline.

By mid-1992 the hollowing out process had accelerated. Turkey's weak coalition government was characterized by populist instincts, old patronage habits, a considerably weaker economic team, and a resurgent parliament. Spending expanded rapidly and inflation reached 78 percent. Increased fear of foreign competition resulting from the earlier reforms led to calls for more protectionism, while the need for other major changes, such as tax reform and privatization, was not confronted. The tension in Turkey between economic and political reform was thus not likely to diminish anytime soon, thereby posing a threat to continued economic transformation.

## The Lost Frontier: Marginalization and Dependence Without Strategic Importance in Africa

Africa is a continent on the edge. It suffers from simultaneous marginalization and increasing dependence. This marginalization is primarily economic, although it has strategic aspects as well: Africa is no longer very important to the major actors in the changing international division of labor of the world economy—to multinational corporations, international banks, or the economies either of the major Western countries or of the industrializing nations such as Korea, Taiwan, Brazil, and Mexico. Africa produces a declining share of world output. The main commodities it exports are becoming less and less important or are being provided more effectively by other Third World countries, such as Indonesia and Chile. Trade is declining; nobody wants to lend, because debt service is not being maintained; and few want to invest except in narrowly defined mineral enclave sectors.

Africa's per capita income levels and growth rates have declined since the first oil crisis in 1973, while its percentage of worldwide official development assistance rose from 17 percent in 1970 to about 30 percent in 1987. Nominal GDP has risen more slowly than that of other developing countries since 1970, despite terms of trade and export prices that have been, on average, slightly better than those for other regions. In fact, African real GNP growth rates have dropped dramatically since 1965. Other developing countries performed better despite the poor economic climate worldwide, especially in the 1980s. African export levels have stayed relatively flat, in some cases actually declining after 1970, while those of other developing countries have risen significantly. The continent's world market share for non-oil primary products declined from 7 to 4 percent between 1970 and 1985. If the 1970 share had been maintained, 1986–1987 export earnings would have been $9 to $10 billion a year higher. Compared to other regions of the world, Africa's average annual growth rates for exports have fared poorly.

Africa's marginalization becomes even more obvious when its performance is compared with that of other low-income countries. This is particularly true in regard to South Asia, with which Africa has the most in common. The difference in per capita GDP growth between the two regions is striking—Africa's has declined dramatically while that of South Asia has risen slowly but steadily. Africa's population growth rate continues to climb while that of South Asia has begun to decline.

The most startling differences relate to the level and quality of investment. Africa's investment as a percentage of GDP declined in the 1980s while that of South Asia continued to increase, despite the difficult economic conditions of the decade. South Asia followed better economic policies, and, above all, provided a much more propitious socioeconomic and political/administrative context for investment. This is most vividly manifested in the comparative rates of return on investment: Africa's fell from 30.7 percent in the 1960s to just 2.5 percent in the 1980s while South Asia's increased slowly but steadily, if only marginally, from 21.3 percent to 22.4 percent.

The consequences of these patterns are very serious. In 1990 a World Bank report indicated that poverty would be in decline by the year 2000 in every region of the Third World except Africa. In Africa poverty would increase significantly. Even with quite optimistic assumptions about policy reform, aid, and world economic conditions, Africa's share of the world's poor would double from 16 to 32 percent. The Bank admits, however, that the outcome could be "much worse."[50]

Given this dismal economic performance, both substantively and comparatively, it is not surprising that world business leaders take an increasingly jaundiced view of Africa. As one business executive expressed it, "Who cares about Africa? It is not important to us; leave it to the IMF and the World Bank." Some observers have referred to this phenomenon as "post-neocolonialism." For the most dynamic actors in a rapidly changing world economy, even a neocolonial Africa is not of much interest anymore, especially after the amazing changes wrought in Eastern Europe and elsewhere beginning in 1989. According to this viewpoint, the African crisis really should be left to the international financial institutions as a salvage operation: if it works, fine; if not, so be it; the world economy will hardly notice.

Yet, despite this marginalization—or rather, perhaps, *because* of its poor economic performance and inability to service its debt—Africa has become extremely dependent on external public actors in the international political economy, particularly the IMF and the World Bank, for resources and in the determination of African economic policy.

In 1974 total African debt was about $14.8 billion; by 1989 it had reached an estimated $143.2 billion. For 1988–1989 alone, it jumped 2.6 percent, compared to 1.0 percent for total Third World debt in the same year. Most of this rise came from the international financial institutions, especially the IMF and the World Bank. Roughly 80 percent of Africa's debt is government or government-guaranteed medium- and long-term debt and thus is rescheduled by Western governments via the Paris Club, not by the private banks as in Latin America. A key norm of the debt regime is that countries cannot obtain Paris Club rescheduling relief without being in the good graces of the IMF and the World Bank.

By Latin American standards, even the total African debt is small change. Despite its small aggregate size by world standards, however, this striking buildup of African debt puts a terrible strain on fragile economies. By the end of the 1980s, the debt was the equivalent of 350 percent of exports or more than 80 percent of total GNP. Africa's debt service ratio averaged nearly 30 percent by the mid-1980s, with some countries having much higher rates. The debt service ratio for 1989 would have been only half as much, however, if African export growth had kept pace with the performance of other less developed countries.

As in other areas of the Third World, this heavy external debt burden, along with the desperate need for foreign exchange that results from it, has made African countries very dependent on a variety of external actors, all of whom have used their leverage to "encourage" economic liberalization. This process has been referred to as "the new neocolonialism"—an intense dependence on the International Monetary Fund, the World Bank, and major Western countries for the design of economic reform packages and the resources needed to implement them. This leverage has been converted into intensive economic policy conditionality: specific economic policy changes in return for borrowed resources. The primary thrust of these reform efforts is to integrate African economies more fully into the world economy by resurrecting the primary product export economies that existed at the time of independence and improving upon them through a more "liberal" political economy—a strategy that could appropriately be called "back to the future."

By the early 1980s the key question was not whether Africa had a serious economic crisis, but rather what to do about it. Avoiding the problem and policy drift were common reactions, despite external warnings and pressures. Much of the African response was to rail against the prescriptions of external actors. For those governments that did decide to attack the problem—out of either conviction or a desperate need for foreign exchange and debt rescheduling—the dilemmas were enormous, the risks great, and the uncertainties pervasive. Throughout the 1980s economic reform did take place in Africa, in large and small ways. A fair number of countries went through the motions or at least appeared to do so, resulting in a series of "small reforms." Few cases of "large reform"—that is, multisectored and sustained over time—appeared, however. By the early 1990s many African countries were still going through the motions, most with quite limited success; collapsed and repeated programs have been the norm. In June 1991, the IMF had 44 programs with Second and Third World countries; 21 of them were with sub-Saharan African countries.

Given the difficulties of reform and the nature of African postcolonial political economies, it is not surprising that there have not been many cases of sustained neoorthodox economic reform on the continent. Ghana, in fact, is the only clear example of sustained progress, an example that illustrates the enormous difficulties involved. A quite rare conjuncture of factors has allowed Ghana's efforts at "large reform," itself still quite fragile, to be successful. This fact has created considerable tension and fostered a sense of betrayal on the part of many Africans. For their part, the IMF, the World Bank, and other external actors helped to generate a crisis of confidence by being unduly optimistic about the expected results in order to sell reform to African governments. As part of a strategy to sustain positive expectations, the fund and the bank fell victim to what I have elsewhere called the "fault of analytic hurry"—wanting to see things as real before they are. They pointed prematurely to "strong" and "weak" performers across the continent.

A backlash from failed expectations should not have been a surprise. In fact, the whole debate about outcomes has been silly. The time frame is too narrow and the data too unreliable; reform measures have not been fully or consistently implemented; and designating "strong" and "weak" reformers, except for an unambiguous case such as Ghana, is arbitrary and misleading. Expectations on all sides about positive outcomes have always been out of line with reality. Even if all reform measures were fully implemented in a sustained manner, the results would not be spectacular; they would be modest at best. Although modest results would be a major accomplishment for Africa, they would unfortunately not be perceived that way by most Africans. The hope, the illusion, of a shortcut persists.

When the economic results appeared to be quite modest indeed, external actors began to argue that politics in Africa was at fault, and they began to call for better "governance" and more democracy. Drawing on vague and suspect lessons that they were applying to Eastern Europe, these external actors added political conditionality to economic conditionality, arguing that successful economic reform *requires* simultaneous political reform. In fact, by 1991 they were also beginning to add security conditionality—requiring that reforming countries should slash their defense budgets in order to pay for simultaneous economic and political reform. We will briefly examine several of the more interesting African cases, starting with its only example of a successful reform program.

*Ghana.* In late 1981, Flight Lieutenant Jerry Rawlings, a young populist military officer, staged his second successful coup d'état in Ghana and promised to make dramatic changes. He did so in the context of a very low level of socioeconomic development, serious economic decline over a 20-year period such that collapse was an imminent possibility, and cycles of ineffective regime change. After trying radical populist mobilization techniques with only modest results, he and his advisors realized that something different had to be attempted. When asked for major help, the Soviet Union suggested that the Ghanaians turn to the IMF and the World Bank. Given their desperate need for foreign exchange, they felt they had little choice but to turn to these international institutions in 1983.

As a result, the IMF and the World Bank jointly played the major formulation role for Ghana's economic reform effort, in conjunction with a very small but capable and stable economic team that received strong and consistent support from Rawlings. He provided this support for economic liberalization according to IMF and World Bank norms with almost no knowledge of economics. After its initial diffuse legitimacy dissipated, however, the new regime found that it had almost no coalitional base for such a strategy. Thus, its delegation strategy was based almost solely on the insulation provided by the military—itself not fully united, as witnessed by several countercoup attempts. By the early 1990s, the result was a remarkably sustained and successful economic recovery program since 1983, in fact, the only major African success story.[51]

Nonetheless, despite the regime's political commitment to a delegation strategy of economic liberalization, which has thus far been successful, the Ghanaian case illustrates tensions inherent in such an approach. One of the strengths of the reform effort in Ghana has been the quite striking stability, quality, and unity of the senior officials involved in it. The small economic team has been loosely but effectively organized, without being very institutionalized. But the pervasive administrative weakness of the Ghanaian state has greatly limited the program. It has affected policy formulation and, above all, implementation. Medium- and long-term government planning has been almost nonexistent. Even basic data gathering, analysis capabilities, and accounting skills are very rudimentary. The most effective reform policies have been those that do not involve direct administrative action on a continuous basis.

Despite these enormous constraints, the Ghanaian economic team learned quickly, and over time it was able to bargain effectively with the fund and the bank and obtain concessions. The Ghanaians often agreed with the principle, but bargained vigorously over scale, speed, and sequence, especially after major unrest in 1986. On a number of issues they formed a coalition with the bank against the fund and were able to carry the day—on the nature and working of the foreign exchange auction, for example.

To compensate for low levels of stateness and cosmopolitanism, the economic recovery program has generated a real and quite visible resurgence of expatriate influence in Ghana—a nearly constant presence of IMF and World Bank personnel, visiting missions, hired consultants, and seconded bureaucrats and managers. The whole recovery effort is a high conditionality process, and the fund, bank, and donor countries believe that expatriate personnel and their skills are necessary to ensure that their funds are used wisely. The World Bank, for example, sent more than 40 missions to Ghana in 1987. While the work of the expatriates has substantially furthered the progress of the adjustment effort, a real political problem has been created in the process. The often intense resentment of the role of expatriates has clearly identified the program with external actors and further weakened its legitimacy among key groups in Ghana. The long-term utility of such efforts is also open to question unless they are supplemented by effective and simultaneous training efforts that are sustained over time.

These difficulties are also directly linked to Ghana's ability to absorb effectively the additional external resources that the sustained success of the program has attracted. The official side of the "implicit bargain" has been fulfilled for Ghana, as bilateral and multilateral resource flows have been relatively high. In fact, given the needs in Eastern Europe, the Soviet

Union, and strategically more important parts of the Third World, it is not clear that such support could be provided to many African adjusters. The private half of the implicit bargain, however, has been close to a complete failure, as direct foreign investment and voluntary international bank lending have been almost nonexistent.

Given its rare conjuncture of favorable factors, and despite the enormous difficulties linked to low levels of stateness and cosmopolitanism, the Rawlings government has managed successfully to pursue a delegation strategy of economic liberalization with an average annual growth rate since 1983 of more than 5 percent. This is a remarkable achievement in the African context, especially given the extent of Ghana's decline. The predatory rent-seeking state of the first 25 years of independence has been held at bay, at least so far. The military government has successfully attacked many of the "easy" adjustment issues; on the other hand, many of the really tough ones remain. Effective privatization, parastatal reform, and a major restructuring of the financial and banking sector are examples of contextual issues that are restricting foreign investment and lending. By 1990 the primary dilemma, however, was still that the impressive success to date had been achieved by the insulation provided by the military regime. The government still lacked major coalitional support or the institutional bases to relink the delegation strategy to society in a way that might sustain the reform effort beyond the life of this regime.

The continued fragility of this successful case was made apparent in 1990, the toughest year since the reform effort began in 1983. Growth dropped to about 3 percent, inflation increased from 25 to 37 percent, the budget deficit ballooned—in part because of a peacekeeping role in Liberia and early fallout from the Gulf crisis—and pressure for political liberalization grew substantially. As a result, Rawlings announced political liberalization measures for 1992. Both cocoa production and revenue, the primary source of foreign exchange, were down in 1990, resulting in great part from a 30 percent drop in cocoa consumption by the Soviet Union, which did not have the hard currency to pay for it. External support continued at high levels, however, from donor countries and institutions. For 1991 the IMF and the World Bank indicated that Ghana would need about $850 million, but it received pledges of $970 million at the May Consultative Group meeting. On the private side, Bankers Trust announced the first voluntary government-guaranteed international loan of $75 million to the National Petroleum Corporation.

Despite these new measures, the primary dilemma remained the clash between economic and political logics. A new constitution was approved overwhelmingly in April 1992, despite the fact that it protects the Rawlings regime from prosecution by future governments. The 11-year-old ban on political parties was lifted the following month, and legislative and presidential elections were scheduled for November and December. Opposition parties still resisted the economic reforms and charged the government with stage managing the transition to protect both itself and the reforms. By midyear Rawlings had not announced whether he would run for president. The primary fear was that even managed political liberalization would erode the hard-won economic changes, as a social coalition supporting them clearly still did not exist. As a result, despite real economic improvement, it is not clear whether Ghana will become Africa's first case of successfully sequencing economic and then political liberalization along the lines of the East Asian dragons.

*Nigeria.* General Ibrahim Babangida's military regime in Nigeria had greater levels of stateness and cosmopolitanism than had the Rawlings military government in Ghana, but these levels were still low by world standards. In 1986 Babangida set in motion a neoorthodox delegation strategy for reforming the quite predatory and rent-seeking Nigerian political economy.[52] Because of intense domestic antipathy toward the IMF, the World Bank quietly played the central role in formulating the structural adjustment program. World Bank personnel worked directly with Nigerian officials in an interministerial committee established by the military regime. They also attempted to engage in extensive "policy dialogue" with influential members of the Nigerian elite. The resulting package was presented by General Babangida to his people as a "homespun" indigenous solution. It was then quietly formalized as an IMF standby agreement, although Nigeria did not draw on the available funds. These were provided by the World Bank instead, again because of political sensitivities. Without its longstanding presence in Nigeria and the key background studies that it had already conducted, the bank would not have been able to play this extraordinary role in helping Nigeria to cope with its comparatively thin (by world standards) technocratic and bureaucratic capabilities and its strong political pressures.

Nigeria's neoorthodox effort at economic reform was supported by a small but capable, relatively stable economic team, by increasingly centralized economic and repressive capabilities, strong political support and insulation by the military regime, and by aggressive executive authority on the part of Babangida. The main dilemma of the Nigerian delegation strategy of economic adjustment was Babangida's promise to return Nigeria to two-party democracy by January 1993. This difficulty arose precisely because, unlike Rawlings, Babangida attempted from the beginning to carry a serious economic reform effort beyond his own regime by using political and institutional engineering. Well aware of the political logics that threaten efforts at economic reform, however, he began to have second thoughts about how freely participatory these new democratic structures should be. He reneged, for example, on a promise to legalize the two strongest political parties that emerged after the lifting of the ban on party activity. Instead he decided that the military government would create two parties that everybody would be free to join.

As the promised return to democratic rule came closer in 1990 and 1991, the economic reform effort began to fray, especially macroeconomic policy, in large part because of the vast corruption of the military regime itself. In mid-1991, the IMF refused to certify that Nigeria was performing adequately under the terms of its January 1991 15-month standby agreement. This put in jeopardy Nigeria's right to reschedule its Paris Club debt again in early 1992. Part of the dispute revolved around the systematic misuse of $3 billion of Nigeria's estimated $5 billion oil revenue windfall from the Gulf crisis.

In March 1992, the IMF forced the Nigerian government to terminate its foreign exchange auction because of abuse and effectively to float its currency, the naira. The exchange rate fell from 10 to nearly 20 naira to the dollar. Major riots broke out in May; they were linked to the renewed sting of the economic reform measures but complicated by ethnic, religious, regional, and political tensions generated by the political liberalization process. The economic reforms were very unpopular, and, as in Ghana, the opposition charged that the military regime was manipulating the transition process in order to protect the reforms and itself. By late June the government still did not have a new agreement with the IMF. Despite these troubles, the Babangida government vowed to continue with the transition timetable and return the country to civilian rule in January 1993. If this happens, the economic reforms are likely to be eroded even more quickly than under the military regime.[53]

## African "Wards" and "Exceptions"?

*Zaire and Zambia.*  At the other end of the reform spectrum are Zaire and Zambia. The rulers of both countries, presidents Mobutu Sese Seko and Kenneth Kaunda, respectively, systematically refused to engage in or support serious economic or political liberalization. Instead, both merely performed the ritual dances of reform for the benefit of external actors. As a result, by the early 1990s, their countries were on the verge of implosion. In the early fall of 1991, major rioting broke out in Kinshasa, the capital of Zaire, leading to intervention by Belgian and French troops. The economy was almost in freefall, the first case in Africa of major Latin American–style hyperinflation. By June 1992, the official exchange rate was 164,489 zaires to the dollar—500,000 to the dollar on the black market. Near political chaos reigned as President Mobutu refused to relinquish power fully, despite frequent episodes of unrest and the demands of a "sovereign national conference" chaired by a Catholic archbishop.

In Zambia in 1991 a carefully constructed package to return the country to international financial legitimacy via the IMF's "accumulation of rights" procedure (discussed earlier in this chapter in reference to Peru) collapsed, as the Kaunda government made no serious effort to implement economic reform in the face of upcoming elections. In late October 1991, in the first free elections since 1968, President Kaunda was overwhelmingly defeated by Frederick Chiluba, a labor leader who had vehemently opposed an earlier attempt at liberal economic reform.

By early 1992 Zambia had pulled back from the abyss, at least temporarily, as the new Chiluba government strove to implement an IMF program while attempting to consolidate its newly acquired democratic authority. It confronted mounting labor protest and clashes with the former ruling party, while serious drought devastated two-thirds of its maize crop. For both Zaire and Zambia, AIDS and the lack of foreign exchange eroded copper production capability, and Indonesia positioned itself to take over their market share. As President Chiluba noted, "The thrill of victory was soon replaced by an ominous realization that the country was not only run down and ravaged by mismanagement, but indeed also that the treasury was bare."[54] President Chiluba would have to work very hard and have considerable luck to keep the economic reform effort from failing.

As a result, these two countries may eventually become social "wards" of the international community, which will provide basic humanitarian assistance but not much more. These are two cases where badly needed political reform and the political struggles surrounding it have seriously aggravated fragile economic bases already at the bottom of the international continuum. But Zaire and Zambia are not the only African cases where the process of political liberalization itself can seriously damage the economy. This is occurring as well in Kenya and Cameroon, both of which once had relatively strong economies by African standards. As one Cameroonian has put it, "In the short term, the opposition has got the upper hand, and [President] Biya seems on his way out. In the long run though, we're sinking further and further into economic chaos."[55]

*Zimbabwe.* Are there major "exceptions" to these African patterns? Two of the most commonly mentioned ones are Zimbabwe and South Africa. The professedly Marxist government of President Robert Mugabe in Zimbabwe did little to undermine the basic health of one of the most developed economies in Africa. But neither did it do much to improve or extend its performance. The Zimbabwe economy, with its legacy of international isolation, remained very protected and technologically backward by world standards, with very little economic reform in the 1980s. Important underlying sociopolitical issues also remained unresolved, the two most important being land redistribution and the possible creation of a formal single-party socialist state. For his part, President Mugabe consigned "teachers of democracy . . . to hell."[56]

After the failure of a "go alone" economic reform program in 1990, the Zimbabwe government agreed to a three-year IMF–World Bank program in 1991. It was a relatively limited and incremental effort, however, especially for trade liberalization—one observer called the move a "controlled liberalization." Nevertheless, by African standards, Zimbabwe is still a "patient with a chance."[57] Whether this chance succeeds depends on a number of unpredictable factors—fear of resurgent South African economic hegemony in the region, unresolved political and social tensions despite the fact that a land redistribution bill was approved in March 1992, and the impact of AIDS. Drought is one of the most unpredictable factors; one of the worst droughts in the history of the region ravaged Southern Africa in 1992, destroying 90 percent of Zimbabwe's maize crop. Economic growth in 1991 was 3.6 percent and was projected to fall 4 or 5 percent in 1992. Like Zambia, Zimbabwe will need hard work and luck, but it has a much greater chance of becoming an exception to the continental norm.

*South Africa* is obviously not typical of the region. It is also a country with a chance, but one characterized by enormous uncertainty. In 1990 and 1991 intense struggles were underway over the nature of economic policy in a postapartheid South Africa; one observer called the negotiations between the African National Congress (ANC) on the one hand and the white government and business community on the other a "dialogue of the deaf." Many in the ANC still viewed capitalism as the arch enemy, the right arm of a racist, fascist state; the white business community and government saw Marxist socialism as a dying dinosaur that could drag South Africa down with it. Serious obstacles confronted vast expectations of change and redistribution. For example, a woman resident of a squatter camp wrote to a Cape Town newspaper in March 1990 asking "Nelson Mandela has been out of jail for a month; where is my house?"[58]

The South African economy lagged in the 1980s, losing much of its nearly world-class status, especially in technology, levels of investment, and labor productivity. In 1990 GDP declined 1 percent and another 0.6 percent in 1991. South Africa is still basically a primary product exporter, with agriculture and mining accounting for 71 percent of exports in 1989; but manufactured exports rose from 18 percent in 1980 to 29 percent in 1989. Very high levels of unemployment constitute a major worry in a situation where the nonwhite labor force is growing by more than 3 percent a year, especially in the midst of a recession. With some form of a political transition on the horizon, stable macroeconomic policy will be very difficult to achieve.

Given this relative strength, but one based on fragile foundations, it is not surprising that contrasting views of the future exist. Some see South Africa as "the Japan of Africa," while others assert, "We aren't potential

Taiwanese or Koreans, waiting to let the tiger loose." As a result, foreign investors and lenders are adopting a wait and see attitude. Despite the 1990 assessment of one respected analyst of the world economy that South Africa is a far better place to invest than Eastern Europe or the Soviet Union[59] (primarily because of the superior overall context), there have been numerous missions, but few commitments. Some see South Africa as a major entry point into the markets of the Southern African region, although it is not clear how much demand the surrounding economies will be able to generate. South Africa can easily become a regional economic hegemon, and it is aggressively and quickly laying the groundwork for it.

In March 1992 a referendum among the white electorate gave President F. W. de Klerk a mandate to pursue major political change. His government then entered into negotiations with the ANC, but they were broken off in June after a massacre in an African township. By midyear the economic rhetoric of the ANC "technocrats" was much more moderate, although it was unclear to what degree these views were shared by powerful factions inside the ANC. It was evident, however, that any postapartheid economy would have several jockeys attempting to control it. As the government's chief economy minister put it in April, the economy has

> too many jockeys. . . . Government is sitting facing forward, hoping the horse will start off moving. The ANC is on it, facing backwards, COSATU (the country's dominant union grouping) is sitting on sideways, hoping to claim the credit regardless of whether it goes forwards or backwards. The private sector is standing holding the horse's reins, but it is bemused by what is happening on top of the horse.[60]

Actually, the private sector was anything but bemused; seriously worried would be more accurate.

Any new South African government will need to find a way to insulate economic policy from powerful postapartheid social pressures, while simultaneously leaving room to buffer them and redistribute wealth and opportunities. South Africa may well be an exception to the African norm, but it has a very long way to go to reach any viable form of embedded liberalism.

Given the enormous obstacles to reform in Africa, with or without political and security conditionality, what are the prospects that many African countries will engage successfully in economic reform and establish more effective linkages to the world economy? The answer appears to be that simultaneous marginalization and increasing dependence are likely to continue, and probably grow worse, for most countries. A few, with hard work, propitious facilitating circumstances, and luck, *may begin to decrease* their marginalization and dependence. Differentiation among African states, already long evident, will increase. A few will stay in the Third World and do relatively better economically, while many will continue to descend into the Fourth and Fifth Worlds—fulfilling the Economic Commission for Africa's own "nightmare scenario." The countries that are likely to do better are those that are already more advantaged economically, partly because of better performance over the last thirty years. These include Kenya, Côte d'Ivoire, Cameroon, Nigeria, Zimbabwe, and possibly Senegal. Even these cases, however, are fragile; political logics may seriously weaken economic strength, particularly in Kenya, Nigeria, and Cameroon. A very small number of countries in serious decline, such as Ghana, may be able to reverse course, but these prospects are even more fragile. The trajectory of individual countries will be affected by a series of interlinked internal and external factors, which will be discussed in the conclusion after we examine the enormous difficulties of transformation in the "new frontier" of the former Soviet Union and Eastern Europe.

## The New Frontier: Marginalization and Dependence with Strategic Importance in the Soviet Union and Eastern Europe

Like the lost frontier, the Soviet Union and Eastern Europe are also now on the edge. While they are seen to be much more important by the most powerful actors in the international political economy because more vital interests are threatened, there may be more similarities between the two frontiers than is commonly acknowledged. In a June 1991 speech, Boris Yeltsin asked an interesting rhetorical question: "Our country had a piece of bad luck: It got chosen for the Marxist experiment. Fate put its finger on us. Why should it have been us and not some African country? At least we proved that communism doesn't work." In fact, fate put its finger on both regions, a point plain to at least some of Yeltsin's fellow Russians. For example, Lyudmila I. Tsegankova, a 69-year-old Moscow street peddler of cosmetics and frying pans, noted, "For the next century our lives won't be as good as in third-world countries in Africa. . . ."[61]

Have these former members of the Second World joined the Third World, with the Second World reduced to China, Cuba, North Korea, and Vietnam? Certainly the major powers and the international financial institutions are treating them like Third World countries by insisting on major economic and political reform supervised by the IMF and World Bank in return for debt relief and new resources. As their membership expands from these two regions, the fund and the bank are now classifying the Soviet Union and the countries of Eastern Europe as "developing countries." In this sense, as the Second World contracts, the Third World, not the First World, expands.

*Soviet Union.* Like the leaders of China, key members of the Soviet elite realized that their economy had to be reformed. Unlike the Chinese leadership, however, President Gorbachev and those around him chose to explore both perestroika and glasnost. The former failed almost completely, while the latter "succeeded" beyond their wildest imaginings, beyond the worst fears of some of them—as the political and territorial fabric of the Soviet Union unraveled with very serious economic and strategic ramifications for the region and the world as a whole.

By the middle of 1991 the de facto collapse of the command economy and the devolution of political and economic power from the center to the republics was nearly beyond control. The institutional framework of the economy and of any political union were in doubt. The money supply was out of control, being nearly double what it had been a year before. Production, especially industrial output, was plummeting; GDP declined 4 percent in 1990 and was expected to fall an additional 10 to 20 percent in 1991 (it fell 14 percent). All financial discipline was gone, and policy chaos reigned. A move to ruble convertibility seemed increasingly problematic, requiring substantial external support. Inflation was soaring beyond 100 percent a year, thus verging on hyperinflation. Budget deficits were doing the same; by late fall those of the various republics approached 15 percent of GDP of the Soviet economy. Unemployment was galloping, while wages were rising well beyond productivity. Social expectations spun out of control. Privatization remained extremely modest while fears of it ran rampant. Most prices remained controlled, and full price liberalization was fought at every turn. Shortages intensified; barter became a major form of exchange, while the progressive deterioration of the transportation and communications infrastructure accelerated.

In addition, trade barriers were rising between republics, and even between regions within them, as goods were held back. International debt was approaching $70 billion while struggles raged over who owed it and thus had to service it. Serious debt service difficulties appeared in the wake of lower oil production and far smaller gold reserves than had been assumed, while desperate maneuvers were undertaken in a frantic search for foreign exchange, such as selling diamonds to DeBeers and withholding hard currency from both state and private firms. Trade with Eastern Europe was plummeting, and import strangulation became a real possibility as foreign exchange became even more scarce. Both internal and external capitalists were looked upon with distaste, and it was not at all clear who owned what property or how contracts were to be established and enforced. Reliable economic data were nearly nonexistent. In short, pervasive uncertainty and near chaos reigned, while no new institutional and attitudinal structure existed to replace the old collapsed one.

The effort to create an economic union treaty emerged to fill the void at the heart of these interlocking dilemmas. The proclaimed imminent signing of such a treaty was one of the key precipitants of the failed August 1991 coup attempt. This failed coup accelerated the economic trends sketched above, however, without resolving the institutional dilemma.

With weak levels of stateness and cosmopolitanism, but pervasive and ineffective statism, the orthodox paradox raised its ugly head: in other words, the capable and knowledgeable state needed to implement economic liberalization did not exist. There was an old political and economic center, but it had no authority; while the former periphery, the republics, had new authority but no structure, just raging sovereignty, wild expectations, and fear of each other and of the old center. In particular, the contest between the old Soviet center and Russia, in part the struggle between Gorbachev and Yeltsin, led to the progressive destruction of the central means to organize economic reform. The political revolution that emerged out of the failed coup attempt brought down the old statist system and made liberal economic reform theoretically possible for the first time, but it also made reform nearly impossible both politically and technically. Reform was now complicated by political, social, ethnic, nationalist, and personal feuds that raged between and within republics.

After the coup attempt, an economic union agreement remained a central issue, but one linked to the other major issues—"Soviet"-Russian relations; linkages with external actors, including the G-7, the IMF, and the World Bank; debt service; attracting new loans and foreign direct investment and, concomitantly, carrying out privatization and technological retooling; and the nature and level of external trade.

Over the previous two years, nine plans for economic union had emerged. While some learning took place, many of these plans resembled, as Boris Yeltsin put it, "a marriage between a hedgehog and a snake." In the month after the coup attempt there were still three major contending plans and many minor ones. Nearly constant pledges to act were never fulfilled. As one Soviet economist remarked, "Virtually all leading politicians in the Soviet republics have their own vision of the system to be built—a tower of Babel of economic reform."[62] Technocratic talent and cosmopolitanism were modest at the center and very thinly and unevenly distributed in the republics.

By late September the dominant plan appeared to be that of Grigory Yavlinsky; it had been drafted in part at Harvard University in the early summer. It garnered considerable external support because it called for a strong central economic union—a common, convertible currency; a single banking system with a powerful central bank; a union budget and taxation system; centrally coordinated macroeconomic policy; a common customs system and free movement of goods, services, and labor; and a firm commitment to private property. These common elements would be run by an "inter-state economic committee" and adjudicated by an arbitration agency. While apparently sweeping in nature, the plan was very skimpy on details, quite intentionally so. While many people in the former Soviet Union appreciated the need for such a structure, and while considerable external pressure was exerted in this direction, the politics of achieving an effective and stable agreement, given the context of the dispersal of sovereignty, were not propitious. As Viktor Gerashchenko, the chairman of Gosbank, pointed out, "Time and life will teach reality. But we are losing time." At one point, Gorbachev asserted that perestroika should have begun 10 to 20 years before it did. Late in 1990 and early in 1991, there were points at which the Soviet officials considered authoritarian market economy strategies, which they referred to as the Pinochet scenario or the Chinese model, but economic ineffectiveness and political events simply outstripped such an approach, leading to what Martin Malia has appropriately termed "revolution by implosion."[63]

On 18 October, only eight republics signed the ambitious but vague union agreement. Yeltsin essentially decided that Russia had to act on its own and immediately. In an emergency session of the Russian Congress of People's Deputies on 28 October, he announced his own version of economic "shock therapy," asked that elections be postponed for a year, and demanded vast new and personal powers to implement the radical economic measures. In announcing these changes, Yeltsin said, "If we enter on this path today, we will have concrete results by the fall of 1992," a prediction belied by the experience of Eastern Europe. He asserted that if radical steps were not taken now, "we will doom ourselves to poverty, and doom a state with a history of many centuries to collapse." Full political liberalization was to be postponed, based on his belief that "it is impossible to hold vast election campaigns and simultaneously carry out deepgoing economic changes." At the same time, he invited the other republics to follow along, but made it clear that Russia would no longer postpone major economic change, noting that "the period for marking time is over. We are on the brink of economic collapse." Finally, he tried to assure Western leaders by pledging that Russia was ready to become "the legal successor to the Soviet Union," while asking for significant external help.[64]

By the end of 1991, the Soviet Union was dead—replaced by a weak Commonwealth of Independent States (CIS). Gorbachev was gone, Yeltsin was in charge, and Yavlinski had been replaced by Yegor Gaidar. Tough stabilization efforts were launched in January 1992, including substantial price increases. Major economic reform had finally started.

After the failures of Gorbachev, the launching of serious economic reform was finally made possible—by the changed political context, by Yeltsin's commitment to reform, the insulation provided by his enormous emergency powers, and by the existence of Gaidar's small but unified and capable economic team. Gaidar offered Yavlinsky a job, but he refused it. The economic team essentially came "ready-made," having its roots in 1980s discussions of the economic crisis. This economic cabinet had six key members, all in their mid-thirties, all of whom had known each other for years; it made Yeltsin's full cabinet the youngest in Russian history.

Given the nature of the Soviet state, that this team existed at all was a miracle and a sign of the terrible crisis. Nonetheless, this stratum of economic technocrats remained very thin indeed, a fact that is likely to pose considerable difficulties down the road. The team was greatly resented by other powerful, and older, members of the new Russian government and Congress of Peoples' Deputies (CPD). One senior CPD official referred to them disparagingly as "the boys in pink shorts."[65] The team was also resented because of its close ties to foreign economic advisors, such as Harvard's Jeffrey Sachs, and for being overly cooperative with the IMF. The government even said openly that it would like to have the central bank run by the fund. In formulating and carrying out the reform efforts, this economic team essentially bypassed the CPD. For example, it attempted to assert control over the central bank, which formally reports to the CPD. At first Gaidar was perceived to be politically illiterate and naive, but he proved to have a prodigious capacity to learn.

The early stabilization shocks were borne amazingly well by the Russian people. Despite strikes and demonstrations, there was no major social upheaval. In the first quarter of 1992 Russia's annualized GNP was smaller than that of Belgium; industrial production was 13 percentage points lower than it had been during the same period of 1991. Little structural change took place, however. The state's vast enterprises were in a sort of catatonic trance, trying to ride out what was expected to be a temporary burst of radical economic reform. As a result, they borrowed rather than changed their behavior, resulting in massive inter-enterprise debt. This in turn made maintaining proper macroeconomic policy very difficult.

Political resistance to the reforms emerged quickly, particularly in response to the fear of industrial restructuring and the mass unemployment it would cause. The central bank resisted efforts to limit its lending to enterprises. Calls for the government to resign by members of the CPD began in February. The confrontation between the Congress and Yeltsin's economic team came in early April, when Congress met for the first time since the collapse of the Soviet Union and since granting Yeltsin his emergency powers. Congress wanted them back. The opposition in the CPD, a loose coalition of communist and nationalist deputies and enterprise managers, wanted to slow or reverse the reforms, and, in order to accomplish this, sought to weaken the two key internal factors making reform possible—Yeltsin's vast powers and the economic team. In short, the deputies sought to undermine the reforms.

Political will, emergency powers, and a good economic team were not enough, however. The new government badly needed additional resources, mostly external ones. The G-7 countries were very slow in putting together a major assistance package. The U.S. government in particular dragged its feet, retarded by the immediate political pressures of an election year and the larger budgetary problems of a declining hegemon. From this hobbled giant, there was to be no Marshall plan that it would plan *and* pay for. At first, the United States even opposed full membership in the IMF for Russia, but it relented when it realized that aid had to come from somewhere. The Bush administration argued lamely that world economic growth was a better way to help and tried to pressure Germany and Japan into reflating their economies. In early March 1992, former president Richard Nixon issued a memorandum entitled, "How to Lose the Cold War," which characterized the U.S. response as "pathetically inadequate."[66] President Bush responded by arguing that the administration did not have a "blank check." At the same time, the U.S. government was also dragging its feet on new resources for the IMF. Finally, on 1 April, only days before the CPD session opened, the G-7 announced a $24 billion aid package for Russia—consisting of IMF, World Bank, and other multilateral forms of assistance, as well as bilateral aid and debt relief. The details were still quite vague, however.

In anticipation of resistance from the CPD, Yeltsin reshuffled his cabinet and eased credit restrictions before its session opened on 6 April. A major political battle ensued anyway. Yeltsin wanted more powers, and the opposition wanted to take away the powers he had. On the opening day, the government barely defeated a vote of no confidence. The opposition then blocked key privatization and bankruptcy legislation. Deputies attacked the economic team, calling it a bunch of disoriented youngsters. On 11 April the CPD voted to reverse the government's reform efforts, demanded a new government, made a long list of contradictory policy demands, insisted that the preliminary IMF agreement be redrafted, and insisted on the power to dismiss the cabinet.

Ruslan Khasbulatov, the powerful chairperson of the CPD, led the opposition and attacked the government in very strong terms. Speaking of Khasbulatov, one cabinet minister asserted, "I think he wants absolute power. He wants to have the government under the full control of parliament, one that is his own."[67] The cabinet and the economic team struck back vigorously, with Gaidar proving that he did indeed have political savvy. In strong terms, he made the government's position clear:

> To put it bluntly, today's decision completely revises the course of economic reform. It is easy by way of minor amendments, compromises, and popular decisions to obtain the kind of change in course that would mean a total paralysis of the possibility to move forward—in essence, a turn toward a rolling back of the reforms, a turn away from them. . . . This is not a Government of capricious boys and girls. We are ready to work, but we need to have free hands and an honest economic policy. . . . Using the pretext of tighter control of the Government by the legislative branch, they in effect deny the Government and the President the possibility of pursuing the policy of economic reforms aimed at the revival of Russia.

> . . . The requirements made by the Congress doom the country to hyper-inflation. The inevitable result of implementing these decisions of the Congress will be a catastrophic decline in living standards, famine, social upheaval and chaos.[68]

Having already threatened that the whole cabinet would resign, Gaidar and his fellow cabinet members stormed out of the CPD session. Two days later the CPD partially backed down from its demands, permitting a messy compromise. The resignation threat appeared to work because the opposition was disorganized, lacked a full alternative of its own, feared losing the $24 billion in external assistance, and, above all, did not want to face new elections or a referendum before mass social discontent was fully ripe *and* organized.

The nature of the messy compromise weakened a number of important policy efforts, especially those dealing with energy prices and credits for industry, thereby fanning external concern that the reform effort was in serious trouble. On the last day of the session, Yeltsin scolded the deputies: "Without a powerful executive branch there can be no reforms, order, nor a statehood befitting Russia, its history and its traditions." At the same time, he partly reorganized his government with appointments that gave external actors a further impression of backsliding. He also took a stronger stand on external dictation of policy: "We do not intend to work to the direct dictation of the IMF. We do not share the views of this organization on everything and we will stick to our point of view."[69]

A powerful example of the nature and depth of Yeltsin's opposition came in an extraordinary article by Georgy Arbatov, the influential director of the Institute of the United States and Canada, published by the *New York Times*. Entitled "Neo-Bolsheviks of the IMF," it asked:

> Are huge sacrifices really necessary to turn the economy around? Don't the consequences make the transition even more difficult? I dislike the style of the I.M.F. bureaucracy and its Moscow buddies. They do not look like promoters of free-market democracy and civilized principles of international relations. Rather, they resemble neo-Bolsheviks who love expropriating other people's money, imposing undemocratic and alien rules of economic and political conduct and stifling economic freedom. . . . Fortunately, alternative ideas for this transition are emerging. . . . In Russia, responsible politicians and economists are questioning I.M.F. and homegrown dogmas and looking for realistic solutions and reasonable compromises.[70]

Yavlinsky and other economists waited in the wings, arguing for more gradual and less deep reform. Thus, the already thin stratum of competent economists was itself now split politically. Mikhail Gorbachev then entered the fray, attacking Yeltsin's slide into authoritarianism, which he vowed to fight, and the economic "shock therapy" that he claimed was leading Russia toward economic and social disaster. He asserted, "The people are on the verge of an explosion." Several days after these remarks, Gorbachev was stripped of his luxurious Zil limousine and given a boxy Volga sedan. Yeltsin's government accused him of stirring up political tensions, while noting that for six years he "could not muster the courage to embark on economic reform" and thus that Russia had to start its reforms "virtually from scratch." "I am convinced," Yeltsin said, "that if we had started three to five years ago, rather than in 1992, we would not face most of the problems we now face in Russia."[71]

Internal political conflict was clearly affecting the course of attempted economic reform. The IMF became increasingly worried, and by late June 1991 there was still no fund agreement with the Russian government; consequently, the new $24 billion assistance package could not become operational. The fund was deeply concerned about the budget deficit, inflation, the money supply, inadequate plans for a unified and fixed exchange rate and a ruble stabilization fund to support a convertible ruble, the failure to remove remaining price controls on oil, debt service, and general economic coordination and implementation, especially in the remaining linkages with the other republics. The Ukraine was a particular problem.

The IMF did not want external assistance to "disappear into a black hole in two days," as one of its officials put it. During his trip to the United States in June, which brought dramatic arms agreements and a plea to Congress for assistance, Yeltsin called for special treatment for Russia, and the Bush administration pressured the IMF to modify its demands, something almost never done for Third World countries. At first the IMF resisted these demands for special treatment, but in late June it agreed to advance Russia $1 billion before a final agreement was reached on a detailed reform program. The fund also dropped some of its stringent policy demands. Russia then floated the ruble on 1 July, but, prior to his participation in the G-7 summit in Munich the next week, Yeltsin declared that Russia would do without the $24 billion rather than capitulate to unreasonable demands: "To force us to our knees for this loan, no. Russia is still a great power; it will not allow itself to do that." He also asked for a two-year extension of the existing nine-month moratorium on interest and principal on Russia's now $74 billion debt. Yeltsin was clearly under increasing pressure from Arbatov and others not to allow the IMF "to treat Russia like a third world country."[72]

By July 1992, Yeltsin's reform effort was both underway and under siege, having achieved some early steps of economic stabilization. Most of the major tasks of structural adjustment still lay ahead, however, including privatization, enterprise reform, the creation of a viable banking sector, a structure of property rights, and the other contextual conditions that would facilitate foreign investment. The list of these major tasks was long, the obstacles numerous, and the technical hurdles staggering. Enormous dangers also lay ahead, especially substantial unemployment. The Russian government had began asking Western countries to accept "guest workers" as a way of easing the political and social impact of unemployment and of earning badly needed foreign exchange. It was far from clear that the Russian state had the capabilities needed to implement neoclassical economic reform.

All of these challenges were further complicated by important political and strategic tasks, such as holding together the Russian federation, coping with turmoil in the other republics, and dealing with the Russians caught in that turmoil. Given the array of forces contesting his economic reforms, Yeltsin could not afford to handle these matters carelessly. To do so might inflame the loose coalition of communists, managers, and nationalists who opposed major economic restructuring.

The tension in the Western vision between economic and political logics, between economic and political liberalization, remained strong and was classically demonstrated by the Russian reform effort. This tension was vividly illustrated by a conversation one Western observer had with one of the most powerful Western officials:

> "I have seen so many pressures in Russia for postponing measures," says Michel Camdessus, the IMF's managing director. While nodding approvingly at the democratic debate in the recent Russian parliament session, Camdessus nonetheless says the debate *must end in one way:* "What is essential is to strengthen the stance of adjustment and not to dilute it if we want to be able to agree as soon as possible" on an IMF loan, the key to a river of other international aid.[73]

Unfortunately, Russia's difficulties extend beyond issues of political structure and involve contextual factors. Attitudes toward external actors will also play an important role, especially regarding their intervention into policymaking by requiring specific reforms in exchange for technical assistance and lending. Attitudes toward foreign investors will likewise be of major significance, especially given fears of "capitalist exploitation." The Chevron corporation ran into substantial problems on this front very early on in a joint venture to develop oil fields in Kazakhstan. In reference to Russian hesitation about the venture, former Soviet Foreign Minister Eduard Shevardnadze noted that fear about capitalist exploitation is understandable, since "it has been dinned into our heads since childhood that capitalists do nothing but rob other states by buying up their wealth for peanuts." One Western observer of the project pointed out, "We're dealing with a classic moving target. The Soviets' learning requirements about capitalism is an enormous task after all the decades of fear and ignorance."[74] A vast gulf of incomprehension does exist and will not disappear easily. Like the nations of Africa, Russia and the other states of the former Soviet Union need the world economy, but they still fear it and frequently run from it. Higher levels of cosmopolitanism and stateness are required, as well as vastly improved contextual variables, such as mechanisms to negotiate, honor, and adjudicate contracts and means to develop viable private capital markets.

The chances of success do not seem high. As in Africa, the economic and contextual tasks are enormous, the politics very difficult. As one senior Russian official complained, the "economy is so far from what should exist in a market economy that we have to recreate the whole economy."[75] The states of the former Soviet Union also resemble those of Africa in that they are suffering from simultaneous marginalization and dependence. A small but vivid indicator of their condition is that they quietly sought and received pledges of assistance from South Korea, the small Gulf states, and Saudi Arabia; and the latter, along with Egypt, offered in addition to send Sunni Islamic preachers to help counter and tame fundamentalist and revolutionary tendencies.

Optimists count on the imperatives of crisis and the incentives of external assistance to force sensible compromise and effective implementation. Pessimists point with increasing frequency to Yugoslavia and, after its October elections, to Poland. Simultaneous economic and political liberalization is a very difficult task, especially given the contextual conditions that will bear on the course of reform in this part of the new frontier. As the IMF now acknowledges, the costs will be "considerably larger" than first expected. This difficult route requires considerable resources for sociopolitical buffering, as well as for the necessary economic and contextual changes; it also requires the ability to insulate economic policy, especially macroeconomic policy, from sociopolitical pressures. Central banks that are at least semiautonomous would go a long way toward providing the resources for buffering and insulation, *if* they could be created effectively. As with Africa, many Western officials fear pouring large quantities of external resources into what may well become an enormous "sinkhole." All of these points are validated by the more advanced efforts of countries in Eastern Europe, to which we now turn.

*Eastern Europe.* This part of the new frontier has a "north-south" split that now runs right down the middle of "Czecho-Slovakia." No vision has more seriously, and tragically, encountered the awful realities of everyday politics than Vaclav Havel's beautiful vision of a free, prosperous, and united Czechoslovakia.[76] On 3 July 1992 his bid to be re-elected president of the country was unceremoniously rejected by a vote of the Federal Assembly. This terrible confrontation between vision and reality has left its mark throughout the region.

Eastern Europe's "north" consists of Poland, the Czech republic, and Hungary; the "south" consists of Slovakia, what is left of Yugoslavia, Romania, Bulgaria, and Albania. East Germany is being reintegrated into a healthy and vibrant First World economy willing, if grudgingly, to bear the burden of reform, although the costs will be much higher and the time frame much longer than initially believed. According to the OECD, for example, it is likely to take 15 years at 7.5 percent annual growth or 30 years at 5 percent growth. For the northern tier, the more developed countries, economic reform is at least possible, although as one observer notes, it is "barely better late than never."[77] For the southern tier, consisting of more heterogeneous, historically less stable, and less developed countries, it is perhaps too late for "better late than never" efforts at economic reform. Yugoslavia has disintegrated into bitter civil wars, fragmentation, and economic collapse, while the other states wrestle uncertainly with enormous obstacles of all kinds. Because it is further along the road of attempted simultaneous economic and political liberalization, Poland will be the primary focus of discussion here. It illustrates most clearly the inherent dilemmas.

*Poland* has been hailed, and properly so, for its significant and radical economic reform measures; they have constituted a serious attempt at economic "shock therapy." This bold effort, however, increasingly confronts serious political obstacles and tensions, while important economic difficulties remain unresolved, both domestically and externally. On the domestic side, the economic pain and political costs have mounted. On the external side, the near collapse of trade with the former Soviet Union and financial tensions with the European Community have posed enormous, and largely unexpected, difficulties. These obstacles challenge the vision of simultaneous, mutually reinforcing economic and political liberalization that is so deeply desired by the Polish people and so loudly trumpeted by Western powers. The major dilemma is the following: Shock therapy makes more sense as a strategy of economic stabilization, but it generates powerful political tensions that are difficult to control under open political conditions. More gradual efforts at economic stabilization, on the other hand, make more political sense but are not as effective economically.

Poland is experiencing this dilemma acutely. The country took much of the painful economic shock therapy in 1990 and was rewarded in April 1991 with an IMF agreement and an unprecedented Paris Club rescheduling (discussed earlier in this chapter). Much of the early popular support for the economic shock therapy came from the common belief that the major economic pain would not last more than six months. It must be remembered, however, that the presidential elections of late 1990 sent up an early political warning shot, when about 40 percent of the vote went to a candidate making highly unrealistic promises of reform without pain. In 1990 GDP dropped by 13 percent.

As soon as the rewards of the spring of 1991 were in place, the political reform effort began to falter as Poland's first free parliamentary elections—in which seats were not set aside for former communists—were postponed from May until late October. In the interim, the economic pain intensified. Much of this period was dominated by parallel but interlocked political and economic struggles. The former were between President Lech Walesa and a parliament increasingly energized by opposition from former communists, farmers, and the more conservative wing of the Solidarity movement; the latter revolved around unsuccessful efforts to maintain macroeconomic stability in the face of the structural constraints and social costs of adjustment.

As opposition mounted, pressures to engage in political buffering increased; in particular, pressure to ease off the shock therapy escalated dramatically, with demands to worry more about the social costs of fiscal austerity and less about hyperinflation. In the first five months of 1991, GDP dropped an additional 14.9 percent after the steep fall of 1990, and unemployment doubled to 1.5 million, or 8.4 percent of the labor force. By late summer a major budget crisis existed, and the IMF had put its agreement with Poland on hold because major performance targets were not met. The slight budget surplus of 1990 became a deficit by the end of May amounting to 10 percent of GDP. The government had planned for a budget deficit of Zl 4,306 billion, but by late summer it was clear that the deficit would probably reach Zl 24,000 billion. A 21.5 percent fall in revenue, resulting mostly from low income from privatization and collapsing trade with the former Soviet Union, meant that a 14.5 percent cut in government spending would have to be attempted, largely through cuts in various subsidies, benefits, pension payments, and government salaries.

At the same time, action on a host of other fronts was being delayed because parliament was slow in passing the necessary legislation. In frustration, the prime minister offered to resign in late August in hopes of getting the special economic powers the government needed to speed up the reforms, but parliament refused to grant them and frustrated other reform efforts as well. In June President Walesa had characterized the dilemma in stark terms: "Very often I have doubts whether evolution from the communist system is possible, or whether different methods are needed—tough, strong, revolutionary methods, using fear to reorient the economy. I don't know yet which it will be."[78] Given all the constraints of the situation in Poland, would a market-oriented authoritarian option really be feasible? Or might an authoritarian nonmarket reaction also be possible? In any case, the need for authoritative decision-making power has remained a preeminent concern.

The more likely intermediate outcome in Poland is political impasse and stalled economic reform. This appeared to be the result of the first really free parliamentary elections, which were held in late October 1991. Nearly 100 parties entered the fray, but few were viable nationally. Prior to the elections, polls indicated that less than 50 percent of the electorate was likely to vote; much of the passion for democracy seemed to have evaporated. There was much concern about growing signs of corruption and income disparities. As one candidate, a former cabinet minister and supporter of reform, noted, "People have stopped believing in democratic mechanisms. That's a great danger to democracy. This campaign is weak because people don't believe that it's going to result in anything good for them. People are waiting for a miracle worker, a strong man." Much of the disillusionment was focused on the costs of the economic reforms. President Walesa remarked, "We have listened to the West and we made too big a leap. . . . We have to produce even expensive things and even worse things because we have to produce, we just have to produce."[79]

Only about 40 percent of the electorate actually voted, and the result was serious fragmentation, with 29 parties gaining seats in parliament. The center-left, proreform Democratic Union, led by the former Solidarity prime minister Tadeusz Mazowiecki, finished just ahead of the antireform Democratic Left Alliance made up of former communists, each with about 12 percent of the vote. The Polish Peasants' Party finished third, with nationalist and Catholic parties also doing well. The Liberal Democratic Congress party, headed by the outgoing prime minister, Jan Krysztof Bielecki—who had attempted to implement the economic reforms—polled only about 7 percent of the votes, while 21 of the parties that obtained seats in parliament received less than 5 percent of the vote each, including the Party of Friends of Beer. Weak and fragile coalition government seemed to be the probable outcome. In an apparent attempt to prevent that result, President Walesa offered to take on the job of prime minister in addition to his role as president. Such an event is not prohibited by the Polish constitution, which gives the president very little executive authority beyond appointing the prime minister. Unlike Yeltsin, who sought expanded powers before full political liberalization had taken place, Walesa did not obtain enlarged powers via this route or any other. The outcome of the voting, then, was a fragile democracy, rising social tensions, and stalled economic reform.

It took nearly two months to form a government after the October elections. At first Walesa wanted a national unity government of nonpolitical technocrats, but a center-right coalition government, headed by Jan Olszewski, was forced on him by the Sejm. By this time the economy was in even worse shape; the GDP for 1991 had dropped 9 percent, and industrial production fell 14 percent, while the trade and current account balances had weakened substantially.

Walesa continued to push for stronger presidential powers as he feuded with the new government, which was clearly not committed to tough economic reform. The new finance minister made this point glaringly obvious when he resigned in mid-February, declaring that the government's economic plans, drawn up by a former central planner, were very weak and inflationary. These plans were a reaction to increased ambivalence about reform and intensified social opposition. Privatization of major state enterprises and the social costs of adjustment remained major obstacles.

In late March 1992 the IMF reluctantly accepted the government's proposed budget—"with disgust" as one Polish official put it. The fund agreement of April 1991 remained in suspension, however. Rumors of a coup d'état circulated in April as Walesa continued his pursuit of a de Gaulle–style presidential system. He asserted that Poland needed a "cabinet of professionals which transcended party divisions."[80] Fears of his authoritarian tendencies made this increasingly unlikely, however.

Late April saw the first major Solidarity protest demonstration since 1989. Then came a court decision upholding the right to inflation-indexed pensions. Attempts to overturn this decision by a two-thirds vote of the Sejm failed—again pointing to the difficulties of untrammeled proportional representation. Prime Minister Olszewski continued to fail in his efforts to broaden his coalition. In early May the new finance minister resigned because of the government's inability to control spending. Meanwhile, relations with all external actors soured, holding up badly needed assistance in the process.

Walesa continued in his efforts to get Olszewski to resign. After seriously damaging himself in a political battle over secret police files, Olszewski was dismissed by the Sejm in early June at Walesa's request, and Waldemar Pawlak, the 32-year-old head of a farmers' party, was appointed prime minister. Following renewed warnings from the IMF, the Sejm reluctantly approved a tough budget for 1992. After four weeks of attempting to form a ruling coalition, Pawlak offered to resign on 2 July, but Walesa refused to accept the offer.

Poland thus continued to be caught in political gridlock, or what Walesa called a "Bermuda Triangle" consisting of the government, parliament, and himself. He noted that reform "cannot all be done by the invisible hand of the market. The economic order is not formed by itself. The state authorities should not steer the economy directly, but should draft a framework of the system." Bielecki, the former prime minister, summed up Poland's situation by noting, "What we have is a victory of political games over any rational approach. Lacking a constitution, and with a very weak government that lacks even a simple majority, you cannot expect all politicians will vote as international institutions would wish."[81]

As in Russia, further difficulties abounded on the external side. The most serious one was the desperate need for trade access to the European Community. The EC began negotiations with Poland, Czechoslovakia, and Hungary over association agreements, but the talks broke down over the issue of agricultural and textile exports by these countries into the EC. These were seen to pose a threat to the Common Agricultural Policy and thus to the stability of embedded liberalism in Western Europe. The major flash point became French opposition to Polish beef exports. Poland could no longer export a large portion of its beef, as it usually did, to the former Soviet Union, and it requested a quite marginal and phased reduction of EC barriers. The French government, which had recently been the target of large demonstrations by farmers, objected vigorously. It received quiet support on these grounds from Belgium and Ireland, but also from Portugal because of related textile concerns. While the issue was eventually finessed by the EC—which agreed to make an effort to send the beef to the Soviets as part of an aid package to help them get through the winter—the dispute remained a dark harbinger of continued EC resistance to a wide range of imports from Eastern Europe.

Thus, despite the new visions, the EC's form of embedded liberalism may well remain a barrier to more open trading relationships. As Jacques Delors, president of the European Commission, noted, "It is no good welcoming the independent countries of Eastern Europe with tears of joy if we do not allow them access to our markets." Another senior European official put it in even stronger terms: "Certain countries make fine statements about Europe and democracy, but when it comes to small concessions and confronting their own vested interests, they behave as if they are living on another planet."[82] While the EC's hypocrisy was obviously not lost on some of its leaders, these issues are nonetheless likely to remain a major structural obstacle to new visions, both for the region and, via GATT, for the world trading system.

In addition to tensions with the EC, trading relationships within Eastern Europe itself are also problematic. Given that these countries are going to find it difficult to compete in Western markets generally, and given the steep decline in trade with the former Soviet Union, tensions among Eastern European countries are likely to increase; moreover, these tensions will affect the willingness of foreign firms to invest in search of new, and secure, markets. In late 1991, for example, Hungary, probably the strongest reformer in the region, was moving to raise protectionist barriers on color television sets and shoes, because Hungarian and joint venture firms were complaining of unfair intra–Eastern European competition. The Hungarian government was also targeting "unfair" competition from subsidized cement in neighboring economies, which were providing inexpensive electricity in the absence of major price reform.

Despite the striking Paris Club and IMF agreements of the spring of 1991, debt service also remained a major problem for Poland. In large part this was because domestic economic performance and external debt service were tightly linked: the implementation of the Paris Club rescheduling was contingent on the continuation of the IMF agreement. The IMF's suspension of this agreement until after the October elections put the Paris Club agreement on hold. In regard to private international bank, or London

Club, debt, the Polish government wanted generous terms similar to those
of the Paris Club agreement. Again the issues were linked: London Club
agreement was complicated by IMF and Paris Club difficulties, by the fact
that debt service arrears on the private debt were over $1 billion by
September 1991, and by a series of corruption scandals involving Polish
debt service officials and institutions—which, among other things, led to
the dismissal of the government's chief debt negotiator.

Trade and debt difficulties, especially when linked to stalled economic
reforms and major political uncertainty, gave external private lenders and
investors great pause about involvement in the Polish economy. Privatization was already in jeopardy because much of the country's capital stock
was almost worthless, and because foreign companies already in Poland
were finding it very hard to do business. With privatization in jeopardy,
the implicit bargain was also threatened, in turn reinforcing—as would be
the case for any country similar to Poland—the increasing officialization
of credit flows. In addition, the preoccupation of the G-7 governments
with events to the east and south added to the concern of Polish officials.
In his visit to the United States in September 1991, Prime Minister
Bielecki urged the major Western governments in very strong terms not to
become overly preoccupied with what he termed "the former Soviet
Union," but rather to maintain more of a sense of proportion.

Beyond these pressing domestic and external difficulties, however, lie
even larger contextual ones that may ultimately be equally important. As a
fine East European joke of the times puts it, "It's easier to turn an aquarium into bouillabaisse than to turn bouillabaisse back into an aquarium."
These issues relate primarily to the need to restructure institutions and attitudes in major ways, and they are nicely illustrated by banking sector reform and privatization. Prime Minister Bielecki was well aware of the
magnitude of the contextual difficulties: "We underestimated two mam-
moth problems. We thought we had a banking system and we had nothing
of the kind, and we thought enterprise managers would respond to market
signals when in fact a lifetime spent in communism meant they were incapable of recognizing market signals, let alone responding to them." Such
a statement holds equally well for the Czech republic and to a slightly
lesser degree for Hungary, because of its earlier reform efforts. It holds far
more intensely, however, for the southern tier of Eastern Europe and the
former Soviet Union. Given Poland's heavy dependence on these latter
markets and given the fear of waves of immigrants from those countries,
the inadequacy of their banking systems and enterprise managers was significant to Prime Minister Bielecki: "When I take these two lessons from
Poland and apply them to the Soviet Union then I am not optimistic."[83]

Many of Poland's problems were mirrored in the other countries of
Eastern Europe, especially in the southern tier states with their more divisive societies and lower levels of development. Struggles for stable gov-

ernance in Romania, Bulgaria, and Albania during 1991 bore stark witness to this fact, but the most wrenching demonstration came with the virtual political, economic, social, and physical self-annihilation of Yugoslavia and its self-management brand of socialism. One Yugoslav historian and sociologist notes that a powerful "megalomania is inevitably accompanied by paranoid delusions about omnipresent enemies and worldwide conspiracies" which are, in turn, supported culturally by "pseudo-romantic nationalist kitsch."[84] The spread of such destructive delusions remains a serious worry for other parts of the region and for the former Soviet Union.

As in Africa then, efforts at simultaneous economic and political liberalization by countries in the new reform frontier of Eastern Europe and the former Soviet Union face staggering odds, given the array of powerful internal, external, economic, political, and contextual obstacles, all reinforced by extravagant popular expectations. As social pressures mount, fragile new participatory structures will come under increasing strain, unless very creative social buffering can be undertaken. The cost of such buffering, leaving aside difficult issues of process and implementation, will be enormous. For example, in late 1990 one Western consulting firm estimated that creating "an adequate safety net" for Eastern Europe over the next five years was likely to cost between $270 and $370 billion; Western countries have pledged less than a tenth of that amount and much of it is slow in coming.[85] Where are these resources to come from and how effectively can they be used under the extremely difficult conditions of the new frontier?

## Conclusion

As much of the evidence presented here indicates, the brilliant vision of global transformation via the magic of the market and the ballot box that has been propounded by Western leaders is flawed. It is flawed in a number of ways, but there are three major ones: (1) it underestimates the role of the state in economic transformation; (2) it misperceives the link between economic transformation and political regime type, especially by assuming that economic reform requires simultaneous political liberalization or democratization; and (3) it seriously underestimates the role and importance of larger contextual factors—i.e., the institutions, knowledge, attitudes, and infrastructures that underpin states, markets, and regimes. These flaws and misperceptions mean that the vision is not likely to be realized in very many places and, thus, that differentiation rather than convergence among regions and countries will mark the coming decade, with confrontational rather than harmonious consequences. Each of these flaws in the vision, and their respective consequences, will be examined briefly in this concluding section.

*Role of the State*

While it correctly captures the fundamental importance of the market and linkages to the world economy, the Western liberal vision has underestimated the role of the state in economic transformation in three major ways: by failing to perceive (1) the existence of the orthodox paradox, that is, that even neoclassical economic reform requires a relatively capable and important state structure; (2) that any state, authoritarian or democratic, but especially the latter, needs to buffer the sociopolitical consequences of transformation; and (3) that the liberal vision of economic transformation itself, especially its stress on minimalist states, the exclusive sway of markets, and correct policy packages, might not be the only possible path to transformation, or even the most common one.

Over the course of the 1980s, Western actors have responded to each of these three problem areas in partial ways. First, in addressing the issue of state structure, they have downplayed the specific type of regime and stressed instead aspects of "governance"—administrative probity and efficiency; effective legal, judicial, and regulatory mechanisms, especially for property rights and contracts; and informational and policy openness or "transparency," including such things as a relatively free press. There is now quite a "laundry list" of relevant factors. Each one of these elements probably is important, but, as the list continues to grow, it is difficult to know which one to target or how to do it. Second, in acknowledging the need for buffering, external actors have increasingly focused on the salience of the social costs of adjustment and policies to deal with them, particularly the creation of a social "safety net" for the most adversely affected groups. For the third problem area, they have recently made a quite interesting but still hesitant about-face, in large part by finally coming to terms with the reality of Korean and other heavily statist cases of transformation: they now admit the possible importance of "market-friendly" forms of state intervention. Each of these responses constitutes an important form of learning. Nonetheless, it remains unclear how centrally and consistently this learning will be reflected in the programs and policies of the major Western governments, the IMF, and World Bank, *and* whether the resources exist to support new approaches.

Since the third change is particularly important, it needs to be explored a little more fully. In its reports on Africa in the late 1980s, the World Bank tacitly began to admit more of a role for the state in economic transformation. With the 1991 *World Development Report,* however, the shift became more explicit. In addressing issues in conjunction with "the remarkable achievements of the East Asian economies, or with the earlier achievements of Japan," the report asks, "Why, in these economies, were interventions in the markets such as infant industry protection and credit subsidies associated with success, not failure?" Their answer is that these

"market-friendly" state interventions were "carried out competently, prag-
matically, and flexibly"; were terminated if they failed or outlasted their
usefulness, did not distort relative prices "unduly"; were export-oriented;
and were "moderate" rather than all encompassing—undertaken reluctantly and openly, and constantly disciplined by international and domestic markets. In sum, according to the bank, these "market-friendly" forms
of state intervention "refute the case for thoroughgoing dirigisme as con-
vincingly as they refute the case for laissez-faire."[86] Until quite recently
then, Western reaction to Third and Second World statism has been what
Tony Killick has nicely called "a reaction too far,"[87] especially when
Western behavior belies its rhetoric. Effective outward-oriented transformation can quite clearly be achieved without following all the liberal economic mantras of the IMF and the World Bank.

In fact, the World Bank's new view still significantly underestimates
the type and degree of state intervention at work in cases such as Korea.
It does represent, however, an important shift toward a more balanced tension between state and market, a relationship that has long been evident
in the practice, if not the rhetoric, of embedded liberalism in northern industrial democracies. This view is not yet fully shared by the IMF or by all
Western governments. It is also not a view shared by many long-time critics of the World Bank, those seeking a "new political economy of development" that continues to stress the state over the market. Their perspective is indicated by the book title of a recent representative attack on
Western "neoliberalism": *States* or *Markets? Neo-Liberalism and the Development Policy Debate*.[88] A more balanced viewpoint would be *States*
and *Markets*.

While all sides still need to seek a proper balanced tension between
state and market, admitting the need for it is an important first step. It
does, however, open up a major Pandora's box, one which Western actors
have wanted to keep closed. Once you concede a serious, nonliberal role
for the state, you then must decide on specific types and instances of state
intervention. This is an enormously difficult thing to accomplish and
clearly constitutes the current policy frontier. The elegant parsimony of the
neoclassical vision has been replaced by messy ambiguity and relativity.
Furthermore, such an admission does not imply that the state capabilities
necessary to engage successfully in such intervention will exist when and
where they are needed.

### Economic and Political Liberalization

The cases presented here for both the Third and Second Worlds, as well as
others, do not support the vision's tight and simultaneous link between
economic and political liberalization. We have seen that insulation, delegation, and buffering have been central to success at economic transfor-

mation. While not impossible, it is very difficult under democratic conditions to achieve or exercise the capacity for these strategies. One analyst points to "the inconclusiveness of the debate" about "the impact of democracy on economic development." While he does admit that "most cases of very high growth rates have involved authoritarian regimes, and authoritarianism may be a nearly necessary, though not a sufficient, condition for rapid economic growth," he asserts that "the economies of many democratic Third World countries have grown at satisfactory rates."[89] Most of his "satisfactory" cases are established democracies, however, such as India and Venezuela; and the Indian case as presented in this chapter does not indicate great potential for major economic reform. He is more pessimistic about the prospects for transitional or newly established democracies facing the tasks of economic restructuring and points to the difficult political logics they confront:

> The capacity of democratic regimes to extricate themselves from social ties so as to restructure the economy is minimal. Generally, only incremental shifts are possible. Moreover, leaders in democracies concern themselves with what appears to be politically 'rational'—namely, how to generate and enhance political support. Thus economic policies often are chosen because of the political benefits they may bring to the leaders. Policy incrementalism and the use of economic resources for sustaining political support generally tend to retard economic growth in democracies.[90]

In another recent study of East Asian and Latin American NICs, it is clear that "authoritarianism contributed to economic growth" and that "crucial policy reforms in the NICs have historically been associated with authoritarian rule; any assessment of the NICs must weigh this high cost of 'success.'" In discussing the bottom line, the author notes,

> One way to circumvent this problem is to go beyond regime type to other institutional factors that have affected the NICs' performance. . . . I have attempted to show how other institutional features of the state, including the organization of interest groups, the centralization of decision-making authority, and the instruments available to government officials, also affected ability to formulate and implement coherent policy. *Yet as the case studies have shown, many of these institutional characteristics were themselves a by-product of the consolidation of authoritarian political power.*

He goes on, however, to express a frequent hope:

> Nevertheless, . . . there are no *theoretical* reasons to think that authoritarian regimes are *uniquely* capable of solving the collective-action problems associated with development. This absence [of theoretical reasons] provides hope that newly democratizing countries will develop institutions conducive to both political liberty and economic growth. . . .

> [A] variety of institutions may be functionally equivalent in their ability to induce restraint from competing social groups.[91]

Thus, in the cases presented here, as well as in other instances, we appear to have a high historical correlation between authoritarian rule and the ability to engage in major economic restructuring in the Third and former Second Worlds, but not a necessary theoretical one. We are left, then, to search for what might be called "effective and sustainable democratic functional equivalents." Institutions and processes of delegation, insulation, and buffering can exist under democratic conditions, as indicated in the first part of this piece, but they are difficult to achieve, and, above all, to sustain over time. If they are to constitute new forms of embedded liberalism, they will need to be supported by relatively high levels of resources. Even then, as in the case of Turkey, the outcome may be very difficult to sustain. The outcome will depend on unpredictable political struggles, especially electoral ones, and on larger contextual factors, all of which can erode reform efforts.

The presumption of the mutually reinforcing character of political and economic reform in the Third and former Second Worlds relies on an extension of neoclassical economic logic, as follows: economic liberalization creates sustained growth, growth produces winners, and winners will organize to defend their new-found welfare and to create sociopolitical coalitions to support continued economic reform. This logic, however, does not appear to hold very often, even under authoritarian conditions, much less democratic ones. Therefore, pushing complete political liberalization, based on faulty assumptions about cause and effect, could be a serious mistake.

The winners of economic reform are often few at first, appearing only slowly over time, and are difficult to organize politically. The neoclassical political logic of reform is too mechanistic; there are real "transaction costs" to organizing winners, and not just infrastructural costs. Direct linkages between economic interest and political outcome are rare, thus making reliable theoretically based predictions about the emergence of support coalitions extremely difficult. Farmers, for example, have complex interests, political loyalties, and histories of organization; direct political organization in immediate response to a given set of economic policies may prove difficult. The 1991 elections in Poland and Turkey show this quite clearly. Farmers have other organizational bases of political solidarity— ethnic, regional, religious, linguistic, and patron-client—that hinder mobilization around policy-specific economic interests. Even where they might so organize, it would not likely be to support the full range of economic measures, thereby threatening the viability of reform. Private sector business actors, domestic or foreign, are also not uniformly supportive of full economic or political liberalization; they can be just as interventionist and particularistic as state actors. It depends on whether or not such intervention and particularistic discretion benefits them.

Political liberalization, then, is not likely to guarantee the appearance of new political alignments that favor sustained neoclassical economic reform. Other issues may be more important, such as the definition of the state and nation or the shape of the political order. The former Yugoslavia and Czechoslovakia are quite vivid examples. Besides, no strong evidence exists that politics in many Third or former Second World countries has shifted from distributional to productionist logics and forms of behavior. Political openness without coalitions supporting a production-oriented rather than a distribution- or welfare-oriented political economy might simply make matters worse. It might end existing reform efforts and make new ones hard to initiate. Openness might simply strengthen elements of the syndrome that dominated the old political economy. Again, the October 1991 elections in Poland are interesting in this regard.

In a passionate discussion of "reactionary rhetoric," Albert Hirschman points to "the thesis of the perverse effect": the situation where, "unwilling to argue directly against reform, opponents of progressive impulses in society have attempted to show instead that reformist measures will invariably have effects that are contrary to the ones intended."[92] Is the version of the "thesis of the perverse effect" presented here—that political liberalization might have a negative impact on the chances for desperately needed economic reform—likely to hold across the board for the Third and former Second Worlds? No, it is not. It is important to assess the cases of particular countries. But a probabilistic rather than a deterministic perverse effect is likely to operate if political liberalization becomes substantive, rather than just rhetorical.

As Hirschman himself finally admits, "There is no denying, to be sure, that the perverse effect does show up here and there . . . I have merely intended to raise some doubts about whether it occurs with the frequency that is claimed."[93] The "here and there" might be more common than we would like to believe. Looking at the evidence, one analyst concludes, "Any justification of non-democratic regimes that relies on their developmental capacities is, at best, weak."[94] Yes, many authoritarian regimes are very poor reformers, but the following has even more basis in fact: any justification of democratic regimes that relies on their developmental capabilities is, at best, weak. It is possible that political and economic liberalization can positively coexist in some transitional democracies, at least for awhile, but it requires a difficult, rare, and fragile conjuncture of factors.

Are we thus to ignore the pessimism inherent in the historical record of the last three decades in the Third World and put our faith in a theoretical vision of widespread democratic functional equivalents? Shall we ignore the historical and analytical pessimism and opt only for policy optimism? It all boils down to how much stock, or hope, we put in democratic functional equivalents and where we place our normative bets.

Paul Collier identifies "agencies of restraint" as one type of democratic functional equivalent for insulation and delegation: "At the macroeconomic level the main function of agencies of restraint is to prevent public expenditure from outpacing public revenue . . . ; the typical business of such agencies is to say no to spending requests or to punish the politically well-connected for abuses of power." As he points out, "For such agencies to function effectively they must be protected from the pressures they are designed to hold in check. They must therefore be autonomous centers of power."[95] But there are attitudinal as well as institutional aspects to the creation and effective operation of agencies of restraint. For them to be most successful, both aspects must be present.

The most common institutional example of an agency of restraint is the central bank. The most typical example is the German Bundesbank, although Chile was the first developing country to establish an effective one. As John Goodman observes:

> Creating an independent central bank can be seen as a way for governments to prevent themselves (and their successors) from pursuing overly expansionary policies. Central bank independence is thus considered a solution to what economists term the dynamic inconsistency of policy. Dynamic inconsistency refers to the inability of politicians to commit to and implement policies that may be best for the economy in the long run, but are politically harmful in the short run.[96]

This is the tension between political and economic logics discussed at the beginning of this chapter.

As part of the conditionality inherent in externally supported economic reform, the IMF and the World Bank can insist on the creation or strengthening of central banks. Such has been the case in a number of Third World countries, Nigeria, for example.[97] In fact, we know very little about how to create viable institutions in contexts where other facilitating factors are absent—a subject to which we shall return shortly. Most central banks in the Third World are weak because they lack autonomy and attitudinal support for generalized restraint.

Collier takes his argument one step further by asserting that "both for fiscal rectitude and adherence to the law, democratic institutions can serve as powerful agencies of restraint" because they can produce "informed domestic constituencies of restraint"[98] at the level of organized social groups and the mass electorate. Most of the evidence from the Third and former Second Worlds does not support such an optimistic conclusion. In large part, this is because powerful populist and distributive political logics are at play; furthermore, much of the debate about the need for economic reform and how to achieve it has been externalized, so that the foreign actors, especially the IMF and the World Bank, have become the lightning rods for opposition to serious economic reform.

In most places, no serious domestic debate about restraint has taken place, and there are few organized social constituencies for such restraint. Indeed, the very political language and set of symbols through which such a debate could take place do not usually exist. Some learning about economic reform and the necessity of macroeconomic restraint has taken place, but the question becomes *who* has learned—technocrats, rulers, military officers, government officials, politicians, leaders of groups in "civil society," or the mass electorate? Thus far, the learning has mostly been at the technocratic level. Collier's "informed domestic constituencies of restraint" are not likely to emerge in very many places.

If effective domestic agencies of restraint do not emerge, then the external conditionality inherent in IMF- and World Bank–sponsored economic reform may become a nasty, second-best, but necessary alternative. Similar problems exist in the United States, of course, where informed domestic constituencies of restraint are also very weak, and where the dominant political logics as well do not bode well for restraint, as David Stockman's brilliant book, *The Triumph of Politics*, so vividly demonstrates.[99] In addition, the United States does not have an external agency of restraint, although it badly needs one.

As this brief discussion indicates, if we place normative bets on the side of democratization as a valued end in itself, we need to do so with our analytic eyes and pocketbooks wide open and our expectations well in check. Following Tocqueville, it is important to bring to democracy neither the enthusiasm of those who expect from it a transfiguration of the human lot nor the hostility of those who see in it no less than the very decomposition of human society. Democracy is risky after all and often lacks brilliance and grandeur.[100] As cases such as Korea, Chile, and Mexico indicate, sequencing economic and political reforms may offer the best chance of sustained transformation, both economic *and* political, but it is very difficult to achieve and normatively risky.

## Contextual Factors

Finally, the Western liberal vision has failed to look in depth beyond policy change and has seriously underestimated the importance of larger contextual factors that facilitate transformation—i.e., the institutions, knowledge, attitudes, and infrastructures that underpin states, markets, and regimes.[101] Its powerful vision of large-scale reform is an amazingly parsimonious one; it asserts that the magic of the market and the ballot box can be achieved merely by changing economic policy and allowing more political participation. It is also an amazingly apolitical vision, as it fails to identify many of the difficulties of implementation and process over time. As a result, the vision has significantly underestimated the time frame and "transaction costs" of transformation. Western actors have suffered from the "faults of analytic and policy hurry," that is, the desire to rush things along, whatever the path, to see things as real before they actually are, to attribute substantive weight to social processes, institutions, and actors who do not possess it.

As a result, they have also created undue expectations about what can be achieved in the Third and former Second Worlds over the medium run. Given the enormous obstacles confronting countries in these regions, overly optimistic expectations can be very dangerous. Slow, steady, consistent progress is far preferable. There are no shortcuts. The lessons of the "development administration" movement of the late 1960s and the 1970s should not be forgotten: that productive change in state capabilities and contextual variables comes about very slowly and unevenly. Change is incremental, uneven, often contradictory, and dependent on the outcome of unpredictable socioeconomic and political struggles. Policymakers, both at the international level and within reforming countries, must try to bring about important changes, but they need to retain a sense of the historical complexity involved. If not, undue expectations can get in the way of making slow but steady progress in overcoming difficult obstacles.

## Differentiation and Regional Redefinition

Because of these flaws and misperceptions in the Western liberal vision—along with the failure of the implicit bargain in most places, the concomitant officialization and politicization of resource flows, and continued difficulties with the openness of trade—it is not likely that the vision will be realized in very many places. The result will be increasing differentiation among countries and regions rather than accelerating convergence. This liberal vision emerged out of the core of the international political economy—the northern industrial democracies—and it is deeply rooted in their sociopolitical realities, dynamics, and weltanschauungs. It is also deeply rooted in the international hierarchy of power, imposed on much of the Third World and accepted voluntarily by parts of the Second World, often for lack of a viable counterfactual backed up by resources. In its contact with these worlds, the vision confronts local and regional realities, logics, struggles, politics, and histories and is frequently deflected by them.

There have always been contending political and socioeconomic definitions of the First, Second, and Third Worlds, and observers have tended to shift back and forth between them easily but often misleadingly. The political definitions are now being replaced by socioeconomic categories based on levels of overall economic development. The First World, essentially the OECD countries, is made up of the capitalist industrial democracies. A new and vigorous Second World is populated by newly industrializing countries such as Korea and Mexico. Much of the old Third World has remained fundamentally unchanged in this scheme, while parts of it suffering from increasing marginalization, dependence, and social decline (for example, large regions of Africa) have entered a Fourth World as wards of the international community.

A powerful "Third Worldization" of much of the former Second World is now underway. With considerable effort, external help, and luck, parts of it may enter the new Second World—possibly Hungary, the Czech Republic, and Poland, for example. A substantial portion of the heart of the former Soviet Union, however, has quickly become part of the Third World, while sections of its periphery may enter the Fourth World as part of a new world underclass. Parts of the Third and Fourth worlds may actually be reconfigured as the result of local and regional conflicts. Evidence of this already exists from Africa, the southern tier of Eastern Europe, and the periphery of the former Soviet Union. This resorting process poses considerable danger, since much of the old Second World retains important military and in some cases nuclear capabilities; the political/strategic consequences could be quite negative.

The resorting process reasserts all the messiness and explosive logics of the traditional state system and is not a sign of any "postmodern" transnational transformation or localization of world politics. Such interpretations arise from the hope for a better world. They often are also the result of believing in the myths we have created about the nature and development of the state system rather than acknowledging its historical realities.

The trajectory of individual countries will be affected by a series of interlinked internal and external factors. On the internal side, relatively high degrees of stateness and cosmopolitanism are central to position a country better in the international political economy; this includes particularly the ability to monitor changes in the world economy and to bargain in a sophisticated way with all types of actors—private business groups, states, international financial institutions, and private voluntary organizations. This is especially true in the areas of trade and credit, since the international political economy has always been more statist on these questions than most analysts are willing to admit. Whether increased stateness and cosmopolitanism will emerge in many places, however, is very questionable. Certainly local and regional political and social dynamics will affect attempts to achieve interlocked balanced tensions between state and market, state and society, and state and the international arena.

At bottom, we still live in a self-help world, and nobody should wait for external miracles that will restructure the international political economy to make it more fair or equitable. Despite all the rhetoric to the contrary, very few Western actors or publics believe they owe the Third or former Second worlds a living. A quietly held but pervasive view in the West is that if the fund and the bank can pull off miracles in the Third World, fine; if not, so be it; there are other places to go. As Peru demonstrates, however, the direct costs of neglect and downward spirals into the international underclass may be very high. Nonetheless, the West doesn't want to hear about and be inconvenienced by these costs. When they can be ignored no longer, resistance rather than assistance is likely to be the dominant reaction, inserting or reasserting malign tendencies into the domestic politics of Western liberal democracies.

Although it is largely a self-help world, external factors are important in determining the trajectories of specific countries. They revolve largely around the degree of openness of the world trading order, the extent to which the implicit bargain is fulfilled, and the stability of the overall political/strategic environment. The first two are very much in doubt, while the third depends greatly on the degree of effectiveness with which the new configuration—of unipolarity without hegemony—functions. It is not likely that embedded liberalism will be extended to much of the Third World. The resources and the will are simply not there. This may not be the case, however, for Russia and parts of Eastern Europe. The economic, political, strategic, and cultural interests of the major industrial democracies in these regions are harder to ignore. This is not to say, though, that Western support will be adequate to the task. Meanwhile, malign mercantilism and malign neglect may well be the fate of much of the Third and Fourth Worlds. The situation will be mitigated only to the degree that individual countries are able to employ self-help to project more effective demand and to use the resources of the state to make the most of existing conditions while attempting to transform them.

Over the course of the 1980s, the IMF, the World Bank, and the major Western countries learned some lessons about the difficulties of implementing the liberal vision. While many more remain to be learned, these lessons now need to be applied systematically to the Second and Third worlds, so that the gap between the vision and reality may be narrowed. This is particularly true for lessons about the implicit bargain, the need to buffer adjustment costs, the enormous challenges of simultaneous economic and political liberalization, the importance of a balanced tension between state and market, and the centrality of stateness, cosmopolitanism, and larger contextual factors. If these lessons are not learned and applied, then the brilliant Western liberal vision will remain seriously flawed and will be undermined by the powerful realities of politics. Whether the lessons can be applied will largely be a function of the domestic politics, resources, and capabilities of the Western liberal democracies themselves. The links between Western domestic politics and an international politics of half-hearted assistance, closure, and malign neglect are likely to be high.

## Notes

For the events of 1990–1992, this chapter has relied heavily on the coverage provided by the London *Financial Times*, the *New York Times*, the *Washington Post*, and the *Wall Street Journal*. I am well aware that some of the events described here, particularly for Eastern Europe and the former Soviet Union, have a short "shelf life," but they are presented here to illustrate both ongoing processes and larger conceptual and analytic points.

1. The concept of "embedded liberalism" is John Gerard Ruggie's; see his "International Regimes, Transactions and Change: Embedded Liberalism in the Postwar Economic Order," *International Organization* 36, no. 2 (Spring 1982), especially pp. 398–399, 405, 413. Robert Gilpin and Barry Buzan both prefer the term "benign mercantilism"; see Robert Gilpin, *The Political Economy of International Relations* (Princeton, NJ: Princeton University Press, 1987), pp. 404–405. I prefer "embedded liberalism" because it more accurately reflects the direction of policy change and the balancing point between state and market. On the Japanese version of it, see Kent E. Calder, *Crisis and Compensation: Public Policy and Political Stability in Japan* (Princeton, NJ: Princeton University Press, 1991).

2. See John Gerard Ruggie, "Political Structure and Change in the International Economic Order: The North-South Dimension" in *Antinomies of Interdependence,* ed. Ruggie (New York: Columbia University Press, 1983), pp. 423–487. I will argue below, however, that the need to extend the compromise of embedded liberalism may be more easily learned by Western governments for the former Second World of Eastern Europe and the Soviet Union precisely because more important interests and consequences are at stake.

3. Parts of the argument presented in this paper were developed as part of my participation in a multiyear, six-person research project on "The Politics of Economic Stabilization and Structural Change in Developing Nations," funded jointly by the Ford and Rockefeller foundations. The project produced three books: Joan M. Nelson, ed., *Fragile Coalitions: The Politics of Economic Adjustment* (New Brunswick, NJ: Transaction Books for the Overseas Development Council, 1989); Joan M. Nelson, ed., *Economic Crisis and Policy Choice: The Politics of Adjustment in the Third World* (Princeton, NJ: Princeton University Press, 1990); and Stephan Haggard and Robert Kaufman, eds., *The Politics of Adjustment: International Constraints, Distributive Conflicts and the State* (Princeton, NJ: Princeton University Press, 1992). I owe a great deal of gratitude to my five wonderful colleagues in this project—Stephan Haggard, Miles Kahler, Robert Kaufman, Joan Nelson, and Barbara Stallings, but they are not responsible for the argument presented here, nor may each of them fully agree with it, particularly in regard to the relationship between economic and political liberalization and the relevance of the argument to the former Second World. On the political economy of attempted neoclassical economic reform in the Third World, also see Paul Mosley, Jane Harrigan, and John Toye, *Aid and Power: The World Bank and Policy-Based Lending in the 1980s* (London: Routledge, 1990); Merilee S. Grindle and John W. Thomas, *Public Choices and Policy Change: The Political Economy of Reform in Developing Countries* (Baltimore, MD: Johns Hopkins University Press, 1991); and Gerald M. Meir, ed., *Politics and Policy Making in Developing Countries* (San Francisco, CA: International Center for Economic Growth, 1991).

4. Max Weber, *General Economic History* (New Brunswick, NJ: Transaction Books, 1981), and *Economy and Society* (Berkeley: University of California Press, 1978); Randall Collins, "Weber's Last Theory of Capitalism," *American Sociological Review* 45 (December 1980): 925–942; Karl Polanyi, *The Great Transforma-*

*tion* (New York: Rinehart, 1944); Alexander Gerschenkron, *Economic Backwardness in Historical Perspective* (Cambridge, MA: Harvard University Press, 1962); Douglass C. North and Robert Paul Thomas, *The Rise of the Western World: A New Economic History* (New York: Cambridge University Press, 1973); Douglass C. North, *Structure and Change in Economic History* (New York: Norton, 1981); Albert O. Hirschman, *The Passions and the Interests: Political Arguments for Capitalism Before Its Triumph* (Princeton, NJ: Princeton University Press, 1977); also see Thomas M. Callaghy, "The State and the Development of Capitalism in Africa: Theoretical, Historical, and Comparative Reflections" in *The Precarious Balance: State and Society in Africa*, ed. Donald Rothchild and Naomi Chazan (Boulder: Westview, 1988), pp. 67–99.

5. On the expanding comparative literature on these East Asian and Latin American cases, see Stephan Haggard, *Pathways from the Periphery* (Ithaca, NY: Cornell University Press, 1990); Frederic C. Deyo, ed., *The Political Economy of the New Asian Industrialism* (Ithaca, NY: Cornell University Press, 1987), especially Peter B. Evans, "Class, State and Dependence in East Asia: Lessons for Latin Americanists," pp. 203–226; Gary Gereffi and Donald L. Wyman, eds., *Manufacturing Miracles: Paths of Industrialization in Latin America and East Asia* (Princeton, NJ: Princeton University Press, 1990); Robert Wade, *Governing the Market: Economic Theory and the Role of Government in East Asian Industrialization* (Princeton, NJ: Princeton University Press, 1990), and "East Asia's Economic Success: Conflicting Perspectives, Partial Insights, Shaky Evidence," *World Politics* 44, no. 2 (January 1992): 270–320; and Ziya Onis, "The Logic of the Developmental State," *Comparative Politics* 24, no. 1 (October 1991): 109–126.

6. For lack of space, the interesting Bolivian case is not discussed here; see James M. Malloy, "Democracy, Economic Crisis and the Problem of Governance: The Case of Bolivia," typed manuscript, August 1989; Catherine M. Conaghan, James M. Malloy, and Luis A. Abugatta, "Business and the 'Boys': The Politics of Neoliberalism in the Central Andes," *Latin American Research Review* 25, no. 2 (1990): 3–30.

7. The Jamaican case is also not discussed here; see Joan M. Nelson, "The Politics of Adjustment in Small Democracies: Costa Rica, the Dominican Republic, and Jamaica" in Nelson, *Economic Crisis*, pp. 169–213.

8. Peter B. Evans, "The State as Problem and Solution: Predation, Embedded Autonomy, and Structural Change" in Haggard and Kaufman, *The Politics of Adjustment*; also see Richard F. Doner, "Limits of State Strength: Toward an Institutionalist View of Economic Development," *World Politics* 44, no. 3 (April 1992): 398–431; B. C. Koh, *Japan's Administrative Elite* (Berkeley: University of California Press, 1989).

9. For contending views, see Jagdish Bhagwati, *The World Trading System at Risk* (Princeton, NJ: Princeton University Press, 1991); Kenneth A. Oye, *The World Political Economy in the 1930s and 1980s: Economic Discrimination and Political Exchange* (Princeton, NJ: Princeton University Press, forthcoming); Gary Hufbauer, *The Free Trade Debate* (New York: Priority Press/Twentieth Century Fund, 1990); Susan Strange, "Protectionism and World Politics," *International Organization* 39, no. 2 (Spring 1985): 233–259; John M. Stopford and Susan Strange, *Rival States, Rival Firms: Competition for World Market Shares* (New York: Cambridge University Press, 1992); John Walley, *The Future of the World Trading System* (Washington, D.C.: Institute for International Economics, forthcoming Winter 1991–1992); OECD, *Trade, Investment, and Technology in the 1990s* (Paris: OECD, 1991); Jock A. Finlayson and Mark W. Zacher, *Managing International Markets: Developing Countries and the Commodity Trading Regime* (New York: Columbia University Press, 1988).

10. In order, *Financial Times*, 18 July 1991, 12 July 1991, 31 July 1991, 12 December 1990, 30 April 1992; also see Ulrich Koester and Malcolm D. Bale, "The Common Agricultural Program: A Review of Its Operations and Effects on Developing Countries," *The World Bank Research Observer* 5, no. 1 (January 1990): 95–121; Richard Arnold and Claude Villain, *New Directions for European Agricultural Policy* (Brussels: Centre for European Policy Studies, 1990); House of Lords Select Committee on the European Communities, *Development and the Future of the CAP* (London: HMSO, House of Lords, 16th Report, 1991); Henry R. Nau, ed., *Domestic Trade Politics and the Uruguay Round* (New York: Columbia University Press, 1988); Leah A. Haus, *Globalizing the GATT: The Soviet Union, East Central Europe, and the International Trading System* (Washington, D.C.: Brookings, 1991).

11. *Financial Times*, 16 June 1992. On the new Europe, see William Wallace, ed., *The Dynamics of European Integration* (London: Pinter, 1991); Gregory F. Treverton, ed., *The Shape of the New Europe* (New York: Council on Foreign Relations, 1991); Alberta B. Sbragia, ed., *Euro-Politics: Institutions and Policymaking in the 'New' European Community* (Washington, D.C.: Brookings, 1991); John Pinder, *European Community: The Building of a Union* (New York: Oxford University Press, 1991), and *The European Community and Eastern Europe* (New York: Council on Foreign Relations, 1991); Geoffrey Garrett, "International Cooperation and Institutional Choice: The European Community's Internal Market, *International Organization* 46, no. 2 (Spring 1992): 533–560; Michael Davenport and Sheila Page, *Europe: 1992 and the Developing World* (London: Overseas Development Institute, 1991); I. William Zartman, *Europe and Africa: the New Phase* (Boulder, CO: Lynne Rienner, 1992); Helen Wallace, ed., *The Wider Western Europe: Reshaping the EC/EFTA Relationship* (London: Pinter, 1990); Willem Molle, *The Economics of European Integration* (Brookfield, VT: Dartmouth University Press, 1990); Jeffrey Harrop, *The Political Economy of Integration in the European Community* (London: Edward Elgar, 1989).

12. For excerpts from a Camdessus speech on the "unwritten contract," see *IMF Survey* 19, no. 7 (2 April 1990): 108–111.

13. Peter Norman, *Financial Times*, 24 May 1991; also OECD, *1990 Report on Development Co-operation* (Paris: OECD, 1990).

14. See, for example, Hobart Rowen, "The Third World's Good News," *Washington Post National Weekly Edition*, 11–17 May 1992, p. 5. Rowen starts off by asking, "Remember the Third World debt crisis that was strangling poor countries and crippling major banks, on the hook for bad loans? It's over."

15. On G-7 coordination, see Paul Volcker and Toyoo Gyohten, *Changing Fortunes: The World's Money and the Threat to America's Leadership* (New York: Times Books, 1992); Ethan Barnaby Kapstein, "Between Power and Purpose: Central Bankers and the Politics of Regulatory Convergence," *International Organization* 46, no. 1 (Winter 1992): 265–287; Wendy Dobson, *Economic Policy Coordination: Requiem or Prologue?* (Washington, D.C.: Institute for International Economics, 1991); Warwick J. McKubbin and Jeffrey D. Sachs, *Global Linkages: Macroeconomic Interdependence and Cooperation in the World Economy* (Washington, D.C.: Brookings, 1991); Michael C. Webb, "International Economic Structures, Government Interests, and International Coordination of Macroeconomic Adjustment Policies," *International Organization* 43, no. 3 (Summer 1991): 309–342.

16. *Financial Times*, 25 September 1990.

17. *Washington Post National Weekly Edition*, 4–10 February 1991, p. 18.

18. Stanley Fischer, now a professor at MIT, *New York Times*, 8 July 1991.

19. B. A. Kiplagat quoted in "Africa Fears Its Needs Will Become Secondary," *New York Times*, 26 December 1989.

20. Most of the data in this section are from two companion reports: World Bank, *Global Economic Prospects and the Developing Countries 1991* (Washington, D.C.: World Bank, May 1991) and World Bank, *World Development Report 1991: The Challenge of Development* (New York: Oxford University Press, 1991); the focus of the latter for 1991 was the record of attempted economic reform in the 1980s. Additional data come from World Bank, *Global Economic Prospects and the Developing Countries 1992* (Washington, D.C.: World Bank, April 1992).

21. World Bank, *Global Economic Prospects 1991*, p. 17.

22. See Appendix D, "The Former Soviet Union in the World Economy," World Bank, *Global Economic Prospects 1992*, pp. 53–55.

23. World Bank, *Global Economic Prospects 1991*, pp. 6, 58 (emphases added).

24. World Bank, *Global Economic Prospects 1991*, pp. 58, 4.

25. World Bank, *Global Economic Prospects 1991*, pp. 6–7, 58–59.

26. World Bank, *World Development Report 1991*, pp. 28–29.

27. *Financial Times*, 19 October 1990, 6 August 1991; on Korea, in addition to the citations in note 5, see Stephan Haggard and Chung-in Moon, "The South Korean State in the International Economy: Liberal, Dependent, or Mercantile?" in Ruggie, *The Antinomies of Interdependence*, pp. 131–189; Alice H. Amsden, *Asia's Next Giant: South Korea and Late Industrialization* (New York: Oxford University Press, 1989); Larry E. Westphal, "Industrial Policy in an Export-Propelled Economy: Lessons from South Korea's Experience," *Journal of Economic Perspectives* 4, no. 3 (Summer 1990): 41–59; Il SaKong, *Korea and the World Economy* (Washington, D.C.: Institute for International Economics, Winter 1991); Jung-En Woo, *Race to the Swift: State and Finance in Korean Industrialization* (New York: Cambridge University Press, 1991); Ji-Hong Kim, "Korea: Adjustment in Developing Industries, Goverment Assistance in Troubled Economies" in *Pacific Basin Industries in Distress: Structural Adjustment and Trade Policy in Nine Industrialized Economies,* ed. Hugh T. Patrick (New York: Columbia University Press, 1991), pp. 357–417.

28. *Financial Times*, 2 July 1991; see Richard Baum, ed., *Reform and Reaction in Post-Mao China* (New York: Routledge, 1991); James A. Dorn and Wang Xi, eds., *Economic Reform in China: Problems and Prospects* (Chicago, IL: University of Chicago Press, 1990); Richard Feinberg et al., *Economic Reform in Three Giants* (New Brunswick, NJ: Transaction Books for ODC, 1990).

29. The head of Hong Kong's Chamber of Commerce, quoted in *Financial Times*, 24 April 1991; also World Bank, *China: Between Plan and Market* (Washington, D.C.: World Bank, 1990); Margaret M. Pearson, *Joint Ventures in the People's Republic of China: The Control of Foreign Direct Investment under Socialism* (Princeton, NJ: Princeton University Press, 1991); Ezra F. Vogel, *One Step Ahead in China: Gwandong under Reform* (Cambridge, MA: Harvard University Press, 1989); Denis Fred Simon, "China in the World Economic System," in *The China Challenge* ed. Frank J. Macchiarola and Robert B. Oxnam (New York: The Academy of Political Science, 1991), pp. 12–29.

30. *New York Times*, 28 June 1991; *Financial Times*, 16 April 1992.

31. See R. William Liddle, "The Relative Autonomy of the Third World Politician: Suharto and Indonesian Economic Development in Perspective," *International Studies Quarterly*, 35, no. 4 (December 1991): 403–427.

32. See Stephan Haggard, "The Political Economy of the Philippine Debt Crisis" in Nelson, *Economic Crisis*, pp. 215–255; Robin Broad, *Unequal Alliance:*

*The World Bank, the IMF, and the Philippines* (Berkeley: University of California Press, 1988); R. J. May, "The Political Economy of the Philippines" and David G. Timberman, "Civil Society, the State and Democracy in the Philippines" (Papers presented at the conference on "Economy, Society, and Democracy," Washington, D.C., May 1992); Paul D. Hutchcroft, "Oligarchs and Cronies in the Philippine State: The Politics of Patrimonial Plunder," *World Politics* 43 (April 1992): 414–450.

33. *New York Times*, 1 July 1992.

34. See Atul Kohli, *Democracy and Discontent: India's Growing Crisis of Governability* (New York: Cambridge University Press, 1991) and "Politics of Economic Liberalization in India," *World Development* 17, no. 3 (March 1989): 305–328; Ashutosh Varshney; "India's Democratic Exceptionalism and Its Troubled Trajectory" (Paper presented at the annual meeting of the American Political Science Association, San Francisco, 1990); Robert E. B. Lucas and Gustav F. Papanek, eds., *The Indian Economy: Recent Developments and Future Prospects* (Boulder, CO: Westview, 1988).

35. *Financial Times*, 22 February 1991.

36. *New York Times*, 25 July 1991, 8 July 1991, 29 June 1991, 26 June 1991; editorial entitled "Perestroika in India," *Financial Times*, 7 August 1991. See John Echeverri-Gent, "Economic Reform in India: A Long and Winding Road" in Feinberg, *Economic Reform in Three Giants*, pp. 103–133.

37. David Housego, "Chances Are Slipping Away," in "India," *Financial Times Survey*, 26 June 1992, p. 1.

38. *Financial Times*, 26 November 1990; on Mexico see Robert Kaufman, "Stabilization and Adjustment in Argentina, Brazil, and Mexico" in Nelson, *Economic Crisis*, pp. 63–111; Stephan Haggard, "Mexico and Brazil in Comparative Perspective," in Haggard, *Pathways,* pp. 161–188; Sylvia Ann Hewlitt and Richard S. Weinert, eds., *Brazil and Mexico: Patterns in Late Development* (Philadelphia, PA: ISHI, 1982); John K. Thompson, *Inflation, Financial Markets, and Economic Development: The Experience of Mexico* (Greenwich: Jai Press, 1979); Leopoldo Solis, *Economic Policy Reform in Mexico* (Elmsford, NY: Pergamon, 1981); Dale Story, *Industry, the State, and Public Policy in Mexico* (Austin: University of Texas Press, 1986). On Latin America generally see Jeffry A. Frieden, *Debt, Development and Democracy: Modern Political Economy and Latin America, 1965–1985* (Princeton, NJ: Princeton University Press, 1991); Barbara Stallings and Robert Kaufman, eds., *Debt and Democracy in Latin America* (Boulder, CO: Westview, 1989); William L. Canak, *Lost Promises: Debt, Austerity and Development in Latin America* (Boulder: Westview Press, 1989); John Williamson, ed., *Latin American Adjustment: How Much Has Happened?* (Washington, D.C.: Institute for International Economics, 1990); Karen L. Remmer, "Democracy and Economic Crisis: The Latin American Experience," *World Politics* (April 1990): 315–335, and "The Political Impact of Economic Crisis in Latin America in the 1980s," *American Political Science Review* 85, no. 3 (September 1991): 777–800. While Professor Remmer, contrary to much of the literature, argues correctly that economic crisis does not necessarily lead to the end of democracy, the argument here is that although, or rather because democracy survives, major economic transformation is made more difficult and thus not very common.

39. Susan Kaufman Purcell, "Mexico's New Economic Vitality," *Current History* (February 1992): 54–58.

40. See Barbara Stallings, "Politics and Economic Crisis: A Comparative Study of Chile, Peru, and Colombia," in Nelson, *Economic Crisis*, pp. 113–167; Sebastian Edwards and Alejandro Cox Edwards, *Monetarism and Liberalization:*

*The Chilean Experiment* (Cambridge, MA: Ballinger, 1987); Barbara Stallings, "The Political Economy of Democratic Transition: Chile in the 1980s," in Stallings and Kaufman, *Debt and Democracy*, pp. 181–199; Pamela Constable and Arturo Valenzuela, *A Nation of Enemies: Chile Under Pinochet* (New York: W.W. Norton, 1991); Carol Graham, "Democracy, Economic Reform, and Civil Society in Chile: The Merging of Democratic and Authoritarian Traditions," and Juan Andres Fontaine, "Economics and Politics in Transition in Chile, 1970–1990" (Papers presented at the conference on "Economy, Society, and Democracy," Washington, D.C., May 1992).

41. For Foxley's own earlier views, see Alejandro Foxley, *Latin American Experiments in Neoconservative Economics* (Berkeley: University of California Press, 1983).

42. IMF, *Managing Financial Risks in Indebted Developing Countries* (Washington, D.C.: IMF, 1990).

43. See Robert Kaufman, "Stabilization and Adjustment" in *The Politics of Debt in Argentina, Brazil, and Mexico: Economic Stabilization in the 1980s,* ed. Kaufman (Berkeley, CA: Institute of International Studies, 1988); Eliana A. Cardos and Albert Fishlow, "The Macroeconomics of the Brazilian External Debt," in *Developing Country Debt and the World Economy,* ed. Jeffrey Sachs (Chicago, IL: University of Chicago Press, 1989), pp. 88–92; Rudiger Dornbush and Juan Carlos De Pablo, "Debt and Macroeconomic Instability in Argentina" in Sachs, *Developing Country Debt,* pp. 37–57; Frieden, *Debt, Development and Democracy*; Ruth Berins Collier and Carlos H. Waisman, "Political and Economic Liberalization in Mexico and Argentina" (Paper presented at annual meeting of the American Political Science Association, San Francisco, 1990).

44. *Financial Times,* 15 May 1992, 29 June 1992.

45. *Financial Times,* 14 May 1992; Juan E. Corradi, "The Argentina of Carlos Menem," *Current History* (February 1992): 80–84.

46. See Stallings, "Politics and Economic Crisis," in *The Peruvian Experiment Reconsidered,* ed. Cynthia McClintock and Abraham Lowenthal (Princeton, NJ: Princeton University Press, 1983); Rosemary Thorp, "Adjustment Policies in Peru, 1978–1985: The Effects of Prolonged Crisis" in *Latin American Debt and the Adjustment Crisis,* ed. Rosemary Thorp and Laurence Whitehead (London: Macmillan, 1987), pp. 117–161; Richard Webb, *Stabilization and Adjustment Policies and Programmes: Country Study, Peru* (Helsinki: WIDER, 1987); David P. Werlich, "Fujimori and the 'Disaster' in Peru," *Current History* (February 1991): 61–64, 81–83; Manuel Pastor, Jr., *Inflation, Stabilization, and Debt: Macroeconomic Experiments in Peru and Bolivia* (Boulder, CO: Westview, 1992), and "Democracy, Distribution and Economic Performance in Peru" (Paper presented at the conference on "Economy, Society, and Democracy," Washington, D.C., May 1992); Cynthia McClintock, "Democracy and Civil Society in the Context of Economic Decline: Peru, 1980–1992" (Paper presented at the conference on "Economy, Society, and Democracy," Washington, D.C., May 1992).

47. Mario Vargas Llosa, "The Road to Barbarism," *New York Times,* 12 April 1992, p. 21; Raúl Alfonsín, "No Excuse for Fujimori," *Washington Post National Weekly Edition,* 27 April–3 May 1992.

48. *New York Times,* 15 April 1992; *New York Times,* 25 May 1992.

49. See George Kopits, *Structural Reform, Stabilization, and Growth in Turkey* (Washington, D.C.: IMF, 1987); Ziya Onis, "Redemocratization and Economic Liberalization in Turkey: The Limits of State Autonomy," typed manuscript, n.d.; Ziya Onis and Steven B. Webb, "The Political Economy of Policy Reform in Turkey in the 1980s" (Paper presented at the conference on "The Political Econ-

omy of Structural Adjustment in New Democracies," Washington, D.C., May 1992); John Waterbury, "The Export-Led Growth and the Center-Right Coalition in Turkey, *Comparative Politics* 24, no. 2 (January 1992): 127–145, and "The Political Context of Public Sector Reform and Privatization in Egypt, India, Mexico and Turkey," in *The Political Economy of Public Sector Reform and Privatization,* ed. Ezra Suleiman and John Waterbury (Boulder, CO: Westview, 1990), pp. 293–318; Roger Leeds, "Turkey: Rhetoric and Reality," in *The Promise of Privatization,* ed. Raymond Vernon (New York: Council on Foreign Relations, 1988), pp. 149–178; Ergun Ozbudan, "Turkey: Crises, Interruptions, and Reequilibrations," in *Democracy in Developing Countries: Asia,* ed. Larry Diamond, Juan J. Linz, and Seymour Martin Lipset (Boulder, CO: Lynne Rienner, 1989), pp. 187–230.

50. World Bank, *World Development Report 1990* (New York: Oxford University Press, 1990) and *IMF Survey* 19, no. 14 (1990): 210–213; also see Thomas M. Callaghy, "Africa and the World Economy: Caught Between a Rock and a Hard Place" in *Africa in World Politics,* ed. John W. Harbeson and Donald Rothchild (Boulder, CO: Westview, 1991), pp. 39–68; and "State and the Development of Capitalism in Africa" in *Hemmed In: Responses to Africa's Economic Decline,* Thomas M. Callaghy and John Ravenhill, eds. (New York: Columbia University Press, 1993), Trevor W. Parfitt and Stephen P. Riley, eds., *The African Debt Crisis* (London: Routledge, 1989).

51. Thomas M. Callaghy, "Lost Between State and Market: The Politics of Economic Adjustment in Ghana, Zambia, and Nigeria" in Nelson, *Economic Crisis,* pp. 257–319; Donald Rothchild, ed., *Ghana: The Political Economy of Recovery* (Boulder, CO: Lynne Rienner, 1991); Jeffrey Herbst, *The Politics of Economic Reform in Ghana* (Berkeley: University of California Press, 1993); Matthew Martin, *The Crumbling Facade of African Debt Negotiations: No Winners* (London: Macmillan, 1991).

52. See Callaghy, "Lost Between State and Society."

53. Thomas M. Callaghy, "Democracy and the Political Economy of Restraint and Reform in Nigeria" (Paper presented at the conference on "Economy, Society, and Democracy," Washington, D.C., May 1992).

54. *Africa News,* 22 June–5 July 1992.

55. On Cameroon and Zambia, see *New York Times,* 5 August 1991; on Zaire, see Thomas M. Callaghy, "The Political Economy of African Debt: the Case of Zaire" in *Africa in Economic Crisis,* ed. John Ravenhill (New York: Columbia University Press, 1986), pp. 307–346, and *The State-Society Struggle: Zaire in Comparative Perspective* (New York: Columbia University Press, 1984).

56. *The Times* (London), 4 June 1991.

57. *Financial Times,* 7 August 1991, 12 June 1991; on Zimbabwe, see Jeffrey Herbst, *State Politics in Zimbabwe* (Berkeley: University of California Press, 1990).

58. Quoted in Patti Waldmeir, "Dark Visions in a Crystal Ball," *Financial Times,* 19 August 1991, which discusses economic scenarios for South Africa.

59. Waldmeir, "Dark Visions"; Elliot Janeway, "The Smart Money Says South Africa," *New York Times,* 19 March 1990.

60. Derek Keys quoted in *Financial Times,* 28 April 1992.

61. *Philadelphia Inquirer,* 9 June 1991; Serge Schmemann, "Soviet Voices Cry Out for Drastic Solutions to the Economic Crisis," *New York Times,* 11 July 1991, p. A8.

62. Leonid Grigoriev, "Soviets Need a *Unified* Free Economy," *New York Times,* 12 September 1991; also see IMF, IBRD [World Bank], OECD, and EBRD,

*The Economy of the USSR, Summary and Results* (Washington, D.C.: IMF, December 1990); Central Intelligence Agency, *Beyond Perestroika: The Soviet Economy in Crisis* (Washington, D.C.: CIA, May 1991); David Lane, *Soviet Society under Perestroika,* 2d ed. (London: Unwin Hyman, 1991).

63. *Financial Times,* 9 August 1991; David A. Dyker, *Restructuring the Soviet Economy* (New York: Routledge, 1992); Ed A. Hewett and Victor H. Winston, eds., *Milestones in Glasnost and Perestroika* (Washington, D.C.: Brookings, 1991); Anders Aslund, *Gorbachev's Struggle for Economic Reform* (Ithaca, NY: Cornell University Press, 1991); Ed A. Hewett, *Open for Business: The Soviet Union and the Global Economy in the 1990s* (Washington, D.C.: Brookings, 1991); John Nellis, *Improving the Performance of Soviet Enterprises* (Washington, D.C.: World Bank Discussion Paper 118, 1991). The term "revolution by implosion" is Martian Malia's, "A New Russian Revolution?" *New York Review of Books,* 18 July 1991, p. 31; while I like his term, I do not agree with his conclusions.

64. *New York Times,* 29 October 1991; *Financial Times,* 29 October 1991.

65. *New York Times,* 2 June 1992.

66. *New York Times,* 2 March 1992.

67. *Financial Times,* 15 April 1992.

68. *New York Times,* 12, 15, 14 April 1992.

69. *New York Times,* 22 April 1992; *Financial Times,* 29 April 1992.

70. *New York Times,* 7 May 1992.

71. *New York Times,* 3 June 1992; *Financial Times,* 12 June 1992.

72. *New York Times,* 16 June 1992; *Philadelphia Inquirer,* 5 July 1992.

73. Steve Mufson, "The IMF Gives Russia a New Lease on Life," *Washington Post National Weekly Edition,* 4–10 May 1992.

74. *Financial Times,* 16 August 1991.

75. *New York Times,* 13 October 1991; *Financial Times,* 5–6 October 1991, 10 October 1991, 9–10 March 1991.

76. On Havel's vision, see "A Dream for Czechoslovakia," *New York Review of Books,* 25 June 1992, pp. 8–13; "The End of the Modern Era," *New York Times,* 1 March 1992; Havel, *Summer Meditations* (New York: Knopf, 1992); for a wonderful review of *Summer Meditations,* see Ralf Dahrendorf, "In Politics Begin Responsibilities," *New York Times Book Review,* 7 June 1992, pp. 1, 29.

77. *Washington Post National Weekly Edition,* 6–12 May 1991; Mark Kramer, "Eastern Europe Goes to Market," *Foreign Policy* 86 (Spring 1992): 134–157; Nancy Bermeo, ed., "Liberalization and Democratization in the Soviet Union and Eastern Europe," a special issue of *World Politics,* 44, no. 1 (October 1991); Ivo Banac, ed., *Eastern Europe in Revolution* (Ithaca, NY: Cornell University Press, 1992); Judy Batt, *East Central Europe: From Reform to Transformation* (New York: Council on Foreign Relations, 1991); Vittorio Corbo, Fabrizio Coricelli, and Jan Bossak, eds., *Reforming Central and Eastern European Economies: Initial Results and Challenges* (Washington, D.C.: World Bank, 1991); World Bank, *Czechoslovakia: Transition to a Market Economy* (Washington, D.C.: World Bank, 1991); Sharon Wolchik, *Czechoslovakia in Transition: Politics, Economics, and Society* (London: Pinter, 1991).

78. *Financial Times,* 3 September 1991; Bartlomiej Kaminski, *The Collapse of State Socialism: The Case of Poland* (Princeton, NJ: Princeton University Press, 1991); Anthony Polonsky and Stanislaw Gomulka, eds., *Polish Paradoxes* (London: Routledge, 1990); Simon Commander, ed., *Managing Inflation in Socialist Economies in Transition* (Washington, D.C.: World Bank, 1991); Mark E. Shaffer, *A Note On the Polish State-Owned Enterprises* (London: Centre for Economic Performance, London School of Economics, Discussion Paper No. 109, 1991); Paul

Hare and Gordon Hughes, *Competitiveness and Industrial Restructuring in Czechoslovakia, Hungary and Poland* (London: Centre for Economic Policy Research, Discussion Paper No. 543, 1991); S. Gomulka, *The Causes of Recession Following Stabilization* (London: Centre for Economic Performance, London School of Economics, Working Paper No. 95, 1991).

79. *New York Times*, 16 October 1991; the Walesa quote is from an editorial entitled "Why Poland Can't Flinch," *New York Times*, 26 October 1991; Simon Johnson and Marzena Kowalska, "The Transformation of Poland, 1989–1991" (Paper presented at the conference on "The Political Economy of Structural Adjustment in New Democracies," Washington, D.C., May 1992).

80. *New York Times*, 19 March 1992; *Financial Times*, 27 April 1992.

81. *New York Times*, 17 May 1992.

82. *New York Times*, 11 September 1991; *Financial Times*, 10 September 1991; Leah Haus, "The East European Countries and GATT: The Role of Realism, Mercantilism, and Regime Theory in Explaining East-West Trade Negotiations," *International Oranization* 45, no. 2 (Spring 1991) 163–182; John Williamson, *The Economic Opening of Eastern Europe* (Washington, D.C.: Institute for International Economics, 1991); John Williamson, ed., *Currency Convertibility in Eastern Europe* (Washington, D.C.: Institute for International Economics, 1991).

83. *New York Times*, 11 September 1991; Susan M. Collins and Dani Rodrik, *Eastern Europe and the Soviet Union in the World Economy* (Washington, D.C.: Institute for International Economics, 1991); Richard F. Staar, ed., *East-Central Europe and the USSR* (New York: St. Martin's, 1992).

84. Aleksa Djilas, *New York Times*, 7 July 1991.

85. A Morgan Stanley report cited in *Washington Post National Weekly Edition*, 7–13 January 1991, p. 9.

86. World Bank, *World Development Report 1991*, p. 5, also see pp. 39–40.

87. Tony Killick, *A Reaction Too Far* (Boulder, CO: Westview, 1990).

88. Christopher Colclough and James Manor, eds., *States or Markets? Neo-Liberalism and the Development Policy Debate* (New York: Oxford University Press, 1991).

89. Atul Kohli, "Democracy and Development" in *Development Strategies Reconsidered,* ed. John P. Lewis and Valeriana Kallab (New Brunswick, NJ: Transaction Books for ODC, 1986), pp. 156, 159, 156.

90. Kohli, "Democracy and Development," pp. 159–160.

91. Haggard, *Pathways*, p. 264 (emphasis added), 256, 267 (emphases added); also see Adam Przeworski, *Democracy and the Market: Political and Economic Reforms in Eastern Europe and Latin America* (New York: Cambridge University Press, 1991); Dietrich Rueschemeyer, Evelyne Huber Stephens, and John D. Stephens, *Capitalist Development and Democracy* (Chicago, IL: University of Chicago Press, 1992); Nancy Bermeo, "Democracy and the Lessons of Dictatorship," *Comparative Politics* 24, no. 3 (April 1992): 253–272; John Dunn, ed., *The Economic Limits to Modern Politics* (New York: Cambridge University Press, 1990).

92. Albert O. Hirschman, "Reactionary Rhetoric," *Atlantic Monthly* 263, no. 5 (May 1989): 63.

93. Hirschman, "Reactionary Rhetoric," p. 70.

94. Atul Kohli, "Democracy and Development," p. 178.

95. P. Collier, "Africa's External Economic Relations: 1960–1990," *African Affairs*, 90 (1991): 340, 339.

96. John B. Goodman, *Monetary Sovereignty: The Politics of Central Banking in Western Europe* (Ithaca, NY: Cornell University Press, 1992), p. 6, n. 12; also

see Stanley Fischer, "Dynamic Inconsistency, Cooperation, and the Benevolent Dissembling Government," *Journal of Economic Dynamics and Control* 2 (1980): 93–107; Ellen Kennedy, *The Bundesbank: Germany's Central Bank in the International Monetary System* (New York: Council on Foreign Relations, 1991); William Nordhaus, "The Political Business Cycle," *Review of Economic Studies* 42 (April 1975): 169–190; Alex Cukierman, Steven B. Webb, and Bilin Neypati, "The Measurement of Central Bank Independence and its Effect on Policy Outcomes" (Paper presented at the Fourth NBER Conference on Political Economy, Cambridge, Massachusetts, 15–16 November 1991). The latter paper, an examination of 70 central banks in both developed and less developed countries, starts with a wonderful quote from Arnold Lobel's *Frog and Toad Together* (1972) which vividly illustrates the paradox of central bank independence:

> "Will power is trying hard *not* to do something that you really want to do," said Frog.
> "You mean like trying *not* to eat all these cookies," asked Toad.
> "Right," said Frog. He put the cookies in a box. "There, now we will not eat any more cookies."
> "But we can open the box," said Toad.
> "That is true," said Frog. He tied some string around the box. He got a ladder and put the box up on a high shelf. "There, now we will not eat any more cookies."
> "But we can climb the ladder."

97. See Callaghy, "Democracy and the Political Economy of Restraint and Reform in Nigeria."

98. Collier, "Africa's External Economic Relations," p. 134, and his talk of the same title (Presented at Center for International Affairs, Harvard University, 6 March 1992).

99. David Stockman, *The Triumph of Politics: The Inside Story of the Reagan Revolution* (New York: Avon, 1987).

100. See Raymond Aron's discussion of Tocqueville's views on democracy in *Main Currents in Sociological Thought*, vol. 1 (New York: Anchor Books, 1968), p. 259; also see Joan M. Nelson and Stephanie J. Eglinton, *Encouraging Democracy: What Role for Conditioned Aid?* (Washington, D.C.: Overseas Development Council, 1992).

101. For a theoretical argument about contextual factors that draws on Max Weber, see Callaghy, "State and the Development of Capitalism in Africa"; also see Douglass C. North, *Institutions, Institutional Change, and Economic Performance* (New York: Cambridge University Press, 1990); Thrainn Eggertsson, *Economic Behavior and Institutions* (New York: Cambridge University Press, 1990).

# 9

# Global Economic Transformation and Less Developed Countries

## Michael Dolan

This chapter investigates the major structural changes of the global economy the last two decades and their impact on developing countries. Looking backward in time over the vast panoply of change that the global economy has undergone, and continues to undergo, two major themes seem to emerge. The first, *globalization,* is quite topical; it refers to the process of gradual elimination of economic borders and concomitant increase in international exchange and transnational interaction. Globalization is a complex and problematic process, however, and this has tended to hinder a precise understanding of the nature of change denoted by the term, despite its popularity. While the term has fairly recent origins, the process has been ongoing for several decades; labels used in earlier periods included international interdependence, transnationalization, and the changing international division of labor. Indeed, one change that is frequently presented as an aspect of globalization, namely regionalization (for example, the increased integration of the European Community), is seen here as a recent protectionist reaction to the onrush of globalization.

The other theme that emerges from the experiences of the last decade has been called the *crisis of hegemony.* Since the Second World War, the global political economy has been dominated by the United States. Although the recent Gulf war evidenced continuing U.S. leadership in military matters, economically, the primacy of the United States has dissipated in the face of Japanese and European development. While debate continues among U.S. scholars and policymakers as to how the United States should react to the relative demise of its economic power, it is not clear that a succeeding hegemony will even be constituted by states rather than by transnational forces. Indeed, the two themes seem to merge in that the resolution of the crisis of U.S. hegemony may be resolved with the emergence of a global hegemony of transnational forces. While I tend to regard this development with extreme suspicion, many globalists support this movement, arguing that the solution to global problems will only appear when state power is subject to transnational control. This subject, however, goes beyond our present concern, which is with the impact of global change on less developed countries (LDCs).

From a perspective that highlights globalization and the crisis of hegemony, we can see several specific structural changes and problems that plague LDCs. The decade of the 1980s saw tumultuous change—the breakdown of socialism in the East, the growth of regional trading blocs across the advanced industrial economies, and the continuing problem of decapitalization of the South due to debt servicing. While the debt crisis obviously involves LDCs, the collapse in the East and the increasing regionalization of world trade also directly affect the Third World. Another structural change is underway, moreover, which, although less visible than Third World debt and the collapse of socialism in the East, may nonetheless be as important as the debt crisis in its impact on industrialization among less developed countries. I am referring to the restructuring of industrial production in the countries of the North. This change from an emphasis on mass production to one of flexible specialization is beginning to impinge directly upon LDCs.

The thesis I develop in this chapter is that the global crisis of the last 20 years has generally inhibited development in Third World countries, and that the immediate future for these countries is bleak. I shall begin with a general explanation of the genesis of the varied structural changes and problems that I have identified. The dramatic events of the 1980s, from the debt crisis to the collapse in the East, as well as less obvious changes—the increasing regionalization of world trade and the restructuring of industrial production—emerged from the general economic crisis of the 1970s. The collapse of socialism is most distant from this general explanation, although it too is related to the structural crisis in the West in the 1970s.

### From Structural Crisis to Structural Change: The Economic Crisis of the 1970s

Although I am primarily interested here in the troubling economic aspects of global change during this period, the crisis can be understood more broadly as well. This is the crisis of hegemony, used in a Gramscian sense—in short, a crisis of legitimacy. This crisis has occurred in different ways both in Western countries and in the former Soviet Union and its satellites. Crisis and transformation in both worlds have a direct impact on LDCs, but because the Third World countries are more closely linked to Western economies and are more profoundly affected by them, I will give more emphasis to Western experiences.

In the early postwar period there was much concern in Western countries that the world would slip back into the prewar depression. Although the causes of the depression were much debated, overproduction or under-consumption was widely recognized as a dominant aspect of the depression, and it became a priority to avoid repeating this calamity. The postwar period thus witnessed the general emergence of a rough compromise across capital, labor, and the state to tie the growth of wages to that of productivity. This intensive mode of accumulation essentially allowed workers in the advanced economies to consume what they produced. The compromise stuck because rising profits satisfied capital, while increasing consumption—and the welfare conditions provided by the state—kept labor quiescent. This emphasis on working-class consumption led to the development of mass production industries that specialized in standardized goods, particularly consumer durables. The regime of accumulation and mode of regulation have become known as "Fordism," after the pioneering work of Henry Ford in establishing mass production methods and the mass consumption patterns made possible by the assembly line.[1]

The implication of this mode of accumulation for trade with the South was negative, in that the producers in the advanced industrial countries did not have to depend on markets in the Third World. In the mid-1960s, the exports of manufactures to LDCs fell to 0.8 percent of GDP in the United States, and 2 percent in the EC.[2] Instead, the advanced industrial countries depended on LDCs primarily for the raw materials and agricultural produce that they could not attain cheaply in the domestic market. This relationship mirrored the "classic" or nineteenth-century international division of labor, although import substitution industrialization in the South began to displace some of the reliance on Northern factories.

The postwar boom and the Fordist compromise began to deteriorate in the late 1960s as the growth of labor and capital productivity slowed.[3] The consumer goods markets in the industrialized countries became saturated through the substantial increase in trade among Western economies, and to a much lesser extent through trade with a few LDCs that were adopting export-oriented strategies. By the early 1970s private investment reacted to the slowed increase in productivity, and eventually with the fall in investment came rising unemployment. Benign neglect of mounting dollar deficits in the United States led to widespread inflation. The situation was exacerbated by the uncertainty of floating exchange rates and then the oil price rise in 1973. The severe recession of 1974 was intensified by deflationary policies instituted across the advanced industrial countries, as well as by the impact of the first oil crisis. Moreover, the nature of the recovery in 1975 and the slow growth exhibited through the end of the decade reflected the fact that the crisis was only deepening.

The changing international division of labor—the movement of LDCs to export manufactured goods—was accelerated in the 1970s by the transfer of investment capital to the Third World to escape the profit squeeze engendered by the slow growth in productivity in the advanced industrial countries. These investments in LDCs occurred variously for reasons of scale, cheap labor, technology, and the import substitution and export substitution polices in the Third World. The capital movement by multinational corporations in the advanced industrial countries was thus complemented by the increasingly popular export strategies adopted across LDCs. The substantial and multifaceted state support in the North for multinational involvement in LDCs was relatively uncontentious until the second half of the 1970s. Thereafter it became increasingly problematic; by then the crisis was clearly no longer a "technical" one. High unemployment, high inflation, and the failed attempts of governments to combat them made the crisis evident to all. Domestic capital and organized labor reacted to the blossoming of the crisis by attacking the "exporting of jobs" abroad. Labor and domestic capital wanted scapegoats and two identifiable targets were multinational corporations and the imports from LDCs.

The alliance between labor and an important fraction of capital proved impossible for the state to ignore. It muted its support for the internationalization of production while it sought to respond to the new domestic pressures raised by these broad segments of society. It attempted particularly to address the needs of those industrial sectors undergoing rapid structural change. State supports for failing industries came in a myriad of ways, but they were of two general types: imports could be restricted, predominately through the "new protectionism," or the industries could be subsidized directly through various forms of state aid. Ironically, the new protectionism forced LDCs to move further into capital- and technology-intensive production much more quickly than they would have done otherwise, exacerbating the crisis and forcing more protectionist measures. In sum, then, the halcyon period for the changing international division of labor in the advanced industrial countries, when it had the active support of states and was actively opposed in only a few industrial sectors, was doomed by circumstance to be a short one. For a variety of reasons, the South was initially better able to avoid the crisis that hung over the advanced industrial countries, but it too eventually fell on hard times.

In the 1980s, the welfare state and labor unions came to be seen in some official quarters as the major contributors to the crisis. Governments in the advanced industrial countries began to withdraw from the postwar Fordist compromise. They moved to relieve the state of responsibility for their economies, suggesting that markets must play a much greater role than they played during the postwar boom. To insulate themselves politically from the vagaries of the market, governments moved to deregulate their economies. Thus, Thatcherism in Great Britain and Reaganism in the United States promoted the ideal of a neoclassical economy that operates largely without fetters (a mode of regulation which Lipietz calls "liberal productivism").[4] Before proceeding, though, to further discussion on changing modes of regulation, I shall outline the structural changes and problems that stemmed from the crisis and their implications for the Third World.

## Third World Debt

Of the several structural problems faced by LDCs that are addressed in this chapter, debt is the most obdurate and long-standing one. Its genesis dates clearly from the crisis of the North in the 1970s. From 1973–1979, manufacturing output in LDCs grew an average 5.6 percent per year, twice as fast as in the advanced industrial countries. (This can be compared to the years 1963–1973 when the South grew more rapidly, at 7.8 percent, but not much faster than the North, at 6.6 percent, and from a much smaller base.)[5] Within the South, the East Asian NICs grew at a pace greater than 10 percent. Undoubtedly these growth rates were achieved because of widening middle and working classes in LDCs, and because of factors that we have already discussed—changing state policy in developing countries and the activity of multinational corporations. After 1975, however, the primary source of capital for LDCs was the huge sums of petrodollars lent to them by Northern banks at moderate interest rates. Ironically, then, the oil price rise and the stagnating economies of the advanced industrial countries provided the capital that was desperately needed in LDCs. The rise in debt was roughly matched by an increase in export earnings, so that debt as a proportion of export earnings, which was around 15.9 percent in 1973 remained at this level until 1977.[6] Interest rates, however, began to rise as a result of state policies in the United States and other advanced industrial countries to reduce inflation, and the debt service ratio began to climb—reaching 19 percent in 1979. After the recession began in 1980, borrowing dropped off considerably (as compared with the period from 1973 to 1979, when it trebled), but this could not prevent a crisis. Interest rates skyrocketed in the early 1980s, so that interest payments became more than 50 percent of the debt servicing. By 1984, as a result of the deep recession and increasing protectionism in the North, debt servicing to export receipts for LDCs reached 33.4 percent, with some countries reaching much higher levels.[7]

Debt was not the only constraint on LDCs. Two other problems were alluded to earlier: On the one hand, markets in the North were becoming saturated, and the "new protectionism" that arose in the 1970s was directed primarily against LDCs. On the other hand, as the statistics indicate, the NICs appropriated much of the South's manufacturing exports. In light of the increasing saturation of Northern markets for consumer goods, the very success of those few LDCs made more problematic the export strategies of the other LDCs.

It would be erroneous, moreover, to argue that it was only external constraints that plagued the export strategies of many LDCs in the 1970s. At least for some countries, the domestic contradictions of export development go far in explaining the failures of the 1970s. These failures occurred because, for particular historical reasons, some states among the LDCs supported multinational corporations whose concerns were with dumping old and excess machinery and to produce for a protected domestic market. In these instances, the LDCs sacrificed support for local capital, which, when it had an interest in developing its own technological capacity, showed that it could export abroad, sometimes despite the international competition for increasingly saturated markets. Finally, mismanagement and corruption in official circles were culpable to some degree.

If the second half of the 1970s signaled a change in the trajectory of the changing international division of labor, the 1980s have certainly confirmed the new trend. In the first half of the 1980s, the economies of the developing countries grew very slowly, an average annual increase of 0.9 percent of GDP and 2.6 percent of manufacturing output.[8] This period of slow growth reflected the depression of 1981–1982 in the North, where exceedingly high real interest rates were used to shake the economies of the advanced industrial countries free from inflation. The North looked to the markets of the developing countries to make up for their own sluggish markets, as they had also done, albeit inadequately, in the 1970s. However, the debt crisis in the South prevented that; unable to pay for imports and needing export earnings to service its debts, LDCs had to establish strong trade balances. Between 1982 and 1989, the Third World had an annual average surplus of $26 billion (the equivalent of 3.3 percent of GDP).[9] These trade surpluses were achieved mainly by the use of austerity programs to squeeze imports; attempts to increase exports were diminished by protectionism and slow growth in the North.

What makes these surpluses more remarkable is that they came in the midst of the relative decline in unit value of the South's exports relative to their imports from the North. The South's terms of trade—except for the NICs that do not rely on the export of primary commodities—deteriorated continuously over the decade. For Africa and the 15 most heavily indebted countries, the terms of trade dropped anywhere from 25 to 50 percent, depending on the country.[10] Nevertheless, these surpluses were needed to help repay Northern creditors. For the first time in the postwar period, officially recorded capital flows to Northern countries exceeded incoming flows.[11] In the 1984–1989 period, Latin America paid Northern creditors $153 billion more than they borrowed from them.[12]

The magnitude of this transfer of wealth to Northern creditors was compounded by a flight of capital from LDCs. In regard to direct foreign investment, the amount of private investment that abandoned the stagnating conditions of the South was greater than the amount of new investment that came in to capitalize them. Since 1982, foreign investment in LDCs relative to that in the North has declined to a level lower than that characteristic of the 1960s.[13] Furthermore, the wealth of Third World elites has increasingly been transferred to Northern countries. The Bank for International Settlements suggests that assets held abroad by Latin American residents may even exceed the region's debt to Northern banks.[14] The total net transfers over the decade of the 1980s constitute an incredible amount of wealth. According to one study, by 1986 LDCs had already transferred over $250 billion—a sum that, when adjusted for inflation, is more than four times the $13 billion of the Marshall Plan.[15]

The implications of this transfer of wealth from South to North are summarized in Table 9.1. Average annual per capita GDP growth in sub-Saharan Africa for the 1980s was a -2.2 percent; for Latin America and the Caribbean it was a -0.6 percent. Only LDCs of East Asia recorded a substantial positive rate of growth. The regions suffering from negative growth rates are those with debt-servicing problems. Sub-Saharan Africa, which includes many of the lowest-income LDCs, has the highest debt *per capita* and debt-servicing ratios, with four/fifths of its debt owed to official creditors. Latin America, containing many of the middle-income LDCs, is the most indebted region, with about half of its debt owed to commercial banks. The East Asian NICs—the high-income LDCs—also found themselves quite heavily indebted in the 1980s, but they were much more successful in reducing their debt load. South Korea, for example, reduced its debt by 30 percent over three years in the late 1980s.

Another impact of the debt crisis has been the decrease of South-South trade, especially in technology-related goods. South-South trade is valuable for development because it is more likely to be technology intensive than are exports destined for Northern markets. Indeed, producers in the South have some advantages over their Northern counterparts vis-à-vis Southern markets because of the similarity of markets as well as greater specialization in technologies that produce simple and robust products. As

**Table 9.1   Growth of Real Per Capita GDP by Period**

| Region | 1965–1973 % | 1973–1980 % | 1980–1989 % |
|---|---|---|---|
| Sub-Saharan Africa | 3.2 | 0.1 | -2.2 |
| Latin America and Caribbean | 3.7 | 2.6 | -0.6 |
| East Asia | 5.1 | 4.7 | 6.7 |
| South Asia | 1.2 | 1.7 | 3.2 |
| Middle East, North Africa, and LDCs in Europe | 5.5 | 2.1 | 0.8 |
| Eastern Europe | 4.8 | 5.3 | 0.8 |

*Source:* Adapted from *World Development Report 1990* (p. 11).

a result of these advantages, South-South trade in the 1970s grew more quickly than North-South trade.[16] However, by the mid-1980s, South-South trade had declined, in some cases rather dramatically.[17] LDCs have been unable to extend necessary export credits. Moreover, they have had to concentrate their exports on countries that would earn them convertible currency for servicing their debt. The use of countertrade has not been sufficient to offset these obstacles.

LDCs have made a sustained effort to reduce their debt, including such conversion operations as buy-backs, debt equity swaps and private sector discounted prepayments. Despite these efforts, the South's debt continues to grow and is expected to reach $1,354 billion by the end of 1991. About half of the debt is held by those with debt-servicing problems. Moreover, commercial debt is falling (ever so slightly), and the percentage of debt owed to public creditors had increased to 42 percent as of 1989; it was expected to grow to 45 percent as of 1991.[18] Finally, except for the lowest-income group of countries, debt-servicing ratios to GDP and exports have been decreasing marginally since 1986.

The response of the North to the debt crisis has been very disappointing. OECD countries have converted about $5 billion from debt to grants; the World Bank and the IMF have instituted special adjustment programs, amounting roughly to $5 billion; and since the Toronto summit of 1988, special concessions amounting to the consolidation of another $5 billion have been made to low-income LDCs.[19] For middle-income LDCs, the Brady Plan has been used to restructure commercial debt in a few countries. Relative to the scale of the debt, the level of assistance has been paltry and just sufficient for debt-ridden countries to avoid bankruptcy. It is difficult to comprehend this failure to help, especially when one considers the tremendous transfer of wealth from South to North over the last decade. Keeping LDCs at subsistence levels internationally has enabled the North to pursue some long-term goals. Northern countries, either directly or through the IMF and World Bank, have used the debt crisis to force many LDCs to denationalize their economies. Import barriers have been dismantled, financial markets have been deregulated, and state-owned enterprises have been privatized. What Northern governments had been unable to negotiate in international trade and financial fora, they have achieved in debt rescheduling.

What does all this mean? What future is there for debt-ridden countries? After the deep recession of 1980–1982, the debt crisis involved both the LDCs *and* the many Northern banks who had overextended themselves in the South. Although there may well continue to be rough sledding for a few commercial banks, most banks have had sufficient time to insulate themselves, while governments and international organizations have helped others enough, so that the crisis in the North has essentially been resolved. However, for the South the debt situation (outside the Asian

NICs) remains critical, despite marginal improvements in many countries. The problem is that the peoples in these poor countries have undergone deprivation for a decade merely to regain their countries' debt situation of about 1982—and many countries have not recovered even to this extent. The living standards for much of Latin America are now lower than they were in the early 1970s; for sub-Saharan Africa, the conditions are close to the 1960s. If these regions continue to transfer wealth to the North as they did in the 1980s, it will be difficult to fathom the additional suffering that they will endure in this decade.

## The Collapse in the East

Of the structural changes and problems identified as having serious implications for LDCs, the political and economic collapse of Eastern socialism is most removed from the economic crisis described above. Nevertheless, while the wholesale changes in the East have been rooted in the particular contradictions of various political economies, the Eastern countries have also been seriously wounded in their relations with the West. While beyond the scope of this chapter, economic development in the socialist countries began to exhaust itself in the late 1960s and early 1970s. These countries had undergone "extensive development"—economic growth through the exploitation of increasing factors of production without an appreciable increase in technology and productivity—which had been fairly successful in the early stages of industrial development, but had now essentially reached its limits. In the 1970s, the East European governments strengthened their ties with Western, particularly West European, companies in an attempt to upgrade their economies' technological base and to borrow heavily from Western banks to buy or license new technologies. The intent of these governments was that exports from their agricultural sector and their newly revamped industrial sector would service the growing debt.

As was the case with LDCs, this intent was frustrated in part by the "new protectionism" in the West. West European governments found it easy to sacrifice imports from the East to protectionist demands at home. Instead of repaying their debts, therefore, East European governments piled up larger and larger ones. Again, in a fashion similar to the Third World experience, when interest rates rose in the early 1980s, a serious problem became a financial crisis. In contrast, though, to the situation in the LDCs, the Eastern European countries were quite successful during the 1980s in reducing their debt to manageable levels. The authoritarian regimes simply cut back on their imports, building up hard currency on their trade surpluses with the West to pay down their debt. The problem with this strategy was that it exacted an enormous cost on the people. While many LDCs also cut back on imports, and incurred a significant social cost, LDCs were not as successful in reducing imports as were the East European governments. The result in the East eventually was a loss of political and economic legitimacy. To a certain extent, people had been willing to accept the scarcity of political freedoms in return for egalitarian economic growth. When economic stagnation was followed by increasingly serious deprivation, the end of authoritarian socialism in the East was near. Actual dissolution came when the Soviet Union—too seriously mired in its own crisis to spare concern for its satellites—finally loosened its grip on them.

It is not clear what the collapse of Eastern political economies will bring. Transformation seems to follow the Western trend of the 1980s toward marketization and privatization, the latter to occur primarily through foreign investment. Until the mid-1980s, little foreign capital was invested in Eastern Europe, but this changed when the U.S.S.R. moved to allow foreign investment beginning in 1987. After fairly dramatic initial increases in foreign participation in the region, growing economic instability and deepening political turmoil have slowed capital inflows considerably since 1990. However, in the long run, huge amounts of foreign investment are anticipated. In the meantime, Western official aid is expected and needed to get the Soviet Union and Eastern European countries through this very difficult period. Western governments and international agencies have been active in their attempts to integrate the Eastern countries into the global economy. To date, the economic assistance has come in the form of debt relief, credit packages, trade liberalization, and training programs; much more will be needed in coming years.

### Implications of the Collapse in the East for the Third World

For the South, the economic implications of structural change in Eastern Europe are generally negative. This assessment is based on an analysis of East-South relations as well as the impact of changing East-West relations on less developed countries.

While not as extensively developed generally as West-South relations, in some respects, East-South ties (before the collapse of the Soviet Union) resembled the former's traditional division of labor. The South predominantly supplied Eastern Europe (particularly East Germany and Czechoslovakia) and the Soviet Union with industrial raw materials in return for manufactured goods, especially machinery and equipment (including military armaments). Overlaying this economic rationale was a political (or strategic) one, as relations were concentrated on a relatively small number of LDCs (this number varying over time as countries fell in or out of favor with the Soviet Union). The countries in this patron-client relationship were also treated to considerable aid, frequently given in preferential trade credits. It has been estimated that the cumulative cost to the Soviet

Union amounted in 1989 to $60 billion, a sum greater than all Soviet hard-currency liabilities.[20]

The East-South relationship has generally diminished in importance since the mid-1970s, and especially in the last decade. For the South's part, it was frustrated in its attempt to substitute manufactures for raw materials in its exports to the East, much as it was with the West. On the other hand, manufactured imports from the East faced increasing competition from Western and Southern countries (especially but not only from the newly industrializing countries). Moreover, because of economic problems outlined above, the East was increasingly unable or unwilling to carry the costs of its informal empire. Politically, as the Cold War dissipated, East-South relations suffered as the Soviet Union and Eastern Europe focused on developing their economic ties with the West. This slipping of bonds was difficult for those LDCs that had grown to rely on Soviet and Eastern assistance and credits.

Exceptions do exist to this secular trend, however, and these bear some promise of a different future for East-South relations. As political and strategic factors underlying East-South relations dissipate, a more sound commercial relationship may develop and help diversify relations. While East-South ties were more trade- than investment-related, a recent study found an increase in Eastern investment activity in the South, perhaps indicating the presence of flight capital in the East, as well as the growth of Southern investment in the U.S.S.R.[21] Regarding trade, to date any increases in exports to the East have been limited to a few LDCs, especially the Asian newly industrializing countries. Only with the development of Eastern markets, as with a similar development in the Asian NICs, will the commodity exporters of the South gain economic benefits from socialist-to-capitalist restructuring.

Changing East-West relations are likely to affect the South even more than shifting East-South ties. As noted above, the East has a tremendous need for capital as the economies restructure into a more capitalist mode. Western governments have been somewhat forthcoming in providing assistance and they are going to be asked to be much more generous as the 1990s progress. Despite some protestations that this aid will not be taken from funds targeted for LDCs, that transfer indeed describes what has happened. For example, the Canadian government has included the Soviet Union and the other countries of Eastern Europe in its new "international assistance envelope." The head of Canadian International Development Agency warned that this economic assistance would most likely come at the expense of LDCs, and that the move could seriously affect the delivery of Canadian aid.[22] Where else can Western governments find money that is unprotected by domestic recipients?

Investment is another source of foreign capital, and here LDCs may not compete well with East European economies. As noted, the countries with debt-servicing difficulties have not been very successful in attracting foreign investment. Eastern European countries have been somewhat more successful because of proximity to Western European markets and because of a generally more developed infrastructure. With many of the restrictions on foreign investment in the process of removal, East European economies are going to be even more attractive to Western investors. However, one study suggests that some Western companies, especially large multi-nationals, approach the East as an addition rather than an alternative to ventures in the South.[23] LDCs may be most severely affected by firms pursuing all-European strategies as a result of Europe 1992.

Finally, there are the trade effects of changing East-West economic relations. Again, the greatest threat to LDCs may be with regard to exports to Western Europe. Although trade between Eastern and Western Europe has been substantial for years, the growth of Western investment in the East will spell more trouble for Southern exporters in the future. As well, Eastern economic liberalization and the proximity to Western Europe will given an advantage to Eastern raw materials and manufactured goods in supplying the economic needs of the new Europe. More generally, one recent study concluded that labor-intensive goods from middle-income LDCs were likely to suffer most from changing East-West relations.[24]

In sum, then, the transformation of Eastern economies offers some promise for LDCs, especially the Asian NICs, but the outlook for the lower- and middle-income countries of the South—that is, the brunt of the Third World—is bleak.

## The Emergence of Trade Blocs

While the collapse in the East and the Third World debt crisis were highly visible in the popular media, the increasing regionalization of world trade is much less well known and understood, and even less so are its implications for LDCs. The GATT—the trade leg of the postwar Bretton Woods economic system—was designed to avoid the regionalization of trade that characterized the depression of the 1930s. And until the 1980s it was successful in this goal, despite some regional tendencies. For instance, the U.S. government in the postwar period encouraged the formation of a trade bloc in Western Europe as well as protectionist-led growth in the rebirth of the Japanese economy. Still, and despite the emergence of the European Community, successive successful trade rounds helped interregional trade to grow even more quickly than the fast growing intraregional trade. Indeed, the emergence of trading blocs can be understood in part as a response to the globalization of trade in the 1960s and 1970s. With the economic crisis came the "new protectionism." While this trade protectionism was directed toward LDCs and the Eastern economies, other advanced industrial economies were also targeted. That this protectionism had a regional character to it began to become apparent in the early 1980s. In November 1983, for example, the *Economist* described the emergence of two trading blocs, one that included Europe and eastern North America (and their respective southern dependents) in an Atlantic bloc, and a Pacific bloc that included Japan, the Asian countries, and western North America. In Western Europe, scholars and economic policy advisers began to advocate proposals that would discriminate against Japan and the Asian NICs.

In the 1980s, it was in the European Community that governments moved first to institutionalize and accelerate the growth of trade blocs. Despite the removal of tariff barriers in the 1960s, which fostered significant increases in intracommunity trade, remaining fiscal constraints and barriers such as restrictive government procurement policies limited this growth. Despite the removal of tariff barriers, much of the European economy, rather than developing as a single market, remained divided into national and regional markets. The returns on the removal of the tariff barriers had reached their limits. Relative to trade with nonmember countries, intracommunity trade stagnated and then declined in the 1970s and 1980s. Obviously, then, if the EC were to continue to develop, major changes were needed. This change came in 1985 when the member states agreed to complete the common market, leading to the signing of the Single European Act in 1987. The treaty commits the twelve member states to remove not only the internal barriers that remained after tariff barriers were removed in the 1960s, but also the many new barriers that had sprung up during the depressed conditions of the 1980s.

Similarly, in North America the United States and Canada agreed to negotiate a liberal trade and investment arrangement, which was also signed in 1987. The immediate impetus in the United States for this treaty came from disappointment with the pace of the multilateral trade negotiations; the impetus in Canada was fear of increased U.S. protectionism. Structural change underlay the free trade agreement. Branch plant production, which traditionally characterized U.S. manufacturing investment in Canada, began to give way to continental production, a shift that began in the automobile industry with the Autopact of 1965. This was a continental manifestation of integrated global manufacturing, discussed earlier in this chapter. Most recently, the United States and Mexico, and now Canada as well, have negotiated a North American free trade zone. One can begin to take more seriously the Bush administration's "Enterprise for the Americas," which would see the North American trade zone expand to include countries from Central and South America.

Institutionalization of regional economic relations in East and Southeast Asia has not proceeded apace of the other regions. The countries of ASEAN, the Association of South East Asian Nations, have been together in their regional body for years, but until very recently the East Asian NICs—South Korea, Hong Kong, and Taiwan—remained aloof from any regional gathering. In addition to the wartime legacy and continued fears of Japanese domination, the special political and legal status of Hong Kong and Taiwan has also made regional gatherings politically awkward. Moreover, until recent years the focus of the Asian countries, including Japan, was the United States. The Japanese market was as difficult for other Asian producers to penetrate as it was for the United States. Raw materials went to Japan, but their manufactures went to the United States. In the 1980s, protectionist measures in the United States, the appreciation of the yen, and the opening of the Japanese market began to change the direction of trade, although the Asian market is not yet as integrated as either the European or North American markets. In November 1989, 12 countries initiated the Asian Pacific Economic Co-operation Forum (APEC), designed to facilitate the flow of trade in the region.

Trade evidence generally supports the regionalization thesis, but the changes in the 1980s were not dramatic (see Table 9.2). Intra-EC trade and intra–North American trade both grew more quickly than did trade between these two blocs. And North American trade with Asia grew more slowly than intra–North America trade. But the fastest growth rate was reported between Asia and Western Europe, partly because of the low amount of trade at the outset of the 1980s.[25] While the figures are not available in the table, the growth rate of intra-Asian trade probably surpassed all of the rates reported there.

**Table 9.2  Intrabloc and Interbloc Trade**

|  | Annual Average Rate of Growth, 1980–1988 % | Share of World Trade | |
| --- | --- | --- | --- |
|  |  | 1980 % | 1988 % |
| European Community | 7.5 | 17.8 | 22.5 |
| North America (United States and Canada) | 8.8 | 3.8 | 5.2 |
| Asia | na | na | na |
| Western Europe (developed market economies) with North America | 2.3 | 3.8 | 3.2 |
| Western Europe with Asia (all countries) | 11.2 | 1.5 | 2.5 |
| North America with Asia | 7.8 | 2.5 | 3.2 |
| World trade | 4.4 |  |  |

*Source:* Adapted from *World Economic Survey 1990* (p. 54).

## Trading Blocs and the Third World

The impact of the regionalization of world trade depends on the balance of trade-creating effects of intrabloc growth versus the trade-diverting effects of new barriers to entry. The trade-diverting trend affects manufactures more than commodities. The European Commission itself has estimated that the removal of internal barriers may reduce Europe's manufacturing imports by 10 percent.[26] Because LDCs are more vulnerable to trade actions, they are more likely to bear a disproportionate share of this reduction. For instance, the EC has recently extended the scope of its antidumping provisions,[27] and antidumping actions have joined VERs as a favorite protectionist instrument to be used against LDCs. Manufacturers in other advanced industrial economies also have the option to relocate production facilities behind the barriers, and indeed North American and Japanese manufacturers (as well as those from the Asian NICs) have rushed to establish factories in Europe. On the other hand, economic growth in Europe could increase the import of primary commodities, which would benefit sub-Saharan Africa and other developing regions.

In North America, both Canada and the United States have developed a formidable array of protectionist measures. The Omnibus Trade and Competitiveness Act of 1988 remains as a potent weapon to be brandished against would-be transgressors. In Asia, as pointed out earlier, the Japanese market has proved to be difficult to penetrate for most exporters. The Asian NICs, moreover, have not abandoned import substitution, despite considerable liberalization in recent years.

Beyond this general impact on the Third World (minus the Asian NICs), regionalization of world trade will have differential effects on LDCs. Essentially, the institutionalization of industrial trading blocs will expand to include nearby LDCs. In North America, as noted, Mexico has joined the United States and Canada in a free trade agreement. And it may be that by the end of the century, the Western hemisphere will be joined in some institutionalized form of trading bloc. Already in Europe, the EC has developed economic and trading relationships with virtually all of the Mediterranean and African countries. In the future, European integration may encompass most of Eastern Europe as well as that part of Western Europe not yet incorporated in the EC. In Asia, it would not be unlikely, also by the end of the century, that Japan, the NICs, and the ASEAN members would be joined in a liberal trade agreement.

The factors behind the regional extension of institutionalized trading blocs are numerous. Frequently, the industrial and less developed countries within regions have historical ties dating back to formal or informal colonial relationships. Economically, the traditional international division of labor, that is, the exchange of industrial goods for primary commodities, began on a regional basis. With the economic crisis in the North, the globalization of production and concomitant search for cheap labor usually started within the region first, and then moved farther offshore. Politically and strategically, the advanced industrial countries are concerned with the stability of nearby countries that are reeling from the economic deterioration of the last decade (Mexico is an obvious example). The effect of this concern, however, is that LDCs located geographically near advanced industrial countries are likely to receive more favorable treatment than more distant but equally distressed countries. Finally, there are some locational effects that stem from the transition of Fordism to post-Fordism, our final structural change to be addressed here.

## From Fordism to Post-Fordism

One of the most notable structural changes resulting from the economic crisis is the ongoing transition in production paradigms. Fordist production concentrates on reaping the benefits of economies of scale through the mass production of standardized goods. It is based on large factories with dedicated machinery that produce large runs. Relatively well-paid workers are semi-skilled and perform single tasks in a long line of tasks. Large inventories of inputs are maintained to ensure that the assembly lines continue to operate. Under this paradigm, price is the primary battleground for competition.

Post-Fordist production focuses on flexible specialization; competition among firms rages over innovation and product differentiation. Production systems include, for example, computer integrated manufacturing (CIM) and just-in-time production (JIT). Post-Fordism makes use of programmable automation, which allows the same machinery to produce a variety of different products, even on the same day, without the expensive shutdown for resetting and retooling that is required in Fordist production.[28] Post-Fordist production also facilitates much more effective quality control than Fordism. To understand post-Fordism in terms of its relevance for LDCs, I shall discuss the nature of the post-Fordist technology and the implications of that technology for the workforce, for the organization and location of production, and for the nature of interfirm alliances.

Perhaps the most important difference between the two paradigms lies in the nature of their respective technologies. As noted, because of emphasis on price competition in Fordist production, when the crisis emerged, most firms attempted to reduce labor costs. They accomplished this through automating production, or decomposing the production process and locating abroad the labor-intensive parts of that process, or a combination of both. Decomposition and relocation became part of the internationalization of production, or global production, that became popular in the 1970s and early 1980s. Fordist automation reduced labor requirements by investing capital in equipment that replaced workers. Post-Fordist technology, in contrast, is used to develop flexibility in the production system. This is accomplished through the use of programmable automation, such as CIM, as well as through new production systems, such as JIT. The use of electronically controlled machinery has progressed from the production to the design and distribution stages, enabling the integration of production from conception to market. The differential impact of the two technologies can be stark. Between 1976 and 1985, U.S. automakers sunk over $100 billion into Fordist-style automation and the development of global production; U.S. auto manufacturing became more automated than its Japanese counterpart, which specialized in post-Fordist methods.[29] U.S. cars are competitive in cost, while Japanese cars now specialize in innovation and quality, and Japanese automakers continue to increase market share. Thus, the key differentiating factor has proved to be the organization of production, which calls upon different technologies, and which makes post-Fordism more competitive in the 1990s.

The labor requirements of post-Fordism are also different, as are the social relations of production. Fordism is based on a large, homogeneous workforce that requires substantial floor management. Workers have little autonomy. The Fordist compromise was that unions were able to get workers relatively high wages in return for sacrificing production control to management. In contrast, workers in post-Fordist production perform multiple tasks within small production groups, and they do so with much greater autonomy. In a sense, they provide their own overseeing. The skill requirements are different in the two production paradigms. There is a certain amount of de-skilling in post-Fordism—for example, in the need for fewer machinists (because with less dedicated production, the number of machines is reduced)—but the maintenance and repair of the new, programmable machinery will require different (and probably even more advanced) skills. Moreover, the duties and responsibilities of the post-Fordist workers are generally greater than their Fordist counterparts.

The production technologies of post-Fordism also affect the organization of production, another important difference between the two paradigms. Post-Fordism is more integrated than Fordist production; large Fordist companies have a hierarchical division of labor within the firm that separates functions within and among the stages of design, production, and marketing. This allows world production and world marketing. Contrastingly, in post-Fordist production, the time and distance between these stages have been reduced. With its emphasis on innovation and product differentiation, post-Fordist production must be very attuned to market changes. Thus, it is advantageous if the design stage is located close to the market. Similarly, production locations should be as close to the final market as possible. Regarding time, with product lives of one or two years, as opposed to the perhaps even 20 years under Fordist production, it is important to reduce as much as possible the traditional divisions within the conception-to-marketing stages. Whereas the logic of Fordist production, when operating *in crisis,* allowed for transferring the labor-intensive segments of the production process abroad, the logic of post-Fordist production is to locate production near the rich markets of the advanced industrial economies.

Finally, the two production paradigms differ in the nature of interfirm relations. Fordism is not notable for the density of relations between firms. Indeed, the way that we think in terms of single firms, with large ones having an internal division of labor, is a Fordist mentality. Suppliers are sometimes integrated vertically into large firms, but frequently subcontractors are "arms length" firms who compete with one another in contracting with downstream producers. Leaving aside informal collusion, horizontal linkages such as joint ventures are frequently associated with market access and technology transfer. In contrast, horizontal and vertical linkages abound in post-Fordism. The needs of just-in-time and quality-at-source production are better served not only by feeder firms that are physically close to producers but also by those that are formally or informally related to the producer. As for denser horizontal linkages, in addition to some of the reasons for interfirm linkages operative in Fordism, the complex knowledge and information technologies that characterize post-Fordism are generally too demanding for single firms. Through "strategic partnerships," many firms collaborate on research and development in an attempt to remain current in markets that compete in innovation and quality.

## Post-Fordism and the Third World

The crisis of Fordism in the 1960s and 1970s and the subsequent globalization of production played an important part in the industrialization of many LDCs. The countries that were most able to take advantage of globalization were those with large domestic markets and import substituting policies, such as Brazil and India, and those with smaller markets that adopted export strategies, such as the Asian NICs. Globalization was most common in the production of labor-intensive products, including clothing, shoes, and consumer electronics, and later in more complex products, such as auto parts and more sophisticated electronics components. A decade ago there was much discussion about the nature and extent of "deindustrialization" in the North. However, the phenomenon of the globalization of production may be short-lived. As early as 1984, Raphael Kaplinsky noted that production costs of semiconductors in Hong Kong in the 1970s were one-third of those in manual assembly lines in the United States; by the early 1980s the use of semiautomatic assembly lines reduced the advantage to 63 percent of U.S. costs, and with the advent of fully automated assembly lines in 1983, the costs were very similar. While, at the time, "reindustrialization" was thought to be based primarily on the increased use of automated machinery, events demonstrated that technology was only one element in reindustrialization, and that in fact a wholesale transition in production paradigms was underway.

How soon and how severely will the effects of post-Fordism be felt? At present, production systems mix aspects of Fordism and post-Fordism. For example, in the electronics industry, some components may be imported and stockpiled from mass production facilities in the Asian NICs and combined with Northern assembly plants that partially use JIT. Hybrid production of one sort or another may prove popular indefinitely. Another determining factor will be how successful post-Fordism will be in comparison to Fordist production. Where cost competition remains a dominant concern, mass production may remain the favored manufacturing paradigm. Thus, it is possible that the exports of LDCs, specializing in low-wage labor and saddled with the old technologies, may not face imminent collapse. However, the best that they may hope for, without restructuring their own production systems, will most likely be a slow deterioration of their export-led growth until the limits of post-Fordism are reached. We must consider, then, the factors that hinder LDCs from adopting the new technologies of post-Fordism. These obstacles will be discussed under three headings: technology requirements, locational criteria, and skilled labor.

In the 1960s and 1970s, the NICs acquired technology from the advanced industrial countries in a variety of ways, such as through direct acquisition, licensing, bringing it in indirectly via foreign direct investment, and "reverse engineering" when necessary. These methods are more problematic in the 1990s. The international climate has become more protectionist and may become even much more so by the end of the decade. Governments in the North, and particularly the United States, seem to be very serious about strengthening intellectual property regimes. Strategic partnering, discussed above, may be one means for some NICs to circumvent new restrictions on the transfer of technology. Those LDCs with large markets may be sufficiently attractive for Northern firms to circumvent transfer restrictions in return for lucrative market access privileges. Access to the North to obtain the new technologies would seem to be critical for LDCs because the knowledge intensity, over and above the capital intensity, of programmable automation exceeds the capabilities of LDCs to develop these technologies on their own—although there are exceptions in some NICs in some industries. Strategic partnerships to date, however, have largely been undertaken among firms of the advanced industrial states, along with a smattering of companies from the Asian NICs and a few other countries.

Even if the problem of technology transfer were removed as a stumbling block for LDCs, the locational criteria of post-Fordist production would still disadvantage most of them considerably. The necessity of locating production facilities near the end markets, as well as the locational dictates of JIT production, will make it very difficult for production in LDCs to compete for Northern markets. Proximity to Northern markets, of course, would advantage those LDCs that were situated nearby. Hence, the *maquiladora* plants in northern Mexico assemble and produce components for export or re-export back to the United States, whose tariff structure encourages globalization of production because only the value added abroad is subject to import duties. Similar arrangements are in place in the Caribbean, and in the EC many manufacturing firms "outward process" production, particularly clothing, to Eastern Europe and to Mediterranean LDCs. While these instances of offshore assembly may involve as much Fordist as post-Fordist production, the implication is that, as post-Fordism becomes dominant, LDCs located close to Northern markets will become even more attractive to Northern producers than more remotely located LDCs. This assumes that JIT production requirements can be satisfied in nearby LDC factories. Border obstacles of any severity may obviate internationalized JIT production. The United States–Mexico free trade agreement will, for example, remove these obstacles. However, even LDCs located near Northern markets may be doubtful sites for post-Fordist production because of the requirements of the labor process.

The implanting of post-Fordism in the South is also made problematic by the labor requirements of programmable automation. As discussed, flexible specialization has variable effects on the skilling of the workforce, but generally greater demands are made of the worker. With exceptions, the low-skilled and undereducated labor force in most LDCs may not be up to the task. The exception, again, is the group of Asian NICs, whose workers are generally highly educated. Indeed, Asian NICs, as in Japan where post-Fordism took hold early, may be well-suited to the unique management/labor relations that characterize this production paradigm.

## Conclusion

As we have seen, the structural changes and transformation of the last decade have serious implications for LDCs, despite the fact that the genesis of change has occurred outside of the South (except in the case of the debt crisis where LDCs are at least partially culpable). Perhaps in the end this is what dependency is all about. Still, the negative impact on the South has affected LDCs differentially. The heterogeneity of the South has been highlighted by observers for years. Partly, emphasis on this theme has reflected a reality, and partly it has been pushed for subjective purposes: the North has feared the possible emergence of an aggressive, unified South. The impact of global restructuring has in fact made the heterogeneous

South even more differentiated. The nature of the difference, however, means that global restructuring threatens some LDCs more than others. My conclusions, therefore, vary depending upon the group or level of LDCs I am addressing. In general, the higher-income, technologically more advanced LDCs are much better placed to accommodate change than are the poorer and less developed ones.

The top performers of the Third World have been the Asian NICs. Least typical of the South, the Asian NICs have thus far emerged from global restructuring much better positioned than other LDCs. While seriously indebted, they successfully avoided the debt-servicing difficulties faced by other LDCs. They are also the only group of LDCs that have been able to take advantage of the marketization and privatization of Eastern Europe. The Asian NICs are seriously threatened, though, by the effects of regionalization of trade and of post-Fordism, especially because of their distance from Northern markets. Some firms from the Asian NICs are locating production facilities in Northern countries, but this may accomplish little for workers in these countries. Thus, the export-led development of the Asian NICs, with its focus on exporting to North America, will not be tenable in the future. A better strategy to pursue would be one in which wages continue to rise in these countries so that domestic demand might approach that of Northern markets. As discussed earlier, the formation of a trading bloc in East and Southeast Asia is developing as companies in the Asian NICs and Japan begin to transfer labor-intensive production processes to the economies of ASEAN. The developing markets in these countries as well as domestic markets may grow to replace those in North America and Europe.

The next level or group includes NICs who have encountered debt-servicing difficulties, such as Brazil and Mexico in the Western hemisphere and the second-tier NICs in Asia—i.e., most of the ASEAN members and the highly populated countries of China and India. All of these countries may be even more threatened than the first group by restructuring in the North and transformation in the East. A strategy of export-led development, particularly with an emphasis on exports to the advanced industrial economies, will become less viable for debt-servicing and second-tier NICs. This group, and the third level, to be discussed momentarily, will be the LDCs most threatened by the new economies of the East. They will suffer in competition with each other in exporting to the East, and their exports to the North will face competition from the exports from the East. The debt-servicing and second-tier Asian NICs will also be forced to compete with Eastern countries for foreign investment and financial assistance from Western countries.

As for the impact of post-Fordism, the NICs with debt-servicing problems simply do not have the capital to adjust to the changing production paradigm. The future for these countries may depend in part on geography.

Those close to Northern markets, such as Mexico and the North African countries, may attempt to integrate more closely with the North. The others will return to regional integration as an alternative to export-led development, but these attempts to date have not proved successful. We saw, for example, how the debt crisis has had an even more debilitating effect on South-South than North-South trade. The United Nations Industrial Development Organization (UNIDO) argues for greater South-South industrial cooperation in subcontracting parts and components for Northern markets,[30] but this ignores post-Fordism and assumes that Fordist production will continue to dominate. As for the second-tier NICs of Asia, they would have been the next group of countries to benefit from the globalization of Fordism. Their alternative has already been discussed; they will constitute an integral part of the Pacific trading bloc.

A third level includes countries that are less industrialized than those of the first two levels; the sub-Saharan countries such as Côte d'Ivoire and Kenya and some of the Andean Pact countries in South America are included here. The prognosis for these countries is even more serious than for those of the second level. They are less advanced technologically, they have less capital for restructuring, and they do not have developed regional markets to target. Moreover, African countries are threatened by the trade diversion that will come from the Europe 1992 movement. Regional integration is a possibility, but these countries face even more serious obstacles here than do the second-level countries. Changes in the East threaten them more significantly in terms of competition for financial assistance than in terms of their ability to compete for investment and markets.

Finally, the least developed countries constitute the fourth level. Because they are not industrialized, they should be least affected by changing production paradigms in the North. But as primary commodity producers, they have suffered badly through the 1980s with depressed prices. While 1986 may have been the nadir for commodity prices in general, the outlook remains very guarded.[31] The new production paradigm is not only less labor intensive but less commodity intensive. Therefore, declining terms of trade are likely to hamper the least developed countries for the foreseeable future. As with the third-level LDCs, these countries will be adversely affected by the competition for financial assistance with the Eastern countries.

## Notes

1. The concept of Fordism was borrowed from Antonio Gramsci and developed by scholars of the French regulation school. The name refers to the mass production system pioneered by Henry Ford and the mass consumption made possible by this method of production.

2. A. Lipietz, *Mirages and Miracles* (London: Verso Books, 1987), p. 69.

3. The origins of the economic crisis are discussed in a number of works, including A. Gamble and P. Walton, *Capitalism in Crisis* (London: Macmillan, 1976); F. Froebel, *The Current Development of the World Economy* (Starnberg: Max-Planck-Institut zur Erforschung der Lebensbedingungen der wissenschaftlich-technischen Welt, 1980); M. Piore and C. Sabel, *The Second Industrial Divide* (New York: Basic Books, 1984); and A. Lipietz, "Behind the Crisis: The Exhaustion of a Regime of Accumulation: A 'Regulation School' Perspective on Some French Empirical Works," *Review of Radical Political Economy* 18 (1986).

4. A. Lipietz, "An Alternative Design for the Twenty-First Century." Paper presented at Carleton University, Ottawa, Canada, July 1987.

5. United Nations Industrial Development Organization, *Industry and Development: Global Report 1985* (New York: UNIDO, 1985), p. 10.

6. UNIDO, *Industry and Development 1985,* p. 15.

7. United Nations Food and Agriculture Organization, *Commodity Review and Outlook, 1985–86* (Rome: FAO, 1986), p. 18.

8. United Nations, *World Economic Survey* (New York: UN, 1986), p. 11.

9. World Bank, *World Development Report 1990* (IBRD: 1990), p. 13.

10. United Nations, *World Economic Survey 1990* (New York: UN, 1990), p. 63.

11. Ibid., p. 38.

12. World Bank, *World Development Report 1990,* p. 14.

13. L. Mytelka, *Technology and the Least Developed Countries: A Background Paper,* LAREA/CEREM, University of Paris, 1989. Draft report.

14. Ironies abound concerning the monies moved abroad illegally by wealthy Southern residents. First, Northern creditors frequently forced Third World governments to nationalize debts even if privately incurred, which allowed the wealthy to avoid responsibility for their debt; then in a contradictory fashion the IMF forced the South to denationalize their economies; and now the fortunes amassed abroad by residents of the debt-ridden countries are being used to purchase non-performing debts at heavily discounted prices, which are then traded for currency, property or equity in privatized state companies, a process called "roundtripping" in financial circles. See A. Hoogvelt, "The Debt Crisis and the Prospects for Socialism in the Third World." Paper presented at the annual convention of the International Studies Association, Vancouver, B.C., March 1991, p. 7.

15. Hoogvelt, "The Debt Crisis," p. 3.

16. I have discussed the pros and cons of South-South trade in M. Dolan, "From North-South to South-South Trade: One View of the Developing Countries' Future," in *Canada Among Nations 1986,* ed. B. Tomlin and M. Molot (Toronto: James Lorimer, 1987). For the advantages of South-South trade, see S. Lall, "Trade between Developing Countries," *Trade and Development* 6 (1985), publication of the United Nations Conference on Trade and Development. For the disadvantages, see O. Havrylyshyn and M. Wolf, "Recent Trends in Trade among Developing Countries," *European Economic Review* 24 (1983).

17. Mytelka, *Technology and the Least Developed Countries,* p. 44.

18. International Monetary Fund, *World Economic Outlook* (Washington, D.C.: IMF, 1990), p. 30.

19. IMF, *World Economic Outlook,* pp. 30–32.

20. C. McMillan, "Foreign Direct Investment Flows to Eastern Europe and Their Implications for Developing Countries," East-West Project, Carleton University, Ottawa, Ontario, March 1991, p. 33.

21. McMillan, "Foreign Direct Investment Flows," p. 30.

22. "CIDA Chief Fears Third World Will Lose Out," *Ottawa Citizen,* 5 June 1991, p. A3.

23. McMillan, "Foreign Direct Investment Flows."

24. Susan M. Collins and Dani Rodrick, *Eastern Europe and the Soviet Union in the World Economy* (Washington: Institute for International Economics, 1991).

25. United Nations, *World Economic Survey 1990,* p. 54.

26. World Bank, *World Economic Report 1990,* p. 22.

27. United Nations, *World Economic Survey 1990,* p. 65.

28. The terms post-Fordism, flexible specialization, and programmable automation are sometimes used interchangably. This practice is acceptable as long as one bears in mind that they refer to different aspects of a new production paradigm. Post-Fordism refers to the paradigm *in toto*, while flexible specialization refers to a capability of the production system, and programmable automation refers to the machine technology of the paradigm.

29. R. Kaplinsky, "Post-Fordist Industrial Restructuring: Policy Implications for an Industrially Advanced Economy." Paper presented at Carleton University, Ottawa, Ontario, April 1990.

30. United Nations Industrial Development Organization, *Industry and Development: Global Report 1989/1990* (New York: UNIDO, 1990).

31. United Nations, *World Economic Survey 1990.*

# 10

## Big Little Japan

### *Daniel Unger*

Concepts for the study of influence must be changed or invented when influence is sought by novel means or under changed conditions. In epochs of rapid development, there is need to reassess the relevance of intellectual effort.[1]

Over the course of a couple of generations, total Japanese production of goods and services has increased from below one-twentieth to about two-thirds that of the United States. How Japan perceives, and acts to bolster, its security shapes the global security and economic environments. It makes no sense, therefore, to think about future international security and welfare issues without trying to anticipate Japan's role. It is not easy, however, to conceptualize that role, given the novelty of the bases of Japanese influence.

In the postwar period, Japan was able[2] to act as a trading state[3] enunciating vague doctrines of "omnidirectional diplomacy" and "comprehensive security." These policies aimed at minimizing Japanese vulnerability to uncontrollable external shocks. Security guarantees provided by the United States enabled Japan to concentrate on economic issues. In Kataoka's contemporary description of the period, Japan "pursues success according to its own definition: in commerce, manufacturing, finance, and high tech."[4]

With the end of the Cold War, Japanese government ministries and their think-tanks envision a bright Japanese future as a culturally based superpower drawing on Japan's economic and technological prowess. Japanese firms, meanwhile, take the lead in buying up overseas assets and spreading Japan's production plant around the world. The capabilities underlying Japan's potential global influence will continue to expand rapidly. The ways in which and the extent to which that influence will be exercised remain uncertain.

While I will not attempt here to explain Japan's rapid growth or to record the indices that reflect its magnitude, it is important to understand that Japan's superior economic performance does not represent any century-long flash in the pan. Some students of Japan now argue that ballooning asset prices and their more recent decline threaten the underlying bases of Japan's economy. Japanese banks, in particular, have suffered major losses and can no longer sustain a dominant international role.[5] Japanese firms have lost their capital cost advantages over foreign competitors. A rapidly changing demographic structure will impose a heavy burden on public finances. Consumerism may lead to further decline in savings rates.[6] Indeed, Japan's economy appears to have entered a new phase marked by lower rates of growth. Nonetheless, the fundamental strengths that underpin the flexibility of the Japanese economy remain: powerful bureaucratic and political elites prone to identify their interests with those of Japanese producers; creativity and flexibility in designing and adapting institutions to serve those interests; and a variety of institutions that train, mobilize, and utilize the broadly distributed skills of the Japanese people. These factors have sustained the resilience of the Japanese economy. Forced to adjust to a rapidly appreciating yen in the late 1980s, the Japanese economy responded with a spurt of growth that, over a six-year period, added to Japan's total product an increment the size of France's gross domestic product.[7] Over the 1980s, Japan's industrial production grew by 54 percent while the comparable U.S. figure was 29 percent.[8] Investment rates in Japan over the late 1980s and early 1990s make it highly likely that Japan's average economic growth rates will continue to outstrip those of other industrialized economies into the next century.

In the following section I review the obstacles, both domestic and foreign, to Japan's assuming a larger global role. I then go on to investigate the ways in which Japan expands its economic influence in East Asia, the region in which its role is most significant. In concluding the chapter, I consider some of the implications of Japan's rising power for leadership in the international system.

## Japan's Global Role: Obstacles and Opportunities

Given Japan's leadership as a supplier of capital internationally, and increasingly as an exporter of manufacturing technology, its economic and political postures inevitably will be important. In the shorter term, Japan will exert growing influence in various multilateral institutions and, in particular, as an exporter of capital to developing countries. One estimate suggests that Japan now provides a quarter of net resource flows to developing countries.[9]

Japan's leadership record in these areas to date has been mixed, yet Japan's importance increases. Reconstruction in the Middle East, restructuring in Eastern Europe and the Commonwealth of Independent States, and ongoing needs for capital in developing countries will place larger demands on Japanese capital surpluses. This becomes especially critical given balance-of-payments deficits in Germany and some of the Gulf states. As the world's leading creditor, Japan helps to sustain the international economy.[10]

Japan and the United States are now the world's leading donors of overseas development assistance; Japan is the leading donor in well over a score of developing countries, including much of Africa. As Japan has increased its development lending, it has also changed the nature of that assistance. A greater share of Japanese aid is now available in the form of grants than in the past; more aid provided on softer terms is going to countries in which Japanese commercial interests are limited; technical assistance is increasing while the emphasis on infrastructure is declining; and Japan is now more prone to exercise its potential influence to shape public policies in recipient countries.[11] Furthermore, reflecting an expansion in its horizons, the Japanese government is providing aid to countries in Eastern Europe and the Commonwealth of Independent States. Japan is also a key player in efforts to alleviate the debt burdens afflicting many developing countries. In pursuing diverse goals through overseas development assistance, Japan seeks to coordinate its efforts with other donor countries.[12]

Nonetheless, where difficult political issues arise, the Japanese penchant for assuming as low a profile as possible is still very much in evidence. This proclivity has been on display during the Uruguay Round of trade talks. Japanese politicians are reluctant to risk the inevitable domestic political reaction to opening up its rice market. Japan has remained thus far on the sidelines, hoping that conflicts between the European Community on the one hand and the United States and other grain exporters on the other will save Japan from having the spotlight of world attention turn to its own protected agriculture markets.

Former prime minister Toshiki Kaifu's botched handling of his initiative to dispatch Japanese Self Defense Agency personnel to Saudi Arabia also revealed the continuing limitations on Japan's capacity to support security measures, even multilateral ones carried out with United Nations sponsorship. Despite a major financial contribution to the allied war effort, Japan's handling of the issue left its allies disappointed and the Japanese themselves frustrated at their inability to gain recognition for their significant role. This experience has had an important influence in Japan, spurring efforts to speed up government decisionmaking,[13] leading to the Diet's adoption of a framework for the dispatch of forces abroad, and, more generally, stimulating Japanese to reflect on their country's place in the international system.

Japan is increasingly active around the world distributing both public and private capital, promoting the United Nations, and assuming a somewhat more visible political profile. In June 1992 Japanese diplomats led donor countries in making commitments for environmental spending at the

Rio de Janeiro Conference on the Environment and Development. A couple of weeks later, Japan hosted an international peace conference on Cambodia at which it pledged major financial contributions. Yasushi Akashi, a Japanese national, heads the United Nations operations in Cambodia. It is likely that the first overseas dispatch of Japanese Self-Defense Forces under the new United Nations peace-keeping forces law will be to Cambodia. During his speech to the United Nations Security Council in January 1992, Prime Minister Miyazawa called for Japan's accession to a permanent seat on the Security Council.

Despite abundant evidence of Japan's more prominent global posture, it remains unclear what kind of role Japan is likely to adopt in the future. Japanese commentators often assume that economic and technological power will prove fungible and enable Japan to become an international leader. Indeed, in the longer run, both the state's capacity to broker agreements among Japanese interest groups and the Japanese political leadership's preference for pragmatic approaches to problems of international cooperation may prove well-suited to an increasingly complex global environment.[14] The Japanese leadership's successful economic record, since the Meiji era, rests in large part on creative institutional design—in Oran Young's words, "a process of steering complex bargaining toward coherent and socially desirable outcomes."[15]

A number of obstacles, however, must be overcome before Japan will be able to emerge as a forceful international actor. Most critical among these is the tradition of weak executives in Japanese government. The Japanese prime minister is constrained by powerful ministerial fiefs, the increasing influence of policy *zoku*,[16] and the slow process of Japanese government decisionmaking. These factors lead to continuing dependence on foreign pressure to initiate major policy shifts.[17]

More generally, elite opinion in Japan must strengthen its consensus that, by its very size, Japan will inevitably be exercising global power. The issue is not whether Japan exerts influence, but whether it acknowledges that power and determines to exercise it in ways consistent with broader goals and aspirations. To date, the Japanese political leadership has not managed successfully to articulate any such vision. Rather, Japan's traditional preference for as invisible a role as possible is still evident. Such a posture, however, is precluded by the dimensions of Japan's economic impact.

## Japanese Isolationism

Rather like the United States in the decades before World War II, Japan has not been much interested in the postwar period in asserting itself internationally. This Japanese reticence is sometimes explained as resulting from traditional social values emphasizing hierarchy.[18] This view holds

that Japan is more comfortable in a position of subordination or domination rather than one requiring cooperation among equals. Clearly, there is
a widely shared reluctance to depart from the broad postwar policy framework emphasizing dependence on the United States. That policy, after all,
has served Japan rather well. Memories of the divisiveness of Japan's
postwar politics—a divisiveness often driven by debates about Japan's foreign entanglements—strengthen the reluctance to move in new directions.
In Japan, the tendency is for politics to start at the water's edge.

Japanese avoidance of international leadership is also explained by
some scholars in terms of Japan's insularity and the force of the ideology
of Japanese uniqueness. In fact, many Japanese, like U.S. citizens before
World War II, are idealists. Today, some Japanese believe that with a
unique culture and history, Japan has transcended the bounds of the de-
pressingly repetitive saga of power politics and the workings of the security dilemma that still shape the foreign policies of other powers.[19] Japan's
status as the only victim of nuclear weapons helps to reinforce the conviction that Japan is a uniquely pacifist nation.

Current institutional weaknesses and popular predispositions in Japan
have parallels with prewar U.S. politics. In the United States, the experience of total war, postwar dominance, and the ensuing Cold War dramatically reoriented foreign policy. Crises served to transform U.S. attitudes
and ushered in a host of new institutions designed to facilitate the exercise of global leadership. Japan, however, will not face a global crisis of
comparable proportions, and its adjustment to new realities is, therefore,
likely to be still more gradual. Japanese foreign policies will shift more
slowly and will do so largely in response to the widening horizons of
Japanese business firms as they expand their interests around the globe.

## Japan in East Asia

Nearly half a century after the end of the Second World War, Japanese security dependence on the United States continues and the United
States–Japan relationship remains at the core of Japan's national interest.
Japan's other principal international interests are in East Asia. Only in
East Asia does Japan have a long record of significant international influence. The importance of Japan's economic ties to the region are growing
rapidly. The threat of protectionism in the markets of the industrialized
countries heightens Japanese interest in East Asia. Accordingly, by reviewing Japan's current posture in the region, it should be possible to suggest the outlines of a future Japanese global role and to assess the degree
to which that role will be concentrated in East Asia. In the following section, I analyze Japanese foreign economic policy in Asia. I then go on to
evaluate the Japanese attitude toward economic regionalism.

Rising Japanese economic power will present more opportunities for exercising leadership. More importantly, that power will make it increasingly difficult to sustain the fiction that Japan does not exercise political influence abroad. Indications of a Japanese willingness to exert leadership are more evident in Asia than elsewhere.

Given the importance Japan attaches to its relations with China, for example, it is not surprising that it was prepared in 1990 to depart from the other members of the Group of Seven in re-establishing its economic assistance to China. Japan had suspended that assistance following the Chinese leadership's crackdown on the Chinese dissident movement. The urgency with which recent Japanese governments worked to win passage of a bill enabling Japan to send forces abroad as part of United Nations peace-keeping operations reflected, in part, a concern to play a direct role in supervising an end to the war in Cambodia. Whether due to propinquity, cultural affinity, or its ability to exercise local economic dominance, Japanese foreign policy has been most active in East Asia. Japan's economic dominance in East Asia may afford us hints of the kinds of policies Japan is likely to pursue in the future in other regions as well.

## Effective Application of Resources to Japanese Foreign Economic Policy Goals

While scholars have paid a great deal of attention to the important part the United States has played in facilitating economic expansion in the East Asian Newly Industrializing Countries (NICs), there has been relatively little analysis of Japan's postwar role in driving the region's development.[20] Japan, after all, was a neomercantilist, dependent state without the strategic concern to stem the spread of Soviet power or the ideological commitment to liberalism that together accounted for the U.S. willingness to keep its markets open to imported manufactured goods and to extend foreign aid. Yet Japan has, in fact, played a critical role in stimulating the region's development.

In 1989, Japanese investment in Asia came to about 16 percent of total Japanese overseas investment.[21] That same year, 43 percent of foreign direct investment by smaller firms went to Asia, down from 73 percent in 1987.[22] Official Japanese aid is helping to facilitate the movement offshore of Japanese manufacturing firms; this movement in turn stimulates Japanese trade with other Asian economies. Intraindustry trade (primarily intrafirm) is increasing rapidly and is producing tighter regional economic integration.

Many foreigners have been unhappy at one time or another with Japanese neomercantilist policies and, in particular, the role of Japan's industrial policy in shaping its trade patterns. These are perceived by many to account for persistent Japanese trade surpluses with most of its trading partners. Japan has by now largely abandoned straightforward policies of protecting its own markets while targeting foreign ones. Yet, as Japan's exports of goods increase and are joined by massive exports of capital and production plant, foreign scrutiny of Japanese foreign economic policies inevitably grows.

Japanese elites have a long, successful record of applying policy instruments rationally to specific tasks, particularly those of catching up with their perceived superiors. The ability to mobilize and apply resources to identified goals was evident in Japanese colonial policies in East Asia early in this century. In Korea, Manchukuo, and Taiwan, Japan laid the groundwork for the later economic development of those areas. Without direct control or coercion, the Japanese are now helping to lay a similar foundation in Southeast Asia. The Ministry of International Trade and Industry (MITI) and other government agencies are attempting to plan and facilitate the integration of the economies of East Asia. Meanwhile, Japanese firms are driving the process forward inexorably.

A comparison of Japan's current policies with those of the prewar period is instructive. In the 1930s, many Japanese hoped to create an integrated East Asian economy. A Japan-led regional economic bloc would be a means of driving the Western powers from Asia, of enhancing Japan's economic security, and of enabling Japan to lead Asians in developing their productive capacities. Realizing these goals would require self-conscious adjustment of Japan's industrial structure—i.e., an industrial policy.[23] Before implementing such a policy, Japan would have to prepare thoroughly:

> A distinctive feature of Japanese colonialism was that its colonial governments, in addition to providing essential services such as law and order, health, education, modern transportation and communication, also actively promoted selected industries, introduced new technology, and funded economic undertakings. The Japanese planned their development programs with considerable care, paying unusual attention to research. They systematically surveyed and investigated economic resources and local customs and planned their economic programs on the basis of these studies.[24]

Japan's approach to its colonies differed fundamentally from that of the other powers. In part because of Japan's proximity to its colonies and also because it was late in joining the game of carving up the world, strategic goals played a particularly dominant role in Japan's colonial expansion.[25] Japan located a great deal of industry and developed infrastructure in its colonies. As in pursuing economic goals in Japan itself, the state was very active in promoting development.

The point is not that Japanese elite goals have remained constant over half a century or that contemporary developments bear more than superficial similarity to those of the 1930s. It is worth repeating, however, that in the 1930s, as now, the institutions of Japan's political economy were distinctive. Those institutions produced an innovative approach to colonialism, just as we are now witnessing an original approach to the problem of exporting productive capacities.

## Japanese Aid

In 1988, Japanese resource flows to developing countries came to over $20 billion, almost half of that from official sources.[26] While Japan is now the world's leading aid donor, critics still charge that Japanese mercantilism is evident in its economic assistance policies. Japanese tend to counter that their aid, unlike that of most other donors, is pointedly apolitical and, therefore, more truly in keeping with the spirit of economic assistance.[27] There is a rough symmetry between these two positions that can be recognized once it is understood that for Japan, economic goals represent "high politics," while for the United States, at least during the Cold War, they represented "low politics." If the United States uses its aid to support its strategic interests in Egypt and Israel, Japan acts in similar fashion in extending its aid to those (East Asian) countries with which it does the greater part of its business in the developing world.

Foreigners as well as Japanese have long criticized Japanese aid for being excessively restricted. Japanese exporters in the 1950s used Japanese assistance, or war reparations, to develop market access and generate orders. Japan not only used to require that aid be used to purchase Japanese goods and services, but aid had a strategic character designed, according to some, to create a Japanese mini-hegemony in East Asia.[28] The popular version had it that Japan was using neocolonial methods to recreate a Greater East Asia Co-Prosperity Sphere. Japanese investment tended to move in tandem with Japanese aid. Gold notes, "from the beginning, the close supportive relationship between the Japanese government and business concerns has been extended to overseas investment."[29]

The nature of the link between government and business in Japan is easily subject to caricature. In fact, government-business cooperation in foreign economic relations has been extensive in the areas of investment, aid, and trade. MITI officials in Southeast Asia attempt to reproduce some of the instruments of industrial policy as practiced in Japan.[30] It is consistent with the general Japanese perception regarding its economic assistance that in Japanese usage the term "economic cooperation" encompasses not only grant aid and concessionary loans, but private loans and investment flows as well. It is significant that both MITI and the Japanese Economic Planning Agency have economic cooperation bureaus. This reflects a basic assumption that it is both possible and desirable for Japan to "harmonize" its economic cooperation activities with the process of adjusting industrial structures in Japan as well as in developing countries.

Japanese officials, particularly in MITI, are trying to create economic complementarities among the smaller East Asian economies and Japan. Not all officials assume that this will result naturally from the play of market forces. In fact, MITI hopes to target particular industries in specific countries of the Association of Southeast Asian Nations (ASEAN).

A couple of Japanese economic assistance institutions help to illustrate the ways in which the Japanese government and private business firms are able to cooperate in providing economic assistance to developing countries.[31] The Japan Overseas Development Corporation (JODC) is funded by the Japanese government and by private sources. It supports a range of services, including sending Japanese technicians abroad to train local workers (the Japan Expert Service Abroad program). It also provides finance for smaller Japanese firms investing abroad, and it finances the import of primary and processed goods that are produced by Japanese joint ventures supported by the Japanese government.[32] Well over two-thirds of the cases of JODC concessional financing through the 1980s were for projects in East Asia, and well over half of those were in the ASEAN countries. JODC also dispatches most of its experts to East Asia. For example, of 880 cases as of the late 1980s, 260 were for the textile industry, and 222 of those went to East Asia—including 88 to Indonesia, 45 to the Philippines, 32 to Thailand, and 27 to Taiwan. The JODC also dispatched many technicians to support the development of wood products (29 to Indonesia), food products (21 to Thailand), ceramics (17 to South Korea), iron and steel (16 to Taiwan), and auto parts (16 to Taiwan).[33]

The Association for Overseas Technical Scholarship (AOTS) was founded in 1959 with MITI backing. By 1989 it had trained over 40,000 workers, the vast majority of them Asians. Three-fourths of the program's budget is funded by the Japanese government, and one-fourth by private industry. The largest numbers of workers trained have been Indonesians, South Koreans, Thais, and Chinese. AOTS training is most common in the transport machinery, electrical and electronics, chemicals, metallurgical, and textile industries.[34] Japanese firms in these industries have been important investors in East Asia.

## Economic Structural Adjustment for International Harmony

By the mid-1980s, a host of Asian countries unhappy with chronic deficits in their trade with Japan were pressuring Japan to adjust its foreign economic policies. Among ASEAN countries, lower commodity prices had drastically reduced growth rates and ASEAN leaders called on Japan to increase its economic assistance at a time when it enjoyed staggering global trade surpluses. The United States, meanwhile, was pressuring Japan to increase its foreign economic assistance. The United States also was urging Japan to implement major structural adjustments at home to alter the Japanese habit of saving more than it consumes.

Along with the other members of the Group of Five, Japan and the United States agreed in September 1985 to seek the yen's appreciation against the dollar as a means of stemming Japan's growing trade surpluses and ever larger U.S. deficits. In response to the yen's rapid rise, MITI devised a regional industrialization plan that responded to foreign pressures while promising relief for Japan's smaller export-oriented industries that were hard-hit by the yen's take-off.

Original proposals called for a "Project for Comprehensive Cooperation and Asian Industrialization."[35] The MITI draft proposal built on a major research project—undertaken by the Overseas Economic Cooperation Fund (OECF), the Institute for Developing Economies (a government think-tank), and the Japan External Trade Organization (JETRO)—that focused on Japanese assistance and ASEAN economic development. The report called for increasing the use of indirect loans to private firms in recipient countries.[36] The MITI plan proposed a rapid increase in Japanese foreign assistance, efforts to increase imports of manufactured goods from developing countries, and assistance for smaller Japanese manufacturers hurt by the yen's steep rise.[37]

The scheme would facilitate adaptive restructuring of Japanese industry but would cope with balance-of-payments surpluses through capital exports rather than simply increasing domestic consumption. It envisioned greater assistance for infrastructure for export-oriented industries, technical cooperation for exporting industries (largely through the Japan International Cooperation Agency, or JICA), investment and financial support for exporting industries, and "cooperation" in liberalizing the tax systems and investment policies of recipient countries.[38] A MITI official described the plan as reflecting "the need for pursuing comprehensive cooperation involving aid, investment, and trade" and argued that Japan "must assist each country in determining which industries will best meet its needs."[39] Japanese aid would be serving, in part, as a subsidy to Japanese firms setting up shop abroad. As an additional benefit, the plan also promised MITI a means of broadening its jurisdiction and boosting budgetary funds under its control, at a time when external and internal pressures had undermined its traditional mandate and instruments of influence.[40]

Japanese aid officials have tended in the past studiously to avoid interference in recipient countries' politics where issues of political participation or human rights have been concerned. The request basis[41] of Japanese aid reflected a similar determination to avoid interference in development planning. Now, however, the Japanese were prepared to lobby for policies that would stimulate inflows of foreign capital.

The MITI proposal called for efforts to "expand economic cooperation to improve the environment for investment in the developing countries."[42] A MITI report on the plan suggested that it is "vital for Japan . . .
to pave the way to enable Japanese enterprises to make direct investments
smoothly in developing countries."[43] The plan was explicit in its call "for
support in cultivating industries that will attract foreign investment from
mainly private-sector sources."[44] This required, however, laying an appropriate groundwork:

> As Japan seeks to expand the flow of capital to developing countries with
> a view toward improving each recipient country's foreign-currency earn-
> ing power, it is important that this flow of capital be accompanied by a
> full complement of service and information-oriented cooperation, ranging
> from consultation regarding economic policy and development project
> planning to transfers of technologies and expertise for specific industrial
> levels. Such cooperation is essential from the perspective of cultivating
> an attractive investment environment which, as mentioned earlier, is a
> prerequisite for expanding the flow of private-sector capital.[45]

The plan differed from most aid initiatives developed by other countries in the extent to which it sought to coordinate public and private initiatives and the fact that it was the product of a trade and industry ministry.[46] Even more striking was the extent to which it envisioned a design
for economic harmony in East Asia. The plan would "devise cooperation
policies that select appropriate industries for each of the developing nations and that include specific industry-cultivation plans."[47]

According to MITI, the plan would help developing countries earn
foreign exchange and assist Japan in developing an "internationally harmonious industrial structure." This would be achieved through the "intensive and systematic input" of economic cooperation; cooperation for "vi-
talization of private industry" in developing countries; and the
participation of private firms from "the developed countries" through investment and trade.[48] The result would be "a desirable horizontal division
of labor . . . [that would] help Japan to shift its industry and trade to an internationally harmonious structure."[49]

The plan represented the clearest effort to date by the Japanese
bureaucracy to coordinate the interests of diverse Japanese actors as well
as those in developing countries. Ozawa suggests that the Japanese approach, a

> new, hybrid form of economic co-operation, a combination of official aid
> alongside private-sector transfers of production capacities . . . which the
> Japanese government has dubbed "a comprehensive development strat-
> egy," is designed to recycle not only surplus capital but also "surplus"
> industrial capacities to those host economies that are capable of absorb-
> ing these economic resources productively.[50]

He goes on to note that the Japanese government "mobilizes and capitalises on the vitality of the country's private sector more extensively than any other donor country in transferring both financial and non-financial (e.g. technical and organisational) resources to the Third World."[51]

### Recycling Japan's Capital Surplus

Beginning in fiscal year 1986, Japan announced a $10 billion capital recycling plan, including both private and government funds. The following year it announced a $30 billion scheme (including the previous one's $10 billion), and this was followed, beginning in fiscal year 1990, with a further $30 billion to be recycled over two years. The bulk of these funds, however, are provided at only slightly concessional rates.[52] These capital recycling measures were announced as measures to help debt-burdened developing countries and were to be channeled through the World Bank, the Asian Development Bank, and the International Monetary Fund as well as the OECF and the Export-Import Bank of Japan.[53] The latter plays a large role in administering the schemes.[54] With the large increase in funds going through multilateral institutions, Japan now employs such institutions to disperse over 30 percent of its economic assistance, well above the average for aid donors.[55] In fact, however, despite the nominal targeting of debt-burdened developing countries, the major part of these funds did not make their way to the hardest-pressed debtor countries, most of which are in Latin America. Rather, consistent with the pattern of disbursement of Japanese bilateral loans, about two-thirds of the recycled capital went to Asian countries.[56] Even as the global reach of Japan's capital exports spreads, the traditional focus on East Asia continues.

### Industrial Policy

The Japanese are not merely strengthening the international extension of their own industrial policy but are also advocating that other countries learn from Japan's successful application of industrial policies. In a 1988 report on economic cooperation, MITI spelled out the role of industrial policy, noting that development does not necessarily result from simply removing government-imposed obstacles. Where risks stem from an "immature market structure," weakness of financial institutions, or market failures, an industrial policy is appropriate, the report suggests—only, however, when based on a fundamental policy of reliance on market mechanisms. Industrial policy should involve consensus between industry and government with "visionary planning" and decisionmaking, enabling the financial system to undertake industrial finance, and helping to upgrade industrial structure. A Ministry of Foreign Affairs official put the issue more baldly: "Laissez-faire can't be recommended. Careful utilization of market forces is always ideal."[57] An official government report, noting developing countries' shift from state-led to private-led development strategies, suggests, "it is debatable whether, without any government intervention at all, sufficient catch-up-oriented economic development can be achieved."[58] In fact, most of the capitalist countries of East Asia have already set about learning from Japan and drawing on Japan's successful experience in devising institutions suited to its developmental goals. Examples range from Thailand's efforts to promote consultation between the public and private sectors to South Korea's creation of general trading companies and the Democratic Liberal party (inspired by the conservative Japanese Liberal Democratic party's success in dominating postwar politics).

## Cooperation Among Private Sector Organizations

Scholars who reject the notion that Japanese state officials, and MITI in particular, played a crucial role in engineering the Japanese miracle are often suggesting that Japanese markets operated much as they do elsewhere, simply more efficiently. This view is consistent with the familiar dichotomization of economies into those in which prices are market determined and those in which they are established authoritatively. Such a clumsy dichotomy, of course, ignores a wide range of intermediate types and often fails to consider the role that private sector institutions themselves play in mediating the ways in which individual firms are able to respond to price signals.

In Japan, a host of private sector institutions facilitate individual firms' efforts to survive. In the context of rapid market growth, survival often has required fast expansion simply to maintain existing market shares. A variety of important private sector institutions also helps Japanese enterprises in seeking export markets or looking to establish production facilities abroad. These institutions include semipublic ones such as the JODC and other financial institutions designed to help smaller enterprises move offshore. Public financial institutions continue to play key roles in supporting smaller Japanese firms.[59] Strictly private institutions also provide critical assistance.

As Japanese firms looked to move offshore in large numbers with the yen's take-off beginning in 1985, Japanese trading companies, insurance firms, and banks were among those to which prospective investors overseas, especially smaller ones, turned for information and services. Trading companies not only provide information services and marketing skills but also help in identifying local partners and frequently take a small equity stake themselves.[60] While the role of trading companies in facilitating Japanese direct foreign investment is declining, their skills in marketing, sales, and distribution remain important, particularly for smaller firms operating abroad.[61]

As Japanese manufacturing firms have moved offshore in larger numbers, Japanese banks also have moved to set up foreign affiliates so as to continue to serve their traditional clients. The banks are positioning themselves to coordinate the interests of diverse private actors while also addressing the desire among Japanese officials to augment the flow of financial resources to developing countries.[62] Another critical example of the reproduction offshore of the institutions of Japanese capitalism concerns the Japanese pattern of subcontracting relations in manufacturing. In many cases, the parent firm's decision to establish production facilities overseas leads their traditional subcontractors to follow the parent firm offshore.

## Regionalism

With its rapidly growing capital exports, including overseas economic assistance, a variety of Japanese institutions are exploring ways in which Japan can use its aid and investment, as well as trade, to further its foreign policy goals. This is a tentative and difficult process given the very limited consensus within Japan concerning its appropriate international role. In the past, most Japanese were content to leave the Ministry of Foreign Affairs in charge of the job of maintaining good relations with the United States, while MITI helped Japanese firms secure access to resources and markets. Today, an increasing number of actors seek to exert or enlarge their influence over Japan's foreign economic policy.

A book edited by Kosaka Masataka, a professor at Kyoto University, presents the findings of the Japan's Choices Study Group, a collection of academics, journalists, and members of business research institutes.[63] They note that technological change and deregulation are resulting in the internationalization of corporate activity. As Japan faces the third technological revolution based on microelectronics, biotechnology, and new materials, it must understand that "the globalization of economic activity has made it impossible to push ahead with economic development within the limited framework of a country defined by strict national boundaries."[64]

With this perspective as a premise, it is inevitable that the various interests and actors that produced the Japanese economic miracle are increasingly turning their attention abroad. It is not so much that Japanese officials and business elites are now pursuing new goals, as that the continuing pursuit of fundamental national interests dictates a more externally oriented posture. This is necessary in part because of the relative decline of the United States. Trade tensions with the United States also encourage Japanese efforts to increase their exports from third-country sites. More fundamentally, however, attention to Japan's place in the broader order of things flows from the internationalization of Japanese firms' production strategies and from the role that the economies of East Asia will play as Japan continuously seeks to upgrade its industrial structure.

Japanese trade with other Asian economies is growing faster than total Japanese trade. With rising trade and capital flows, Japanese firms are integrating the region's economies. For Japan to realize the goal of becoming "a culturally oriented industrial state" (the status of a major power without inordinate military power), the Japan's Choices Study Group suggests that Japan will have to work to create new economic relations with its Asian neighbors "based on a well-coordinated horizontal division of labor."[65]

Another Japanese study group, the Asian Forum Japan, operates under the auspices of the Forum for a Liberal Society. Its members include ruling party politicians, government officials, academics, and chief executive officers from major banks, securities, insurance, and trading companies.[66] The organization looks toward establishing branches in all Asian countries and includes among its goals: increasing Japanese technical assistance and exchange programs with Asian countries; establishing an international development university; strengthening Japanese education on Japan's relations with Asian countries; fostering education programs in Japan concerned with development issues; promoting the study of Asian languages; assisting foreign students to study in Japan; providing internships in the private sector for foreign students; increasing the number of Japanese serving in international organizations; and attracting greater numbers of Japan Overseas Cooperation Volunteers.[67]

As in the past, most of the recent initiatives concerned with reshaping Japan's international role are focused on enlarging Japan's role in Asia. Japanese have had greater exposure to Asian countries than to other developing countries, and Japan already has well-developed economic and political ties with the countries of Asia. Many Asians predictably harbor uneasiness with Japan's increasingly dominant regional role. At the same time, however, Japan's image in the region is much better than it was two decades ago. This shift in Asian views of Japan reflects the attraction of power, increasingly sensitive Japanese diplomacy, Japan's promise as a source of needed capital and technology, and growing annoyance with U.S. foreign economic policies. Furthermore, the nature of Japan's economic links with East Asian developing countries has been changing quickly—for example, Japanese imports of manufactured goods have been increasing rapidly. The prime ministers of both Malaysia and Thailand have been particularly vocal in expressing their support for an increasing Japanese role in the region.

Nonetheless, there is concern in Japan about pushing too energetically for the creation of an Asian economic grouping. Japanese officials worry that doing so could accelerate tendencies afoot in North America and

Western Europe to emphasize regional economic associations at the expense of multilateralism. The Bush administration was very direct in voicing its opposition to any East Asian economic grouping that does not include the United States. Japanese are also nervous about being seen by other Asian countries as overly aggressive in promoting any schemes over which Japan will inevitably loom as the dominant actor. Some of these neighbors recall Japan's earlier empire when, in the interests of being self-sufficient within its East Asian sphere of influence, Japan worked "to develop the industrial resources in her colonies and to rearrange the division of labor between her industries at home and those in the colonies."[68]

Given this concern, Japanese officials were pleased in 1989 at the generally favorable response in Asia to a proposed Asia-Pacific political and economic grouping (to include Japan, China, the Asian NICs, the ASEAN countries, Australia, New Zealand, Canada, and the United States).[69] Australian initiative[70] helped to calm disquiet stemming from the perception that such an organization would serve as a Trojan horse for still greater Japanese economic dominance in the region. Ding Xinghao, of the Shanghai Institute of International Studies, expressed such anxieties: "Japan's view is always a flying goose formation with Japan as the head goose. Our memories are long, so we aren't about to fly in Japan's formation."[71] By and large, though, political and economic elites across Asia find they gain more than they lose by joining the flock. For example, in December 1990 Prime Minister Mahathir Mohamad of Malaysia proposed the creation of an East Asian Economic Group, and Prime Minister Goh Chok Tong of Singapore subsequently endorsed the idea.

Proposals for an Asian economic organization have been booted about for quite some time. Japanese politicians have been expressing interest in such an idea since the 1950s. Economists Okita Saburo and Kojima Kiyoshi championed the cause of an Asian economic grouping in the early 1960s. The notion is gaining salience recently because of nervousness about possible further limitations on East Asian access to European and North American markets. A similar stimulus-response dynamic was evident in the late 1950s when the signing of the Treaty of Rome aggravated Japanese fears of isolation and prompted initial research into the feasibility of an Asian economic community. Such a response was also evident in prewar Japan. In 1941, former Japanese foreign minister Arita Hachiro wrote:

> When the doctrines of freedom of communications and trade prevailed the world over . . . it was possible even for small nations . . . to maintain a respectable existence side by side with the great Powers . . . Now, however . . . with the great Powers' closing or threatening to close their doors to others, small countries have no other choice left but to strive as best they can to form their own economic blocs . . .[72]

Japanese officials recognize that a world of regional economic groupings is a distinctly inferior option for Japan. Japan remains too big for Asia
and its extensive economic links with other regions, primarily North
America, argue for maintaining global patterns of trade and investment.
As a study by the Foundation for Advanced Information Research (a Ministry of Finance think-tank) suggested, "The EC integration and US-
Canada free-trade agreement are moves that cannot be stopped. But Japan,
the NICs, ASEAN, and Oceania should not succumb to the temptation of
promoting their own integration as a countermeasure."[73] All the same, the
report went on to detail the many areas in which research could be carried
out to stimulate regional integration. Leaders in other Asian countries are
concerned that the United States and West European nations will be increasingly preoccupied with events in Eastern Europe, the republics of the
former Soviet Union, the Middle East, and Latin America. On the one
hand, these Asians fear that the result will be the absence of any challenge
to Japan's economic supremacy in East Asia. On the other hand, they want
to assure that their future fortunes are tied to those of the Japanese economy. In the words of the former prime minister of Thailand, Chatichai
Choonhavan, "The World Economic War is over. Japan has won."[74] Japanese officials, for their part, recognize that the importance of Japanese links
with East Asia is growing rapidly.

Japanese foreign economic policy involves close coordination among
both private and public economic institutions. The Japanese facility in designing such mutually supportive arrangements could ease the task of ac-
commodating a world of economic blocs. Indeed, many Japanese have
long anticipated a world in which international economic ties would increasingly be managed among public institutions. In 1964, Hiyama Hi-
roshi, then head of Marubeni trading company, asserted that "ultimately
there will be an arranged division of labor among the advanced countries
in terms of categories of products."[75] Reflecting a similar view, Kojima
once wrote an article entitled "An Approach to Integration: The Gains
from Agreed Specialization."[76] Leon Hollerman's study of the Japanese
Ministry of Finance argues that the vision of the global future among
Japanese bureaucrats involves far-flung Japanese affiliates and sub-
sidiaries "controlled and coordinated by Japan's international financial institutions and its trading companies" in concert with Japanese bureaucrats.[77] MITI's efforts to coordinate Japanese firms' movement offshore
and to create complementary industrial structures in East Asia reflect an
impulse to manage even the most fundamental economic transitions. While
expressed in a radically different institutional idiom, and reflecting defensive moves to ward off threats of instability rather than any innate hubris,
the "can do" spirit of the Japanese today echoes that of earlier generations
of Americans.

## New Directions in Japanese Aid

Of its total foreign aid in fiscal year 1992 of over $7 billion, Japan has targeted an increasing share at environmental issues (about one-eighth of total project loans in 1991 according to one estimate).[78] Japanese leaders discussed late in 1991 the possibility of imposing new taxes in Japan as a means of supporting larger global spending on environmental projects.[79] Such initiatives are aimed in part at enhancing the perception abroad that Japan is assuming a more "responsible" international profile.

Japan has in fact moved rapidly to increase its contributions to Eastern European countries, despite the very limited degree of prior Japanese experience with or interest in that region. In 1990, Poland ranked among the top ten recipients of Japanese ODA, the only non-Asian country among that group.[80] With growing Japanese aid commitments to Eastern Europe and some Central American countries, Asia's share of total Japanese aid has been in decline, falling below 60 percent.[81]

Japan's contributions to the Commonwealth of Independent States are compromised by the ongoing dispute between Japan and Russia over the islands north of Hokkaido that the Soviet Union seized in the closing days of World War II. Late in 1991, Japan committed about $2.5 billion in the form of investment guarantees and trade credits. Other donor countries have been pushing Japan to increase its contributions. Perhaps at the prompting of Prime Minister Miyazawa, Chancellor Helmut Kohl of Germany complained in May 1992 about the level of Japan's assistance:

> Now especially it is time for Japan, an exporting nation, to assume a larger share of the West's common responsibility and, in keeping with her economic strength, to help insure the success of reforms in Central, Eastern, and Southeastern Europe and in the Commonwealth of Independent States.[82]

In Asia, it now appears likely that for the first time in nearly half a century, Japan will be sending its forces overseas, in this case as part of United Nations peace-keeping operations in Cambodia. Indeed, Japanese diplomats have been active in seeking a solution to the Cambodian conflict. The number of Japanese delegations traveling to Vietnam also is increasing as Japanese firms anticipate the re-establishment of U.S.-Vietnamese diplomatic relations and the resumption of Japanese aid to Vietnam.[83]

In April 1991, then Prime Minister Toshiki Kaifu outlined a new framework for Japanese ODA. According to this scheme, Japanese development aid will increasingly be linked to recipient countries' levels and types of military expenditures as well as their commitments to political and economic liberty. It is too early to discern the extent to which these guidelines will in fact shape Japanese policies. To date there is little evidence that this framework guides Japanese policies in either Burma or China. Nonetheless, we should not expect commitment to such a policy to lead to highly visible pronouncements by Japanese leaders condemning the policies of recipient countries. In any case, enunciation of the new guidelines clearly represents an effort to imbue Japanese ODA policy with greater coherence and a more explicitly political content.

## Conclusion

Differential rates of economic growth lead, over time, to an altered hierarchy of power among nations. Wars generally have been necessary in the past in order to assure that the objective distribution of power is reflected in international institutional arrangements and the subjective hierarchy of prestige.[84] Japan today lacks the military power or the desire necessary to challenge the United States for the position of dominant global power, and nuclear weapons deter the fighting of wars to establish new hierarchies of prestige.[85] In the realm of ideas, Japan has yet to offer a striking ideological stimulus to emulation or followership.[86]

A further factor arguing against Japanese efforts to establish fundamentally new international institutional arrangements stems from the nature of international economic liberalism. When the possession of dominant overall power dictated relations of economic tribute, power to create the rules of the game was critically important. Within the framework of economic liberalism, however, it is less clear that a rising power needs to challenge the institutional arrangements created by a status quo power. Hence, when the United States asserted its postwar global leadership, it sought to recreate at least some of the norms of the earlier Pax Britannica.[87] Similarly, growing Japanese power is likely to aim at strengthening existing international economic institutions rather than fundamentally altering them.[88] As the international system's heir apparent, Japan has an interest, as U.S. officials repeat ceaselessly, in supporting that system.

The challenge to Britain by the United States for international leadership in the first half of this century and to the United States by Japan and Germany in the 1980s and into the 1990s proceeded at a slow pace. The nature of liberalism as an economic system, particularly its relative openness resting on decentralized markets rather than authoritatively determined decisions, may help to account for this.[89] If the nature of liberalism does help to account for changes in the nature of leadership succession in the international system, significant movement away from the norms of liberalism toward those of neomercantilism in the form of managed trade may have consequences far greater than the loss of economic efficiency.

Japan may be precipitating just such a shift, both directly and indirectly: directly, in that its approach to economic development at home and abroad reflects a less than wholehearted commitment to arms-length market-based transactions; indirectly, in that its superior economic performance is provoking defensive responses, particularly in the United States, the former champion of international economic liberalism. Japan's flexibility, then, is a double-edged sword. On the one hand, it may enable Japan to adapt rapidly to changes in the structure and norms of the international economy. Its institutions facilitate mutual adaptation among a variety of economic organizations, helping to secure social stability. On the other hand, Japan's flexibility may hasten movement away from those norms that help to depoliticize international succession issues. As a result, Japan may undermine flexibility at the level of the international system.

Japanese officials want their economic assistance to serve Japanese interests, including recognition by other countries that Japan is doing its part to support the international system. They are also aware of Japan's special responsibilities as a capital surplus country. While many Japanese commentators began expressing concern as early as the mid-1980s about a possible erosion of Japan's industrial structure, major Japanese capital outflows, including direct foreign investment, are certain to continue in the years ahead. As a result of liberalization of capital controls, Japanese ministries are less able to regulate such outflows than in the past. Japanese firms, therefore, will respond to cost factors as well as protectionist pressures by moving their production offshore. In any case, Japanese direct foreign investment as a share of gross national product remains relatively low, amounting to only 4 percent in 1988.[90] Offshore production by Japanese manufacturing firms as a share of their total production stood at some 3 percent in 1986. The Economic Planning Agency estimates that this figure will rise to 20 percent by the end of this century.[91] The latter figure is roughly comparable to that for the United States today.[92]

A MITI report issued in 1987[93] features a section entitled, "Expectations of Japan and Lessons from History," which warns against Japan's following the path taken by the United States in the 1930s, when

> the United States, oblivious of its responsibility as the world's largest creditor country, pursued a protectionist trade policy by imposing high tariffs on imports, and . . . thus undermined the ability of debtor countries to earn dollars to service their debts to the United States.[94]

The report suggests that Japanese officials are intent on having Japan follow the more enlightened policy of Great Britain in its heyday. Britain "abided by the principle of free trade" and the capital it exported to European countries and the United States was

> employed to finance the construction of infrastructure, was instrumental in integrating the recipient economies and developing regional econo-

mies, while the technology transferred to them in the form of industrial facilities accelerated the industrial revolution in these countries.[95]

It remains to be seen, then, whether on balance Japan will emerge as a supporter of the norms of international economic liberalism or will help to undermine those norms. Changing structural realities argue for Japan to support those norms. If, as the aphorism has it, a strong trader is a free trader, Japan certainly should be a free trader. This conclusion, however, ignores the critical element of social policy that informs Japanese economic policymaking.[96] The political arrangements that support cooperative social and economic arrangements within Japan may be difficult to sustain with the increasing globalization of Japan's productive structure. The global interests of Japan's business firms may run counter to those of smaller import-competing businesses and agriculture.

Furthermore, Japanese leaders are not comfortable exercising their enormous influence. Most continue to cling to the fiction that Japan does not act as a political power abroad. They appear to prefer a "leadership role that will be technical and sector-specific rather than broadly political."[97] This involves, for example, pursuit of comprehensive development strategies that require coordinating the export of surplus capital and surplus capacity.[98] While many of Japan's allies welcomed Kiichi Miyazawa's recent assumption of the position of prime minister, it remains to be seen whether his tenure will signal a bolder Japanese international leadership. When asked whether it would be appropriate for Japan to be more assertive abroad, Miyazawa responded, "I think that perhaps—perhaps once in a great while—we perhaps should make ourselves more clear. Not perhaps every day. Once in a while is enough."[99]

It appears odd on the face of it that the same Japan that wins renown for the strategic nature of its industrial policies seems incapable of adopting a long-term view of its global political interests.[100] As economic tensions between Japan and the United States increased in the 1980s, many Japanese told U.S. business and political leaders that Japan wanted to see an economically resurgent United States. Such expressions reflect a sincere hope that Japan, somehow, will be spared the necessity of having its political power emerge naked before the eyes of foreigners and, more importantly, before the Japanese themselves. Many Japanese continue to hope that political unrest in Eastern Europe, instability in the Middle East, and the disintegration of the Soviet Union can be left to the care of the United States. And many in the United States would prefer that Japan continue to signal a willingness to finance a U.S. global role that requires resources greater than either Japanese political or U.S. financial capacities.

Japan's leadership increasingly has been willing to support the United States and other countries in sustaining existing international institutions, primarily through financial contributions. Japanese leaders, however, still seek to avoid leading in new directions or in any way challenging U.S. global supremacy. Japanese business firms, on the other hand, with support from government ministries, will lead the way as Japan searches for means of institutionalizing a broader global role reflecting its rapidly changing interests.

It is worth recalling that the Japanese conservative ruling party implemented a rapid increase in spending on social services over the 1970s. Kent Calder suggests that because the fragility associated with high levels of debt in corporate Japan induced an especially sharp aversion to potentially destabilizing influences, business interests supported preemptive social policies.[101] In the 1990s and beyond, Japanese corporations will push the Japanese government to assume a larger international role so that it can serve those firms' interest in a healthy global economy.

## Notes

1. Harold D. Lasswell, cited in David A. Baldwin, *Economic Statecraft* (Princeton, NJ: Princeton University Press, 1985), p. 29.

2. Tetsuya Kataoka argues that the United States was at least equally complicit in creating a mercantilist Japan. See *The Price of a Constitution* (New York: Crane Russak, 1991).

3. See Richard Rosecrance, *The Rise of the Trading State* (New York: Basic Books, 1986).

4. Ibid., pp. 2–3.

5. *Financial Times*, 15 January 1992, p. 19.

6. See Bill Emmott, *The Sun Also Sets* (New York: Simon and Schuster, 1989).

7. Kenneth Courtis quoted in *New York Times*, 6 October 1991, p. E3.

8. William J. Barnds, "The United States and Japan: A Time of Troubles," The Asia Foundation's Center for Asian Pacific Affairs, Report Number 2, June 1991.

9. Japan Institute of International Affairs, *White Papers of Japan, 1988–1989* (Tokyo: Japan Institute of International Affairs, 1990), pp. 24–27.

10. For a discussion of the significance of Japan's creditor status, see Richard Rosecrance and Jennifer Taw, "Japan and the Theory of International Leadership," *World Politics* 42, no 2 (January 1990): 184–209.

11. For example, in May of 1990, Prime Minister Kaifu was in South and Southeast Asia, urging the countries of those regions to address problems of environmental degradation, terrorism, population growth, and development policy reform.

12. Takashi Inoguchi, "Japan's Global Role in a Multipolar World," p. 22, and Julia Chang Bloch, "A U.S.-Japan Aid Alliance," p. 81, both in *Yen for Development*, ed. Shafiqul Islam (New York: Council on Foreign Relations Press, 1991).

13. One of the results of this episode was a high-level advisory commission study of the Ministry of Foreign Affairs. The commission's initial draft recommendations called for steps that would have further weakened the ministry. The report's final version, reflecting ministry lobbying, was far more circumspect. Interview with Ministry of Foreign Affairs official in Tokyo, August 1991.

14. On the factors giving rise to negotiated institutional arrangements, see Oran R. Young, *International Cooperation* (Ithaca, NY: Cornell University Press, 1989), particularly pp. 81–108.

15. Young, *International Cooperation*, p. 230. For a discussion of Japan's postwar institution building, see Chalmers Johnson, *MITI and the Japanese Miracle* (Stanford, CA: Stanford University Press, 1981).

16. Liberal Democratic Diet members' familiarity with specific issues and the concerns of private interests over which they have jurisdiction enhance the former's influence.

17. For a discussion of the reactive state, see Kent E. Calder, "Japanese Foreign Economic Policy Formation: Explaining the Reactive State," *World Politics* 40, no. 4 (July 1988): 517–541.

18. See, for example, Herbert Passin, "Sociocultural Factors in the Japanese Perception of International Order," *Annual Review* (1971): 51–75. Publication of Japan Institute of International Affairs.

19. See Donald C. Hellman, "Japanese Security and Postwar Japanese Foreign Policy," in *The Foreign Policy of Modern Japan*, ed. Robert A. Scalapino (Berkeley: University of California Press, 1977), pp. 321–340. Like many traditional U.S. isolationists concerned for the integrity of democratic values at home, some Japanese fear that a more active foreign policy will endanger Japan's own democratic institutions. See Masaru Tamamoto, "Japan's Search for a World Role," in Scalapino, *The Foreign Policy*.

20. The particularities of Japan's prewar colonial policies are emphasized by Bruce Cumings, "The Origins and Development of the Northeast Asian Political Economy: Industrial Sectors, Product Cycles, and Political Consequences," in *The Political Economy of the New Asian Industrialism*, ed. Frederic C. Deyo (Ithaca, NY: Cornell University Press, 1987), pp. 44–83.

21. Ministry of Finance figures.

22. Small and Medium Enterprise Agency figures.

23. Samuel Pao-San Ho, "Colonialism and Development: Korea, Taiwan, and Kwantung," in *The Japanese Colonial Empire, 1895–1945*, ed. Ramon H. Myers and Mark R. Peattie (Princeton, NJ: Princeton University Press, 1984), p. 351.

24. Ho, "Colonialism and Development," p. 355.

25. See Cumings, "Origins and Development of the Northeast Asian Political Economy."

26. Japanese Institute of International Affairs, *White Papers of 1988–1989* (1990); OECD, *Development Cooperation*, 1988.

27. Japanese war reparations launched Japan's economic assistance programs. The Japanese have used a "request-based" system of yen loans in which the initiative for projects is supposed to come from the recipient government.

28. Jon Halliday and Gavan McCormack, *Japanese Imperialism Today: Co-Prosperity in Greater East Asia* (New York: Monthly Review Press, 1973); Phillip McMichael, "Foundations of U.S./Japan World Economic Rivalry in the 'Pacific Rim,'" in *Journal of Developing Societies* no. 3 (April 1987): 61–77.

29. Thomas Baron Gold, "Dependent Development in Taiwan" (Ph.D. diss., Harvard University, 1981), p. 178.

30. Interview with MITI official in Bangkok, December 1990.

31. The Overseas Economic Cooperation Fund and the Japan International Cooperation Agency distribute the great bulk of official development assistance.

32. *Japan Overseas Development Corporation*, English Edition.

33. Ibid.

34. *Guide to AOTS, 1989*.

35. *Asian Wall Street Journal*, 5–6 September 1986.

36. Interview with official at Keizai Doyukai (Organization for Economic Cooperation).

37. Interviews with officials at Keidanren, MITI, and Ministry of Foreign Affairs.

38. MITI, *New Aid Plan* (June 1987).

39. Nangaku Masaaki, "Japan's Economic Cooperation to Support the Industrialization of Asian Nations" (Paper presented at the conference on "Global Adjustment and the Future of Asia-Pacific Economies," hosted by the Institute for Developing Economies and the Pacific Development Centre, Tokyo, 11–13 May 1988).

40. Leon Hollerman also notes that liberalization has restricted bureaucratic turf in Japan, which has prompted more bureaucrats to turn abroad. See his study of Japanese economic influence in Brazil, *Japan's Economic Strategy in Brazil* (Lexington, MA: Lexington Books, 1988), p. 99.

41. The request basis of Japanese aid is supposed to depend on the initiative of the recipient country in identifying projects.

42. MITI, "The Present State and Problems of Economic Cooperation," Foreign Press Center, Japan, 1986.

43. Ibid.

44. Ibid.

45. Ibid.

46. Alan Rix, "Japan's Aid Leadership" (Paper presented at annual meeting of the Association of Asian Studies, Washington D.C., 17 March 1989).

47. Kosaka Masataka, ed., *Japan's Choices: New Globalism and Cultural Orientations in an Industrial State* (New York: Pinter, 1989), p. 41.

48. MITI, "Economic Cooperation," pp. 26–27. This has been achieved, in part, by diverting Japanese exports with Japanese firms now serving the same markets but from new export platforms.

49. MITI, *New Aid Plan.*

50. Terutomo Ozawa, *Recycling Japan's Surplus for Developing Countries* (OECD Development Centre Studies, 1989), p. 11.

51. Ozawa, *Recycling Japan's Surplus.*

52. Hasegawa Junichi, "Japan's Official Development Assistance and an Analysis of the Macroeconomic Effects of Aid," United States–Japan Occasional Paper, Harvard University, June 1989, p. 8.

53. For details see the Ministry of Trade and Industry's "Present State and Problems of Japan's Economic Cooperation: 1987," Foreign Press Center, Japan, June 1988, p. 26.

54. Kurosawa Yoshitaka, "Japanese Capital Flows to the Third World: Problems and Prospects," United States–Japan Program Occasional Paper, Harvard University, March 1989, p. 18.

55. Rix, "Japan's Aid Leadership." Personnel shortages help to explain Japan's heavy dependence on multilateral institutions to disperse its aid.

56. Japan Economic Institute, 20 May 1988.

57. Quoted in *Asian Wall Street Journal*, 20 August 1990, p. 1.

58. Japanese Institute of International Affairs, *White Papers of 1988–1989*, pp. 126–127.

59. Jung Taik Hyun and Katherine Whitmore, *Japanese Direct Foreign Investment: Patterns and Implications for Developing Countries* (The World Bank Industry and Energy Department, 1989), p. 38.

60. See Yoshihara Kunio, *Japanese Investment in Southeast Asia* (Honolulu: University of Hawaii Press, 1978); M.Y. Yoshino, *Japan's Multinational Enterprises* (Cambridge, MA: Harvard University Press, 1976), pps. 95–125.

61. Hyun and Whitmore, *Japanese Direct Foreign Investment*, pps. 24–28.

62. Ozawa, *Recycling Japan's Surplus*.

63. Masataka, *Japan's Choices*.

64. Ibid., p. 6.

65. Ibid., p. 41.

66. Promotional publication, *Asian Forum, Japan Conference 1988* (Tokyo, n.p.).

67. Asian Forum Japan, *The Asian Era—Theme and Prospect*, Asian Forum Japan Commemorative Symposium, 30 November–1 December 1988.

68. Ho, "Colonialism and Development," p. 351.

69. At the meeting in Canberra in late 1989, China, Hong Kong, and Taiwan were excluded. The grouping subsequently settled on a formula for their inclusion.

70. Prime Minister Robert Hawke proposed consultations with Japan on creation of an Asia-Pacific grouping during Prime Minister Takeshita's visit to Australia in July 1988. In 1980 Prime Minister Ohira made a similar proposal to his counterpart, Malcolm Fraser, resulting in the creation of a Pacific Basin study group and the first meeting of the Pacific Economic Cooperation Council in Canberra that year. The group held its seventh meeting in November 1989.

71. Quoted in Chalmers Johnson, *The Problem of Japan in an Era of Structural Change* (Graduate School of International Relations and Pacific Studies, University of California at San Diego, Research Report 89–04, June 1989).

72. Quoted in Joyce Chapman-Lebra, *Japan's Greater East Asia Co-Prosperity Sphere in World War II* (New York: Oxford University Press, 1975).

73. Foundation for Advanced Information Research, Ministry of Finance, Tokyo.

74. Quoted in Bruce Koppel and Michael Plummer, "Japan's Ascendancy as a Foreign Aid Power," *Asian Survey* 29, no. 11 (November 1989).

75. Quoted in a report by the Foundation for Advanced Information Research on the future of the Asia-Pacific Region.

76. In *Essays in Honor of Roy Harrod*, ed. W.A. Eltis (Oxford: Clarendon Press, 1970).

77. Leon Hollerman, *Japan Disincorporated* (Stanford, CA: Hoover Institution Press, 1988), pp. xix–xx.

78. *Far Eastern Economic Review*, 12 March 1992, p. 39.

79. *Japan Economic Institute Report*, No. 16B, 24 April 1992.

80. *Japan Economic Institute Report*, No. 1B, 10 January 1992.

81. Ibid.

82. *New York Times*, 6 May 1992, p. A1.

83. *Far Eastern Economic Review*, 30 January 1992, p. 41.

84. See Robert Gilpin, *War and Change in World Politics* (New York: Cambridge University Press, 1981).

85. As suggested briefly at the outset of this paper, I do not believe that Japan's period of rapid growth relative to its referent group is drawing to a close.

86. On followership, see Andrew Fenton Cooper, Richard A. Higgott, and Kim Richard Nossal, "Bound to Follow? Leadership and Followership in the Gulf Conflict," *Political Science Quarterly* 106, no. 3 (Fall 1991): 391–410.

87. For a discussion of the differences between the two eras of international liberalism, see John Gerard Ruggie, "International Regimes, Transactions, and Change: Embedded Liberalism in the Postwar Economic Order," in *International Regimes*, ed. Stephen D. Krassner (Ithaca, NY: Cornell University Press, 1983).

88. While international economic management under the leadership of different countries would influence the respective roles of different currencies, the shift in the international roles of those currencies is likely eventually to reflect un-

derlying structural realities, even if existing institutions are not fundamentally altered. Increasing acceptance by other countries of the yen as a reserve currency will bestow upon Japan some of the "exorbitant privilege" currently enjoyed by the United States, although the departure from a fixed-exchange-rate regime makes this less significant.

89. Security issues have, of course, been more significant in explaining these developments. In any case, the argument is not the traditional liberal one that interdependence removes or overcomes the sources of international conflict. Rather, the point is that conflict and adjustments in hierarchies may not necessitate major institutional overhaul.

90. Young-Kwan Yoon, "The Political Economy of Transition: Japanese Foreign Direct Investments in the 1980s," *World Politics* 43, no. 1 (October 1990), p. 5.

91. Yoon, "The Political Economy of Transition," p. 17.

92. Hyun and Whitmore, *Japanese Direct Foreign Investment*, p. 4.

93. MITI, "Present State and Problems 1987."

94. Ibid., p. 21.

95. Ibid., p. 19.

96. See Peter Drucker, "Japan's Choices," *Foreign Affairs* 65, no. 4 (Summer 1987): 923–941.

97. Calder, "The Reactive State," p. 541.

98. Richard P. Cronin, "Japan's Expanding Role and Influence in the Asia-Pacific Region: Implications for U.S. Interests and Policy," Congressional Research Service, Library of Congress, Washington, D.C., 7 September 1990.

99. *New York Times*, 26 September 1991, p. A4.

100. Calder, "The Reactive State," addresses some of the reasons for this apparent anomaly. Briefly, throughout the postwar period Japan's most polarized politics have tended to start at the water's edge.

101. Kent Calder, *Crisis and Compensation* (Princeton, NJ: Princeton University Press, 1988).

# PART 4

## CONFLICT AND ITS RESOLUTION

# 11

## Conflict and Change
## in the International System

### *Robert O. Slater*

The international system is transforming at a rate not witnessed since the end of the colonial era with the emergence of newly independent states. The unwinding of the Cold War and the breakup of the Soviet Union have unleashed another array of newly independent states, many of whom are virtually unprepared to deal either with transforming their domestic political and economic systems or with a highly complex and competitive global political and economic system.

Describing and characterizing the global transformation of the 1990s and defining the context of future conflict, particularly as it might pertain to the Third World, is a matter of some consequence. Politicians and scholars alike have struggled to explain changes and to describe the future prospects for the international system. Some have been led to focus on the new world order which they now believe exists—or would like to imagine exists. This new world order is characterized by the failure of the Soviet model and the ultimate triumph of liberalism; it is taken to its furthest point, perhaps, by Fukuyama and those who subscribe to his famous (or infamous) "end of history" thesis. Others *prescribe* a new world order—an order with great possibilities for the rule of law and for the renewal of the role of international and regional organizations. Still others see a remarkable opportunity for a Pax Americana—a U.S. resurgence in world politics in response to a vacuum left behind by the demise of the Soviet Union. To proponents of this latter school of thought, the demise of the Soviet Union and centrally planned economies came as a welcome relief from the doomsday theories of Paul Kennedy, who argued that the decline of the United States was due to military spending and imperial over-stretch.[1] Students of political science tend to view the changes in purely political terms; students of political economy see a far different world of competing national and regional economies.

Unfortunately, reality dictates caution. The world of the 1990s is one of continued violence coupled with marginalization and even potential elimination not only of Third World states but of many ethnic minorities.

Much of what takes place seems beyond the influence, scope, or even interest of major powers. Certainly, events warrant optimism in relation to the role of international organizations (specifically the United Nations) in resolving state, regional, and international violence (more regionally based organizations, though, have demonstrated little effectiveness in conflict mitigation and resolution). But one need only look at the respective cases of Yugoslavia in 1991, or Somalia, or the Kurds as evidence of the apparent incapacity or unwillingness of the new international system to address the clash of ethnic groups unleashed within this new world order.

To be sure, the world of the 1990s will be a combination of multiple perspectives. The complexity reflects a world dominated by the less developed and highly troubled nations or states, whose numbers within the international system are increasing, and a challenge to major powers in determining what role they can and need to play. As Stanley Hoffman has stated, "If, in a world of shaky regimes, contested borders, and ethnic upheavals, aggression requires the mobilization of three-quarters of a million troops, many sent across the seas to face well-armed troublemakers and obtain their unconditional surrender, there will be very few cases of collective security."[2]

The world of the early 1990s has been punctuated by highly intense and deadly conflict and is likely to be further defined by forms of ethnic conflict and retribution that have not been matched in intensity at least since the origins of the Cold War and quite possibly since the *inter*national bickering that preceded World War I and World War II. Not only does the nature of conflict require re-examination but the roles noncombatants might play in its resolution requires redefinition. Indeed, as the *Economist* recently reported, "Since the Gulf War there have already been four western interventions; forcible, by America and Europe in defeating Iraq, to help the Kurds; peaceable, by American diplomats to wind up Ethiopia's civil war; feeble, by EC ceasefire monitors in Yugoslavia; firm, by European soldiers in Zaire."[3]

How is this conflict controlled? How are decisions to be made concerning which conflicts represent threats to the stability of the international system or threats to national security interests? Who is to control the conflict—powerful states, regional centers of power, or international organizations? What is certain is that conflict is inevitable for the 1990s. Almost as certain are some of the forms it will take. Uncertain, however, is how the new international system will cope with old and new forms of conflict.

The objective of this essay is to explore alternative and in some ways less orthodox characterizations of the new international system, a system distinguished by fundamental changes in the rules of the game and in how we may define such commonly accepted concepts as sovereignty and the nation-state. These rules and definitions will clearly bear a relationship to the forms of conflict that will be manifested in the new system, but debate about these forms cannot be resolved unless we come to terms with the structure of the international system within which they will emerge.

## The Viability of the "Sovereign" State in a Transformed Global System

The sovereign nation-state, dating from the 1648 Peace of Westphalia, is commonly seen as the factor that has successfully guided the international system through the last three and one-half centuries:

> The chief characteristic of power capabilities in the modern world system is their fragmentation, their dispersal among many centers of authority. Westphalia's genius lies in its having made the best of that situation by creating a system of order that derives from fragmented capabilities rather than trying to overcome them through centralization.[4]

Miller continues by asserting that in theory, the Westphalian concept of order needs "no central authority, no governmental institutions, to maintain acceptable social order among the component units."[5]

Modern world politics has been guided by a reliance on the nation state as the primary unit of analysis. Prior to World War II and the advent of the Cold War, the nation-state was seen as the unifying concept in an overall Westphalian system of order. Without the nation-state, chaos would reign. The Cold War brought about a change in the attitude toward the concept of state—the state became the centerpiece of major power politics and rivalries. In many ways what Miller calls the "laissez-faire" quality of the Westphalian order broke down because there was no environment conducive to the free development and growth of sovereign states.

The postcolonial era, coupled with the Cold War, further eroded the Westphalian sanctity of the nation-state. External interference in the Third World led to support for insurgencies in states already lacking legitimacy, thereby undermining the ability of the state to survive over the long term. Support for insurgencies in Southern Africa—particularly Angola and Mozambique—and in Central America—contributed to the erosion of the concept of nation-state. Weak states searched for models for economic, social, and political development. In a bipolar, ideologically charged environment, states gravitated either toward Marxist-Leninist or democratic models.

It is likely that the end of the Cold War has resulted in a radical change in the endurance of the nation-state in world politics and in the potential for more specialized forms of conflict that challenge its legitimacy. More precisely, the era of global transformation has brought about a profound change in the sanctity of the nation-state *and* its associated borders, as defined by colonists and often by the vagaries of the post–World War I and World War II periods. It is true that external support for insurgencies has largely evaporated; there is little interest or perceived necessity on the part of any major power to support insurgencies. But it is also true that these major powers have left behind, for example in Eastern Europe and Africa, either the legacy of a fractionalized state—ruled by a weak central authority that has survived over time primarily because of external military and economic support—and/or an insurgent group now operating on its own to challenge the legitimacy of the central "authority." Unfortunately, it is also quite apparent that the abundance of weapons supplied by these external forces will continue to fuel insurgencies for years to come.

Global transformation causes us to examine what has all too often been ignored in the consideration of international issues—that the problems of the state from *within* dominate international politics. While the traditional challenges to the state—insurgency, revolution, and territorial challenge—still exist, we must also begin to examine the critical relationship between state and civil society, which affects the capacity of the state to be constituted by legitimacy and to achieve some degree of harmony *within* its national borders.

Clearly the traditional notion of sovereignty, as Miller and others would admit, is under tremendous stress. The very notion of sovereignty, however, and the ways we perceive sovereignty, may be inadequate to grasp the fundamental changes occurring in the international system of the 1990s. The rather commonplace analyses of world politics, lost in the time warp of Westphalia and the centuries following, are no longer sufficient.

Scholars, primarily theorists of international relations, have focused on the "state as actor." Now, faced with a major global upheaval that causes us all to rethink most concepts and much conventional wisdom, many are willing to dismiss the concept of the state because it "gets in the way when we analyze the processing of real political issues."[6] They argue for a "new research agenda" and continue to search for patterns of "authority" in interactions among states or among other entities that either replace the state or rival the state for authority. Ferguson and Mansbach, for example, and James Rosenau in his recent major effort addressing this very issue, argue for the recognition that there are authority patterns that are both vertical (e.g., territorially defined entities) and horizontal (e.g., class, religion).[7] Such diversity in authority patterns *is* and has been the reality of international politics long before the transformation that has characterized the late 1980s and 1990s. Unfortunately, those who study international relations have missed the boat by focusing almost exclusively on state-to-state patterns, leaving to other disciplines the complexities of cross-cutting religious, sociocultural, and economic issues that shape the patterns that develop *within* states. Now, acknowledging that contemporary global politics is rapidly changing, they strive to capture this transformation by arguing that the "state" is rather trivial "because it obscures the equally important fact that humanity is divided in many other ways as well."[8]

It is erroneous to dismiss the state as the central locus of authority in what remains a predominantly Western-dominated international political and economic system, though it is clear that the state is confronting considerable challenge and stress. Significant new entities are emerging— some representing regional cleavages within a former state (e.g., Serbia and Croatia from Yugoslavia and Eritrea from Ethiopia) and others representing re-emergence of states lost in the shuffle of World War I, World War II, and the Cold War (e.g., the Baltic states and other former states of the Soviet Union). Many of these re-emergent states actually represent a new and final wave of decolonization as they spin off from Soviet control. Regardless of the circumstances of their emergence, these entities immediately search for security of borders (the critical component of the state in the "modern Western" system) to establish the necessary prerequisites of a "state." They want to be recognized as states because the new order into which they are emerging still contains a state system, one that rewards the state. The posturing that characterizes the chaos in Yugoslavia is of vying for state recognition from the European Community. The European Community will not "do business" with a nonstate actor, nor will the World Bank or the United States. The Commonwealth of Independent States that formerly comprised the Soviet Union is unequivocal in its structure, which is designed to command respect and full diplomatic recognition for each of its component independent states. New leadership attempts to display control and authority in order to demonstrate to the world "community" that it is deserving of de facto, if not de jure, recognition as an independent *state*. What we must recognize is not that the state paradigm is at an end, but that we must begin to tolerate, as Jowitt so vividly points out, more irregularity in the state system with the appearance and disappearance of states and the changing of international boundaries.[9]

A single and rather parsimonious definition of the state is no longer possible in the complex international system of the 1990s. As Higgot notes, "States are not, and have never been, the only major units of identification and interest in global politics." Furthermore, "sovereignty as a normative and legal concept may circumscribe a territorially defined legitimacy, but has only limited utility for an understanding of the nature and practice of world politics in the 1980s and 1990s."[10] Higgot refers here to a form of sovereignty both less hegemonic and less parsimonious than previous forms, but reflecting the far more complex nature of within-state and state-to-state relations. This form of sovereignty addresses the paramount issues of state-society relations instead of focusing on the state as a monolithic actor in a rational model of international politics.

What, then, is the point of all of this? First, we must recognize that the "state"—and the sovereignty associated with it—of the 1990s requires defining in ways that scholars have previously dismissed, for reasons of parsimony as well as adherence to a neorealist model of international politics, which demands that we treat the state as a unified, rational actor. Second, if we recognize the "state" differently, i.e., as an entity undergoing considerable challenge to its legitimacy and sovereignty, then we must consider a new set of significant and probably rather sophisticated challenges to popular conceptions of international politics. Indeed, the most significant challenge for the international system of the 1990s—and the single greatest source for potential conflict within it—is the evolution of the legitimacy of the state and the viability of the state itself.

## The Challenges of Conflict

Challenges to the state and to sovereignty, while they do represent significant challenges to domestic and regional stability—and in some cases to international stability—do not represent threats to the fundamental viability of the state as central to the order of the international system. Instead, the challenges to the state force us to re-examine the nature of conflict in the international system and its susceptibility to management, mitigation, and resolution at some international level. State systems that endured during much of the twentieth century are faced with latent challenges from *within*. These systems were manufactured, often artificially, to consolidate large territories and disparate populations; they were held together by authoritarian or totalitarian rule; and now the glue has simply lost its grip. Democratization, while seen by many as a positive force in the international system, fosters ethnic self-consciousness, a clear and present danger to the survival of the multiethnic "state." The pressure to liberalize economic systems, meanwhile, sometimes stands in stark contrast to a democratization process that erodes centralized authority; the result is even greater tension with the state.[11] Thrust into an international system requiring more viability than previously as an international political *economic* actor, Third World states find it more difficult to "deliver the goods" and discover little assistance coming from the external environment. Soviet client states, having adopted a Marxist-Leninist model, are cast adrift, unable to function in a more competitive, open market system. Indeed, as Callaghy has discussed in Chapter 8 of this volume, many Third World states are now being further marginalized, constituting a Fourth World of international "basket" cases of interest only to nongovernmental organizations. All of these conditions mitigate *against* the survival of states and their ability to control their domestic populations, leading to significant potentials for conflict.

What types of conflict are likely to persist in the international system of the 1990s? If we acknowledge the importance of the challenge from within, we must focus primarily on challenges to the legitimacy of the state. Schutz and Slater, in a recent work on revolutions in the Third World, characterize seven primary types of movements that have challenged state (or regime) legitimacy.[12] Although their work focuses on the challenge of revolutions to regime legitimacy, the movement types they identify highlight the changes that have taken place in the international system as well as their implications for conflict.

Type 1 is the "collapse of monarchical legitimacy." The classic case is Ethiopia. There remain but a few contemporary monarchical regimes that are vulnerable to such collapse and potential conflict; Saudi Arabia stands out as such a possible case. Certainly, one must consider the impact of a resurgence of democratic movements on the ability of traditional monarchical regimes to survive during the 1990s. Type 2 is Islamic resurgence. Iran, of course, endures as the classic contemporary case. Islamic influence is pervasive throughout much of the Middle East and South and Central Asia and remains a potential threat to the survival of certain states and to the stability of regional politics. It is not likely, however to be a pervasive cause of conflict in the international system. Type 3 is the classic "Eastern" type of revolutionary movement identified by Huntington, which begins with peasants in the countryside. These cases seem rare and are limited to Peru and possibly Colombia. With the diminishment of Marxism-Leninism as a force in the international system—and the absence of external support that has sometimes been associated with Marxist-Leninist models—it is hard to imagine a significant and ideologically based threat from this type. Type 4 is represented by revolutionary mobilization against soft "illegitimate" regimes. Central America and the Philippines are the classic examples here. We will return to this type later in this chapter, as it is likely to persist in a somewhat modified form as a catalyst for conflict in the globally transformed system of the 1990s. Types 5 and 6, anticolonial revolutionary nationalism and anti-Marxist insurgencies, seem likely candidates for elimination from the international scene. Classic colonial cases where movements challenge settler/colonial rule (Algeria, Kenya, and Rhodesia) are rare. Only South Africa and the Israeli-PLO case seem to remain as possibilities for explosive violence. Insurgencies based in anti-Marxism have virtually passed from the scene since, with the remarkable changes in Eastern Europe, the Soviet Union, Ethiopia, etc., there are few cases of Marxist authority to be challenged. One could argue, however, that the cases of China, Cuba, and North Korea remain volatile. Type 7 includes movements that are ethnonationalistic and oriented toward secession, boundary alteration, or a rearrangement of state power. Recent historical examples include the Eritrean People's Liberation Front in Ethiopia, the Sudanese People's Liberation Army in Sudan, and the Kurdish movements of Iran, Iraq, and Turkey.

Two types of movements, then, seem to represent both the greatest challenge to the central authority of the state and the most likely catalyst for conflict in the international system. "Soft" illegitimate regimes, in some cases now deprived of support from a dominant external power, remain vulnerable to crisis and conflict. This is the case throughout Eastern Europe and in the former republics of the Soviet Union. Furthermore, such regimes will face new challenges to legitimacy as the expectation that they must "deliver the goods" intensifies in an increasingly competitive international political economic system. Third World states will experience such pressures as well, as they attract less attention from the developed world and as economic failures leave them vulnerable to internal decay. Cuba stands out as a classic case of an increasingly soft regime whose weaknesses are highlighted by a lack of support from external sources.

*Ethnonationalism* presents the most dramatic potential for conflict—and for dramatic violence that can spill beyond the state and attract regional and international attention. As Jowitt discusses in Chapter 2 of this volume, the vastly transformed international system will result in new and bold challenges to the territories and boundaries of an earlier system.[13] Many of these territorial and boundary issues are highly related to the displacement of ethnic groups, an issue which often dominated "modern" world politics but which took a back seat to the political posturing and maneuvering that characterized the bipolar international relationships of the Cold War.

While the potential for conflict is worldwide, it is most concentrated in two "regions"—the African continent and the states of Eastern Europe and the former Soviet Union. African states, marginalized even during much of the Cold War, have been cast aside to confront their problems head on. Not surprisingly, for example, President Mitterand of France made it clear to leaders from French-speaking African states, that France would no longer prop up dictators in the name of stability. The pull-out precipitated a breakdown of "authority" in Zaire; most analysts do not foresee a revolution in Zaire, but unrest is likely to continue.

No region is more emblematic of changes in the international system than the Horn of Africa. No longer possessing any strategic value (in contrast to Zaire, which has vast supplies of cobalt, copper, and diamonds), the Horn of Africa has been marginalized to a clearly Fourth World status. The intense East-West rivalry that fueled the Soviet advance into Ethiopia and the U.S. buttressing of Somalia and Sudan has unraveled the region. The end of the Cold War has brought about isolation of the region and an era of civil war and famine. The failure of the Somali state has been pervasive and has led to a bloodbath of monumental proportions. Samatar[14] describes the Somali debacle, but his words are applicable more generally:

> While the peoples of Eastern Europe, in their search for democratic socialism, victoriously bring down one oligarchic collectivist regime after another, the struggle for genuine democratic rights and humane gover-

nance in most Third World societies is rather grim. Whether in Central or South America, North or Sub-Saharan Africa, the Near or Far East, the humane impulse toward liberty, sustenance, and equity is as contentious as ever . . . But it is in Africa . . . in the northeast part . . . where some of the most gruesome contradictions of development are being played out.

In Eastern Europe, the case of Yugoslavia represents dramatically not only the pressures from within that imperil the sanctity of the "state" but also the obvious inability of the international system to solve the problem. The conflict between Serbia and Croatia has shown no signs of abatement and has remained impervious to outside influences. Moreover, the efforts at peaceful resolution are plainly indicative of a continuing attempt to apply pre-1990 conceptions of the viability of the state and its sovereignty to a post-1990 crisis. For example, a European peace plan proposed during the fall of 1990 attempted to move Yugoslavia toward a loose association of sovereign republics with a currency union. The plan called for no internal border changes except by mutual agreement and for the demilitarization of disputed areas inhabited by ethnic minorities. Clearly, such a plan has not worked, and its potential for success is further dimmed by a more careful examination of other tensions underlying the Yugoslav "state." Tensions in Bosnia between Serbs, Croats, and Muslims further threaten the viability of the state. Albanians, the dominant population in the southern region of Kosovo, are anxious to move away from Serbian rule. Finally, Macedonia has already declared its independence. Clearly, Yugoslavia will not survive in its previous state.

The Soviet Transcaucasus constitutes another region of ethnic strife. The region includes Armenia, Azerbaijan, and Georgia; the population is comprised of dozens of ethnic groups belonging to three orthodox churches (Armenian, Georgian, and Russian) as well as both branches of Islam. A writer for the *Economist* observes "At the meeting-point of the Russian, Turkish, and Persian empires, it seems things have changed little since Pliny said: 'We Romans did business there with the aid of 130 interpreters.'"[15] The *Economist* goes on to report that the case of Armenia is yet another example of conflict waiting to begin. In the Nagorno-Karabakh region, a heavily Armenian enclave in Azerbaijan, CIS troops seem to provide the only protection from war.

Underlying the tremendous potential for domestic ethnic conflict is the significance of the displacement of minorities. While they were often lost in the shuffle of Cold War politics, the international trend toward democratization has served as a catalyst for ethnic minorities to reassert themselves in ways that threaten the survival of the state. While the ethnic minority problem is not new, it is emerging now as the most salient threat to international stability. Gurr suggests an explanation for the significance of ethnic conflict:

Political conflicts among warring ethnic groups are not new, but they have proved to be more perplexing and intractable for those concerned with global security than were the guerrilla wars of national liberation and revolution of the Cold War era. They are perplexing, because the motives of the contending parties cannot be reduced to the familiar categories of nationalism and Marxist-Leninist revolution. They often appear intractable because the well-worn policy tools of economic reform and counterinsurgency neither satisfy nor suppress the underlying desires of the protagonists to protect and assert their group identities.[16]

Gurr's landmark study of "minorities at risk" raises a number of key issues that are indicative of the volatility of ethnic issues in international politics:

1. Most of the world's 170 independent states have significant ethnic and regional cleavages.
2. There are as many as 5,000 distinct communities in the contemporary world that might claim to be national peoples or "ethnics." The 230 distinct minority groups identified by Gurr in his study total about 900 million (in 1991) or slightly more than 17 percent of the world's population.
3. Most ethnic groups are concentrated in one or several adjacent regions; conversely, relatively few of the groups are widely dispersed. More than a third of the groups have kindred distributed across three or more countries, with the most widely dispersed groups concentrated in Latin America and the Middle East (in Latin America, blacks and Indians and in the Middle East, Kurds, Shiites, and Palestinians).
4. Fifty-one of the 230 groups have supported serious insurgencies and 142 have taken some kind of violent political action against authorities; 176 groups have at some time mobilized and used nonviolent protest.

It has taken a long time for political scientists and policymakers to realize, if they actually yet realize, that ethnicity challenges the existence of the state itself. Lessons from observing the breakup of the Soviet Union serve to clarify an issue that has existed in states as diverse as Nigeria, Malaysia, India, and the new states of Central Asia. Brown argues this point

It has been argued that . . . the state possesses some degree of "relative autonomy" whereby the imperatives of statehood lie behind the expansion of bureaucratic and ideological control over society. From this perspective, it is the state bureaucracies that seek to expand their influence, not so much from self-interest per se, but more from the necessary concern of the state, and especially the new post-colonial state, to seek the order, national cohesion, and economic development necessary to secure the preservation of the system. Most of the literature on the politics of development has tended to assume that, apart from a few exceptions, the governments of most Third World states were ethnically neutral, at least at the level of ideology and intent. Given their multi-ethnic societies and generally "artificial" borders, it was widely assumed that the ethnic loyalties and inter-ethnic rivalries of their citizens constituted "problems" which the state-regimes had to resolve.[17]

Finally, as Weiner suggests, "In country after country, a single ethnic group has taken control over the state and used its powers to exercise control over others . . . In retrospect there has been far less "nation building" than many analysts had expected or hoped, for the process of state building has rendered many ethnic groups devoid of power or influence."[18]

The challenge to state authority and to the viability of states will come from these ethnic groups interested either in challenging the legitimacy of the central authority or in asserting their autonomy. How the international system recognizes and deals with these challenges—some of which responses may clearly amount to genocide—is one of the great challenges of the 1990s.

In sum, I have identified in this discussion the possibility that we may be in many ways returning to patterns of violence and conflict similar to those that highlighted earlier twentieth-century and pretwentieth-century world politics. It is a system that can be surprisingly consistent with some of the major precepts of Westphalian order—tolerating, in fact fostering, the proliferation of new sovereign states. The search for new alliances among states—political, military, and economic—is already underway, and these alliances are likely to be based less on the perception and identification of an external (and ideological) threat than on the international economic realities of a highly competitive and fight-for-survival system. States will be most threatened from *within* by opponents (1) who are disenfranchised and, in some cases, displaced and threatened ethnic minorities or (2) who raise challenges—essentially nonideological—to a weak and ineffective central authority. For example, in early 1992 in the former Russian republic of Georgia, a traditional power struggle has emerged among groups who seek to control the government but do not necessarily have strongly divergent ideological viewpoints. In stark contrast to the Georgian case stand Yugoslavia and potentially other states in Eastern Europe North Africa, parts of Latin America, and Central and South Asia, where there is genuine hostility between ethnic majorities and minorities. Thus, the romanticism of returning to a pre–Cold War environment, without the danger of nuclear holocaust or major power confrontation (whether direct or through surrogates) is tempered by a world of disintegrating states, which are threatened by an incapacity to build a viable political/ economic central structure and by a volatile social/ethnic structure.

## Challenging Conventional Wisdom

The challenge of the 1990s will involve both mastering the characteristics of a transformed international system and coming to terms with the changing nature of conflict. Unfortunately, the catalysts for conflict—nationalism (more precisely, ethnonationalism), democratization, and the instability created by eroding the central political authority while attempting to successfully liberalize the economic sector—are not well understood. The manner in which these catalysts interact to create the potential for state and regional conflict is particularly unclear.

Equally important will be discriminating between "good" and "bad" regimes not on the basis of ideology but more on the evidence of "good" or "bad" government. As Thomas Friedman argues,

> In the post–Cold War era, Washington is going to have to wrestle with the complexities of a world governed increasingly by its own values, or at least imitations of its own values. In such a world, America will increasingly have to acknowledge that elected tyrants—like Mr. Gamasakhurdia [in the former Soviet Republic of Georgia]—are scarcely better than unelected ones, and it will have to choose its allies not by choosing between dictators and democrats, or between friends and foes in a Cold War, but between so-called democrats and genuine democrats.

Quoting U.S. Congressman Les Aspin, Friedman goes on, "The emerging world is likely to lack the clarity of the Cold War, and to be a more jungle-like world of multiple dangers, hidden traps, unpleasant surprises and moral ambiguities. The old world was good guys and bad guys. The new world is gray guys."[19]

How well equipped is the international system—and particularly the United States—to deal with a revamped world in which conflict cannot readily be categorized as "good" against "evil"? Unfortunately, the record would suggest that much ignorance is combined with a considerable dose of unwarranted idealism. Gelb states,

> The generation of Cold War experts who guided the post–World War II era, and who still hold sway in Washington and the various sanctum sanctorums of foreign policy, inevitably carry the baggage and blinders of their experiences. . . . Almost without exception, they missed or misunderstood the revolutions that were transforming world politics—in Iran, the Soviet Union, and Eastern Europe. Their eyes were closed to the Iraqi threat. They simply did not grasp the new power of nationalism, religion and democracy. With few exceptions, they know little about economics or the new-agenda issues. Even those who are experts on the Soviet Union are really experts on Moscow, not on the Soviet republics and their enormous variety of languages and cultures.[20]

To be sure, our conclusions should not be entirely pessimistic about the transformed global system and its potential for order. With few exceptions (i.e., Iraq), conflicts will rarely be seen as candidates for significant spillover into regional and international politics. Iraq's incursion into Kuwait was seen by some as challenging regional stability, necessitating an "international response." Certainly, a conflict within South Asia involving India and Pakistan would be seen as having regional and international ramifications. But beyond a few key examples, most conflicts appear to be more localized and to involve challenges to the legitimacy of a central authority—challenges that are more likely to be either ethnic or economic than ideological in origin. Even the highly charged and depressing conditions of the Horn of Africa are likely to be destabilizing only for a narrowly defined region. This not only provides an opportunity for a more orderly world system but creates occasions for international efforts at mitigation and resolution.

There remains, unfortunately, a highly discouraging aspect to this analysis that cannot be dismissed. We run the risk of marginalizing Third World conflict based on its lack of impact on international security. No problem is a better example of this than the international response—or lack thereof—to Iraqi assaults on the Kurds.

We have entered an era of change, unbridled by direct interference from East or West. This era of change will involve, as Jowitt has suggested in his essay in this volume, changes in borders and territories as well as movements of populations. Such changes are likely to continue well past the end of the century, and weak states are likely to stumble in their attempts to liberalize both the political and economic sectors.

The globally transformed system abounds with promise. Conflicts are no longer necessarily the result of the clash of ideologies and the interference of external powers. Resolutions can be achieved based on influence of the international community. But conflict in the international system remains inevitable. Threats to the viability of the state are equally likely. In the long run, the international system, along with the state as its central focus, will survive. The challenge is to understand the nature of conflict in the 1990s and to structure approaches that grasp this reality.

## Notes

1. See Paul Kennedy, *The Rise and Fall of the Great Powers* (London: Allen and Unwin, 1988).

2. Stanley Hoffman, "Avoiding New World Disorder," *New York Times*, 25 February 1991, A19.

3. *The Economist*, "A New World Order: To the Victors, the Spoils—and the Headaches," 28 September 1991, p. 22.

4. Lynn H. Miller, *Global Power: Values and Power in International Politics* (Boulder, CO: Westview, 1990), p. 27.

5. Miller, *Global Power,* p. 27.

6. Yale H. Ferguson and Richard W. Mansbach, "Between Celebration and Despair: Constructive Suggestions For Future International Theory," in *International Studies Quarterly* 35, no. 4 (December 1991): 382–383.

7. James N. Rosenau, *Turbulence in World Politics* (Princeton, NJ: Princeton University Press, 1990).

8. Ferguson and Mansbach, "Between Celebration and Despair," p. 381.

9. See Jowitt's essay, Chapter 2 in this volume.

10. Richard Higgott, "Toward a Nonhegemonic IPE: An Antipodean Perspective," in *The New International Political Economy*, ed. Craig Murphy and Roger Tooze (Boulder, CO: Lynne Rienner, 1991), p. 102.

11. See Callaghy's essay, Chapter 8 in this volume, for an outstanding discussion of the tensions in the international political economic system.

12. See Barry M. Schutz and Robert O. Slater, *Revolution and Political Change in the Third World* (Boulder, CO: Lynne Rienner, 1990), pp. 12–16.

13. See Jowitt's essay, Chapter 2 in this volume.

14. A. I. Samatar, "The Contours of Contemporary Somali Politics," in *The Horn of Africa and Arabia* (Washington, D.C.: Defense Intelligence College, 1990), p. 27.

15. *The Economist*, "A Mess on a Map," 28 September 1991, p. 56.

16. Ted R. Gurr and Monty Marshall, "Ethnopolitical Conflicts Since 1945: Report of a Global Survey," Draft Project Report, September 1990, p. 8.

17. David Brown, "Ethnic Revival: Perspectives on State and Society," *Third World Quarterly* 2, no. 4 (October 1989): 9.

18. Myron Weiner, "Political Change: Asia, Africa, and the Middle East," in *Understanding Political Development*, ed. M. Weiner and S. P. Huntington (Boston, MA: Little Brown, 1987), pp. 36–37.

19. Thomas L. Friedman, "A New U.S. Problem: Freely Elected Tyrants," *New York Times*, 12 January 1992, p. E3.

20. Leslie Gelb, *New York Times*, 29 December 1991, p. 54.

# 12

# Changing Forms of Conflict Mitigation

## I. William Zartman

Global restructuring removes global restraints and releases regional conflicts.[1] As a result, it gives national, regional, and global level participants a broad opportunity either to pursue untrammeled their own interests in the conduct of conflict or to see their interests in conflict's management. The very act of changing structures allows for and even occasions conflict. Old limitations and possibilities break down, and parties scramble to seek new ones. The search for the new is itself conflictual; while some parties are contending over the nature of the replacement for their own benefit, others are seeking to take advantage of the transition, also for their benefit. The new structures, once established, may yield greater possibilities for conflict management, but in the meantime, conflict is inherent in the transition.

Conflict, it should be understood, is inherent in any politics, as is cooperation. Conflict is often functional and even enjoyable, and cooperation is often conflict-driven.[2] Political structures regulate its conduct and also determine many of its ingredients. To expect that any structures will exorcise conflict and install cooperation is illusory; the best that can be sought is that rules, relations, and procedures will be established to render that conflict as productive and constructive as possible. The condition, however, is that it remain political. The rules, relations, and procedures should permit conflict to reach a satisfactory conclusion without resort to violence. In brief, then, conflict reduction means the establishment of institutions to contain conflict and to eliminate or replace violence.

Conflict comes in many types from many sources, but certain assumptions must be spelled out about its nature before the question of its mitigation and management can be confronted.[3] Regional conflicts can be categorized in several ways. By target, they are either centralist or provincial, depending on whether they seek to enlarge or replace the central government of an entire state or simply to achieve self-determination in a part of it. By social base, they draw on either ethnic or class grievances, organized into political movements. The line between the internal and international aspect of regional conflict is too thin to be perceived by the human eye; whether the conflict has domestic or foreign origins, it relates to a domestic target and social base and to neighbor states' interference. Unfortunately, none of these distinctions relates exclusively to cause but all are involved, so that a neat categorization of the etiology of regional conflicts is impossible. Neighboring states' claims, popular grievances, and government ineffectiveness can constitute either alternative or reinforcing causes of conflict among Third World states.

Third World regional conflicts form part of the broad condition of underdevelopment, in that they are symptoms of still incomplete state definitions and capabilities. The uncertainty in regard to basic aspects of state formation—the rules and institutions of governance, citizenship and boundaries, state ability to respond to citizen expectations, and patterns and hierarchies among members of the region—is the basic component of political underdevelopment and the cause of Third World conflict.

In prospect, the current political restructuring contains the potential for deep change in the case of all three levels of participants. Nationally, there is a resurgence in democratic ideals and in the belief that legitimacy as well as stability can only be found in popular participation in politics and governance. Globally, the structures of bipolar conflict have collapsed, although it is far too early to say that a new system of world order is being created.[4] In between, on the regional level, the most immediate effect of the two surrounding levels of change is to liberate regional structures and patterns of interaction from their global constraints. Eventually, other structures, and even institutionalized arrangements for conflict management, may emerge, but there is no resurgence of regional organization and integration at the moment.

These, then, are the major elements of global restructuring discernible in regard to regional conflict. The period we are drawing on stretches from the recent past into the immediate future, covering the very early years of the collapse of the bipolar system of world order. To assess the impact of this collapse should not be merely an exercise in prediction, but rather an analysis of the logical possibilities and empirical probabilities of taking certain actions rather than others in regard to conflict. It should also be an occasion for creativity and innovation, so that the opportunities that open up are used to their greatest potential.

## Domestic Restructuring and Conflict Management

Studies of conflict reduction usually address only conflicts in their course, to the neglect of the important prior topic, the prevention of conflict. The greatest contributor to the prevention of violent conflict is an effective and established mechanism for handling domestic grievances, generally agreed to be the practice of governance by democracy. The most important impact of global restructuring on the national level is the ascendancy of democracy as political legitimization. Democracy contains two elements that work to prevent conflict: (1) elects officials according to the interests and demands of the citizenry at any given time, so that current issues are on the table and the governors are chosen in the light of their apparent competence and concern for these issues; and (2) it holds those governors responsible for living up to their promises and therefore accountable in case of weakness. The general trend of democratization is evaluated in Chapter 3 of this volume, by Larry Diamond, but its potential for conflict reduction and conflict prevention can be assessed here.

Democracy can reduce the chances of violent conflict and can be an element in its successful resolution in a number of ways. The first is the engagement of collective responsibility and the alignment of expectations about national government programs that would otherwise occasion serious protest. It has frequently been claimed that structural adjustment demands democratic participation, so that the citizenry feels that the necessary measures of austerity are their own decision rather than being imposed on them; studies have shown that "IMF riots" are less likely to occur where the affected citizenry feels closely involved with its government.[5] While South Africa represents a sui generis conflict, it shows in an extreme case that the resolution of conflict depends on the installation of a democratic system of government, and furthermore that this must be done by a representative democratic process, not by minority fiat.[6]

A second role of democracy is to provide representation for various opinions through multiparty competition. Even though an aggrieved group is not in charge of governance, the fact that it can compete for election and can make its voice heard through representatives in coalition, or even in the opposition, transfers conflict from the violent to the political arena. The resolution of the longstanding conflicts in Angola and Mozambique, as stipulated in the 1991 Estoril Agreement and the Rome negotiations, respectively, provided for a system of multiparty democracy, just as the effective outcome of the Nigerian civil war was a multiparty system within a federal structure.[7] Multiparty competition converts violent conflict to politics, and multiparty representation gives minorities and causes an officially recognized voice. There is no magic in this conversion; political competition may be almost as debilitating for national governance as military conflict, although less costly in human lives, and representation in the opposition may be no more effective in securing redress of grievances. But the political process contains a potential that can long be pursued.

A third contribution lies in the short-term operationalization of self-determination, through referendum.[8] Current norms in international relations hold that territory shall not change sovereignty except by expressed consent of the governed. Self-determination, as specified in U.N. resolutions, can take many forms, but the most frequent and most legitimate is that of a popular vote. Other methods are possible, including outright conflict and conquest, but the resulting lack of legitimacy renders the results challengeable and inconclusive. Referendum is one-shot democracy. The Western Saharan dispute was won diplomatically by the Polisario Front and militarily by Morocco, but confirmation of one victory or another and an end to the conflict was possible only through the political solution by referendum eventually provided by the U.N. Mission for the Referendum in Western Sahara (MINURSO) in January 1992.[9] The conclusion of the conflict in Namibia, like that in Zimbabwe, was provided by a similar vote of self-determination.[10] Competitive elections are the key element in the agreements designed to end the conflicts in Cambodia, Angola, and Afghanistan. The business of agreeing to and setting up the referendum is a matter of complex political conflict, in which violence often stands not only as the alternative means to the end but also, by the threat of that action, as the goad to keep negotiations on track.

The fourth contribution lies in the long-term operationalization of self-determination, through regional autonomy or self-governing arrangements. Self-government, of course, need not be democratic, any more than any other government. But the term does imply participation in government, and the practice usually follows and extends a participatory decision, either through referendum or through conflict. The Addis Ababa Agreement of 1972 ended the southern Sudanese conflict by granting regional autonomy to the southern provinces; it is ironic that the arrangement collapsed a decade later, in part because it was sabotaged by its northern author, Gen. Jaafar Numeiry, but also in part because the removal of the northern enemy opened up southern politics to debilitating internal rivalries.[11] Democracy, the experience reminds, can perpetuate conflict in such a way as to reopen the question of violence if democratic practices are not protected.

Internal restructuring can act as conflict reduction by either prevention or resolution. Since this is an internal response to internal conflict, it is often impervious to external efforts at conflict management, but not entirely. Large and middle-sized states outside the conflict can play a role in establishing democratic practices and solutions by making democracy the criterion for resolution, as seen in previous examples, and by pressing for democratic practices as conditions, among others, of their programs of economic aid and political support. The shape of a solution in Eritrea and Mozambique was determined in part by the conditions that outside, interested states would accept as the form of resolution and the price of noninterference, just as free elections were held to be the key to the solution in Nicaragua. Arguably the largest failure in U.S. African policy in the 1980s was U.S. unwillingness in 1985 to stick to its criterion of free and fair elections for continued support for the Doe regime in Liberia. Five years later, the chickens came home to roost for both Doe and the United States; Liberia was plunged into a bloody rebellion and social chaos, and the United States was blamed for inaction. It was the international community's insistence on a referendum in the Western Sahara that kept one side or the other from running off with half a victory. It was the absence of democracy in Kuwait that soured the U.S.-led liberation of that country in early 1991, and it was the continued presence of a dictator in Iraq that caused even greater problems for the world coalition than the previous warfare. Both regional and global powers have a role to play in bringing in democratic practices as a way of domestic restructuring for the purposes of conflict abatement and resolution.

## Regional Restructuring and Conflict Management

A major characteristic of political development in interstate relations is the rise of conflict over the patterns of rank and relations within regions, including the notions of membership in the region itself. Thanks to the odd shapes into which continents have been poured and the curious patterns into which geography has channeled human settlement, states tend to conceive of relations in their immediate international region as areas of common belonging and to identify with them. Some regions are clearly better defined than others, and some states have a possibility of selecting their regions or "moving" from one to another. Within the regions, states need to regulate expectations, to know their enemies and their friends, and also to know the pecking orders of rank and power that will give structure to regional relations. Often, these needs and expectations are long-term affairs, not easily resolved in the short run and not easily accepted even when apparently established.

The "struggle for Syria" between Iraq and Egypt as the basis of the structure of the Arab East, squared more recently by the entry of Saudi Arabia as a power, is an example of both a regional structure and its inherent instability.[12] The central position of India in South Asia and of Ethiopia in the Horn of Africa, about which lesser powers gravitate when they are unable to form an alliance among themselves, is another characteristic regional structure;[13] South Africa in Southern Africa is in a similar position, although the lesser neighbors have been able to make an alliance. The Maghrib's bipolar rivalry between Morocco and Algeria is both complicated and balanced by the recent rise of Libya and by the uncertainty of its membership in the regional system. A particularly delicate structure is the tripartite counterbalancing stability in the Gulf based on Iran, Iraq, and Saudi Arabia, which depends on the success of each member's efforts to balance the other two and the inability of any two to ally against the third.

These are structures of conflict, although the conflict is not always violent; to the extent that such structures lead to cooperation, through checking and balancing alliances, cooperation is conflict-driven. When regional cooperation becomes the means of integration, the old structures still serve as the basis of alliances and coalitions within regional organizations, often even after other interests dictate other patterns of affinity. Classically, conflict arises over a need to protect a distinctive identity and sovereignty against neighbors growing more powerful or to extend one's growing power over weaker neighbors.

Regional restructuring, then, means not simply a new set of alliances or ranking patterns within a region—characteristics that are part of the inherent fluidity of the old structures of conflict—but rather a change to cooperative structures and more institutionalized regional relations. Like other political changes such as the wave of democratization, interest in regional organization and integration seems to come in waves, although no one has identified its mode or dynamic. Within any region, the escalation of conflict to the point where it threatens to break up the region or destroy its members frequently leads to a rise in the attraction of integration, just as an external threat can also produce the same result. There may be some contagion effect between regions, but not enough to explain the waves' rise and fall.

The late 1980s and early 1990s do not appear to be a time of regional restructuring. While some regions, such as the Maghrib or Southeast Asia, have indeed adopted or reinvigorated a regional organization during this period—for example, the Arab Maghrib Union (UMA) and the Association of South East Asian Nations (ASEAN)—the new institution has not been durable or the new level of activity sustained. For the most part, regional organizations have been significant failures in organizing economic cooperation, leaving the trend of the decade as a collapse of regionalism rather than its increase. The decline in economic growth in most developing countries has led leaders to think of protecting rather than combining sovereignties, and continental organizations have been more successful in defending members' independence than in promoting their interdependence.

This trend has significant effects on conflict reduction. Regional organizations have shown a marked inability to mediate conflicts, to reduce tensions, and even to maintain their own cohesion in the face of conflict among their members.[14] There does not seem to be any significant difference in capabilities from region to region, nor any cultural characteristics that make an organization in one region stronger than one in another. Not only are such organizations incapable of conflict management; they themselves become victims of conflict. The collapse of the Gulf Cooperation Council (GCC) and the Arab League (LAS) upon the annexation of one of their members by another in 1990, the paralysis of the Arab Maghrib Union (UMA) by continuing conflict between two members in 1990–1991, the involvement of some members of the Economic Community of West African States (ECOWAS) in the civil war of a member state against the will of other members in 1991, and the inability of the Organization of African Unity (OAU) to resolve or even reduce conflict among a number of pairs of members throughout the 1980s are only some of the recent cases of regional organizational weakness. In each case, the old, fluid structures of conflict have prevailed, uninhibited by the structures of co-operation that they eventually destroy.

Adding to the challenge is the fact that regional organizations cannot be sponsored by outside powers; they must be the result of regional activities, since their identity and integrity are tied to their regional autonomy. States can help states, but only with difficulty can they help organizations; only organizations—such as the U.N., for example—can help organizations. The four subregional cooperation agreements in West, Central, North, and East-Southern Africa resulted from the initiatives of the Economic Commission for Africa (ECA), and not of outside states. The U.N. carried out the referendum operations in the Western Sahara for and with the OAU in 1992, but the peace-keeping operations of the African organization in Chad collapsed in 1982 because of insufficient cooperation from the global organization. There may be a few slight exceptions: the Inter-Governmental Agency on Drought and Development (IGADD) in the Horn of Africa turned some helpful mediation efforts to the Somali-Ethiopian conflict (under pressure from the Italian government, among others) in 1986–1988, and the West African Economic Community (CEAO) has benefited from French impetus. Nonetheless, in the absence of a long-standing or postcolonial relationship, organizations remain hard to influence from the outside.

There is a great deal that regional organizations could do to reduce conflict. They can perform a range of mediatory functions, establish principles to focus and limit conflict, organize peace-keeping forces, and provide occasions and procedures for managing conflict and reducing chances for violence, among others. But to do this they must be established, cohesive organizations engaging their members' commitment as a valued arena of interaction. This does not mean that the basic structures of conflict need to be abolished or that all conflict need disappear for such organizations to work; it only means that the members need to agree to play their politics within the region and act to maintain their regional identity. Unfortunately, for the moment, these organizations are caught instead in a vicious circle. Regional organizations are not considered useful, because of the effects of regional conflict structures, and so are not cultivated as useful organizations to handle regional conflicts.

Along with a galvanizing event, what is required to break the circle and manage conflict is a revised perception of the value and usefulness of institutionalized regional cooperation. Such a change occurred in Southeast Asia when it was confronted with the longstanding Cambodian crisis; likewise a more momentary shift occurred in North Africa when it was confronted with the Saharan dispute in the context of domestic weakness and the European challenge. This change may have also occurred in West Africa with the civil war in Liberia, and in the Horn during the protracted conflict along the Somali border, but the change does not appear to have been conclusive as yet. Not surprisingly, the classical conclusion is reinforced by these experiences: the more durable cohesion is produced by an external challenge, whereas internal conflicts tend to reduce cohesion. Yet the coming age is one where external challenges are in decline.

## Global Restructuring and Conflict Management

The end of the Cold War has several clear implications for both conflict and conflict reduction. First, along with bipolar conflicts, bipolar constraints on conflict are reduced. Where earlier regional conflicts tended to escalate rapidly to bipolar dimensions, there was a concomitant pressure to keep them under control lest their escalation run out of hand. In this sense, the effects of the Cold War were nearly identical to those of the earlier colonization of the Third World. Once, local conflicts became global or were squelched; now, neither takes place. External sources of power have little interest in involvement in Third World conflicts, either by lending strength to Third World clients in order to pre-empt and defend space from global opponents, or by actively reining in adventuresome clients in order to avoid entanglement in a Cold War proxy encounter.

Second, superpower mediation is less readily offered and less readily accepted. Superpower mediation has largely been U.S. mediation; the U.S.S.R. has mediated little and with little success. The absence of Cold War competitive bidding removes some of the appeal that superpower mediators once had. When they competed as mediators (actively or tacitly), they would deploy efforts and resources to make their actions successful; when they cooperated, the novelty itself was appealing. In the current era, even the United States often lacks the four basic ingredients of leverage—willingness to persuade, ability to extract an appealing offer, and resources for side payments, resources with which to shift weight between the parties.[15] Its record as ombudsman as well as gendarme has been uneven in the brief post–Cold War era: extraordinary diplomatic neglect of the Iraqi threat followed by extraordinary military engagement when it materialized, unusually tenacious diplomatic commitment but with little leverage to mediate the Arab-Israeli conflict; willingness to take on the Cyprus dispute; important support for others' efforts to mediate in Angola and Mozambique; understandable failure for lack of leverage and ripeness in Eritrea and Cambodia; disinterest in Sri Lanka and Yugoslavia. Although there are many lessons to be learned (for both participants and observers) from the Gulf war of 1990–1991, it would be a mistake to take it as typical of U.S. policy toward Third World conflicts, largely because such blatant aggression and uncompromising absorption of a neighboring country is itself not typical of Third World conflicts.

Still, there are important things that can be accomplished as a result of global restructuring, many of them illustrated by the Gulf war. The first is the return of the world organization to its conflict management vocation. Unlike the regional organizations on their level of operations, the United Nations has emerged from global restructuring strengthened in its potential. The rise of other strong members alongside the "superpowers" and the decreasing gap between the superpowers and other states has increased the participation of member nations, and the passing of superpower competition has removed the hidden agenda that skewed all other debates. The elimination of bipolarity has resulted in political space that the Secretary General can fill to the satisfaction of his own criteria, without having to be primarily concerned about the superpower dimensions of his position. The Reaganite campaign against the U.N. was effective in weakening its most vociferous and least responsible organ, the General Assembly, without hurting the rest of the organization. As a result, the other two branches of the U.N.—the Secretariat and the Security Council—increased their role.

The former secretary general, Javier Perez de Cuellar, and his representatives were particularly effective in the Namibian and Saharan conflicts. In both cases, their role was the same—the provision of technical assistance to the political conflict management efforts provided by an interested state or states. In Namibia, the prime mediator was the United States, with some little help from the Soviet Union; in the Sahara it was Saudi Arabia with some little help from Tunisia.[16] Yet the secretary's role was not just in some incidental technicalities; it was in providing an organized, comprehensive capability for the implementation of the political decision—a technical "how" to the political "what." This assistance was particularly important because in both cases the solution required a referendum, in line with the current democratic focus of domestic restructuring. In the previous decades, the focus had been on peace-keeping forces (PKF), leaving the move from conflict management to resolution to the parties' ulterior efforts; currently both the peace-keeping and the resolving functions comprise the U.N. mandate. In a third case, the Iran-Iraq war, the Secretariat assumed an additional role as catalyst for the political decision, a role that was played by states in the other two cases. In a slightly earlier phase of the Cold War's waning, the secretary general was also important in mediating the end of the Afghan occupation, a case of disengagement rather than resolution that illustrates another type of role. The increased latitude and activity of the secretary general was a primary ingredient in the search for an appropriate successor to Perez de Cuellar.

The role of the Security Council has been more static, focusing on decreeing the conditions that limit the conflict and determine its resolution, a role it played to the hilt in the Gulf war. The U.N. Security Council is not a mediator, nor as an international body can it be one. It sets standards, provokes reactions, and evaluates performance, not just for the conflicting parties but also for its agent in resolution, the secretary general. As such it is a locus where member states can harmonize their policy and give the coordinated result an international legitimacy. Major powers as well as lesser states have an interest in channeling their policy through U.N. legislative/diplomatic organs, of which the Security Council is the most powerful (in that it has the largest range of permissible means of action). For example, to U.S. policy it gives international legitimacy and shares the burdens of its implementation, as the Gulf war showed in the extreme.

Separate conflict management designates a U.S. role, one for which it had an incentive during the Cold War, but for which there may be less interest as the United States is undergoing its own structural adjustment. The United States had compelling interests in reacting to the Iraqi invasion of Kuwait in 1990–1991. One interest was the perceived need to keep oil supplies in friendly and diversified hands, and another was of course the need to respond decisively to blatant aggression. But a third, sui generis and decisively exorcized, was the perceived need to banish the ghosts of Vietnam, once and forever. That degree and conjuncture of compelling needs is unlikely to be repeated. A separate U.S. role almost necessarily means a leading but not a solitary role; in role played by the United States in conflicts from Namibia to Kuwait, Washington was surrounded by a number of other states in ancillary roles. What those roles are to be and how they can be coordinated is a major challenge of global restructuring.[17]

Setting standards is an indirect conflict regulating mechanism that narrows the field of resolving outcomes. The action can range from setting the terms of trade that comprise the formula for settlement, as the United States did when it posited "Cuban withdrawal for South African withdrawal" as the linkage formula for a Namibian-Angolan settlement; to endorsement of a particular criterion for a solution, as it did by designating independence as the only acceptable outcome in Zimbabwe. Setting the terms of trade shades into direct mediation and even negotiation as a party, whereas endorsing a criterion keeps the standard setter outside the fray but influential over the final settlement. The United States already plays this standard-setting role in a number of current conflicts, by a variety of measures. The Comprehensive Anti-Apartheid Act of 1986 set the standards for the removal of sanctions on South Africa and hence for a settlement in that country. The United States used the U.N. Security Council to set unconditional Iraqi evacuation and restitution as the standards for a settlement in Kuwait, not as a mediator or external guardian but as a participant and protagonist.

Standards have been less clear in a number of other conflicts, such as Mozambique, Palestine, Cyprus, and the Horn of Africa. In the latter, a joint U.S.-Soviet statement supporting the OAU position on African states' territorial integrity and indicating the unacceptability of secessions as in Ethiopia would have been particularly useful during the Carter mediation (although it would not have been sufficient to produce success). With the collapse of the Ethiopian government and the victory of the Eritrean separatists, such a statement is probably irrelevant, again indicating the limits of major-power roles in regional conflicts. A similar statement on the terms of a Palestinian settlement, also at a strategic moment, could have had a guiding impact on the search for a solution; in this case, the association of other parties could help broaden the base of the statement and establish its legitimacy more firmly.

The other role that major powers can play in the new global structure is that of mediator—alone, together, or in concert with others. These roles have already been played in 1990, in the beginnings of the new era, although their lack of success to date also illustrates some of their problems and limitations. A former U.S. president attempted to mediate the Ethiopian civil war with the Eritrean and other liberation movements; it was a private effort at unofficial diplomacy, but was viewed by the parties as having official sanction if not official sponsorship. Both the U.S. and the Soviet governments were kept informed and did what they could to support the effort. But the war was spreading, the fortunes of the parties shifting, and the moment was not ripe. When the U.S. government took over the initiative in October 1990, the conflict was poised on the verge of victory, not of reconciliation; and the U.S. role in the end, in London in May 1991, was merely to host a meeting of the winners.[18] Official mediation was underway in the Angolan civil war between the MPLA and UNITA since the beginning of the Bush administration, at which time the U.S.S.R. played alternately an adversarial and a cooperative role. The United States had some potential leverage in its "covert" aid to UNITA and the possibility of opening diplomatic relations with Angola; the U.S.S.R. was able to complement this leverage with its own assistance programs to the Angolan government. In the event, none of this leverage was applied very vigorously, if at all, and pure persuasion was not pressed either. Over the year, the conflict was moved ever so slowly toward an agreement under the joint sponsorship of the two powers, in parallel with the gradual perception of an inability by either side to escalate the war to victory. Finally, it took the intervention of a third party, the former metropole—Portugal—to bring about an agreement in Estoril in May 1991.[19]

Official mediation was practiced by the U.S.S.R. in the Gulf crisis between Iraq and the U.N. allies led by the United States, without making any dent in the hardline positions of the two sides. The pressure that U.N.

sanctions were intended to produce had not yet taken hold in Iraq, and various other internal pressures on the cohesion of the alliance had not yet produced any hurtful effects. When the U.S.S.R. returned to the conflict as it drew to a close in February 1991, the pressures of war and sanctions had only confirmed Saddam Hussein's stubbornness; the best that can be said is that the Soviet mediation prepared for final Iraqi surrender a few days later. The conflict illustrates the fact that a mutually hurting stalemate takes a long while to register on the parties' perceptions, even when its objective elements have long been in place, and that the parties will seek to reinforce the other's perception of a stalemate while avoiding their own, even when they cannot escalate their way out of the mutual constraint.

These cases of superpower mediation bring out two aspects of the mediating role—the stalemating side and the persuasion/leverage side. Stalemating, as seen, is a long and difficult process, dependent on perceptions more than simply on the sources of arms. As shown by timely Soviet arms supplies to Angola in the mid-1980s, U.S. arms supplies to Israel in 1973, U.S. arms to Morocco in 1980, and Israeli arms supplies to Ethiopia in 1989, timely shipments can keep a party in the game when it otherwise might have fallen out, but such supplies may break a hurting stalemate as well as create one. If the end of the Cold War means the end of competitive arms supplies, there may be some benefit for conflict management. But the presence of large stocks and alternative suppliers, as well as commercial interest in staying in the arms trade, tends to make that benefit marginal indeed. Major powers retain their potential for persuasive mediation, but even here, as seen, the potential for leverage is reduced. Studies of mediation have shown that both the third parties' interest in mediating and the conflicting parties' interest in accepting mediation is often tied to the latters' interest in maintaining good relations with the former.[20] If the conflicting parties no longer have the competitive clout they gained from the Cold War, the external powers' interest in preserving a good relationship is diminished accordingly. Major powers must think of new ways to make themselves attractive to conflicting Third World countries— and preferably not just as arms suppliers—in order to buttress their mediating role.

Regional disputants will thus be looking for other benefits for giving up their conflicts and superpowers will have a harder time making peace and order interesting. Even European states are more actively focused on their own integration than on the substantial engagement in Third World conflicts that mediation requires. Japan is far away. The United States is left, custodian of multilateral as well as bilateral economic assistance, wearing a reputation for successful conflict management, condemned to play the role in the future. It is the very desire of most leading powers not to be too deeply involved in Third World conflicts that can also be used by an active U.S. leadership to constitute collective support and pluralistic alternatives within a broad collective concert system. Cooperation in arms controls, coordination in mediation efforts, and an alertness to propitious stalemates would be the hallmarks of such a system, in which Europe, Russia, Japan, and possibly China would participate. Its leadership and orchestration will have to come from a United States newly aware of a commitment to a primary role of mitigating conflict and enhancing the conflict management potential of democratic governance.

## Notes

1. This study is part of a larger project on Conflict Reduction in Regional Conflicts (CRIRC) supported by the Carnegie Corporation, whose assistance is gratefully acknowledged.

2. Lewis Coser, *The Functions of Social Conflict* (New York: Free Press, 1956).

3. For more detailed discussions, see I. William Zartman, ed., *Negotiating Internal Conflict* (New York: Oxford, 1992); I. William Zartman, ed., *Resolving Regional Conflicts: International Perspectives, The Annals of the American Academy of Political and Social Sciences,* 518 (November 1991); I. William Zartman, *Ripe For Resolution: Conflict and Intervention in Africa* (New York: Oxford University Press, 1989); Joseph Montville, ed., *Conflict and Peacemaking in Multi-Ethnic Societies* (Lexington: Heath Lexington, 1990); Manus Midlarsky, ed., *Internationalization of Communal Strife* (New York: St. Martin's, 1992); Francis Deng and I. William Zartman, eds., *Conflict Resolution in Africa* (Washington, D.C.: Brookings, 1991).

4. See I. William Zartman, "World Order Systems and Conflict Reduction," in *Cooperative Security: Reducing Third World Wars,* ed. Zartman (New York: Oxford, 1992).

5. Joan Nelson, "Short-Run Public Reactions to Food Subsidy Cuts in African Countries," Overseas Development Council, Washington, D.C., 1985.

6. Donald Horowitz, *A Democratic South Africa?* (Berkeley: University of California Press, 1991); Chris Heymans and Gerhard Totemeyer, eds., *Government by the People?* (Johannesburg: Juta, 1988).

7. See I. William Zartman, ed., *The Political Economy of Nigeria* (New York: Praeger, 1983); John Paden, "National System Development and Conflict Resolution in Nigeria," in Montville, *Conflict and Peacemaking.*

8. Benyamin Neuberger, *National Self-Determination in Post-Colonial Africa* (Boulder, CO: Lynne Rienner, 1986); Lawrence Farley, *Plebescites and Sovereignty* (Boulder, CO: Westview, 1986).

9. Bruce Maddy-Weitzmann, "Conflict and Conflict Management in the Western Sahara," *Middle East Journal* 4 (Fall 1991); Zartman, *Ripe for Resolution,* Chap. 2.

10. Zartman, *Ripe for Resolution,* Chap. 5; Stephen J. Stedman, *Peacemaking in Civil War* (Boulder, CO: Lynne Rienner, 1991).

11. Dunstan Wai, *The African-Arab Conflict in the Sudan* (New York: Africana, 1981); Francis Deng, "Negotiating Identity Conflicts in the Sudan," in Zartman, *Negotiating Internal Conflict.*

12. Patrick Seale, *Struggle for Syria* (New York: Oxford, 1965) ; Malcolm Kerr, *The Arab Cold War,* 3d ed. (New York: Oxford, 1971); Alan R. Taylor, *The Arab Balance of Power* (Syracuse, NY: Syracuse University Press, 1982).

13. Howard Wriggins, ed., *Regional Structures Around the Indian Ocean* (New York: Columbia University Press, 1992).

14. Sam Amoo and I. William Zartman, "Mediation in Regional Organizations: The OAU," in *International Mediation,* ed. Jacob Bercowitz and Jeffrey Rubin (London: Macmillan, 1992).

15. Saadia Touval and I. William Zartman, "Mediation in International Conflicts," in *Mediation Research,* ed. Kenneth Kressel and Dean Pruitt (San Francisco, CA: Jossey Bass, 1989).

16. On both, see Zartman, *Ripe for Resolution.*

17. See Zartman, *Cooperative Security.*

18. Terrence Lyons, "The Transition in Ethiopia," *CSIS Africa Notes*, no. 127, 27 August 1991.

19. Shawn McCormick, "Angola: The Road to Peace," *CSIS Africa Notes,* no. 125, 6 June 1991.

20. Saadia Touval and I. William Zartman, eds., *International Mediation in Theory and Practice* (Boulder, CO: Westview, 1985).

# 13

## The Role of Region in a Restructured Global System

*Barry M. Schutz*

As I ponder the changing global landscape from Maputo, the besieged capital of Mozambique, I perceive two competing tendencies: on one side, active, multilevel concern on the part of national governments and regional or international institutions, sharpened by the acute analyses of academics such as Chester Crocker and William Zartman, and on the other side, a bursting of raging and senseless but increasingly organized violence within countries of the Third, (former) Second, and even the First World. The capacity of great powers such as the United States or the ability of collective efforts on the part of the G-7 democracies to deal with these pervasive insurgencies and fire zones has to be questioned and investigated before engaging in the extensive and increasingly self-congratulatory campaigns of optimism often exhibited in official circles of the collective powers and within the organs of the United Nations.

This chapter sets out to explore three distinct cases of endemic internal conflict in Third World countries—Nicaragua, Cambodia, and Mozambique—with an analysis of the means that have been pursued to mitigate these conflicts. In each of these cases, dynamics toward mitigation have been pursued, at various levels, with actors in conflict within the country presuming the ultimate resolution of that conflict through actions being taken at higher levels, e.g., superpower or U.N. intervention. Experts such as Crocker, Touval, and Zartman tend to perceive successful mitigation through a "supermediator" who would represent the international system as a power-packed emissary from its most politically and militarily powerful country. They comprehend the solution for successful mitigation as an extension of the power constellation within the international system. One person fortuitously skilled in mediation and arbitration techniques at the level of international politics is the sufficient, although not necessary, cause for resolution. Ironically, this belief itself becomes systemic, and soon the Third World country, where such conflict continues, begins to see its salvation in the arrival of the supermediator from The Hegemon.[1] The single example of mitigation in Angola/Namibia appears to have promoted this belief. However, it will be argued here that "the significant action" is more regional than hegemonic-international. This signifies that the necessary cause for mitigation is more often identified in regional dynamics than in hegemonial or international organizational "super-mediation."

## Region

The significance of the regional subsystem has not only been stipulated in the academic literature.[2] The enunciation of the U.S. Nixon Doctrine in 1970 actually went so far as to try to incorporate the regional subsystemic perspective into U.S. foreign policy. During the 1980s the concept of "region" became relegated to tertiary status in the new bipolar crusades mobilized in Washington. The Gorbachev era only served to reinforce this tendency. A new tripartite type of regionalization has now become a fashionable concept in which the European Community, Japan, and the United States each ostensibly dominate their own hemispheric blocs. Again, the concept of region, as it was understood in the early 1970s, got lost in the focus on Great Power politics.

Part of the problem with the concept of the regional subsystem is that it is difficult to know the geographical boundaries—or even the functional boundaries—of any given region.[3] If Jowitt is correct and we are indeed in an era of Genesis, then perhaps even the conceptualization of regions is merely an academic exercise. However, we can observe in the dynamics and mechanics of conflict mitigation that the tendency is for contiguous or proximate states to get involved in the process in an effort to either maximize or protect their own interests. It is, therefore, not merely the figment of some analyst's imagination that projects regional configurations in the international system. It is nonetheless important, however, to recognize the malleability of regional subsystems and, therefore, not to concretize any given region unduly. Overconceptualizing regions leads to the angels-on-the-head-of-a-pin inquiry that focuses on questions of country inclusion in one or another specific regional subsystem (e.g., Is Mexico part of the Central American regional subsystem or the North American regional subsystem? Is Zaire part of the Central or Southern African regional subsystem? etc.).

The concept of regional subsystem, however, has no automatic relationship to conflict mitigation. To assume that regional states have interests biased toward conflict mitigation is dangerous and myopic. States within regional subsystems are just as likely to be oriented toward regional power politics and even subimperialism as they are toward conflict mitigation. In the three cases under review here, South Africa, until 1990, was more interested in conflict than conflict mitigation within Southern Africa.

Mozambique was an unfortunate recipient of this policy choice. In Southeast Asia, Vietnam, until recently, had not displayed a preference for conflict mitigation in Cambodia except under the aegis of Vietnamese subimperialism. Central America is a somewhat different case because of the pre-existence of U.S. hegemony in the region. However, an argument can be made that Cuba's interests in Central America and the Caribbean have been subimperial, thus dragging those states, and especially Nicaragua, into a confrontation between traditional U.S. imperialism and emerging Cuban subimperialism in the Central American regional subsystem.

## Regimes

The conceptual projection of regional subsystems is not in itself, however, a sufficient basis for generating an adequate explanation for conflict mitigation (or promotion) at the level of region. Something quite essential needs to be added. This directs us to regime theory as elaborated by Krasner, Jervis, Osler Hampson, and others.[4] Regimes fundamentally can be defined as "sets of governing arrangements that include networks of rules, norms, and procedures that regularize behavior and control its effects."[5] Keohane and others also stress that regimes are more than just agreements, although they tend to facilitate agreements. Furthermore, regimes are more than mere conveniences for the purpose of the short-term interests of states. Krasner points out that regimes, like friendship, contain more than simply the elements of direct mutual exchange but are governed by principles and norms that generate something akin to trust. At any given moment, regimes will not provide exactly balanced exchanges of interest between states, but over the long run these states assume that such interests will "balance out."[6]

However, regional conflicts in the Third World do not lend themselves to comprehensive regime arrangements as was the case with Soviet-U.S. arms control regimes. Fes Osler Hampson proffers a more appropriate conceptual scheme, which he labels the "partial security regime." Hampson argues that "in places like Southern Africa where the creation and support for such security arrangements reinforces the status quo and disarms the forces of change, they may not be a desirable objective."[7] He then elaborates four kinds of partial security regimes conducive to a regional subsystemic setting: (1) confidence-building regimes; (2) self-help conflict regulation regimes; (3) multilateral arms control regimes; and (4) bipolar crisis management and crisis prevention regimes. The first type of confidence-building regime derives from the Stockholm Conference on Disarmament in Europe, which was signed in September 1986 by the 35 members of the Conference on Security and Cooperation in Europe. A recent conference in Maputo, Mozambique, sponsored by two German institutes and the Mozambican Higher Institute of International Relations, was dedicated to the exploration of transferring the fruits of the Stockholm agreement to the conditions existing in Southern Africa in late 1991.[8] However, confidence-building regimes—such as the one established during the transition of power in Namibia in 1990—comprise peace-keeping, fact-finding, and observation forces, ostensibly furnished through the auspices of the United Nations. International peace-keeping is the key ingredient and that demands an entirely new set of criteria. The possibility of peacekeeping forces not succeeding because some of these criteria cannot be met makes the achievement of this type of partial security regime somewhat risky.[9]

The second type of partial security regimes, the self-help conflict regulation regimes, are "cooperative security arrangements organized by regional groupings with the aim of ending interstate *and intrastate* conflicts [emphasis added] while limiting the influence of external, usually superpower, actors in the region."[10] The critical component of this regime type, especially with regard to our own regional focus in this study, is that the response or initiative is regional (or local). Nicaragua represents an especially poignant example of a conflict promoting this type of partial security regime. As we shall explore later in this essay, the emergence of the Esquipulas II Accord provided a Central American regional initiative in resolving the Nicaraguan conundrum, in excluding a unilateral intervention by the United States, and in inviting other states as part of a third party monitoring and verifying mission under the auspices of the United Nations. However, this development has been more problematic in the Cambodian imbroglio where, until late 1991, the ASEAN states had not been the primary impetus in generating a regionally self-centered partial security regime dynamic.

The final case of Mozambique has presented an even knottier set of regionally centered problems. Chris Brown has suggested that the hegemonial, exploitative subimperial presence of South Africa in the Southern African regional context imposes serious limits to forming a self-help conflict regulation regime that could mitigate the pervasive internal conflict in Mozambique.[11] However, the Southern African region is presently a rapidly changing regime. Internal change is taking place inside South Africa. And while this change is internally conflictual, it is generating a different set of interests and policy orientations inside South Africa. As of late 1992 it has become increasingly clear that South Africa has moved away from its established inclination to intervene militarily in its neighbors' affairs. Perhaps some "gun-running" persists but it is doubtful that these possible activities have the approval of the government of Pretoria at its highest official levels. What seems clear is that a governing consensus in Pretoria is building toward total stabilization of the region. Maputo now houses an extensive, and growing, official compound of South African business and political interests. Under these circumstances, it is highly unlikely that Pretoria will continue to provide support for RENAMO (the Mozambique National Resistance) operations.[12]

Hampson lists two other partial security regimes. The multilateral arms control type of regime has more relevance in Central America than in Southeast Asia or Southern Africa, although it has had some impact in the mitigation of conflict in Angola. Major power, if not superpower, involvement is essential here, in that this type of partial regime focuses on the regulation of technology transfers that could be destabilizing to Third World countries. This type of regime, however, would seem most appropriate to the countries and conflicts of the Middle East, where superpower and great power arms sales have been the heaviest and where the conflicts themselves appear most directly linked to the acquisition of such arms. Keith Krause has argued that the sine qua non for the establishment of this type of regime is the willingness of the suppliers to cooperate.[13] For this sort of cooperation to ensue, there must be shared agreement on the primary significance of international mutual security. On this basis, the regime operates more at the global than at the regional level.

Hampson's last partial security regime type, superpower crisis management and crisis prevention regimes, is the sort alluded to by Crocker, and to a lesser extent, by Zartman. Hampson refers to this as "regime building from the top down."[14] In this type, bipolar superpower agreement extends to rules in which the limits of each superpower's interests in any given regional conflict are understood and actually communicated. Much of Crocker and Zartman's advocacy for supermediation relies on the development of this type of regime. Even when bipolarity was operative, this regime approach lost impact in conflicts so local and in which causes were so diffuse that respect for the superpowers, or The Superpower, diminished to the point of insignificance. It is in these types of regional conflict, like that in Mozambique, that confidence building and regional self-help have more appropriate application.

In our analysis of the cases of Nicaragua, Cambodia, and Mozambique, we shall apply a common framework of inquiry. Our basic question asks for the distinction within each of these countries, between the nature of the conflict before the end of superpower rivalry and since that rivalry has been terminated. We shall use the critical year of 1989 as the cut-off point for the Cold War. Specifically we shall ask the following questions: What was the nature of the conflict in each country before 1989 and since 1989? Who was/is in conflict with whom? What were/are the actors' objectives? What was/is the level of intensity of the conflict? What efforts were made/are being made at the global or international systemic level to mitigate the conflict? What efforts were made/are being made at the regional level to mitigate the conflict? Finally, which of these levels has provided the most substantial progress in mitigating these conflicts? What conclusions can we draw from these inferences regarding the prospects for effective mitigation in each of these conflicts?

## Nicaragua and Central America

During the Cold War Nicaragua remained locked into a regional security regime that was characterized by external hegemony by the United States and a collection of mostly authoritarian governments dominated by the military in the Central American states. Nicaragua's major attempt to reform from within was repressed earlier in the century by overt U.S. military intervention. The hero of that struggle was Augusto Sandino. The Marxist-Leninist reformulation of that movement in the early 1970s was named for this historical martyr. The ultimate collapse of the U.S.-supported Somoza regime in 1979 brought the Sandinistas to power. This development essentially vitiated the U.S.-dominated security regime and presented to U.S. policymakers the prospect of a second Cuba in a traditional U.S. sphere of hegemony.

The threat to the old U.S.-dominated security regime began to preoccupy U.S. policymakers even before Ronald Reagan was elected president in 1980. However, after that election and the appointment of William Casey as director of central intelligence, the United States commenced with an obsessive policy to uproot the new Sandinista government in Nicaragua and to re-establish militarily and politically the old Central American security regime.[15] Swimming against the current of a new regionally based Central American self-help conflict regulation regime, the United States consistently tried to extirpate the Sandinista regime in Nicaragua and to obliterate the Faribundo Marti National Liberation Front in El Salvador by creating and supplying new antirevolutionary insurgency elements such as the Nicaraguan contras and by pouring military personnel, supplies, and money into what the Reagan administration perceived as the Central American breach. The failure of this "last ditch" attempt to reconstruct and to strengthen the old security regime accelerated the formation of the new self-help regulatory regime initiated among the Contadora group in 1983 (comprising Colombia, Venezuela, Mexico, and Panama) and culminating in the formalization of Esquipulas II in August 1987.[16]

The Central American conflict, focused on the U.S.-backed contra insurgency in Nicaragua, was mitigated by its sudden "ripeness," by the accelerating conclusion of the Cold War, and by the transformation of political forces within key Central American countries and within the branches of power in the United States.[17] For example, the election of the Social-Democratic Oscar Arias as president of Costa Rica in 1985 swung the Central American states to a majority favoring the establishment of a new regional regime not submitting to U.S. domination. Arias provided the impetus for his own "Arias Plan," which not only won over other Central American states that were "on the fence" (e.g., Guatemala), but also helped transform internal U.S. politics on the issue, winning over the House majority leader, Representative Jim Wright of Texas, and much of the Democratic majority in Congress.

In our introduction, we also suggested that Cuba never relinquished its regional interests. Whether Cuba should have been classified as a potential subimperial power might be open to question, pending empirical analysis. However, there is no doubt that the mere perception of Cuba as *actively* sympathetic toward the Sandinista government and other anti–United States movements in Central America alarmed some U.S. policymakers and analysts while encouraging national liberation movements within Central America. Thus, the termination of the Cold War released the United States from this fear and transformed the internal national consensus toward acceptance of the new Central American regime instituted by Esquipulas II.

Since 1989, our arbitrary year of distinction, the new self-help conflict regulation regime in Central America has gained momentum. Even the Conservative ARENA regime in El Salvador, under Alfredo Cristiani, has come to support the new regional regime. In October 1991 the Salvadorian Supreme Court rendered a verdict of guilty against some of the military officers involved in the murder of six Salvadorian Roman Catholic clerics in 1989. The winds of change are also affecting Guatemala and Honduras. Only the peculiar and frustrating effects of the U.S. intervention in Panama in 1990 have reminded the Central American actors of lingering U.S. power. However, the Panamanian case has a number of exceptional circumstances that separate it from the traditional cohesion of the other Central American states.[18]

In 1990 Nicaragua experienced a remarkable event, which, we would argue, further confirms the concrete reality of the new regional regime in Central America. The Sandinista government of Daniel Ortega was defeated in a critical, "free and fair" election monitored and supervised by a United Nations observer group (ONUCA). This event actually serves to legitimate the system. By electing the government of Violetta Chamorro, Nicaragua has, at least for the time being, gotten the U.S. behemoth off its back. The critical test comes with the next election. If the Sandinistas are elected to return to government, it will be interesting to see the reaction of the U.S. administration. This event also epitomizes the wave of political liberalization sweeping the region (although this must be seen in regionally relative terms). Whereas during the last phase of the Cold War, during the 1980s, internal conflict characterized the political configurations of Nicaragua, El Salvador, Guatemala, and, in a subsidiary sense, Costa Rica and Honduras, since 1989 all of the Central American states have become more politically open, and their internal conflicts have been mitigated regionally and de-emphasized internationally. The Nicaraguan contras cling to the hope that Violetta Chamorro's not completely *simpatico* government will maintain power—but the contras are not organizing nor being organized. The Sandinistas can no longer count on military support from Cuba or a Soviet system of states. Their political power is increasingly drawn from the politics of internal mobilization and labor action. They are also much more accountable for the political or economic excesses of any of their members or followers. The decline, though not disappearance, of U.S. political will toward direct military intervention in Central America has emboldened popular movements in these states to pursue more political and less paramilitary means in their efforts to broaden their bases of power.

Finally, the impact of the international system in effecting change in Central America needs to be addressed. While we have argued that the primary thrust toward the construction of a new regional regime came from the regional states themselves, one cannot discount the fact that France, the other Western European states, Canada, the Socialist International, and the U.N. contributed important support for the Contadora group and its support group. These states and nongovernmental organizations blunted the singular efforts of the Reagan/Casey cohorts to divide, control, and intervene in the affairs of Central America. In this sense the Monroe Doctrine was whittled down to size. It is ironic that it was a U.S. administration determined to return that hoary doctrine to the center of U.S. policy that ultimately opened the door to the support and concern of nonhemispheric interests (with the exception of Canada, of course).

The Central American self-help conflict regulation regime has not brought this historically troubled and dominated area to a new golden age. U.S. interests have not disappeared. The Panama exercise serves as a reminder that there is still a U.S. capacity for intervention in the region. However, without the persistence of internal conflict in these states, there is less "material" for any hegemonic or subimperialist state to work with in its efforts to dominate the region.

## Cambodia and Southeast Asia

While the conflict in Nicaragua helped to catalyze the formation of a new self-help conflict regulation regional regime, the Cambodian internal conflict has had the opposite effect in the Southeast Asian region. The Cambodian conflict—partly a legacy of ancient history, partly the product of the U.S. war in Vietnam—has brought into contention not only four distinct internal groups but also two blocs within the Association of Southeast Asian Nations (ASEAN). It also brought into conflict China vis-à-vis the

Soviet Union, as the ideological claimant to world Marxism-Leninism, and China vis-à-vis Vietnam as the hegemon of Indo-China. The fact that these multilevel conflicts have become intertwined in Cambodia has made prospects for mitigating this conflict even more problematic.

Cambodia, also known as Kampuchea, was one of the first plums to be picked off by the newly victorious Socialist Republic of Vietnam in late 1978. However, before assuming the worst about this rather unsubtle maneuver in regional subimperialism, it must be recalled that the Khmer Rouge under Pol Pot was the government being replaced. Soon Vietnam established what appeared to be a satrap by installing Heng Samrin, a disillusioned ex–Khmer Rouge, as the new president of the People's Republic of Kampuchea (PRK). As a result of this sudden and decisive turn of events, Vietnam created three new political facts:

1. China was astounded to see its own regional protégé, the Khmer Rouge, who had proudly proclaimed themselves Maoists—so rudely routed. Furthermore, China saw this regional expansionism as a regional power play by its global adversary, the Soviet Union.
2. Because Vietnam did not establish total control over Cambodia in the first few weeks, the Khmer Rouge succeeded in reorganizing and maintaining their presence in the country while operating from Thai sanctuaries.
3. The ASEAN states strongly opposed the Vietnamese operation and began channelling this concern through the United Nations. This provided the Khmer Rouge with unanticipated support as the legitimate government of Cambodia.[19]

By 1982 China and ASEAN coordinated their common disdain for Vietnam's occupation of Cambodia and proceeded to sponsor a coalition opposed to that rule. The Coalition Government of Democratic Kampuchea (CGDK) comprised Prince Sihanouk's Cambodge neutre, pacifique et coopératif (FUNCIPEC); the Khmer People's National Liberation Front (KPNLF); and the Khmer Rouge of Kampuchea (DK). Under the leadership of Prince Sihanouk and Son Sann, the prime minister, the CGDK commenced harassment operations against the government of the People's Republic of Kampuchea (PRK).

In this nearly bizarre multilevel standoff, no one seems to mind being hurt. Indeed China and the ASEAN states each seem content to allow this situation to persist. No one wants the PRK to stay in power; no one wants the Khmer Rouge to return to power (not even their erstwhile patrons in China); and no one seems that anxious to encourage the heretofore problematic Prince Sihanouk to regain his previous dominance. The Soviet Union furnished critical military and political backing to the PRK while it was still a global player. China confronted the Soviets to the north and the

Vietnamese to the south. Thailand and Singapore within ASEAN wished for a plague on the PRK, Vietnam, and the Khmer Rouge. Malaysia, and especially Indonesia—the two other ASEAN players—feared China more than Vietnam and so looked to bridge the gap between the PRK and the CGDK. Finally, the Western powers, and especially the United States, saw every outcome as worse than the status quo. They refused to recognize the Vietnam-implanted PRK government; they tended to quietly encourage Chinese opposition to both the Soviet Union and Vietnam; and they supported their ASEAN allies.

ASEAN tried to internationalize the conflict and its resolution through the U.N. Vietnam tried to internationalize the conflict by co-opting third party mediation from Japan, Australia, Indonesia, and anyone else who might be interested. Japan, adhering to its general policy, eschewed a political role, preferring to remain a strictly economic actor. The Australian Labour government, anxious to pursue a renovated foreign policy that focused on Australia more as an Asian actor, responded to the Vietnamese call. Recent Labour governments in Australia have taken a strong interest in becoming a more active Asian actor and in settling the Cambodian problem, going so far as to contribute peace-keeping forces there.

In late October 1991 the five permanent members of the U.N. Security Council—the United States, the Soviet Union, China, France, and Great Britain—agreed to a timetable for a multiparty election to be organized, verified, and monitored by the U.N. Clearly, the Soviet Union by that time was no longer interested in playing regional politics in Southeast Asia. The Vietnamese themselves seem uncertain now of their own political path, and while they are not abjuring their concern with China, they do not seem quite as keen to maintain control over Cambodia at all costs. A less direct method of influence might seem more attractive at this point. However, the pacification of the internal conflict might be less realizable and more expensive than anyone would be willing to admit. Controlling the Khmer Rouge with international peacekeepers is a forbidding thought. The Khmer Rouge, even in their present disposition, are ideological kinfolk to Peru's Sendero Luminoso. They more appropriately fit Ken Jowitt's characterization of "movements of rage."[20] Unless the Khmer Rouge have been transformed into a legitimate political party, Cambodia is faced with more internal violence.

Perhaps even more than in Nicaragua, the end of the Cold War has changed the nature of the conflict in Cambodia. Without Soviet backing of Vietnam, Cambodia's nasty and complex little war pales into irrelevance. Only China continues to benefit from the prolongation of this conflict. Yet the "hurting stalemate" has not provided sufficient cause for the mitigation, much less resolution, of the conflict.[21] Here, perhaps more so than in Central America, Ken Jowitt's "new world disorder" seems to be not merely a cliché. Anti-Chinese feeling, anti-Vietnamese feeling, and the existence of what might be labelled euphemistically "a Chinese Monroe Doctrine in Indo-China" insure continual war and social disruption inside this unhappy country.

## Mozambique and Southern Africa

The internal conflict in Mozambique has exhibited elements deriving from all three levels of impact: global, regional, and domestic. However, it is at the regional level that the greatest leverage appears to have been applied and where the greatest results have been attained. Chris Brown, in his most recent interpretation of events in the Southern African regional complex, argues that South Africa's internal struggle is "freeing" domestic actors to determine their own fate.[22] Events in South and Southern Africa have been unfolding at such a rapid rate during this period that Brown's reassessment is understandable. However, it is does not necessarily follow that because Pretoria is internally involved, that it has abdicated or even relegated its regional interests. What is becoming clear is that South Africa is making adjustments based on developing global and regional trends.

Mozambique is one of the major conflict zones within this region. It was the recipient of a "White Redoubt" strategy deriving from the Central Intelligence Organization of Rhodesia in 1976, then under White rule. This strategy was aimed at weakening the insurgency of the Zimbabwe African National Union (ZANU), which was given sanctuary by newly independent Mozambique and its ruling revolutionary party, FRELIMO. Rhodesia chose to create a Mozambique National Resistance (RENAMO) composed of revanchist elements from the Portuguese-led preindependence army and from varied and assorted dissident elements within Mozambique, including those unhappy with the orthodox Marxist program of the new FRELIMO government. Some commentators have argued that RENAMO picked up where the Revolutionary Committee of Mozambique (COREMO) and other anti-FRELIMO and ex-FRELIMO splinter groups left off.[23] Indeed, whether the dynamic foundations of RENAMO's origins were internally impelled or externally concocted (or, as I suspect, both), RENAMO became a serious force within Mozambique; its evident success has been as much a consequence of growing internal disaffection toward FRELIMO among the diverse population groups in rural Mozambique as a result of sustained South African military support and RENAMO's own brutal terrorist tactics.

Giving these domestic considerations their due, the regional dynamic must be evaluated. There is no doubt that whatever misgivings that were felt by sections of the traditional Mozambican population, RENAMO could not have generated the level of terror and destruction inside Mozambique without the steadfast support of an actor capable of providing and transporting arms and military supplies to them. Ian Smith's Rhodesian intelligence operation initiated that support, and after Zimbabwean independence in 1980, South Africa's increasingly mighty regional military machine sustained and enlarged that support. Moreover, the disgusted and revanchist Portuguese emigres from Mozambique settled in South Africa by the hundreds of thousands. Like the Cuban settlers in Miami, these emigres increasingly pressured the Pretoria regime to teach FRELIMO and its popular and Marxist-inclined president, Samora Machel, a lesson. On two distinct occasions, South Africa officially proclaimed renunciation of this support—once, in the Nkomati Agreement of 1984, and again in a clarifying commitment that P.W. Botha, the president of South Africa, made in 1988 to the Mozambican president, Joaquim Chissano (who had succeeded Samora Machel, killed in a somewhat mysterious airplane crash in 1986). In that commitment, Botha admitted that "technical violations" continued; these renunciations lend evidence to those who argue that South African military support to RENAMO had lingered even into the de Klerk era.[24] On the other side, Zimbabwe's crucial military support in protecting its own supply lines to the Mozambican port of Beira (up to 12,000 troops), Tanzania's intermittent military support, and clear support for FRELIMO by the Southern African Development Coordinating Conference (SADCC) illustrate the pervasive regional cleavage that was manifested in the Mozambican conflict.

At the global level, increasing concern was expressed over the extent of the conflict and its cost in human and economic terms to Mozambique. After the Soviet Union and the Eastern bloc declined to accept Mozambique into COMECON in 1983, the country increasingly veered away from its socialist plan. Even before Joaquim Chissano succeeded Samora Machel in 1986, the trend away from the Eastern bloc formula was evident. At about the same time, the United States made a commitment to aid Mozambique. By 1985, such anti-Communist stalwarts as William Casey and former national security advisor William Clark were gone or in decline. At that point, the former assistant secretary for African affairs, Chester Crocker, was able to assert his own policy toward the countries of Southern Africa without having to abide by the reflexive anti-Marxism of Casey and Clark. He very quickly ended any prospect of U.S. sympathy, let alone support, for RENAMO. Increasingly, U.S. concern for Mozambique coincided with Mozambique's disenchantment with Marxist-Leninist formulas for development. In the meantime, the International Monetary Fund (IMF), World Bank, United Nations Development Program (UNDP), and numerous other intergovernmental organizations as well as the states of the European Community (EC) and Sweden channelled resources into Mozambique.

At the same time, the search for mediation was being carried out at all levels. On the local level, President Chissano put forth serious efforts to reach and conciliate RENAMO. However, FRELIMO constituted the government and possessed the commanding political heights in regard to these contacts. RENAMO, in consequence, remained highly suspicious of these efforts. At the regional level, Mozambican contacts with official and un-official South African sources continues. There is no obvious evidence of continuing South African support for RENAMO. However, RENAMO is still reasonably well supplied, so that suspicions persist regarding a sus-tained South African support role. Recent allegations by Nico Basson, a former South African serviceman, and Adrian Maritz, an imprisoned far-right activist, support these suspicions.[25] Until 1992, all attempts to forge a mediation formula at the all-African level had failed. In 1989 Presidents Daniel arap Moi of Kenya and Robert Mugabe of Zimbabwe were asked to mediate with the assumption that Moi had closer links with RENAMO while Mugabe's were with FRELIMO. However, despite progress in en-hancing FRELIMO's legitimacy to RENAMO as the government of Mozambique and RENAMO's legitimacy to FRELIMO as a bona fide po-litical party, the talks foundered on Moi's transparent affinity to REN-AMO and Mugabe's lack of credibility with RENAMO.[26] Finally, Presi-dent Chissano and Alfonso Dhlakama, the leader and spokesperson for RENAMO, agreed to an offer by the Santo Egidio Community, an Italian lay group associated with the Vatican, to host the talks.

The result of several rounds of talks between FRELIMO and REN-AMO under the aegis of this particular Italian patronage was the creation of a technical verifying mechanism, the Joint Verification Commission (JVC). This body successfully monitored the six-month ceasefire that was agreed to in December 1990. In the meantime RENAMO held a first party congress and is continuing to try to make efforts to achieve some measure of internal and external legitimacy. The mutual suspicions persist and RE-NAMO terrorism continued into 1992. However, in late October 1991 an-other breakthrough seemed to occur in another round of meetings in Rome. It was at this point that "ripeness" began to emerge. Both sides are hurting. RENAMO has convinced FRELIMO and everyone else that it could para-lyze Mozambique, threaten Maputo (the capital), and even "connect" with the variegated grievances of rural Mozambicans.[27] FRELIMO, meanwhile, realized that it could not continue to govern a city-state (i.e., Maputo) while claiming to represent a country. Its own legitimacy was being ques-tioned by many Mozambicans. Thus, the moment was approaching for a "win-win" solution to the conflict.

To emphasize the significance of conflict mitigation at the regional level, a breakthrough bolted not out of South Africa, but out of Zimbabwe. Beleaguered by drought and its increasingly costly occupation of the Beira corridor, Zimbabwe pressed strongly for a meeting between Chissano and RENAMO's Dhlakama. Finally, at a meeting in Botswana in July 1992, Zimbabwe's president, Robert Mugabe, was able to convince Dhlakama that he should accept a meeting with President Chissano for the purpose of reaching an agreement to end the civil war in Mozambique. In August 1992, Chissano and Dhlakama met in Gaborone, Botswana's capital, to establish a ceasefire in Mozambique on October 1, 1992.

At the same time, South Africa faces the consuming problem of focusing on the settlement of its own internal conflict. At the regional level, not only is South Africa making serious efforts to use carrots principally in rebuilding its regional image, but it now sees its own future as a multiracial state with a multiracial government integrated into a formal regional regime, perhaps SADCC.[28] Clearly, the transformation of the global structure has distinctly affected policy in Southern Africa. However, the impact of global events would not be so significant were it not for the even greater impact of South Africa's internal transformation and the greater confidence of Zimbabwe and the other actors within the Southern African region.

## Conclusion

Each of these case studies from three distinct Third World regions suggests that the end of the Cold War has had an ameliorating impact on the management and reduction of at least some conflicts. However, this relationship is not direct in at least one of the cases and has had only a delayed effect in another. In each of these three cases, the significance of regional impact—and particularly the reformation of regional regimes—has been the most salient, and perhaps most decisive, factor in conflict reduction. At this writing, the first case, Nicaragua and regime formation in Central America, has had its internal conflict mitigated by a decisive restructuring of the Central American security regime. While the hemispheric power of the United States still looms large over the region, the collective ability of the Central American states to coordinate their political, and perhaps even economic, resources toward some modest regime autonomy has been impressive. Moreover, the diminution and eventual collapse of Soviet interest and involvement in the Western Hemisphere accelerated the process objectively by reducing military and economic assistance to Cuba and subjectively by obliterating the perception shared by both the United States and the Central American governments that external (Soviet-derived) demons were continuing to instigate and inflame revolutionary movements in Nicaragua and Central America.[29]

In the case of Cambodia, the regional factor has been, until October 1991, a retardant to conflict mitigation. Vietnam's successful execution of its war(s) against France and the United States furnished the Vietnamese with momentum and confidence, if not arrogance, to assess its opportunities and act accordingly in the Southeast Asian region. Exploiting nearly universal distaste with the bloody Khmer Rouge regime of the mid-1970s

(China excepted), Vietnam proceeded to invade, occupy, and establish satellite control over Kampuchea. This control persisted in the face of pervasive regional opposition. The Vietnamese consummately manipulated the interests of such peripheral regional actors as Australia and Japan in deterring effective congealing of regional/Chinese efforts to force them out of Cambodia. In this case, 1989 was indeed a watershed. The decline of Soviet capacity to patronize its clients perhaps affected Vietnam more than any other Third World state. Confronted with the reality of dissipating Soviet support, Vietnam executed an orderly exit from Cambodia, finally effected in early 1991. The end of the Cold War thus created an opening in the Cambodian imbroglio that was quickly entered by the United Nations, pushed by the joint interests of ASEAN and China. However, it is not yet certain whether the Cambodian conflict is internally "ripe" for resolution. The Khmer Rouge continues to press-gang recruits from its sanctuary on the Thai border and in its occasional forays inside Cambodia. If Khmer Rouge remains committed to coercion and terrorism, then the efforts by any U.N. or regional peace-keeping contingent to enforce the Security Council resolution of October 1991 are going to be politically and financially very costly. In this case, the efforts of the regional actors to "shut down" the operations of Khmer Rouge are going to be critical.

As in Cambodia, the case of Mozambique provides another example of Jowitt's "movements of rage." Again, however, it is the regional dynamic that is critical. As in Cambodia, the process *appears* to be heading toward resolution. In August 1992, a ceasefire, effective October 1, was agreed to by President Chissano and RENAMO leader Alfonso Dhlakama. This turn of events reflects, more profoundly than anything else, the diminution of South African support for RENAMO within the Southern African region. The "hurting stalemate" between FRELIMO and RENAMO endured from 1989. However, RENAMO resisted FRELIMO's claim to be the legitimate government of Mozambique until well into the details phase of the peace talks in Rome in 1992. And South Africa's own preoccupation with its questions of internal legitimacy have left RENAMO dangling without a decisive regional supporter. Kenya attempted to replace South Africa as RENAMO's prime sponsor, but Kenya's lack of proximity to Mozambique and its lack of *bona fides* as a regional actor minimized the effectiveness of its support. But it was Zimbabwe, which was also hurting, that finally acted to break the stalemate. The end of the Cold War no doubt accelerated the search for resolution of this conflict—particularly at the global level. However, the Soviets and the Warsaw Bloc began to disengage their support for Samora Machel and FRELIMO as early as 1983. Concomitantly, the United States, the EC, the Scandinavian states, and the IGOs increased their support for the FRELIMO government at about the same time. Thus we cannot infer here that the end of the Cold War was decisive in turning around events in Mozambique.

These three cases provide persuasive evidence that the regional context is not only important but is decisive in establishing the necessary conditions for the mitigation of internal conflict. A foundation for an effective regional security regime must be laid before one or more of the internal combatants become convinced that the "hurt" is greater than the enticement of the goal. Thus, we might add an important proviso to Zartman's thesis of "the ripe moment" for resolution. We are convinced that such "ripeness" *must* exist in the regional subsystemic context before it can be internalized by the domestic combatants or be programed by the actual or potential global mediators. Thus the hurting stalemate must especially hurt the regional actors before the internal combatants will holler "ouch!"

## Notes

1. See Chester A. Crocker, "Conflict Resolution in the Third World: The Role of Superpowers" and Saadia Touval and I. William Zartman, "Mediation: The Role of Third-Party Diplomacy and Informal Peacemaking" (Papers presented to conference on "Conflict Resolution in the Post–Cold War Third World," U.S. Institute of Peace, Washington, D.C., October 1990). See also Chester A. Crocker, "Southern African Peacemaking," *Survival* 32, no. 3 (May–June 1990): 221–232.

2. For the classic statement on the importance of region in international politics, especially as it relates to the Third World, see Larry W. Bowman's "The Subordinate State System of Southern Africa" *International Studies Quarterly* 12 (September 1968).

3. For an excellent discussion of this problem in conceptualizing region, see Kenneth W. Grundy, "The Impact of Region on Contemporary African Politics," in *African Independence: The First Twenty-Five Years*, ed. Gwendolen M. Carter and Patrick O'Meara (Bloomington: Indiana University Press 1985), pp. 97–125.

4. See especially the groundbreaking work of Stephen Krasner, ed., *International Regimes*, especially the chapters by Krasner, "Structural Causes and Regime Consequences: Regimes as Intervening Variables," Robert Jervis, "Security Regimes" and, more critically, Susan Strange, "*Cave! hic dragones*: A Critique of Regime Analysis" (Ithaca: Cornell University Press, 1983). More specific to our focus on the Third World—and more contemporary as well—is the thematic issue of *International Journal*, Spring, 1990, devoted to regional conflict and conflict reduction, especially the concluding piece by Fen Osler Hampson, "Building a Stable Peace: Opportunities and Limits to Security Co-operation in Third World Regional Conflicts," pp. 454–489. The latter source has furnished much of the stimulus for this chapter. My thanks to Roger Rieber, University of Utah, for his guidance in this direction.

5. Robert O. Keohane and Joseph S. Nye, *Power and Independence* (Boston, MA: Little, Brown 1977). Quoted by Krasner, *International Regimes*, p. 2.

6. Krasner, *International Regimes*, p. 3.

7. Fes Osler Hampson, *International Journal* (Spring 1990). The author states "Regional co-operation and security regimes may also freeze the status quo in ways that are morally and politically undesirable," p. 485.

8. The Workshop on "Cooperation and Security in Post-Apartheid Southern Africa" was held in Maputo, Mozambique, 3–6 September 1991. There was more

than just an unconscious effort to apply the regime dynamics of the Council on Security and Cooperation in Europe (CSCE) to the evolving regional dynamics in Southern Africa, and especially to the mitigation of conflict in Mozambique. Invited to the workshop were officials, academics, party activists, and business people from South Africa as well as from SADCC, EC, and the United States. No ideas or perspectives were excluded.

9. I have tried to present a comparative perspective on this problem as it has affected sub-Saharan Africa in my "Peacekeeping in Africa: Breakthrough Politics as Usual?" *TransAfrica Forum* 8, no. 3 (Fall 1991) 49–60. Hampson lists some of these criteria for effective U.N. peace-keeping:

> more comprehensive and regular meetings in the Security Council for monitoring the world security situation, earlier treatment of disputes and questions of peace and security, a more regular use of regional organizations in the overall international system for peace-keeping and peace-making, firmer links between conflict control and the negotiation and settlement of disputes, more positive support for United Nations peace-keeping and peacemaking efforts, more systematic earmarking of materiel and logistical support for peacekeeping, standardization of equipment, creation of naval peacekeeping forces for conflicts which encompass international waterways . . . , creation of a formal military peacekeeping force, and establishment of a United Nations multilateral war risk reduction center.

Hampson borrows these measures from a paper presented by Brian Urquhart, *International Journal,* pp. 461–462.

10. Ibid., 464. It should be noted that such self-help conflict regulation regimes can be directed against a perceived subimperial or hegemonial-exploitative state *within* the region, e.g., the Southern African Development Coordinating Conference (SADCC) organizing to deal with South Africa.

11. See Chris Brown, "Regional Conflict in Southern Africa and the Role of Third Party Mediators," *International Journal* 45 (Spring, 1990): 340ff.

12. However, South Africa has already developed a track record for applying both carrots and sticks to its regional neighbors. The twin poles of reform and repression especially characterized the regional destabilization policies of the P. W. Botha regime during the 1980s. Given these policy orientations, a milder version of that policy may very well still be in effect during the de Klerk policy of the early 1990s. For reference to the carrot-and-stick regional policy of the 1980s, see Chris Brown, "Southern Africa in the Post-Apartheid Era," *International Journal* 46 (Spring 1991): 275–279. For comprehensive documentation and analysis of the regional destabilization policies of the 1980s, see Joseph Hanlon, *Beggar Your Neighbours: Apartheid Power in Southern Africa* (Bloomington: Indiana University Press 1986).

13. See Keith Krause, "Constructing Regional Security Regimes and The Control of Arms Transfers," *International Journal* 45 (Spring 1990): 386–423.

14. Hampson, "Building a Stable Peace," 471–473.

15. For an insightful assessment of Central American regime transformation in the 1980s, see Liisa North and Tim Draimin, "The Decay of the Security Regime in Central America," *International Journal* 45 (Spring 1990): 224–257.

16. North and Draimin, "Decay of the Security Regime." Also see William M. LeoGrande, "Regime Illegitimacy and Revolutionary Movements: Central Amer-

ica," in *Revolution and Political Change in the Third World,* ed. Barry M. Schutz and Robert O. Slater (Boulder, CO: Lynne Rienner, 1990), pp. 142–159.

17. For an elaboration of his theory of "ripeness," see I. William Zartman's essay, chapter 12 in this volume and his landmark *Ripe for Resolution: Conflict and Intervention in Africa* (Oxford: Oxford University Press, 1989). For a comprehensive case study applying and refining these concepts, see Stephen J. Stedman, *Peacemaking in Civil War: International Mediation in Zimbabwe, 1974–1980* (Boulder, CO: Lynne Rienner, 1991). Stedman emphasizes the often overlooked dynamic of political change within the political units engaged in the regional process of conflict mitigation.

18. Panama is close to being a U.S. settler-colonial vestige. That political memory and the perceived strategic significance of the Panama Canal revive the imperialist impulses of many U.S. citizens, especially those on the political right.

19. Gerard Hervouet, "The Cambodian Conflict: The Difficulties of Intervention and Compromise," *International Journal* 45 (Spring 1990): 258–260. Much of this section derives from this comprehensive analysis.

20. Ken Jowitt, "The New World Disorder," *Journal of Democracy* 23, no. 1 (Winter 1991): 17–19. Jowitt's chapter in this volume does not include that acute perception.

21. Zartman, *Ripe for Resolution.*

22. See Chris Brown, "Southern Africa in the Post-Apartheid Era." The author's earlier pessimism on this question, pervasive in his article of the previous year, "Regional Conflict and Third-Party Mediators," is here greatly diminished.

23. Including Stephen Weigert, Department of State, who has an unpublished manuscript, "Traditions of Peasant Warfare in Africa and The RENAMO Insurgency in Mozambique," arguing that RENAMO is not all that external nor abnormal in the context of African and Mozambican organized peasant violence. Many Mozambicans share this belief.

24. For an excellent summary and analysis of these events, see Witney W. Schneidman, "Conflict Resolution in Mozambique: A Status Report," *CSIS Africa Notes,* 121, 28 February 1991.

25. The interview with Maritz appeared in the (South African) *Weekly Mail,* 25 October 1991.

26. Schneidman, "Conflict Resolution in Mozambique."

27. See Karl Maier, "The Revival of Tradition," *Africa Report* (July–August 1991).

28. These thoughts are more than speculative. The appearance and statement of N. P. Van Heerden, the South African director general of the Department of Foreign Affairs, at the Maputo conference on "Regional Cooperation and Security in Post-Apartheid Southern Africa," confirms these interests from Pretoria.

29. See William J. Foltz, "Dynamics of Revolutionary Change: External Causes—Who First Seduced Them to That Foul Revolt?" in Schutz and Slater, *Revolution and Political Change,* especially pp. 54–57.

# PART 5

## CONCLUSIONS

# 14

# Global Transformation and the Third World: Challenges and Prospects

*Robert O. Slater*
*Barry M. Schutz*
*Steven R. Dorr*

We began this effort with an inquiry into the state of global transformation as it pertains to the status of those states that we have traditionally labeled the Third World. Even as we ponder these issues, the structure of interstate relations continues to evolve and is likely to continue to change during at least the remainder of this decade. In particular, those problems that we thought of as belonging to the Third World have now spread to the Second World:

> The start of the 1990s has thus witnessed the culmination of the decolonization process that began at the same time as the Cold War and has now pushed it to one side. Fifteen years after the last Western empire—that of the Portuguese—collapsed, the post-1945 Soviet acquisitions were liberated. . . . From an oasis of stability in an unstable world, Europe has become among the most turbulent of continents. Old states are falling apart and new ones are being created, all sharing economic fragility but varying greatly otherwise in culture, tradition, and potential international weight. . . . In some areas violence is becoming endemic and routine. . . . In this way problems that once seemed quintessentially "Third World" are becoming common in Europe.

This analysis by Lawrence Freeman echoes the less than sanguine warnings voiced by Jowitt in his opening chapter for this volume. The processes of fragmentation and reordering of state boundaries and identities are likely to continue unabated; as these processes unfold in Europe and the former Soviet Union it also becomes increasingly likely that the Third World will experience greater marginalization. This marginalization is a double-edged sword, as it provides a degree of insulation for Third World

359

countries from the meddling in domestic affairs to which they were so often subject previously, yet it isolates them in an increasingly interdependent, multipolar, and highly competitive international system.

As outlined in our introduction, the challenge to the Third World is found in three critical areas: (1) the expanding range of choices of political systems; (2) the changing international political economy; and (3) the changing nature of conflict and its mitigation. The analyses that comprise these efforts lead to a number of important conclusions and speculations about the changing international system.

It seems apparent that we will continue to witness a world more inclined to experiment with different forms of democratic rule. The pressure toward democracy is worldwide and its successes will be varied. It is not clear, however, whether this is truly a worldwide movement or whether it has been precipitated by the events in the former Soviet Union and in Eastern Europe. Remmer, for example, provides compelling analysis that the most recent "wave" of democracy in Latin America was partly attributable to economic rather than political or ideological origins; and that these economic origins relate to the oil and debt crises of the 1970s, long before the breakdown of the Berlin Wall. Meanwhile, Bernstein and Dorr see extremely limited prospects for democratization in China and the Middle East. Their optimism is frustrated by the lack of preconditions within the political and socioeconomic systems of the countries and their insulation from events in other parts of the world. Thus, while there are conspicuous instances where the global transformation has provided an impetus toward democratization, the depth and breadth of the process remains in doubt.

It also seems apparent that we will confront a world of rampant conflict, albeit of a different variety than the conflicts that characterized East-West rivalry. Unfortunately, this difference may actually be manifest, as in Yugoslavia and Somalia, in levels of violence and genocide not witnessed during much of the Cold War. Slater suggests a return to patterns of conflict and violence that highlighted the late nineteenth and early twentieth centuries. Zartman sees a world of continuing conflicts among Third World states and an international and regional system not well prepared to mediate and mitigate. Zartman also sees, however, a United States "wearing a reputation for successful conflict management, condemned to play the role in the future," while Schutz argues that the "significant [conflict mitigation] action is more regional than hegemonic-international."

These, and other, debates concerning the viability of democratization and the future of conflict in the Third World remain compelling. Nevertheless, the most pivotal and complex dimension remains that of the political economies of the Third World and former Second World, not only in terms of the link between the political and economic liberalization but the very capability of many states to survive in a transformed global economy. It is clear, throughout the analyses, that the extreme dilemma faced by the

Third World is the challenge of making the transition to a new type of political system and then sustaining that system, while coping with the demands of an extremely complex international economy. One also has the sense that the harsh political realities resulting from the demise of the Soviet Union and of Marxism-Leninism mask the more serious challenges of a transforming global economy—a transformation that certainly predates the stark events of the end of the Cold War. Dolan points out that, while the effects of the collapse in the East have direct and potentially negative impact on the middle- and lower-income countries of the South, the structural and "less obvious changes involving the increasing regionalization of world trade and the restructuring of industrial production" impinge directly on the Third World's abilities to compete.

There remain clear differences among scholars concerning the antecedents to the current "wave" of democratization—particularly whether in fact there is a "wave" and whether it has been precipitated by the disintegration of the Soviet Union and the collapse of Marxism-Leninism. This latter relationship is intricate and has been addressed consistently. To add to this perspective, Diamond ponders whether fragile states will be capable of preserving democracy in the face of difficulties in "delivering the goods." Remmer's conceptual framework for analyzing democratization in Latin America addresses economic rather than political or ideological factors as pre-eminent in terms of the international system's impact on political systems. She cites the oil shocks of the 1970s, the related expansion of international lending, and the debt crisis as the most influential developments in the rather enduring transfer to broad electoral participation that has typified Latin American politics.

A critical relationship that emerges here as worthy of examination is the neoclassical link between political pluralization/democratization and economic liberalization. In the neoclassical view, economic liberalization provides the impetus for evolving sociopolitical changes. As Callaghy states: "The presumption of the mutually reinforcing character of political and economic reform in the Third and former Second Worlds relies on an extension of neoclassical economic logic. . . . This logic . . . does not appear to hold very often, even under authoritarian conditions, much less democratic ones." Callaghy sees a rather "perverse relationship" between political liberalization and economic reform.

In the final analysis, the remarkable global transformation of the 1980s and early 1990s appears to have left much of the Third World out in the cold. To be sure, there are cases of considerable accomplishment, including the increased viability of democracy throughout much of Latin America and the success of the Newly Industrialized Countries (the NICs). But these accomplishments, while in some cases fueled by the global transformation, predate the events of the 1980s. For those countries who comprise much of the Third and Fourth Worlds, the picture remains bleak.

For every success there is a Peru or Somalia, marginalized and neglected by much of the First and Second Worlds. As we suggested in our introduction, the Third and Fourth Worlds are indeed laboratories for developing responses to a reordered international system. There are tremendous obstacles to overcome as countries attempt to deal with an uneasy mix among political, social, and economic variables in a global system that isolates and marginalizes the most burdensome cases.

# About the Contributors

**Thomas Bernstein** is professor of political science at Columbia University. In 1989/90 he was a visiting scholar at the Center for International Security and Arms Control of Stanford University. He is the author of *Up to the Mountains and Down to the Villages: The Transfer of Youth from Urban to Rural China* and numerous other articles and essays on political and economic issues affecting China. Dr. Bernstein serves on the editorial boards of *China Quarterly* and *Chinese Law and Government*.

**Thomas R. Callaghy** is associate professor of political science at the University of Pennsylvania. He has taught at several other universities including the University of California, Berkeley, and Columbia University, where he was also associate director of the Research Institute on International Change. Dr. Callaghy is the author of *The State-Society Struggle: Zaire in Comparative Perspective* as well as a number of articles and coeditor of several volumes dealing with political and economic conditions in sub-Saharan Africa.

**Larry Diamond** is a senior fellow at the Hoover Institution on War, Revolution and Peace at Stanford University. He is coeditor of the *Journal of Democracy*. Previously Dr. Diamond was assistant professor of sociology at Vanderbilt University. He is author of numerous books and articles on democracy including *Class, Ethnicity and Democracy in Nigeria: The Failure of the First Republic* and coeditor with Juan J. Linz and Seymour Martin Lipset of *Politics in Developing Countries: Comparing Experiences with Democracy* and the four-volume *Democracy in Developing Countries,* covering Latin America, Asia, and Africa.

**Michael Dolan** is a professor of political science and director of the Institute of Political Economy at Carleton University in Ottawa, Canada. His current research is on the political economy of European integration and the external economic relations of the European Community. Dr. Dolan has published numerous articles in such professional journals as the *International Studies Quarterly, International Organization,* and the *Journal of Conflict Resolution* and has received numerous grants and professional honors for his work on European economy and integration.

**Steven R. Dorr** is a program manager, director of conferences, and occasional teacher of a Middle East course at the Defense Intelligence College in Washington, D.C. He has conducted research under a Fulbright-Hays Fellowship in London, Lebanon, and the Gulf states of the Arabian Peninsula. For ten years he was on the staff of the Middle East Institute in Washington, D.C., serving variously as librarian, book review editor of *The Middle East Journal,* director of programs, and secretary to the board of governors. He was a research fellow at the Woodrow Wilson International Center for Scholars of the Smithsonian Institution and is the author of their *Scholars' Guide to Washington, D.C. for Middle Eastern Studies.*

**Kenneth Jowitt** is professor of political science at the University of California, Berkeley, where he is also dean of undergraduate academic life. Dr. Jowitt has written numerous articles and monographs including: *Revolutionary Breakthroughs and National Development: The Case of Romania, 1945–1965, The Leninist Response to National Dependence,* and, most recently, *New World Disorder: The Leninist Extinction.* His articles have appeared in such journals as the *Journal of Democracy* and *Eastern European Politics and Societies,* of which he serves on the editorial committee.

**Karen L. Remmer** is a professor of political science at the University of New Mexico in Albuquerque. Dr. Remmer has published extensively on politics in Latin America, including scholarly articles in *World Politics, Comparative Politics,* and, most recently, "The Political Impact of Economic Crisis in Latin America in the 1980s," in the *American Political Science Review.*

**Barry M. Schutz** is on the faculty of the Defense Intelligence College, where he teaches African Studies and Third World related courses. Dr. Schutz was a Fulbright Lecturer at the Higher Institute of International Relations in Maputo, Mozambique during 1991/92. He has also been an adjunct professor at Georgetown University and a senior fellow at Columbia University's Research Institute on International Change. He has also taught at the University of Zimbabwe in Harare, the University of Lancaster in England, and Trent University in Canada. Dr. Schutz has published on Southern Africa with an emphasis on Zimbabwe and he is coeditor of *Revolution and Political Change in the Third World.*

**Robert O. Slater** is presently on the staff of the National Security Education Program. Previously he was director of research at the Defense Intelligence College, where he was also the director of the Defense Academic Research Support Program. Dr. Slater is a scholar of international politics and has published in major journal including the *American Political Science Review.* He is coeditor of the *Defense Intelligence Journal,* and coeditor of two recent books: *Current Perspectives of International Terrorism* and *Revolution and Political Change in the Third World.*

**Daniel Unger** is assistant professor of government at Georgetown University and is affiliated with the Program on U.S.-Japan Relations at Harvard University. He previously taught Japanese political economy at the Fletcher School of Law and Diplomacy. A Southeast Asian specialist fluent in Japanese and Thai, Dr. Unger has delivered papers and lectures in both the U.S. and Japan. He has also served on the editorial staffs of *Foreign Policy* magazine and the *Woodrow Wilson Quarterly.*

**Claude E. Welch** is a distinguished service professor of political science at the State University of New York at Buffalo. His numerous publications have focused on Africa, human rights, and the political role of the armed forces. Among his recent books are: *Asian Perspectives on Human Rights* and *No Farewell to Arm? Military Disengagement from Politics in Africa and Latin America.* Dr. Welch edits *Armed Forces and Society* and serves on the board of Africa Watch.

**I. William Zartman** is the Jacob Blaustein Professor of International Organization and Conflict Resolution and director of African studies at the Nitze School of Advanced International Studies of the Johns Hopkins University. Dr. Zartman has taught at New York University and the American University in Cairo and has lectured at a number of universities in Europe, Africa, and the Middle East. He has written extensively on North Africa, sub-Saharan Africa, and in the field of negotiation analysis. Among his many publications are: *New Issues in International Crisis Management, Ripe for Resolution: Conflict and Intervention in Africa,* and *The 50% Solution.*

# Index

Africa: authoritarian rule, 33; debt service, 210, 211; dependence on IMF and World Bank, 212; dependence on major powers, 209–221; economic growth in, 183, 185tab, 209–221; economic marginalization in, 209–221; ethno-nationalistic conflict in, 318; investment in, 210; Japanese assistance in, 285; marginalization of, 180; per capita income, 182, 210; population growth, 210; post-neocolonialism in, 211; primary product exports, 212; trade decline in, 210; United Nations intervention in, 181; World Bank assessment of reform in, 182–183
African-American Institute, 57
African National Congress, 219, 220
Agriculture: commercialization of, 106; decollectivization, 114; in European Community, 171
AIDS, 218, 219; effect on political alignments, 21; polarizing effects, 21
Albania: democratization in, 52; as Third World state, 2
Alfonsín, Raúl, 92, 169, 193, 202, 206
Algeria: democratization in, 38, 52, 132–133, 135, 136, 137–138, 143, 149; economic crisis, 137; effect of fundamentalist Muslims, 20; elections in, 149; Islamic election victory, 137; Islamic movements in, 149; political reform in, 143
Alliance for Progress, 105
Angola: civil war in, 34, 56, 327; conflict mitigation in, 7; membership in IMF, 177–178; withdrawal of Soviet assistance, 45, 87
Apartheid: international pressure for abandonment, 51; legalization of opposition to, 33
Aquino, Corazon, 56, 192
Arab Maghrib Union, 330
Arab Organization for Human Rights, 149–150
Argentina: authoritarianism in, 44; debt crisis, 204; democratic transfer of

power, 92; democratization in, 41tab, 91; dependence on IMF, 203; economic crisis, 100; economic growth in, 100, 183, 202–205; international pressure on, 49; military regime in, 87, 102; per capita income, 98; popular support for democracy, 94; religious opposition to authoritarianism, 57; reversal of democratization, 91
Arias, Oscar, 344
Aristide, Jean-Bertrand, 34
ASEAN. See Association of South East Asian Nations
Asia: co-prosperity sphere, 173; democratization in, 35–38. See also East Asia
Asia Foundation, 57
Asian Development Bank, 294
Asian Forum Japan, 297
Asian Pacific Economic Co-operation Forum, 272
Association of South East Asian Nations (ASEAN), 271, 291, 298, 330, 347, 348
Authoritarianism. See Regimes, authoritarian
Autonomy: in civil society, 46–47; embedded, 169, 189; movements, 196
Aylwin, Patricio, 94, 200, 202

Babangida, Ibrahim, 216
Bahrain: political reform movements, 141; prospects for democratization in, 139, 141
Baker, James, 206
Baltic states: democratization in, 41tab; integration with Europe, 33; links with European Community, 173; membership in IMF, 177–178
Banda, Hastings, 34
Bank for International Settlements, 173, 174–175, 177, 265
Banking: centralized, 200, 201, 204, 223, 243; international, 106, 210; reform, 188, 236; subsidized, 200
Bank of Credit and Commerce International, 174

# About the Book

Much has been written already about the changed international system of the 1990s projecting the configuration of a restructered Europe, the future role of the United States and the emergence of a multipolar world with or without a dominant hegemon. In the search for new structures and explanations, however, it is too often assumed in error that these apply to what we label the "Third World" in the same way that they do to the "North" or the "West."

This book explores the phenomenon of global transformation in the context of the Third World, looking specifically at the preference for more democratic political systems, the emergence of a new international economic order, and the changing forms of conflict, its mitigation, and its resolution. The contributors provide major theoretical analyses of these three trends, as well as in-depth case studies that explore specific developments.